The Sorcerer's Oath Series
Book 3: The Lost Forest

The Lost Forest

Jenny Ealey

Eskuzor Publishing

ᴇꜱᴋᴜᴢᴏʀ ᴘᴜʙʟɪꜱʜɪɴɢ
1 Monash St,
Melton South,
Victoria, Australia 3338

www.jennyealey.com

Published by Eskuzor Publishing 2015

© Copyright J. J. Ealey 2015

The Author asserts the moral right to
be identified as the author of this work

ISBN 978-0-9876017-5-9

Printed and bound by Ingram Sparks, Australia

Acknowledgements
I would like to thank Paddy Mary Stentiford who,
from the other side of the world, painstakingly edited
my novels with me through all their myriad drafts.
I would also like to thank my father Tim Ealey who
painted the eerie background forest for the cover and my
sister Wendy Ealey who created the cover and designed
and typeset the book.

DEDICATION

To all those people who have had to leave behind their homes, their day to day lives, their hopes and aspirations to become strangers in new lands.

May we welcome them into our hearts and our communities.

West Sea
Encampment
Infestation Damage
Forestals
Dark Beech Forest
GREAT WEST R
Valley of the
Dry Mile
Lord Tolmad's Estate
Grasslands
Mountain Folk
Night in Trees
Western Forest
Hails Cliffs
Top of Range
Black Lion Cave
Lake
Montraya Castle
Falling Rain's Swamp

Wood Nearing
Wooding Deep
Wolves Burial
First Firesite
Borovan's Ride
Ancient Elm's Firesite
Eagle Cliffs
GREAT WEST ROAD
TORMADELL CASTLE
Second Firesite
N
Not to scale

Characters

SORCERERS

Tamadil Royal Family:
King Markazon (deceased)
Queen, Markazon's wife
King Kosar, eldest son of King Markazon
Prince Jarand, second son of King Markazon
Prince Tarkyn, third son of King Markazon

Courtiers:
Danton Patronell, Lord of Sachmore, Tarkyn's friend from childhood
Andoran and Sargon, friends of Tarkyn at court
Stormaway Treemaster, wizard for Prince Tarkyn and King Markazon
Journeyman Cloudmaker, Prince Jarand's wizard
Sergeant Torrigan

Thieving Family:
Old Ma
Gillis, Old Ma's son
Tomas, Old Ma's son
Morayne, daughter of Tomas
Charkon, son of Tomas

Grasslands:
Tolward, Lord of Middle Grasslands
Juniper, his wife
Eidelweiss, his daughter
Winguard, his son
Karlian, his healer

Trappers:
String and Bean
Pipeless, wizard trapper (deceased)

Scorcerers of the South:
Captain Harkell
Kayama, Harkell's wife
Sorrell, Harkell's son
Marema, Harkell's daughter
Colonel Charford
Captain Guerion
Davorad, Lord of Stansbeck, financier of Jarand's encampment
Greyskies Swampwatcher, independent wizard
Captain Sotrain
Lady Jirriel
Mirallee

WOODFOLK

Wanderers:
Waterstone
Sparrow, Waterstone's daughter
Autumn Leaves
Thunder Storm
Creaking Bough, Thunder Storm's wife
Rain on Water, Thunder Storm's son
Rustling Leaves
Grass Wind
Lapping Water
Summer Rain, healer
Falling Rain, Summer Rain's exiled brother
Autumn Storm, Autumn Leaves and Thunder Storm's grandfather
Twig Snap
Leaf Fall

Forestals:
Raging water
Falling Branch, his son
Sun Shower, Falling Branch's wife
Rainstorm, Falling Branch's son

Gatherers:
Ancient Oak
Tree Wind
North Wind
Running feet

Mountainfolk:
Dry Berry
Woodfolk near Tormadell
Ancient Elm
Blizzard
Cavern
Dripping Rock
Melting Snow
Hail
Midnight, Hail's son, Tarkyn's ward

Captured Woodfolk:
Golden Toad
Rushwind
Ibis Wings

Woodfolk of Lost Forest:
Singing Bird
Borovar, Sorcerer from Lost Forest
Orolan, chief of bandits

The story so far...

BOOK ONE

In Eskuzor, land of sorcerers, nineteen year old Prince Tarkyn is brought up on unjust charges by his twin brothers, King Kosar and Prince Jarand. He throws up a magical shield and escapes, inadvertently leaving a trail of death and destruction. A family of thieves try to rob him but then help him to flee the city of Tormadell.

After days on the run, Tarkyn wanders into the woodlands in the company of an old wizard, Stormaway Treemaster, only to find himself unable to leave. Woodfolk attack him and he retaliates with threatening displays of magic. But Tarkyn is then horrified to discover that he is unwelcome, bitterly resented liege lord to these elusive people who fear sorcerers and whose oath to him has been spellbound to the welfare of their forest.

Before the woodfolk can take adequate measures to protect him, bounty hunters capture Tarkyn. In the chaos of his escape, the prince is severely injured. While Tarkyn lies unconscious, Stormaway, disguised as the prince, leads the bounty hunters far from the forest.

For more than a week, the prince lies unconscious, while one woodman, Waterstone, stays by his side talking quietly to him and bringing him back to an awareness of his surroundings. As he recovers, Tarkyn, raw from his brothers' betrayal and wary of the woodfolk's resentment, gradually develops an uneasy friendship with Waterstone.

Woodfolk can hold conversations and send images mentally to each other, an ability not shared by sorcerers and wizards. Gradually, Tarkyn discovers that he can receive and send images and feelings, but not words. In fact, sometimes Tarkyn's strong feelings transmit to other people without his knowledge or control.

When a hunting party of the king and Prince Jarand enter the woods, Tarkyn's reaction to seeing his brothers overwhelms Waterstone's daughter, Sparrow, and she blacks out. Waterstone is furious, hurling threats at the prince and trying to attack him. The woodman's behaviour breaches the oath, causing an area of forest to be seriously damaged before Tarkyn curtails the destruction by giving Waterstone permission to attack him.

Tarkyn discovers that the healer's brother, Falling Rain, was exiled twelve years ago for revealing the woodfolk's presence to the king. Some woodfolk wish him to return. Some don't. Struggling with the politics surrounding the prince and the potential damage his own anger could cause, Waterstone almost abandons his friendship with Tarkyn.

Tarkyn offers to help repair the forest, by holding up branches while woodfolk bind them, amazing Waterstone that sorcery has more than martial uses. Stormaway returns and rails at the prince for not behaving in a manner due to his station, until Tarkyn treats him to a dose of royal hauteur. Later that evening, Stormaway informs the prince that the bounty hunters who had captured him were Andoran and Sargon, Tarkyn's erstwhile friends. As Tarkyn wanders down near the river thinking about this further betrayal, an attacking wolf is stopped by Waterstone's arrow. Then, from a viewpoint above him in the trees, Tarkyn sees another wolf approaching behind the woodman. Tarkyn shouts a warning and uses shafts of magic to kill the wolf.

Because Tarkyn's ability to trust has been damaged by betrayal, Waterstone allows Tarkyn free access to his memories to establish his own trustworthiness. However, Tarkyn delves too deep and when Waterstone has fled, finds himself confronted by Autumn Leaves who intervenes angrily on his friend's behalf.

Stormaway lets slip that seven years before, he had used mind power on Falling Rain when the woodman was held captive by the king. This knowledge expiates Falling Rain's guilt and revokes his exile. As reparation for the wrong done by sorcerers, Tarkyn resolves to trek across the mountains to find Falling Rain and bring him back to the fold.

Tarkyn discovers that, unlike the woodfolk, he can also share images and emotions with birds and animals, and uses this discovery as a reason to approach Waterstone and repair the rift between them. As he talks with Waterstone and Autumn Leaves, it becomes increasingly obvious to Tarkyn that the egalitarian woodfolk have a very different concept of service from him and that he must work out how much to modify his expectations.

While he is mulling this over, an eagle shares with him its view over the forest of an impending, large-scale wolf attack. Tarkyn warns the woodfolk and allows them the use of his powers.

Soon after the wolf attack has been averted, Stormaway notices green shoots appearing on Tarkyn's walking staff and upon investigation, finds that the trees Tarkyn helped to repair have recovered unnaturally fast. Much to his embarrassment, Tarkyn learns that his newly discovered powers of healing and communing with animals define him as a legend in the woodfolk lore; the guardian of the forest, who appears among the woodfolk to aid them in times of great strife.

Celebrations of the advent of the Forest Guardian go late into the night but next morning, Tarkyn and the woodfolk come back to the reality of considering where the source of the danger might be. The survival of the woodfolk depends on their ability to stay hidden. They realise that a hunting party will be coming to find the wolves they killed but instead, will find the dismembered, cleaned wolf carcases that will betray the woodfolk's existence.

As they prepare to face this threat, Waterstone's resentment of the oath surges up, leading to a fight between Tarkyn and himself. As a result, one of Tarkyn's broken ribs punctures his lung and only his healing powers as Guardian of the Forest, supplemented by the life force of the woodfolk, save him. Through this experience, Tarkyn discovers that he can also draw on the power of the forest itself through the trees to heal himself.

After helping the woodfolk avoid a hunting party, Tarkyn becomes aware that his group of woodfolk have been concealing the existence of woodfolk who had not sworn the oath. He feels betrayed, especially by Waterstone, and using an owl as a guide, leaves them to find his way to a community of oathless woodfolk.

He offers this community of woodfolk, the forestals, the opportunity to kill him to release their kin from the oath and to ensure that oathbound woodfolk do not have to fight oathless woodfolk to protect him. Despite their initial hostility, the forestals decide it would be dishonourable to help their kin to betray their oath, so they cannot kill the prince. During this confrontation, Tarkyn finds a feisty ally in a rebellious young woodman, Rainstorm.

Autumn Leaves trudges into the forestal's firesite and with Rainstorm's help, faces a resistant Tarkyn. When Autumn Leaves explains that all woodfolk are sworn to conceal their kin, Tarkyn concedes the need for their duplicity, but is left feeling separate from them.

Unwittingly, Tarkyn's resigned acceptance of his isolation rolls around the woodfolk camp, causing the forestals to reconsider their attitude to him. During the following week, woodfolk gather from all parts of the forest to discuss the unknown threat. In recognition of his demonstrated commitment to them, the woodfolk decide to accept Tarkyn as a member of the woodfolk nation in a ceremony during which he becomes Waterstone's blood brother and by association, Ancient Oak's brother and Sparrow's uncle.

Tarkyn's unreserved acceptance by the woodfolk is short lived. As they discuss ways to meet the impending threat, resentment against the prince resurges and the opinions of the group who stayed with him, the 'home guard,' are not respected. Eventually, Tarkyn decides to assert his authority temporarily, but unequivocally, in the interests of protecting the woodfolk in the face of the impending threat, reasoning that he intends to leave the next day anyway so it won't matter if he upsets a few people.

However, when morning breaks, an enormous magic-driven storm threatens to cause widespread flooding and to force the woodfolk onto open higher ground. Tarkyn harnesses the power of the forest to channel magic into Stormaway who orchestrates the dissipation of the storm.

In the wake of Tarkyn's suggestion of a stocktake of people's whereabouts, woodfolk establish that three of their kin are missing and are possibly being held by sorcerers. A power play amongst rival factions leads to decisions being made more on the basis of whether they support Tarkyn rather than on the issues themselves. Tarkyn confronts the worst of the factions and neutralises their antagonism.

Once the course of action had been decided, Tarkyn links his mind with a field mouse to reconnoitre the sorcerer's encampment. The woodfolk are gravely shaken when he discovers that the woodfolk are indeed being held at the encampment and at least some people from outside the forest know of their existence.

With the aid of an eagle owl, Tarkyn spots a shadowy figure skulking in the nearby woods. The woodfolk capture the intruder, who turns out to be Danton, an elite palace guard and Tarkyn's childhood friend. But having been betrayed before, the prince is wary of trusting him. Only after testing Danton's loyalty to the prince, do the woodfolk allow him to stay in the woods with them. But Danton brings the expectations of the Royal Court with him, leading to disputes between several woodfolk and himself, and making Tarkyn re-evaluate his relationships with the woodfolk.

When the prince stops a fight between Danton and Rainstorm, the young woodman turns his attack on Tarkyn. The wind thrashing through the trees makes Tarkyn realise that Rainstorm and the oathless woodfolk have somehow become subject to the sorcerous oath. Despite their friendship with the prince, Rainstorm and Waterstone are horrified when they discover that the oath has spread and it is decided to keep it from the others until after the rescue of the imprisoned woodfolk.

The woodfolk all insist that Tarkyn should not take part in the rescue because they must ensure they protect him. Because Tarkyn was also vowed to protect the forest, he cannot risk them refusing his orders and destroying the forest. So he does not insist on going with them but takes part from a distance.

Danton and Stormaway infiltrate the sorcerers' camp, in preparation for the woodfolk mounting a rescue. They run into Sargon and Andoran, forcing Danton to assume the appearance of disloyalty to Tarkyn to conceal his role in the rescue plot. Once Stormaway is reassured that Danton is merely playing a role, the wizard and Danton concoct a series of unpleasant revenges on Sargon and Andoran, involving hallucinogens, itching powders and slow working non-lethal poisons.

Meanwhile Tarkyn discovers that Waterstone's objections to using horses for the impending raid stems from his fear of them. In the ensuing conversation, Waterstone becomes aware that Tarkyn is distressed by Danton's possible betrayal and the accumulation of people's horrified reactions to the oath. He reassures Tarkyn of his enduring commitment to him, as both friend and brother, and Rainstorm bravely goes swimming in an icy creek with the prince to cheer him up.

Once the campsite has settled for the night, the woodfolk use their deadly hunting skills to knock out the boundary guards and throw the chained woodfolk onto horses, which are being remotely guided by Tarkyn. As the horses carry them safely into the woods, a strong, fear-filled image makes Tarkyn realise that Autumn Leaves has been captured by Andoran and Sargon. Tarkyn translocates into the sorcerer's encampment and rescues him. On his return, angry woodfolk confront him for putting himself at risk but he asserts that he will no longer allow them to dictate to him.

Danton's association with Andoran and Sargon causes Tarkyn and the woodfolk to lose faith in him and take him captive. Danton refuses to defend himself and insists they trust him. When Tarkyn relents, Danton then avers that Tarkyn is the only true hope for the future of Eskuzor, a sentiment that Stormaway reinforces saying:

"Your destiny is written in the stars and lives deep within the trees of the forest.

It has been clear from the day of your birth for all to see who have knowledge of such things. Your father and I always knew. That's why you had to be protected. You are not only the guardian of the forest. You are the one true hope for the future."

Book Two

In the face of Stormaway's avowal, Tarkyn declares he has no wish to be king; to drag Eskuzor into civil war. Stormaway tells him that there are already rumours of civil war brewing between his brothers and that the encampment is a recruiting station for vigilantes wishing to fight the lawlessness created by King Kosar's incompetent rule, funded by Lord Davorad, one of Jarand's cronies.

To the woodfolk's relief, only a few sorcerers have seen the captured woodfolk but one of them is Stormaway's erstwhile apprentice, Journeyman Cloudmaker, now Prince Jarand's wizard. Woodfolk want Tarkyn to protect them against whoever is hunting them; Danton and Stormaway want him to protect sorcerers against his brothers. Tarkyn decides to prioritise finding Falling Rain and protecting the woodfolk before addressing the wider issues of the sorcerers.

Using his powers as forest guardian, Tarkyn tries to heal the rescued woodfolk's mindtalking ability, an effort that goes disastrously wrong; destroying a swathe of forest and nearly killing him before he uses rage-driven power to burn out the infection. Tarkyn repels a squadron of soldiers by sending mental images of attack to their horses and subjugating the leader of the wolf pack that runs with them. But his use of power threatens to distance him from his woodfolk companions and Waterstone accuses him of breaking the wolf's spirit.

Tarkyn wakes despondent about the damage to the forest and at the reactions of the woodfolk to his magic. However, the woodfolk recognise the extreme efforts he made to save the forest and celebrate with him. He discovers Tree Wind's ongoing antagonism stemmed from the fact that she had intended to wed Falling Rain who was exiled as a result of King Markazon discovering the existence of woodfolk. Waterstone takes issue with Danton over the fact that Danton used to report Tarkyn's actions to the king, angering him so much that Danton hits him. Sorcerer protocol demands that Tarkyn preside over a trial for Danton attacking Waterstone, now a member of the royal family. Waterstone is horrified. Tarkyn discovers he is sovereign lord of the forests, according to Stormaway, and as such, is able to commute the usual death penalty for such a crime to a lesser punishment.

As the woodfolk prepare to cross the Great West Road, a family travelling along the road are attacked by brigands. Tarkyn uses his magic to burn the arrows and place a shield around the family to protect them. The family are fearful of him at first, since he has been branded a rogue sorcerer by his brother. At Tarkyn's request, they tie up the brigands and continue on their way as soldiers crest the rise and Tarkyn disappears back into the forest. The soldiers recognise the brigands as fellow soldiers. Stormaway breaks cover and acts as witness that Tarkyn protected the family. He then challenges the King's version of events at the tournament asking how Tarkyn could have won a tournament he was supposed to have destroyed.

Tarkyn realises that Falling Branch is the only one among them who is unknowingly affected by the spread of the sorcerous oath. He sees him privately to tell him, endures his reaction and discovers he is Rainstorm's father. Falling Branch goes off to talk to his woodfolk friends while sending Tarkyn off to talk to Danton. Tarkyn clarifies his expectations of Danton, as a sorcerer living among woodfolk.

When Tarkyn explains the spread of the oath and the concept of mutual obligations to the rest of his home guard, they offer to support him when they encounter the mountainfolk.

They travel across the open grasslands by night, with Tarkyn using his mind link to quieten the guard dogs. When two riders thunder through the night to arrive in haste at a homestead, Danton investigates and sees two young sorcerers lying mortally wounded, surrounded parents and farm hands. Against opposition from the woodfolk, he enlists Tarkyn's assistance. Tarkyn and he enter the sorcerers' house and Tarkyn heals the children amidst a mix of suspicion, because he has been declared a rogue sorcerer, and obeisance, because he is a prince. Lord Tolward tells Tarkyn that lawlessness is rife, that bloodhounds are now being recruited at the encampment and there is talk of a secret army. Tarkyn promises to return to them in the spring and leaves, feeling even more torn between woodfolk and sorcerers.

The mountainfolk appear friendly but drug Tarkyn's companions before tying Tarkyn's hands behind him. In order to check whether the mountainfolk are subject to the sorcerous oath, two thugs hit Takyn but continue to belt him when their blows do not cause damage to the forest, despite Dry Berry's efforts to stop them. Tarkyn sends out a mental scream for help to which firstly a mountain eagle, then other birds of prey respond by fighting off the thugs and keeping the mountainfolk at bay until his home guard recovers. He then orders Danton to kill the two assailants. Remorseful, the mountainfolk offer to take the oath, but Tarkyn says he does not want them as liegefolk and would not to entrust the forest's welfare to their honour. With help from Autumn Leaves and Rainstorm, Tarkyn bathes in an icy stream to clean his bloodied hair and talks to the woodfolk about his decision to execute the thugs.

Danton, Summer Rain and Rainstorm are then taken hostage by the mountainfolk and Tarkyn must use shields and eagles to protect his home guard and coerce the mountainfolk into returning his friends. Eventually, a compromise is reached and the mountain folk swear allegiance to Tarkyn without any sorcerous sting to the oath. However, Tarkyn still does not trust them and is unable to sleep. He gets up in the middle of the night only to find Waterstone and Autumn Leaves keeping watch over him. In the morning Rainstorm tries to teach Danton how to be less lethal with his magic and Thunder Storm demonstrates his mastery with a slingshot by making line of different sized rocks gently sway. Eventually Waterstone helps Tarkyn deal with the intrusive images of the attack so that he can concentrate on healing himself.

Tarkyn joins the target practice and makes the rocks sway by hitting the stump underneath them. The mountainfolk take Tarkyn and a few friends for a tour of their cellars. In the caves, they find a little neglected boy who is despised by the mountainfolk. The Mountainman, Blizzard, holds the boy down by putting his foot on his chest and does not release him at Tarkyn's request. Tarkyn bellows at Blizzard who explains that he thought he was supposed to protect the prince. Tarkyn takes the tatty little boy, Midnight, under his wing and Midnight swears allegiance to him. Midnight is deaf and mute but can exchange images and emotions only with Tarkyn. Midnight is mistrustful of people, continually tests Tarkyn's commitment and is ready to run at the slightest provocation.

Word comes through that bloodhounds are tracking Tarkyn from the encampment and his tracks will lead them to Lord Tolward's house and then to the mountainfolk camp. After various suggestions and tensions, Tarkyn agrees to contact the lead wolf, only if Waterstone is linked in to check that he doesn't damage the wolf's spirit.

The woodfolk cover their tracks, travel south and spend the night high in trees. Tarkyn has trouble sleeping until Waterstone ties him to the trunk. Midnight realises he has left a bracelet he made for Tarkyn in the clearing and rushes back to find it, with the hunting party less than an hour away. Tarkyn and Danton translocate to the clearing, find Midnight and ensconce him high in a tree before outfacing the hunting party using Tarkyn's ability to fire through his own shield as he clings to Danton's back in mid-air. Journeyman Cloudmaker, the hunting party's leader, realizes that Tarkyn is not a rogue sorcerer and says "This changes everything," but does not explain why. Midnight is so upset that he refuses to come out of the tree. So Tarkyn levitates to grab Midnight from behind and carries him safely to the ground.

Tarkyn, Danton and a few woodfolk find shelter from a storm in a shallow cave. They decide to operate on Autumn Leaves' injured nose but when Thunder Storm uses his slingshot to knock him out, Midnight attacks him, thinking he is trying to hurt Autumn Leaves. When Midnight realises his mistake, he cowers into the corner clearly waiting to be beaten. Thunder Storm reassures him while Summer Rain and Tarkyn continue the operation on Autumn Leaves' nose. They debate whether there might be some sort of evil loose among the mountainfolk for someone to have mistreated Midnight so badly.

The woodfolk flick into hiding, instructing Tarkyn and Danto to raise their shields as two scruffy old trappers enter the cave. String and Bean are laconic, clever and love guessing games. Because Tarkyn uses the word 'firesite' and is dressed in woodfolk garb, they know that Tarkyn knows about woodfolk. So they eventually admit that they do too. Three woodfolk return to speak to them. When Midnight returns with some others, he does a double take and greets the trappers effusively. Bean tells them that Midnight's mother Hail was caught in a landslide eight years ago and Pipeless, a wizard, rescued her. He felt in love with her but, frustrated by her not returning his affection, raped her. When String and Bean rescued her, she threw a knife at Pipeless, fatally wounding him. As the wizard died, he muttered an incantation that Bean carefully remembered. Hail always hated Midnight and was frustrated because he couldn't hear. Since she wouldn't allow String and Bean to adopt him, they talked her into giving Midnight to the mountainfolk but they too neglected him. String and Bean were the only people he ever saw who were kind to him.

After a mental debate with all other woodfolk, a faction wants to kill Midnight saying he is an abomination. Tarkyn says they are under oath and must protect Midnight. The woodfolk then agree to allow the trappers to live, as long as they reside with them for six months as surety.

Stormaway returns and explains that his care for Tarkyn comes before his care for Eskuzor. Meanwhile Waterstone and Danton lead a group of woodfolk in tracking down two members of the hunting party who are sneaking through the woods looking for Tarkyn. When they are captured, Tarkyn is not pleased that he was not informed of the threat earlier. He sends Journeyman's sorcerers on their two day journey back to the encampment on foot, with their hands tied behind them, but exacts no other punishment.

Midnight is missing. Stormaway says that Pipeless' last words are a curse: Midnight will breed resentment in his mother's people and this resentment will slowly corrupt them all. He leaves to consult his books, admonishing them not to interfere without his direction. Tarkyn is worried that Midnight's death may be needed to release the curse. A mental cry for help is received from Blizzard. When they arrive, they find an unconscious Midnight tied to a sapling with half the mountainfolk trying to attack him and the other half trying to prevent them from attacking. Hail arrives then verbally and mentally abuses the crowd. A brawl breaks out but Tarkyn merely stands watching them with arms crossed. Gradually they settle, stand straighter and look towards Tarkyn who has been sending waves of faith in their integrity. Tarkyn immobilises Hail who blocks his way with knives. He uses his power to heal Midnight, who vomits all over him as he regains consciousness. Stormaway says if Tarkyn had rescued Midnight, it would have further undermined the mountainfolk's belief in their integrity but now they are temporarily better able to fight the curse. He adds that if Midnight had died, the curse would have been irreversible and eventually all woodfolk would become corrupted by the curse. The curse can only be lifted in the place it was created by the curser or his direct descendant, Midnight.

High on the mountain, Hail and all her kin, the mountainfolk and woodfolk trappers, gather to have the curse lifted. Tarkyn must ask Midnight, with no compulsion, to help the mountainfolk who have reviled and maltreated him all his life. Midnight misunderstands and thinks that Tarkyn has faith in the mountainfolk and therefore not in him. He runs off and it takes the combined efforts of Tarkyn and Ancient Oak to resettle him. Midnight refuses to help but when, true to his word, Tarkyn remains his friend, he changes his mind and agrees to assist.

Stormaway realises that although Midnight can lift the curse from the mountainfolk, he first must be free of the curse. However, he cannot lift the curse from himself. They need Pipeless who is dead, to do that. Stormaway tells them that a forest guardian once drew the parts of a dead person back into one place and resurrected that person but many onlookers were killed. Tarkyn is horrified and fearful at the prospect but agrees to try, provided there are precautions.

With everyone else safely within Stormaway and Danton's shields, Tarkyn reaches his power deep into the forest and draws together the remains of Pipeless. He thrusts his hands before him and Pipeless, ten feet tall because he is not fully concentrated into one spot, towers above him and still as angry as he was at the moment of his death, sends forth a destructive power ray. Tarkyn just manages to raise his shield in time then demands that Pipeless acknowledge his authority as prince. Pipeless, bewildered by the sudden change in his circumstances, calms down and rues having created the curse. He meets Midnight, his son, and raises the curse from him. Then Midnight sends forth all his memories of his treatment by the mountainfolk and, as a cloud of Pipeless's blue magic swirls over the mountainfolk, the warped memories are challenged and dispelled. Just before he dissipates back into the earth, Pipeless says that it was too soon for Hail and him. Then, glancing at Lapping Water, the nearest woodwoman, he suggests that Tarkyn may do do better in the future.

A wild wind swirls up the valley and the earth reverberates as the Mountainfolk's oath is tied to the welfare of the forest. Tarkyn waits tensely for their reaction but their gratitude overrides any resentment.

Next morning, Midnight emerges to find an array of special foods, especially laid out for him by the mountainfolk, and each of them pats or touches him to welcome him back into the fold. He then plays with the other children using his magical shield. Sparrow discovers that now the curse is no longer isolating him, he can use mind images, although still no words, to communicate with her.

Ancient Oak talks to Tarkyn and Rainstorm talks to Lapping Water, as part of an ongoing plan to get Lapping Water and Tarkyn together. They also remonstrate with Tarkyn about being too controlling when Waterstone and Danton had overseen the hunt for Journeyman's sorcerers.

Meanwhile Danton tells the woodfolk that he had served as Tarkyn's whipping boy from the age of eight and that Tarkyn, as a six year old had become distraught whenever Danton was punished, forcing members of the Royal Family to be summoned to override him. Eventually, on an occasion that King Markazon had been summoned, Tarkyn threw up his shield and cut his arm until the king ordered the flogging stopped, earning Danton's lifelong devotion.

When Tarkyn joins the others, he has to apologize all over again and walks off, annoyed. Because he is still very tired, he stumbles over a small cliff and knocks himself out. He follows a silver fox who leads him down the mountain to a group of sorcererswho are escaping from Jarand's press gangs. To Tarkyn's surprise they are honoured, rather than frightened, to meet him and he discovers that Stormaway's machinations have turned public opinion in Tarkyn's favour. However, Tarkyn makes it clear that he does not wish to become king.

With the help of a crow, his woodfolk find him. Tarkyn writes a letter of introduction for Trey and his family to go to Lord Tolward before he leaves them. A celebration for his efforts with Pipeless await Tarkyn on his return.

Waterstone asks Tarkyn why he doubted Danton's loyalty after having saved him from being a whipping boy when he was little. Tarkyn can't see why Danton should be grateful for facing only consequences for his own actions like everyone else. He adds that when they were older, their first loyalties was to the king. So when the king turned on Tarkyn, he couldn't assume where Danton's loyalties lay. Remembering how much Danton loved the glitter of court, he revokes his requirement that Danton wear woodfolk garb. Danton is moved by his acknowledgement but does not revert to his own clothes

At the end of the evening, Midnight comes to sit on his lap, sad that his mother has still avoided him even after the lifting of the curse. He tries to get away to lick his wounds in private but Tarkyn holds him close even while he thrashes about, kicking and punching, in his distress. When he has settled, Tarkyn sends out a query about Hail's whereabouts. Just as he is discussing it with woodfolk trappers, he receives a strong feeling of desperation and determination; Hail is at the edge of a nearby cliff about to throw herself off. Tarkyn sends her a command to wait before running with several others to try to stop her.

As they come into sight, she lets herself drop off the cliff but Tarkyn sends out a shaft of magic and pulls her back onto safe ground. Between them, they talk Hail into living with how she had treated Midnight under the curse.

Next day, as they continue their journey across the mountain, Waterstone is angry, thinking that Tarkyn risked the woodfolk and forests by commanding Hail when she was so emotionally unstable. Tarkyn reminds Waterstone that he refused one of Tarkyn's commands with a minimal consequence of wind through the trees. However, Tarkyn points out that nearby trees are turning mouldy because everyone has been doubting Tarkyn's competence behind his back.

Realizing that Stormaway lied when he said that he would refuse a direct order to defuse the oath, Tarkyn quietly commands the wizard to retract the sorcery in the oath. Stormaway bows and obeys. He had promised Markazon to maintain the sorcery in the oath but had failed to mention that this was only until directly ordered to release it by Tarkyn.

The woodfolk are so relieved their forest are now safe, many are in tears. Ancient Oak pulls Tarkyn into the family celebratory hug and reconciles him with Waterstone. Tarkyn remonstrates with woodfolk for talking about dissatisfaction behind his back instead of to his face. They tell him, not unkindly, that he is irritable, autocratic and intimidating so that they hesitate to bring issues up with him. Hail stands up for him saying she is grateful that he is so interfering.

Looking out over the plains to the distant walled city of Montraya, Jarand's seat, Danton betrays his disdain after he has had to explain to

Rainstorm what a ball is. Danton is surprised Rainstorm isn't offended but the woodman says that disdain and amusement are both ways of reacting to seeing another person's culture through their own values, which makes Danton realise that he has underestimated Rainstorm.

As they descend the mountain, snow starts to fall. String and Bean lead Tarkyn's home guard, which is double the size it was at the beginning, to a cave on the lower plateau. The trappers express concern that a mountain lion has been in the cave recently.

Suddenly a deep throated roar and two streaks of gold resolve themselves into a huge mountain leaping at the children playing in the back of the cave. Midnight throws his dark green shield over the children and himself and backs away from the lion until Tarkyn places his shield over the lion. While the other children run crying to their parents, Midnight walks quietly over to Tarkyn who realizes the little boy is shaking with fright.

Tarkyn uses his forest guardian powers to create a standoff with the mountain lion but rather than subjugating it, he uses images of wolves to show that his woodfolk are lethal to mountain lions in a pack, just as wolves are.

They discuss how to locate and talk to Falling Rain, knowing that Falling Rain will not reveal himself to any of sorcerers because of the woodfolk's bond of secrecy and won't reveal himself to any of woodfolk because he has been exiled. Ancient Oak and Rainstorm have manoeuvred Tarkyn and Lapping Water to sit next to each other but Tarkyn and Lapping Water are both assiduously trying to act casually.

The home guard work out that Falling Rain will have to be in an area that is inhospitable for sorcerers. String and Bean think of the swamp. With the search area specific, Running Feet guides Tarkyn until he connects with an egret to look for Falling Rain. At first the bird is protective of Falling Rain but eventually takes Tarkyn on a mind journey to Falling Rain's hideout halfway up a tree in the middle of the swamp.

The woodfolk travel the rest of the way down the mountain and set up camp on the banks of the lake, less than a mile from Falling Rain's hideout. Summer Rain climbs onto Stormaway's back, Tree Wind onto Danton's and Waterstone onto Tarkyn's. They levitate their way through the swamp. As a warning, an egret flies straight at Tarkyn's head, rising just high enough to miss him, at the last minute.

As they come into Falling Rain's view, Tarkyn uses his *Shturrum* spell to immobilize the exiled woodman before dropping Waterstone off next to him and then retreating to sit among the egrets in a nearby tree. Once Summer Rain and Running Feet have been dropped off too, Tarkyn replaces the *Shturrum* spell with his shield, which prevents

Falling Rain from flicking into hiding. Once Falling Rain is reconciled to them, the four woodfolk head off through the trees to explore Falling Rain's domain.

The sorcerers are left behind and eddies of discontent and the odd ripple of anger. whirl through these flooded forests, signalling that Tarkyn is offended at not being introduced. The woodfolk return and once they have repaired their omission, Tarkyn unbends and feeds Falling Rain's pet egret mentally asking her to accompany Falling Rain when they leave.

Falling Rain is shocked by the changes of twelve years. In a confrontation with Stormaway, it becomes clear that other sorcerers knew of Falling Rain's presence when he was held captive by King Markazon. Falling Rain only agrees to share his memories with Tarkyn so that he can identify these other sorcerers, on the condition that Tarkyn share painful memories with him. Amid protests from his woodfolk, Tarkyn agrees.

Falling Rain and Tarkyn engage in a furious mind duel, during which Falling Rain realizes that Tarkyn is not like his father King Markazon. Tarkyn shows Falling Rain the scene after young Tarkyn stood up to his father to stop Danton being flogged: Markazon hugs Tarkyn as he cries himself out, then says, "You are the best of us but you will suffer for it. And in the end, you must be the one to bring hope to our nation and save us from ourselves."

To everyone's amazement, Falling Rain and Tarkyn return as friends. The woodfolk are horrified to learn that it was Kosar, Jarand and Journeyman who had discovered Falling Rain's existence, and thus the existence of woodfolk and the oath. Having experienced Tarkyn's memories, Falling Rain tells them that Tarkyn will not be able to stand by and watch sorcerers suffer under Kosar's reign. The woodfolk agree that he has earned their support to help sorcerers.

Part 1: The First Encounter

CHAPTER 1

The little grey-robed wizard skittered across the polished floorboards on his knees, propelled by the boot of a heavy guardsman. He came to a halt, discomforted and irascible, at the feet of a strongly built man in his mid-twenties dressed in finely embroidered dark red robes, seated on a carved wooden chair with the arms of the Tamadil line emblazoned on its back rest.

Prince Jarand raised an eyebrow as he stared down at the dishevelled wizard, "I believe you have something of interest to report?"

"Yes, Your Highness, although I would have been quite capable of presenting myself to you without the assistance of that oaf." Without presuming to raise his head, the wizard sent a poisonous look over his shoulder at the guard, who was now standing imperviously at the door.

"Perhaps it was your reticence in coming forward with this information that misled him into thinking you unwilling." The Prince was gently tapping his finger on the arm of the chair, making the wizard nervous.

The wizard shifted his position slightly on the floor to ease his sore knees. "Your Highness, I did not realise that my observations would be of interest to you…and to tell you the truth, even if I had, I would not have known how to gain access to you. It is a great honour for me to meet you and I am more than willing to speak with you."

Jarand waved a lazy hand at the guard, "You may leave us, Gorval." When the guard hesitated, the prince's voice sharpened, "I am sure this wizard you have brought me is aware that his life is forfeit, should he make any move on my person. Now leave us."

The guard bowed and withdrew, closing the great carved doors behind him. The dull thud reverberated into silence as the prince was left alone in the huge reception hall with the wizard at his feet. After a few moments, Jarand said quietly, "You may rise." When the wizard was standing before him, he waved at a nearby chair, "Please be seated. I can see the hard floor is causing your knees some discomfort."

The wizard picked himself up, brushed off the front of his long grey robes and backed onto the chair, keeping his eyes trained on the prince. "Thank you, Your Highness."

"And you rejoice in the name of Greyskies Swampwatcher, I believe?" asked the prince, the faintest of derisory smiles lifting one side of his mouth.

The little wizard nodded his head, "Indeed, Your Highness."

"So. Tell me of this strange sight you thought so unnoteworthy."

"Oh, it was not unnoteworthy, but I didn't think that it would interest the likes of you who have travelled so broadly, Sire." As the prince began to lose patience, Greyskies hurried on, "I saw three sorcerers gliding between the trees in the swamp, quite high up. And each of them was carrying another sorcerer on their back."

The prince raised his eyebrows. "Really? And are you sure they were sorcerers?"

The wizard looked confused, "What else could they be? Actually, now you mention, I think one of them may have been a wizard – hard to tell without talking to them."

"And how close to you were they?"

Greyskies tilted his head to one side as he considered, "At least a hundred yards away. I really only caught a glimpse of them deep within the swamp. I was wading around in the shallows collecting some particular herbs that can only be found there. Normally, I stay on dry ground - too many nasties in those waters – but now and again I risk it."

"So, do you think these people are living within this swamp of yours?"

Greyskies coughed to clear his dry throat, "I wouldn't think so. Too many insects. Nowhere to live except in trees and I would have expected to spot them from time to time if there were a number of people living there."

"Hmm. I see you have thought this through."

Greyskies coughed again, "Plenty of time for thought in your cells, Your Highness. Nothing else to do."

The prince stared at him for an unnerving moment before saying mildly, "You may help yourself to a drink, Greyskies. I will have one too." He waved at a small table to the side that bore a large cut crystal jug of water, several glasses and an array of fruits and small, exquisitely decorated cakes.

The wizard bobbed his head, "Thank you, Sire." As he poured the water Greyskies, who had not been given anything to eat or drink since he had been dragged in just before midnight, looked longingly at the food but kept carefully away from it. Once he had handed the prince his glass and sat down, he gulped his water in one draught. "Ah, that's better," he sighed, wiping his mouth with the back of his hand. "Thank you." He glanced uncertainly at the empty glass in his hand, wondering what to do with it.

The prince raised his eyebrows, "Would you like another glassful?"

Greyskies hesitated as he considered whether he risked overstepping the prince's goodwill by accepting.

Correctly interpreting his hesitation, Jarand said, "I would not have asked you, had I not wanted you to have it. You may take another." As the wizard reached the table again, he added, "And you may bring me that platter of cakes. I believe I am a little hungry."

Looking resolutely ahead, Greyskies offered the heavy platter to the prince. Jarand took his time choosing before waving the wizard away. Just as the wizard was about to return with his water to sit down, Jarand said, "You may choose something for yourself also, Master Greyskies."

Despite the prince's apparent courtesy, Greyskies could not help feeling that he was being toyed with. He sat nibbling on his cake, keeping his eyes warily on the prince. For a few minutes, Jarand seemed to have forgotten him but as soon as the wizard dropped his guard and addressed himself more fully to his cake, he looked up to find the prince's grey eyes studying him. He jumped with fright and crumbs of cake bounced onto the floor.

"I beg your pardon, Your Highness," mumbled the wizard through a mouthful, "I did not mean to keep you waiting."

Surprisingly, the prince smiled, "Don't panic, Greyskies. I am not going to eat you. When you are ready, you may tell me how these men were dressed."

Deciding to take the prince at his word, Greyskies finished off the last mouthful of cake, drank the rest of his water and stood up to brush himself down. Then he sent a trickle of grey magic to place his glass and the prince's empty glass on the table. Once everything was back in place, he sat down again and answered, feeling much more at ease now that he was no longer so hungry, "That is an interesting question, my lord. Five out of the six of them were dressed in similar clothing. The sixth wore green robes. He was the one I thought might be a wizard."

"Interesting. So they were wearing uniforms, were they?"

The wizard shook his head. "No, sire. I would not describe them as uniforms. They were wearing light brown shirts and leggings. They were not tailored as uniforms are. More like the sort of clothing worn by farmhands but not quite."

"I see. That is very interesting indeed."

"Is it, Your Highness?" As the princes eyebrows snapped together, Greyskies realised he had been over-familiar. "I b-beg your pardon. I should not have asked that." The wizard noticed with some irritation that he was trembling.

After subjecting the wizard to a few seconds of silent scrutiny, the prince continued, "And do you remember anything else about these men?"

Greyskies swallowed, "They were a good distance away but I think at least one of them may have been a woman, sir."

"What? Dressed in leggings?"

"Possibly, sir. I could have been mistaken."

"Hmph. Anything else? Could you see their eyes, hair colour, size?"

Greyskies shook his head dubiously, "Not really sir. Certainly not eyes at that distance." He frowned as he tried to remember, "Most of them seemed to have brownish coloured hair. One of them had hair that looked a bit lighter but it was hard to tell amongst the shadows. And one definitely had black hair." The wizard shrugged. "That's about it, I think. I couldn't tell how tall they were. I only caught a glimpse of them between the trees.

The prince leaned forward, suddenly intent, "So when did you see the people?"

"Towards evening, yesterday."

Suddenly the prince's hand slammed down on the arm of his chair, making the wizard jump in fright.

"Blast it! Why am I surrounded by incompetents? Why did they not bring you to see me last night? Now we have lost precious hours." Jarand pulled a cord at his side that brought guards running into the room. "Gorval, tell Captain Harkell to prepare eighty men to be ready to leave within the hour, armed and provisioned for several nights away. Find a horse for our wizard friend here and have Storm saddled and ready for me at the front gates in one hour."

The guard bowed with his hand over his heart, "Your will is my command, Your Highness."

Without even acknowledging the guard's response, the prince turned to the wizard and snapped, "You will be coming with us to guide us and give us your local knowledge. I am appointing you as my personal wizard until Journeyman returns."

The wizard stood and bowed, "Thank you, my lord. It would be an honour." In actual fact, the last thing he wanted was to have his peaceful, generally solitary lifestyle disrupted but he bowed to the inevitable with the best grace he could muster, aware that any hesitation on his part would be foolhardy.

Chapter 2

By mid-afternoon, the column of soldiers headed by Prince Jarand, Captain Harkell and the little wizard had reached the edge of the forest. After a brief consultation, the column turned to the right and travelled parallel to the base of the mountains until it reached the point where the forest edge swung around to the right, away from the foothills.

At a nod from Jarand, Captain Harkell raised his hand and brought his men to a halt. The captain swivelled in his saddle to address the wizard. He noted with wry amusement that the wizard was looking even more dishevelled than when they set out.

"Not used to horses?" he asked with some sympathy.

Greyskies drew himself up. "No sir, I am not. And I made the reverse journey late last night with my hands tied to the pommel. My legs are killing me."

The captain flicked a warning glance in the direction of the prince, "But no doubt you feel honoured to be able to serve your prince?"

"Of course I do," grumbled the wizard. "But it doesn't stop my legs from hurting."

"A twenty minute break, I think," said the prince, "while Grumble Guts here advises on the terrain and our next move."

"Dismount," ordered the captain, springing lightly from his horse.

Before the suffering little wizard had time to lift his leg over his horse's back, the captain was at his side taking most of his weight as he more or less fell out of the saddle. When he hit the ground, the wizard's legs crumpled beneath him but the captain's strong arms held him until he had recovered himself.

Greyskies huffed, "Thank you, Captain. That was most kind of you. It would have done my dignity no good at all to have landed in a heap in front of your men."

The captain gave a friendly laugh, "All of us know what it feels like to be stiff after a long ride, and for someone who has never ridden, you have done a lot of hours in a short time."

"When you are ready, wizard," said the prince dryly, "perhaps you can spare us some time to explain where you saw these people and in which direction they were heading."

"I beg your pardon, Your Highness." Greyskies took a swig from his waterbag before sweeping his arm around from straight in front of him to the right. "The swamp is in that general direction, following the line of the Montraya River south for the first five miles or so. If we enter the forest here, we will come to the edge of the swamp in another three or four miles. There are only narrow tracks through this part of the forest. Not many people live near the swamp. There is a wider road that leads to the lake at the foot of the mountains where the river has its source," he indicated slightly to his left, "but the people I saw were travelling away from the mountain."

"And where did you see these people?"

"More or less straight in from here, perhaps a little to our right."

The prince turned to Captain Harkell. "So is it reasonable to assume that they would continue in that direction?"

"Failing any other sightings or information, yes. I don't know what manner of people you are hunting, my lord, but do you have any idea where they might be heading, and whether they would wish to remain concealed in the forest or break out into the open?"

The prince's grey eyes narrowed. "As you so rightly assume, the nature of these people is none of your business. In answer to your questions, I do not know their intentions or where they are heading but I would like to find out. However, unless they had a particular reason for doing otherwise, I would expect them to stay within the bounds of the forest." He turned to the wizard, "Does the forest extend further south beyond the end of the swamp?"

"Yes, Your Highness. The swamp finishes where the river cascades through rapids into a steep, narrow, heavily wooded valley that continues for another couple of miles. Although there are farmlands on either side, the valley itself is too steep to sustain any type of agriculture. After that, the river spreads out, and there are farmlands right up to its banks."

"Thank you, Greyskies. Your knowledge of the area is very comprehensive."

The wizard flushed with pleasure and bowed. "A pleasure, Your Highness."

"So, do you have any idea what might lie at their journey's end if they continued in that direction?"

Greyskies' brows crinkled in effort but after a few moments, he shook his head regretfully. "No, Sire. I do not know enough about what lies deep within the swamp and I can think of nothing remarkable in the surrounding bushlands."

After several minutes of silence, during which the prince thought through possibilities, Jarand galvanised into action, "Right. Can we cross this river at any point?"

"Only by skirting around the lake at its source or by ferry which is at least... hmm… sixteen miles south of here. And there is, of course the bridge right back at Montraya."

"Then we shall travel to this lake, send half the men around to the other side and keep half on this side. Then we will travel along both edges of the swamp towards the south and hopefully trap them within the swamp or in the bottleneck of the steep valley. Captain, I want you to ask through the ranks for any sorcerers who are adept at levitation and bring them to the front. Clear? We leave in fifteen minutes."

Prince Jarand's decision directed his troop straight towards the woodfolk's firesite near the lake.

Chapter 3

After careful discussion, the woodfolk had decided that the return trip up the exposed part of the mountain's slope should be undertaken after nightfall. It would be easier to keep one's footing travelling back up the mountain and quite possible to do so in the dark. And even though everyone was anxious to put more distance between themselves and the sorcerers in the nearby farmlands, they decided it was better to travel under cover of darkness. So as Jarand's troops approached, they were still sitting around the firesite, discussing the upshot of Falling Rain's memories.

"Now that's another strange thing," mused Danton "Do you remember when Tarkyn and I faced off that hunting party? And Journeyman said, 'That changes everything'?"

Tarkyn stared at Danton, "Oh, I see. I've just realised. Not only did he know about the oath, he and the twins really did think I was a rogue sorcerer before that, didn't they?"

Danton shrugged, "Possibly, unless Kosar and Jarand didn't tell Journeyman everything. After all, from what you've told me, your brothers left the Great Hall a long time before the end. They wouldn't have known for sure, one way or the other. For all they knew, you could have caused all that destruction in an ungoverned fit of rage."

Tarkyn turned impulsively to Falling Rain, "I didn't though, did I? You saw my memory."

Falling Rain shook his head, "No, you didn't."

Tarkyn ran his hand through his long hair, "But it was my unruly emotions that made the shield reflective. So I and my emotions did cause all that destruction."

"Settle down, Tarkyn," said Waterstone gently. "We have all seen your shield become reflective. It is not an act of aggression. If no one attacks you, nothing happens at all."

"Anyway," said Danton, "the point is that Journeyman now knows that you are not a rogue sorcerer and that therefore the oath will have been invoked."

"So where does that leave us then?" asked Autumn Leaves. "From what I understand of sorcerer politics, Journeyman may not tell both brothers. So possibly only one will find out that Tarkyn has become the woodfolk's liege."

"And that one brother is probably, but not necessarily, Jarand," said Danton thoughtfully. "After all, the wizard could be ostensibly working for one, while actually working for the other or he could be working for both."

"Or he might just keep that information to himself for his own advantage," put in Stormaway.

Falling Rain boggled, "I see what you mean about sorcerers' manoeuvrings. How do you know you can trust this lot then?" He asked Tarkyn, waggling his thumb at all four sorcerers.

Tarkyn laughed, "String and Bean are not interested in politics. Poor Danton has had to prove himself over and over again. And Stormaway… well, he couldn't lie straight in bed. So I know I can't trust him unless I give him a direct order."

"You do realise," said Stormaway, ignoring this little gambit, "that from Kosar's point of view, now that he has alienated you, these forests are effectively a foreign country under foreign rule, right in the middle of his kingdom?"

"And they're a good size, aren't they?" mused String. "What do you reckon, Bean? I'd say they account for a good third of the kingdom, maybe more."

"Ooh, at least that much, String." Bean turned to look at Tarkyn. "I'd say you've got yourself a bit of a problem here, Your Highness. I may know nothing about politics but I can tell you right now; if I were a king, I wouldn't want a foreign country sitting in the middle of my kingdom."

String scratched his head. "No. I'd be taking it over, quick as a flash."

Tarkyn's face tightened, "If I had meekly accepted imprisonment, I would never have been seen again… and the sovereignty of the forest would have reverted to Kosar." He looked at Stormaway, "Is that right?"

"Only your death can release the sovereignty of the woodlands." The wizard shrugged, "But that can easily be arranged in prison, should the need arise. So, I would say you're probably right."

"And so, Tarkyn," said Waterstone firmly, "as I have always said, your safety is paramount to all of us. We don't want King Kosar hunting us down to rule us."

"But if they know of you, I'm afraid String is right. They will do just that, whether I am here or not," Tarkyn looked at Stormaway, "Your plans have gone sadly awry, Stormaway. Instead of providing me with a safe haven, you may have made these forests and the woodfolk within them a target for both brothers' ambitions, particularly if they now know that I am safely ensconced here as sovereign."

"I admit it is not ideal, Your Highness." Ignoring Rainstorm's look of derision, Stormaway bowed his head, "I apologise, sire. King Markazon and I did the best we could under the circumstances but alas, we did not know that others had seen Falling Rain while he was in my chambers."

Tarkyn waved his hand dismissively, "It can't be helped, Stormaway. I know you did not intend any of this" His brow crinkled, "Hmm… Something is nagging at the back of my mind about all this. Where could I have heard something that has a bearing on it?…" Suddenly Tarkyn sat bolt upright. "Oh no! I know what it was. Lord Tolward told me there were rumours of a secret army that the people at the encampment were planning to enlist to their cause."

"Oh no! That's us, isn't it?" exclaimed Lapping Water. "They are hunting us to make us fight for them."

"Us, an army? How exciting!" Rainstorm's eyes shone. He was immediately beset on all sides with strictures to stop being silly and to be quiet.

When the fuss had died down, Tarkyn said quietly, "Rainstorm, that was one of your less well judged remarks. Even with my powers, I would not be able to heal enough casualties quickly enough after a battle to save everyone. Most would die or live the rest of their lives maimed. I know that, under the oath, I could ask you all to fight for me but I would not do it, at least not in open combat. And we must make sure that no one else is ever in the position to force you into fighting on their behalf."

Danton poured two cups of tea and brought one over to the prince, "That was why Journeyman wanted to be able to contact you, wasn't it? He, and presumably Jarand, want to enlist you and the woodfolk to their cause against Kosar."

Tarkyn gave a grunt of laughter, "Optimistic, to say the least. Jarand conspires to throw me into prison and then hopes to enlist my help less than two months later."

"He may be hoping to have something or someone with which to force your hand," said Danton gently.

Two miles away, deep within the swamp, three egrets flew in to perch among their colony. Suddenly there was mayhem as the entire flock took to the air, calling to one another as they circled each other and swooped in and around the trees before resettling in their original position. Moments later, back at the firesite, Falling Rain's egret launched herself upward, locking Tarkyn's mind into hers as she climbed.

The conversation continued undiminished as, for several minutes, no one realised that Tarkyn had fallen silent.

As Elsie rose over the treeline, a cloud of dust came into view. Then, as she flew towards it, Jarand's column of soldiers appeared in the distance.

She soared above them before, at Tarkyn's request, gliding in lower over the front of the column.

As Tarkyn recognised his brother, a wave of fear and hatred rippled out into the people around him at the firesite. The conversation stopped and Waterstone put a hand on Tarkyn's knee, sending a query into his mind. In response, Tarkyn managed to link Waterstone to the egret's images. Elsie flew in a wide circle above the column of soldiers, giving Waterstone a clear view of every angle, before heading back into the forest and cutting the connection.

Of the people in the column, only the little wizard noticed the flight of the egret. He thought her flight pattern unorthodox and watched her until she disappeared behind the trees. But knowing nothing of Tarkyn's ability to connect with animals, he forbore to mention something that seemed unlikely to be relevant.

"What was that all about?" asked Autumn Leaves.

"Waterstone, you share the image with the woodfolk while I tell the sorcerers," suggested Tarkyn.

As soon as the danger was understood, everyone sprang into action, ready to disappear. But Falling Rain didn't move, saying, "I know you are intent on avoiding these soldiers, but we have just said we will help Tarkyn to resolve the situation among the sorcerers. Perhaps we should take this opportunity to learn more about Jarand's knowledge and intentions."

Everyone stopped dead in their tracks and stared at him. Then they transferred their gazes to Tarkyn who shrugged, "Well, he does have a point but do we have long enough to plan? We need to sort out who can see Jarand, what they are permitted to tell him, how we are going to isolate him…"

"I would say we have about forty minutes, at the outside," answered Waterstone decisively. "We only need another couple of minutes to dismantle the firesite and flick into hiding but you sorcerers will need a lot longer to disappear."

"I can always spook the horses if we need a bit longer," offered Tarkyn.

After a short mental conference, most woodfolk continued to clear up while a few gathered around to work out a plan.

"First question; are we willing to do something like knocking out soldiers that will alert them to our presence and to the fact that we are working with Tarkyn?" asked Tree Wind.

"Second question; who will confront Jarand? Don't forget, Tarkyn can't lie to save himself. So he may be a bit of a liability in that situation," pointed out Autumn Leaves.

"Do we want to keep the presence of the other sorcerers secret so we can use them later in different situations?" asked Summer Rain.

"How are we going to get Tarkyn and the rest of the sorcerers away afterwards if we don't knock out all the soldiers?" asked Lapping Water.

Waterstone looked wryly at Tarkyn, "I think you may have to spook the horses. This is going to take a while."

Tarkyn smiled, "Let's give ourselves ten minutes. Then I will intervene if we look as though we may need longer." Once this was agreed, he continued, "Let's get it straight in our heads; What does Jarand definitely already know?"

Falling Rain answered, "He has definitely seen a woodman before; to be exact, me."

"He will know by now that Tarkyn is not a rogue sorcerer because Journeyman and those hunters we allowed to return unharmed, will be back at the encampment by now," added Danton.

"He will know that a groundswell of support is running through the land because, according to Trey and the sorcerer family that Tarkyn met when he fell from the path, everyone is talking about Tarkyn having been set up by his brothers," said Stormaway with some satisfaction.

"Hmm, that's bad not good, I think," mused Tarkyn. "Competition brings out the worst in my brothers."

"He knows Stormaway is involved with Tarkyn because he saw Falling Rain in Stormaway's rooms," said Tree Wind.

"Not necessarily," Rainstorm pointed out. "He may not have overheard anything about the proposed oath. Possibly only Journeyman knows that. But Jarand is aware that Stormaway knows about woodfolk."

Danton glanced at Waterstone, "And if he has heard about my sudden disappearance from the encampment on the night we rescued Golden Toad and his family, then he will guess that I am involved with woodfolk, assuming he knew that Golden Toad and his family were being held captive in the first place."

"Jarand must know about Golden Toad," Stormaway was firm, "Journeyman could not afford to take the enormous risk of secretly imprisoning people within Jarand's encampment for an extended period of time and not tell the man himself."

"So String and Bean are the only two sorcerers he could come across, without connecting them with Tarkyn," concluded Tree Wind.

"But if we use them that would mean that from here on, we would have no one without a known connection to Tarkyn, which is less than desirable in my opinion," said Stormaway. "We need to keep an ace up our sleeves for a more urgent situation."

"So, if he saw Stormaway or Danton, would he try to arrest them?" asked Rainstorm.

"Almost certainly, I would say," answered Tarkyn. "Now that they are known associates of mine. To lead him to me, if for nothing else."

There was a short silence while everyone mulled over the significance of their information.

Then Tarkyn looked around the group with a slight smile, "Do you know what I would like? I won't insist on it but I would like to meet my brother face to face."

"On your own?" asked Waterstone, carefully controlling his initial adverse reaction.

"Ideally. If I have someone with me, then he would need someone with him not to feel intimidated. Then we couldn't ask him what he knows about Falling Rain." Encouraged by the fact that the woodfolk had not yet jumped down his throat, he continued, "I would have my shield up at all times, of course. And the rest of his troops would have been immobilised somehow. And you would be all around me, hidden in the trees."

"And how could you escape afterwards?" asked Lapping Water.

"If he becomes threatening, we will need to find some way to hold him where we meet until I back off into the woods and translocate once I'm out of sight."

"And the rest of us?" asked Stormaway.

"Can you translocate?" asked Tarkyn.

Stormaway shook his head.

"Neither can we," chorused String and Bean.

"Then you three had better work with the woodfolk to ensure you stay concealed, until the soldiers are out of the area," said Tarkyn firmly.

The three sorcerers glanced at the woodfolk for their opinion. Tarkyn frowned but managed to resist his urge to assert his authority.

"I agree with Tarkyn. We don't want to risk you being captured. You will endanger us all if you are found," said Tree Wind.

Tarkyn blinked at Tree Wind's support. She caught his expression and gave a short laugh. "Stop it Tarkyn. I don't oppose you as a matter of principle, as least not anymore."

Tarkyn smiled at her before saying, "This will mean I can't use Stormaway's shield but even using only Danton's, I think I have the makings of a plan that will not reveal woodfolk presence and that will keep us all safe."

CHAPTER 4

Prince Jarand's column moved at a gentle trot along the road to the lake. As they entered the forest the road surface deteriorated, and they had to slow their horses to a walk. All around them, the forest watched and waited. Captain Harkell sent two soldiers to scout ahead. The birds fell silent as they passed and the sound of their horses' hooves seemed unnaturally loud. It was not long before soldiers began to exchange furtive glances and to peer anxiously into the gloom between the trees. The trees on either side loomed over tangled bushes and it was hard to see more than a few yards into the woods. Even the little wizard, who was used to living in these woodlands, was unnerved.

After a while he kicked his horse and managed to raise a trot to bring himself up alongside the prince. Once he had reined in to a walk and had stopped bouncing around in the saddle, he addressed Jarand, "Your Highness. There is something amiss. The woodlands are unnaturally quiet."

"I would agree, sire," said Captain Harkell, trotting up to join them. "How many do we seek? Perhaps they are planning an ambush. Something is not right. Perhaps I should send a few more scouts up ahead."

But already it was too late. Behind them, exclamations arose as some of the soldiers' horses, unprompted by their riders, quickened their pace to draw alongside other soldiers' horses. Before anyone understood what was happening, the column was crammed side by side in rows of six, taking up the full width of the road. A shield of aqua slammed down around the first four rows, bringing them to a heaving halt. Startled horses plunged and sidestepped into each other until their riders calmed them. Prince Jarand, the wizard and the Captain were left alone and unguarded out in front. Jarand immediately raised his dark red shield around the three of them. The remaining horsemen could not reach the front of the column to protect their prince other than to leave the road and thread their way between the trees. Any desire they had to do this was thwarted by the fact that their horses would not move.

Before they had time to dismount, Tarkyn appeared, walking calmly down the middle of the road towards them, surrounded by the bronze haze of his shield.

"Good afternoon, brother. Would you please tell your men, particularly those at the rear, that any attempt by them to leave the road will result in them being picked off one by one? I do not intend to hurt them or you, so heroic gestures will be quite pointless."

Prince Jarand's face suffused with rage but he knew an impasse when he saw one and nodded curtly to his captain. Tarkyn waited while the order was given for the men to remain where they were, before he continued, "And now, if you could ask one or both of your companions within your shield to raise their own shields, then that will free you up to accompany me without them. However, if neither of them can raise a steady shield, it matters little as I have no intention of harming them. You, naturally, will wish to maintain your own shield around yourself."

"Your Highness, I must come with you," protested the captain. "You can't go alone into an enemy camp."

Jarand raised his eyebrows and, receiving a slight shake of the head from Tarkyn in response, replied, "Captain Harkell, I think you have demonstrated your ineptitude sufficiently for me to dispense with your services. My shield will protect me."

While Tarkyn waited for them to sort themselves out, he sent a query to Rainstorm to pass on to Danton checking that he was comfortable with maintaining his shield around so many. In return, he received an assurance that as long as the troops were stationary, it was no strain. He refocused to find Jarand trying unsuccessfully to urge his mount forward to accompany him. With a slight smile, Tarkyn gave Jarand's horse exemption from the request to stand still. He did not want to humiliate his brother any more than he already had done.

Tarkyn nodded courteously to the wizard and the captain, before turning to walk beside the horse carrying his brother. Nothing was said until they rounded the bend out of sight of Jarand's troops. Then Tarkyn stepped off the road into the trees at a point where Jarand's horse could follow and led him back around to the firesite. In fact, the firesite was not far from where Jarand's troops waited and was close enough for Danton to overhear the conversation while maintaining his shield.

"Here we are," said Tarkyn. "I have a fire waiting with a kettle boiling. I thought you might like a cup of tea. I'm afraid I don't have enough for your entire troop but at least I can offer you something."

Jarand's glare was wasted because Tarkyn didn't look at him while he expanded his shield over the fire and set about making cups of tea.

"Most kind of you," said Jarand at last, with heavy irony.

Finally Tarkyn straightened up and looked at him, "So. Are you going to come down or do you need the comfort of your horse? I would prefer to talk to you face to face but I will leave it up to you."

Jarand shot him a poisonous look before dismounting. Tarkyn placed a cup of tea on a stump some distance away so that Jarand could retrieve it without needing to lift part of his shield near his brother.

Tarkyn sat himself down against a log and gestured casually for Jarand to join him.

Jarand was outraged, "How dare you seat yourself while I am standing?"

Tarkyn smiled up at him, quite unmoved. "For three reasons, but for now I will only tell you two of them. Firstly, I care less than I did for protocol and secondly, since I am no longer a member of sorcerer society, I no longer acknowledge your superior rank."

Jarand choked on his tea and spent the next few minutes in the throes of a coughing fit. Tarkyn waited patiently, sipping his tea.

When he had recovered, Jarand eyed him, "You seem very sure of yourself for a hunted felon."

Despite his outward calm, Tarkyn stomach turned over at these words. He sipped his tea to maintain his equilibrium and said, "If I am a hunted felon, I have only you and Kosar to thank for it. But I am sorry that you think of me in that way."

"Why have you brought me here?" asked Jarand suddenly.

"Why have you come?"

"To recapture you, of course, and have you brought to justice."

Tarkyn shook his head. "We both know justice has no place in this. If you must maintain this pretence, do it with people who will believe you. Don't waste my time and yours."

Jarand stared at him. "Kosar was right. I didn't realise what a threat you were until now. You were never so strong, so sure of yourself at court."

Tarkyn raised his eyes to look at his brother, "I have had to learn a lot in a short time. And Kosar was wrong. I was never a threat to you or him. Not then. Maybe not even now. We'll see."

His older brother frowned, "What do you mean, 'We'll see'?"

Suddenly Tarkyn grinned, "I mean, I will see whether you two can sort yourselves out or whether I need to intervene."

Jarand gobbled. "You arrogant little upstart! What do you think you're doing - sitting in judgement on your older brothers?"

Tarkyn shrugged, still smiling. "You did it to me with far less cause. I'm just returning the favour."

Jarand was so agitated that he sprang to his feet and began to pace. Tarkyn simply watched him until he settled down. Eventually Jarand's brain clicked back into gear and he turned to Tarkyn and asked, "So, alone and exiled, how are you proposing to present a threat to either of us?"

Tarkyn's eyes twinkled, "In case you hadn't notice, I have just overcome eighty of your men and isolated you with, to be honest, minimal effort."

"You haven't overcome me. I am safely within my shield."

"So you are," said Tarkyn spuriously.

Jarand did not feel at all reassured. After a moment, Tarkyn asked, "Have you spoken to Journeyman since he attempted to capture me?"

Jarand waved an impatient hand, "Not in any detail. I received a garbled message from him trying to give excuses for his abject failure. I am a little disappointed in him, I must say. The man seems to be a lunatic. Some of the things he said were laughable."

"I see."

Jarand stopped and glowered down at Tarkyn with his hands on his hips. "What do you mean, 'I see'? You have become unbelievably irritating."

Tarkyn laughed and stood up to face his brother. "I beg your pardon. I really did not bring you here, just to irritate you." He paused while he thought through the wisdom of verifying Journeyman's story, "Well, I might as well tell you myself, because sooner or later, the evidence from Journeyman and the other hunters will make you realise that he's not fantasizing."

"Tell me what?"

"Well, let me see. I would say the things he told you that you didn't believe were that my shield had become reflective in the Great Hall when all those people were killed and that I can perform more than one spell at once." Tarkyn paused, "Would that be about right?"

"Yes. It would."

"All true, I'm afraid."

Jarand let out an impatient sigh. "Oh my stars! I'm surrounded by idiots."

Tarkyn didn't bother answering but merely murmured "*Liefka*" and sent a small stream of bronze to lift the kettle off the fire and bring it through his shield to him. When he had settled it safely on the ground, he looked at Jarand with a shy, proud smile on his face.

Suddenly all Jarand saw was his younger brother, having done something clever, hoping that his older brother would applaud him. Despite himself, he smiled and shook his head. "Very clever, Tarkyn. Very clever indeed."

Tarkyn beamed, "Thanks. More tea?"

They both laughed but it was not long before Jarand's smile faded as he thought through the implications of Tarkyn's skill.

"Can you penetrate my shield?"

"No."

"Hmm. But if what that wizard says is true, you were able to protect yourself while forcing the hunters down a path they didn't want to take, weren't you?"

Tarkyn nodded as he finished making a second cup of tea. As before, he placed Jarand's cup safely away from him. Finally, he looked up, "Jarand, you are safe with me. I will not hurt you, not at this time and in this place, anyway. But I could."

The calm certainty in Tarkyn's voice sent a chill down his brother's spine.

"And why did you want to see me?" asked Jarand after a pause.

"To talk about Falling Rain."

"Why? What about it?"

"Not what, who. Falling Rain is the person captured by Markazon and Stormaway all those years ago. You knew about him and visited him when Stormaway wasn't there… Didn't you?"

Jarand looked stunned, "How do you know all these things? You were only little at the time. Who told you? Stormaway didn't know. Even if you had spoken to this Falling Rain character, how would he have known who I was?"

Tarkyn shook his head, smiling, "I'm afraid there are some things I don't feel at liberty to discuss with you. But do you know who Falling Rain is?"

Jarand waved his hand, "Not really. I couldn't get a word out of him. I didn't even know that was his name. He's obviously from some other country. Those soft green eyes and that strange light brown hair. No one around here looks like that. In fact, no sorcerer I know of has green eyes." He shrugged, "But other than that…"

Tarkyn was a little perplexed by his brother's answer. It was not at all what he had expected. After a moment he tried another tack, "You realise that I am not a rogue sorcerer?"

Jarand's eyes narrowed, "I do now. Journeyman said you weren't but I didn't believe him. I thought you must have gone berserk with rage after Kosar and I left the Hall. Tell me what happened."

"Because of the intensity of my feelings, my shield changed its consistency and reflected back all the guards' power beams. If their rays were lethal, they died at their own hands. Many of the beams ricocheted around the hall and gradually the walls and pillars disintegrated under the assault of the palace guards. I didn't fire on anyone. I just stood within my shield while the world collapsed around me."

"How did you get away?"

"Through the mayhem," replied Tarkyn shortly.

"You realise there is nothing I can do about the charges facing you?"

Tarkyn shrugged. "I would never trust either of you enough to return, anyway. I do not want or need your charity."

"And why did you not flee the country all together? Surely that would be safer than remaining within the borders of Eskuzor."

Tarkyn suddenly felt a void opening at his feet. A wave of encouragement from Waterstone steadied him and he realised that safety lay in taking the high moral ground. "I could never leave Eskuzor unless I was sure her people were safe. At the moment, they are not."

Jarand smiled patronisingly, "I know that lawlessness is rife. That is why I am recruiting people to combat the renegades."

"Your press gangs are as fearsome as the outlaws. Some of them are brutal and uncompromising, and force unwilling sorcerers to abandon their farms and businesses, to become vigilantes." When Jarand frowned at him, Tarkyn continued, "And let us be frank. You care much more for undermining Kosar than you do for preserving law and order."

Jarand made a sudden move towards Tarkyn, "You young upstart! What would you know about the politics of this nation? I am striving to mitigate the deficiencies in Kosar's rule, supporting him to manage an unruly nation."

Tarkyn met his eyes and held them. "If that is indeed the case, you will have nothing to fear from me. But I have heard very different stories from many different sources and gullible though I may be, I struggle to believe you."

"How dare you doubt me? I could have you…"

"What, Jarand?" Tarkyn's voice cracked like a whip as his carefully controlled anger threatened to overwhelm him. "What could you throw at me that you haven't already? I have been outlawed and face execution for trumped up charges. You have nothing left to threaten me with. And I warn you, a person with nothing left to lose is a dangerous person to cross." Deliberately insolent, Tarkyn threw himself down to lounge against the log while Jarand stood above him, fuming.

After a minute, Tarkyn found himself a stick and began to break pieces off it methodically to calm himself down. When he next looked up, Jarand was watching him quizzically, "Do you know, you've always done that when you're upset or thinking? Broken little bits off a stick or a biscuit, or torn little pieces off bread?"

Tarkyn managed a tight smile, "Have I?" Suddenly he began to remember all the times they had played together when they were younger and unbidden, tears sprang to his eyes. "Blast you, Jarand! Why did you throw it all away? Why did you throw me away? I was never going to hurt either of you." He brushed his hand angrily across his eyes and stood up, "And now… Now, nothing will ever be right again and I am left to be Eskuzor's constant watchdog to ensure that between you, you don't destroy her."

Jarand's grey eyes narrowed, "I do not know what power you think you possess or what you think you can do to interfere in the affairs of our nation but let me assure that I too have Eskuzor's best interests at heart. Perhaps when you are a little older and wiser, you will understand how I am striving to secure Eskuzor's future." He turned and walked to his horse. As he straightened the stirrup strap, he said casually over his shoulder, "In fact, if you really care for Eskuzor, you could consider joining forces with me to help me to bring law and order to our suffering nation."

Tarkyn gave a short bitter laugh. "I can't see how you could justify me riding by your side in a vendetta against lawlessness, if I myself am a wanted felon."

Jarand waved his hand impatiently, "Not openly, of course. At least, not at the moment. No, you and your associates could work in subterfuge to bring those renegades into line." He raised his eyebrows, "In fact, I did hear that you were instrumental in bringing a band of outlaws to justice on the Great West Road. I didn't credit it at the time, but perhaps I do now."

"What associates?" asked Tarkyn tightly.

A knowing smile played around Jarand's lips. "Interesting clothes you're wearing. I understand from my new little wizard that a few people around here sport that type of clothing. He's right. It doesn't look like a uniform but rumours have reached me of some secret army. You wouldn't know anything about that, would you?"

Tarkyn's eyebrows shot together in consternation. He took a deep breath before replying. "I have also heard of some secret army. I think the rumours originate from your encampment up near the Great West Road." He paused and asked as casually as he could muster, "Where did your wizard see these other people dressed as I am?"

"Gliding through the swamp. On reflection, I think you may have been one of them… the black hair, you know."

Tarkyn let out a breath and, taking a great leap forward for his woodfolk, did his best to lead Jarand astray, "Yes. That was I and a few other people who have since moved on. This is no uniform that I wear. It is merely that clothes such as these are practical for life in the forest and a lot of displaced people wear them."

"I see. That explains why that Falling Rain fellow had similar clothes. I was wondering about that." Jarand frowned, "And what on earth were you doing in that godforsaken swamp?"

Tarkyn shrugged, "We were searching for something precious they had left there."

"And did you find it?"

"Yes, we did." Tarkyn grimaced. "You couldn't land anywhere. Horrible, dank-smelling place. And now it is empty except for the egrets."

"Hmm. So. Mystery solved and almost the outcome I was hoping for." Jarrand smiled wryly, "But not quite. I was hoping to meet up with you but with the expectation that I would hold the balance of power."

"And that you would drag me back to your dungeons?"

"Perhaps. Or perhaps come to some arrangement. I meant what I said. I would value your support in protecting this country." Suddenly Jarand came to a decision. He straightened up and drilled Tarkyn with his hard grey eyes. "So, whether you wear a uniform or not, you do have at your command a sizeable force, if I'm not mistaken. You are clearly not a rogue sorcerer and from all I know of you, you will have had enough integrity to galvanise that oath that Stormaway devised so long ago. Correct?"

Tarkyn, caught out completely by Jarand's sudden change of tactics, simply nodded. For several long seconds, they stared at each other in silence. Then Tarkyn found his voice and asked, "How many people know about this?"

Jarand's eyes narrowed as he considered the reason for the question, but eventually he shrugged and answered, "Other than our father and Stormaway, only Journeyman and I knew about your Falling Rain. And only Journeyman and I knew about that strange family that we captured and held at the encampment. A couple of other soldiers knew of them but they have since, unfortunately, perished." He raised his eyebrows and smiled slightly, "Would I be right in thinking that you have those strange people from the encampment back in your fold?"

Tarkyn nodded.

"Hmm. Interesting. Of course, I think the rumours of your little secret army may have sprung from the hunters who accompanied Journeyman in his efforts with the wolves to track down your unusual friends." Jarand sipped his tea before asking conversationally, "So, do they have a collective name or are they just sorcerers like the rest of us but living within the woods?"

"They are called woodfolk," said Tarkyn shortly. He took a deep breath, squared his shoulders and said resolutely, "*We* are called woodfolk."

"Are you indeed?" said Jarand mildly, as he mulled over the significance of this defiant statement. "So, will you do me the courtesy of introducing me to these people, since presumably I am in their midst?"

"No. Not unless they make that choice themselves."

"Oh, so you are not in command, as I first thought. What happened to the oath they swore?"

Tarkyn's mouth quirked, "It's complicated. And not something that you would easily understand."

As he stood there, even though he couldn't understand the words, Tarkyn could feel the debate raging through the minds surrounding him. Suddenly Waterstone appeared by his side. Jarand jumped in fright while the woodman bowed deeply and straightened without a word.

Tarkyn suddenly realised that Waterstone had remembered the sorcerer protocol about not speaking first and was waiting to be introduced.

"Your Royal Highness Prince Jarand, may I present Waterstone, woodman of the forests of Eskuzor and my bloodbrother… and by virtue of my relationship with you, also your bloodbrother."

For a moment, Jarand just stood there, stunned. Then, with a visible effort, he pulled himself together and, using every ounce of his courtly training, nodded graciously in return. "It is an honour to meet you Waterstone. I am, I admit, a little surprised to discover that I have another brother. I have always found two of them enough to handle."

"So I gather," said Waterstone with a courtly smile. "You also have a fourth brother, Ancient Oak, and a niece; my daughter, Sparrow."

"Have I indeed? Well, this certainly is a day for surprises." Unconsciously ill at ease, Jarand folded his arms, "And will I have the honour of meeting the rest of my unexpected family?"

There was a protracted silence. Jarand frowned as he noticed the woodman's eyes go out of focus. He leaned towards Tarkyn and murmured, "What's wrong with the man? Is he drunk?"

Tarkyn laughed and shook his head, "No. He's arguing with his brother. Just wait."

Suddenly, Ancient Oak appeared with Sparrow tightly holding his hand. Ancient Oak bowed and Sparrow, watching out of the corner of her eye, bowed also.

Tarkyn smiled reassuringly at them, and waved a hand casually at the prince. "This is Prince Jarand," he turned to Jarand, "And this is my brother and yours, Ancient Oak and our niece Sparrow. If you would be kind enough to give your word that you will not harm any of us, we could dispense with our shields for a while. I give you my word that none of us will harm you if you do not attack. Agreed?"

Jarand nodded shortly and waved away his shield. Tarkyn followed suit.

Immediately Sparrow ran and jumped up into Tarkyn's arms and hugged him. Then she twisted to face Jarand and frowned fiercely at him from the safety of Tarkyn's arms. "You were mean to Tarkyn, weren't you?

You made him very sad, you know. I don't know how you could be so mean to your own family."

"Sparrow," hissed Waterstone sharply, clearly flustered by his daughter's faux pas, "That is no way to speak to an adult. Now, apologise."

For a moment Sparrow looked mutinous. But then she gave a little sigh and said, "I beg your pardon. I shouldn't have said that." Then she flicked a very naughty glance at her father before adding, "But it's still true."

Tarkyn gave her a couple of taps on the end of her nose with his finger. "Young lady, you are embarrassing everybody, including me. We all know what has happened and must live with it, as best we can. Nothing will be gained by ramming it down Jarand's throat. If you want to help me, please be polite to my brother. Can you do that?"

Sparrow nodded, and swallowed, "Sorry, Tarkyn. Sorry, Your Highness."

Tarkyn gave her a squeeze and breathed a little sigh of relief that she had used the right form of address for Jarand. "Good girl."

Within Jarand, outrage was warring with diplomacy. Despite his best efforts, some of this showed on his face. Waterstone said kindly, "Don't worry. We know you will be horrified by all of this. I think you are doing a very good job of disguising your consternation. Even after all this time, Tarkyn still struggles to quell that marvellous, inbred Tamadil disdain. We are doing our best to follow your etiquette. You may notice, we all bowed. That was a big effort for us. Ask Tarkyn."

Jarand was so stunned at being spoken to like this that he went beyond anger. He blinked and looked around at Tarkyn, "I feel as though I have just walked into a dream… Or is it a nightmare? I'm not sure which yet." He frowned suddenly, "I hope this level of familiarity is only amongst your adopted family. Even for family members, it is well beyond the bounds of propriety, but for those outside… well! It would be unconscionable."

With a sense of inevitability, Tarkyn watched as Rainstorm appeared beside him grinning cheekily and said, "Hi, Prince. Going to introduce me to your brother?"

Tarkyn gave his head a little shake and sighed. With a wry smile, he waved his hand from one to the other, "Prince Jarand, Rainstorm."

When Rainstorm made no move to bow, the prince's grey eyes glittered dangerously, "I see these ill-educated people have no understanding of the niceties of a civilised society. Your behaviour, young man, is a disgrace. If you were in my court, I would have you flogged for insolence."

"Lucky I'm not then, isn't it?" retorted Rainstorm. "And after the way you treated Tarkyn, you will get no respect from me."

"Rainstorm," said Tarkyn firmly, but not unkindly, "Please at least respect me and back down a little. We do not want outright war here. We are merely trying to exchange information. And remember, Jarand is now one among many. That gives us an unfair advantage."

"Good!" Rainstorm glowered at Tarkyn for a moment before waving a hand in the air, "Fair enough. Sorry. I'll back off." Matching actions to words, he turned and patted Tarkyn on the arm on the way past as he walked away to stand a little behind them all, arms folded.

For several long seconds, a fraught silence reigned. Then Ancient Oak broke the impasse by crossing over to Jarand's horse and stroking its neck in long calming movements. "This is a fine stallion you have here, my lord. Is he fast?"

Jarand stared at him for a moment before gathering his wits to reply, "Yes. He combines speed and stamina. I have had him since he was a foal." He walked over to stand beside Ancient Oak. The stallion tossed his head and butted him gently. "I don't suppose you have any carrots?… or apples?"

Surprisingly, Rainstorm produced an apple from his pocket and held it out, saying gruffly, "Here."

Jarand's eyes narrowed but after a moment he accepted the gesture for what it was and said, "Would you like to feed it to him?"

Alarm flickered in Rainstorm's eyes, "What about you, Ancient Oak? Don't you want to feed him?"

Ancient Oak gave a wicked little smile, "No Rainstorm, I couldn't deprive you of the pleasure."

"What about you, Prince, I mean Your Highness? Don't you want to feed your own horse?"

Jarand realised an opportunity for a small revenge had just presented itself and shook his head, "No. I would be honoured if you gave him the apple yourself."

"Oh my stars! What have I let myself in for?"

Rainstorm looked in panic at Tarkyn who laughed and said, "Just put the apple in the palm of your hand and hold it out in front of him. He won't hurt you. Promise."

Rainstorm took a deep breath and did as instructed, holding his hand as far away from himself as he could. The great black stallion gently mouthed the apple out of his hand and munched it. Rainstorm straightened up and began to strut around the clearing, "Did you see that? Easiest thing out. I think your horse likes me."

Tarkyn looked at Sparrow and asked her, "Do you want to pat the horse?"

She considered for a minute then nodded, "Don't put me down, though."

As Tarkyn walked over within patting range of Storm, Jarand said, "I gather you woodfolk don't ride, as a general rule?"

"No sir. Not in the normal course of events," replied Ancient Oak.

"Only when you are mounting a raid on my encampment?" asked Jarand silkily.

Ancient Oak kept a perfectly straight face and nodded inconsequentially. "Yes. That would be one of the rare times we have used horses." He shrugged and grinned, "But if you don't want us letting your horses loose again, you'll just have to make sure you don't take any of us prisoner again."

Jarand raised his eyebrows, "Then you will have to make sure that you don't cross me."

Waterstone, standing a judicious distance away from the horse, said, "I don't think we are even close to being able to agree that. However I think we can guarantee that if you do take any of us again, the disruption to your troops and horses will be more severe." In response to Jarand's frown, Waterstone shrugged, "Now that we know that you know about us, we can afford to be less cautious in future, if we need to be."

Jarand looked down his aristocratic nose at Waterstone, "You do not look like fighting men, if I may say so."

"Certainly you may say so," said Waterstone airily. "Say what you like. After all, your men clearly have it all over us, don't they?"

"Unless I'm much mistaken, I believe that is the work of sorcerers, not you people," replied Jarand disdainfully.

Tarkyn intervened hurriedly, flicking a warning glance at Waterstrone, "Much as I hate to disrupt this game of one-upmanship, I'm sure Jarand is anxious to return to his troops and begin his long trip back to Montraya."

Ancient Oak frowned and looked from one royal brother to the other, "So, what have we gained from all this? Are we any further forward?"

"I think so," answered Tarkyn, looking at Jarand. "We now know that Jarand and Journeyman are the only people from the encampment who know about woodfolk and that they want to keep it that way in case they can enlist our help at some time in the future. They also know about the oath." Tarkyn did not go into any detail about the deficits in their knowledge.

"For my part," continued Jarand, "I now know that Tarkyn is not a rogue sorcerer and that my press gangs are making me unpopular. So, since that is counter-productive to my purpose, I may have to modify their behaviour. I have also discovered the presence of two adopted brothers and an adopted niece, none of whom, I hasten to add, has a legitimate claim to the throne, even if all three of us, Kosar, Tarkyn and I, should die. That being the case, I can acknowledge our relationship with some degree of equanimity but strictly, of course, within the forest." Jarand gave a condescending smile, "Obviously, I could not possible countenance it beyond, once I leave this fairytale nightmare to return to reality."

Jarand gathered the reins and as Ancient Oak moved out of the way, swung himself into the saddle. He looked down on them all and continued, "I now have the rumours of a secret army under Tarkyn confirmed but, having met some of you and gauged your calibre, I am not as concerned as I was previously, nor as anxious to recruit you to my cause."

Waterstone stepped forward and gave an ironic bow, "Your lack of courtesy is breathtaking compared to ours. For our part, it is of great interest to us to meet someone so wholly lacking in moral fibre that he could betray his own brother. But at least you kept your word not to attack us."

Jarand raised his eyebrows haughtily, "Of course I did. Mind you, I would have been a fool to attack you when I was so heavily outnumbered." He turned his attention to Tarkyn, "Now, are you going to release my men? Poor Danton will soon tire of holding his shield over so many, won't he?"

Tarkyn flicked him a querying glance then answered his own question, "You recognised the colour of his magic, didn't you? Yes, I had better rescue him soon. I will walk you back. Do I have your word that you will leave us in peace and return to Montraya?" asked Tarkyn.

Jarand nodded shortly, "To quote you, 'At this time and in this place', you have my word. Beyond that, I will make no undertakings."

"No more will I," countered Tarkyn.

When they returned to Jarand's troops, Tarkyn sent Danton a message via Rainstorm to change the shield from a dome over the ranks of horses to a wall between the troops and the three at the front of the column. Then he released the horses and waited until Jarand had ordered their return to Montraya before allowing Danton to drop his shield altogether.

As the troops manoeuvred their horses around in the tight space, Tarkyn asked, "Before you go, Jarand, perhaps you would be kind enough to introduce me to your companions."

Jarand raised his eyebrows in surprise, but complied with formal courtesy, "Tarkyn Tamadil, Prince of Eskuzor, let me introduce you to Captain Harkell of the Royal Montrayan Guard and Greyskies Swampwatcher, wizard of these parts."

"It is an honour, Your Highness," murmured the wizard and the captain, both bowing from their seated positions.

"Captain Harkell, you will find the two soldiers of your vanguard back down the road a little and may retrieve them on your way past. Because they are unconscious, we have tied them to their horses but they will recover shortly and you may then do with them as you will." Tarkyn smiled gently at them, "I beg your pardon for your wasted journey. But unfortunately, I am unwilling to return with you. I wish you a safe journey back."

With which, the fugitive prince turned on his heel and, still within his shield, walked back down the road without a backward glance.

CHAPTER 5

As they rode towards the forest's edge, Jarand kept himself tightly under control. But those who knew him could see from his glittering eyes and his thinned lips that he was furious.

"Captain Harkell," he said tightly, "I want you to pick out your two toughest, strongest men. I don't want anybody who is the slightest bit squeamish. Do you understand? And they must be unquestionably loyal to me."

"All the men are loyal to you, Sire. We all are."

"Excellent. Because I am about to test that loyalty."

At this point they broke out of the cover of the forest into farmland. The prince pointed to a lone tree standing two hundred yards from the forest edge.

"When we reach that tree, bring those two men to see me and then ask your troops to dismount and gather around so I can address them."

"Yes, Your Highness." The captain glanced at him uneasily, aware that the prince's rage was bubbling just beneath the surface.

Ten minutes later, the soldiers stood in a semicircle around the prince, shuffling a little in anticipation of a dressing down. They were all embarrassed to have been caught out so easily and knew that, although he was disguising it, the prince would be smarting at being shown to disadvantage by his younger brother.

His voice, when he addressed them, was calm and matter of fact. They found this even more unnerving than if he had ranted at them. As it turned out, they had every reason to be unnerved. "Soldiers of Montraya, as you are aware, the penalty for attacking a member of the Royal Family of Eskuzor is death." Jarand paused until most of his audience had nodded or given some form of acknowledgement. "Of course none of you has attacked me." Up to this point his voice was still pleasant. But now it hardened. "But the second most heinous crime is a failure to protect me." Prince Jarand swept his gaze around the soldiers standing around him. "And in varying degrees, all of you are guilty of that." He let his words hang in the air for a few moments.

Then Jarand turned and placed his hand on Captain Harkell's shoulder, "But above all, your captain is responsible for the deployment and performance of his men."

The captain kept his eyes forward and his face expressionless but his heart was thumping unpleasantly in his ears.

"Now, Captain Harkell has kindly identified these two men," here Jarand waved at two powerfully built, tough looking soldiers who were standing by his side, "who are renowned for their strength and loyalty. So to them, I give the honour of providing a just punishment to your negligent captain." Jarand thrust the captain into the arms of the two men and barked, "Tie his hands. Secure them above his head against the tree."

The watching men stilled with shock but no one moved to intervene. Captain Harkell's hands were bound in front of him and then he was thrown face first against the tree and his arms yanked above his head. A rope was tied between his wrists and the other end thrown over a high bough. Then he was dragged upward so that his feet barely touched the ground. The little wizard looked on in horror, remembering the kindness the captain had shown him.

"Strip off his shirt," ordered Jarand. "Now, I want him flogged within an inch of his life."

Both men took off their long leather belts and held them by the buckles ready to begin.

"Oh no," said Jarand softly, "I think we'll have the buckle on the business end. Smooth leather is too easy. Forty strokes to begin with. Alternate strokes, so that you don't tire. I want a gap between each stroke so that there is plenty of time for anticipation and I want each stroke to be given full measure." He looked around at all the soldiers, "And if I see one of you avert your eyes, you will share his fate." He waved a hand, "Now, begin."

In the deadly quiet of the countryside, all that could be heard was the thwack of the leather hitting flesh and the grunts of effort from each of the guardsmen as they put their full weight behind each lash. The captain set his teeth and not a murmur broke from his lips. After ten lashes his back was lined with red streaks and pockmarked with gouges where the buckles dug in with each stroke. After twenty strokes, the red weals were weeping as the leather bit repeatedly into the same places. At thirty strokes, his back was raw and running with blood where the buckles had gouged deep lines along the whip marks. The captain had long since lost all sense of time and space and his world had contracted to an all-encompassing sensation of rhythmic, brutal pain. At thirty six strokes, he lost consciousness and so was unaware that, after the fortieth stroke fell, his troop was ordered to remount, leaving him hanging by his hands from a tree in the middle of nowhere as they headed back to Montraya without daring a single backward glance.

CHAPTER 6

As Tarkyn stepped back into the trees, he said to Waterstone who appeared at his side, "I don't think we need to rush off. Jarand will keep his word."

The woodman shook his head, "I don't see how you can trust him to keep his word when he is totally unscrupulous in other respects."

"Didn't like him much, did you?"

"He was deliberately belittling and offensive."

Tarkyn smiled, "Well, if he goes away thinking that you lot are harmless, we will have done a good day's work."

"Hmph. Just as well you hauled me in. I was ready to tell him how deadly we really are."

Tarkyn gave a short laugh, "I know. Your temper was getting the better of your judgement."

"You did us proud," said Ancient Oak, joining them. "You stood up and told him you were one of us and then acknowledged us as your family."

"Of course I did."

Autumn Leaves frowned, "Now Tarkyn, that's not like you. There was no 'of course' about it. I saw you steeling yourself to say '*We* are woodfolk'."

"Just because I had to steel myself to deal with Jarand's reaction, doesn't mean there was any doubt that I would say it."

Autumn Leaves smiled, "I see. Fair enough."

"I'm not sure how wise it was to hit Jarand with the double whammy that not only do we exist but he now has an extended family. Just meeting us might have been enough for the first time," mused Waterstone.

Tarkyn shrugged, "Well, I didn't know what you were expecting and I thought you might have been offended if I left out the little detail that you were my brother."

"I can't say I'm proud to have him as a member of the family," said Waterstone, shaking his head.

Tarkyn grinned, "No. Even though most people in Eskuzor would be overcome with the honour of being able to claim relationship to the heir to the throne, I can see your point."

Ancient Oak waved his hand around airily, "Why would we be honoured by him? After all, we have the King in our family too, and the sovereign lord of the woodlands. And if they are not enough, we also have Waterstone and Sparrow."

"Not to mention Ancient Oak," added Tarkyn with a slight smile.

Just as he finished speaking, Tarkyn turned pale and sat down suddenly. He ran a shaking hand across his forehead.

Autumn Leaves leaned over him, "What's wrong?"

"Aagh. Such anguish. Such pain," breathed Tarkyn, closing his eyes. "I don't know this person's mind like I did yours, Autumn Leaves, but someone is in terrible trouble. Ooh, he's enduring, he's enduring. No! He's gone. He's either dead or passed out." Tarkyn ran his hand over his face and took a shaky breath.

"But where is he? How can we help him if we don't know where he is?" demanded Autumn Leaves.

Tarkyn shook his head slowly. "I don't know."

"Were there any images?" asked Waterstone.

Tarkyn took a deep breath as he thought about it, "Yes… Yes. There was the bark of a tree close up. That was nearly all I could see. Hmm, a flash of deep brown to one side. Wait on. Let me focus on that… Yes. It's a ploughed field. I can't see it properly." He groaned, "Mostly I can feel the pain. My wrists are hurting but my back feels like as if it's on fire. Worse than that. It's absolute agony."

Summer Rain appeared beside him and placed a firm hand on his shoulder, "Tarkyn, come out of it. You're taking on the hurt."

The youngest prince shook his head to clear it, "Sorry. It is the intensity of the experience that has connected me to this person, whoever it is."

"So it must be in farmland somewhere," said Danton prosaically, handing Tarkyn a cup of cold water. He glanced at Tarkyn, knowing he was about to upset him further. "Hmm. I would say that someone has just paid for our success. What you're describing is how it feels to be flogged."

Danton carefully didn't meet anyone's eyes and an awkward silence ensued until it was broken by Rainstorm striding over and giving Danton a few hearty slaps on the shoulder, "Well, you'd know, you poor bastard. So we'll have to take your word for it."

A ripple of relief and appreciation for Rainstorm's forthrightness drifted through the group.

Danton gave a gentle smile, "Thanks Rainstorm."

Tarkyn sat in the middle of it, feeling sick with someone else's pain and inundated with a deeper horror of what his friend had been forced to endure as a child on his behalf.

"Excuse me," he muttered and blundered off into the undergrowth to vomit. He stood leaning over with a hand against a tree, breathing deeply and trying to pull himself together enough to help the person who had been flogged.

A few moments later, Falling Rain appeared next to him, "I bet you're feeling dreadful about Danton."

Tarkyn nodded mutely. He ran his hand through his hair, "And for this poor unknown. All because of me. If I hadn't captured Jarand, he wouldn't have wreaked his revenge on this hapless individual."

"On the other hand," responded Falling Rain, "If you hadn't captured Jarand, he may have captured you or one of us." The woodman put his hand on the prince's shoulder, "And if you don't mind, you should give credit where credit is due. We were all party to the plan to capture Jarand. If we hadn't knocked out the vanguard and been waiting in the bushes to pick off the soldiers, it might not have worked, especially with your non-talent for bluffing. We all took part and are equally responsible. And this man's fate was decided by no one but Jarand." He shrugged, "And perhaps by the man himself. After all, the risks associated with serving the royal family are blindingly obvious."

With an effort, Tarkyn straightened up, "Ugh. I feel awful. But I'd better go and see if I can find this man."

Falling Rain put a restraining hand on his arm, "No need. The others have already gone."

Tarkyn managed a crooked grin, "There I go again. Trying to take over when there is no need."

Having worked out the probable cause of Tarkyn's image, it was not difficult to determine where to find its source. Danton and a group of woodfolk stood within the trees at the edge of the forest looking out into the open fields along the side of the road back to Montraya. In the distance they could see the cloud of dust that was the only sign of Jarand's troops.

"He'll be somewhere along that road, I expect," said Danton.

Waterstone's eyes swept anxiously across the flat open landscape. "There is no cover anywhere. It may be a trap." After a moment, he shook his head slightly. "No. Can't be. No one would know that Tarkyn would pick up that man's distress. There might still be some soldiers lurking though. What do you think, Danton?"

Danton considered. "Unlikely. Either they have cut down the man down and taken him with them to throw him in the dungeons at the other end or they will have left him to his fate. Jarand won't waste precious manpower on standing guard over him."

Autumn Leaves shook his head, "He could be anywhere along that road."

"No, he couldn't," said Rainstorm decisively. "They hadn't been gone for long when Tarkyn went all shaky."

"True." Danton shaded his eyes against the setting sun as he peered out along the road. "Tarkyn saw rough bark close up, didn't he? So this man is probably tied to a tree somewhere. There are a couple of trees dotted along the roadside. I guess we can start by checking them." There was a strained silence. He looked around and found himself surrounded by anxious faces. "You don't want to go out of the forest, do you?"

They all shook their heads. "The only place we ever break cover is to cross the grasslands and only then, at night."

Danton put his hands on his hips. "Well, I guess that leaves us with these choices; I go alone, some of you break with tradition and come with me now, or we wait until dark. What do you want to do?"

There was an intense silence as they conferred with each other.

Eventually Waterstone cleared his throat and asked, "Do you think you could carry him on your own?"

Danton shrugged, feeling a little disappointed. "If it's not too far. I can use magic to transport him back. It would probably hurt him less if I did that, anyway." He waited but no one said anything else. "So, is that your decision?"

They nodded, looking a little shame-faced.

"We will wait here and if you really need us, we will come," said Waterstone. "I'm sorry, Danton. I can see you feel let down but I, we, have never been outside the forest in broad daylight. Even at night, we feel exposed and unsafe, just going through the grasslands that are deep within the forest's boundaries, let alone here."

Danton sighed, "I understand. More or less." He took a deep breath. "So be it. Wish me luck." With that he gave Waterstone a pat on the back and headed out of the trees.

He walked unhurriedly over the fields to the road and sauntered along in the late afternoon sunshine, having decided that a slow pace would attract less attention if anyone happened to be watching. He breathed in the air and savoured the tang of newly turned soil on the wind. He gazed around at the open space, realising what a relief it was to be out of the constant confines of the trees. But his enjoyment was short lived. Before long, he was close enough to see the inert body of a man hanging by his tied hands from a large horse chestnut tree further down the road. Despite his intentions to the contrary, Danton broke into a run.

When he reached the tree, his eyes widened as he saw the damage that had been inflicted on the man's back. The man's head was lolling to one side and Danton's first move was to check for a pulse. After several attempts, he eventually found a blood vessel in the man's neck that betrayed a fast shallow beat. Danton put his arm around the man's lower body to take his weight while he reached up with his other hand to cut the ropes. With some frustration he realised he couldn't reach. Inwardly cursing woodfolk as timorous cowards, he lowered the man and thought about what to try next.

"You could use your magic to hold him up while I cut the ropes," came a voice behind him.

Danton whirled around to find Rainstorm standing there, grinning. The sorcerer's movement brought the man's back into Rainstorm's view and the young woodman blanched. "Oh my stars! Oh, that's horrible. Is that what happened to you?"

Danton shook his head. "No. Nothing nearly as bad as this." He gave a derisive smile, "No. This would have ruined their carpets in the palace. They usually stopped when my back began to weep."

Impulsively, Rainstorm put an arm around Danton's shoulder as they stood looking at the whipped man. "Well, let's get this poor bugger down, shall we?" He gave Danton a pat and withdrew his arm, "So, what do you want me to do?"

"Your suggestion about using my magic was a good one. I'll levitate him while you cut him down. Ready?"

Suddenly a crow cawed overhead as it flew in to perch in the branches of the tree. Danton found himself talking to empty space. He rolled his eyes, "Rainstorm, it's just a crow."

A voice somewhere above him gave an embarrassed chuckle, "Whoops. It's a bit scary out in all this space." Rainstorm reappeared at his side, grinning sheepishly.

Danton gave his head a little shake and continued where he'd left off, "So will you cut him down while I hold him up?"

Rainstorm nodded and sidled around the man, eyeing the wounds on his back as he came closer. He took a deep breath, "Right. Are you ready?" The woodman reached up and cut through the large rope that held the man aloft. Danton's magic held and although the man's arms dropped, the rest of him stayed where he was. Rainstorm swiftly cut through his bonds and stepped back. Danton turned the man into a horizontal position in the air, face up.

"Rainstorm, can you just loop a bit of rope around his arms to hold them together on his stomach while we're moving?"

"I shouldn't have cut his bonds."

"Oh, I think you should have. They were shockingly tight. The circulation was cut off from his hands. Look. They're all blue. Either those bastards tied them too tightly in the first place or his weight dragged them tighter."

Rainstorm did as he was asked and stood back quickly. "Right. Are we off?"

Danton could hear the tension in the young woodman's voice. "Thanks, Rainstorm, for coming."

Rainstorm nodded briefly, his eyes never leaving the injured man so that he didn't have to see the wide space he was walking through. "Will he survive, do you think?"

Danton shook his head, "If we can get him back to Tarkyn in time, he might stand a chance. He's pretty far gone, though."

Woodman and sorcerer walked together through the orange rays of the setting sun, the injured man floating beside them. Around them, yellow grasses around the fields' borders glowed deep gold but the young woodman only had eyes for the forest ahead.

By the time they reached the forest's edge, Rainstorm's message had been relayed and Tarkyn was waiting for them. A flat grassy space had been cleared far enough inside the forest for safety and laid with furs and cloth. Rainstorm undid the ropes holding the man's arms and manoeuvred them out of the way as Danton turned the man over to lay him face down on the ground. Gasps and exclamations of horror erupted around him. A few furtive, speculative glances were directed at Danton but he decided he would deal with them later. A slight release in tension around him made him realise that Rainstorm had dealt with it now.

As soon as the man was settled, Tarkyn sat beside him, placed his hand on the man's shoulder and sent his life force into him. After a few minutes, nothing had changed. Tarkyn let himself flow down his arm into the man beside him. He found himself surrounded by abject misery, not of flesh but of spirit. The power he brought with him flowed passively through, but little was absorbed by the man's body. Tarkyn opened his eyes and frowned. "There seems to be some sort of resistance. My power isn't working on him." He looked around for the woodfolk healer, "Summer Rain, could you do what you can for him, while we try to work out what is going on?"

"Maybe you can only give this life force of yours to woodfolk?" suggested Falling Rain.

"No. It's not that," replied Autumn Leaves, "Tarkyn has healed Danton a couple of times."

"Well, maybe he has nothing left to live for, no life to go back to, if his prince has rejected him," said Lapping Water slowly. "He's probably as good as dead in your sorcerer society, anyway. He won't a have a position to go back to. Will he?"

"Not as captain of the guard, he won't," agreed Tarkyn.

"Oh. Is that who he is? That makes sense." Danton shrugged, "He may well feel that he has lost his honour by failing Prince Jarand as he did."

Waterstone rolled his eyes, "Only you could think like that, Danton."

Danton gave a slight smile, "In fact, he may well believe that he deserves to be punished."

"But not like this!" exclaimed Autumn Leaves hotly. "This is barbaric."

"No," said Tarkyn softly, "Not like this." The prince looked at Summer Rain who was gently wiping away the worst of the blood with a soft, damp cloth. "Is there any chance that he may regain consciousness without my intervention?"

Summer Rain felt his pulse and lifted an eyelid to peer closely into his eye. She straightened up and said, "He is in shock but he is strong and fit. In themselves, his injuries are not life threatening. It is the shock or infection that could kill him. If we take care of him, keep him warm and make sure he takes in fluids, I think he will recover over time. We will have to guard against infection, though. If his wounds fester, without his resistance he might succumb. But on the short run, once the worst of the shock has passed, he should regain consciousness."

Even as she spoke, the man groaned and grimaced with pain as he moved.

"If he's about to open his eyes, we'd better think about whom we want him to see," said Tarkyn.

There was a short mind conference. "Whatever happens, he's going to have stay with us until he recovers unless we just decide to abandon him," reported Waterstone. A glance around indicated that no one was thinking of this option. "So, from our point of view, we will allow him to see us. From his point of view, he may find a group of new people a bit threatening in his present condition."

After a minute's thought, Danton said, "Let me deal with this. At least, let me try. Your Highness, if you could sit out of his vision but be ready with your hand on his shoulder, I will speak to him when he comes around. I think you're right, Waterstone, that the rest of you are probably a surprise he may not yet be ready for."

Tarkyn nodded, smiling to himself that Danton had used his title to offset the fact that he giving him instructions.

"Tarkyn, do you know his name?" asked Danton.

"Captain Harkell."

"Thanks."

For a while nothing happened. Everyone sat out of the captain's line of vision and waited. Eventually, the captain stirred again and groaned.

Danton leaned over him and lifted him a little to give him a drink. The captain let out a gasp of pain. Most of the water dribbled onto the ground but a little found its way between his lips. Danton let him gently down again.

"Captain Harkell. Captain, can you hear me?"

There was an almost imperceptible nod.

"Captain, your punishment is now complete. His Royal Highness would like you to recover so that you may serve him in the future. Do you understand?" All around him, eyes widened. Tarkyn frowned.

The captain nodded again.

"Are you willing to do your best to recover to serve the royal family of Tamadil?"

A whisper issued from the injured man's throat. Danton bent closer so that he could hear. When he straightened, he gave a slight smile, knowing how the woodfolk would react, "Your Highness, the captain said, 'I live to serve'."

Looks of disbelief passed among the assembled woodfolk.

"The man's mad," mouthed Rainstorm.

Danton returned his attention to his task. "Captain, in a moment, you will feel a warm wave of strength entering your body through your right shoulder. I want you to take that strength and send it into the damage on your back." When Danton looked up to nod at Tarkyn, he found a pair of very angry amber eyes trained on him. Danton held their gaze steadily and added mischievously, knowing he would pay for it later "When you are recovered, the prince will wish to speak with you."

Tarkyn's eyes narrowed but, as the suffering captain nodded and gave another slight groan at the pain the movement cost him, the prince resolutely turned his attention to the healing and, taking a deep breath, channelled his life force through his hand into the man's shoulder. Tarkyn flowed his consciousness down into the injured man and directed his power to repair the gouged, stressed flesh. The damage to the man's back was extensive and it took close to an hour for the last and deepest of the weals gradually to close over and fade. When Tarkyn took his hand away, Captain Harkell's back was criss-crossed with pink scars and there was some residual bruising but he was healed.

"That was the easy part," mouthed Tarkyn. "This man is going to want to kill us all when he finds out what stunt you've pulled."

Danton gave a slight shrug and tore his eyes away from Tarkyn to lean close to the captain, "Captain Harkell, your back is looking a lot better now. Unfortunately, you will carry the scarring for the rest of your life but other than that, it is repaired. You may find it a little stiff to begin with.

When you are ready, you can sit up and I will give you some water and then some tea to revive you."

As the man began to move, Danton waved frantically at everyone. The woodfolk grinned at him and disappeared in one easy flick. Tarkyn rose to his feet and stood uncertainly, wondering whether or not to stay. Before he could decide, a strong arm grabbed him and pulled him behind the bushes at the edge of the clearing. He frowned and looked around to find Autumn Leaves next to him, with Tarkyn's sleeve gripped firmly in his hand.

"I might have known it was you. You always seem to be the one manhandling me in these situations," whispered Tarkyn. "I could kill Danton. That man is going to hate me."

"And who knows what manner of man he is. He could be an out and out thug, for all we know."

Back inside the clearing, Captain Harkell was looking around himself with dawning suspicion, "Why are we back within the forest? I had thought His Highness intended to return to Montraya."

Danton handed him a cup of tea before sitting down beside him. "Prince Jarand has indeed returned to Montraya, as far as I know." Danton gave the captain a little while to digest this information before saying, "I was impressed by your devotion to the royal family, even while you lay there suffering."

Harkell sipped his tea, "I am lucky to be alive after giving such poor service."

After a pause, Danton said slowly, "I'm afraid to say that I don't think Prince Jarand cares one way or the other whether you survive."

"I don't understand. Were you not speaking to His Highness? Didn't you say he wanted to speak with me?" The captain frowned, "I see… Is he now planning to send me on some impossible mission where my life will virtually be forfeit? Is that what it is?" The captain sighed and sipped his tea. "At least then, I may have the chance to redeem myself in his eyes."

"No, I'm afraid your situation is both better and worse than that." Danton glanced at him, "You may still serve the royal family but not as you have been used to."

"Am I to become a servant then? For mercy's sake, man. Spit it out. What is my fate to be?"

Prince Tarkyn walked out into the clearing, "Your fate, should you choose it, is to serve me."

The captain threw down his cup, scrambled to his feet and, despite his warring emotions, bowed deeply. He stayed bent over, hand on heart until Tarkyn permitted him to rise. When the captain straightened, he swayed slightly, still weak from his injuries, but his face was an impassive mask.

"You may be seated before you fall over. Danton, you may procure us both another cup of tea since Captain Harkell seems to have thrown his last one away." Tarkyn paused. "Out of interest, did you check whether the captain was armed?"

Danton bowed his head in apology, "No, Your Highness. I did not think of it."

Tarkyn looked at Harkell, "I will depend on your honour to answer me truthfully. Are you armed?"

After a fractional pause, the captain answered, "Yes, Your Highness. I am carrying a small knife inside my left ankle."

"Be so good as to hand it to Danton, if you don't mind."

"I would prefer to keep it, Your Highness."

Tarkyn gave a gentle smile, "I'm sure you would. However, despite the wording, that was not a request."

"I beg your pardon, Sire. Here." Captain Harkell drew out his knife and handed it to Danton with a hand that still trembled from the aftermath of the attack on him.

Tarkyn watched the man closely, checking for any signs of subterfuge, trying to gauge his calibre. The captain was in his mid-thirties. His dark wavy hair was matted with sweat and his soft brown eyes roved the clearing looking for clues about his location and the threats facing him.

"Captain Harkell, I am sorry that Danton misled you into thinking that my brother had returned for you. I myself do not like to deal in such subterfuge. However, we feared you had lost the will to live and so, Danton gave you a reason to recover. He did not so much lie as word things ambiguously. I beg your pardon. As his liege lord, I must take responsibility for his behaviour." Tarkyn threw Danton a look of displeasure while he waited for the soldier's reaction.

The captain was not yet able to deal with the subtleties of Danton's veracity. He frowned, "So how long have I been here? I must have been here for weeks. My back has already healed."

Tarkyn smiled and shook his head, "No. Danton cut you down from that tree less than two hours ago. I healed your back. Remember the stream of strength that came into you through your shoulder? That didn't take weeks. It took less than an hour."

"Did you do that? That's amazing. Hmm." The captain accepted another cup of tea from Danton with a nod of thanks. "So, why would you help someone who had ridden out to capture you? At least, I presume that's what we were doing. Prince Jarand didn't say more than that we were trying to track down some sorcerers that Greyskies had seen in the swamp. But when you turned up, I assumed that must have been what we were doing."

"I sensed your pain." Tarkyn shook his head and grimaced, "Your suffering was so intense that it transmitted itself to me."

"That doesn't mean you had to do anything about it," said the captain stiffly, embarrassed at having shared his experience.

Danton glanced at Tarkyn and smiled, "You don't know this prince. It absolutely meant he had to do something about it, especially when it was our ploys that made you fail to protect Prince Jarand."

"And so now what?" asked the captain, "Will you force me to stay here and serve you as some sort of prisoner of war?"

"I thought you were honoured to serve the royal family," said Danton dryly.

The soldier ran his hand through his matted hair. "I am… or I was. I still am. But I have always served Prince Jarand." Harkell brought his eyes up to meet Tarkyn's. "If you and he are in conflict, what sort of loyalty is it that changes horses in mid-stream? One can no longer simply say, 'I am loyal to the royal family.' You can't be loyal to all members of the royal family at the same time anymore." He dropped his head into his hands. "I'm confused," he mumbled.

After a moment, he raised his head. "So, before I confuse myself further trying to decide what to do, do I in fact have any options? Or it is as I suggested, that I am being held prisoner?"

"Hmm, Interesting question," said Tarkyn. "No. You are not being held prisoner. But what your options are, I have no idea. I would not bank on a warm welcome back in Montraya but you must be the judge of that. Perhaps you can roam the countryside and pick up work elsewhere. Perhaps you could become a mercenary away from Jarand's eye. I am not well versed in these things." The prince shook out his cup and stood up. He gestured to indicate that Captain Harkell could remain seated. "However, I do not want you by my side unless I have your full support. If you stay with me, you must swear an oath of fealty to me. I will not endanger the people I am with, by countenancing the presence of someone with uncertain loyalties. If you cannot give me your pledge, you are free to go."

A look of panic passed across the soldier's face. "Your Highness, must I decide so soon? My world has been turned upside down and I need time to think. My loyalties, my beliefs and my honour are dragging me in all directions. I can't think straight. Even the information I have about you is in complete conflict. On what am I to base my decision?"

Tarkyn stood glowering down at him, "You could start by considering that Jarand had you flogged and I healed you."

Harkell shook his head, "It is not as simple as that. It was inevitable that I face the consequences of my failure."

Tarkyn threw up his hands impatiently. "I am not going to vie with my brother for your loyalty. I will say this one thing, even though you may place little value on it. No one in my service would ever be treated like that, no matter what they had done. I have had two men killed who tied me up and beat me, nearly as badly as you were flogged. Other than that, the worst anyone has endured is a tongue lashing."

"I need time," reiterated the captain stoically. "I would not wish to give you my service half-heartedly. I need to be certain."

"You have two hours," said Tarkyn shortly. "After that, I leave and you will remain. Danton, stay with Captain Harkell and give him whatever assistance he may require." Just as he was about to leave, the prince turned back and said, "And Danton, since our friend's sojourn amongst us may be unexpectedly short, I urge you to remember your vow of secrecy."

Danton bowed his head, "Yes, Your Highness."

The two ex-guardsmen were left alone in the clearing.

Captain Harkell glanced sideways at Danton, "You must think I am ungrateful not to jump at the chance of serving your prince after he has put himself out to rescue me and heal my wounds."

"I think Tarkyn values honour and will respect your decision, whatever it is." Danton shrugged, "You could have thanked him for his efforts. I think that would not have been too much to ask. And me. I am the one who cut you down and carried you back." Danton made a mental note to apologise to Rainstorm for not acknowledging his contribution at this point.

"I'm sorry. I was overcome with confusion when the wrong prince appeared. I do thank you both. Without your intercession, I think the crows would have picked the flesh off my back while I hung there."

Danton gave a shudder. "What a ghastly thought. How is your back now?"

Harkell moved his shoulders back and forth experimentally. "Not bad. A bit stiff but not bad." He looked at Danton. "So tell me. What do you think I should do?"

Danton knew he was being asked as a fellow officer who would understand loyalty, not as Tarkyn's liegeman. "I can't decide for you. Ostensibly, I too have changed loyalties. I was a palace guard in Tormadell and loyal to the king until he turned on Tarkyn. But in reality, I grew up with Tarkyn and have always served him, body and soul."

"And what would you have done if he had flogged you and left you for dead?"

Danton frowned, then shook his head. When he had repeated this sequence, Harkell asked what he was doing.

Danton smiled wryly, "I am trying to imagine Tarkyn doing that to me. I just can't. I've been whipped scores of times, but not at Tarkyn's instigation. He fought to save me. He is my liege lord and as such, I trust him and expect him to look after me, even as I look after him. If he did anything like that to me, I could no longer feel safe around him."

Harkell gave a short derisive laugh, "I have never felt safe around Jarand. I never expected to. So his actions today have not betrayed my trust in him because I never had any."

"So why do you follow him?"

"Because he is my prince. Because my family have lived on his lands for generations. Because that is what you do, if you live near Montraya."

"In other words, you never thought about it."

"No, I didn't. And even after the flogging, if I had survived, I wouldn't have. It is only because you and your lord challenge me now, that I even begin to think about the possibility of a different life." The captain stared into the shadows of the surrounding trees, "So what sort of life would I expect if I chose to stay?"

Danton's eyes narrowed, "I find your question offensive. A life of service to His Highness is not designed around your comfort. I will not try to entice you or dissuade you, based on the lifestyle." He shrugged, "That may change anyway. It has certainly changed radically for me. You must make your decision purely on the basis of whether you can commit to Prince Tarkyn."

"I can't think. Am I permitted to walk around?"

Danton waved his arm, "Be my guest. You can go wherever you like. You can start walking back to Montraya now, if that is your wish."

Captain Harkell got to his feet and looked down at Danton, "You don't like me much, do you?"

"Not yet. I may come to like you, if I get to know you. At the moment, after all I have heard of the way Prince Jarand's troops behave, I am very wary of anyone associated with them, let alone one of their officers." Danton stared back up at him, "I may have helped to save your life but that was not because we need your support. We can do quite nicely without a man of uncertain character and uncertain loyalties in our midst."

The man's faced darkened. "I am not a man of uncertain character. If I were, I could easily pay lip service to your prince. I have never been brutal in the discharge of my duties other than to flog any man in my troop who was. But I'm talking about three to five lashes, at the outside ten. Not forty. And not with a brass buckle on the end of the whip." He bowed slightly, "You have made your position clear. I will not stay for someone's charity. I will relieve you of my presence." He turned away a little too quickly and swayed. After taking a few moments to recover, he strode off towards the last of the light glimmering through the trees that showed him the way to Montraya.

"DANTON!"

The blonde sorcerer's head whipped around at the sound of Tarkyn's angry voice and he scrambled to his feet. One look at the prince's face and he was bowing in apology before he could stop himself. "I beg your pardon, Your Highness. I can see I have angered you."

The extent of Tarkyn's anger soon became evident when Danton began to straighten up.

Tarkyn's voice was like ice, "I did not say you could rise. You have well and truly pushed the limits today, Danton. Firstly, you misrepresented me and forced me into the position of having to apologise for your behaviour. Then, you turn away a man who has nowhere to go and no one to serve. Now, get up, and go and fetch him back. Tell him I would be honoured to accept his service, if he would be willing to give it to me and that I would value his experience. He still has time to decide one way or the other. Make sure you do not force his hand again." He waited until Danton met his eyes. "Are we clear? Now go."

Minutes later, slightly out of breath, Danton drew up alongside the captain who had just broken through the cover of the trees and was striding angrily across the fields towards the road. He put a restraining hand on Harkell's bare shoulder. "Stop."

The soldier twisted his shoulder from under Danton's hand and kept walking.

"Please stop, Captain Harkell. I apologise for what I said. Prince Tarkyn is very displeased with me and I must try to make amends."

The appeal of one liegeman's plight to another worked, and the captain slowed his pace, "Hmph. You may walk with me. I may decide to return. I may not."

"Captain Harkell, His Highness has charged me to say that he would be honoured to accept your service if you choose to give it and that he would value your experience. He reiterated that you still have time to decide."

The captain stopped walking and turned to look at Danton. "I gather he overheard our exchange?" When Danton nodded, a slow smile appeared on the soldier's face, "He is very kind, this prince of yours, isn't he?"

Danton, who was smarting from his recent encounter with his liege, took a moment to agree. Then he shrugged and smiled, "Yes, he is. He is kinder than I. But I am more protective of his person than he is. So perhaps that is why."

"And he said he would be honoured to accept my service, did he? Honoured? Wow. That is really something. Prince Jarand does not feel honoured by anyone's service. He just takes it for granted." The captain frowned, "But perhaps your prince is just lying to lure me back so he can use me to find out about his brother." One look at Danton's face was enough to tell the captain that this train of thought was incorrect. He put up his hand, "Sorry. I can see I have offended you again."

Danton took a tight breath, "Prince Tarkyn does not say things like that lightly. He once rejected a whole community of people who would have sworn their fealty to him. He said he would not feel honoured to have them as liegemen and women and so rejected their offer." Aware that he must not misrepresent Tarkyn's affairs, he added, "Later on, things were resolved between them and he did accept their oath."

"Hmm. So he would not just accept anyone?" The captain turned and continued his walk away from the forest's edge. "So why would he accept me?"

"Rightly or wrongly, he has formed a good opinion of you and is willing to give you a chance."

"He does not have much to go on."

"No, he doesn't," said Danton dryly. He thought about it for a minute, "Hmm. Perhaps he gets a feel for people when he heals them. I know the person being healed usually gets to know about him. So presumably the reverse is true." Danton glanced at the captain, waiting for his reaction but received only a thoughtful silence.

At this stage, it was clear that they were heading for the tree where the captain had been tied and beaten. Nothing further was said until they arrived. In the last of the light, Harkell walked up to the great tree and placed his hand on its trunk. He leaned forward and studied the splashes of blood on its bark, and ran his hand over the rusty patches he found. He squatted down and ran his hand over the little patches of dried blood in the dust at the base of the tree. Then he straightened and looked up at where the rope had been flung over the bough above him. Rubbing his wrists in memory, he turned and looked behind at where all his men had stood and watched silently as he had endured, before turning back once more to the tree. He gazed around the horizon at the bleak lonely landscape filled with ploughed furrows but no people. Suddenly, he gave an involuntary shudder down the whole length of his body.

"I will follow your prince," he said shortly.

Chapter 7

Tarkyn stood just within the woods watching their return. He waited until their eyes had adjusted to the gloom and they were standing before him in the small clearing.

"And so, Captain Harkell, now that darkness has fallen, we must leave. What is your decision?"

The captain dropped to one knee and placed his hand over his heart. "Sire, would you do me the honour of accepting me into your service?"

"What of your loyalty to my brother?"

Without raising his head, he replied, "Sire, I have been back to the place of my punishment. It is clear that Prince Jarand has completely forsaken me and so, with a clear conscience I can forsake him. He did not expect me to live to serve him further. And so my life is my own to do with as I wish."

"And would you throw away your newly found freedom so easily? You do not have to exchange one life of service for another."

Despite himself, the captain rocked upright in surprise. "Yes I do, Your Highness. One cannot live completely unbonded."

Knowing he was surrounded by incredulous woodfolk, Tarkyn smiled and said, "I think you will find that some people think you can. Although perhaps they are bound to each other."

A note of uncertainty entered the captain's voice, "Your Highness, I understood that you would be willing to accept me."

"Captain Harkell, look at me. If you are sure, I will feel truly honoured to accept you into my service."

The captain met Tarkyn's eyes unwaveringly. "I am sure, Your Highness. You have my pledge that I will honour and serve you, body and soul, to the end of my days."

"Captain Harkell, I give you my vow that I will protect and support you, as your liege lord." Tarkyn took a breath, "And if I ever treat you as you have been treated today, your oath to me will no longer bind you. You may stand."

Once the captain was standing face to face with him, Tarkyn smiled, "And now, we must soon be on our way. We do not have ranks among us here, except of course, for mine. So, are you happy that we address you simply as Harkell?"

"Your will is my command, Sire."

"Harkell, I am giving you a choice," said Tarkyn dryly, thinking he was going to have to train up another guardsman not to use too much protocol. "Are you happy with being called Harkell?"

"Yes, Your Highness."

"Good. Now, before you meet everyone else, I'm afraid I must ask you to swear another oath."

Harkell immediately dropped to one knee in preparation.

"Harkell, you must swear, on pain of death, never to reveal the presence of the people you are about to meet."

"Your Highness, you have only to ask and it would carry as much weight. But I give you my oath as you require."

"Thank you. You may rise."

In the next instant, the woodfolk appeared around them and Stormaway, String and Bean walked out from between the trees. Lapping Water came forward carrying a light brown shirt and jerkin.

"Harkell, you must be freezing by now. I'm afraid we only have the one colour but it will keep you warm. I am Lapping Water."

Harkell's eyes darted around him, taking in his first view of the woodfolk. However he brought his soft brown eyes to bear on Lapping Water and thanked her.

She smiled at him, "You have lovely coloured eyes. Very good for camouflage." She sent a mischievous grin at the prince, "Not like Tarkyn's. His are like beacons."

Harkell noted with interest that she had called the prince by his first name. He was even more interested to see that the prince had coloured slightly.

"You may struggle to remember everyone's names at the beginning," said Danton, "And even if you do remember them, you probably won't be able to tell one person from the other for a while. But in the interests of your safety, you had better meet and remember Waterstone, Ancient Oak and Sparrow." He indicated them as he talked and they came forward. "Waterstone and Tarkyn are blood brothers. So these three are, to all intents and purposes, members of the royal family."

Harkell immediately bowed deeply.

Waterstone waved an irritable hand, "No. Cut that out. I won't have people bowing to me. It is outrageous. Now stand up straight and let me talk to you properly."

As Harkell straightened, he said, "I beg your pardon, Your Highness. I did not mean to offend you."

Surrounded by the grins of woodfolk, Waterstone rolled his eyes and continued, "And before we go any further, you have my permission to attack me if you need to. And Ancient Oak's." He smiled, "I'm not so sure about Sparrow. I don't think I could let you attack her."

As Harkell was looking totally bewildered at this point, Tarkyn intervened, "Harkell, let me introduce the woodfolk to you. They do not believe in hierarchies and only accept my rank because I insist upon it. So my woodfolk brothers will not accept any sign of respect commonly due to a member of the royal family. You will only make them feel uncomfortable if you bow to them or address them by title."

"Absolutely correct," confirmed Ancient Oak.

"And you are only bound to serve me, not them."

Waterstone looked revolted, "Yes. Don't even think about it. You treat us on equal terms or not at all."

Tarkyn smiled sunnily, "But despite our differences, we all get on remarkably well, don't we, young Sparrow?" He looked around, "And where's Midnight? He's been a bit left out of all this."

Hail, who was standing at the back of the throng well away from the new sorcerer, pushed Midnight forward as Tarkyn sent him a request to come. Midnight's face lit up and he took a running jump into Tarkyn's arms.

Tarkyn gave him a squeeze and then swung around so that Midnight was facing Harkell. "And this is Midnight, who is my ward. He's deaf but very clever." Tarkyn beamed at the little boy, "Aren't you, mischief?"

Midnight grinned back and waved at the soldier.

Summer Rain came forward and said, "Since it is so late, I think we should have something to eat before we go. Would you like something, Harkell? I am Summer Rain."

Harkell nodded, "I am nearly faint with hunger."

"Of course you are, after what you have been through this afternoon," said Summer Rain kindly. "Just a minute, I'll fetch you a tonic while some of the others prepare the food."

"Oh no. Now that's not a kind way to welcome Harkell. Your tonics taste terrible," said Tarkyn lightly.

Summer Rain threw him a minatory look, "Tarkyn, I'm sure Harkell will have the fortitude to endure the taste, to gain the benefits."

Harkell watched and learned that Tarkyn accepted what he would consider to be an impertinence. Tarkyn caught his glance and said quietly, with a twinkle in his eyes, "And not only will I endure a scolding from her, I never learn that she has no sense of humour whatsoever." He became serious, "But Summer Rain is a very skilled healer. She spread salves on your back when you first arrived in the woods and advised us on how to manage your shock."

"But I thought you healed me, my lord."

"Oh, I did, once Danton overcame your resistance. But Summer Rain has the knowledge ...and Stormaway, now I come to think of it. I only have the power." He turned to the three sorcerers waiting quietly to one side, "This is Stormaway Treemaster, my personal wizard, as he was my father's before me.

Stormaway smiled warmly, clearly pleased by this form of introduction. He inclined his head, "It is a pleasure to meet you."

"And these are trappers, String and Bean, who are living with us for a while."

Harkell frowned at them, "Didn't I see you two down in Montraya about six or eight months ago?"

String and Bean looked at each other and back at Harkell, "Might have done."

"Pub brawl, wasn't it?" asked Harkell.

"Might have been," said String.

"Bad luck. Can't do anything about it now," added Bean, with a wicked grin.

"What would you have done, Harkell, as a matter of interest? I am Autumn Leaves."

Harkell suddenly felt himself to be on trial but he answered honestly, nevertheless. "Had I caught them at the time, I would have thrown them in the lock up for the night until they sobered up, and sent them off with a stiff warning the next day." He gave a short laugh, "If you imprisoned every pub brawler for more than a few days, there wouldn't be many people left walking the streets." He paused. "And now, eight months later, I would have given them a mild warning." He looked around, "Do I pass muster?"

Waterstone smiled and clapped him on the shoulder, "You'll do. Come and have something to eat."

Part 2: Harkell

CHAPTER 8

The cold night air cut into their lungs as the little troop of woodfolk and sorcerers threaded their way up the steep mountainside between huge tumbled boulders. Because the woodfolk's night vision was better, the sorcerers were spread among them so that they could be guided through the more difficult passages. As they rose higher, the valley floor spread out below them in a black carpet, dotted with warm golden lights pinpointing the location of the various farmsteads. Away in the distance, part of the horizon glowed from the strength of hundreds of lamps in Montraya.

At the rear of the line, Autumn Leaves and Running Feet kept an eye on Captain Harkell in front of them. After they had seen him stumble for the second time, Running Feet pulled up alongside him and realised that the soldier was gasping for breath as they climbed. The woodman relayed this information forward and a halt was called. As Tarkyn appeared from further up the line, a look of apprehension crossed the soldier's face and he made every attempt to straighten up and present a strong front. But the darkness did not hide his labouring breath as he fought to regain his strength.

"Here," said Autumn Leaves, handing him a cup of water.

The captain accepted the cup with a hand that shook so much, some of the water spilled. He eyed Tarkyn, waiting for a derisory remark.

"Harkell, I presume you are not usually so unfit."

"No, my lord." Harkell gave a slight bow, and took another couple of breaths. "I apologise for holding you all up."

"No. It is we who should apologise for force-marching you when you are still not fully recovered. Anyway, the children could do with a break." He considered the soldier for a minute. "Would you agree to me giving you a little more *esse*? I think that will help to shore up your reserves of energy."

"Of course, Your Highness. If that is your will."

Tarkyn shook his head, "No, Harkell, that is my offer. You may accept or not as you choose."

"I'd accept, if I were you," said Autumn Leaves. "We still have a long way to go."

"But what about you, Your Highness? Will it not weaken you?"

"Don't worry about me. I replenished my power after healing you before and there are plenty of trees around. But a small boost to you will not tax me, anyway."

"I'm not sure what trees have to do with anything, but thank you, I will accept your offer."

Tarkyn placed his hand on the man's shoulder and sent a wave of strength coursing through him. When he withdrew his hand, the prince looked thoughtful as Harkell gave a slight bow and thanked him.

"What are you leaving behind you, Harkell?" asked Tarkyn slowly. "Some of your physical distress is coming from a reluctance to move away from that valley below us."

Harkell took a deep breath, "I am leaving behind my wife and two small children, Your Highness."

"Oh no! Blast it!" exclaimed Tarkyn. "After all this, I still haven't learnt to consider people beyond their relationship with me."

"Yes, you have," said Autumn Leaves, giving the young prince a pat on the shoulder. "It just takes you a while to think of it sometimes."

Harkell watched this over-familiarity with interest but thought it would be a long time before he himself could trust this prince enough to similarly push the boundaries. He realised Tarkyn was speaking to him.

"I am sorry, Harkell. Did you realise you would be leaving the area when you made your pledge to me?"

Harkell shook his head, "No, Your Highness. But Danton made it clear that I must decide regardless of where it would lead me or what type of life it committed me to." He gave a sad smile, "I did not think serving a fugitive prince would lead me back into the arms of my family, no matter how much I might wish for it. But now that I have fallen from Prince Jarand's grace, nothing would."

"We can't leave them believing that you have died, though," said Tarkyn decisively. "At the very least we must get word to them that you are safe. Then, in time, we will consider how to reunite you." He smiled at the nearby woodfolk, "Of course, I have no idea how we can achieve any of this but it will give us something to think about as we climb, won't it?"

With that, he gave Harkell a final pat on the shoulder and climbed his way between the resting woodfolk nearer to the front of the file. Unconsciously, Harkell let out a sigh of released tension as Tarkyn disappeared into the darkness ahead.

"I know what you mean," said Running Feet, as though he had spoken. "The first time I met Tarkyn, he shot me up into the air with his magic and threatened to drop me."

"Don't be unfair, Running Feet," protested Autumn Leaves. "You know he had just discovered he couldn't leave the forest and was scared and angry. He hasn't done anything like it since. And now I think about it, Tree Wind had just pinned him down with an arrow to his throat and tried to use mind control on him. So it was not surprising that he was a bit edgy."

Harkell looked from one woodman to the other, "Things have not always been so harmonious between you then?"

"Oooh no," replied Autumn Leaves. "We woodfolk have never had leaders, never sworn allegiance to the king or anyone, until we were forced to by Markazon, twelve years ago. Even after that, we carried on as before until Tarkyn turned up two months ago."

Harkell raised his eyebrows, "Well, I suppose I don't know how you all behaved before he arrived, but I must say that your culture seems to be the prevailing one. He has clearly not imposed the expectations of our culture on you all."

"Except that we must 'serve, honour and protect' him and we have never done that for any man or woman in our entire history," said Autumn Leaves. "It is totally alien to us."

"Not even for a forest guardian," added Running Feet. "Not officially anyway. In reality, I suppose people would have done all that for a forest guardian, but it was their choice."

"We have just spun off onto some strange trajectory here. What is a forest guardian?" asked Harkell.

"In our myths, a guardian of the forest is someone with extraordinary powers who appears among us in times of strife to guide us through whatever ills beset us. Their appearances are very rare. Once every four or five hundred years."

Harkell took a sip of water and frowned as he tried to understand, "And you wouldn't even swear your allegiance willingly to someone like that?"

"Tarkyn is someone like that," said Autumn Leaves shortly.

"Hmm," Harkell's gaze travelled between the two woodmen as he slowly sipped his water.

After a couple of minutes, when Harkell said nothing further, Running Feet asked, a little belligerently, "What do you mean, 'Hmmm'?"

Harkell gave an apologetic smile, "I was wondering whether you thought the prince had extraordinary powers simply because he is a powerful sorcerer and you people are not sorcerers. Then I remembered you have Danton and Stormaway with you who are also powerful sorcerers. So I wondered whether you considered them to be forest guardians as well. On balance, I thought probably not, because it sounds like the appearance of this forest guardian of yours is a very unusual occurrence." His smile broadened, "And then, having come that far, I was wondering what extraordinary powers were possessed by the prince that went beyond normal expectation…but I had decided not to ask because at this stage, you may not yet trust me enough to tell me."

"You are very phlegmatic about the possibility of not being trusted," commented Autumn Leaves, "Danton was very unhappy about it when he first arrived."

Harkell noted that his unasked question had been avoided, "If Danton grew up with the prince, he would have expected to be trusted. I, on the other hand, have met none of you before and have clearly just changed alliances. So, it would be foolhardy to trust me at this stage." Seeing movement further up the line, he drank down the rest of his water, stood up and handed his cup to Autumn Leaves with a nod of thanks, before adding, "Particularly if you yourselves have little experience of the value of oaths of allegiance."

Autumn Leaves' eyes narrowed, "We know exactly how much value to place on an oath and it is our own honour that binds us to Tarkyn. The question is more how much faith we should place in the honour of sorcerers."

"I see," said Harkell slowly. Without another word, he hunched himself deeper into his cloak and turned to follow the rest of the woodfolk up the mountainside.

CHAPTER 9

As they rose higher, the wind became bitter and white flakes began to spiral down among them. They tried to quicken their pace but there was only so fast they could negotiate the steep, rocky terrain in the darkness.

"I hope you think this is worth it, to put a greater distance between sorcerers and us," grumbled String to any woodfolk within earshot.

"Yeah. As far as I could see, there were only harmless farmers near the woodlands anyway," added Bean dolefully. "Your danger from a storm on the mountain is far greater."

"One of those harmless people told Jarand we were there," pointed out Tree Wind.

"Huh." There was a short pause while String hauled himself up over a large boulder. "So what he's going to do that he hasn't tried already?"

"Watch out," rumbled Thunder Storm, "There's a sheer drop on your left along this next part. Keep against the right hand side of the path."

"Why don't we talk about this when we don't need our breath for climbing?" said Tree Wind trenchantly. "We have enough to contend with at the moment."

Slowly the wind picked up, driving the snow against their faces in sharp stabs of ice. The littlest children were struggling and had to be carried. Midnight stomped stoically between Hail and Tarkyn but his teeth were chattering and his laboured breathing hurt his chest. His foot slipped on an icy rock and he came down hard on his hands. As he scrabbled to get up quickly so that he didn't hold everyone up, he felt strong hands grab him from behind and he was swung up into Tarkyn's arms. Breathing a sigh of relief, he snuggled into the warmth of Tarkyn's shoulder as he was borne up the mountain.

For two more long, cold hours the little troop struggled through the darkness, over icy rocks and along slippery paths, not daring to stop. The wind and snow made them miserable but did not develop into a storm. Sometime after midnight they reached the cave they had left two days before. Once on the narrow plateau, String and Bean led everyone to the entrance that was just beginning to disappear under a thin covering of snow and swept it clear with their arms.

Woodfolk and sorcerers gathered around but did not enter.

Tarkyn peered down into the pitch darkness of the cave's entrance. "I had better go in first, I suppose."

"I'll come with you," said Waterstone.

"And I," added Danton.

Harkell wondered in the darkness why it fell to their liege to go first into an uncertain situation. He would have expected others to protect the prince by exploring any possible dangers and reporting back. The three volunteers disappeared into the darkness and after a moment a dim light could be seen emanating from within the cave.

Suddenly an angry roar shook the night. Without hesitation, Harkell pushed his way through the waiting woodfolk and rushed into the cave to the aid of his new liege.

"No. Harkell. Don't go in," shouted Autumn Leaves. "You don't know what you're dealing with." He turned to Running Feet. "I don't think he's even armed."

Harkell landed breathlessly within the cave to be confronted by the sight of Prince Tarkyn, standing face to face with a huge black mountain lion. As the mountain lion spotted the sudden movement out of the corner of his eye, he snarled and rushed at the new intruder. A shimmering wall of bronze slammed down around the lion just as it was about to launch itself at Harkell. The soldier found himself just feet from the enraged animal.

Waterstone raised his hand slowly to tell him to stay where he was. Bearing in mind that for all his reticence, Waterstone was Tarkyn's bloodbrother, Harkell followed his request without question, against instincts that screamed at him to back away.

"I think this has just become more difficult," said Tarkyn quietly as he walked over slowly to join Harkell in front of the mountain lion. He expanded his shield so the cat had room to move.

Tarkyn stood firmly before the mountain lion, emanated waves of greeting and apology while he sent images of the wolf pack interspersed with images of the woodfolk waiting outside, into the mountain lion's mind. The great animal paced back and forth, lashing his tail and growling deep within his throat. Whenever the lion faced him, Tarkyn held his eyes unwaveringly and although he made no attempt to simulate an answering growl, slowly increased the sense of inherent threat in his images. Suddenly, the huge cat came to stand eye to eye with Tarkyn. After several fraught moments, the lion tilted his head back and let out a mighty roar that reverberated around the walls of the cave. Then, satisfied that he had affirmed his strength, he turned away and sauntered to the furthest reach of the shield where he lay down with his back to them, put his head on his paws and, to all intents and purposes, went back to sleep.

Tarkyn let out a sigh of relief, "Whew, he's an ornery bastard, isn't he?" He ran the back of his hand over his forehead, "I might just maintain my shield for a little longer until we are sure he is settled. It's safe for everyone to come in now. They must be dying to get in out of the cold."

"Well done, young one," said Waterstone, patting Tarkyn's shoulder on the way past, "I'll bring in the others."

Harkell moved aside to let Waterstone through, "I am sorry, sire. I gather my entry was not helpful. When I heard that first roar, I rushed to your assistance. I can see I should have been more cautious."

Tarkyn shook his head, "No Harkell. You did as you should. Thank you for coming to my aid. How were you to know if no one thought to tell you?"

Harkell would have asked more but again did not wish to appear too curious. His eyes roved around the cave, checking for hidden crevices. He looked briefly at Danton and then returned his gaze to the prince to find himself being watched quizzically.

"I am a little surprised, Harkell. I expected you to ask me what it was that no one had told you."

Harkell cleared his throat, "It is not that I am not curious, my lord..."

"I can see that," said Tarkyn with a smile. "Your eyes don't stay still for a moment."

"No. But I do not want you to think that I might be spying for your brother. So I do not want to pry too closely and arouse your suspicions any more than I presume they already are."

"Very wise," said Danton firmly from the side.

Tarkyn raised his eyebrows, "Danton, that is not kind."

Danton gave a short laugh, "It depends on how you look at it. It is kinder to be forewarned than to wake up one morning and find one's arms pinioned behind one's back, facing charges of betrayal."

"Is that what happened to you?" asked Harkell.

Danton gave a short nod.

Tarkyn looked at him, "Danton, you told me that you were willing to stake your life on your belief that my integrity would overcome my fear of betrayal. Yet when I offer my faith to someone new, you warn them off."

Danton gave a slight bow, "I apologise. But the fact that I would stake my life did not necessarily mean that I was sure that I would win the bet. It meant that I thought you were worth the gamble."

As they spoke, the woodfolk were spreading out into the cave, setting up places to sleep and setting a fire in the middle.

Tarkyn waved his hand in irritation at them both before walking away, "Do what you like then, both of you. If you can't trust my faith in you, then so be it."

Harkell was left standing uncertainly near the doorway. Danton glanced at him but feeling that Harkell's presence had already soured his relationship with Tarkyn enough for one day, turned away from him and left to set up his own bedding.

The soldier stood watching the woodfolk chatting amongst themselves, saw String and Bean already lying down ready to sleep and Tarkyn speaking briefly with Stormaway before collecting Midnight to find a place in the corner to settle down. Harkell had never felt more alone. He edged slowly towards the entrance, then turned and climbed up the short slope to stand outside in the darkness. The wind had dropped and only the odd white flake drifted down. He hunched his cloak around him and walked across the narrow plateau to a small group of bushes. He peered into them and after a backward glance at the mouth of the cave, crawled in between the close-knit branches of the shrubs and lay down. He hugged his cloak around him, closed his eyes and tried to block out the events of the day.

A few minutes later, a voice close to him, whispered, "Hey, are you awake?"

After a moment's thought, Harkell whispered back, "Yes. At least, I am now."

"Sorry. I didn't mean to wake you. I'm on lookout duty."

"I am not intending anyone any harm, if that's what you're wondering."

"No. I can see that. I was just wondering if you were warm enough or needed another cloak over you if you're staying out here for the night. I am Rainstorm, by the way."

"No, I'm fine. I'm used to sleeping outside."

"You may be warm enough," replied Rainstorm, "But you're not fine. Otherwise you wouldn't have come out here on your own when it's obviously warmer and safer in the cave."

"Hmph."

"Come on," cajoled Rainstorm, "Why don't you come out and talk to me and help me with lookout duty?"

Harkell let out a long sigh and roused himself to crawl out from within the bushes. The clouds had cleared and the moon shone strongly down on the scatterings of snow. He could see Rainstorm's silhouette, sitting on a rock near him, scanning the trees nearby. When the woodman turned his head, the light was strong enough for him to see the green of his eyes.

Rainstorm patted the rock next to him, "Here. Plenty of room for two."

Harkell glanced at the entrance to the cave but it was quiet and dark, only a slight orange glow from the fire inside showed through the doorway. "Won't it get smoky in there with that fire going through the night?"

"No," replied Rainstorm, "Stormaway has a neat little spell for directing and hiding smoke. Sorcerers have their uses, I must say. Danton can direct smoke too, but he has to concentrate on it whereas Stormaway can set up the spell and it will look after itself."

"They've all gone to sleep then?"

Rainstorm smiled in the darkness, "Yes, now that they know you're safe."

"No one came out after me."

"No. But when they realised you weren't there, they checked with the lookouts and I told them where you were."

Harkell mulled over this information, "So, were they alarmed for themselves or for me? And how did you speak with them? I didn't hear voices."

"We mind talk," said Rainstorm matter-of-factly. "And they were alarmed for you, not for us. As you see, we have lookouts. We know when danger approaches. We are all armed and we have powerful sorcerers in our midst."

"Are you giving me a warning?"

Rainstorm looked surprised, "No. I am trusting you with knowledge about us and proving that it was you and not us that we were worried about."

"I see." The soldier ran his hands through his hair. "I'm sorry. I feel so jarred after the events of today. The hideousness of that flogging, with all my men watching; losing my whole way of life and all my years of training and experience as a soldier; gone in one quick afternoon."

"You have had a pretty tough day, haven't you? And now you find yourself among people you don't know." Rainstorm smiled encouragingly, "But you still have your training and experience behind you. They haven't gone. You just have to use them for someone else."

"No. You don't understand. Everything I have learnt of how to fight an enemy has been turned upside down. You people defeated eighty of my well-trained troops without a shot being fired, with no one being killed and with complete ease, as far as I can see. And there are how many of you?"

"Forty-four," replied Rainstorm. "Forty-six now, with the sorcerers, you and Falling Rain."

"Hmm. Roughly two to one. Not a great effort on my part, I would have to say."

"Rainstorm grinned, "Well, to set the record straight, we did shoot your two frontrunners but only with slingshots so that we didn't kill them. But I am afraid to say, that with the way we set our trap we could have immobilised you all with – let me see – less than ten, I think."

Harkell scratched his head, "But I still don't understand how it happened. One minute we're riding along in neat pairs. The next minute, the troops were bunched up right across the road, jostling for space. Good use of a shield, though. Shields have only ever been used for defence before, you know. This will revolutionise warfare."

"A shield wouldn't have trapped you so effectively without Tarkyn's intervention first," said Rainstorm with some satisfaction.

Harkell frowned, "What did he do?"

Rainstorm smiled, "He asked the horses to bunch up and stop. He's the guardian of the forest, you know. He can communicate with animals." He nodded towards the cave, "You saw him doing it just now with the mountain lion."

Harkell eyes grew round, "Oh, I see. That is amazing. I saw him with the mountain lion but I just thought he must be intimidating it somehow."

"He was," chortled Rainstorm, "He was using images of a wolf pack. That poor deluded mountain lion thinks we're all a strange type of wolf."

For the first time, Harkell smiled, "I can see we are, in a way. The mountain lion could defeat one man, but not a pack of us."

"True. So you see, Tarkyn used images of a wolf pack to say that." He glanced sideways at Harkell, "Tarkyn could simply have defeated the lion outright but he chose not to. To preserve the lion's autonomy… and to keep Waterstone happy."

"Why would that please Waterstone?"

"Waterstone doesn't like the fact that Tarkyn could break that mountain lion's will if he wanted to." Rainstorm shrugged, "Waterstone is fiercely independent and it has been hard for him, and for all of us, to accept a liege. But even without the oath, Tarkyn's power is so immense that he could break any of us if he chose to." Rainstorm brought his eyes up to meet Harkell's, "But he doesn't choose to. If you must follow someone, you have found yourself a great person to follow."

"Hmm, so I am beginning to think. And I don't feel quite so bad now about failing Prince Jarand as I did. I didn't realise the extraordinary power I was up against. The ability to control our horses is like having our forces riddled with enemies. It is an enormous advantage. In fact, since the horses effectively changed sides, we were outnumbered."

"I don't know why you care that you failed Jarand. The man is an out and out bastard."

"I care because I had undertaken to serve and protect him, whatever his worth. I failed myself when I failed him."

Rainstorm smiled and gave him a pat on the shoulder, gently in case it was still tender, "I see. Fair enough, I suppose. I would not feel good about failing to keep an oath either."

Harkell looked away out across the light dotted blackness below. "Somewhere out there are my wife and children whom I may never see again. Do you think Prince Tarkyn will really let them know I am safe?"

"If he said he would, he will"

They sat in companionable silence for a while until Harkell said quietly, "Thanks, Rainstorm, for making the effort to talk to me."

Rainstorm smiled at him, "After such a terrible day, you needed to talk to someone. I helped rescue you from that tree, you know. And we all saw the state of your back."

Harkell frowned, "I didn't realise that anyone other than Danton and the prince was involved. Danton didn't mention you."

"No, he couldn't at the time, because you didn't know about us then."

"I see. Then thank you for that as well." Harkell thought for a minute, before saying slowly, "Since I have never seen you people, would I be right in saying that you never leave the forest?" When Rainstorm nodded, the soldier asked, "So was it nerve-racking, going out into the open?"

"Yes, very. I have never been out in the open in daylight before. I jumped a mile when a crow cawed near me." He gave a soft laugh, "Well, actually, I jumped about seven feet. That's a little something we woodfolk can do that you sorcerers can't."

"Really? Show me."

A voice called out quietly from behind the bushes he had lain in, "Over here."

Harkell swung around to see Rainstorm waving from behind the bush. In the next instant he was sitting back at his side on the rock.

Harkell grinned, "That's marvellous. So you people have your own special powers, mind talking and…I don't know what you'd call that… it's like short distance translocating but quicker and easier. It doesn't seem to make you feel sick in the same way."

"No, it takes no effort at all. Tarkyn calls it flicking."

"Can he do it?"

"No, only born woodfolk can." Rainstorm considered him for a minute, "So, I understand sorcerers all have different sorts of power. What about you?"

Harkell shrugged, "I can't do much. I come from a long line of blacksmiths. So I can bend and shape metal to some extent and sharpen blades."

Rainstorm beamed at him, "Can you? You're going to be in great demand here. We all have knives, and then there are arrow tips that need sharpening. I come from a long line of artisans myself. My people are forestals. They tend to stay in or near one particular area of the forest and craft weapons, bowls, utensils, clothing… all sorts of things. Do you have any magical fighting skills? We always thought, before Tarkyn came, that sorcerers only used power to fight with."

Harkell raised his eyebrows in surprise, "Really? How odd. Hardly any sorcerers do. I certainly don't. I live and die by the sword."

"What about shields? Can you make a magical shield?"

The soldier grimaced, "Under extreme circumstances and for a very limited period of time. But it takes all my effort and concentration and leaves me exhausted after only a couple of minutes. So, if the danger hasn't passed by then, I'm a sitting duck."

"Hmm. String and Bean aren't very good at shields either but Danton, Stormaway and Tarkyn can hold them up for hours."

"Really?" Harkell frowned, "I would have expected Prince Tarkyn to be able to because he is renowned for his skill as a tournament fighter and I would have expected a wizard to be able to. But what do you know about Danton?"

Rainstorm shrugged, "Not a lot. He is apparently an elite guard and his full name is Danton Patronell, Lord of… Hmm, I've forgotten where he's lord of. Not lord of us, that's all I care about."

"Oh, I see. He's a lord, is he? And he has an honourific. He must be bloody good."

"What's an honourific?" asked Rainstorm.

"It is a title that can be carried down through the generations. Like Tamadil. The royal family's second name denotes that their line is very strong in magic. One of their ancestors will have earned it. If you achieve a very high level of magical use and fighting skill, you are granted a second name in recognition of your achievement. That's why wizards all have two names, although both of theirs are honourifics. With these elite sorcerers, the honourific is added to the name that they already carry."

Rainstorm became thoughtful, "Perhaps if I had known this, I might not have tried out Danton's skills so casually." He shrugged and grinned, "But then again, I knew he was an elite guard. That's why I was testing him." He stilled. "Hang on," he said quietly, "There's something in that tree over there."

He sent out a message to the other lookouts and received back a reply from Grass Wind that an owl had just flown from her area into his.

"Don't worry. It's just an owl," said Rainstorm. "Owls and eagles are always hanging around and keeping an eye on Tarkyn. The whole forest protects him."

"Not the mountain lion apparently."

"No. Some of the more predatory animals need a bit of persuading." His eyes went out of focus for a moment before he turned to Harkell, "That was Waterstone relaying a message from Tarkyn asking whether you are all right. Why don't you come back inside when I finish my shift? You can stay and chat with me until then. What do you think?"

Harkell smiled, "It is a novelty having my liege care what happens to me. Could you thank him and Waterstone for their concern and say that I will do as you suggest."

CHAPTER 10

"Morning, Harkell."

Harkell opened an eye to find the prince standing over him holding out a cup of tea. As a look of alarm passed over his face and he scrabbled to get himself upright, Tarkyn gave a friendly laugh and put out a restraining hand.

"No, Harkell. Don't rush to get up. I'm just bringing you a cup of tea. You may lie there and drink it, if you wish. We won't be leaving for another hour or so."

Harkell accepted the tea and thanked him, watching warily as the prince sat down, cross-legged, beside him and picked up his own tea.

Tarkyn took a sip then turned to look at the uneasy soldier. "I'm sorry we treated you so poorly last night that we forced you out into the cold. Everyone was cold and tired and perhaps a little too focused on their own needs."

Harkell sat himself up and pulled his cloak around himself with one hand while he held his tea in the other. "It was not that anyone did anything unkind…"

"I know. It's just that we didn't do anything kind either, when you needed a little kindness."

Harkell was intrigued to hear the prince including himself as being at fault. He smiled, "No harm done. Now I have made a friend in Rainstorm. He put a lot of effort into drawing me back in."

Tarkyn smiled, "Rainstorm is great. He is one of my best friends. Sharp as a tack, which doesn't always go down well with his elders."

Harkell's eyes watched the prince over the rim of his cup as he sipped his tea.

"Now Harkell," continued Tarkyn, "I shouldn't have said, 'So be it,' last night. I suppose I too, was tired. I am not content that you may think I don't have faith in you. You and I both made a decision yesterday to commit ourselves to each other. As far as I am concerned, that decision is final. So, feel free to ask me anything you would like to know. If there are things I don't want to tell you, I will explain why, but it won't be because I don't trust you. Clear?" Suddenly he laughed and patted the soldier on the knee, "Harkell, you have the most speaking eyes I have ever seen. They are always darting around taking in information or focusing on people as you weigh up what is being said to you against what you are seeing. It is most unnerving."

Harkell lowered his cup and felt at ease enough to smile, "I beg your pardon, my lord. I did not mean to scrutinise you."

"It's fine. Don't stop. I'll get used to it." Tarkyn sipped his tea, "So, come on Harkell. What would you like to know? I gather Rainstorm filled you in on a few things last night but there must be some other questions you would like to ask."

There was a short silence before Harkell smiled ruefully, "There is so much I want to know that I don't know where to begin. I suppose I am most interested in your extraordinary powers that everyone is talking about. And you being this character out of woodfolk mythology. How mystical are you and how does it feel to be a walking legend?"

Tarkyn smiled warmly at the captain, "I can see I am going to grow to like you very much. Not many people stop to wonder how I feel about all this. Probably only Lapping Water, Waterstone and Rainstorm. And to answer the last of your questions first, I find it constantly embarrassing because it is not my legend and so I am something to the woodfolk that I don't fully understand. And, as their forest guardian, I am expected to save them all and it is not clear to me whether this is an ongoing avoidance of disasters or whether I have already fulfilled it by saving them from the curse." He waved his hand, "I'll tell you about the curse later, or someone else will."

"And how did they decide that you were a forest guardian?"

Tarkyn glanced sideways at him, "There are particular powers that denote a forest guardian which I developed after I entered the forest. You have seen them already. The power to heal and promote growth, and the power to share images and feelings with animals."

"So, are those your only extraordinary powers?"

"No. There is one more but it has nothing to do with being the forest guardian. I can perform two spells at once. In fact, if I concentrate hard, I can do three at once but not for long." Tarkyn sat back looking smug, "Even Jarand was impressed by that."

Harkell smiled, "I can see *you* are, whatever anyone else thinks."

Tarkyn exploded with laughter, sending a mouthful of tea shooting all over himself. As he put down his cup and wiped himself down, he was still grinning, "Well, yes I am, Harkell, as it turns out. But thanks for pointing it out."

Harkell grinned in return.

Tarkyn sent a message to ask Midnight for a cloth before adding lightly, "It's those eyes of yours. I knew they were seeing more than other people bother to notice." He became serious, "You are very courageous, aren't you? You're lucky to have survived as long as you did with Jarand."

"I would never have said anything like that to your brother. I like to think I combine courage with careful observation and sound judgement." He shrugged, "With the obvious exception of my failure yesterday."

Midnight arrived with a cloth and Tarkyn took a moment to thank him and ask for two bowls of porridge. Midnight beamed at him and trotted off.

"Such a cute boy," Tarkyn murmured quietly, watching him thread his way over to the fire. He brought his gaze back to bear on the captain, "But now you understand from Rainstorm, don't you, that you could not have predicted the forces you were up against."

Harkell nodded slowly, "Do you all talk about each other all the time? Will all my conversations become public knowledge?"

"Not all the time. I have it on the good authority of Waterstone that they talk about me constantly, much more than they do about each other. Of course, for the moment, you have taken centre stage as a new arrival, but with any luck it will wear off in time." Tarkyn smiled as Midnight and Sparrow arrived bearing two bowls each. They distributed the porridge and then sat down on either side of Tarkyn to have their own breakfasts.

"Morning, Sparrow."

"Hello, Tarkyn…and Harkell," said Sparrow cheerily. "Is your back better now, Harkell? It looked terrible yesterday. It must have hurt like anything."

Harkell finished his mouthful of porridge before replying, "Yes, it did hurt like anything. But thanks to His Highness, my back is feeling nearly as good as new."

Sparrow turned to her uncle, "Tarkyn, why does Harkell have to keep calling you Your Highness?"

The prince frowned at her, "Young lady, you are beginning to become quite a handful. You were rude to Jarand yesterday and now you are embarrassing me in front of Harkell. It is my choice how I am to be addressed, not yours."

Sparrow seemed quite unmoved by his displeasure. When she had finished her next mouthful of porridge she said calmly, "I wasn't telling you what to do. Even I would be careful about that. I was just asking. That's all."

Harkell's soft brown eyes watched as he ate his porridge.

Tarkyn smiled ruefully at him, "Harkell, I was going to say at some stage, before I was so rudely pre-empted, that you may call me Tarkyn, as everyone else does." He frowned down at Sparrow, "And just so that we are clear, Sparrow, I would appreciate questions like that being discussed with me privately first. You know perfectly well when something you say is going to be awkward. You are not as stupid as you are pretending to be."

Sparrow finished her porridge, put her bowl down and hopped into his lap, "Sorry Tarkyn. I'll try to be trickier next time."

Tarkyn put his bowl down so that he could wrap his arm around her, "Hmm, I'm not sure that I just won that argument. I think you're an out and out scoundrel."

Sparrow chortled and sent Harkell an impish grin. Moments later, he felt a tug on his leg and looked down to see Midnight pointing at him, then at himself, followed by wrapping his hands around each other. Then the little boy tilted his head to one side.

"He is asking whether you would like to be friends with him," interpreted Tarkyn. "He has also just double-checked with me his understanding that you are now isolated from your own people and wants you to know that he, too, was isolated for a long time and so understands how you feel. I think, if you don't mind me suggesting it, that he would accept an invitation to sit on your knee as a seal of friendship."

Harkell smiled, pointed at Midnight and then patted his cross-legged lap. Midnight grinned and climbed into the nest created by Harkell's legs.

"There is a little team of us who are or have been exiles," said Tarkyn as he returned Midnight's satisfied smile. "Four of us who were forced into it; you, me, Midnight, and Falling Rain. And then there is Danton who chose it, to be with me. Midnight and Falling Rain are now back with their people but you and I, my friend,…" Tarkyn shrugged, "Well, these are my people now. And maybe one day you can return to yours, though perhaps not beneath the walls of Montraya."

"Hmm, I would like to be reunited with my family, but for the rest I am less concerned. I can't see how I could ever return and remain true to my pledge to you, if you remain in exile."

Tarkyn gave his head a slight shake, "There are many types of service, Harkell. They do not all involve being by my side."

Harkell was slowly stroking Midnight's hair. "My son is about the same age as Midnight. He has my colouring and his name is Sorrell. My daughter is only three and she is called Marema."

"And your wife?" asked Tarkyn.

"My wife's name is Kayana. She has dark hair, almost black and the most vivid turquoise eyes you have ever seen."

"And who will look after them while you are gone?"

A shadow crossed the soldier's face, "I suppose they will get no more money from Prince Jarand. But my brother will take care of them and

I'm afraid Kayana will have to work. It will not be easy with a three year old and a six year old to look after but they will get by."

"Hmm, that's something else we should have told you before you made your decision. None of us has any money. Well, actually, there may be some stashed away somewhere in the forest that Waterstone knows about, and perhaps Stormaway has some, but anything that I rescued from the ruins of my previous life is hidden somewhere between the forest and Tormadell."

Harkell stroked Midnight's hair a couple of time before looking up and saying, "Lord Danton would not allow me to choose on the basis of anything other than being willing to follow you. So I had no chance to ask about money or to count it as a factor."

Tarkyn frowned, "I can't help feeling that Danton was very hard on you, insisting that you make such an enormous decision with so little information."

"He was tough," said Harkell, "but he was right. If I chose to follow you for the money or the lifestyle, what would happen when they changed, or a better offer came up?" His eyes wandered over to watch Danton chatting to Waterstone near the fire. "Saying that, Lord Danton did make it clear that he didn't like me much. He has tarred me with the brush of Prince Jarand's misdeeds." He sighed, "I suppose only time will change his mind."

"Harkell," said Tarkyn quietly, "Since I have given you leave to call me by my first name, you may not use Danton's title. It would be unseemly to show him more respect than I am requiring for myself."

The soldier's cheeks darkened, "I beg your pardon, Your Highness." When Tarkyn raised his eyebrows, Harkell added, "I am not quite ready to address you informally, if you don't mind. I will practise on Danton first."

Tarkyn smiled, "Good start. You'll get there." He stood up, shedding Sparrow as he rose, "Now, we have a bit of work to do, you and I." He called Falling Rain over, "Before we get too far away, do you think your egret might be able to fly an errand for us?"

Falling Rain shrugged, "I have no idea. I can't speak to her. But if you are asking me whether I'm willing to allow her to, the answer is yes."

"Thank you." Tarkyn stood with his hands on his hips, frowning. "Hmm. Now how are we going to do this? I'll need Harkell to explain to Running Feet where his family lives and then Running Feet will have to connect to me so that I can transfer to Elsie the images of where to go."

"You don't need Running Feet. I can do it," protested Falling Rain.

"Oh. Are you good at directions then?"

"Good enough. Better than you, by the sound of it. And I would like the chance to connect with Elsie."

Tarkyn smiled, "Of course you would. I should have thought of that. Very well. Harkell, ask Stormaway for a small piece of parchment and write your message to your family. When you've done that, meet us outside."

Twenty minutes later, Harkell emerged with a small roll of parchment that he handed to Tarkyn. Harkell noted that Tarkyn did not even think of looking at it to check what information it might contain.

"Now Harkell, give Falling Rain clear directions on how to reach your family. Use as much visual information as possible, landmarks, buildings, roads…whatever will guide an egret to find her way."

While Harkell talked to Falling Rain, Tarkyn requested the egret to come down out of the trees and checked with her that she could carry the message comfortably in her beak. When all parties were ready, Tarkyn held out the parchment to Elsie, who grabbed it firmly in her beak and, with a few strong beats of her wings, rose slowly into the air. "Ready, Falling Rain. As you connect to me, you will see the world through Elsie's eyes. Don't forget. Elsie can't receive words and I am very bad at interpreting directions. So if you can, use pictures or feelings."

Moments later, Falling Rain was seeing the mountainside from twenty feet above. As Elsie scanned the mountains and plain below her, he saw Montraya and by sending encouragement, guided her towards it. For nearly an hour, Tarkyn and he joined her in her flight across the plains. As she neared the first buildings of the city, Falling Rain looked down through her eyes, sending her an image of a small winding dirt road leading off to the left out into the fields beneath the southern end of the castle. Falling Rain's imagined street was not too dissimilar from the original and Elsie soon homed in and directed her flight towards Harkell's home. The egret scanned the area until Falling Rain spotted a stone cottage that fitted Harkell's description, set back from the road in a little garden used mostly for growing vegetables, with a pear tree in the corner against the wall

Without losing contact with the egret and Tarkyn, Falling Rain asked carefully, "Do you have an orange and white striped cat?"

"Yes, we do!" exclaimed Harkell. "Well, actually it belongs next door but it's always in our yard."

"Okay. Elsie has landed in your pear tree," reported Falling Rain. "How is she going to deliver the message from here?"

Harkell's eyes were shining with excitement, "Tell her to go around the back. The back door is always open. Do you think she would actually go inside the house and leave it on the kitchen table?"

"I don't know. I'll suggest it when she gets there," said Falling Rain.

As it turned out, Harkell's wife came out of her back door with a load of washing under her arm just as the egret swooped down. Kayana backed off in fright, dropping her washing and waving her arms at Elsie to frighten her away. Elsie screeched and nearly dropped the parchment. Flapping her wings hard, she gained enough height to take her far from the frightening woman. Tarkyn sent her a wave of reassurance and praise and when she was calm enough, directed her back to circle the back yard of the house well out of Kayana's reach. Eventually patience was rewarded and Harkell's wife noticed that Elsie was carrying something in her beak. Tarkyn could see her focusing in on the egret. Sending another calming wave, he asked Elsie to fly lower and drop the parchment into the basket of washing. Elsie retreated to perch on the back wall of the garden and watch.

Kayana reached down and picked up the parchment. Then, after directing an appraising look at the egret, unrolled it and began to read. As she read, she put her hand over her mouth and an expression of joyful astonishment crossed her face. Tears sprang to her eyes and she smiled and cried all at once. As soon as she had finished, she held her hand up to ask Elsie to wait and rushed inside. Tarkyn interpreted her gesture for the egret. A few minutes later, she emerged with a new piece of parchment, rolled up and ready to go. She held it out and walked slowly, tears still shining in her eyes, towards Elsie. The egret shuffled along the wall uncertainly but Tarkyn's calming presence kept her from flying off. As Kayana neared the wall, Elsie turned her head to one side and eyed her carefully. When Kayana made no sudden moves, the egret opened her beak and accepted the new message. Kayana backed off and pointed to herself, the egret and then her heart. As the egret rose ponderously into the air, Kayana, tears flowing down her cheeks, blew a parting kiss.

"Elsie will know…" Tarkyn found he had a sudden frog in his throat. "Harumm, Elsie will know how to get back here, won't she?" he asked, blinking away some moisture that had gathered in his eyes.

"Yes. She'll be fine," answered Falling Rain.

Tarkyn sent the egret a final query and thanks before cutting the connection. He heaved a deep sigh, "Well, that was long." He looked quizzically at Harkell, "Did you say anything in your note about us seeing through Elsie's eyes?"

"Yes, but I also told her not to tell anyone."

Tarkyn waved his hand, "Oh, I'm not worried about that, although perhaps I should be. No, it's just that I think I have received a message that was directed at you, not at Elsie. Would you agree, Falling Rain?"

Falling Rain grinned, "Yes. I would say so. Clever woman, your wife. She blew you a kiss and said she loved you." He repeated the gestures that Kayana had made.

Harkell smiled broadly, "Thank you so much for doing that. It means a great deal to me. I wish I could have seen her but now, at least, you have. So you will know what she looks like when I talk about her. And she will know I'm alive and safe."

CHAPTER 11

efore they set out, the woodfolk gathered around the fire to discuss all that had happened and what they intended to do next. Up to this point, they had been driven by putting distance between themselves and the sorcerers in Jarand's valley but now that Falling Rain was once more in their midst and they were on their way back over the mountain, they had no particular plan ahead of them.

"Let's make this quick," grumbled String, "We've already been here too long. It's madness to be on these mountains so late in the season. The sooner we get over them and down the other side the happier I'll be."

"Yeah, true," chimed in Bean. "Hail knows what we're talking about. I love the mountains but you have to treat them with respect."

Hail nodded curtly in agreement.

"Well, I suppose to some extent, the decision rests with Tarkyn since we said we'd help him to sort out his brothers," said Waterstone.

Harkell couldn't help blinking in surprise at this statement. However, he made no comment but just watched and learnt.

"So. We all heard Jarand yesterday saying he was planning to support Kosar by fighting lawlessness. Do we believe him?" asked Autumn Leaves.

"Not for a second," said Tarkyn firmly. "Unless he's had a complete personality change in the last two months, he will be planning to show up Kosar and undermine his rule."

"Tarkyn! Such scepticism!" said Lapping Water, shaking her head.

Tarkyn gave a slight smile, "When it comes to sorcerer politics, I don't trust anyone an inch."

Danton threw Harkell a speaking glance.

"Well, I certainly wouldn't trust Jarand," said Ancient Oak. "He's the most offensive person I've ever met."

"I don't think one necessarily implies the other," pointed out Bean.

Ancient Oak shrugged, "He kept saying we were strange. How bloody rude!"

"And he said he'd never seen a sorcerer with green eyes… Well, I don't know where he's been. Look at Stormaway," said Rainstorm disparagingly.

Suddenly there was an arrested silence. All heads turned to look at the old wizard. His face was expressionless but a certain stiffness betrayed his tension.

Danton spoke slowly, "Jarand is right. There are no sorcerers with green eyes. I hadn't thought of it before."

"But Jarand has seen Stormaway before, when I was there." protested Falling Rain. "And Stormaway would have been around a lot as he was growing up," He shook his head as he tried to remember, "Now I think about it, I don't remember Stormaway's eyes as green. Hmm. I'm not sure what colour they were... maybe brownish."

"Stormaway can change his eye colour," said Tarkyn slowly. He addressed the wizard, "So which is your true colour, Stormaway? I require an honest answer. Beyond that, you may keep your own counsel."

"I have green eyes, my lord."

Tarkyn frowned, "But didn't you say that it takes you quite an effort to maintain a disguise? Surely you couldn't have managed it for all the years you were at the palace?"

"I thought you said I could keep my own counsel."

"I meant I wouldn't command you to answer. I can still ask, though, and leave it up to you whether you answer."

After a moment's thought, Stormaway replied, "I will answer this much at least. A full disguise requires considerable effort. A simple eye colour change, especially to non-descript brown, is easy and becomes habit after a while."

There was a strained silence.

Finally Rainstorm exploded with exasperation, "Stormaway, you can't leave it there. Are you a woodman?"

"His hair is darker," pointed out Tree Wind.

"So is Midnight's," said Harkell quietly.

"You're half woodman, aren't you?" exclaimed Rainstorm, "Like Midnight. And if he's a wood sorcerer then you must be a wood wizard. No wonder your second name is Treemaster! Come on Stormaway. Tell us. We know anyway now. Tell us!"

"Oh for pity's sake! Save me from badgering young men who don't know when to mind their own business and let well alone," muttered Stormaway. He pulled his cloak around himself and stared stonily into the fire.

"Are you embarrassed to be a woodman?" asked Lapping Water quietly, the hurt clear in her voice.

The wizard cocked his eye at her for a moment before replying, "No, Lapping Water. Within myself, I am quietly proud of my heritage, on both sides."

"Why didn't you tell us?" asked Waterstone. "All those years living amongst us. None of us has been outside the woods so we didn't realise the significance of your green eyes." He, too, sounded upset.

Stormaway straightened up and sighed. "I was protecting my father's reputation. He betrayed your oath of secrecy and was forever haunted by it. He did not want to hurt his kindred by tarring them with the ignominy of his duplicity. Even though he is now dead, I have stayed true to his wishes through all these years."

"But that has caused you to be isolated among us," protested Waterstone.

Stormaway raised his hands then dropped them, "I would have been isolated anyway. My mother was a wizard and I do not think woodfolk were ready for the likes of Midnight back then. Even now, it has been controversial, to say the least."

"But a lot of the reaction to Midnight was the effect of the curse, wasn't it?" asked Melting Snow in her tinkling voice.

Waterstone cleared his throat, "It was, but I think Stormaway is probably right. Until Tarkyn arrived and we had a chance to get used to sorcerers, we wouldn't have been very open to the concept of someone from mixed backgrounds," he eyed the wizard, "especially if that person was the product of a betrayal of our woodfolk bond."

Stormaway returned his gaze steadily but with a hint of defiance.

"But," said Waterstone, relenting, "I hope I would never knowingly lay blame at the wrong door. Even you, Stormaway, as old and authoritative as you are, cannot be held accountable for your parents' actions."

Waterstone stood up, walked around the fire to sit beside the wizard and patted him on the knee, "Come on, my friend. Tell us your story. Your kindred, whoever they are, will have to cope with an old scandal. A family's first responsibility is to its living members. All of us believe that."

Stormaway, usually so remote and self-assured, took a long breath to steady himself and began to speak, "My mother's name was Blueskies Herbgrower. She lived near the forest's edge in the south east of the country. She lived alone, and was young and very beautiful when my father first saw her. He studied her for weeks from within the trees and gradually fell in love with her. Eventually, his feelings became too much for him and one evening, just as the first star appeared in the soft orange sky, my father appeared in her garden." Stormaway harrumphed, "That may sound uncharacteristically poetic to you but that is how my mother described it to me. She was surprised but not frightened. She welcomed him into her garden and showed him the herbs she was growing, and talked to him about their particular uses. In return, he told her of the seasons of the forest, where to harvest the best fruits and how to brew elderberry wine. They came to love one another deeply and in time Blueskies bore him a child.

"My father never lived with my mother but he came regularly to see her until, during one particularly cold winter, she caught some illness and, between one of my father's visits and the next, died. I was twelve. A passing tinker found me alone in the house and, despite my protests, bore me off to Tormadell. Knowing that my mother had been a wizard, he kindly but firmly found me an apprenticeship with the court wizard and set me up so that I would be cared for. But an apprentice has very little freedom to roam unsupervised and I could not find my way back to my mother's house to wait for my father and tell him what had happened. Even if I had found my way back, he was unlikely to be there and I did not know where to find him."

"That is such a romantic story," sighed Lapping Water. "But so sad."

"Did you ever see him again?" asked Ancient Oak.

Stormaway shook his head, "No. I nurtured a faint hope that I might when I first came to live among you but he had died many years before."

"So who was your father?" asked Lapping Water quietly.

"I think I know," said Summer Rain unexpectedly, directing a look of enquiry at the wizard."

Stormaway nodded, "Yes, I think you do." He gave her a slight smile, "His name was Autumn Storm. Autumn Leaves and Thunderstorm are his grandsons."

Autumn Leaves and Thunderstorm looked across the fire at each other then, without a word, walked over to stand before Stormaway.

Waterstone also stood and placed his hand under Stormaway's arm to direct him to stand up, "Come on, Stormaway. Having come this far, you must now go the rest of the way."

The other woodfolk and sorcerers stood up in a circle around the fire, while Creaking Bough and the two little ones came to join Stormaway at the front.

When everyone was ready, Waterstone began their ritual, "All woodfolk must be a member of a family. Your blood relations must now be acknowledged."

Auutmn Leaves and Thunderstorm glanced at each other, before Autumn Leaves stepped forward and spoke formally, "Stormaway Treemaster, I offer you membership of our family that you may share with us the joys and trials of kinship and that we may call upon each other's strength in times of need. Do you accept?"

The usually phlegmatic Stormaway nodded, his eyes shining with tears, "I would be honoured to become a part of your family."

Autumn Leaves grasped Stormaway's arm near the elbow and as Stormaway returned his grasp, intoned, "We are of one blood. My kin are your kin. My ancestors are your ancestors. Creaking Bough, Thunder Storm and I welcome you as an uncle. Rain on Water and Trickling Stream welcome you as their great uncle."

Stormaway, who had seen ceremonies such as this before, replied unerringly, "We are of one blood. My kin are your kin. My ancestors are your ancestors. I welcome Creaking Bough as my niece, and Thunder Storm and you as my nephews. I welcome Rain on Water and Trickling Stream as my grandnephews."

As the cheering erupted, an almighty roar issued forth from the shadows at the rear of the cave. Barely missing a beat, Tarkyn flicked his wrist to send a bronze barrier down around the grumpy mountain lion, murmuring. "I'll deal with him later."

In true woodfolk fashion, everyone made sure that they patted Stormaway on the arm or shoulder and said some word of welcome.

When Summer Rain's turn came, she said, "Your father was my mentor. When he saw my interest in herbs and healing, he taught me all he knew. We would gather herbs together and he showed me how to make tonics and ointments. It never occurred to me to wonder where his knowledge came from. I always assumed that it was just woodfolk knowledge being handed down through the generations." She gave one of her rare warm smiles, "And now I find I have been working alongside his son. Our future work together will be laced with our shared knowledge of Autumn Storm."

Eventually the fuss died down and everyone returned to sit around the fire, except that this time, Autumn Leaves and Thunderstorm sat on either side of their new uncle.

"But now, Stormaway," said Waterstone firmly, "there must be a reckoning. Since, at the time, you were not acknowledged as a woodman, your actions then are not accountable to woodfolk law. But we still need an explanation. Were you so angry with your father that you took out your revenge on his, your own, people? Or did you learn your loyalty to your new providers so well, that all past associations became irrelevant? I remember you saying once, 'I do not know or trust the woodfolk well enough to break faith with Tarkyn's father.' What drove you to betray us? You alone knew who Falling Rain was and where he came from. Without your interference, none of this would have happened."

Stormaway looked silently at him for several long seconds. Then he said quietly, "Think what you are saying, Waterstone. You are absolutely right. I could simply have let Falling Rain go. And in all this, that is my one true regret; that Falling Rain was exiled. But for the rest, no." He gave Waterstone time to think before continuing, "I forced you to accept Prince Tarkyn. But I knew enough of your society from my father to be fairly sure that only force would make you accept an outsider, especially one in authority. And I knew enough about Tarkyn to know that as your liege lord, he would give you everything he had, to support you. I told you I knew of the portents concerning Tarkyn." He glanced briefly at the prince before returning his gaze to Waterstone. "I gave you Tarkyn. You needed him just as much as he needed you."

The cave shuddered as a quickly curtailed wave of outrage reverberated through the rock. Falling Rain and several others glanced anxiously at him but Tarkyn sat there impassively while the silence of mind talking ensued.

Eventually Waterstone cleared his throat and asked, "So whose side are you really on, Stormaway? Or *were* you really on?"

Stormaway looked at Tarkyn, "Sire, I have always been true to you, but in being true to you, I have also been true to my woodfolk heritage. The words in that oath were designed by me to reflect the truth: Your cause is their cause and your fate is their fate. After all, you *are* the guardian of the forest."

"Whoever or whatever I am, I was not yours to give." The prince spoke quietly, but all who knew him could feel the undercurrent of anger. He stood up slowly and swept the woodfolk with his gaze. He looked as though he would say something further but after a moment, simply waved his hand dismissively at them and strode off out of the cave.

As the prince disappeared from sight, his shield around the mountain lion winked out. That he had left without considering their safety shocked them all. With as little fuss as possible, Danton flicked his own aqua shield over the mountain lion and resigned himself to holding it in place until his liege had calmed down.

"Well, that was an error, if ever there was one," stated Rainstorm baldly, "How would you like it if Tarkyn has said he'd given you to us?" He shrugged, "He was absolutely right. He was not yours to give."

Stormaway looked flustered, "I didn't mean it like that. Trust a bloody Tamadil to get the wrong end of the stick. I meant I was bestowing an honour on you, not an imposition."

"No," said Bean shaking his head decisively, "Tarkyn was not an honour that was yours to bestow. Whichever way you look at it, you can't just commit someone's life like that without asking them."

"But at seven, he was too young to make that choice for himself," protested Stormaway.

"Then you should have worded the oath differently," said String.

"Or waited until he was older," added Bean.

"We couldn't wait. It was our one chance. I would never have found you people again. Any other time you would have flicked away into hiding." Stormaway shrugged, "I suppose I could have made his part of the oath less binding. But you think about it. When things went wrong, it was only because Tarkyn was bound by his commitment to you that he stayed."

"And that will be the only reason he's staying now," said Rainstorm unexpectedly. "I'll bet he wants to get away from everyone and think all of this through."

"I'm just staggered that he didn't turn on you," said Harkell, shaking his head. "I can't even imagine anyone saying anything like that to Prince Jarand."

Waterstone looked worried, "No. He took it very calmly, I must say. I didn't even think about it from his point of view at first. I was just trying to work out where Stormaway stood."

Autumn Leaves frowned in thought, "There was a short blast of outrage, wasn't there? He cut it off but it was very intense. The whole floor shook."

Harkell's eyes grew round, "That was the prince??"

Rainstorm grinned at him, "Yep. He has very active feelings sometimes."

"He didn't mention that special power," said Harkell, still in awe.

"It's not a special power." Waterstone gave a short laugh. "It's a liability. His feelings sometimes betray him when he doesn't want them to."

The soldier looked thoughtful but said nothing more.

Outside the cave, the lookouts were keeping a careful watch on Tarkyn, having been briefed about the occurrences inside. He did nothing more than wander about gathering wood for the fire. Perhaps some of the branches were broken with slightly more force than necessary but other than that, there was nothing to betray that he was upset. Once he had a good sized load, he returned inside and tossed the wood against the wall. Then he walked over to the mountain lion and, after thanking Danton quietly, reinstated his own shield and focused his attention on the animal until he had quietened it. With all eyes on him, he resumed his seat at the fireside and said nothing at all.

In the ensuing conversation, he was polite but non-committal, leaving the decision about their onward journey to the woodfolk's discretion. The previous conversation was not alluded to and Tarkyn was quietly courteous to everyone, including Stormaway.

But by the time they had reached the top of the mountain in the late afternoon, the woodfolk were becoming distinctly uneasy. Several people had walked beside Tarkyn and tried to talk to him but although he had seemed to respond, no one felt that they had really succeeded in connecting with him. Even Midnight was treated with friendliness but no exuberance. Intrigued, Harkell watched the quiet, concerted effort being made to draw the prince out.

As they crested the top of the ridge, Harkell took one last look behind him and, with a sigh, turned his head resolutely forward to join the woodfolk as they broke for a rest.

After a brief discussion, they moved off quickly in order to reach the tree line further down the northern side of the mountain range before nightfall.

Once shelters had been constructed and a meal of snow hare, almond meal cakes and berries had been prepared, the woodfolk relaxed around the fire, tired but pleased that they were on their way down out of the mountains. But as the evening progressed, the effort to maintain their usual conversation around the firesite became more and more strained. People began to realise just how much their evenings were usually spiced by Tarkyn's humour, irascibility and liveliness. Now, although they couldn't fault him, his responses were friendly and courteous but lacking in spark.

Finally Waterstone could stand it no more. He asked Tarkyn to come with him away from the firelight. With the same quiet courtesy he had shown all day, Tarkyn rose without protest and went with him.

As soon as they were out of earshot, Waterstone exploded, "Tarkyn! You are driving us all crazy!"

Tarkyn raised his eyebrows and asked mildly, "Why?"

"Because…because you should be upset by what Stormaway said." When Tarkyn didn't respond, the woodman continued, "Anyway, we know you are because the whole cave shuddered."

Tarkyn put his hands on his hips and said calmly, "I don't know what you're worried about. I may have had an initial reaction but I challenge you to bring forth anyone who says I have been angry or even irritable since."

"That's exactly the problem. You're being too nice."

"That is an unusual complaint to level against someone." Tarkyn dropped his arms to his sides and gave a slight smile, "Perhaps I should be offended that you don't usually find me so congenial."

Waterstone nearly stamped his foot in frustration, "Now stop this nonsense! We all care about you. If you feel betrayed by Stormaway, if that's your problem, then have it out with him. Don't take it out on all of us. We were no more a party to his scheming than you were."

Tarkyn regarded him for a moment, the faintest hint of disdain in his face, "I don't think I have so little judgement that I would lay the blame for his duplicity at your door."

"Then stop punishing us!" exclaimed Waterstone angrily.

Tarkyn turned away to lean his elbows on a large boulder and look out into the darkened trees below. After a moment, Waterstone took a breath to rein in his temper and joined him. Together they gazed into the looming shadows.

"There is a small herd of deer down through those trees, about fifty yards away," said Tarkyn quietly. "Just below this rock, there is a little mouse scurrying across a small patch of open ground. She'd better hurry because in that larger tree off to my left is an eagle owl." He shrugged, "Mind you, his attention is trained fairly exclusively on me. So I expect he is on guard duty!" He glanced wryly at Waterstone, "You're not the only ones worried about me."

Waterstone shook his head, "You have such a different view of the world. Not just in your connection with the wildwood. You see everything differently; us, sorcerers, animals, the relationships of woodfolk to sorcerers, and how they all relate to you."

"I do. You're absolutely right, I do." Tarkyn studied Waterstone's profile, then took a deep breath, "And at the moment, my whole understanding of myself and my life up to now has been rocked to its core. And no one else has been in the same position." He leant further onto the rock, and lowered his chin onto his crossed arms, "I'm really not trying to punish anyone, you know. But inside myself, I am drowning in confusion. I am not even trying to hold anyone at arm's length. I am merely trying to stop myself from falling apart."

Tarkyn felt Waterstone's arm come down to rest across his shoulders and heard his reassuring voice say, "Tarkyn, I do not have to be you, or to see the world from your viewpoint, to understand you. Everyone sees the world differently – perhaps not as differently as you – but differently, nevertheless. Talk to me about it. If you fall apart, I undertake to pick up the pieces and put you back together again."

And breathing a sigh of relief, Tarkyn knew that Waterstone would do just that, if it were needed. So, finally, he began to talk. "I am so confused I don't know where to start. So much has happened in such a short time. Jarand, Harkell, Stormaway…"

"Falling Rain…"

"Yes. I relived all the horror of the infection and the mountainfolk's attack on me with him and all of Danton's punishments. Then to have Harkell, flogged half to death, thrust into our midst…" He sighed, "But that's not really the problem. I didn't like Jarand calling me a hunted felon. That really upset me and gave me a new, unwelcome view of myself. I know, officially, that's what I am. It's just that hearing my own brother call me that… " He shrugged, "I don't know. It somehow gave it substance."

Waterstone resisted the impulse to reassure him that woodfolk didn't think of him like that, knowing Tarkyn would know that and that it would distract him. Instead he said nothing and waited patiently.

Tarkyn looked sideways at Waterstone, "And I could have died of embarrassment at the way Jarand treated you and Ancient Oak as he left. I am truly sorry, Waterstone, that I have such an ill-mannered lout as a brother. I probably should have intervened and said something but at the time, I was focused on keeping the lid on his antipathy."

"You acted wisely. There is a time for getting up on your hind legs and braying but that was not one of them." Waterstone patted Tarkyn's shoulder before taking his arm away. "We knew we had your support. You had already made that perfectly clear."

"Well that's good then. It was hard being in the middle of all that, with each side hating the other."

"You weren't in the middle. You were on our side," said Waterstone firmly.

Tarkyn smiled, "Yes. I was. Unequivocally. But managing the clash of cultures was tricky. You managed it. You were superb at it. Ancient Oak was brilliant too. But Rainstorm and Sparrow were a nightmare."

Waterstone gave a wry grin, "Yes, that daughter of mine has a mind of her own. But they were both just sticking up for you, weren't they?" When Tarkyn had nodded, the woodman continued, "So now that we have wandered our way through the appetisers, shall we move onto the main course? How are you feeling about being Stormaway's gift to the woodfolk?"

"Totally confused. On the one hand, I understand what Stormaway was really trying to say. But on the other hand," Tarkyn suddenly heaved a deep breath, "on the other hand, I feel like an absolute idiot. Instead of being your benign ruler, I am in fact your vassal. At the age of seven, I was delivered to you, lock, stock and barrel and have been bound to serve you ever since." Tarkyn stared steadfastly out into the trees, "I feel nearly ill with embarrassment. And I don't know if I can come to terms with it. And yet I see no way out. I have always told you I couldn't accept equality but now I find it is even worse than that. You people are effectively my masters and I am supposed to be your faithful hound, chained by my oath to protect you."

"Hmm, I can see why you were a bit distant today," said Waterstone slowly, giving himself time to think.

Tarkyn pushed himself upright and pushed his hair back over his shoulders, "And for all that Stormaway may avow that he is true to me, his view of reality is coloured by his past and he has justified his betrayal of me by quoting obscure portents that no one else has had the chance to interpret. For all I know, he may have connived with my brothers to ensure my downfall. Stormaway's network is wide and insidious. If he had chosen to do that, he could have." He gave a forlorn smile, "And even though I may have argued with him, I thought he was a rock on whom I could depend. And now, once more, I am wading through quicksand." He wrapped his arms around himself. "And so, you see," he said tightly, "I am completely undone."

Waterstone straightened up and faced him, "Tarkyn, my young brother, all of us were outraged by Stormaway's words. No one owns you but yourself and the forest. You do belong to us but only in the same way that we belong to you, as part of one family. And we all belong to the woodfolk people but we are not owned by them. We may be guided and supported by them and in turn, support them but we are not owned by them." He grasped Tarkyn's arm, "And Tarkyn, Stormaway's interpretations may have been swayed by his woodfolk origins but whatever the portents say, your powers do define you as our forest guardian."

After a pause to give Tarkyn time to consider what he had already said, Waterstone continued, "You were right. You were never his to give, but neither were we, and he gave us to you. But since you are the forest guardian, you would somehow have found your way to us, sooner or later." He gave his warm, strong smile, "So we belong to each other, just as we are, in our present roles with our present responsibilities. Don't let the incautious phrasing of an emotional old man confuse what we have developed together."

Tarkyn let out a gusty sigh, "Oh Waterstone. What would I do without you?"

Waterstone smile broadened, "You big galoot. Come here." He dragged Tarkyn into his arms and wrapped him in a bear hug, "You have put yourself through the wringer again, haven't you?"

Tarkyn nodded, "I have. I knew I wasn't angry with any of you but I didn't know how to act. And, believe it or not, even though I feel uncertain about him, I didn't want to detract from Stormaway's advent as a woodman. So I retreated." He gave Waterstone a final pat on the back and pulled back, "Thanks Waterstone. It's hard to break back through, once I've withdrawn. Thanks for persevering."

Chapter 12

Waterstone and Tarkyn walked back into the firelight.

"Hi, everyone," said Tarkyn cheerily as he sat down. "My older brother here has been sorting me out. Now, tell me where we're going tomorrow."

Running Feet laughed, "I didn't think you were listening properly this morning. Although why you want to know is beyond me, since it will definitely be beyond you with your awful navigational skills."

"Rude, isn't he?" said Tarkyn in an aside to Harkell, before returning his attention to the woodman. "Just the general direction will do for now. Are we dropping in on the mountainfolk on the way past?"

"You weren't listening at all, were you?"

Tarkyn grinned, "Possibly not. So, have we decided to head for Lord Tolward's or the encampment?"

"We will retrace our steps so that you sorcerers can visit Lord Tolward on the way back to the encampment, even though he isn't expecting to see you until spring. We will go via the mountainfolk so that we can pick up provisions and deliver anything they may want to send to other woodfolk that we visit on our journey. That is, after all, part of our job as wanderers."

"What? Not exclusively to pander to my wishes?" chortled Tarkyn.

"You are happier, aren't you?" observed Ancient Oak dryly.

The prince settled down a little, "Yes, I am. And thank you to all of you who tried to talk to me today without success. I do appreciate your concern. I just wasn't able to respond at the time."

"We should just have sent in Waterstone from the start," said Ancient Oak.

Tarkyn shook his head, "Nothing would have worked at the start. I needed time to get my thoughts in some sort of order." He glanced at Waterstone with a slight smile, "Although I think the order I eventually put them in was still very confused."

Waterstone gave a brief nod and a smile.

Taking his cue from his brother, Ancient Oak changed the subject and asked Tarkyn, "Do you think we can ask Harkell what he knows of Jarand's intentions and whether he thinks there will be a need for us to intervene?"

Harkell watched all this with a half frown, not having been a party to the conversations Tarkyn had had with Jarand and not really understanding why Ancient Oak hadn't addressed him directly.

Seeing his uncertainty, Tarkyn explained, "Ancient Oak does not want to make you feel uncomfortable by asking for information about Jarand that you may feel reluctant to provide. Not being totally clear on our sorcerer hierarchical system, he is asking me where I think you stand, now that you are sworn to me." The prince smiled, "My response is; that while I could demand that information from you, I will not, at this stage. I think it is only fair that you first understand what our intentions are. After all, your wife and children are down amongst Jarand's troops."

Harkell's eyes flickered around the circle of woodfolk and sorcerers, taking in their expressions and demeanour, before bringing his eyes back to meet Tarkyn's. "Your Highness, I mean Tarkyn, I will answer whatever you request. I do not think you people are planning mass murder of Jarand's troops. You had eighty of us at your mercy yesterday and killed no one. In fact you didn't even give anyone a permanent injury." He shrugged and smiled, "Admittedly, there are thousands of his troops who would have come seeking revenge. So perhaps mercy was the better part of wisdom. But still, I think I trust you."

"I hope that trust is not based on an under-estimation of our skills," said Tree Wind sharply. "I am Tree Wind," she added.

Harkell tilted his head to one side as he considered her, "I admit freely that I have no knowledge of your full fighting strength. But it is your intention, not your potential threat on which I base my judgement. And I think, whatever your skills, you are not a warlike people."

Tree Wind glared at him for a moment before shrugging, "True. We are not. But we are lethal when we choose to be."

"Have you quite finished now, Tree Wind?" asked Tarkyn. "I can understand why you gave me such a hard time but Harkell has done nothing to you. Give the poor man a break."

Tree Wind crossed her arms, "Just as long as he knows that if he ever tries to leave, he won't get out of the forest alive. That's all."

"Tree Wind, a new age is dawning. There will be some sorcerers who, having seen you, will still leave the forest alive. String and Bean have already done that in the past." Tarkyn avoided mentioning Stormaway since the issues surrounding him were too vexed. "Danton and Harkell may need to travel among sorcerers on our behalf at some stage. Force of arms alone will not ensure their silence once they leave the forest. We must depend on their honour." He turned to the soldier, "Harkell, although we appreciate your willingness to answer our questions, you will give us more useful information if you first know why we are asking." Tarkyn shrugged, "Besides, being under oath to me does not generally require blind obedience. You have every right to raise questions and speak your mind. It is very rarely that I will give you a direct order."

"Yeah, true," said Bean. "Our prince here is not as bad as we were expecting."

"Though I'd have to say Jarand *was* as bad as we were expecting," added String.

A murmur of agreement rose from the circle.

Unusually, Danton took over, "Harkell, this is our understanding of the situation. Eskuzor is suffering under the distracted rule of King Kosar. Jarand works with his allies to undermine everything the king does. So, no new projects are started. Building works are held up by worker discontent or sudden lack of supplies. Kosar is constantly faced with complaints and deputations that take up so much of his time that he can't think clearly enough to address the needs of his military forces. Recruitment has dropped over the last few years because conditions in the forces are poor and requests for arms and equipment are continually sidelined by more pressing issues. Consequently, the crime rate has risen and people are taking the law into their own hands."

Just as everyone was thinking that Danton's attitude towards Harkell had mellowed, Danton took a sip of wine and asked in a patronising tone of voice, "With me so far?"

A faint tinge of colour on Harkell's cheeks betrayed his irritation. "Yes thank you, *Danton*."

Danton's eyes narrowed and he was about to insist that Harkell use his title when he realised Tarkyn was watching him, waiting for him to make the breach of etiquette.

The subtleties of title use were well beyond the ken or care of the woodfolk, but String and Bean watched the manoeuvring with great interest.

"Slight class issue here, I think," whispered String to Bean.

"Yep. Danton's a bit of a snob at heart. I'm surprised he didn't think to put us in our place," whispered Bean.

"Yeah. I'll think about that," said String quietly, his mind wandering off into his own little world of surmise.

Danton was saying, "Now, as far as we know, Jarand is setting up vigilante groups across the country. Despite what he said to Tarkyn yesterday, we believe his sole purpose is to undermine Kosar by setting himself up as the saviour of law and order. Beyond that, I don't think we are sure how far he will go." He raised his eyebrows enquiringly at Tarkyn.

"No. Even I do not know whether he is prepared to go as far as trying to depose Kosar."

"Rumours abound at the encampment," said Stormaway, entering the conversation but not meeting Tarkyn's eye, "of an impending civil war."

"And many sorcerers," continued Danton, "headed by Lord Tolward, have organised themselves in the past to follow Tarkyn as an alternative to his two brothers and would still like to support him. In fact, they were nearly ready to stage an uprising when Tarkyn was arrested."

"But to make it perfectly clear to you, Harkell," Tarkyn leaned forward and laced his arms around his raised knees, "at no time, either then or in the present, have I harboured a desire to be king."

Harkell's eyes had been flitting around the group watching not only the speakers but also other people's reactions to what was being said. He brought his eyes back to bear on the prince, "In that case, what is your interest in their affairs? I would have thought you were safe enough within the woods."

Tarkyn smiled self-consciously, "You may think my ambition is a little grandiose but my concern is for the sorcerers of Eskuzor. I cannot stand by and allow them to suffer as Kosar's rule is made inept by the machinations of his twin."

"So you think you can do better?" asked Harkell, a certain dryness in his tone betraying his belief that, despite his protestations, Tarkyn was presenting a rationale for aspiring to be king.

Tarkyn shrugged, "Possibly. Possibly not. I have no experience of kingship. But I certainly have no intention of finding out. I want my brothers to sort themselves out. How we achieve this, I have no idea. But I do know that it will not be by me becoming king."

Harkell's eyes gleamed as he watched Tarkyn. Suddenly he transferred his gaze to Rainstorm and said, a slow smile dawning, "You were right, Rainstorm. I have found myself a truly great lord to follow."

For different reasons, the colour heightened in both Rainstorm's and Tarkyn's faces.

Finding himself surrounded by grinning faces, Rainstorm hissed fiercely, "Har*kell*, you weren't supposed to tell anyone that."

Harkell laughed, "Sorry. But it's so obvious that I just assumed it would be openly acknowledged among you all."

"Finally Harkell," said Danton, amidst exchanged glances and mind talking among the woodfolk, "I begin to warm towards you."

Thunder Storm cleared his throat and rumbled, "No, Harkell, we do not acknowledge it. Although in truth, I think you are right. Already some of Tarkyn's deeds among the woodfolk will become part of our folklore in the generations to come. But his greatest accomplishment may not." At a look of query from the soldier, Thunder Storm went on, "His greatest accomplishment has been to overcome our resentment - I would even go so far as to say our *hatred* - of having to accept an overlord."

Harkell looked around at them thoughtfully, "Yes, I gather that has been hard for you. An achievement indeed, to have reconciled you." He smiled, rather mischievously, at Tarkyn who was looking thoroughly discomforted, "Your greatness becomes more apparent by the moment, my liege."

Tarkyn rolled his eyes, "I don't know how much more of this I can take. You are excruciatingly embarrassing, Harkell."

"He is, isn't he?" agreed Rainstorm.

"Well, you can't talk," retorted Tarkyn. "You started it, by the sound of things." He cleared his throat, "So, getting back on track… what do you know about Jarand's plans?"

"He has not spoken to me of his plans. So I can only give you my observations and the information gleaned from listening to conversations." Harkell paused and thought a moment, "And my conclusions, if they would be of interest."

"Of course they would," said Waterstone decisively.

Harkell gave a brief nod, "Then I will tell you that I think the whole vigilante angle is just a pretext for gathering troops. I think Prince Jarand is preparing for war. Our troops have been taking part in training and drills that have no bearing on maintaining law and order in peaceful times."

"What type of drills?" asked Danton.

"Advancing in close formation with shields raised – real metal shields, not magical ones. Charging on foot and on horseback. Hand to hand combat and long distance target practice." He glanced around the group, "You don't need much more to arrest people than skill with a sword and some knowledge of hand to hand combat. In the towns, you would rarely shoot for fear of some innocent walking into the flight of the arrow." He shrugged, "I suppose there is some justification for shooting if we find ourselves dealing with organised bands of brigands but no stretch of the imagination can justify the advancing in close formation – not with the numbers of soldiers involved in these drills. Not unless these bands of robbers number several hundred," Harkell shook his head, "and nothing I have heard leads me to believe they do."

"What about weaponry?" asked Danton.

Harkell nodded, "That's the other thing. The manufacture of swords, lances and arrows has escalated." He glanced at Rainstorm with a quick smile, "I think I was lucky to avoid redeployment into the armouries. I don't think the prince was aware of my father's trade."

"Ah, that's right. You come from a blacksmithing background, don't you?" said Falling Branch. "I will be very interested to talk with you about that. Rainstorm may have told you; we forestals are also craftsmen. I am Falling Branch, his father."

Harkell inclined his head in greeting.

Lapping Water held out a hunting knife, hilt first, "Harkell, do you think you could show us how you sharpen knives? We would all like to see how you do it."

Harkell smiled at her as he took her knife. Then he frowned and held the knife up so that he could see it more clearly in the firelight. He ran his finger along the flat of the blade and when he felt a roughness near the hilt, studied it more closely.

"Where did you get this knife?" he asked quietly.

Lapping Water shrugged, "I don't really know where the blade comes from. Stormaway brings us blades and we fashion the handles; some from leather, some from wood and some from bone or horn. Then we keep what we need and he sells the rest in exchange for other goods." She gave a quietly proud smile, "I made the handle on this one. Like Rainstorm and Falling Branch, I too am a forestal, although I have been travelling with wanderers for quite some time now."

Harkell transferred his attention to the handle of the knife, "Hmm. Very fine work. What type of wood is it?"

"Thank you. It is sycamore wedged between layers of hammered deer hide."

Harkell's eyes shone, "My father and my brother run a smithy. One of them made this blade. I can't quite tell which of them made it, in this light. But between you and someone in my family, you have created a beautiful weapon."

Lapping Water's smile broadened. "Your family made this blade? That's amazing. I will treasure this knife doubly now."

Even as she spoke, there was the whispered hissing of blades being drawn from sheaths all around the firesite. Suddenly Harkell found himself surrounded by naked blades as fascinated woodfolk studied their own and each other's knives.

"What does your family mark look like?" asked Thunder Storm.

"It is a horseshoe crossed diagonally by a sword. It's quite small, and will be near the hilt." He pointed to its position on Lapping Water's knife. "There is a slight variation between my brother's and my father's insignia but you will only be able to discern it in daylight."

"How about in this light?" asked Tarkyn, raising a soft orb of sorcerous light.

Harkell held the blade up. After a moment of squinting, he said, "Yes. I can just make it out. The guard on the sword in my father's insignia is slightly flared while my brother's is dead straight." He smiled, "This blade was made by my father."

Several people discovered that they too had blades that had been fashioned by Harkell's family.

"Do you recognise the marks of other blacksmith's?" asked Autumn Leaves.

"Some, but not all," replied Harkell. "I am more familiar with the blacksmiths who live around Montraya. I probably wouldn't recognise the origin of work from Tormadell."

A lengthy discussion ensued during which everyone's blades were inspected by Harkell or each other, until they had learned the origin of most of them. Stormaway was also consulted but he usually obtained the blades through agents and so did not know the makers directly. Eventually, when the topic was exhausted, attention returned to Lapping Water's request that Harkell demonstrate his powers.

He placed her knife on a rock and murmured "*Feeyen*", as he ran his finger along the flat edge of the blade. Deep purple sparks sprayed off into the darkness. Then he turned the knife over and did the same on the other side. He smiled and handed back the knife. "There. See how that is."

Lapping Water felt it gingerly with her thumb. Ancient Oak threw her a piece of hare skin which she sliced with ease. She raised her eyebrows, "Very impressive. I can see you are going to be a great asset, if you will allow us to use your skill."

He gave a slight bow and a smile, "It would be my pleasure." After a moment, he returned to the original topic and asked, "So what do you intend to do to prevent Prince Jarand from throwing the country into civil war?"

"I think we should have kept hold of Jarand while we had him," said Autumn Leaves. "We've lost our chance now."

Tarkyn raised his eyebrows and asked with a slight edge to his voice, "Really? And what would you have done with him?" The gap, that was never quite closed, suddenly yawned between them.

Autumn Leaves frowned, "Oh no. Don't tell me your rules about attacking a member of the royal family apply to your brother? What if we went to war against him?"

"Of *course* those rules apply to my brothers."

Waterstone threw up his hands, "Well, that's it then. You've just lost us. How can we protect you if you might turn on us for harming them? This is crazy, Tarkyn."

Harkell's eyes moved from speaker to speaker, taking in the flow and ebb of these exchanges.

Tarkyn gave a slight smile, "I have no intention of harming my brothers… not at this stage, anyway. And I would not expect you to take it into your own hands to hurt either of them either. If ever we come to the situation where one of them is threatening you or me, I would expect you to use the least force possible and would not hold you to account for it. Beyond that, it will be under my orders only."

"Is that because they are your brothers or because they are royal?" asked Lapping Water calmly.

"Both." Tarkyn looked around the group, "Is that reasonable enough for you?"

Waterstone nodded shortly, "It will do. Anyway, if we had kept hold of Jarand, we wouldn't have done anything to him without everyone consulting on it. We may not acknowledge his rank amongst ourselves but we do understand his significance to sorcerers and to you."

A little cough interrupted this. "May I suggest," said Bean, "that we leave these discussions until we are down off the mountains? We need to leave early in the morning." He shivered and pulled his furs around himself, "I can feel the bite of bad weather coming. We still have a long way to go to reach safety."

As the woodfolk packed up and headed into their shelters, soft white flakes began to drift down out of the darkness between the trees.

Chapter 13

Tarkyn awoke in pitch darkness, frozen to the bone. He realised that a little bundle of warmth, in the shape of Midnight, lay curled up asleep against his chest and stomach. He smiled, knowing that Midnight must have crawled in under his wolfskin cloak at some time during the night while he was asleep. He wondered what time it was and what had woken him. As he listened, he could hear the wind whistling through the trees outside.

Gradually, he tuned into a debate raging through the minds of the woodfolk. He could feel their indecision and anxiety but could not hear what they were saying. He sent a query and received back an image of their shelters buried under snow drifts. Then he received pictures that alternated between huddled waiting within the shelters or fighting their way against the wind as they battled their way down off the mountain. He sent back images of Hail, Blizzard, Melting Snow, Cavern, String and Bean querying their opinions.

A few minutes later, he heard sounds of scrabbling as snow was brushed aside. A shaft of light broke through the roof of his shelter followed by the precipitous entry of Lapping Water and Melting Snow, who landed in a laughing wet heap on the soft pine needles on the floor of the shelter.

"Oh whoops," tinkled Melting Snow, as she picked herself up. "We meant to let you know we were coming in."

Lapping Water brushed herself off, grinning, "Yes. Sorry about that. The snow has piled up unevenly and we didn't realise we were digging right on top of your shelter. We thought we were coming in from the side."

Then the girls caught each other's eyes and went into gales of laughter.

It was still snowing gently and the wind that followed them in brought the temperature down even lower. Tarkyn pulled the wolf skins and eiderdown closer around him as he blinked in the sudden light. He waited patiently until the girls had regained the power of speech, before saying dryly, "Good morning, you two. I gather we are leaving?"

Lapping Water nodded, as she wiped tears of laughter from her cheeks and looked around. "Where's Midnight? I thought he was with you."

Tarkyn peeled back the wolf skin to reveal the little boy curled up against his side.

Lapping Water beamed, "Oh, isn't he a cutie? Well, at least he was warm last night. I was absolutely freezing."

"Yes. So was I," said Tarkyn.

As they spoke, a little hand came up and firmly pulled the wolf skin back down.

Tarkyn smiled, "Sensible boy. But I'm afraid you're going to have to get up, young one." Tarkyn matched images to the words for Midnight as he spoke. "What about the others? Do you need help to dig other people out of their shelters?"

"If you're willing," replied Lapping Water. She grinned, "It will warm you up, anyway. Then, when everyone is out, we can huddle around the fire to thaw our hands and eat our breakfast before heading off."

"Right!" With great resolution, Tarkyn sat up, brushed his long hair back and threw off the wolfskin. Midnight immediately grabbed it and a short tug of war ensued which ended in the little boy being tickled mercilessly by Lapping Water and Tarkyn. Melting Snow stayed judiciously to one side until one of Midnight's flailing legs caught her solidly in the thigh. With lightning reflexes, she grabbed his leg and, dragging him out of the wolf skin, tickled the bottom of his foot.

Suddenly the light was blocked and the gruff voice of Blizzard growled at them, "What on earth is going on here? Heavy storms are coming. We can't stay in the shelters. We'll be buried under feet of snow. We have to get down off the mountain. Hurry up!"

As Lapping Water turned to face him, Blizzard realised the prince was among them. The mountainman's glower froze, "I beg your pardon, Your Highness," he said stiffly but after a moment added, "But what I said still stands."

"We're coming," said Tarkyn cheerfully. "You can blame Midnight. He's the one who's hard to budge."

Blizzard gave a little cough, "Actually, I'd rather not, if it's all the same to you. I think we've all blamed him far too much in the past."

Tarkyn laughed, "I suspect he'll sneak his way into people's bad books from time to time, no matter how lenient you are. He's a naughty little mischief… aren't you, rascal?"

Midnight beamed up at him as he pulled his boots on.

Within an hour, the entire company of woodfolk and sorcerers was packed, fed and on their way down the mountain. Thick purple-grey clouds hung low in the sky and a constant flurry of snowflakes whirled down around them. The wind streamed down the mountainside and strengthened as the morning progressed. The snow was deep and soft, hindering their progress and blurring the landmarks. String and Bean constantly threw anxious looks at the sky and urged people to stay close together.

When the storm hit, they were crossing an open, treeless area, exposed to the full force of the gale.

"Run!" bellowed String. "We need the cover of those trees."

"Keep hold of each other," yelled Bean.

The raging wind threw sharp snowflakes into their eyes and faces. Visibility was reduced to a few feet and although it was almost noon, the day was as dark as dawn.

And in the swirling stinging whiteness, stumbling through knee-deep snow, some fell and lost their hold.

By the time the travellers reached the relative shelter of the forest edge, the raging gale was lashing the tops of the pine trees, bending them almost horizontal. The roar of the wind through the pines was almost deafening. The branches above the woodfolk provided scant cover and only standing in the lee of the trees reduced the force of the icy wind.

But when the woodfolk and sorcerers, frozen and wet, took stock, they realised that nearly a quarter of their number was missing. String and Bean gathered them together, urging them to stay within the tress and wait for the others. They peered out around the trees but the storm was at its height and only a haze of driven snow greeted their eyes.

String shook his head and shouted above the noise of the storm, "There is no point in going back out into that. Look! Our tracks are almost gone already. You won't find them and you will become lost yourselves."

"Let's hope they are all together and will find their way to shelter," yelled Bean. He looked around, "Who's missing?"

Tree Wind replied but her voice blended in too well with the wind to be heard. When String shook his head and put his hand to his ear, Thunder Storm repeated what she had said, his voice rumbling loudly against the noise of the storm.

"Tarkyn's missing. Midnight, Waterstone, Lapping Water, Melting Snow, Running Feet, Falling Rain… What about Sparrow?"

"I'm here," came a small voice from the back. When everyone looked around, they saw her clinging determinedly to Creaking Bough's hand.

"Anyone else?" yelled String.

"Harkell," bellowed Danton.

Falling Branch pushed to the front, "Rainstorm's not here either. Neither is Autumn Leaves."

"What are we going to do?" demanded Danton. "We can't just sit here letting them freeze out there." He turned to the old wizard, "Stormaway, Can you do anything to get rid of this storm?"

The wizard shook his head, "This storm is huge. It would take me over an hour to have any effect on it…even then I'm not sure that I would have enough power."

"Tree Wind, Thunder Storm, can you contact them? Can you direct them towards us?"

The woodfolk went out of focus, sending their minds out to find the others. After a few minutes, Thunder Storm breathed a sigh of relief and reported, "It's all right. A couple of them lost their footing and the others stopped to help them up and lost contact with the rest of us. They are all together and just approaching the tree line now."

But the minutes ticked by and still there was no sign of them. Another round of mind talking produced the information that the lost group had reached the tree line. But still they were not in sight.

"They must have veered off slightly and have entered the forest either above or below us," shouted Bean.

Suddenly, an image of huge, twisted, deciduous trees, untouched by the raging wind, came through to the woodfolk from Melting Snow. The images meant nothing to most of them but galvanised Hail and Blizzard.

Blizzard shouted at String and Bean, "They're lost. They are nowhere near us. Somehow, they have entered the Lost Forest"

String stared at them, "I didn't know that was real. I thought it was a myth."

Hail glared back, "It is a myth. But so is Tarkyn."

"So what do we do?" shouted Bean.

"We seek shelter." Hail's voice brooked no argument. "There is nothing we can do for them."

Part 3: The Lost Forest

CHAPTER 14

Just as the first woodfolk reached the tree line through the raging wind, Running Feet, further to the rear, stepped awkwardly on a hidden stone and fell heavily. The land dropped away steeply to their left towards the edge of a sheer cliff, and having lost traction, the woodman began to slide sideways down the steep slope. Tarkyn and Midnight, following right behind, threw themselves at him to save him but were unable to reach him and instead, began to slide themselves.

Tarkyn managed to grab hold of Midnight's arm as they slid together down the slope and shouting *"Maya Reeza Mureva,"* rose into the air, with the little boy dangling below him.

As he rose higher, Tarkyn pulled Midnight up until the little boy was able to scrabble up and hoist himself onto Tarkyn's hip where he clung, wild-eyed, his heart beating tumultuously.

But Tarkyn had no time to reassure him. Stabilising the first spell in his mind, he pointed at the fast disappearing Running Feet and shouted, *"Ka Liefka!"* A bronze beam of power shot forth and lifted the woodman up into the air just as he careened out into the empty space over the lip of the cliff. Tarkyn swung Running Feet around in an uneven arc through the buffeting wind, to deposit him back on the trail in the midst of the remaining woodfolk, making sure they had a firm grasp of him before releasing him. Then, in fits and starts amidst the turmoil of the storm, the sorcerer, with his long black hair whipping around his face, floated back up to the trail himself with Midnight tucked firmly within the circle of his arm.

When Tarkyn landed, Running Feet was leaning against someone's rucksack in the snow, white-faced with shock, surrounded by anxious woodfolk.

"I think his ankle may be broken," shouted Waterstone above the gale.

Tarkyn shook his head, "I can't fix it out here in all this wind. We'll have to brace his leg and get to shelter first." He deposited Midnight and squatted down in front of the ashen woodman, "Running Feet, I will lift you up again and carry you through the air so that your ankle doesn't jar too much." When the woodman's eyes flared in alarm, he added kindly, "I won't drop you, I promise. I never have yet, even though I may have threatened to. It will be easier than trying to walk." When Running Feet nodded reluctantly, the sorcerer gave a little smile, "Maybe this time, I won't leave you with nightmares!"

Running Feet gave a weak smile in response but was in too much pain to reply. He gritted his teeth as Waterstone and Harkell strapped knives wrapped in padding to either side of his ankle as a temporary brace while the others clustered around him as a wind break.

But when they stood up ready to move off, with Running Feet floating above the ground on a strand of bronze magic, no one could see which way the others had gone. The trail had blown away and the tree line was obscured by the dense, driving snow.

They knew they had to keep the downward slope on their left but, because they had become so conscious of the sheer drop that lay at the edge of the slope, they instinctively veered slightly to their right. After a few minutes, they came up against a sheer wall and realised they had come too far across. As they huddled together, working out what to do next, the first message came through from Thunder Storm and the others. At this stage they were fairly sure they could simply readjust their bearings and rejoin the rest of the group already sheltering in the forest, so they sent back a reassuring response.

As they tried to work out which way to go, Tarkyn became aware of a silver fox standing only a few feet away, watching him with its light grey eyes. Oblivious to the howling wind that ruffled the fur along its back, the fox focused exclusively on the forest guardian until it had his attention.

Tarkyn received a clear message from the fox to follow him, which he relayed to the woodfolk, gesturing the request for Harkell's benefit. The group fell in behind Tarkyn and, protecting their airborne companion against the buffeting wind, followed the fox into the swirling whiteness. Among them all, only Melting Snow felt some uneasiness about the silver fox but she was still not sure enough of herself around the prince to say anything.

In minutes, the tree line loomed before them and they quickened their pace for one last push. In response to a query, Autumn Leaves informed Thunder Storm that they were in sight of the forest edge.

In the next instant, the air around them thrummed, shifting their perceptions. There was a lull in the storm and suddenly it was not a forest of tall pines lashed by the wind they were approaching, but huge, gnarled old trees, bared of leaves, yet dense enough overhead to filter out most of the light. As they followed the silver fox into the woods, Melting Snow just had time to send Blizzard her image before all communication with the other group was cut.

Within the ancient woodland, no breath of wind stirred a single twig. No grass or plants grew underfoot beneath the dense canopy. The only colours that met their eyes were shades of brown. The silver fox trotted up ahead, completely unaffected by the sudden change. When Tarkyn explained the need to stop and attend to Running Feet, the fox sent an image of a circular clearing up ahead filled with grasses, mosses and small shrubs, protected by overhanging trees. Tarkyn shrugged and relayed the fox's image before continuing to follow.

Melting Snow, in a surge of determination, ran to catch up with the prince and, as she drew alongside him, said quietly, "Your Highness, please stop and listen."

Tarkyn, who knew how shy Melting Snow was, stopped without hesitation and looked enquiringly at her. The silver fox sat down a little way ahead and watched.

Melting Snow took a breath and continued, "Tarkyn, we have entered the Lost Forest." At her words, a ripple of consternation passed through the woodfolk. "At least, I think that is where we are. No one in living memory has been here but it fits the description in our myths."

Tarkyn's eyebrows snapped together, "Are we in danger?"

Melting Snow gave her head a little shake, "I don't know. But that silver fox is also part of legend. It is said that it can lead you to destruction or salvation. There have been trappers in the mountains who saw it as they sat with their companions around a firesite. They followed it out into the night and were never seen again. But there have been times when a lost mountainman has followed it back to safety."

Tarkyn's eyes narrowed as he considered the silver fox sitting quietly watching him, well within range of the woodfolk's arrows. He could feel no threat or compulsion or ill will emanating from it. "A silver fox, possibly this one, looked after me once before. My instinct is to trust it. It has, after all, led us out of the storm into shelter."

Melting Snow looked anxious but didn't say anything further.

"Melting Snow, don't stop now. You are the only person with experience of the mountains among us. I am not dismissing what you are telling me. I am thinking it through. What of this forest?" asked Tarkyn, sending her a wave of calm as he spoke.

Lapping Water walked up to stand beside her friend. She put an encouraging arm around her shoulder, her soft green eyes shining up at Tarkyn, making his stomach contract. "Come on. Tell Tarkyn about the Lost Forest. It is one of your mountainfolk legends. So you will remember it better than the rest of us."

Melting Snow wrinkled her brow, "It's hard to explain. The Lost Forest exists within the pine forests, on the mountainside, within the northern forests nearer to Tormadell, in the south-western forests of the wolves. It exists everywhere and nowhere. None of us could look for it with any hope of finding it. And I doubt that any of us here could find our way out of it even though we have just entered it and are near its edge. No one alive today has been in the Lost Forest."

Tarkyn frowned, "Is that because they died within the forest or because no one has found it in the first place?"

Melting Snow shook her head, "I don't know. Some people disappear on the mountains without trace. Who knows what happens to them. But the legends of the Lost Forest have been passed down through generations, by people who have been here and returned."

"So not everyone dies who enters here," prompted Tarkyn.

"No. But not all have returned."

"And what did they have to say?" asked Tarkyn, carefully staying patient.

"That within the forest, the past and future come to haunt you. You will face your greatest fears, and how you deal with them will determine whether you leave weaker or stronger. Sometimes, if the fears have been too great, people have chosen to stay forever within this forest to avoid returning to face them… and sometimes, the forest has refused to let them go."

Tarkyn ran his hand through his hair, "Oh marvellous! So we now find ourselves within some sort of a mystical courtroom that determines our futures based on how we deal with our fears." He shrugged, "Well, we are where we are." The prince turned to the rest of the party, "So, as a first step, will we continue to follow the silver fox? My opinion is that we should, but with so much at stake I will not insist."

"I cannot see the point in doing otherwise," replied Ancient Oak. "If Melting Snow is right and we can't find our way out, there is little point in trekking off on our own with no clear destination." He shrugged,

"Besides, I have faith in your instincts, Tarkyn. You are, after all, our forest guardian." He grinned suddenly, "You're a myth yourself. So you'll fit right in with all these other myths."

Tarkyn rolled his eyes and shook his head, "Very funny. You make it sound as though I'm about to fade into the mists of time before your very eyes." He folded his arms and said firmly, "I am not a myth. I am a normal, solid person like the rest of you. I am just following in the footsteps of other people who have become legends."

Harkell watched with his soft brown eyes and, having just seen the prince use two simultaneous spells to rescue Running Feet and having experienced the healing himself, decided that whatever else he was, Tarkyn was not just a normal person like the rest of them.

However, Waterstone laughed and walked forward to pat the prince on the back. "Yes. Solid as a rock. You haven't started to fade away yet." He looked around at everyone, "Shall we go?"

By general consensus, they turned once more to follow the silver fox but Harkell didn't miss the look of gratitude that Tarkyn threw Waterstone before he moved off.

For another twenty minutes they followed their guide through winding earthen pathways past exposed gnarled roots and giant trunks. Overhead, the branches laced in a dense covering. What could be seen of the sky was grey but there was no way of knowing whether the storm still raged outside. No wind or snow penetrated the Lost Forest.

They rounded a bend and found themselves at the edge of a beautiful little clearing, a bright, chuckling stream running through the midst of the greenery and flowers of a spring meadow. Light streamed down from a gap in the clouds, uncannily lighting only the clearing and none of the surrounding forest. A quantity of logs and kindling was piled up near the stream.

Tarkyn sent an image of a fire with a query. He didn't want to assume anything in this strange place. The silver fox sent back a picture of the woodfolk and sorcerers seated around the fire, eating and drinking. Then the little fox trotted over to a large, green drawstring bag that was lying under a large old sycamore and gave a sharp yap. When Tarkyn approached to investigate, the fox shied away but stayed close enough to watch.

Within the bag, wrapped in damp cloths, were pheasants and woodcock, plucked and ready to cook. Tarkyn pulled them out and laid them on their wrappings in a row along the ground. At the bottom of the bag, he found cups, plates and cooking utensils. He felt around and found a large covered bowl containing nuts and dried fruits and a sack filled with root vegetables and greenery. As the bag was emptied, a large barrel of wine, which had been sitting behind it, came into view.

Tarkyn sent his thanks to the fox before looking around at the others with a smile, "Over to someone else. This is definitely the makings of a lovely dinner and I am definitely not making it. Emptying that sack is the closest I have ever come, or ever want to come, to cooking." He grinned, "Besides, Running Feet needs me."

Waterstone shook his head smiling and walked over to inspect the bounty. "Go on then. Go and help Running Feet. He is in a lot of pain, I think. I will start preparing a meal."

Without a word, Lapping Water began to set the fire while others spread out wet clothes to dry. Harkell hovered near Running Feet, quietly marvelling that Tarkyn had left him floating in the air with no apparent effort while he had unpacked the green bag.

Tarkyn came to stand looking down at Running Feet, whose face was pinched with pain. "Are you ready to be lowered onto the ground? I'll ask Harkell and Rainstorm to hold your leg so it doesn't jar too much as you land. I'll hold your shoulders to make you feel safe."

As Running Feet landed gently on the ground, he let out a sigh of relief.

"Oh come on, Running Feet." protested Tarkyn. "You should know me better than that by now."

Running Feet managed a wan smile, "I do, but there is nothing quite as comforting as solid ground under you."

"Hmph."

Running Feet's smile broadened despite the pain, "Don't take offence. None was meant. And thank you for all you have done for me, even if swinging out over that void did scare the living daylights out of me."

Rainstorm laughed, "I think the alternative of plummeting to your death would definitely have been worse."

"Yes, it would. I'm just bloody lucky you were nearby when it happened, Tarkyn."

Tarkyn just gave a slight smile and changed the subject. "Now you two, take the bracing off his leg and lay his leg out straight. This will hurt, Running Feet. Do you want someone to knock you out?"

Running Feet shook his head decisively, "It's not safe enough here. I need to stay as alert as I can, in case we have to leave suddenly." He looked at Harkell, "You'd better give me something to bite down on though, and be ready with a large glass of wine afterwards."

Harkell nodded calmly and prepared a tightly rolled up piece of cloth, which he gave to the woodman. Then he sat cross-legged on one side of him, holding his shoulder. Rainstorm sat on the other.

"Right. If you two are going to stay there, I'll need two more to manipulate Running Feet's ankle," said Tarkyn sitting with the woodman's head on his lap.

"I will," offered Lapping Water, leaving a small but well-established fire behind her for others to tend.

"And I," said Ancient Oak.

"Do any of you have experience of setting bones?"

"I do," replied Harkell. Before Tarkyn could ask, he swapped places with Ancient Oak. "His boot will have to come off, you know. You can't set it like this. If we cut it off carefully, perhaps Falling Branch could mend it?" Tarkyn noted with approval the calm manner in which Harkell gave out orders almost without seeming to do so. "If I hold his leg still, can you cut through the leather, Lapping Water?"

Even with the boot cut down the side to its sole, it was still difficult to manoeuvre it off Running Feet's foot. By the time they had succeeded, his face was beaded with sweat. Harkell felt gently all around his ankle, carefully testing the movement and pain levels.

After a few minutes, he straightened up, "Hmm. Hard to say. I think there may be a hair line fracture just above the ankle," he pointed to the spot, "just about here. We may be able to simply brace it without manipulating it. I wish I could be more sure."

Tarkyn gave a little smile, "Don't worry. I can go in and check. Ready, Running Feet?" He drew on his power and sent his focus down through his arm into the shoulder of the woodman. From there, he coursed through the woodman's body until he reached the part of his leg that was strained and swollen. Although the sorcerer was unsure when he was in the place indicated by Harkell, he compromised by searching up and down all the nearby bones. None was broken right through, but he found one that was cracked but still straight. He fed his *esse* into the bone, knitting the fibres back together. This bone was smaller and less damaged than Winguard's femur had been and the two surfaces were touching, so Tarkyn was able to repair it in a relatively short time. When he had finished, he sent a surge of *esse* flowing through Running Feet's body, leaving his body to choose how to direct it. Then he travelled back up his own arm into his own body and opened his eyes.

Tarkyn took a breath to re-orient himself, "How's that?"

Running Feet let out a long breath, "A lot better. Thank you. And thank you to everyone for your help." He wriggled his foot experimentally, gradually increasing the movements. "It's still quite sore but the swelling is going down and it's nothing like as painful as it was."

Tarkyn looked at Harkell, "You were right. It was only cracked."

Harkell frowned, "He shouldn't walk on it though, for a couple of weeks at least."

"Oh, I think he'll be all right," said Tarkyn airily. "Since it was only a slight fracture, I was able to mend it straight away."

"What?" asked Harkell. "Can't you mend compound fractures? Disappointing."

Tarkyn, who had been expecting some appreciative astonishment, did a double take.

Rainstorm chortled, "You should see your face."

Tarkyn tried unsuccessfully to suppress a grin. "I'm beginning to think that Harkell's mission in life is to take the wind out of my sails."

Harkell laughed, "I shouldn't tease you. You have every right to be proud of your skills, particularly when you use them so judiciously."

A dry cough interrupted them. "Tarkyn. We have company," came Waterstone's voice, carefully pitched to blend with the stream, so only those used to it could hear him.

"Company," hissed Tarkyn to Harkell, knowing he would not have heard. The prince disentangled himself from Running Feet, stood up slowly, careful to make no sudden movements, and swung around to face the newcomers

Four green-robed, ephemeral figures stood on the other side of the stream; two male sorcerers, a woodman and a woodwoman. All were grey haired, their faces lined with age.

"Greetings," said Tarkyn formally, giving a slight bow. "I am Tarkyn Tamadil, Prince of Eskuzor and Guardian of the Forest."

"We know who you are," The woodwoman's voice, although only a whisper, could be heard clearly.

The four bowed slightly in return, giving no more respect than they had received. After a few moment's silence, Tarkyn asked, "Would you like me to introduce my companions?"

The whisper came again, "There is no need. We know you all."

"I see," said Tarkyn slowly, not seeing at all. "And would you be kind enough to introduce yourselves to us?"

A deep sighing voice emitted from the sorcerer with chestnut eyes. "Between us, we have been the guardians of the forest for nearly two thousand years."

Tarkyn bowed low. "I beg your pardon. I did not realise your stature."

"You do not need to bow to us. You are one of our number." The chestnut-eyed sorcerer gave a slight smile, "And there is no point in your companions bowing, as it would only be an empty gesture on their part, since they do not hold with such conventions. I am Moridan Tamadil."

Before Tarkyn had time to ponder the connection he had with this man or why Harkell had been included in this description, the whisperer added, "And your Captain Harkell will do what he must to get by, but in his heart, he meets men eye to eye. He bows because he must, not because he believes in another person's superiority." She smiled at the soldier, "Harkell, my name is Nightwind. You should have been born a woodman."

Harkell flicked an uneasy glance at Tarkyn before inclining his head and saying, "Coming from a woodwoman, I will take that as a compliment."

"Waterstone," hissed the green robed woodman, his voice sending shivers down everyone's spines. "Come and stand before us. I am Grass Snake."

In the quiet of the clearing, Waterstone walked stoically over to stand, head held high, beside Tarkyn.

"Waterstone," hissed the forest guardian, "you, above all others, have held true to our woodfolk belief in the worth of all men. Others have followed in your footsteps but from the start, you fought against your anger and your prejudice to treat Tarkyn as fairly as you would have treated any woodman or woman. Your actions are honoured by us."

"Thank you," replied Waterstone gruffly, not knowing what else to say. He glanced sideways at Tarkyn and a smile passed between them.

The final guardian of the forest, his royal blue eyes shining, spread his arms wide and addressed Tarkyn in a surprisingly gentle, lilting voice, "Tarkyn Tamadil, we welcome you to the Company of Guardians of the Forest. When your life among the living has finished, you will join us here at the end of your days. I am Windchange Treewarden."

Tarkyn felt the blood drain from his face and his stomach knot. These figures who faced them were dead. And he was horrified by the prospect of being condemned to dwell with them in this eerie forest.

Nightwind gave a gentle laugh. "Do not look so stricken, young guardian. We are not such bad company and this forest is not so dire as it would first appear."

"I beg your pardon. I do not mean to offend you."

"Tarkyn, you are not yet ready to join us. One day, when the time is right, you will be."

Tarkyn, from the standpoint of a nineteen year old, privately thought this was highly unlikely but had no intention of saying so. As he stood facing the unnerving forest guardians of old, Midnight crept over to him and clung to his leg. Glad to have something to distract him, Tarkyn bent down and swung the little wood sorcerer up onto his hip. He smiled at Midnight and tousled his hair.

"Tarkyn Tamadil," came the voice of Moridan, "You have said you have no wish to be king."

Tarkyn reluctantly dragged his eyes from Midnight to face the ghostly figures. "Yes. That is true. I possess neither the skill nor the inclination to deal with the intrigues of the Royal Court."

"Yet you have taken upon yourself the guardianship of the whole of Eskuzor, have you not?" pressed Moridan.

Tarkyn nodded a little uncertainly.

"Do you not think that a little presumptuous?" whispered Nightwind.

Tarkyn's eyes flicked from one to the other before replying tensely, "Very presumptuous. I have effectively placed myself in judgement over the king and the crown prince, while in the eyes of the law outside the forests, I no longer have any status at all." He drew a breath, "And yet I cannot stand by and watch my brothers destroy people's lives."

The guardians exchanged glances and a small smile passed between them. Tarkyn was not sure whether it was a smile of satisfaction or derision.

"The task you have taken upon yourself is both difficult and dangerous," came the deep voice of Moridan. "We would help you on your journey."

There was an appreciable pause before Windchange murmured, "You have skill in magic but not in intrigue."

"You have great courage, Tarkyn, but not in all things," whispered Nightwind.

"The woodfolk support you within the forest but not without," hissed Grass Snake.

"And you are a true guardian of the forest but you do not yet know what that means," completed Moridan.

"To help you with intrigue, I give you this knowledge," Windchange, the wizard guardian, smiled, "Trust Stormaway. He has always been true. Equally should you trust Danton. They will guide you through the webs of dissemblance."

In Tarkyn's head, the voice of Nightwind sighed softly, "To give you courage in love, I say this; to have a chance at happiness you must risk pain. Nothing is certain, but if you do not risk pain, you will have no chance at all."

To Harkell and the watching woodfolk, there was a period of silence during which the colour in Tarkyn's face heightened. Then Grass Snake's voice hissed forth.

"And to support you beyond the forests' boundaries, I turn to the woodfolk." Grass Snake's gaze swept across the woodfolk gathered around Tarkyn. "There will be sorcerers beyond the forest who support Tarkyn.

But you are now his people and it is your support that he needs. If you truly wish to work by his side, you must be prepared to venture forth. Rainstorm has done it already. It will not be easy and it will not be often. But there will be times when you must break beyond the forest's borders."

His piercing green stare made the woodfolk shuffle uneasily. "If Tarkyn fails, the woods will ring with the clash of blades and the screams of wounded men dying. The fight for the supremacy of Eskuzor will invade the forests and leave havoc in its wake." He paused for effect. "He has sworn to make your cause his own. But the converse is also true. Tarkyn's cause is your cause. You and he are one people and the future of Eskuzor depends on you all."

Harkell have a quiet cough, "And what of me, my lords and my lady?"

Nightwind smiled and glanced at Moridan, "You see what I mean. In less awe of us than anyone."

Moridan frowned, "Harkell, you are the wild card in the pack. Jarand made a grave mistake when he let you go. You are so strong and true that none of us foresaw that you would change sides. So if we say that you will stay true to Tarkyn, we may be equally inaccurate a second time."

Harkell bowed his head, "I know my actions condemn me and bring further undertakings into question. But had there been any indication that Jarand planned to return for me, I would have stayed true to him, however I felt about him and his treatment of me." He raised his head, "Perhaps it is the quality of Tarkyn's strategy and power that were unforeseen by you, for they are what led to my downfall in Jarand's eyes."

The four wraiths looked at each other, before Windchange spoke, "You argue well on your own behalf." He sighed, "But we are not here to condemn you, Harkell. It is just that we do not know what you will bring into the future conflict. If all is as it seems, the fact that you stand beside Tarkyn instead of beside his brother will strengthen the chances of bringing a productive peace to Eskuzor."

The guardians transferred their gazes back to Tarkyn, and Moridan's voice resonated deeply around the clearing. "And now we give you the greatest of our gifts; the knowledge that you are Guardian of all Eskuzor. Your concern for the welfare of all sorcerers is not just a passing fancy, or the sanctimonious posturing of a presumptuous young brother. It is your birthright and your destiny to protect and support all the people of Eskuzor – not as their king but as their guardian."

"Tarkyn, the power of the forest guardian runs strongly within you. In past times, the forest covered all of Eskuzor," hissed Grass Snake.

"And so," said Windchange, "the guardianship of the forest was synonymous with the guardianship of Eskuzor. Your instincts guide you truly. You are, in truth, Guardian of Eskuzor, not only of the remaining forests. And it behoves you to protect all people, both sorcerers and woodfolk from the folly of your brothers."

Suddenly, it felt to Tarkyn as though an idea he had simply been playing with, had been dropped as a heavy burden onto his shoulders. He let Midnight slip gently to the ground and stood straight before them, his hand on Midnight's head, for several silent seconds. Finally, he let out a long sigh, "Thank you for your gifts. You have given me a great deal to think about." He gave a little smile, "I am glad that Stormaway is true." Tarkyn glanced at Waterstone standing stalwartly beside him and said wryly to him, "Despite your best efforts to protect me, the impossible burden has now been placed firmly on my shoulders."

Waterstone smiled, "Yes, it has. But you were bearing it anyway. And now you have our full support, not just an indulgent gesture of gratitude."

"Your fight is our fight, Tarkyn," said Lapping Water, smiling up at him. "Your purpose is now one with ours."

Autumn Leaves clapped him on the shoulder. "For your sake, for our sakes and for the sake of the forests."

"And for *all* people of Eskuzor," said Harkell firmly, standing a little apart, his arms crossed protectively and his stance stiff with defiance.

Seeing his unease, Tarkyn met his eyes. "Harkell, I have given you my faith. I will trust you."

"Thank you, my lord." Harkell gave a wistful little smile, "But that would mean more if you were better at intrigue."

Tarkyn gave a short laugh. "I can only do my best with what I am."

He turned back to ask how long they would remain within the Lost Forest but only the burbling stream and the meadow met his eyes. The guardians of the past had vanished.

Chapter 15

Tarkyn put his hands on his hips and stared for long minutes at the empty space in front of him. Then he scrubbed his hands over his face, pushed back his hair and turned around. "So now what?"

"Now we have lunch," replied Waterstone prosaically, "and accept the hospitality of the Lost Forest and its guardians."

Tarkyn gave a wry smile, "I didn't even have time to find out who Moridan Tamadil was." He walked back over to Running Feet and with Harkell's assistance, helped the injured woodman to his feet.

"Perhaps you can ask the king when you meet him," suggested Harkell casually.

The prince glanced sharply at him from the other side of Running Feet before relaxing into a smile, "Perhaps I can."

"Just a moment," interrupted Autumn Leaves. "Did I miss something?"

Ancient Oak grinned, "No. I think Harkell has just divined Tarkyn's intentions before Tarkyn was even aware of them himself."

"Obviously Tarkyn will have to talk to Kosar if he is trying to resolve the sorcerers' plight, won't he?" said Lapping Water calmly. She gave a little smile, "We'll just have to find a way to trap him, too."

"Hmm. I doubt that it will be as easy a second time," pondered Harkell. "If the king has found out about your last effort, either directly from Jarand or by word of mouth from his men, he will not enter the forest with unshielded troops."

As Running Feet was lowered to the ground, Tarkyn smiled cheerfully, "Never mind. I'm sure we'll figure something out." He transferred his attention to Running Feet, "How's your ankle feeling?"

Running Feet leant forward and rubbed it, "Not bad. I think I'll be up and hobbling in no time."

Rainstorm came over and handed glasses of wine to Running Feet and Tarkyn, "So what did Nightwind say to you?"

Tarkyn regarded him quizzically, "If she spoke to me so that you couldn't hear, don't you think that might mean it was for my ears only?"

Rainstorm shrugged and smiled sheepishly, "No harm in asking. You looked a bit worried, that's all. I just don't want you having to manage something hard on your own, if you don't have to."

Tarkyn smiled, "Thanks Rainstorm." After a moment he added, "But I'm afraid there are some things that only I can do."

An air of constraint fell around the group as they, who were so used to sharing all their thoughts, wondered what secret Tarkyn had been told. Tarkyn sat staring into the fire, a little smile playing around his lips.

Finally he threw his hands up. "All right. I can see this is going to prey on your minds. There is something I must do before I tell you. But I will contract to tell you what Nightwind said before we leave the Lost Forest," he said, thus setting himself a deadline to approach Lapping Water. "It is nothing that endangers my life. So don't worry about my safety. And my reticence does not spring from a lack of trust in you." He looked around, "So. Can we leave it for now?"

The woodfolk took a collective deep breath and resolutely turned their minds from the conundrum. Harkell, who was used to living surrounded by state and personal secrets, watched them and smiled.

Chapter 16

In the hour before dawn, four woodfolk awoke with a start. Waterstone, Autumn Leaves, Melting Snow and Ancient Oak could just make out each other's features in the fading darkness. In this strange Lost Forest, they had not built shelters because no weather penetrated its dense canopy.

Waterstone sat up and looked around, running his hands back and forth through his hair to wake himself up. "Where are the others?" He looked around more carefully, "In fact, where are we?"

"We are near the edge of the forest," said Autumn Leaves, pointing through the trees at a far horizon glowing orange behind wide, open fields.

Ancient Oak scratched his head, "I don't recognise this at all. This isn't the grasslands and it isn't the fields where they hung Harkell up."

"It might be near the road to the northwest but I'm not sure." Waterstone frowned, "But I'm more worried about where Tarkyn and the others are."

"Tarkyn is out there," whispered Melting Snow, pointing to a lone figure walking quickly along a path parallel to the forest but a hundred yards distant from its edge.

Even as they watched, two figures rose up out of the grasses and fell in quietly behind the lone sorcerer.

"What is he doing?" whispered Watersone urgently. "Why is he out there alone? I will wring his neck for putting himself in danger like that."

"If you can get him back in one piece," added Autumn Leaves dryly. "Unless I'm much mistaken, those people following him are carrying drawn swords."

"Come on. We'll have to close in to get a clear shot at them," urged Ancient Oak.

The four of them slid through the trees until they were at the very edge of the woodland. Waterstone shook his head, "We're going to have to break cover to get close enough. Come on. Stick together. We can flick back into hiding, if they look around."

Just as they broke out into the open, the first rays of the sun lit up the sky and they found themselves caught in broad daylight. Before thought, they had all flicked back into the cover of the woods, breathing hard with fear.

"Come on. Not good enough," hissed Autumn Leaves. "We have to try again. We have to get close enough. Quickly. They are closing in on him."

"I'll send him an image to warn him," suggested Ancient Oak. When the others looked at him, he added hurriedly, "Don't worry. I'm coming too."

"So, are we flicking back out? It will be quicker," asked Melting Snow.

The whole concept of flicking *out* of hiding was so alien to them that it took a few seconds for the possibility to sink in.

"Yes. Good idea." So saying, Waterstone was gone and reappeared well beyond the tree line, his bow already in his hands, blinking in the harsh early morning light.

Ancient Oak appeared beside him, frowning furiously against the sun, "Oh my stars, it's bright out here. I can't reach Tarkyn's mind. It's something about this strange forest. It hinders mind communication. I'll try again now that we are in the open."

Autumn Leaves and Melting Snow appeared and the three of them advanced behind Tarkyn's shadowers while Ancient Oak tried once more to warn Tarkyn. This time he was successful and Tarkyn turned to face his shadowers. As soon as they saw him turn, they rushed at him, trying to reach him before he could raise his shield. Woodfolk arrows thrummed through the air and the shadowers fell, long before they came anywhere near the prince. Tarkyn ran his hand through his hair and smiled his thanks. Suddenly his face shifted, his hair became lighter and his glowing amber eyes changed to green. The face of Grass Snake surveyed the four woodfolk appraisingly. At his feet, the bodies of the shadowers faded and disappeared.

"You have done well. Not flawlessly, but well enough." The ghostly woodman waved his arm in a wide circle around him, "Now, look around yourselves. See and feel what it is like to be outside the forest while the sun brightens the sky. And remember. If you have done it once, you can do it again."

"And where is Tarkyn?" asked Waterstone tightly.

"He is back in the Lost Forest, asleep in the clearing," Grass Snake hissed, "but you are not. You are where you appear to be, exposed in the middle of a field. There are no sorcerers nearby, you are quite safe and you may return to the Lost Forest at any time before the sun reaches the top of its travel. After that, you will not be able to re-enter." His mouth broadened with a smile that did not reach his eyes, "But I doubt that you will want to remain out here for so long. If you care for Tarkyn as you seem to, stay as long as you can endure, to become used to it. Then if the need arises, you may be able to act more decisively next time."

The four woodfolk were left with the sneer in his voice ringing in their ears as he faded from sight.

"I think he was a bit tough on us," said Autumn Leaves after a minute.

Waterstone shrugged, "Our reflex to flick back into the woods could have meant Tarkyn's death in some circumstances."

By common, unspoken agreement, they stayed out in the open standing with their backs to each other so that they could watch all four quadrants. Every so often they would rotate so that they could watch and become used to a different view of the wide open spaces. After two long hours, well before the sun had reached its zenith, they had had enough. As they entered the cool dimness of the Lost Forest, they breathed a collective sigh of relief.

Autumn Leaves peered at the other three, "I think you're all sunburnt. I expect I am too. We're not used to undiluted sun like that."

Just as Waterstone was wondering how they were going to find their way back, the silver fox came trotting up a path from within the forest. As soon it was clear they had seen him, the fox turned, assuming they would follow him.

CHAPTER 17

"I hope you are not a hypocrite, Harkell," said Tarkyn, sipping his tea as he waited for the woodfolk to return from wherever they had disappeared to. Strangely, he didn't feel any concern for his or their safety, and was sure they would return when they were ready.

Harkell eyed the prince as he leaned forward to poke the fire, sending a shower of sparks scattering into the air. "I wondered if Nightwind's words would come back to haunt me."

"And were her words true?"

Harkell gave a smouldering black piece of stick to Midnight so that he could use it to draw on a nearby tree trunk. Then he stood up on the other side of the fire, arms akimbo, to face his liege. "Yes Sire, they were."

"So, if in your heart, you see all men as equal, does that not make your gestures of respect rather hollow?"

"Sire, custom dictates that I bow to men of higher rank. Had I not done so in Jarand's court, I would have died long ago. It is not hypocritical to acknowledge another's superior rank and yet to believe them to be your equal in value. The rules of our society are that I must act in certain ways to men of higher status. The sanctions for disobeying those rules are severe. If I were to flout those or any other rules, there would need to be a good reason to do so."

Tarkyn sipped his tea, never taking his eyes off his newest liegeman. "And why, then, did you profess the need to be bound to me? You could have become a free man."

"Freedom would have come at too high a price. I am used to being part of a unit; giving and accepting support. The only unbonded people I know of are drifters and renegades." Harkell smiled slightly, "I do not want to drift." He hesitated, but instead of saying anything further, he set about offering the prince another cup of tea.

When he had accepted it, Tarkyn said with a slight smile, "And you were about to say…?"

Harkell considered the prince for a minute before saying, "What I was about to say, I have thought better of."

"I see. And is that because it was unkind or because you do not trust my reaction?" Despite his best effort, a note of reserve had crept into Tarkyn's voice.

"Tarkyn, you told me that you give people the freedom to speak as they wish. If that is the case, is it not also true that we have the freedom to hold silent if that is what we choose?"

Now Tarkyn's voice was definitely cooler, "Not to the same degree. I do not expect the woodfolk to discuss important issues among themselves without keeping me informed. However, I do not intend, in this instance, to force you to say something you would rather not."

Harkell's soft brown eyes watched every nuance of Tarkyn's mood. "You have become too used to the open style of the woodfolk and my reticence is now making you withdraw. Although you permit me to remain silent, I can see that it will be at a cost."

Tarkyn frowned a little as he considered Harkell's words. "Possibly, but I will not stay withdrawn. That will pass. And the chance to get to know each other better will come again, perhaps when you have more experience of me."

Harkell relaxed back and smiled broadly. "I really do like you, Tarkyn," he said, much to the prince's surprise. "You have great generosity of spirit." He threw a hand up, "When you put it like that, I might as well tell you now, as later. It is the sort of thing one confides at the end of a long wine-soaked evening. So it is bound to come out sooner or later." He looked into his cup of tea for a minute to compose himself before raising his eyes to meet Tarkyn's. "Actually, no it isn't. It is the sort of thing one holds close to one's chest." He gave a slight smile, "It is this; that I am, and have always been, very ambitious. There are very few men from a tradesman's background who rise to become Captain of the Guard." He shrugged, "It took years of hard work and I knew that, for someone from my background, it was risky. If I had been a lord, I doubt that Jarand would have left me behind, tied to that tree. I gambled, and in the end, I lost."

Harkell picked up a stick and started making patterns in the dirt with it. Tarkyn did not speak, knowing that Harkell had not finished. After a few minutes, the deposed captain lifted his eyes to lock them once more with Tarkyn's. "I do not want to be a drifter, a person with no influence and no allegiance. I want to have an influence on the affairs of our nation, to feel that my actions are affecting people. I tried, as Captain of the Guard, to keep the peace and maintain control for the benefit of the townspeople. And I would have hoped to be involved in any wider conflict that arose."

"And what of right and wrong? What if Jarand waged war for his ends only?"

Harkell turned his attention to his doodles in the sand, "Sire, I had given him my vow. His cause was my cause. If he asked for Eskuzor on a platter, I would have fought to give it to him." He shrugged, "There is not always room for conscience in the wages of war. I would never have advocated extremes of retribution or destruction but on the other hand, I doubt that I would have had enough influence to stop them, except possibly among my own troops." He looked up at the prince. "When you give someone your oath, you give your conscience into their keeping. I never had a choice with Jarand. I was born and bred to serve him. But I did have a choice with you."

Tarkyn gave a wry smile, "It didn't sound as though you thought you had a choice when you said one cannot live unbonded."

Harkell shook his head, "You and Jarand were not the only choices. I could have sought service with a powerful lord, far from Montraya, or even with the king. That was one reason that I needed time to think."

"And what of your ambitions? How did you expect to have any influence in the affairs of the nation in the company of a fugitive prince? As it happens, you well may have, but you didn't know that then."

"Hmm. To be honest with you, there were many signs that suggested that you would be pivotal to the future of our nation. Firstly, I knew of the groundswell of support for you which, even now, is sweeping through the nation. I could already tell that you were not a rogue sorcerer, as had been previously thought. And finally, Danton made me realise that I had learnt the power and quality of you during my healing." He looked up and smiled, "Once I understood where my impressions of you were coming from, the last alone would have been enough."

"So, do you follow me now, only to fulfil your own ambitions?"

Harkell smile faded and he ran his hands back and forth though his hair until it stuck up in a dishevelled mess. "You can see why I didn't want to tell you this. You, also, need more experience of me." He stood up and began to walk distractedly back and forth. Eventually he stopped and stood with his hands on his hips, facing the prince.

"I would not have allied myself with a paltry, powerless lord, no matter how nice he was. But equally, with the choice in my hands, I would not have allied myself with someone who placed ambition above conscience." Harkell grimaced and dropped his arms, "I should have endured your withdrawal and kept quiet." He heaved a sigh, "Tarkyn, it is not a crime for people who are not of noble birth to be ambitious, to wish to move from the station into which they were born and to have their opinions considered by those born above them. My ambition is not all that drives me. In you, I felt an integrity that mirrors my own. And without wishing to be too presumptuous, I think you and I are alike in many ways. Obviously, you have vastly more power and status than I, but I have more experience." He shrugged, "Anyway, I have made my choice and now you know me better than I would wish. If you side-line me, I will be disappointed but I will stay true to you."

Tarkyn picked up a stick and set about breaking bits of its end. "I'm sorry, Harkell, that my behaviour pressured you into saying more than you felt comfortable with. You have shown me great honour and trust in speaking so openly. I will not abuse it by thinking less of you. In fact, it makes me realise how hard you must have worked, and how talented you must be, to have reached the position you were in." He looked up and gave a wry smile, "I'm sorry I blew it all away in one afternoon. You are right. You have every right to your ambition. I might not have said that six months ago, but I do now." His smile broadened, "And I have no intention of side-lining you. Among the woodfolk, you will not be able to gain greater status than theirs, but you will have equal status and we will all give your views due consideration, just as we have up until now. I hope that is sufficient for you?"

Harkell's face lit up, "It is far more than I ever had before in Jarand's service. That puts me in the highest rank of the service, below royalty. I couldn't ask for more than that."

Tarkyn laughed, "Of course, you will be sharing that rank with all the woodfolk of Eskuzor."

The captain grinned, "They deserve it. And what matters to me is being listened to and having some influence, whatever my rank."

"And you have picked the right camp for the maximum influence on the affairs of Eskuzor. Not only that, but if you can come up with some grand plan to sort out my brothers, we will be only too happy to heed it."

Harkell jumped to his feet and started pacing energetically back and forth, "You have no idea how excited I am about all this. It feels as though a huge barrier that I have been pushing up against all my life, has just evaporated. I have suddenly bobbed to the top of the ocean." He waved a dismissive hand. "There are lots of other little corks bobbing around but that's fine because we're all up there together."

"And where am I in this seascape of yours?" asked Tarkyn, grinning at the captain's excitement.

"Hmm. I don't know. Maybe a bigger cork? The bottle? A bird flying overhead? A boat? I don't know. I'll have to think about it."

Tarkyn laughed, "Don't spend too long on it. Put your effort into the plight of Eskuzor."

Harkell spread his arms out wide. "You see? How marvellous is this? If I come up with a plan, you will actually take notice of my ideas."

"Of course we will," said Rainstorm, entering on the scene at this moment and blithely assuming that Harkell meant everyone and not just the prince. He rolled his eyes, "They even listen to me sometimes and I'm still too young to be taken seriously most of the time."

"Stop being a drama queen, Rainstorm," laughed Lapping Water, following him into the clearing. "People listen to you more now because you've stopped being so belligerent."

"Well, you can thank Tarkyn for that. He had the good sense to take me seriously right from the start."

"Once I'd sorted out your manners," added Tarkyn dryly.

"There's no point in being cranky if someone is listening to you."

Falling Rain and Running Feet appeared from between the trees and came to sit around the fire while Rainstorm and Lapping Water busied themselves with preparing lunch. A general air of constraint hung around them.

"Your ankle seems a lot better," observed Harkell. "You are barely limping now."

"Yes. It's feeling better. I will be able to keep up when we leave this ghastly place."

Harkell directed a frown of query at Tarkyn who just shrugged and raised his eyebrows.

Shortly afterwards, four very disgruntled woodfolk stomped into the clearing from the other direction, just as lunch was being served. Without comment, plates of cheese, bread and dried fruit were handed to them. After a few minutes, Rainstorm asked, "So how did you get on then?"

"What do you mean, 'How did we get on?'" growled Waterstone.

Rainstorm grinned. "Did you rescue Tarkyn or did you leave him to die?"

Waterstone scowled. "How do you know about all this?"

"We have all been through it, Waterstone," said Lapping Water gently. "Only Tarkyn, Midnight and Harkell were exempt. Even Rainstorm, who has already braved the outside, was forced to prove his willingness to protect Tarkyn beyond the forest edge."

"These bloody old forest guardians," grumped Waterstone. "What are they all doing, still hanging around after all these years? They should keep their noses out of it and let us get on with it as well as we can. If we're not good enough, then bad luck."

"Yes, he does have quite a sneer to his voice, doesn't he?" sympathised Rainstorm, cutting to the heart of Waterstone's displeasure.

"Yes, he bloody does." Waterstone picked up a stone and hurled it in anger across the stream. "And what's worse, he was right. We hesitated when it could have meant life or death. Our instincts overrode our intentions." He picked up another rock and hurled it after the first.

When he brought his eyes up to glance shamefacedly at Tarkyn, he found the prince watching him. "And it's just as well that wasn't really you out there," he snapped belligerently. "I'd have wrung your bloody neck for putting yourself in danger like that."

Tarkyn wisely chose not to react and simply met his eyes silently.

Finally, Waterstone heaved a sigh and ran his hand dispiritedly through his hair. "I'm sorry. I'm just disappointed in myself. I know it wasn't really you out there, but if it had been, I would have let you down."

Tarkyn spoke quietly, "Waterstone, you could never let me down. You would always do the best you could, in any situation. If your best means dealing with your instincts, then that is what it is." He smiled, "Perhaps those bloody old forest guardians have helped after all. I'm sure you would prefer to learn how to fight your instincts on a practice run, rather than actually lose me while you were learning."

"Yes, I would. You know I would." Waterstone cleared his throat. "So, how did everyone else go when the sun suddenly shot up over the horizon?"

"Is that what happened?" Tarkyn couldn't help smiling. "No wonder you ducked for cover."

Rainstorm chuckled. "Yes. I think we were all back in the trees before we knew what had happened." Without exception, all the woodfolk nodded. "But we all ventured forth the first time and then came out again after we had recovered from the shock of the rising sun. So our intentions were good even if our execution needed refinement."

"I never doubted you for a second." Tarkyn's smile broadened, "You do realise that I knew nothing about this. Harkell, Midnight and I have been sitting around idly all morning, wondering where on earth you had all disappeared to."

"By the way, Tarkyn," said Harkell in a total non-sequitor. "I think you must be the sky."

Surrounded by confused faces, Tarkyn blinked in astonishment. "Stars above, Harkell. You are nowhere near as egalitarian as woodfolk.

Harkell grinned, "Yes I am. But I just know greatness when I meet it."

Tarkyn had no idea whether to take him seriously nor not.

CHAPTER 18

Late in the afternoon, as the yellow of the sun's rays turned darker gold between the trees, Harkell and the woodfolk sat deep in discussion trying to figure their way out of the Lost Forest. This was too navigational for Tarkyn to be very interested. Besides, he suspected that they would only be able to leave when it suited the forest guardians. So when Midnight scampered off out of the clearing in pursuit of a blue and gold butterfly, Tarkyn headed after him.

At first, they followed the path of the stream in amongst the gnarled old trees, the butterfly dodging and dipping, always just beyond Midnight's grasp. As they drew away from the clearing, the trees seemed to close in around them and before long Tarkyn could no longer hear the voices. The butterfly led them away from the stream and into the depths of the forest, through hanging creepers and under low twisted branches. Then with a few flicks of its wings, the little creature disappeared out of sight up into the higher branches of the trees.

Midnight and Tarkyn stood side by side, hands on hips, gazing up into the dense branches above, trying to spot the gold and blue of the butterfly's wings. Gradually it dawned on them that it was gone for good. They smiled at each other and shrugged. Tarkyn tousled Midnight's hair and turned back the way they had come. They ducked under a low bough and pushed their way between a couple of creepers before coming to a fork in the indistinct path. Tarkyn looked at Midnight and raised his eyebrows. Midnight screwed up his face in thought and eventually pointed uncertainly to his left. With his head slightly to one side, Tarkyn frowned at the little boy. In response, Midnight grinned and shrugged.

Tarkyn rolled his eyes. "Oh good. So we're lost. Wait on. I'll send them a message to come and find us."

But his mind images did not penetrate far through the strange atmosphere of the Lost Forest. He felt the resistance and knew he had not been able to contact anyone in the clearing.

Just as he was wondering what to do next, Tarkyn heard rustling from along the left hand fork of the path. Instinctively, he grabbed Midnight and drew back into the shadows of the vines, his hand ready to flick up his shield if the need arose. A moment later, Lapping Water appeared from between the trees and looked around briefly, before walking unerringly to their hiding place.

Her soft green eyes shone through the gloom. "Hello you two. What are you doing in there? I thought I had lost you for a while there."

Tarkyn and Midnight emerged, smiling sheepishly.

"We were hiding from whatever was rustling down that path," replied Tarkyn, his eyes twinkling. "I presume that was you." He frowned, "But why could I hear you? You usually move silently."

Lapping Water smiled, "I was letting you know I was coming. Just as a person might knock on a door in your palace. I didn't want to walk in unannounced."

"Oh. I see. And why were you following us?" he asked.

"To protect you. Even though there aren't enough of us to set up lookouts, we still take it in turns to be vigilant. I saw Midnight and you head off. So I followed after you at a distance, to keep an eye on you." She grinned, "I thought you might get lost."

Tarkyn grinned back, "We had just worked out that we were."

Lapping Water chortled. "Huh. I love it."

"You do?" asked Tarkyn, his heart turning over.

"Yes. Well," Lapping Water gave a little self-conscious cough. "What I meant was that it is fun to see you at a loss when you are often so strong."

"Oh. I see."

Lapping Water put her hand impulsively on his arm, "No. You don't see. I didn't mean to be mean. I meant I like the way you go from one extreme to the other. Supremely capable to absolutely useless and back again from one minute to the next." She smiled, "It is …nice" she finished lamely.

Tarkyn gave a short laugh, "Huh. It is inconvenient, sometimes."

As they turned to begin the walk back, Tarkyn drew a deep breath and took the plunge, "Do you mind if we sit here for a while, before we return?"

Lapping Water frowned a little but nodded and sat down, "As long as it doesn't get too dark. I don't know these woods."

The sorcerer sat down with his back against a gnarled old tree, "I have my light if we need it."

Midnight looked from one to the other, saw they weren't in the mood to play and busied himself by climbing up into the tree above them.

Tarkyn could feel his heart beating slow and hard in his chest but he was determined to heed Nightwind's words. He took another deep breath and asked, "Lapping Water, do you think a sorcerer might ever be able to have a partner from among the woodfolk?"

Lapping Water glanced at him, her cheeks tinged with sudden colour, before looking steadfastly away into the depths of the trees. "Stormaway's parents seem to have managed it," she said carefully, "although they never actually lived together."

"Hmm. Were you shocked to hear Stormaway's story?"

The young woodwoman shook her head. "No. I was saddened but not shocked… Saying that, I think Waterstone was right. I would have been shocked if I had heard that story a year or two ago." She brought her green eyes to bear on Tarkyn, "But a lot has changed since then."

Tarkyn couldn't quite hold her gaze. He looked down at his hands for a few seconds before resolutely bringing his eyes back up. "Lapping Water, I know I am a bit hard to get on with at times, and my eyes are too bright and my hair is too black… and sometimes I turn green." He gave a wry smile. "I know I am very big and I scare people sometimes, like Melting Snow, and Running Feet when I first met him but…well, I was wondering whether *you* liked me at all?"

Lapping Water stared at him for a long moment before carefully hedging her bets by asking coolly, "And why would you want to know that?"

Tarkyn stared back at her, a small puzzled frown on his face. Then, despite his tension, he broke into a grin, "Oh sorry. That's not the way it should go, is it?"

Suddenly, he jumped to his feet and paced up and down a few times before flinging himself back down, "Okay. Now, please understand that I don't know all your customs yet and if I say something wrong, it will not be out of disrespect…" He frowned and shook his head, "I can see I should have prepared myself better for this. There were plenty of people I could have asked and didn't!"

He gave his head another little shake. He stood up once more, before lowering himself slowly onto one knee before Lapping Water, who recoiled a little, "Lapping Water, whatever your feelings for me, I think I love you…In fact, I'm sure I do. My heart turns over every time you come near me and my breath catches in my throat. I love your wit and practicality, your calm sense of self and your amazing woodfolk abilities. If you could consider it, I would be honoured if you would consent to becoming my wife." Seeing the woodwoman blink in surprise, he rushed on, "You are under no compulsion to agree. It is entirely up to you."

"Tarkyn, please stand up or sit down or do something else. You are confusing me."

Tarkyn jumped up and took several long strides before turning to face the woodwoman from a noticeable distance away. "I beg your pardon, Lapping Water. I did not mean to make you feel uncomfortable," he said stiffly.

Lapping Water smiled and stood up, coming over to stand beside him and link her arm through his. "I am pleased with what you said. I just felt awkward with you kneeling over me."

Tarkyn looked down at her, "Oh."

She tilted her head up and gazed into his eyes, her long shining hair falling down her back. "Tarkyn, I love your burning amber eyes and your black hair. I love watching you swing between hauteur and humour. I love your strength and your weakness. You don't frighten me at all." She smiled, "And I would love you to be my husband."

Tarkyn's face lit up. "You would?" He disengaged his arm and placed both arms around her instead. Then he pulled her gently towards him and smiled down at her, "And is it within your customs for us to kiss?"

Lapping Water smiled warmly up at him and nodded. Tarkyn bent his head and, after a few first-time falterings, all their uncertainties dissolved as their lips met.

Suddenly, Tarkyn broke away and sent a shaft of bronze spearing past Lapping Water's shoulder to intercept a dark green ball that was flying out of the tree above. Muttering "*Ka liefka*", he lowered Midnight, encased in his green shield, gently to the ground. In response to an angry query, Midnight sent back an image of himself bouncing along the ground within his spherical green shield.

Tarkyn shook his head and smiled wryly before returning an image of Midnight hitting the ground hard within his shield. "It doesn't work like that, Midnight," he said, sharing the images with Lapping Water.

"Oh look! Now he's all upset," Lapping Water walked over to Midnight and waited until he flicked away his shield before scooping him into her arms. The little boy clung to her and cried with fright, occasionally sending poisonous glares in Tarkyn's direction.

Tarkyn looked bewildered. "I don't know why he's angry at me. I just saved him from a nasty fall."

Lapping Water laughed, "You got angry with him when he'd just had a fright. He'll get over it." She concentrated on sending Midnight images explaining how Tarkyn had saved him. After a few minutes, Midnight sniffed and held out his hand to Tarkyn who came over and tousled his hair.

"Give him to me," he requested, taking the little wood sorcerer out of Lapping Water's arms. He swung him onto his hip and gave him a hug. "Friends again?" he asked, matching words to gestures. Midnight nodded and gave a few more pathetic sniffs. Tarkyn sent Midnight an image of the little wood sorcerer encasing himself in his green shield and jumping off a low rock to experiment rather than out of a high tree. Midnight nodded and as the light in his eyes reignited, he wriggled out of Tarkyn's grasp and shot off.

Tarkyn sighed, "What a pesky boy!"

Lapping Water smiled as she watched him disappear between the trees, "But cute."

"Oh yes, very."

Lapping Water hooked her arm into Tarkyn's. "Come on. Let's go back. I don't want to be away from the others in the dark."

"Me or the forest?"

Lapping Water laughed and shook her head. "The forest. I told you, I'm not scared of you."

Tarkyn smiled as they turned to walk back to the clearing. "I don't have a vested interest in thinking you are. It's just that in my society and especially at my rank, an unmarried woman would not be left alone with a man, even if they were promised to one another."

Lapping Water's eyes crinkled with amusement, "How peculiar. But you and I have been alone before…or just with Midnight."

"I know. But I thought you might feel…" Tarkyn shrugged, "I don't know…more worried now that you know how I feel about you. And I don't know what your protocols are."

The woodwoman laughed, "Tarkyn, you should know by now that we all trust each other. And I trust you or I wouldn't have come to love you. As for protocols, there are no restrictions on us being together. And in a year from today, the day we have declared our love for each other, we can marry and mate."

"A *year*?" Tarkyn's voice came out as a strangled squawk.

"Yes. A year." Lapping Water gave him a playful punch in the stomach. "Don't look so horrified. Our love has to stand the test of time before we can marry."

"I give you permission to attack me," he said quickly, pretending to double up in pain.

Lapping Water stood back and looked at him, "You're only half joking, aren't you?"

"I'm not joking at all about giving you permission. I *am* joking about being hurt."

"Hmm. Interesting," mused Lapping Water.

The prince eyed her, aware that the whole issue of royal protocol and the oath was hanging in the air.

"Don't look so worried, Your Highness," she said lightly. "I know where you stand. I have spent many hours talking through how to manage it with Rainstorm and others."

Tarkyn frowned in astonishment, "Have you?"

Lapping Water grinned. "Yes, Tarkyn, I have. That is why I was able to accept your proposal so easily. I have already thought through all the doubts."

"Ooh dear. Well, I'm not sure that I have… at least not in terms of how the oath and royal protocol affect us." He glanced down at her, "So, what conclusions did you all come to?"

"The biggest stumbling block is the fact that in woodfolk marriages, the man and the woman are equal partners. And although you may accept that for other woodfolk, you will always insist on having your higher rank acknowledged. So our partnership is unequal in your eyes."

The prince nodded uncertainly. "That would be true with whomever I married, in either society."

Lapping Water gave him a warm, strong smile, "I have watched how you treat people and I know how you have treated me up until now. You listen to other people's opinions and usually try to reach a consensus. Sometimes you are too autocratic and your actions are less than ideal." She shrugged, "But no one is perfect. I love and accept you for who you are." She grinned, "If Waterstone can deal with being your best friend and brother on unequal terms, I can deal with being your wife."

Tarkyn frowned quizzically, "Why do I feel as though I am being humoured?"

Lapping Water spluttered with laughter, "We are not *just* humouring you… although only you believe in rank." She sobered up, "But sometimes you insist on the inequality becoming a reality. So, if I accept you, I must at least acknowledge your view of things and expect that it will affect me."

"Thank you, Lapping Water," said Tarkyn quietly. He raised his hand and dropped it, "I begin to see what a courageous decision this has been for you to make, above and beyond the fact that I am a sorcerer and not a born woodman. I would say that I will try to be fair and negotiate with you but I can see that you already know that. Just as you know that I will not always succeed." He smiled gently and hugged her to his side, "Thank you for your strength and courage in accepting me. As I told Harkell yesterday, I can only do my best with who I am. I can't be anyone else."

Lapping Water smiled and hugged him back, "That's all right. I don't want anyone else." The night was beginning to close in. Suddenly she shivered, "This forest is creepy and I don't know my way around it or what its particular dangers are."

"Do you want me to put up my shield?"

"No. I've managed without it so far. I think I would prefer to keep managing unless there is something tangible to worry about." The woodwoman looked around. "Where has Midnight gone?"

"Don't worry. Ever since his running off forced Danton's and my confrontation with hunters, he has always stayed in sight of me. I may not be able to see him but I bet he can see me." Tarkyn sent out a little query. "Yes. He's just up ahead behind those bushes. He's given up on jumping and is busy collecting snails at the moment."

CHAPTER 19

By the time they reached the clearing, darkness had fallen and only the fact that Lapping Water had been able to contact the group as they neared the clearing had prevented the other woodfolk from mounting a search party.

Without a word, Tarkyn and Lapping Water separated on arrival to sit on opposite sides of the fire while Midnight trotted over to show Rainstorm his collection of snails. When the fuss had died down and everyone was installed with a glass of wine and something to eat, Tarkyn cleared his throat to gain everyone's attention.

"As you may recall, yesterday I promised that before we left this forest, I would tell you what Nightwind had said to me." He let his gaze travel slowly around the gathered audience, "What I had to do alone, I have done. So now I can tell you." He smiled at their anticipation. "Nightwind urged me to take a chance if I wanted happiness. The lack of courage she was talking about, related to my reticence with…hmm… how shall I put this?… my reticence with romance."

Tarkyn grinned as Ancient Oak's and Rainstorm's eyebrows snapped together. They looked at each other and then swung their gaze from the prince to a smiling Lapping Water.

Tarkyn laughed out loud, "Yes, Rainstorm and Ancient Oak, my wicked, conniving friends. I have finally come up to the mark. I have the honour and pleasure of announcing that Lapping Water and I intend to marry."

Anything further he might have said was drowned out in the general uproar that met this announcement. Drinks were refilled and toasts proposed. Midnight looked around himself in confusion. Tarkyn tried to explain but Midnight couldn't see what was different about Tarkyn and Lapping Water being together because, from his point of view, they had always spent time together around him. In the end, the little boy just shrugged and smiled with everyone else.

Melting Snow's eyes were wide with admiration for her friend's courage. "Lapping Water," she whispered, "You didn't just say yes because you had to, did you?"

"Stop it. Of course I didn't. Would I be looking this happy if I had been forced into it?" Lapping Water leant in towards her friend to say quietly, "Anyway, it's about time you started to give Tarkyn a break. He has never done anything to you to warrant your fear of him. If he looked like Running Feet, you wouldn't think twice about him."

Melting Snow subsided to think about her friend's words, knowing she had pushed as far as she could without risking their friendship. She looked up to see Tarkyn watching her across the fire, clearly aware of her misgivings. Instead of being angry, he sent her images of how he had proposed to Lapping Water up to the point where he had put his arms around her. Although there were no words, Melting Snow could see that there had been no coercion and that, in fact, Tarkyn had been the more nervous participant. Her face relaxed into a smile and she mouthed her thanks across the fire to him, both for his reassurance and for his generosity in sharing those images with her.

Waterstone kept patting Tarkyn solidly on the back and speaking in words that became more slurred as the evening progressed. "Tarkyn, it's an honour to have you as a brother… Not because you're a prince, of course. You already know my views on all that…but because you have shown us all how much a person can change his way of thinking. To want to marry one of us, well, to start with, it shows good taste, especially Lapping Water but also… well I don't know. It just seems to be one step further than being a bloodbrother…to have chosen a wife from among us when you could have had any sorcerer woman." He eyed Tarkyn, "Well possibly not any sorcerer woman, given your present circumstances, but I suspect with your peculiar social bigotries, many of your women would still feel enormously honoured to catch a prince, even if he is a fugitive."

Tarkyn smiled and caught Harkell's eye, "I'm not too sure that most sorcerer women would appreciate living in the woods, even to become a princess."

"Oh, I think you underestimate the allure of a title and, of course," Harkell's eyes twinkled, "your own personal charm."

"Hmph. But since I have never been in day-to-day contact with sorcerer women in the same way that I have with woodwomen, it is inevitable that I have lost my heart to a beautiful green-eyed woman of the woods… and in particular to Lapping Water, the most down-to-earth, pragmatic, athletic, self-assured, witty woman I have ever met."

Somehow, as this little speech progressed, everyone stopped talking and unashamedly listened in.

Melting Snow sighed, "Oh. He does love you, doesn't he?"

Tarkyn snorted, "Of course I do. I wouldn't have proposed to her, otherwise."

Lapping Water smiled broadly, "He just hid it well until now."

"No, he didn't," chorused Rainstorm, Ancient Oak, Harkell and Waterstone.

"You just refused to notice, in case you got it wrong," added Rainstorm.

"You're the one who hid it well. Poor Tarkyn had absolutely nothing to gauge your feelings by."

Suddenly Nightwind appeared among them, glimmering in her long green robes. Tarkyn's and Midnight's eyes both homed in on a blue and gold butterfly that was sitting quietly on her right shoulder.

She smiled privately at Tarkyn, "Everyone needs a bit of help. It is hard to find time alone in a close-knit group such as this." Nightwind brought her arms up and spoke in her eerie sighing voice. "Lapping Water and Tarkyn Tamadil. You both show openness of mind and great courage to venture where none have gone openly before. You will need courage to face your critics from both societies but you will have each other and you will have your stalwart friends to support you. I wish you well on your journey through life."

As the ghostly forest guardian faded from sight, the butterfly remained and flitted off into the darkness.

"What help?" asked Lapping Water suspiciously.

Tarkyn grinned. "The butterfly. Midnight and I were chasing that butterfly when we lost our way."

Part 4: The Rift

CHAPTER 20

Lying in the darkness, the woodman found himself awake. He listened intently, waiting for a repeat of the sound that had woken him. After a few moments of silence, he heard a quiet snuffle in the corner. He listened again to be sure, then slowly pushed back his bedding, before moving silently across the cave to put his hand on the little girl's shoulder. At his touch, Sparrow turned a tear-stained face to look up at him.

"Come here, little one," murmured Thunder Storm gently, gathering her into his arms.

Creaking Bough appeared beside him and stroked Sparrow's hair as she buried her head into the woodman's chest and let the sobs come.

"Don't worry," crooned Creaking Bough, "We will find them somehow… or they will find us. They will all keep each other safe. No forest will harm a forest guardian and he can look after your dad and your uncle. We just need to be patient."

"Tomorrow morning, when it's light," rumbled Thunder Storm, "Stormaway will look up his books and see what he can find out about this Lost Forest. At least we know they made it out of the storm, don't we?"

Sparrow nodded and gave a few doleful sniffs. She gave a shuddering sigh and leaned in harder against Thunder Storm. Then she thought that maybe she would never see them again and her tears ran silently down her face.

"Come on," said Creaking Bough quietly, "You come in with us for the rest of the night. We can't have you out here on your own, feeling miserable."

Around the cave, disturbed by Sparrow's tears, several people stirred and sent her mind messages of encouragement. She settled in under the down-filled covering between Thunder Storm and Creaking Bough, but lay awake for a long time thinking about Waterstone, the rock of her life. Then she thought about Ancient Oak with his gentle humour and Tarkyn being bossy and only a huge effort stopped her from crying again until eventually, the rhythm of breathing around her lulled her back to sleep.

When she awoke the next morning, Sparrow found herself curled up in the crook of Creaking Bough's arm. Everyone else was up and about, and the smells of bubbling porridge and tea were wafting from a cheery fire crackling away in the middle of the cave.

"Good morning, young ladies," rumbled Thunder Storm, bearing down on them with cups of tea, "Stormaway is already hard at work looking through his books. He will let us know the minute he finds something."

As the morning progressed, various people wandered over to the wizard to peer surreptitiously over his shoulder at whatever book he was studying or to ask how he was going. Without exception, they were all sent on their way with a pithy comment.

On the other side of the cave, like water finding its own level, the people who had knowledge of the mountains congregated to pool their resources, trying to figure out how to find the Lost Forest.

"Come on, you mountainfolk. Tell us what you know and we'll see if any of it sounds familiar," said Bean.

"Yeah," added String, "We might have our own version of it."

Blizzard, Hail and Cavern looked at one another until, by mental agreement, Hail began to speak, "None of us has been there. Until now, it has lived only in our stories." She shrugged, "But then, so has the forest guardian. Maybe one triggers the coming of the other. I don't know."

"You cannot enter or leave the Lost Forest by choice. The forest decides." Cavern's voice echoed eerily around the cave. "That is why Hail said there was nothing we could do for them."

"And do people return?" asked String.

Hail nodded, "Yes. How else would we know of it? … But they do not always return. In the Lost Forest you must face your fears and if you cannot, then you will not return. That, at least, is my understanding of it." She looked to Blizzard for confirmation.

"I'd say that's about right." Blizzard grimaced. "The Lost Forest is a pretty grim place, by all accounts."

Cavern sent him a look of reproof. "All who went in there are strong. I am sure they will return."

"But what should we do?" asked Danton who, in his restless pacing, had listened in to most of this conversation. Tarkyn's fiercely devoted liegeman was showing signs of strain. His eyes were heavy, underlined with purple shadows. He couldn't sit still and he alternated his time between pacing the cave or walking outside to scan the sky and surrounding forest in the faint hope that he might see something useful. It had taken enormous persuasion to keep him from rushing back out into the depths of the storm the day before to search for his liege. "Do we just sit here and hope this Lost Forest spits them out conveniently at our feet or do we go back to where we lost them, now that the weather has eased, or do we continue our journey, assuming they will know to find us with the mountainfolk?" The blonde sorcerer threw his hands up. "What if they are gone for months?"

"Well," drawled String, "You'll go mad, for a start."

"And we'll all go mad putting up with you," said Bean laconically. After a moment, he added, "Come on Danton. Sit down. You are distressing all of us. Have a little care for your fellow man. We are all worried. Not just you. Pull yourself together or you'll work yourself into a frenzy and be no good to anyone."

"Yeah Danton," String patted the ground next to him, "Sit down and gather your forces. Think about how Tarkyn would want you to act. He wouldn't want you to be winding everyone up."

Danton threw himself down next to them, "No, he probably wouldn't." He gave a little smile, "But he would know that's exactly what I'd be doing, nevertheless." He looked around at them all, "So, what are we going to do?"

"We wait," said Blizzard stolidly. "We wait until Stormaway has had a chance to look through his books. Then we decide." He turned his attention firmly to Bean, "So, do you sorcerers have any legends about a strange forest? Maybe people disappearing for a while?"

"No, not that I can think of."

"I did meet a chap once," put in String, "before I met you, Bean, who said he'd lost his way for a while and had wandered through an old dark forest. When I asked him where it was, he had no idea." He grimaced, "Now, when you think about it, that's a bit odd, because we old trappers are pretty good at finding our way around."

"Did he seem changed at all?" asked Cavern.

Strung shrugged, "I don't know. I didn't know him before. He did seem a bit …hmm…preoccupied, you might say. But maybe that's because he was still trying to figure out how he'd become lost."

Suddenly a bellow emitted from the other side of the cave, "I'VE FOUND IT!"

As the entire company converged on the wizard, he added, "Well, I think I have. It's not called the Lost Forest in the sorcerers' history but it sounds much the same." Like bees around a honey pot, the company of sorcerers and woodfolk swarmed around him until Stormaway flapped his hands swatting them away, "Shoo. Get back, all of you. You're in my light. How can I see what I'm doing?"

When they had all fallen back to sit or squat in a ring around the wizard, Danton urged, "So come on Stormaway, what have you found?"

Stormaway threw him an irritated glance that was, surprisingly, laced with understanding, "Young man, I am trying to tell you. If you can stop yourself from interrupting, I might have a better chance."

"Sorry."

"It is referred to here as the Forest of Yesterday Today and Tomorrow." Stormaway glanced at Hail, "Ring any bells?"

Hail thought for a moment but shook her head.

"Hmph. Anyway, this forest was a place to which wizards of old could banish people who had faltered in their service to the king… not who had failed exactly but who had not lived up to expectation. It was a punishment of sorts but if they returned they were accorded great honour because it was recognised that they must have overcome something fearful to return. Apparently many men asked for the privilege of going to prove themselves. Hmm. In fact, in earlier times anyone who wanted to serve the King personally was sent there as a matter of course, to have their merit tested. It seems to have been rather like sending someone on a stringent training course from which they might not return."

Danton frowned, "It sounds like sending a champion on a dangerous quest to prove himself."

Stormaway's brow cleared, "Exactly. That describes it well."

"And why the long-winded name?"

Stormaway smiled. "Because wizards are fond of the grandiose, my dear. I expect Yesterday Today and Tomorrow means that the fears that must be confronted may come from a person's past, present or future." He shrugged. "Or maybe they have to deal with all of these. It's not clear from this text."

"So who has sent our people into that forest and why?" asked Thunder Storm. "They did not need testing, in my view, and they certainly didn't ask to be tested."

"In our stories, no one sends people into the Lost Forest," said Hail. "The forest chooses. Anyway, how do you know this forest of yours is the same as our Lost Forest?" asked Hail.

"It is no more my forest than the Lost Forest is," said Stormaway quietly. "It is the sorcerers' forest. Or, if you want to look at it another way, both of them are my forests." When Hail looked puzzled, he added, "Both the Lost Forest and the Forest of Yesterday Today and Tomorrow are part of my heritage."

Hail, usually so acerbic, gave a little grimace, "Sorry Stormaway. I did not mean to offend you. I merely meant the forest that you had found in your book."

The wizard gave a wry little shrug, "Hmph. Perhaps I am still a little oversensitive on the subject. Anyway, to answer your question; one mystical forest is unlikely enough. Two would beggar belief. Besides, in essence, they seem to be the same. Both versions of this forest confront people with their worst fears and demand that they overcome them."

"Hmm. I think the Lost Forest sounds more intimidating," mused String, "if that's what the wizards were trying to achieve."

"Perhaps, but it wasn't lost to them. They knew how to send people into it."

"Aah," rumbled Thunder Storm. "But did they know how to get them back out?"

Stormaway scanned the rest of the relevant pages before shaking his head regretfully, "No. One way trip, I'm afraid. Those banished there had to find their own way out."

Danton threw up his hands "Yes, but the point is that you can send us into the Lost Forest...can't you Stormaway?" He stood up and resumed his pacing.

"Can you, Stormaway?" asked Creaking Bough. "And if so, will it be safe for the children?"

Danton stopped dead and swung round to confront the woodwoman. "I would think you should be more concerned about protecting your forest guardian." said Danton sharply, "... and being true to your oath."

Thunder Storm rose slowly to his feet. Something about his stance reminded Danton that this woodman was the fastest, deadliest marksman among them. "Danton, you are not the keeper of our honour." A note of anger vibrated through the woodman's voice. "Creaking Bough and I have children who look to us for their life and safety. We have already taken them through dangerous situations in support of your prince. Taking them somewhere where their presence may hinder our actions will help no one. This oath of ours has a whole nation of people to fulfil it. Be careful that your attitude does not turn away those of us who have stood by Tarkyn's side from the beginning."

Danton locked stares with the woodman. Then with a visible effort, he breathed out and relaxed. Giving a small bow, he smiled ruefully and said, "Thunder Storm and Creaking Bough, I apologize for my words. I should never have spoken them. You have indeed always stood staunchly beside Tarkyn and it is not my place to question you. I fear I am a little overwrought." He ran his hand through his blonde hair, "I feel that I have let my liege down and it does not sit well with me."

"It does not sit well with any of us," replied Hail. "You should know that by now. So come on, Stormaway. Answer Creaking Bough's question."

Stormaway raised his eyebrows and looked around to make sure no one else was going to interrupt him, "Yes, in answer to the first part. I think I can send us into the forest. And in answer to the second part, I don't know for certain but I hope so, because Midnight is in there."

It was a couple of minutes before String was able to make himself heard above the general hubbub that greeted this. "Stormaway, is there any advantage in us going in after the others?"

Stormaway gave a wry smile, "Watch out. You'll have Danton on your back if you're not careful." The wizard thought for a moment, "To be honest, I doubt it. I think we will only be assuaging our own anxieties by following them into this forest. Once they entered the Lost Forest, the die was already cast."

"But how else can we meet up with them again?" asked Bean. "Or will they find us?"

Stormaway shrugged, "I don't know how big this Forest of Yesterday Today and Tomorrow is. Just because we enter it, doesn't necessarily mean we will find them."

Danton jumped up and started pacing again, "Come on Stormaway, we have to try, don't we?"

The wizard felt a small hand clutching at his robe and looked down to see Sparrow gazing up at him, "*Please* Stormaway,"

Stormaway glanced around the company, "I will leave it in your hands. You may choose to go individually or as a whole group. You all talk about it while I work out how to do it. Let me know in an hour or so. I should have figured out what to do by then."

Sparrow walked over to Danton and took his hand as he strode past for the umpteenth time. She looked up at him and smiled shyly, "We will go, won't we?"

Danton stopped and looked down at her, realisation dawning, "Oh Sparrow, I'm sorry. All I was thinking about was that I had let down Tarkyn. I didn't even think about your whole family being lost." He gave her a little smile, "Yes, Sparrow. We will go, no matter what, whether it is sensible or not."

Sparrow nodded and smiled. "Do you want to go for a walk outside while the others are talking? We could collect some wood."

"Good idea. I can't sit still anyway."

The two of them emerged into the glare of midmorning. Low white clouds and snow piled in drifts against the trees reflected the light into their eyes. Sparrow stepped out into deep snow up to her thighs, making her wobble and giggle, "This is fun. But I don't know how we're going to find any wood. We'll have to feel around with our feet."

"Just be careful you don't stand on a branch and twist your ankle. I don't fancy facing Waterstone with a damaged daughter in tow." Danton gave her a warm confident smile and she beamed back at him, suddenly sure that Danton would help her find her father.

Now that Danton had realised her plight, he was determined to help Sparrow, his liege's kin, as much as he could. Together they ploughed through the snow, laughing as they tripped over the logs they were looking for and throwing snowballs at each other. By the time they returned to the cave with a good load of wood, they were wet through but relaxed and even cheerful. Sparrow and Danton shook themselves off and stood over the fire to dry themselves.

While they had been outside, the rest of the company had decided that they too would enter the Lost Forest in search of Tarkyn and the others. It was still well within the wizard's stipulated hour so everyone packed up while they waited patiently for Stormaway to prepare himself.

Suddenly a tremor shook the ground and the sky outside darkened.

"What was that?" exclaimed Hail.

"Well, it wasn't Tarkyn getting angry this time," rumbled Thunder Storm, "because he's not here."

"It might be a thunder storm," suggested Golden Toad.

"Bloody enormous thunder storm to shake the whole mountain," responded Blizzard derisively, "Besides, I didn't hear any thunder, did you?"

"Avalanche?" suggested String.

Bean shrugged, "Could be. One in the distance somewhere, maybe. It can't be close by or we would have heard the roaring."

"And unless we've been buried by it, that doesn't explain the darkness outside," objected Blizzard.

"Maybe there was an avalanche somewhere else and the weather is closing over here," suggested Creaking Bough.

"Why don't we go outside and have a look?" asked Danton dryly. "That will at least eliminate some possibilities." He smiled at Sparrow and held out his hand, "Coming?"

Danton, Sparrow and Thunder Storm walked to the cave's entrance and looked out. The conifer forest and the snow was gone. Old gnarled twisted trees, densely entwined overhead, met their gaze. After a few moment's silence, Danton said slowly, "Hail, could you come here please?"

"No need," said Thunder Storm calmly, "I have already sent her the images - and yes, it is the Lost Forest."

"Well, blast it all!" came an explosion of irritation from behind them. "I was looking forward to trying out some new magic."

Hail grunted, "I told you. The Lost Forest finds you."

Chapter 21

"Okay. So what do we do now?" asked Danton of the gathered company who were standing around him outside the cave, all packed up and ready to begin their journey.

Stormaway scratched his head, "Well, there seems to be a bit of a path wandering into the forest just ahead of us. We might as well follow it. When we come to a fork, we'll have to rethink."

"I don't suppose you woodfolk can just mind link with them and find out where they are, can you?" suggested Danton, without too much hope.

Thunder Storm smiled understandingly, "No Danton. You will be astonished to know we actually thought of that ourselves and have already tried. But our mind talking isn't working beyond the people in our immediate vicinity within this forest."

Danton flashed him a smile and shrugged, "Sorry. I thought you would have, but I just had to ask."

Thunder Storm grunted, "Well, in fairness, we should have told you, shouldn't we?"

They set off along the path but it was not long before they found themselves at a crossroads with nothing to indicate which way they should go.

"This is worse than a fork. This gives us three choices," grumbled Tree Wind.

Everyone pondered in silence until Stormaway suddenly snapped his fingers. "I know what we'll do. Now, what did Tarkyn say all those months ago when he first entered the forest? He said, 'If all roads lead nowhere, choose the road with heart'." The wizard beamed. "Okay everyone. Close your eyes, think of whoever you're closest to amongst the people we seek, and let your heart choose."

A chorus of voices said firmly, "Left."

Stormaway smiled in satisfaction, "Left it is, then."

Each time they came to a fork or an intersection, they repeated this process and each time there was a consensus on which road to take. As they progressed, the forest closed in around them, brown and seemingly lifeless, with only glimpses of grey sky overhead. But still they persevered, keeping close together for safety and reassurance. They stopped for lunch at a dusty widening of the path beneath great twisted tree roots. No one knew whether Stormaway's plan was getting them any closer to their lost companions and only the fact that they continued to agree on the direction kept them at all convinced that they should continue with it.

As they set off after lunch on yet another of their hunches, Bean grumbled, "If this is the sum total of Tarkyn's navigational skills, no wonder he gets lost all the time."

"I bet he doesn't even do this," drawled String. "I think he just goes blank and gets other people to navigate for him."

"Prince's prerogative," said Danton shortly, "No reason why he should do it himself if he chooses not to."

"Oh, put a sock in it, you feisty bastard," snapped Bean. "No one's sniping at your precious prince. He's just entertaining, that's all."

"Hmph."

"And another thing," chipped in String, "Why are you so haughty around Harkell and not around us? If you're going to be a snob, at least be consistent about it."

Danton subjected him to a frosty glare. After a noticeable pause, he said tightly, "You two do not play the games of royal favour. You are no threat to me or to Tarkyn. Harkell, on the other hand, has risen well beyond his birthright. That will not have happened by accident. Whether he has learnt from Jarand's treatment of him to accept his place in life remains to be seen, but otherwise his intentions may threaten my place at Tarkyn's side or threaten Tarkyn himself, if our blacksmith captain decides to further his own cause by undermining the people close to the prince."

Bean let out a low whistle, "Stars above, Danton. I did not know you could be so unkind."

"If you really care for Tarkyn, shouldn't you accept it if he prefers someone else at his side?" pressed String.

Danton threw his hand up in disgust. "You two are such babes in the wood. It's patently obvious that you have been out of circulation for years. Before you start slamming into me, take a bit of time to think. Do I begrudge Waterstone his close relationship with Tarkyn? No… Or Rainstorm? No. I kept a very low profile for the weeks after I first arrived… barely went near the prince at all. But if this social climbing, ambitious upstart usurps me, will it be because he cares for Tarkyn or cares for himself? I want to stay by Tarkyn's side so I can shield him as the groundswell of support draws devious sorcerers in, with plans to use him for their own ends."

String glanced at Danton then looked quickly away. The trapper almost winced, as he said determinedly, "I hope Jarand's treatment has not resigned our Captain Harkell to thinking himself tied to his birthright. It would not be just for such treatment to affect a man's opinion of himself."

"And yet that is exactly what it does," Danton said bleakly, "I learnt my place in life over and over again, until Tarkyn stood up to his father. I was nothing more than a means of control over the prince." For the first time, a flash of anger crossed Danton's face "Who I was or what I felt or thought, mattered not at all. They didn't even bother to watch me as they whipped me. They watched only Tarkyn."

"So do you want Harkell's flogging to have beaten the spirit out of him?" asked Bean, with a frown of concern.

"In one way, yes, because then he won't pose a threat." Danton sighed, "But in truth, no. Anyway, I know it didn't. He accepted the flogging for having failed to protect Jarand. What shook him was being abandoned afterwards. He knew that was the punishment for having made an error when he had risen so far above his station." The young lord shrugged. "He was left to die in the field. I was ignored as they whipped me. Both of us have been shown how little we matter. Even though I am a lord and he is a only a tradesman, we have both endured the same annihilating disregard from those above us."

"Except from Tarkyn," said String.

"Exactly," agreed Danton, "Which is why I will do everything in my power to make sure that he doesn't fall victim to the wiles of predatory sorcerers."

"Assuming Harkell is one," Bean sounded dubious.

Danton gave his head a little shake, "I will assume he is, until I am convinced otherwise.

String shook his head dolefully. "Poor Harkell," was all he said.

A little further along the path String, who had been pondering over their conversation, asked another question, "Why didn't you stay beside your prince when you first entered the forest? Surely, when everyone else was strange to you, that would have been when you needed his companionship the most?"

"I did not want it to become sorcerers versus woodfolk with my advent, so I kept my distance." Danton gave a little grin, "I would always put the prince's needs before my own. The woodfolk tease me about it mercilessly."

"That and the bowing," put in Thunder Storm, coming alongside. He gave a deep chuckle, "You should have seen Danton when he first arrived – bowing all over the place and getting red in the face and telling us off when we didn't."

String's eyes widened, "Ooh. That must have gone down well!"

Thunder Storm nodded. "Yes. It wasn't long before Danton found himself flat on his back under the impetus of Rainstorm in a towering rage."

"That was a pretty poor effort for an elite guard, Danton," said Bean derisively. "I wouldn't have expected young Rainstorm to down one of Eskuzor's best."

Danton's eyes twinkled. "When you speak of Eskuzor's best, you have to remember that none of the woodfolk has ever entered the lists. Thunder Storm here is streets ahead of any of us in marksmanship."

Bean looked at Thunder Storm with new respect. "Is he? Hmm."

The woodman cut in before he could ponder this for too long. "I might just point out, since Danton doesn't seem to be going to, that when Rainstorm downed our loyal guardsman here, Danton was under strict orders from Tarkyn not to use any violence whatsoever against any of us."

Danton chuckled, "Thank you, Thunder Storm, for springing to my defence."

"You seem very unconcerned about your reputation as a fighter," observed Bean.

Danton shrugged, still smiling. "My name and the fact that I'm an elite guard say it all. I don't need to keep proving something that has already been acknowledged." He gave a short laugh. "I'm just glad I didn't spout off about my prowess. Most woodfolk are as good as, or better than me in most areas."

Tree Wind considered the matter, "Stealth, tracking and marksmanship possibly. But not hand to hand fighting, I think you'll find."

"But I thought you managed to flatten Tarkyn and hold an arrow to his neck when he first arrived," protested Danton.

Tree Wind dismissed this with a wave of her hand. "I only managed that because he was caught completely unawares and jumped back in fright when he saw my reflection in the water. And he only let me stay in a commanding position because he knew he was surrounded by other woodfolk." She grimaced, "If I had known then what I know now about his power, I would never have done it – Anyway, the point is that we woodfolk have never had the need for hand to hand combat because we hide. If we're seen, we fire an arrow or throw a knife. Simple as that."

"Some people wrestle," added Thunder Storm, "but it's mainly for entertainment and the odd personal fight. It's not part of our stringent survival training. No point."

Danton's brow creased as he thought about it. "What if someone sneaks up on you when you are on your own?"

"Wouldn't happen," said Falling Branch with complete conviction. "The only person who can sneak up on a woodman is another woodman. And even if it did happen, we'd just send a mind message and someone else would shoot them." He shrugged, "Besides, we have lookouts."

"What about lone trappers like Hail?" asked String.

"Yeah. They have to sleep sometime," pointed out Bean. "And they don't have lookouts."

Danton raised his eyebrows with a grin, "Besides, I slipped past your lookouts."

"Yes, true. You did. We were impressed by that," conceded Thunder Storm. "But if you had attacked anyone, the sudden movement would have given you away and you would have died in a hail of arrows."

"So have there ever been any occasions where woodfolk died at the hands of outsiders?" asked Danton.

"Sadly yes," said Falling Branch. "But the intruders have never made it to the forest edge alive. And the occurrences are so rare that we feel our present skills are enough to keep us safe."

"You may need more if you go among sorcerers in support of Tarkyn." Danton had bent over to pick up a stick and so only caught the end of a glance that passed between the woodfolk. "I beg your pardon," he said stiffly. "I was not presuming to tell you what you should do. I was merely discussing it with you."

As Danton turned to stride on ahead, Thunder Storm caught up with him and clapped him firmly on the shoulder. "Danton, my young friend, do not be so quick to take offence. The look that passed between us was not resentment of you. It was a shared fear of venturing among sorcerers."

The tension drained out of the young man and he gave them a rueful smile, "Sorry. I'm a bit edgy at the moment."

By tacit agreement, the entire company gathered in support around Danton before moving off once more.

"Come on Danton. Have faith in your liege. He can look after himself," said Stormaway bracingly.

Danton grinned, "You're right. He can. It's me I'm worried about."

This was so patently untrue that everyone laughed. For the next few hours they travelled deeper and deeper into the ancient forest, at each parting of the ways using their unanimous vote to choose their next direction.

But late in the afternoon, something changed.

As they came to a fork in the path, Stormaway took them once more through a routine that had now become established. "Close your eyes. Focus on someone you hold dear… Okay. Which way?"

For the first time, the vote was split. They looked at each other in confusion before turning to Stormaway.

"Try again," said Tree Wind, speaking for them all.

But a repeat of the exercise produced the same result.

"Blast it!" swore Stormaway. "This was going so well too."

"Well, you don't know it was," objected Bean. "All you know is that we agreed with each other."

"Yeah," chimed in String. "We might have been agreeing to go around in circles."

"After all," added Bean dryly, "This *is* Tarkyn's navigational system."

"Perhaps we need to think about why it's different this time," suggested Tree Wind.

"Is there anything different about this part of the woods?"

The woodfolk scrutinized the area, seeing through their eyes things that the sorcerers would miss.

"There doesn't seem to be anything unusual. There are a few more oaks and horse chestnuts off to the left and a couple of vines," said Falling Branch slowly. "While off to the right, we can see more beeches."

Danton, who thought all leafless trees looked the same, blinked. "Well, the things I don't see," he drawled. "Hmm. But without wishing to be dismissive, that doesn't seem to have helped us much. Has it?"

Tree Wind smiled, "No, not that I can see."

"Who said 'left' and who said 'right'?" asked String, suddenly animated. When everyone answered at once, he requested people to separate into the two groups. Then he asked each person who had chosen left, to say on whom they had been focussing.

"Tarkyn," replied Danton predictably.

"Midnight," replied Hail and Bean.

"Tarkyn," said Summer Rain, Golden Toad and his family.

String added, "I also chose left and was thinking of Tarkyn." He turned to the group who had chosen the right hand path.

"Rainstorm," said Falling Branch, his father.

"Autumn Leaves," said Thunder Storm, his brother.

"Waterstone," said Sparrow, his daughter.

"Falling Rain," replied Tree Wind, his fiancee.

String held out his arms in triumph. "And there you have it. Tarkyn and Midnight have separated from the others."

Amongst the general hubbub that greeted this, Stormaway exclaimed, "Well done, String! You're a genius!"

String shot a glance at Bean, who muttered dryly, "He knows." After a moment he added gruffly, "It's the only reason I put up with him. Couldn't conceive of spending those endless hours in the mountains with a dullard."

Once the initial reaction had passed, the company was left with the problem that had emerged from the solution of the previous one.

"So, who will we seek out? Tarkyn and Midnight? Or the rest of them?" asked Summer Rain.

"I think we should wait here for a while," replied Stormaway. "With any luck, Tarkyn and Midnight haven't separated from the others permanently."

"True. Chances are that Tarkyn may just have gone for a walk with Midnight," said Creaking Bough. "After all, they only separated from the others sometime in the last hour because we had a consensus at the previous intersection."

"And we must be quite close to them now, for the short distance between them to show up as a different direction," concluded Bean.

Once everyone had thought through the logic of Bean's statement, they felt encouraged.

"We could just go straight to the bigger group and wait there with them for Tarkyn and Midnight to return," suggested Tree Wind. "Then at least we would know what was happening and we could follow Tarkyn and Midnight if they needed us."

Stormaway smiled understandingly. "Your idea has merit, Tree Wind. But I suspect there are some among us who would struggle with knowingly walking away from Tarkyn."

Danton said nothing, looked down at the ground with his arms folded and waited.

"In my opinion," said Thunder Storm ponderously, "If no one but Midnight is with Tarkyn, it behoves us to head in his direction to make sure he is protected."

"But we might be leaving our kin, those we hold dear, in danger," protested Tree Wind who had so recently reunited with Falling Rain after twelve years apart.

"And even though I love Tarkyn, I want to see my dad," said Sparrow anxiously.

And suddenly the choice stood starkly before them: to fulfil their oath or to go to the ones they loved. Never before had they been in a position where they had to choose between them. An intense silence of mental debate filled the air.

Still with his arms folded, Danton glanced at String, Bean and Stormaway before dropping his eyes back to the ground at his feet.

Stormaway watched the woodfolk closely as the debate raged. Anxiety, frustration and irritation followed each other across their faces, but interestingly, not resentment. Nevertheless, for a while, the distance between woodfolk and sorcerers widened perceptibly.

Eventually the parade of expressions subsided and, after what seemed like an interminable length of time, Tree Wind asked Danton tightly, "What if we told you that we wanted to return to our kin?"

Keeping his voice carefully neutral, Danton replied, "As Thunder Storm pointed out earlier, I am not the keeper of your conscience. It is entirely up to you what you choose to do."

"And what if we insist that we should all stick together?" continued Tree Wind.

"I am not a woodman. You have not included me in your discussions so far and I feel no compulsion to stay with you if I feel obliged to follow a different path." He actually managed a slight smile, "But should it occur that the parting of our ways were permanent, I would miss your company."

Uncharacteristically, Thunder Storm strode over to Danton and wrapped him in a big bear hug. "She's teasing you, Danton. Well done. You coped admirably." He smiled as Danton's wired up body relaxed. "I think we could, and did, argue either course of action and even possibly justify it in terms of holding to our oath but we won't because we know you would find it too hard to go in the direction away from Tarkyn, and we want to stick with you even if you are willing to part from us."

Danton patted the woodman on the back before pulling away and smiling wryly, "I would not willingly part with you but I couldn't live with myself if I didn't go after Tarkyn."

Hail grunted, "Anyway, it wasn't just about you. We decided that, in all honesty, if Tarkyn is unprotected, following him was the only truly honourable course of action."

"It would not feel good to return to our kin having done less than our best to uphold our people's oath to him," said Tree Wind. "Besides, we care about him too."

"But sometimes being honourable is a bit hard," said Sparrow with a sniff, "And sometimes I could almost wish Tarkyn hadn't come."

Instead of taking offence, Danton crossed to squat down in front of Sparrow. "Little one, as soon as we have met up with Tarkyn and made sure he has someone to protect him, we can continue on to meet up with Waterstone and Ancient Oak and everyone else." He smiled at her and wiped away her tears with his finger, "And you know, if we don't go and find him, he might get lost on his own in a big forest, mightn't he?"

Sparrow giggled through her tears, "Yes. In fact he probably will because he doesn't know about our tricky way of finding people, does he? … even though he invented it. And he's sure to get lost if he is away from the others because he always does." She nodded and gave a final sniff, "Yes, I can see we had better go and rescue him. Dad's much better at looking after himself and he'll be waiting for us… won't he?"

"Yes," said Creaking Bough, "I'm sure he will."

Chapter 22

Had they but known it, their intention of offering Tarkyn protection would have been most unwelcome at that stage of the young prince's life, bent as he was on declaring himself to Lapping Water. But luckily, long before they caught up with him, Tarkyn was back in the circular clearing with the others of his party, celebrating his betrothal to Lapping Water.

Their celebrations were still in full swing when, between one sentence and the next, the woodfolk around Tarkyn and Harkell fell silent. When Tarkyn went to speak, Waterstone held up his hand and rose silently to his feet. Quietly, the woodfolk unsheathed their knives or reached for their bows. Some stayed close to Tarkyn while others melted into the surrounding trees. Then a little figure came running into the clearing.

"Dad! Dad! We're here. We've found you."

"Sparrow!" In one fluid movement, Waterstone sheathed his knife and swept his daughter up into his arms. Under the influence of an evening's hard celebrations, he staggered a little under the impetus, but held upright and hugged Sparrow close to him.

Danton, now that he knew his liege was safe, held back at the edge of the clearing as woodfolk and sorcerers swirled around each other. He felt he had rather overstepped the mark already and did not want to make a further exhibition of himself. So he wrapped his arms around himself and watched in satisfaction as the others celebrated their reunion. Suddenly the crowd parted and Tarkyn walked towards him.

Danton unwrapped his arms and gave a slight bow.

Tarkyn kept walking until he stood right in front of the blonde sorcerer. He smiled, "Danton, my oldest friend, I hear you have been driving everyone to distraction and yet here you are, standing on the periphery so that I have had to come to greet you."

A look of uncertainty crossed Danton's face but as he began to apologise, Tarkyn interrupted him, "I have something of great importance to tell you, my friend." He glanced back over his shoulder before meeting Danton's eyes once more. Then Tarkyn beamed. "Lapping Water and I are to be married."

Danton blinked as his mind adjusted. Then seeing the happiness in Tarkyn's face, he thrust aside any doubts he might have about the implications of the match and, throwing caution to the winds, threw his arms around his liege in an enthusiastic embrace. "Congratulations. I am so pleased for you. I know you would not give your heart lightly.

So this must have been a momentous decision for you. I wish you all the happiness you both deserve."

Tarkyn returned his embrace with a warmth that sprang from years' of shared experience, "Thank you, Danton." And into his ear, he added, "And thank you for so quickly adjusting your expectations. I promise you, I will never abandon sorcerers."

When they parted, Danton's eyes were shining with emotion. "Sire, I cannot tell you how proud I am that you would consider my feelings at a time like this."

Lapping Water walked over to join them and smiled at him, unusually for her, a little shyly. "Hello Danton."

Danton took her hand and kissed it with great gallantry, "Congratulations, Lapping Water. You have found yourself the finest man in all of Eskuzor. And Tarkyn, if Lapping Water, who has no interest in rank, is brave enough and clear-sighted enough to see past your fearsome power and accept who you really are, then you have found yourself a true partner."

Tarkyn and Lapping Water put an arm around each other as they stood facing Danton and a glowing look passed between them.

"Thank you, Danton," said Lapping Water quietly. "I was a little worried that you might not approve."

"Lapping Water, it is not my place to approve or disapprove."

"Everyone has an opinion, Danton, whether they should or not."

Danton shrugged, "I admit I have some qualms about the road ahead of you but none that you won't have considered yourselves." He grinned, "And I would be very churlish to disapprove of something that is so patently bringing such happiness to my liege… and to you." He gave a little bow, "And I am truly honoured that either of you should care about my reaction."

Lapping Water put her hand impulsively on Danton's arm, "Of course I care and of course Tarkyn cares. You are his oldest friend and you are also my friend. I cannot understand why you would consider yourself of so little account."

Danton met Tarkyn's eyes, as he said, "Tarkyn understands." He returned his gaze to Lapping Water and tried to explain, "The royal family does not look to its retainers for approval of its actions. Tarkyn is a very unusual prince."

"More unusual than he used to be, I suspect," replied Lapping Water acerbically.

Danton thought carefully before replying slowly, "Yes. That is true. And although his underlying integrity has always been the same, I doubt that you would have fallen in love with him at court."

"I'll just leave you two to dissect my character, shall I?"

The dryness of Tarkyn's tone brought Lapping Water and Danton's heads whipping around.

"I beg your pardon, Your Highness. I forgot myself," said Danton stiffly.

"Oh stop it, Danton!" exclaimed the prince impatiently. "This has nothing to do with rank. I just don't like being talked about as though I'm not here."

"You're right," said Lapping Water, with a twinkle, "We should wait until you aren't here to discuss you, shouldn't we?"

Tarkyn's eyes narrowed and for a moment, the issue hung in the balance. Then he shrugged and smiled, "Yes, you should. Or include me in the discussion about myself when I am present."

Danton frowned as he thought, then rephrased his previous remark, "And so Tarkyn, do you think Lapping Water could have fallen in love with you in the persona you portrayed at court?"

Tarkyn glanced at the woodwoman and gave a shy smile, "I'm surprised she grew to like me out here in the woods when I've been trying to be conciliatory, let alone in my previous life when I was unquestioningly autocratic." He shook his head, "So no, I don't think she would have… Do you, Lapping Water?" he added, meticulously not falling into the error he had just objected to.

Lapping Water did not answer immediately. She studied him as she tried to imagine what his life had been like before. Finally, she shook her head, "In all honesty, I couldn't say. I can't imagine you were autocratic all the time. You must have had times where you were just chatting or laughing or… I don't know… whatever princes do at court." She smiled, "I think your kindness must have shone through because otherwise, Danton wouldn't have stayed so devoted to you, no matter what you did for him when you were younger. And if you weren't so kind, you wouldn't have bent over backwards to come to terms with us." She smiled up at him, "I might have grown to love you, you never know, but it sounds as though you would never even have known I was there. So it's just as well it didn't happen like that, isn't it?"

They turned to find Danton smiling benignly at them. "You do understand him, don't you?" he said, unconsciously giving the match his final seal of approval.

As soon as they returned to the main body of the party, Waterstone sought Danton out. He handed the young sorcerer a glass of wine with one hand while still holding Sparrow on his hip with the other. "Here. You have this one. I'll get another." Almost like clockwork, another glass of wine appeared in his hand from a passing Rainstorm, who was off to chat with Tarkyn. He smiled his thanks and, signalling to Danton to follow him, found a comfortable place to sit where Sparrow could sit on his lap and settle against his shoulder while he talked.

"So, my young friend, I hear you and Sparrow have been looking after each other."

Danton smiled and interpreted this for what it was, a vote of thanks, disguised because of Sparrow's presence. "Yes. I think we two found the separation the hardest and so we ended up supporting each other. Didn't we Sparrow?"

Sparrow smiled and nodded sleepily.

Waterstone nodded over at Tarkyn, "You took Tarkyn's betrothal extremely well, considering your concern for your fellow sorcerers."

"I would never stand in the way of Tarkyn's happiness." Danton sipped his wine and commented on its quality before saying, "It did come as a surprise to me, I must admit. I had seen some signs that Tarkyn liked Lapping Water but it is a long step from that to contemplating marriage." He smiled, "But Tarkyn has never been anything but totally serious about women. He has never seen them as a form of entertainment as some of the young lords did and he always held himself aloof from any gossiping about them. He only spoke to women himself, very formally in strict social settings."

"Ancient Oak told me that Tarkyn was nervous about approaching Lapping Water," said Waterstone, smiling.

Danton grimaced, "Some of the young lords thought Tarkyn was a sanctimonious prig. But I don't think it was that. I think it was more that his duty lay heavily on his shoulders and he really did disdain disrespectful discussions about anyone."

"Anyone?"

"Well, anyone of rank. But even those more lowly born. He might inadvertently have treated people of lower birth with disdain by not being aware of their existence but he never set out to be unkind."

Waterstone shook his head, smiling to himself

"And on the other hand, Tarkyn knew he would be expected to marry to suit the kingdom and, as a prince, he expected himself to behave with decorum and to set an example." Danton smiled wryly. "I'm afraid the whippings I had to endure had the desired effect on Tarkyn. He never intentionally stepped out of line."

Waterstone put his head on one side, "And so, do you think he is marrying Lapping Water to suit the kingdom?"

Danton grinned, "Oh no, not at all… which just goes to show how far he has come." He shook his head, "I don't know how he managed to ask her, really. He has had so little experience of conversing with women, at least until he came to the forest."

"Yes, I think it may have been one of his biggest challenges." Waterstone smiled. "But I'm so glad he did. Ancient Oak and Rainstorm are delirious with happiness, of course."

"Why?"

Waterstone grinned, "Because they have been conniving for weeks to get Lapping Water and Tarkyn together."

Danton laughed. "Have they? Hmm. Well, it is good to know that they think enough of Tarkyn to entrust one of your women with him."

"Why wouldn't they? *You* think Tarkyn is the greatest thing on two legs, don't you?"

Danton grunted with laughter. "Oh, *I* do. But I am not such a fool that I expect everyone to think as I do. It's one thing for me to expect a certain form of behaviour around the prince. It's quite another for me to expect you people, who have had to accept him unwillingly, to actually want him to marry one of your own."

"You know," said Waterstone, "I said almost the converse to Tarkyn. I think it shows that he really respects us as a people to have chosen a woodwoman when he could have had his pick of any of your women."

Danton's smile slipped a little. "Yes, clearly he does. I have known that for a long time. You know, he whispered to me before, that he wouldn't ever abandon sorcerers but... I can't help thinking that I am fighting a losing battle as he becomes more and more a part of you woodfolk."

Waterstone shook his head decisively, "Never doubt your liege, Danton. I am surprised I should have to say that to you." He stroked Sparrow's head and bent down to give her a kiss. "Poor little girl. She's sound asleep now. She must have been so distressed to lose us all at once." He looked back up, "Thank you for looking after her."

Danton shrugged, guiltily aware that he had been a bit slow to recognise her need, "Thunder Storm and Creaking Bough looked after her too, you know."

"Anyway, Danton, while we have been here in this forest, it has been made very clear to all of us that Tarkyn is not just Guardian of the Forest. He is Guardian of all Eskuzor." Waterstone shook his head dolefully, "Such a young man to have such a heavy weight on his shoulders. But we will not let him bear it alone." He smiled gently, "He will never be king, as may have been your fond wish, but not his. But he is, and will be, greater than that."

Seeing Danton's uncertain frown, Waterstone went on to tell him of their encounter with the forest guardians of old. When he had finished he added, "And so my friend, you and I are no longer rivals for Tarkyn's services. We are united in supporting him and he will be working to protect all of us, sorcerers and woodfolk alike."

CHAPTER 23

Not having the advantage of mental communication, Danton was not privy to the same level of information about their surroundings that the newly arrived woodfolk were. So, being a dedicated protector of his liege, Danton headed out before breakfast the next morning, to scout around and get a feel for the area. As soon as he left the clearing, the greenness disappeared and he found himself once more surrounded by brown, leafless trees. He skirted the clearing in a wide circle, studying the tracks into it and looking for signs of other people having been there. Now and again, he waved to a lookout as he passed.

Suddenly, he bent down to look more closely at the dusty surface of a small path that led to a tunnel through the dense twiggy undergrowth. He ran his hand gently over the dirt and rubbed his fingers together to feel the consistency of the soil. His eyes narrowed and he transferred his attention to what he could see of the path as it disappeared into the shrubs. He got down on his hands and knees, and crawled quietly along the low passage beneath spiky plants.

The path led him around a long left hand turn, down a short slope before climbing in a right hand curve. It crested a small hill, curving once more to the left. Up ahead of him, Danton could now see the brightness at the end of the brush tunnel. He slowed down to creep the last thirty yards more quietly. As he reached the end, he stayed hidden within the bushes while he took stock of his destination.

He was looking down over another small circular clearing. But no stream ran through this one. Instead, soft greenery and reeds led to a perfectly round pool that nestled at the bottom of a small waterfall cascading from the rocks above it. Danton caught his breath at the beauty of it. As his eyes adjusted to the light, he realised that a young woman was sitting on a ledge overlooking the pool. He gazed slowly around the whole clearing before carefully sliding his way from bush to bush until he was near enough to get a better look at her.

The young woman was dressed in a long kingfisher blue robe that reflected the colour of her eyes. Her feet, clad in soft blue suede boots, hung over the edge of the ledge. Her soft strawberry blonde hair cascaded in a shimmering sheet down her back. She turned her brilliantly blue eyes towards his hiding place and said in a deep, self-assured voice, "Lord Danton, you may approach me."

Danton straightened immediately and walked down to stand before her, looking up at her from the other side of the pool. He bowed low, responding to the authority in her voice. "I beg your pardon, my lady. I did not mean to spy on you. I merely wished to ascertain your intentions in order to protect my lord."

The woman smiled slowly, "Which, if you did not intend to alert me to your presence, amounts to spying."

"My lady, I had not yet formed my intention one way or the other. I have yet to establish what power you possess and whether, or how, you intend to use it."

The young woman raised her eyebrows in delicate amusement, "You could be waiting a long time before I choose to use my power. Would you have watched me in subterfuge until then? You may have seen more than I would choose to show someone I do not know."

Danton coloured, "I beg your pardon, ma'am. I can assure you that I have only just arrived."

"I know you have," she replied coolly. "One does not live for years in these woods without knowing the meaning of every little sound. The birds alerted me to your presence when you were halfway along my tunnel. I have been waiting for you to emerge."

"I see." Danton gave a rueful smile. "The longer I live in the woods, the less I think my training has been adequate. I used to believe I could approach a person unawares but such is patently not the case." He hesitated, "Would you do me the honour of telling me whom I am addressing?"

"Some of who I am you may know and some I will not yet tell you. My name is Stillwaters Pathfinder." The woman smiled, "This is the Forest of Yesterday, Today and Tomorrow. Who I was, is not who I am now. And who I am now, is not who I will be. But for now, in this time and in this place, I am Stillwaters Pathfinder."

Danton inclined his head, "You are young to be a wizard, my lady."

One eyebrow rose, "Do you doubt me, sir?" She took obvious pleasure in Danton's hasty reassurance before relenting, "I began my training when I was very young. The circumstances were... unusual." She gave a delicate shrug, "Besides, Stormaway's mother was not much older than I, when she became a fully-fledged wizard."

Danton looked surprised, "Did you know her, my lady?"

"Just how old do you think I am, Lord Danton?" Her laughter tinkled at him when he coloured with embarrassment. "I would have to be, let me see... I would have to be well over sixty years old to have known Stormaway's mother. Have I aged so badly?"

Danton was beginning to find her constant teasing wearing, and so was less gallant than usual in his reply, "It is hard to say, my lady, since

I do not know your age… I would not have thought you to be sixty, however."

The smile wiped off Stillwaters' face. Her eyes glittering with anger, she said cuttingly, "I had heard that you were a courteous, gallant lord. Obviously my sources were mistaken."

"Obviously, my lady." He gave a slight smile, "I am as you find me."

"I had thought that the expectations of court would have whipped you into shape." There could be no doubt that her wording was not coincidental.

Anger flickered in Danton's eyes but he merely bowed and replied, "I am sorry to disappoint you, but the protection of my liege has meant that my unmannerliness has been able to flourish unchecked."

Stillwaters glared at him long and hard before surprising him by saying, "I beg your pardon. My last remark was uncalled for. I should not use as a weapon something of which I do not approve."

Danton stood stiffly before her but made no reply. Despite her apology, he was still angry and did not want to lay himself open to any more of her shafts. After a moment, he took a short breath and said tightly, "My lady, I will not pollute your morning any longer with my presence. Do I have your assurance that you have no ill intentions towards Prince Tarkyn?"

The young woman considered him in silence. Eventually she said softly, "Lord Danton, I can see that I have seriously offended you. For that, I am sorry." She pulled her shining hair over her right shoulder so that it trailed down on one side almost to the ground. She ran her hands through it, watching the light catching the ripples in it. After a moment she looked back up at him. "I will give you the assurance you request, but you and I both know that I could answer the same way whether I meant your prince ill or not." For the first time, she looked a little uncertain. "My lord, before you go…" She raised a hand and dropped it. "My lord Danton, please don't go…Not yet. I have so many things I would like to ask you and I do not want you to leave, thinking so ill of me."

Danton was quite unable to resist such a straightforward plea. He gave a slight bow, "I would be honoured to answer any questions you would like to put to me."

Stillwaters looked back down at her hair as she stroked it and asked inconsequentially, "Tell me of your travelling companions."

As Danton drew breath to answer, a yawning pit opened before him and he realised he could not tell her. After the slightest hesitation, he answered, "I travel with Prince Tarkyn, his wizard Stormaway Treemaster, a Captain Harkell and two trappers who go by the unlikely names of String and Bean."

She tossed her hair back over her shoulder and sat up, "Lord Danton, it cannot be comfortable for you to be standing there crooking your neck to look up at me. If you intend to humour me by staying a while longer, you might like to take the small path you will find to your left and come up here to sit beside me. If you do that, I will undertake to provide us with cups of the purest water delicately flavoured with mint and heather."

Danton smiled his thanks and by the time he had made the short journey around the pool and up between the tumbled rocks, she had indeed procured him the refreshment she had promised. As he sat down beside her and took his first mouthful of the drink, she asked casually, "And what of the woodfolk?"

Danton promptly choked and Stillwaters had to assist him by hitting him heartily on the back before he could catch his breath again. When he had recovered, he eyed her and suggested, "Perhaps you should tell me what you know first."

She nodded approvingly, "I am pleased you did not give away the presence of the woodfolk." She smiled, "Despite my previous words, I do believe you to be an honourable man. But I know of their presence in general, and of their presence with you and your prince in particular. So you are free to speak with me about them. I know there is one called Waterstone who was singled out by the forest guardians for his dedication to woodfolk lore in befriending your prince. There is a strange, darker coloured little woodman who is constantly at your prince's side and yet does not seem to be his servant."

Danton grinned, "That will be Midnight. He is Tarkyn's ward. He is half woodfolk and half sorcerer, like Stormaway. But unlike Stormaway, little Midnight was the product of a rape and has been reviled by the woodfolk for most of his life."

Stillwaters frowned, "I had not thought the woodfolk so cruel."

"They are not. Midnight's father cursed him and all of his mother's people. Tarkyn, with Stormaway and Midnight's help, saved them all from a slow descent into evil." He went on to tell her the whole story of the curse.

"Your young prince takes much upon himself, adopting a child."

Danton smiled broadly, "Yes, he does, especially if you know anything about Midnight. But Tarkyn loves him to bits. I think it must be like having a constant shadow around, by now."

"And what of this woodwoman who *dares* to marry a sorcerer prince?" asked Stillwaters, a note of disdain back on her voice.

Danton glanced at her and chose to answer, as though her question had been complimentary. "Yes, Lapping Water must be very courageous,

I think. Tarkyn is a handful for those of us who understand and accept his status, let alone for someone who does not. She, who sees everyone as her peers, must go into this marriage knowing that he will not, *cannot*, see her as his equal, and knowing that he wields far more power than she does."

"She is not his equal. He is of the royal line of Tamadil." The young woman's voice had become severe. "I hope she recognises the great honour the prince does her, in deigning to accept her as his wife."

"I don't think either of them sees it in quite that way." Danton gave a slight smile, "Don't tell me you're jealous. You don't have designs on him, do you?"

Stillwaters looked profoundly shocked. "I? I would not marry Prince Tarkyn if he were the last man on earth."

Danton reeled back. He stood up and glared down at her. "No one, no one speaks to me of the prince like that. If you were a man, I would have knocked your teeth out for that."

"If I were a man, I wouldn't have said it," riposted Stillwaters, completely undaunted. She patted the ground next her. "Now come on. Sit down. I apologise if I have upset you… yet again."

"What do you have against Tarkyn?" he asked, scowling at her as he reluctantly resumed his seat.

She considered him for a minute before replying. "I do not have to have anything against him, not to want him for a husband." She patted Danton's hand in what he considered to be a patronising manner, "I think your prince is a fine young man. I can see why you are proud and protective of him. But he is too young, too volatile and too arrogant for me."

"You're not short on arrogance yourself," retorted Danton, and then immediately wished he hadn't, as those harsh blue eyes turned to stare at him.

But after subjecting him to a period of discomfort, Stillwaters merely replied, "Exactly. And I have no doubt he and I will struggle to deal well with each other, when eventually we meet."

This last remark gave rise to so much speculation within Danton that for a while he was silent, lost in his thoughts. Eventually he asked, "Why would you meet? And if you would meet, why wouldn't you meet now?"

Stillwaters hesitated as she decided what to say. "We will meet when I choose to and not before. He may be a prince and Guardian of Eskuzor but I am not beholden to him and I will choose the time of our meeting. There are many things I know that he does not. But one thing is sure; he must, and I know he will, do everything he can to bring about peace between his brothers. When he has done that, I will come to him."

Danton frowned, "I don't think you answered my question. I asked, 'why?'"

The mysterious woman smiled slowly at him. "So you did. And yet I have given you all the answer I intend to."

Danton hit his knee in frustration. "You are the most irritating woman I have ever come across."

"Danton," she said reproachfully, "Don't be so churlish or I will think I was right in saying you lack manners."

"If I do, I think you are at least partly to blame for it."

"Definitely an ungallant thing to say," said Stillwaters mournfully, a quiet twinkle in her eyes.

Danton regarded her with a puzzled frown creasing his brow, "Who are you? What are you doing in this forsaken forest? Have your fears forced you to stay here? Somehow I don't think you are just a lost soul wandering this forest."

A note of reserve returned to her voice. "If you remember, I told you at the beginning that I would tell you some, but not all, of who I am. That still stands. I have lived in these woods for many years and I will not leave them until the time is right. For now, that must be enough."

In response to her cooler tone, Danton also withdrew. "My lady, I believe we have spoken enough. I must return to my liege."

The woman smiled, "You may tell Tarkyn of our meeting and assure him that I intend no one in your party any harm."

Danton blinked in surprise at the notion that he might not tell Tarkyn. But before he could reply, she continued, "And you may tell Stormaway Treemaster…no, don't tell him anything in particular…yes, wait a minute. Tell him my mother will forgive him when she knows what he had done."

Danton eyes grew round, making Stillwaters laugh. "And no, I am not going to put you out of your misery by telling you any more than that." She became serious, "And one more thing before you go. We have spoken of Prince Tarkyn's companions and of the prince himself and a little of myself. But we have not spoken of you."

"Except to comment on my lack of manners," put in Danton dryly.

Stillwaters gave a gentle laugh. "It wasn't fair of me, was it? But Lord Danton, I want to thank you. In your different ways, Stormaway and you have worked for Tarkyn's welfare and, with his welfare, for the future of Eskuzor. I could not ask for a more devoted, passionate man than you to stand by… Prince Tarkyn's side as the future unravels itself. You are a staunch ally at his shoulder and he is lucky to have you."

Although a part of his mind wondered at the slight hesitation, Danton was overcome by her accolade. "Th-thank you," he stammered. He smiled shyly at her, "But he has earned my devotion, you know. He was prepared to give his life to protect me and I would give him mine without a second thought. As a young child, he stood up to Markazon and let his life blood drip onto the floor until the whipping stopped."

Danton saw that Stillwaters had gone white. She shook her head a little, "I did not know of this. Tell me what happened."

When Danton had told her the whole story as he knew it and as Falling Rain had added to it, her eyes shone. She shook her head, "Such chances have been taken with the future of Eskuzor." She smiled at him, "But I am glad he did that. You are worth taking chances for."

This took Danton's breath away. He had always seen the incident as proof of Tarkyn's courage, not of his own value. He looked out across the pool to the reeds on the other side and watched little birds flitting in and out of the long stalks, as his place in the world made a slight shift.

Finally, he let out a long sigh. "I must go. You are deliberately enigmatic and frustrating to converse with, but on balance, I have enjoyed our time together," He gave a sudden grin, "Perhaps that is because you are so generous with your compliments." He shook his head and said seriously, "No, it is not that. You have an underlying strength and a quick wit that is entertaining to cross swords with. I am not sure how well you would go down at court. Perhaps a little too forthright and sharp, to appeal to many of the male courtiers. But you appeal to me." He stood up and shrugged, "Anyway, perhaps I will never see you again. Or not until that time far in the future that you spoke of, since I will always be at the prince's side."

She smiled, "You are not at the prince's side now and you may not always be, even though you continue to serve him."

She stood up and held out her hand. Danton bent over, took it in his hand and kissed it. "It was a pleasure to meet you, Stillwaters Pathfinder."

"And it was a pleasure to meet you, Danton Patronell, Lord of Sachmore."

CHAPTER 24

As Danton entered the clearing, Tarkyn strode up to him and roared in his face, "Where on earth have you been?"

Danton recoiled, "I was scouting out the surroundings, Your Highness."

"Don't lie to me, Danton," snapped Tarkyn. "The lookouts reported you missing three hours ago."

Waterstone came up to Tarkyn and put a hand on his arm, "Tarkyn, what is wrong? All of us went missing yesterday for several hours and you were completely unconcerned. Why does Danton now earn the brunt of your wrath?"

Tarkyn turned and glared at him, "Have a care. Do not interfere in what does not concern you."

Waterstone's eyes narrowed but he kept himself in check. He said evenly, "Injustice always concerns me, *Your Highness.*"

Tarkyn's eyes flickered with anger, "I *will* not have people uniting against me every time I express my displeasure. Danton is my liegeman. He is accountable to me for his behaviour. Let him speak for himself."

"Fair enough," said Waterstone, but making no attempt to move away.

Tarkyn returned his attention to Danton. "Well? What do you have to say for yourself?"

Danton glanced around the clearing, discomforted by being berated in public and yet reluctant to wrongfoot Tarkyn with people watching. "Sire, I have several things to say. Firstly, I did indeed go out scouting the surroundings this morning, as a result of which I found something of interest that I was coming back to report to you. Secondly, I had not realised how much time had passed and thirdly, I was not aware until now that I required permission to leave your side." He bowed, "I will ensure in future to keep you in constant cognisance of my whereabouts."

Tarkyn folded his arms and stared at his liegeman, quite unconcerned about the audience. When Danton straightened, purple eyes met amber steadily but the guardsman offered no further explanation. Finally Tarkyn broke the impasse by running his hand through his hair and exclaiming, "Blast you, Danton! I was worried sick about you." He waved an irritated hand at Waterstone, "I know I wasn't worried about you people yesterday but all I can say is that it felt different today. There is something or someone strange out there. I can feel a great power and I was worried about you." He blew out a long breath. "I'm sorry I yelled at you," he added shortly.

"And I apologise for not letting you know where I was, but when I left this morning you were asleep."

Tarkyn waved his hand dismissively. "You know perfectly well I don't want to know your every move. Stars above! We would bore each other rigid if I insisted on that."

When Danton smiled slightly, Tarkyn relaxed and gestured towards the fire. "Come on. Let's get a cup of tea and sit down, and you can tell us what you found." He glanced around at the watching faces. "Where's Stormaway? I think we will need him. And can someone fetch Danton some food while we talk, please? He's missed lunch."

Waterstone grinned. "Lovely to see you at your peremptory best, Tarkyn,"

Tarkyn grunted, but said in a friendly enough tone, "Where did I go wrong, that I allow my liegemen to comment on my every move?"

At being called a liegeman, Waterstone grin faded. Between one step and the next, he melted from Tarkyn's side, veering off to find others to talk to.

Tarkyn rolled his eyes, "Oh no. I've upset him now. Blast that stiff-necked brother of mine. I make every conceivable concession but still he wants more."

Danton shook his head, "No Sire. I think Waterstone is mainly content. It is just that he can't abide being referred to as a liegeman. It makes him feel that you see him as some type of servant, as one of many anonymous faces. It reduces his own particular importance to you."

Tarkyn frowned, "And so, does it not upset you if I call you my liegeman?"

"No, Your Highness. We come from completely different directions on this, Waterstone and I. He feels it anonymizes him. I feel it singles me out from the general populous as having been granted special recognition."

Tarkyn thought hard. Eventually he said, "In a sense, you are both right. Among sorcerers, I do have very few liegemen now. But the oath makes all woodfolk my liegemen." He sighed, "I should be more careful. I know woodfolk do not appreciate being liegemen and women. And when I call Waterstone my liegeman, I remind him of the oath and our differential status which he prefers to forget." He glanced sideways at Danton, "In fact, he once told me that the only way he could remain my friend was to keep the oath out of his mind as much as possible." The prince gave a wry smile. "He deserves that accolade given to him by the forest guardians. From his perspective, he has had to work hard to have a friendship with me."

Tarkyn looked across at Waterstone who was talking with Autumn Leaves and Rainstorm. A slight rigidity in his body gave away that he was still smarting. Tarkyn sent him over a wave of friendship and apology, thinking as he did, that if any sorcerer in his service at court had reacted in that way, he would have been dismissed and quite possibly punished.

Tarkyn did not have time to see the effect of his apology because Stormaway arrived at this point. The wizard gave a shallow bow, "You asked for me, my lord?"

"Yes. Take a seat, Stormaway. Cups of tea are on their way." Tarkyn looked from Danton to Stormaway. "I have not had a chance to speak to you about our encounter with the forest guardians of yore, although no doubt others have filled you in."

Stormaway shook his head regretfully, "That is one of the great regrets of my life; that I missed seeing them all."

Tarkyn gave a little smile, "I suppose it would be. You were so excited when you discovered that I was a guardian of the forest, weren't you?" He shrugged in sympathy. "Anyway, there is one thing I wanted to say about it. They stated very clearly that I could trust you, Stormaway, and you, Danton." He smiled, "I thought I knew that, but because I am bad at discerning intrigue, I could never, until now, be sure. So it is a great relief to me and I'm sure, to you, that I can now let down my guard with you."

"Your Highness, I bitterly regret saying that I gave you to the woodfolk," said Stormaway anxiously, "… and the fact that I kept from you that I am part woodfolk. I feared you would turn me away completely after that."

Tarkyn looked into the wizard's green eyes. "I nearly did, Stormaway. I nearly did… And because you are one of the rocks of my existence, it shook me to the core when I thought that you had manipulated me for your own ends." He sighed, "But I have been giving this a great deal of thought and now I think I understand. The welfare of Eskuzor, the woodfolk and I cannot be separated. So, in supporting one, you automatically support the others. When you were working for Eskuzor's future before I was born and when I was young, Stormaway, you were already supporting me."

Stormaway's face relaxed into a smile. "Yes, Sire. You do understand. If I have manipulated you in the past, it has been for the cause that you yourself support wholeheartedly. I would never work against your happiness or your beliefs."

Tarkyn smiled, "Good. So, now we have that sorted, you can stop waiting anxiously to see if I am about to send you away. I am not and will not. I depend on both of you to unearth any conspiracies or undercurrents among sorcerers that I may not pick up."

"On which topic," said Danton slowly, "I have some serious qualms about your Captain Harkell."

A look of apprehension flickered in Tarkyn's eyes, "Do you? On what grounds?"

"Captain Harkell is an ambitious man, Sire. He must be, to have risen so far. You might not, perhaps, have thought of that. And so, his rationale for serving you must be called into question, particularly since he has recently changed allegiances."

"Is that your only reason for doubting him?" asked Tarkyn.

"So far, yes, Your Highness."

Tarkyn leaned forward, "My Captain Harkell, as you like to call him, has been subjected to considerable scrutiny in your absence." He found himself a stick and began to break bits off one end. After a while he looked up at Danton, "And as to being ambitious, you are absolutely right, he is. But he told me that himself. And yes, I know he could be double bluffing but he was quite clinical in his explanation of why he chose to give his oath to me." Tarkyn threw away the end of the stick and smiled, "And his greatest ambition is to have an influence on the future of Eskuzor…"

Danton snorted derisively, "High ambition indeed for a mere blacksmith."

Tarkyn kept speaking as though Danton had not interrupted him, "…and to have his ideas considered. He does not care whether he leads the charge or commands troops of men. He just wants his opinions to count." Tarkyn smile broadened. "When Rainstorm assured him that we would listen to his ideas, you should have seen him. He was so excited. He said that raised him to the level of everyone else, like corks bobbing around on the ocean, all on one even level."

"And where were you in all this?" asked Danton scathingly. "Not bobbing around too, I hope."

"Oh no." Tarkyn chortled, "I was the sky!"

"The man's a toadeater," spat out Danton in disgust.

"No, he's not, Danton," said Tarkyn gently. "At least, if he is, he is extremely skilful at it, because he was quite forthright about his reasons for joining me." The prince paused to give weight to what he was about to say, "Danton, I have said I will trust you to unearth conspiracy and disingenuity but I will not abide witch hunts. You are welcome to talk to Harkell and take him through his paces but don't badger him or be unnecessarily unkind. Don't forget he is new among us. The forest guardians said that if he can be trusted, his presence on our side could swing the balance. So treat him with care. Do you understand?"

Danton took a deep breath, "Yes sire. I will do as you wish." He gave a rueful smile, "I have already been berated by String and Bean and although I was able to justify my attitude to them, maybe I *am* a little worried about having my position threatened by another sorcerer."

Tarkyn smiled warmly. "Danton, my friend, you have no need to worry. No one could ever take your place."

Danton let out the breath he had been holding in and smiled, "Thank you, my lord. With those words, you have probably saved Harkell from a fate worse than death."

Cups of tea arrived and with them, Waterstone. He sat down without reference to his previous displeasure and said, "So come on Danton, tell us what you found on your travels this morning."

"I found a sorceress. A wizard woman, to be exact."

Waterstone let out a low whistle, "Did you now?"

"There you are, you see," said Tarkyn triumphantly. "I told you I could feel a strong power around."

Danton glanced at this liege, "She knows a great deal about us all, but not everything. She assured me that she meant none of us any harm and that she would meet up with you, Tarkyn, when it suited her which, from what I can gather, will be quite some time into the future."

Tarkyn raised his eyebrows, "And why will she not meet with us now?"

Danton shook his head, "I have no idea. I asked her and she refused to answer. She was a very irritating woman in many ways."

"And how old is this martinet? What was her name? What did she look like?" asked Stormaway, rapid-fire.

Danton took a moment to picture her. "She would be in her early to mid twenties, I would say. She has hard, kingfisher blue eyes and very long, pale red hair, almost to her thighs. She may be a martinet but she was strikingly beautiful. But for some reason, she seems to have a transient name." Danton frowned in irritation. "Her conversation was full of obscure insoluble riddles. Her name is Stillwaters Pathfinder, at least for the time being."

Stormaway chuckled in appreciation. "Good name. Good name. Full of ambiguity. Full of mystery. She is a tricky one, isn't she?"

Danton, who had long since run out of patience with her trickery, asked acerbically, "*What* are you talking about?"

The wizard grinned, "Well, Stillwaters probably means that she can calm rough seas or disturbed waters on a lake or river, if she's good at her craft. Very handy for sailors, to have someone like her on board in rough weather. But it also means that there is more beneath the surface than meets the eye. You know. 'Still waters run deep'? Well in her case, I suspect they run very deep."

"And Pathfinder?" asked Waterstone.

"Again ambiguous," replied Stormaway with great satisfaction. "Is she one who can find her way along a dense forest path? Or is she someone who can help people into a better future by finding the way through present dilemmas?"

"Well, I hardly think she is going to help people to solve present dilemmas. She presents many more conundrums than she solves," said Danton crossly.

Waterstone glanced at him, "She seems to have got under your skin, well and truly."

"Yes, rather like a prickly burr or a grass seed," retorted Danton. "Oh yes, Tarkyn, I nearly forgot. You'll be pleased to know she gave me permission to tell you about her. Oh, yes and something else. I was charged with an obscure message for Stormaway. She asked me to tell you that her mother would forgive you when she found out what you had done." He folded his arms, "So, I hope that means something to you because it doesn't to me."

Stormaway went very still. His face tightened as he thought back through the past. After a minute or two he gave himself a little shake and refocused on those around him. A slow smile dawned on his face, "So this is where she has been all this time. I wonder how she got here. Danton, now I am going to drive you crazy too. I do know what she means, although I am not sure that she is right. And now, I do know who she is, but I am not going to tell you until I have her permission."

Tarkyn raised his eyebrows and said with a note of censure. "Might I remind you that you serve *me*, not her? Who is *she* to give you permission?"

"Sire, you may indeed force the information out of me, if you insist. But should you not grant a lady the right to her privacy if she feels the need for it? If I thought she were a threat to you, you know I would tell you without a second thought."

"Hmph." Tarkyn folded his arms and glanced at Danton. "I see what you mean. A very irritating lady."

"Yes she is." Danton hesitated, "But she did say one nice thing while I was there. She was shocked that you had risked the future of Eskuzor, as she put it, to stop me from having to endure those whippings." He gave a shy smile, "But she said I was worth it."

Tarkyn smiled and shook his head, "She is right. Of course you are worth it. I didn't do it as a matter of principle, you know. I did it for you."

As Danton coloured faintly and stared steadfastly at the ground, Waterstone met Tarkyn's eyes and a slight smile passed between them. Then, to assuage Danton's embarrassment, Waterstone gave the guardsman a gentle prod in the ribs and said, "You like her, don't you?"

Danton glanced at him briefly and grimaced. "Yes and no. She can be engaging when she chooses to be but she is incredibly annoying and very arrogant. She is not an easy person to be with, by any means."

"No," said Stormaway thoughtfully, "I could imagine she might be a bit of a handful."

At this juncture, Waterstone raised his hand in a warning gesture. "There is a stranger approaching," he said quietly. A minute later, he added, "More than one."

The others waited while he went out of focus. Around them, they could see woodfolk melting into the surrounding trees, weapons appearing in their hands.

"Tarkyn, we are being approached on all sides. I do not know that any way is safer than any other, for you to hide. I think perhaps you had better put up your shield."

Tarkyn nodded decisively, "Danton, Stormaway. Move away from me. I want you to be able to offer cover to woodfolk and other sorcerers, should they need it. And I want to be able to act unhindered, should the need arise. Danton to my left. Stormaway to my right. Waterstone, stay with me…*please*," he added as a concession to Waterstone's pride before continuing to issue orders. "Tell everyone that my first priority is their safety. If we are being approached from all sides, they already know we are here, so your subterfuge may not be as effective as usual."

After a few moments, Tarkyn asked, "What manner of people are they? Are they sorcerers, woodfolk? Are they armed and if so, are their weapons drawn?"

In response, Waterstone sent the prince an image from the lookouts of a curved line of men and women approaching, slowly but quite openly. All were armed, swords and knives held firmly in their hands or arrows notched on bows. Sorcerers were interspersed with woodfolk but they seemed inured to each other, focusing their entire attention on reaching the clearing.

"Waterstone, I want everyone to…" Tarkyn's voice trailed off as he caught sight of Waterstone's face, set in an expression of resigned endurance. "No. Rescind that. You people decide and let me know how I can help." He gave a wry grin at the look of surprise on the woodman's face. "We do have an agreement, as I have just recalled, that we negotiate rather than me taking over. True?"

"True." Waterstone sprang into action. "Tell me what you were going to *suggest*," he couldn't resist a touch of irony, "so that I can enter your ideas into the lists with ours."

"I wanted everyone under shields."

While Waterstone relayed his message, Tarkyn spoke to the two sorcerers. "I think we need at least Harkell, String and Bean under shields. Otherwise, their need for protection may put others at risk."

Waterstone nodded abstractedly to indicate he had heard that, even though he was mind talking with the others. Moments later, Harkell, String and Bean emerged at a run from within the trees to stand beside Danton. Almost immediately afterwards, woodfolk flicked into the clearing next to Danton and Stormaway.

"Is everybody here?" asked Tarkyn. "Where's Midnight?"

"He's here," called out Sparrow from beside Danton.

"We decided to keep a few people scattered through the trees," reported Waterstone, "Mainly as lookouts for further arrivals. Other than that, everyone is here."

"Thanks. Danton, Stormaway, raise your shields."

Three large domes, aqua, green and bronze, blossomed in the clearing just as the first of the strangers could be heard pushing through the undergrowth. Moments later, the intruders appeared in a solid ring around the edge of the clearing, their eyes dull and faces expressionless. They kept closing until they had surrounded each of the three shields.

For several minutes, no one spoke. The faces of the armed men and women outside the domes flickered with the faintest traces of animation as their eyes moved slowly from person to person inside the domes drinking in the details of their dress and demeanour. Some of them frowned at the enigmas presented by Midnight and Stormaway.

Eventually Tarkyn, for whom a prolonged silence was an impossibility, spoke in a low, courteous voice. "I am Tarkyn Tamadil, Guardian of the Forest. Who are you and why have you come here? And what do you hope to gain against our shields?"

"I am Boravar and we are the Lost," replied a large burly sorcerer with a bushy beard. His voice was flat, as though he had long ago lost hope. "There are many of us and few of you. So we can outlast you." He gazed at each of the domes and said gloomily, "In truth there are only three of you holding us at bay. And as soon as any one of you grows weary, your protection will falter." He shrugged dismally. "When your strength reaches its end, we will be waiting."

"Waiting for what?"

The burly sorcerer's voice boomed out eerily, "Waiting for those of you who fail to face your fears, to join us."

To everyone's surprise, Tarkyn sat down unconcernedly within his bronze dome and gestured to Waterstone to join him. Then he said flatly, "No. You are mistaken. We have already succeeded."

Boravar opened his mouth to speak and then shut it again.

Tarkyn smiled patronisingly at him, "Let me explain. All of us here have already had to deal with our worst fears. I have twice lived through my worst fear," here he smiled across at Lapping Water, "which was *not* proposing to Lapping Water. I have a much greater dread of betrayal. Harkell's worst fear has recently materialised; that all his efforts would come to nothing. Midnight's whole life has been anybody's worst nightmare. Falling Rain lived through twelve years of being reviled by his people …and, worse than that, agreeing with their judgement. Stormaway has lived in dread all his life of having his heritage discovered and now it is out in the open. String and Bean lived through having their knowledge of woodfolk exposed.

"And these woodfolk?" With a final flourish, Tarkyn swept his hand around him at his woodfolk, who had followed his suit and seated themselves within the other domes. "All of them live and breathe daily their worst fear - the loss of their independence."

The prince smiled sympathetically as his eyes travelled around his woodfolk, "So much so, that some of them had to choose me above their kin yesterday, and some have acted against their very nature to venture out of the forest in broad daylight to protect me."

Outside the domes of colour, looks of uncertainty passed between the armed intruders. But uncertainty was followed by a look of resigned despair on Boravar's face. "Brave words," he said heavily. "But it is not up to you to decide the nature of each person's greatest fear."

Tarkyn stood up slowly and folded his arms across his chest. Although Boravar was big, the prince met him eye to eye. The sorcerer shifted uneasily beneath the challenge of Tarkyn's stare. Then Tarkyn spoke quietly, but with a warning note of anger, "You forget yourself, Boravar. You are speaking to a prince of Eskuzor and the present Guardian of the Forest. You will address me with due respect and you will not presume to dictate to me."

Boravar's eyes widened and he bowed awkwardly. "I beg your pardon, Your Highness. I was giving you information, not dictating."

As he stood facing the burly sorcerer, Tarkyn became aware that a quiet debate was taking place between Harkell and String. After a few minutes, the ripples of discussion eddied out to include everyone within Danton's shield. Harkell moved to the edge of Danton's shield so he could then confer quietly with Stormaway and his companions. The wizard frowned thoughtfully before quietly offering an opinion, which triggered the return of the debate to those with Danton. With a slight smile and complete disregard for Boravar, Tarkyn watched the progress of this discussion with interest.

At a gesture from Harkell, Waterstone walked to the edge of Tarkyn's shield closest to Danton's to hear the outcome of the debate. What he heard made him first grin with amazement then nod in vigorous approval. Waterstone returned to the prince's side and murmured, "Your Highness, if I could have a private word with you?"

Tarkyn walked away from Boravar to listen to Waterstone's quietly delivered message. When he had been apprised of the gist of the discussion, Tarkyn sent a nod of appreciation to String and Harkell before at last returning his attention to the people lining the outsides of the shields.

Tarkyn looked them over pityingly. "You are those people who have been trapped by the forest, are you not? And you have been trodden into the ground by your failure."

Shamefaced nods answered this question. "Some of us have chosen to stay to avoid the world outside. Some of us cannot find the path out. All of us have a fear we cannot face," said Boravar heavily. "We are bound within this Forest by our failure, Your Highness." The burly sorcerer bowed his head in shame.

"The lore of both sorcerers and woodfolk is that this Forest may keep you here indefinitely if you are unable to face your fears." The prince let the silence develop before announcing, "But I tell you now that I, Guardian of the Forests of Eskuzor, do not accept that premise."

Looks of confusion gave way to uncertain hope dawning on the faces of the Lost.

"Boravar, you must look me in the eye when you speak to me. You must be aware that it is a rare privilege to speak with a prince of the realm." Tarkyn's voice was gentle but his words were breathtakingly arrogant. "You should hold your head up with pride that you have been accorded that honour. I expect all of you to meet my eyes unless I specifically say otherwise." He let his gaze run across all of the Lost, meeting the eyes of each of them. He nodded his approval, "When you have put away your weapons, I will honour you with my trust by removing my shield."

Tarkyn's home guard watched in stunned silence as the Lost meekly sheathed their swords and knives and replaced their arrows in their quivers, all keeping their eyes on the prince's face. With a wave of his hand, Tarkyn released his shield, leaving Waterstone and himself standing unprotected in their midst.

"Thank you." The prince smiled benignly at them. "Now, let me be clear on my position. Your fears are your own to face, or to avoid, as you choose. The world is full of people who avoid their fears and yet are strong productive members of their communities. One failure does not require an eternal loss of freedom."

He gave them time to absorb this before continuing, his voice just patronising enough to keep them keenly aware of his status, "I will now accord you the honour of introducing yourselves individually to me, and to my brother Waterstone." For a moment, his mouth quirked as he thought how outraged Waterstone would be at people feeling honoured to meet him. He bent slightly to murmur a request into Waterstone's ear. Waterstone's eyes narrowed but he knew that now was not the time to take issue. So, with a semblance of willingness, he relayed Tarkyn's message to Stormaway.

In response, Stormaway began to issue formal instructions, "Woodfolk and sorcerers of the Lost Forest, you have been granted the favour of a Royal Audience. When you approach the prince, you must bow and await his word to rise and introduce yourself. He will want to know your name, where you came from, what you did before coming to this forest and how long you have been here. You may then greet Waterstone and move on." He swept his hand around, "Boravar, you may begin."

The process of introductions was long and tedious. Over one hundred people waited patiently in line for their minute of favour with the prince, not once begrudging the time or their tired backs and legs. To Waterstone's disgust, even the woodfolk among them were eager to pay their homage to Tarkyn. Within the aqua and green shields, the home guard soon lost interest and talked quietly among themselves. Not once did Tarkyn falter in his concentration as he meticulously accorded each person his undivided attention. Beside him, Waterstone stood rigid with contained fury.

After nearly two hours, when the last person had filed past him, Tarkyn made one final address. "You have my word that it will be your choice whether you stay or leave this forest. Woodfolk of the Lost Forest, I depend on you to keep in contact with your kin. Sorcerers, ask the woodfolk to relay messages on your behalf. Do not go too far away so that we may keep in contact with you. Many of the workings of this forest are still a mystery to me but one thing is certain, you will have your freedom." He waved his hand in dismissal. "You may now leave us. Should any of you wish to visit us again, you may request my permission to do so, *before* arriving."

Without demur, the Lost left the clearing, with heads held higher and more assurance in their steps. As the last of them disappeared into the trees, the aqua and green shields wavered and disappeared.

Tarkyn turned to find Waterston's baleful green eyes glaring at him.

"Don't you *ever* do that to me again." The woodman's voice was husky with rage.

He spun on his heel and, shrugging off the hand that Tarkyn's put on his shoulder to restrain him, stalked off across the clearing. Tarkyn caught up with him and turned him around roughly to face him. "Now, just a minute. Don't walk off on me like that."

Waterstone hit Tarkyn's hand away. "Leave me alone. Much more of this and I'll regret ever asking you to be my brother."

Tarkyn pushed him in the shoulder. "So, what do you think? Do you think I am so vainglorious that I need the adulation of those people? Is that what you think?"

By now, they were both so angry that the world had contracted to the space around the two of them and they were completely oblivious of the whole home guard watching them.

When Waterstone refused to reply but just stood glowering, Tarkyn snapped, "Have you ever seen me do that before? Did I do that to you? No!" He pushed Waterstone hard enough to send him stumbling backwards. "No!" Tarkyn repeated. "So why did I do it, do you think? Was it because I'm ruthless and demand total submission? Is that why I did it, do you think?"

"Whatever your reason, you didn't have to include me," retorted Waterstone stubbornly.

Tarkyn waved his hand, "No. I could just have let them think you were my lackey. And if I hadn't introduced you, that is exactly what they would have thought, especially the sorcerers among them. Would you have preferred that?"

"You're a bastard, Tarkyn. Don't involve me in your games."

Tarkyn folded his arms across his chest, and said tightly. "Waterstone, you are so angry, you're not even thinking straight. I wasn't playing a game. I was trying to restore their self-respect. Perhaps your pride won't bend enough to let you help these people, but mine will. I don't care if they think I'm an arrogant, supercilious scion of the House of Tamadil. I just want the honour of meeting me to make them feel that, despite their past failure, they are of value."

"You see?" spat out Waterstone. "It is a game. You are not showing them who you really are."

"Yes I am. That is part of who I am. It is not a game," insisted Tarkyn steadily. "And it was certainly not for my pleasure. They were deadly serious and so was I. Had I been anything less, it would have been the height of cruel japery." He raised his eyebrows, "And I think, even *you* will admit, that I am not cruel."

"You come bloody close, forcing me to endure that. You have no idea how excruciating that was for me, watching all those people being *grateful* for the chance to be subservient. It was disgusting. And then to be forced to be a party to it…" Waterstone shook his head, his eyes still glittering with resentment, "And *you*, telling them what an honour it was for them to meet you. Well, your arrogance just takes my breath away."

Infuriatingly, Tarkyn just smiled, "I wasn't being arrogant. I'm just being realistic. In the eyes of everyone but you woodfolk, meeting me is a great honour. I'm not bragging when I say that. I'm just stating facts. Whether or not I believe it, is irrelevant. It is what they believe."

"Hmph." At last Waterstone was mellowing. He crossed his arms and looked up at his unusual friend, "But do *you* believe it?"

Gradually, a huge grin spread across Tarkyn's face. "Yes. I'm afraid I do."

"That's it!" exclaimed Waterstone, half serious, half laughing. He threw himself at Tarkyn and the pure impetus of his rush bore them both to the ground. Tarkyn blocked a punch and thrust the woodman far enough off, to throw himself on top of him. Waterstone dug his knuckles into the prince's ribs and then, as Tarkyn flinched back, drew his legs up into the space between them. The woodman kicked upwards into Tarkyn's gut as hard as he could and thrust Tarkyn up and to one side. Fast as lightning, Waterstone was on his feet and shoving Tarkyn down onto his back.

Beside Danton, a melee broke out as Harkell tried to rush to the prince's aid. A succession of determined woodfolk were hit or kicked as Harkell tried desperately to break away from them. Finally, someone grabbed his arms and another bound his hands behind him. Then they shoved him to the ground and Rainstorm sat on him so that they could watch the rest of the spectacle in peace.

By now, the combatants were both looking the worse for wear. They were breathing hard and both of them had cuts and grazes that were smearing blood all over them. They rolled their way across the clearing as one after the other gained the ascendancy. Suddenly, the impetus of a lunge by Tarkyn threw them both over a ledge and into the air. With a resounding splash, they found themselves in the stream. The searing cold of the water shocked the fight out of them and they sat next to each other in the shallow water, gasping for breath and laughing.

Rainstorm chortled before looking down at the glowering sorcerer lying awkwardly beneath him. "So. Your prince has survived the lethal attack. Are you ready to get up now without killing any of us?"

"There is nothing funny about this," gasped Harkell under the weight of Rainstorm sitting on his chest. "Don't you realise? Waterstone faces the death penalty for this…And even if he did attack the prince, I like Waterstone. It's a bloody tragedy."

Rainstorm smiled and gradually eased his weight off the sorcerer, "No, he doesn't, Harkell. Someone should have told you. Tarkyn has specifically given some of us permission to attack him to avoid that very problem."

Harkell sat up and leaned forward so that Rainstorm could untie him. "Thanks," he grunted ironically, as his hands came free. "You certainly should have told me. If I could have got a clear aim at Waterstone, I'd have thrown a knife at him and he might have been dead by now."

Rainstorm glanced at him, all joking past, "Harkell, I think you should accept that all of us with Tarkyn are completely trustworthy. You don't need to protect Tarkyn against us. Concentrate on outsiders." He thought back to the time when Rushwind attacked Tarkyn under the influence of the rampart virus running through her and added a rider, "Or at least, if you are worried about one of us, aim to disarm, not to kill."

Harkell smiled at him, "You are very sensible for one so young."

"You should have realised, Harkell." Rainstorm gave a grunt of laughter. "Tarkyn could have put up his shield at any time there was a space between them. Or he could have hit Waterstone with one of his nasty bronze shafts or immobilised him. And Waterstone could have flicked into hiding anytime Tarkyn wasn't actually holding him. They were both fighting because they chose to be."

Harkell rubbed his wrists as he watched Tarkyn and Waterstone wade out of the water, still smiling. "Tarkyn must indeed trust you to allow actual physical attack. It is unheard of among sorcerers except perhaps for closely supervised practice fights. Even then, I can't imagine anyone would feel free to give it their all." He shook his head, "Even if Tarkyn gave me permission, I don't think I would ever feel free to attack him as Waterstone just did."

Rainstorm laughed, "You're probably not as bad tempered as Waterstone."

As they spoke, Tarkyn and Waterstone walked up, still smiling, and breathing heavily. Tarkyn waited until he was close to everyone to shake his head and send water spraying over those nearest to him. Amid shouts of protest, as he straightened up grinning, he began to notice that several people around him were also sporting bruises and cuts.

As Autumn Leaves limped up with towels for them, Tarkyn nodded his thanks and frowned, "What happened to you?"

Autumn Leaves jerked a thumb in Harkell's direction, "Your feisty new recruit was bent on wading into the middle of your fight with Waterstone. Eventually we subdued him, and Rainstorm sat on him so we could watch in peace."

"Ooh dear," Tarkyn smiled at Harkell, "Sorry about that. We should have told you. And sorry to anyone else who got hurt. I will give you some life force if you need it. Just ask."

"I think we can manage," said Autumn Leaves. "After all, a bit of pain is interesting, as long as it's not too severe and you know it isn't going to last too long."

As Tarkyn and Waterstone's faces bore red blotches and were still running with red rivulets of water mixed with blood, Summer Rain came forward with salves and bandages to inspect the protagonists and make running repairs on them.

Suddenly the air thrummed and the four guardians of old appeared on the other side of the stream. They were not looking pleased. Tarkyn stayed where he was, sitting on a log, while Summer Rain tended his scrapes, merely nodding to acknowledge their presence.

"Tarkyn Tamadil," boomed Moridan Tamadil's voice, thick with reproof, "There is a sad lack of discipline among the members of your home guard. I am disappointed to see you forgetting so easily what you owe your heritage. Do you think your father would approve of your riotous behaviour? Or the present king? You seem to have forgotten the expected behaviour of a prince of the realm and his retinue."

Tarkyn gave a quiet chuckle. "You caught us at a bad moment, I must say." He tilted his head to consider the guardian who must, in some way, be related to him. "Moridan, quite clearly Kosar disapproves of me since he has condemned me to face the death penalty. My father would be horrified by my over-familiarity. On the other hand, my brother Waterstone was disgusted by my excessive formality earlier when I met with the Lost. And only days ago, all these woodfolk told me how difficult I am and regaled me with my shortcomings." He thanked Summer Rain as she finished, before turning back to Moridan to add, "And now you, too, condemn me." He shrugged, "So amidst censure from all sides, all I can do is tread my own path."

"Unless in the presence of the king, a prince of the realm's behaviour is what he chooses it to be," said Danton, stoically coming to Tarkyn's aid. "Prince Tarkyn has no need for court protocol."

Waterstone, now taking his turn to be administered to by Summer Rain, blinked in surprise at Danton foreswearing protocol and sent him a smile of approval.

"And we are not Tarkyn's retinue," said Autumn Leaves firmly. "Stormaway, Danton and even Harkell may be, but we are not. And how any of us behaves, is between Tarkyn and ourselves."

Rainstorm came over and put a friendly arm around Tarkyn's shoulders.

"And we take exception to our prince being told off by someone who has been long dead and should keep his nose out of the affairs of the living."

Tarkyn rolled his eyes and smiled wryly, shaking his head at his feisty allies. After a moment, he returned his attention to the past guardians, "I am glad that you four have arrived. I did not know how to summon you and I needed to speak with you." He glanced across at his wizard with a mischievous smile, "And Stormaway was sorry to have missed you."

The wizard threw the prince a pained look that Tarkyn missed as he bent down to pick up his towel. As Tarkyn rubbed his hair dry, he continued, "Were you watching our earlier encounter with the Lost?"

"That is why we are here," Windchange's voice vibrated with disapproval.

Tarkyn smiled casually, "That's what I expected. So you just thought you'd use the opportunity to rebuke me while you were at it, did you Moridan?"

Tarkyn was being so patently and uncharacteristically disrespectful that the woodfolk and sorcerers around him exchanged surreptitious glances of speculation. Rainstorm's eyes lit with appreciation.

"You are becoming a little too cocksure, my young lad," retorted Moridan. "You may be of our company but we deserve a certain level of recognition for our age and greater experience."

"Do you know," said Tarkyn, "that was just what I thought myself when I first met you." He unhurriedly put down his towel and pushed back his damp hair before finally rising slowly to his feet. Suddenly, all insouciance gone, he spoke quietly, "But that was before I realised your cruelty and thoughtlessness in condemning a host of unquestioning, unexceptional people to wander your forest, bowed down with shame." He studied them, as though gauging their calibre, his amber eyes reflecting the sun setting behind the trees. "How could you allow such injustice to continue?"

"And just who do you think you are, to disturb the order of things?" snapped Windchange.

"You know who I am. I am your undisputed successor." Tarkyn said slowly. "And before I leave this forest, those people will be freed."

"We could just catapult you out of this forest right now," hissed Grass Snake. "Then you'd be crowing to an open field."

Tarkyn smiled with an infuriating lack of concern. "So I would. But Stormaway would catapult us straight back in."

"We could keep you here for eternity, just like the Lost," threatened Moridan.

"So you could," agreed Tarkyn, completely unfazed. "But unfortunately for you, despite your thoughtless cruelty, I know that your life and even your death's work has been to protect Eskuzor. Without my intercession, you know my brothers will wreak havoc."

"You could just have asked us courteously for this favour," sighed Nightwind.

Tarkyn shrugged, "Perhaps if you had treated me with more respect, I may have done so, but Moridan berated me as though I were a schoolboy. When I first met you, you said I was one of you. But if that is so, why do you presume to pass judgement on my actions?" He gave a tight humourless smile, "I do not react well to attempts to belittle me... But more than that, you have let those poor people wander in dejection for their failure, some of them for centuries, when it must be within your gift to stop it."

"It was the king's will," said Windchange firmly. "I created this forest and the spell that binds them, according to the king's will."

"Yes, but which king?" asked Stormaway, finally entering the lists. "The practice of sending people to the Lost Forest by the king died out centuries ago. For a short time, some chose to pit their strength against the Forest. Since then, the Forest appears to have accidentally absorbed passersby, both woodfolk and sorcerers, and then sat in judgement on them."

"Windchange, why did you not revoke your spell?" asked Tarkyn, having reverted to his usual courteous manner.

"I do not have the authority to revoke a monarch's command, Your Highness."

"Moridan? You are a Tamadil. Could you not have revoked it?"

Moridan shook his head. "I precede the king in question." He shrugged, "Besides, I am the younger brother, not the monarch."

"So too am I," said Tarkyn thoughtfully. He frowned down at the ground for a minute or two, before raising his head and glancing at Stormaway, "However, I am sovereign lord of the forests of Eskuzor."

"Is this true?" asked Windchange, looking to Stormaway for confirmation.

"Signed and sealed by King Markazon himself." Stormaway gave a little bow. "And witnessed by me."

Windchange looked back at Tarkyn to find himself under the glare of amber displeasure.

"I am not accustomed to being doubted," said Tarkyn frigidly. "I may be young, but I am the sovereign lord of these forests and the present guardian of Eskuzor and I am becoming very tired of being underrated by you four." He put his hands on his hips. "Now, Windchange, would you please revoke the spell that holds people in this Forest."

Windchange gave a nasty little triumphant smile, "Unfortunately, despite my wishes to indulge Your Highness, I am dead and so cannot revoke a spell I made in my lifetime."

Tarkyn smiled sweetly back, "That presents no problem. I can summon your remains to stand before me and then the particles that were once you, will be able to revoke the spell."

Windchange looked panic-stricken. "No. Don't do that. No, the very thought makes me feel ill."

"But you are aware that I can do it, aren't you?" insisted Tarkyn. "I have done it before."

Windchange turned to Moridan, his eyes wide with fear, "I thought you tried that and it went disastrously wrong."

"Yes, I did." Moridan grunted, "Bad moment, that. Inadvertently wiped out a small community of woodfolk."

Tarkyn frowned at his ancestor in confusion, "If you lived with woodfolk yourself, why would you expect me to insist on court protocol? Surely you would know how uncomfortable that would be for them?"

Moridan waved a hand dismissively. "Never gave it a second thought. Not my job to worry about their feelings. Their job to worry about mine. End of story. Anyway, I wasn't their liege. I wasn't exiled like you. So I only visited the forest in my free time, so to speak. I was struggling to prevent a sickness running rampage through the forest. It was killing all the oaks and beeches and beginning to affect other trees. So I thought I would ask a past guardian for help. So I summoned…what was his name? The wizard guardian who knew a lot about trees."

"Scarecrow Treehealer," supplied Stormaway. He frowned, "Why is he not here?"

"Harrumph," Moridan looked uncomfortable, "I'm afraid my re-summoning didn't go to plan in many ways. Scarecrow came blasting forth and was so irate…he died in rather unfortunate circumstances, you know…that he let rip with a huge blast of power that not only fried all the woodfolk in sight but also blew himself apart, reformed particles and spirit. Luckily I managed to get my shield up, just in time."

Stormaway found himself the subject of one purple, one amber, forty green and a couple of grey stares.

"What on earth were you thinking, allowing me to do that?" demanded Tarkyn.

The wizard gave a weak smile and shrugged, "I did warn you and we prepared adequately. And if you hadn't summoned Pipeless, the curse would still be destroying the mountainfolk."

A shudder went down the length of Tarkyn's spine, "And now I must do it again." He grimaced, "I can't say I'm looking forward to it." He raised his eyes to meet Windchange's. "Where did you die and where are you buried?"

Windchange folded his arms, "I find this whole conversation very macabre. I may choose not to tell you."

Tarkyn looked at the old Guardian sympathetically, understanding his distaste but at the same time wondering the best approach to gather the information he needed.

Suddenly Danton spoke, "Windchange is lying, Your Highness. I am fairly sure that he can revoke this spell without any need for you to re-summon his body particles." The blonde sorcerer smiled sideways at his liege, "After all, the reason you summoned Pipeless' body back was to address his spirit, wasn't it?"

Tarkyn nodded his acknowledgement and turned back to Windchange, "You spoke truly when you said that Stormaway and Danton would guide me through intrigue." He paused and asked quietly, "Why did you lie to me, Windchange? Do you want these people to stay trapped within this forest?"

"I don't like being dictated to by a young whippersnapper, any more than you like being dictated to by us. I'll put you through your paces any way I can."

Tarkyn gave a lopsided smile, "I think there are many of us here who don't like to be dictated to. I did ask you courteously, though."

"After you had called us cruel and thoughtless. Whatever our failings, I think we deserve better than that, at least a hearing before the judgement." The wizard guardian shrugged, "After all, we did have a legitimate reason at the beginning."

Tarkyn threw his hands up. "Fair enough. I'm sorry. May we start again? I was wired up after fighting Waterstone and after Moridan berating me." He hesitated and glanced at the people around him before asking, "Guardians, would you mind if I spoke privately with you for a while?"

The four guardians nodded and suddenly they were somewhere else in the forest, with none of the home guard in sight. Tarkyn looked around him and then gestured at the logs scattered around the small clearing in which he found himself.

"Do you people ever sit down? Or are you constantly formal?"

"We can sit down if it puts you more at ease," murmured Nightwind.

Tarkyn smiled, "Thank you. Yes, it will."

"And so, young sorcerer," hissed Grass Snake as he appeared to seat himself on a mossy log. "Why do you wish to speak privately with us?"

Tarkyn grinned, "Because, despite the fact that Moridan tried to tell me off and I then tried to dictate to you, you are the first and only people I have ever met who are actually my equals. Regardless of our origins, all of us are above and beyond any hierarchies." He shrugged. "I did it all wrongly. Windchange, I realise now you don't need me to counter an order from some past king, as I'm sure you well know. You can do as you like. You are beyond the authority of kings…as we all are." Another smile chased across his face, "This feels so strange. My father and brothers were ranked higher than me and everyone else was ranked lower. No one else was ever on a par with me before."

Grass Snake watched him, his green eyes gleaming, "Remember this, Tarkyn. This is how it feels to be woodfolk…or did, until you came along."

"They still feel like this among themselves," returned Tarkyn. "Waterstone and I come close to feeling equal, but we both know that I can insist on his compliance if I choose to." He let his eyes travel around the four guardians. "I find this rather unsettling. In the past, if I were with someone of higher rank, then I would know where I stood and would do his bidding," he gave a wry smile, "well, except on the odd occasion. And if I am with people of lower rank, I know where I stand because they will do *my* bidding. But with you people… I don't know what the outcome will be."

"You seem to be pretty good at forcing the issue," observed Moridan dryly. "Threatening to remain in the forest and threatening to re-summon Windchange. Both very effective means of control. I congratulate you."

"I apologize. I am used to controlling or being controlled. It is not within my experience simply to leave the outcome dependent on the opinions of others when it matters so much to me. I do negotiate with the woodfolk but I do so, safe in the knowledge that I can pull rank if I feel the need to. Even now, I am not sure that I can trust your judgement to the extent of relinquishing control."

"By meeting like this, you are already showing a willingness to deal on equal terms with us," sighed Nightwind. "And you know, Tarkyn, I don't think your threats would stand much scrutiny."

"I don't know about that," interposed Windchange stringently. "You had me worried at the thought of a re-summoning."

Tarkyn smiled, "I don't like re-summoning any more than you do. But I wouldn't have let you blow yourself apart. I wasn't threatening you with annihilation. I wouldn't dream of it. I was merely trying to make it possible for you to revoke that spell." He turned back to Nightwind, "What do you mean, my threats wouldn't stand much scrutiny."

Nightwind smiled gently, "Think about it, Tarkyn. You said that we wouldn't be able to endure having you remain within the Lost Forest while your brothers run riot. You're quite right. We couldn't. But neither could you."

Tarkyn smiled sheepishly, "I was hoping you wouldn't think of that."

"Huh!" Moridan gave a shout of laughter. "You cheeky bugger!" He leaned forward, chuckling, "Tarkyn, my many-times-over great nephew, I would pat you on the back or put my arm around you, but my hand would go straight through you and you might find that a bit unnerving. So I will restrain myself and simply say that I'm sorry I came on so strongly before. You would think, after all this time…"

"He means fifteen hundred years…" hissed Grass Snake with a snigger of mirth.

"…that I would have learned to accept that there are many ways of behaving, but still I struggle." finished Moridan, ignoring the woodman guardian's interjection.

Tarkyn gave a wistful smile, "Thank you for that. It would be nice if someone among the Tamadils supported me."

Nightwind frowned at him in motherly concern, "You are very young to be managing all of this. Guardians of the forest usually come into their powers later in their life. And none of us has had to placate a mob of resentful, oathbound woodfolk." She frowned severely at Moridan, "You should know from being with Grass Snake and me how hard that must have been for Tarkyn."

"But you two are forest guardians," protested Moridan.

"We are no more or less in our attitudes than all woodfolk" hissed Grass Snake. "Tarkyn has had to work with hundreds of people who have the same pride and self-assurance as us." He glinted at Moridan, "Can you imagine how you would fare if you tried to tell either of us what to do?"

Windchange and Moridan both looked at Tarkyn with new respect.

"But will they obey your orders?" asked Moridan.

"Yes. Never doubt their honour. They have sworn an oath to me and they will uphold it." He smiled wryly. "But I try very hard not to give them too many orders. It doesn't come easily, but I do try."

Nightwind folded her arms and looked in triumph at Moridan, "So now, think about the level of camaraderie you saw and don't just forgive it, applaud it."

"Tarkyn, I will revoke the spell of the Lost Forest," said Windchange, his words an acknowledgement of Tarkyn's achievement. "You are right. We were cruel to allow the situation to continue unchallenged."

"That spell has become part of the definition of the Lost Forest," said Moridan. "And we forgot that it could be changed."

Grass Snake hissed thoughtfully. "I still quite like the concept though. Perhaps you could just force them to stay a year if they can't face their fears, rather than indefinitely."

"A year is forever in the life of young people," protested Tarkyn. "I have not yet been with the woodfolk for a year and it feels like a lifetime… What about a month? That would give them time to reflect but would return them to their lives without too much disruption."

"Done!" smiled Windchange, banging his knee but making no noise at all. "A month it is! All agreed?" He frowned thoughtfully, "I think I will make it that they have to see two full moons…something like that. More poetic, you know. One full moon is too short, could be the next day. And we need time to test them, after all. Two would mean the longest stay is two months. Besides, I need a trigger for releasing the spell for each person. The moon would be more elegant than counting thirty days."

Tarkyn frowned. "Two months is a long time," he said uncertainly.

"But think about it," hissed Grass Snake. "It's a story they can tell their family and friends. After all, we do need some people to tend to our lady wizard."

"Why?" asked Tarkyn sharply. "Can't she look after herself?"

"Could you?" asked Nightwind gently.

Tarkyn folded his arms and stared at them belligerently. After a moment, he grunted, "Hmph. Perhaps I would have a few difficulties." He unfolded his arms and waved them around, "All right. No, I couldn't. You know I couldn't. But I have only just come into the woods. Hasn't she lived here for many years?"

"Yes, on and off. But her skills and her nature do not lend themselves to self-sufficiency, as those of many other wizards do," said Windchange.

"Do not fear," hissed Grass Snake. "The Lost are paid in kind for their services."

"So are slaves," retorted Tarkyn.

"I think you are digging yourself into a hole, Tarkyn," warned Nightwind. "What do you pay Lord Danton? Or any of your companions, for that matter. You expect their service but I have not yet seen any payment exchange hands."

"I pay them with my support and protection," replied Tarkyn slowly, realising where this was going.

"You pay them in kind, don't you?" hissed Grass Snake.

"Hmm." Tarkyn looked around until he spotted a thin dry branch on the tree behind him. He broke it off and set about breaking it methodically into little pieces. When he had finished and brushed his hands off, he looked up, his eyes troubled. "They are not slaves. Any of them. They are free to leave me if they choose. There is nothing to spend money on within the forest. But if any of them wished to go forth and needed money, I would find a way to retrieve some of my wealth and give it to them."

"Do they know that?" asked Windchange.

"Mm, not exactly." Tarkyn grimaced, "I'm not very good with money. I have never had to deal with it myself." He gave a little grin. "In fact, I've never bought anything or paid anyone in my life. So it's hardly surprising, is it, that I haven't sorted it out with Danton and Harkell… or with Stormaway for that matter…although I suspect he's richer than all of us, having been the sole agent for the woodfolk for the last twelve years."

"I think I should just mention to you," said Nightwind quietly, "that offering to pay the woodfolk, should it cross you mind to do so, would offend them so deeply that it would fundamentally change your relationship with them."

Tarkyn smiled, "Yes, I noticed Autumn Leaves was very quick to point out that they were not my retinue. I'm lucky to have got away with calling them my home guard even if it is only a nickname, aren't I?"

"Yes and no," hissed Grass Snake. "Your skill at walking the tightrope between friendship and dominion is breathtaking."

Tarkyn laughed, "I don't feel very skilful. I seem to spend my life rubbing people up the wrong way."

Nightwind smiled, "You may not be perfect at it, but it was never going to be plain sailing and you are doing better than anyone could have imagined."

"Thanks," There was a short companionable silence until Tarkyn rose to his feet. "I suppose I should go back. Midnight will be getting anxious by now if he can't see me."

"They all are," laughed Windchange.

"There is one more challenge that one of you must endure before you leave. But whatever the outcome, you may all leave the Lost Forest in three days' time," said Moridan.

Tarkyn raised his eyebrows, "And why not now?"

Moridan grinned at the other three, "Don't you love that Tamadil hauteur that you know so well?" He turned back to Tarkyn. "Nephew, if you insist, we will allow you to leave now. But your followers have been travelling for months now, with very little respite and through many uncertainties and dangers." He smiled, "Don't forget, you are younger and stronger than most. Let them rest. If they know when they are leaving, they will not fret at the delay…and you will leave the Forest nearer your destination. So you will not lose precious time."

Tarkyn's face relaxed into a smile, "Thank you. That is most kind of you. And what of the Lost?"

"They may leave any time they like. You can tell them or they can find out for themselves, whichever you prefer. Nothing will stand in their way when they choose to leave." Windchange shrugged, "Mind you, they always could have left. In this Forest, we deal only in words and illusions. But you have to be able to see through them."

"Oh no," breathed Tarkyn, filled with consternation. "Don't tell me this private meeting is an illusion and we have said all of this in front of everyone."

As Windchange faded away, he gave a broad smile and Tarkyn just managed to hear "You're quick. I'll give you that."

Tarkyn blinked as he found himself seated among the woodfolk, Rainstorm squatted in front of him and Danton leaning over him, both looking into his eyes with some concern. Midnight was standing on the other side of him, tugging at his sleeve.

"Did you hear what I said to the Guardians?" demanded Tarkyn immediately.

Danton breathed a sigh of relief. "Waterstone, he's back."

"Well?" insisted Tarkyn.

"And his usual peremptory self. He must be all right then," said Watestone, coming around to stand in front of him next to Danton. "You gave me an awful fright. I thought I must have hurt you badly again, knocked your head or something. You've been sitting there like a stunned mullet for at least five minutes. Ever since the guardians left."

Tarkyn's eyes narrowed. "Did you hear what I said to the guardians?" he asked slowly and clearly.

Danton and Waterstone looked at each other and then back at Tarkyn.

"No," said Waterstone finally. He frowned, "Are you sure you're feeling all right?"

Tarkyn's face relaxed into a smile. "Yes, I'm fine. Don't worry Waterstone. I'm fine. It's just the guardians playing games. That's all." He smiled down into the anxious face of Midnight before swinging him up onto his lap. "Hello, scruff. Don't look so worried. It's all right." Once he had Midnight in his arms, Tarkyn realised the little boy was trembling and his eyes were bright with unshed tears. Tarkyn hugged him close and sent him waves of reassurance. "Poor little one. It doesn't take much to rock your precarious little boat, does it?"

"You see? You will have to keep yourself safe. Forget about us. Forget about Eskuzor." Lapping Water smiled from where she stood a few yards away, leaning against a tree with her arms crossed. "You have to keep safe because the whole happiness of that little seven year old depends on it."

Tarkyn raised an enquiring eyebrow and Lapping Water laughed, "Yes. All right. Mine would be severely dinted too, if anything happened to you." She hesitated then decided to say nothing further.

Tarkyn laughed, "Lapping Water, I know what you're thinking. That it wouldn't devastate you as it would him." He dropped his eyes to his armful of mischief and sighed, "She's not very romantic, is she rascal?"

Although Midnight had no idea what Tarkyn was saying, he smiled back, just happy that everything was all right in his little world again.

Chapter 25

oridan had been right. The home guard did need time to rest, take stock and make running repairs. Tarkyn did not arrange to meet up again with the Lost and instead left it to the woodfolk to communicate the outcome of his meeting with the Guardians. He felt that he had already grandstanded enough and that the salutary privilege of meeting him would be diminished if he made himself too available.

He did wonder how the Lost would manage in the world outside the Forest. Time seemed to have stood still for them and for some of them, generations of their families would have lived and died in their absence. No one they had known would be awaiting their return. Tarkyn was fairly sure that the sorcerers would find this more difficult than the woodfolk. From what he had seen, the woodfolk would welcome their strays back and make sure they had families to belong to.

As it turned out, this was the least of the Lost sorcerers' problems.

The exodus of the Lost was gradual. They had lived within the Forest for a long time and many were settled and tied by their accumulated possessions. During the following day, woodfolk and sorcerers could be seen occasionally trudging through the nearby woods. Now and then huge warhorses, carrying warrior sorcerers and their belongings picked their way slowly between the intertwined trees. Some carried the goods of a whole household if a warrior had paired up with a lady during their sojourn in the Lost Forest.

The first sign of trouble was a riderless horse cantering wild-eyed into the clearing. Woodfolk scattered as the huge animal swerved back and forth, sending packs and equipment flying.

Danton and Harkell between them herded it into a corner where it stood, sides heaving, eyes flared in alarm. Tarkyn approached slowly sending waves of calm and reassurance. Gradually the great horse settled and allowed Harkell close enough to take hold of its reins. In answer to a query from Tarkyn, all the horse could provide was the sound of a dull thwack, a grunt and then the feeling of the rider's weight slewing off its back.

"This horse's rider had been attacked," said Tarkyn. "I can't tell by what or by whom."

"I can tell you that," replied Tree Wind, walking up to stand near Tarkyn but a safe distance from the horse. As she spoke, Waterstone and many others gathered behind her. "We attacked him."

Tarkyn frowned, "What do you mean, 'We attacked him'? You've been here in the clearing."

A triumphant little smile played around Tree Wind's lips, "I mean we woodfolk attacked him. We are all one people. That sorcerer, and all the Lost sorcerers, have seen woodfolk. None of them can leave the forest alive."

Tarkyn threw his hands up, "And what happened to negotiation and talking things over with me?"

Tree Wind folded her arms, "We were waiting to see if you would be true to us and remember."

Tarkyn stared at her. "So you watched me clear a path out of the Forest for these people, knowing I was sending them to their death and didn't even have the decency to warn me?"

"You should have known. You're a woodman. You should start acting like one."

Anger warred with chagrin within Tarkyn. He realised, with a dawning sense of panic, that his impetuous decision to free the Lost had now led to a serious impasse. And suddenly all his woodfolk appeared to be against him. He could command his home guard to ensure the sorcerers' safe passage but then they would be fighting the Lost woodfolk. What was worse, if he insisted that the sorcerers should go free who knew of their existence, he would not only betray his woodman's oath, but would also cause irreparable damage to his relationship with the woodfolk.

His distress radiated outwards, causing the great horse to rear up, jerking the reins out of Harkell's hands. Tarkyn had no attention left to spend on calming it down again so, as the horse's forelegs hit the ground, he waved his hand casually and muttered, "*Shturrum*".

"Tree Wind," he said formally, ignoring the horse entirely, "Would you please request that the Lost woodfolk only knock the sorcerers out with slingshots, rather than kill them, until we reach a resolution? If you feel this will be too much of a betrayal of your principles, I will not insist but you chance losing my goodwill even further than you already have."

"We can accommodate that, as long as they don't leave the Forest. In fact, so far, that is all that has happened." she replied, equally formally.

"Is there only one way open out of the Forest or are people leaving in every direction?" the prince asked, as though speaking to a stranger.

"So far, only one path has opened up." Tree Wind pointed to her left. "It is in that direction."

"Thank you."

As he turned to follow her directions, she and several other woodfolk fell in behind him. Tarkyn turned back to survey them all, "None of you may accompany me. And that is a command." He looked until he spotted Ancient Oak in the crowd, "This, Ancient Oak, is what I meant all that time ago. I am now dealing with a hostile crowd and we have all ceased to exist as people to each other. I want none of you with me."

As he turned away, he said to Danton, "Hold the horse's bridle. I will release the spell as I leave. You sorcerers must also stay behind." He hesitated and then turned back, "However, I want Midnight and Stormaway to accompany me. The rest of you, stay within this clearing until I return."

With that, he turned and strode out of the clearing, Midnight holding one hand and Stormaway walking on his other side, both running a few steps now and then to keep up.

It was not long before they came across angry sorcerers who, seeing what was happening to their companions, had turned back to take issue with Tarkyn. As soon as they saw the prince, they surrounded him and his two companions, some mounted and some on foot. For several minutes, angry voices berated him from all sides. Tarkyn swung Midnight up into his arms and waited until they gradually ran out of words. Then he spoke quietly into the hostile silence.

"Sorcerers of the Lost Forest, the Forest is allowing you to leave, as I promised, but unfortunately the woodfolk are not. Their code of secrecy demands that no one who has seen them can leave the forest alive… Presumably, while you remained within the forest, you were able to live side by side. But now that you are going your separate ways, the old rules once more apply."

"Then we are trapped, just as surely as we were before," shouted one sorcerer, looking around himself for support. "And you have misled us."

Tarkyn gave a sharp flick of his hand to raise his shield, "Please don't turn this into a brawl. Until you calm down, I will keep my shield raised. I too am angry at what has happened so I will warn you that, should you attempt to fire on me, your arrows, stones or shafts of power may reflect back and kill you."

Boravar pushed to the front and stood belligerently, arms folded. "So what do you propose to do about it?"

Tarkyn's eyebrows rose and when he next spoke, his voice was edged with disdain, "I? I intend to do nothing about it until you remember whom you are addressing and treat me with due deference."

When Boravar hesitated, Tarkyn sent a shaft of bronze spearing through his shield to hit the big sorcerer just below the knee. Boravar's leg collapsed and he found himself kneeling. Tarkyn's eyes swept around the rest of the crowd.

"I am waiting," was all he said.

One by one, the sorcerers knelt and placed their hands over their hearts. Those on horses dismounted so that they too could demonstrate their respect. Unlike Harkell or Danton, none of them bowed their heads, remembering Tarkyn's previous stricture that they should meet his eyes. For several long minutes, Tarkyn let his gaze wander across all of them in silence. Then he said quietly, "Do not forget again what is owed to me as your prince. If we were at court, your threatening, unruly behaviour would be enough to have you flogged or even hanged. Just be glad that I mete out my own justice and that I am prepared to overlook your behaviour this one time…You may rise."

"Your Highness," asked a middle aged woman clutching a child in her arms, "Please. Can you help us?"

"Your name?" asked the prince peremptorily.

"Karrin, Your Highness."

"To be honest with you, Karrin, I don't know." Tarkyn's voice was aloof but not unkind. "But I will certainly try." He looked around, "Who among you has friends among the woodfolk?"

"We all do, Your Highness," said Boravar, standing with his hand on his neighbour's shoulder to keep the weight off his injured leg. "That is what makes this so shocking."

"Will they come to meet with you and me, if you ask them?"

Boravar shook his head despondently. "Maybe, Sire. I don't know. We could try."

"Your Highness," said Karrin, "Could you not ask your woodfolk to contact them?"

The prince frowned. "No," he said shortly.

A thin man with long fingers that constantly entwined themselves, said haltingly, "Your Highness, can you not demand that they obey you, just as you have done with us? They are subjects of Eskuzor, just as we are, after all."

Tarkyn stared at him while he thought about it. The thin man, misunderstanding the prince's stare, stammered, "I beg your pardon. My name is Steriza."

Tarkyn nodded briefly in acknowledgement and continued to keep his eyes trained on him. The thin man shifted uncomfortably. Finally the prince's mind came back to his surroundings. "Steriza, your point is a good one. However, woodfolk can choose not to be found, which makes them difficult to deal with. I could force them to come here. I could ask the eagles to round them up and bring them before me but by the time they arrived, I cannot imagine they would be keen to negotiate with me."

"But Your Highness, can you not demand that they allow us to leave?" asked Steriza.

Tarkyn shook his head regretfully. "No. It is not as easy as that. I am sworn to protect woodfolk and keep their existence secret. I cannot allow the risk of the knowledge of their presence spreading throughout the land, any more than they can. Their whole way of life and their safety depends on it."

As he spoke, Tarkyn gradually became aware that the trees around them were filled with hidden woodfolk, listening in on their conversation. He acknowledged their presence and invited them to join the sorcerers around him. He felt the buzz of a mental conference all around him. Then suddenly they were there, standing around the outside of the group, arrows notched, aimed at the Lost sorcerers.

Instantly, Tarkyn waved his hand and muttered, "*Shturrum.*" In the next instant, he moved his shield so that it was between the sorcerers and the woodfolk. A ring of angry green eyes looked at him out of still faces.

"Woodfolk of the Lost Forest, you have no reason to threaten these sorcerers until they attempt to leave. I will not condone wholesale slaughter, either now or as they try to leave the Forest. Now, until I know you better, I expect the same degree of respect from you as I have demanded from the sorcerers. I will release half of you from the spell. The other half are hostages to your good behaviour. When you have given me adequate assurances that you will stay but not attack, I will release the other half. When I have had assurances from all of you, I will remove the shield. Are we clear?"

Tarkyn waved his hand and those standing along his left hand side regained the power of movement.

"Put your weapons away please," said Tarkyn. "I will permit none of these sorcerers to attack you, under pain of death. But the same also applies to you. I can and will hunt down anyone who attacks another while we are together negotiating." As the woodfolk lowered their bows, Tarkyn continued, "Will you give me your assurance that you will stay and not attack anyone so that we can sort out this mess?"

After a brief mind discussion, the woodfolk nodded. As Tarkyn released the other half of the woodfolk, they immediately lowered their weapons and nodded their agreement. As Tarkyn looked around at them, debating with himself whether to force them to kneel, they sank to their knees and answered his debate for him. He inclined his head. "Thank you. You may rise. And thank you for coming here." He waved away the shield. "Shall we sit down? This could be a long tiring session."

The prince sat down cross-legged in the middle of the dusty road with Midnight on his knee and Stormaway by his side. When everyone else was settled, he addressed the woodfolk, "Some but not all things have changed among woodfolk since you last walked through the outside world. I, a sorcerer prince, am also a woodman. Waterstone, whom you met yesterday, invited me to become his bloodbrother so that I could become a true member of the woodfolk nation." He indicated Stormaway and Midnight. "These people have one woodfolk parent and one sorcerer parent. Stormaway has lived for many years in both of these communities. So far, Midnight has only lived among woodfolk and with me. I have lived most of my life among sorcerers but am now betrothed to a woodwoman and intend to live with the woodfolk." Tarkyn carefully masked his present feelings towards the home guard as he said this.

"And what of the other sorcerers who travel with your woodfolk?" asked a tough, wiry woodman. "I am Scraping Boughs."

"Good question. Two of them, String and Bean, have known of woodfolk for twenty three years and never breathed a word to anyone until they met me. They only talked to me about it because they realised that I knew of woodfolk. My woodfolk decided to let them live, on condition they stayed with us for six months to gauge their trustworthiness." Tarkyn smiled, "After that, they will be free to go back among sorcerers."

"And the blonde one?"

"He is my lifelong friend. But that alone was not enough. The woodfolk agreed to let him stay because they needed him to help them rescue some woodfolk who had been captured by sorcerers."

Seeing the woodfolk's eyes widen in alarm, Tarkyn smiled, "Yes. We have had some major disasters to overcome. Those woodfolk are back with us now and, as far as we know, only two sorcerers knew of their existence. Both of them are still roaming free but, for their own reasons, are unlikely to divulge your existence. Before the rescue, Danton and Stormaway both went unaccompanied into a sorcerer's camp and did not betray the presence of woodfolk. Stormaway has been back and forth between woodfolk and sorcerers for twelve years now and never mentioned woodfolk to sorcerers."

"And the dark haired sorcerer?" persisted Scraping Boughs.

"He has recently arrived among us and we have not yet gauged his suitability for returning to sorcerer society," replied Tarkyn calmly, glad that Harkell could not hear what he had just said.

There was a protracted silence as the woodfolk indulged in a lengthy mind discussion.

Eventually, an older woodwoman asked, "Even if these sorcerers were permitted to swear an oath of silence to you, how would we know that they would keep it? I am Calling Bird."

Tarkyn raised his eyebrows in surprise, "But surely many of you have been living in close proximity for years. Surely you know each other's calibre by now?"

"But in here, we forgot that we were woodfolk and sorcerers. It is different outside."

"It may well be different outside," countered Tarkyn, "but you will not be. Who you are now is who you will be. These sorcerers do not become big bogeymen the second they step out of the Forest. They will be the same people they always were." He waved his hand around to encompass all the sorcerers. "I cannot tell you who among them is trustworthy. I don't know them. But you do."

"But with the best will in the world, some of us may swear to keep quiet and then inadvertently slip a reference into a drunken conversation in six months' time," said Boravar, shrugging self-deprecatingly.

Tarkyn smiled at the woodfolk, "Well, you can obviously trust him, if he's going to incriminate himself like that."

"He does have a point, though," said Calling Bird, with a hint of regret that gave Tarkyn hope.

"Yes, he does," answered the prince. "But if you have the will to work this out between you, perhaps you can concoct a story to cover any inadvertent slips. After all, the sorcerers have only met you in the Lost Forest, which is known to be legendary and untraceable. So you people could simply be part of that myth."

Slowly, very slowly, smiles spread around the faces of the woodfolk.

"We will need some time," said Scraping Boughs. "to work out the finer details but overall I think we can do it. With your help, if you don't mind, Your Highness. We need you to take their oath, if they agree to do it."

"It would be my pleasure," replied Tarkyn. "I will leave you all to sort it out. You can send an image directly to me when you need me and I will return."

"One small thing," said Stormaway, as he struggled stiffly to his feet. "I have a wide ranging intelligence service at my disposal. If there are any sorcerers who need to be watched, let me know. My agents are everywhere." The wizard smiled as he felt a wave of approval from the prince.

CHAPTER 26

As soon as they were out of earshot, Tarkyn said, "Thank you Stormaway. I hope you didn't mind being used as an exhibit. But I noticed the woodfolk's interest in you two the other day and I thought it might help to break down the barrier."

"For a specific reason such as that, you are welcome."

Tarkyn gave a short laugh, "Point taken." He glanced sideways at the wizard, "I don't want to go back there, you know."

Stormaway patted him on the back, "No. I could imagine you wouldn't want to, at the moment."

"Do you think you could go back and fetch Danton, Harkell, String and Bean and meet me out here somewhere? Make it clear that the others are still under orders to stay in the clearing. I think I've had about enough of woodfolk for the time being. I could do with a good dose of normality."

"And Midnight?"

Tarkyn grinned, "Midnight had nothing to do with all of this. Anyway, he's a little sorcerer, as much as he's a woodman, aren't you?" Tarkyn sent him images to match what he was saying and Midnight nodded back.

Back in the clearing, Waterstone was livid that he and the other woodfolk had been forced to obey an order, particularly when it meant that Tarkyn had left to face the Lost without adequate protection. Tree Wind was quietly pleased that she had shown Tarkyn up to disadvantage but was annoyed not to be present when he had to face the sorcerers.

The gap between woodfolk and sorcerers was so palpable that String and Bean joined Danton and Harkell in looking after the horse, to give themselves something to do away from the woodfolk, even though the horse had long since calmed down and was tied to a tree on the edge of the woods, happily munching grass.

When Stormaway returned, and made it clear that the sorcerers had been asked to gather elsewhere while the woodfolk were still confined to the clearing, Waterstone's eyes glittered with anger.

"What about the lookouts?" he demanded tightly. "Or are we supposed to forego our defences to please His Highness?"

The wizard thought for a minute, "I think the important part of Tarkyn's order is that you stay away from him. So I think deploying your lookouts would still be within the spirit of his instruction." He grimaced as he left, "I hope you are pleased with your efforts. You have well and truly alienated him this time."

Half an hour later, Stormaway returned to the prince, bearing a bag full of food and wine and accompanied by the sorcerers of the home guard.

"Woohoo," whooped Danton as he arrived. "You've really put the cat among the pigeons now. They're furious."

Tarkyn waved his hand angrily. "Blast the lot of them! I will not be taught lessons by sanctimonious woodfolk. A bit of kindness would have gone a long way. I have too much to think about, to get everything right all the time." As he ranted, waves of anger blasted out from him, rocking the sorcerers surrounding him and swirling off through the forest. "Their whole bloody culture is so alien. I spend my life pandering to their peculiar egalitarian beliefs. And how was I supposed to know that woodfolk, who have lived harmoniously with sorcerers for years, were going to turn on them the minute they left the Forest? I credited them with some common sense and integrity. Obviously, both are sadly lacking. They are rigid and dogmatic. Supercilious. Stiff-necked. Excessively proud. They are frightened little rabbits," he continued, blithely contradicting himself. "Won't take chances with anything. I don't know why I put up with them."

He glowered around at his fellow sorcerers who were doing their best not to laugh. "And another thing. Months of hard ground for beds. The only soft bed was in the first few weeks and even that was piles of bracken. Only one style of clothing. Wolf stew, for heaven's sake! And a bloody wolfskin cloak! When I think of the beautifully cut, embroidered cloaks I left behind, I could cry. And the food… Unbelievable! Nothing but meat, fruit, bread and nuts. Where are my chefs? My delicate dishes? The exquisite sauces? Where are the priceless wall hangings and paintings? Generations of artwork and portraits?" He waved his arm around, "Nowhere, that's where."

By this stage, his audience was doubled up with laughter. He stopped and frowned at them, with a half-smile on his face. "You lot are hopeless. Here I am, drastically upset and all you can do is laugh. I'm not even treated respectfully among sorcerers anymore."

"Ah, Tarkyn. That was great," laughed Danton, tears rolling down his cheeks. "I've been so carefully correct for so long. It's such a relief to let go."

Stormaway unpacked his bag and handed around wine and food. For the next few hours, the six of them drank themselves into oblivion telling stories of sorcerer life and tales of court intrigue while Midnight gradually fell asleep. When the call came for Tarkyn to take the Lost sorcerers' oaths, he was completely past it and had to postpone it until the morning.

A short distance away, in the circular clearing, the mood among the woodfolk was sullen and defensive. Out of all of them, Ancient Oak was the least comfortable with what had happened. When he was quizzed about Tarkyn's remark to him, he replied, "He said that to me in the oak tree when we were all arguing over whether to cooperate with him when he first became a woodman. He said that when you are the centre of attention, no matter what you do, there will be someone who doesn't like it. And he said, when people get heated up they forget that he even exists as a person." He glanced at Waterstone and Tree Wind, "Well, I haven't forgotten. But I think some of us are serving up consequences instead of helping someone who is new to our ways."

"If he wants to be a woodman, he has to learn to behave and think like one," said Tree Wind.

"No, he doesn't," replied Ancient Oak firmly. "He will never think and behave in the same way as we do. He has too much more to live up to. Tarkyn is my brother and I am proud of him, just the way he is."

Since Ancient Oak very rarely spoke up, his words had considerable impact. Into the thoughtful silence that followed, Ancient Oak continued, "You all know how much it will affect him if he has inadvertently caused the deaths or suffering of any of these sorcerers. These are people like Tarkyn who may be killed. You can't keep writing them off as the faceless enemy. Those days are gone. We know some sorcerers now. And they all seem pretty nice to me."

"You're forgetting Jarand," Autumn Leaves pointed out. "And there are still thousands unaccounted for." When this last remark did not raise its usual smile, he added, "All right. I concede. Most of them are probably nice enough."

"But they do get caught up in all that etiquette stuff, don't they?" said Rainstorm with a slight grin.

"And they couldn't hide themselves in the dark, let alone in the daylight," rumbled Thunder Storm.

"And you can hear them coming for *hours* before they arrive," chortled Grass Wind.

Waterstone gave a slight smile, "And they bow at the drop of a hat, and kneel to Tarkyn, regardless of whether the ground is dirty or muddy. I wouldn't want to have to keep their clothes clean."

"And when Tarkyn is angry, his eyes flash," laughed Melting Snow, "and I'm sure you could see them for miles around."

"And we are forever having to remember to keep them in on the conversation because they can't mind talk," added Creaking Bough.

Rainstorm chuckled, "And I think we should call String and Bean the Doleful Duo."

And gradually, as the night wore on, the woodfolk too revelled in the chance to have time away from the constant presence of sorcerers.

Chapter 27

Tarkyn awoke the next morning, lying on a soft grassy verge, his head throbbing with the aftermath of the wine. The other sorcerers had taken turns in guarding him throughout the night but now only Harkell and Midnight were awake. The night before had released a lot of the tension but he still hadn't forgiven the woodfolk for their cavalier treatment of him. After a bit of vengeful thinking, he sent a message through to the Lost woodfolk that the sorcerers should meet him in the circular clearing in two hours' time.

"Good morning, Sire," said Harkell with a smile. "I've seen you looking better. Would you like a cup of tea?"

Tarkyn scratched his fingers through his hair. "Yes thanks. A leisurely breakfast, I think. Then a dip in the stream to brighten me up before we return to the clearing." He smiled sweetly, "That should wind them up beautifully, having to wait so long before they can go anywhere. Then I will make a big show of accepting the Lost sorcerers' oaths. If they don't dislike me now, they will by then."

Harkell hesitated, then said what was on his mind, "Tarkyn, don't you think that you may have wound them up enough already, staying away from them last night?"

Tarkyn shook his head and then wished he hadn't. "Ow. Just a minute. I've had an idea." He shut his eyes and, drawing on his life force, sent a warm wave of it around his hung-over body. He opened his eyes and smiled, "That's better. A benefit of being a forest guardian. Fixed my own hangover. Marvellous." He frowned, "Now, you were saying?"

"That you may have punished them enough."

"Ah, yes." Tarkyn accepted a cup of tea and took a sip before saying, "No. I haven't even begun. They want me to start acting like a woodman? Well, I have tried…at least to some extent. But no more." He grimaced, "Trouble is, I can't really force all that court etiquette on them. It would be too unkind, even for revenge. But I will make them endure the spectacle of the Lost sorcerers swearing their oaths and I will remain aloof for a long as I can manage it." He gave a little grin, "I managed it for years at court. So it could be a while. I will make them sorry that they were so unkind, if it's the last thing I do."

Harkell eyed him but said nothing further.

Two hours later, Tarkyn walked into the clearing with his retinue of sorcerers just minutes before the Lost sorcerers arrived. When woodfolk approached him, he held up his hand, "I am busy at the moment. Talk with me afterwards, if you have something important to say."

The Lost sorcerers arrived and Tarkyn took their oaths of secrecy as they knelt before him. When he had finished, he asked them to rise and after a short address, accepted their thanks and sent them on their way. At the last minute, he called Boravar back.

"How is your leg?"

Surprise showed on Boravar's face. "The pain, although intense at the time, did not last more than a couple of hours. I thank you for your clemency, my lord."

Tarkyn waved his hand dismissively. "And where will you go when you leave here?"

Boravar shook his head. "I have no clear plan, Your Highness. I will wander the world until something or someone attracts my interest, I suppose. There will be many new things to see after so long." He hesitated, "It has been a privilege to meet you, my lord, and I will carry your memory to my grave."

The prince smiled, "Good luck Boravar. You are a man of great strength and integrity. The world needs people like you."

The burly man coloured beneath his beard, "Thank you." He bowed, his hand over his heart, before turning to follow his companions.

For a few minutes, Tarkyn stood watching the departing sorcerers. Then, leaving Stormaway and Danton with instructions to bring provisions and follow him, he levitated himself and the other sorcerers one at a time across the stream to sit well away from the woodfolk.

Needless to say, Stormaway and Danton were beset on all sides as they gathered together the required provisions.

"What on earth is he playing at?" asked Waterstone crossly.

Stormaway glanced at him, "I did warn you. He is still extremely angry."

Danton grimaced, "I think he has decided that if you feel he is not doing well enough as a woodman, he will no longer make the effort and will revert to being purely a sorcerer. Speaking for myself, I think you placed him in a very dangerous, embarrassing situation yesterday and it was only his negotiating skills, combined with judicious, skilful use of magic that pulled him through."

"He should have let us come with him," protested Tree Wind.

"No. I don't think so." Danton, now that he had been confronted about it, realised that he too was angry on Tarkyn's behalf. "If you are not going to keep him informed as agreed, then you place him at risk." He straightened up from packing his bag and looked Tree Wind in the eye, "In fact, what you did yesterday came very close to betrayal. I can't see him trusting you for quite some time after this."

"Letting those sorcerers go into the world knowing about woodfolk also amounts to betrayal. If anyone but he had done that, they would have been exiled. We are not the only ones at fault, you know," she insisted stubbornly. "He needs to learn the woodfolk code."

"Then teach it to him until he can recite it backwards. Talk to him about it. Don't ambush him with it." He closed his bag and swung it onto his shoulder. "You have destroyed in one day, months of goodwill between us. Congratulations." He turned away and headed off to join his liege.

But woodfolk are naturally gregarious people so it was not long before the barrier of the freezing stream was breached. Rainstorm and North Wind waded across, groaning and laughing at the icy water soaking through their leggings.

With his characteristic lack of ceremony, Rainstorm plonked himself down on the grass next to Tarkyn and said cheerily, "Hi prince. In a huff, are you?" He helped himself to a piece of fruit and continued, unabashed by the silence, "Don't blame you, really. I think risking people's lives to teach you a lesson is a bit rich. I don't know what they were thinking." He took another mouthful and munched it down before adding, "Actually I think it's a bit rich teaching you a lesson at all. I think you're doing fine, myself."

"You should have heard Ancient Oak," put in North Wind. "He stuck up for you. He told them all that you were his brother and that he was proud of you just the way you are."

"Yeah," agreed Rainstorm, "And when Tree Wind said you had to start thinking and acting like a woodman, Ancient Oak said no, you didn't. He doesn't usually say much, Ancient Oak. So he must have felt strongly about it."

"He did not come over with you, however," said Tarkyn dryly.

Rainstorm looked at him, "Hmm. I don't know if you've noticed, but Ancient Oak is a bit shy. I think he would find it hard to come over here and outface a hostile group of sorcerers."

"Whereas you don't?"

Rainstorm took another bite of apple and munched it before replying, "Actually, for the first time, I must admit I did feel a bit nervous coming over here. It's never been so 'you and us' before and you all have bags of magic and we don't. Even without the magic, you're all older, bigger and angrier than we are." He shrugged, "But there you go. Sometimes you just have to get on with it, don't you?"

Despite his best intentions, Tarkyn broke into a smile at this guileless little speech. "Thanks Rainstorm, and you too, North Wind. I did want to stay aloof but I didn't mean to make anyone nervous." He sighed, "Perhaps enough is enough and we had better cross back over into the fold. What do you think?"

Rainstorm shrugged, "Up to you, prince. I wouldn't bust your guts for them after yesterday. But if you are going back sometime soon, I wouldn't mind a lift over, partly for the fun and partly because my leggings are just starting to dry off."

Tarkyn chuckled, "I think we can do that for you."

Chapter 28

Once everyone was safely back across the stream, Tarkyn asked Rainstorm to send a request for all the home guard to gather around him. This was achieved in very short order since they had all been watching and awaiting his arrival.

Tarkyn took a deep breath, stamped on his pride and said quietly, "I am sorry that I disappointed you. When I saw woodfolk and sorcerers living side by side, I forgot that the sorcerers could not be allowed to return to the outside world to spread word of woodfolk as it suited them." He let out his held breath, "And I am sorry that you felt the need to humiliate me as you did. If you were trying to teach me a lesson, you succeeded, but a quiet word in my ear would have served just as well."

He looked around at all of them, "And if you were trying to knock me off my pedestal, you also succeeded in that. I have never been more mortified than I was yesterday at the mess I had created. And I am sure you are pleased, Tree Wind, that I was also berated by an angry rabble of sorcerers." He raised a hand and dropped it. "And all of this could have been avoided if you had had the kindness to forewarn me."

He spread his arms wide. "So. I hope you are satisfied. I have taken my punishment since I had no choice but to repair the damage I had done. But don't ever talk to me again of equality. You have demonstrated clearly how little you think of us. You would never have risked woodfolk like that."

With that, Tarkyn pushed through the crowd, helped himself to a cup of tea and retreated to visit the horse that was still tethered to a tree at the edge of the clearing. He stroked its shiny dark brown neck with long calming movements that gradually relaxed the turmoil inside himself. When the great horse nuzzled him, he sent a request for an apple to Midnight.

A few minutes later, a voice behind him said, "Here."

Tarkyn turned in surprise to see Waterstone standing close behind him, holding out an apple. Tarkyn met his eyes steadily. After a minute, he asked, "Do you want to try feeding the horse yourself?"

"If that is what it takes to mend the rift between us, I will." Waterstone gave the ghost of a smile, "But I would rather not."

Tarkyn thought about it, knowing how great the gesture was that Waterstone was offering. After a minute, he said, "Put out your hand flat, with the apple on it. I will place my hand under yours and we will feed him together. Take a few deep breaths and try to relax. Otherwise your fear may frighten it."

Waterstone did as requested, his heart thumping hard in his chest. Together they held out the apple. With its soft velvety mouth, the horse gently lipped the apple out of Waterstone's hand and munched it inconsequentially. Waterstone was so relieved he blew out a stream of air, which startled the horse and made it snort. Instantly, the woodman was several yards away, gasping in fright.

Tarkyn smiled, "Come back here. You just gave it a fright. Come on. Try again. It's not going to hurt you. I'm here. I'll protect you." Gradually Tarkyn talked Waterstone back to stand once more beside him. "Here. Try patting it."

The sorcerer demonstrated, all the while sending calming waves to the horse to counteract the woodman's fear. Slowly Waterstone, his forehead beaded with sweat, reached out and gingerly began to stroke the horse's neck.

After a few minutes of endurance, he glanced at Tarkyn and said tightly, "I think I've had enough for now. Can I stop?"

Tarkyn gave quiet laugh. "Of course you may stop. You never had to start, if you didn't want to. I think you have done very well for your first time. Maybe you can try again later or tomorrow if it is still here."

Waterstone stepped back a good distance this time before releasing his sigh of relief.

Chapter 29

Some time later, Tarkyn lay on his stomach, his head propped on his hands, gazing into the waters of the shallow stream and watching a tortoise swimming through the flowing plants on the bottom. He was just about to try to connect with it when he realised someone had sat down quietly next to him. He looked around and met the steady green eyes of Tree Wind. For a moment he thought of ignoring her and reverting his attention to the tortoise but, on balance, he decided that it would be better to sort out whatever had driven Tree Wind to be so dogmatic.

So he turned on one side and asked gently, "Are you still punishing me for Falling Rain?" Before she could reply, he continued, "Tree Wind, no matter how you exact your revenge, neither you nor I nor anyone else can do anything that will bring back the twelve years with Falling Rain that you have lost. I am truly sorry for your loss but there is nothing I can do to restore it."

"No Tarkyn, Falling Rain has forgiven you and so have I." She gave a wry smile, "Not that it was your fault in the first place. But feelings are not always logical." She pulled up a stem of sweet green grass and began to suck on it as she talked. "No. It was as I said. We all thought that you would realise before it was too late. The Lost woodfolk didn't believe you would do anything about the sorcerers, but we assured them you would. We lost a bit of face over it, actually. They were ready to kill every sorcerer who stepped out of the Forest but we persuaded them to use only slingshots and to give you a chance to sort it out."

"Oh." After a moment to adjust his thoughts, Tarkyn frowned, "But why did you seem so pleased with it all?"

"You should know me by now. I am always proud of the fact that we woodfolk, so lacking in power, can defeat sorcerers if we choose to. And I think it right and proper that we defend our borders, so to speak. But we had already made sure no one would be killed."

"So you weren't looking triumphant at showing me up?"

Tree Wind gave a short laugh. "No. I was just stating facts. You should have known." She looked sideways at him. "I suppose I was a bit angry because I knew that you would be inviolate if you had allowed those sorcerers out into the world whereas Falling Rain had been so severely punished for a similar offence. So I took some satisfaction in your discomfort, but it was not the driving force."

Tarkyn studied her for a minute as she found another juicy strand of green grass, pulled it up and sucked on it.

"I would not have been inviolate, you know," he said quietly. Tarkyn waved his hand dismissively. "From exile or from legal punishment perhaps, but not from myself or even from you. How could I have lived with myself if I had betrayed you, us, like that?" He rolled back over onto his front. "I was angry with myself as much as I was angry with you."

"But no matter how angry you were, Tarkyn, you should not have rejected our assistance."

Tarkyn looked up in surprise when he realised the speaker was Lapping Water who had finally decided to come over and talk to him. As she sat down on the other side of Tree Wind, he met her eyes, trying unsuccessfully to gauge where she stood in all this. After a moment he said, "I may have been angry and I did assume that you were all angry with me, but I didn't leave you behind because of it. I left you behind because I didn't want a host of wound up woodfolk at my back when I met the Lost sorcerers. That would have turned it into a confrontation. They were angry enough as it was."

"So we saw," she said shortly.

For a moment Tarkyn's eyebrows twitched together, thinking his woodfolk had disobeyed his order. But then he realised that the Lost woodfolk must have relayed the events to them.

"No, *Your Highness*," replied Lapping Water dryly, in answer to his expressions, "We did not forget our oath, much as we would have liked to." She shrugged and smiled shyly at him, "But you did pretty well on your own."

"Yes, you did," Tree Wind patted him on the shoulder, "So, in the end, you justified our faith in you."

"Just a bit slow on the uptake, really," said Lapping Water, with a twinkle in her eye.

Soon after this, Tree Wind found an excuse to leave so that Tarkyn could be alone with Lapping Water.

Tarkyn sat up and looked at Lapping Water, taking in her long soft brown hair and her mischievous smiling eyes. After a while he asked, "Why didn't you come over the stream with Rainstorm and North Wind? You haven't taken my breath away with your support."

Lapping Water's face crinkled in feigned concentration. "Hmm. And I don't seem to remember an invitation to join your precious sorcerer club last night."

"Would you have come if I had asked?"

Lapping Water coloured slightly. "Actually, I would have found it very embarrassing to be singled out…and I would have been just the tiniest bit scared. So I'm glad you didn't."

"Ever since the night of our betrothal, you seem to have faded into the background." Tarkyn kept his eyes firmly on a blade of grass he had found himself to fiddle with. "Are you regretting your decision?" He raised his eyes to look at her.

The colour in her cheeks deepened and she did not return his gaze. As she drew a deep breath to reply, Tarkyn's heart almost stopped beating. Finally she lifted her eyes to meet his. "No… No… I do love you." She smiled gently. "I love you so much it almost hurts. But I don't know how to act in front of everyone."

Tarkyn let out a pent up breath and smiled. "Come here." He pulled her gently over to him to sit within the circle of his arms and kissed the top of her head. "You know I nearly died just then, waiting for your answer?" He stroked her hair as he talked. "I suppose it is awkward for you, isn't it? If you align yourself too closely with me, you risk losing your equality with your fellow woodfolk." He kissed the top of her head again. "This was never going to be easy, was it?"

Lapping Water tilted her head up and smiled up at him, "No, not easy. But worth it."

This time, he kissed her lips.

CHAPTER 30

Sometime later they were disturbed by the sounds of an intense discussion that increased in volume as it drew nearer. Tarkyn and Lapping Water looked up to see Rainstorm, Blizzard and Melting Snow bearing down on them with Ancient Oak and North Wind bringing up the rear. Ancient Oak kept tugging at Rainstorm's sleeve in an unsuccessful attempt to halt his progress as he remonstrated with him. Rainstorm just kept smiling and pulling Ancient Oak along with him until they all arrived in a chaotic mass around Tarkyn and Lapping Water.

"Hi Tarkyn, Lapping Water," said Rainstorm breezily, sitting himself down right next to them.

Ancient Oak rolled his eyes, "I tried to stop him. I thought you'd like a bit of peace and quiet. But the boy has all the subtlety of a rock."

Tarkyn smiled, "Since you're here, you might as well stay." Lapping Water made to pull away but Tarkyn gave her a reassuring squeeze and kept his arm around her. "I don't suppose anyone brought something to drink, did they?"

"As it turns out, you're in luck," said Rainstorm, triumphantly producing a flask and some mugs from his bag. "Blizzard?"

"Yes, I've brought the bread and cheese," replied the mountainman, as he emptied his bag and distributed the contents on the ground around him.

"And I've brought some lovely little berries that only seem to grow in this forest," added Melting Snow. "Look! They are bright yellow and very sweet."

Lapping Water's nose crinkled up, "Are you sure they're all right? How do you know they're not poisonous if we haven't eaten them before?"

Melting Snow waved her hand airily, "Don't worry. There are still Lost woodfolk around, you know. They haven't all chosen to leave. So when I found the berries, I asked. They call them sun berries." She smiled, "Suits them, doesn't it?"

Tarkyn noticed Ancient Oak was still hovering uncertainly on the outskirts of the group so he gestured to him, "Come on. Sit down and join in. You might as well. This lot aren't going away in a hurry. You tried your best. Now just give in with good grace and have some fun. You too, North Wind."

For the first half an hour, Tarkyn could feel the tension in Lapping Water's body as she leant against him in the midst of her friends but gradually, as the wine, talk and laughter relaxed them, she forgot to be self-conscious and began to laugh and joke with them, starting to feel at home within the circle of his arms. He too found it difficult and had to work hard to appear relaxed at the start. He was acutely aware of his arm in contact with her and kept monitoring his muscles to keep them from tensing up and making her more nervous. After a while, he realised that when he focused hard on the conversation, he was able to stop thinking about being on show with Lapping Water and could just relax and be himself. A few wines and a couple of hours later and they were well on their way to feeling natural about it.

Gradually, as the afternoon progressed into evening, Danton, Harkell and other woodfolk drifted over to chat for a while or to stay.

And suddenly, into a lull in the conversation, came Ancient Oak's voice, "Fair enough, Rainstorm. I concede. You were obviously right."

Tarkyn looked at Ancient Oak quizzically. "About what?"

Rainstorm shrugged and tried to look innocent, "Oh, nothing much."

Tarkyn frowned smilingly, "Come on Rainstorm. What are you up to?"

Rainstorm gave a slight smile that gradually turned into a large grin, "I just thought you two might be finding it a bit hard knowing how to act with everyone around you. After all, I reckon that Lapping Water has spent less time with you in the last two days than she has for ages. So I thought we should grab you while you were together and force the issue." He laughed and looked sideways at Ancient Oak, "As you may have gathered, Ancient Oak didn't agree."

Lapping Water choked with laughter and buried her face in Tarkyn's chest. Tarkyn smiled broadly as he looked down at her, "Now look what you've done, Rainstorm! She's going to dribble all down my front, if I'm not careful."

Lapping Water dug him hard in the ribs and gurgled into his shirt front, "Stop it. I am not."

"Oof! Not happy with dribbling on me, now she's attacking me."

Lapping Water gave Tarkyn one last jab before sitting up and straightening her hair. "Rainstorm," she said primly, "I don't know whether I should hug you or hit you."

As Rainstorm looked horrified, Tarkyn grinned evilly, "Oh. Hug, definitely."

CHAPTER 31

Very early the next morning, Danton crept out of the firesite, unknowingly disturbing nearly all the woodfolk as he passed. Even Harkell heard him pass and, being a habitual early riser, decided to follow him to see what he was up to.

As soon as they were out of earshot of the sleeping woodfolk, Danton turned around and said, "Come on. You might as well catch up and talk to me, if you're going to follow me. I may not be able to detect a woodman but I can certainly hear you."

Harkell came out from behind a tree he had been hiding behind with an embarrassed grin on his face. "Morning."

Danton stood with his hands on his hips. "So, what are you up to? Surely you don't think I can't be trusted? Especially after what the guardians said."

Harkell shook his head, smiling. "No. I just thought you might be off to find this wizard lady you spoke of and I wouldn't mind meeting her."

"Wouldn't you now?" Danton gave a short laugh. "Well, if you're looking for a bit of female sorcerer company, I think she may be a little above your touch."

Harkell stared stonily at him before saying, "That was offensive in so many ways I don't know where to begin." He ticked the points of on his fingers as he continued, keeping his anger very tightly in check, "Firstly, I am not some sex-starved low life desperate for a quick fling. Secondly, I am quite content with the company of woodwomen. Thirdly, I am married and that matters to me, even if it does not matter to you and fourthly, I am well aware of my origins and, having met Falling Branch and Rainstorm, am beginning to be proud of them. After all, a craftsman is a far greater asset to society than many aristocrats I can think of."

"I see. So am I to understand from that, that you consider me to be of no value to society?" asked Danton icily.

Harkell looked startled, "You in particular? No. I don't think that of you." He smiled slowly, "Unlike you, I take each person on their merit." He thought for a moment, "Actually, that isn't quite fair. You seem to take most people on their merit – all the woodfolk and the trappers, although I gather you had a few issues with the woodfolk when you first met them. But now? Now you only seem to have an issue with me." He shook his head and smiled, with just a hint of regret, "But no matter how much you goad me, or deride me, or needle me, or try to intimidate me, I will not fight you. I have endured treatment like that ever since I left the smithy and set out to make my fortune in the armed forces. I have had twenty years of practice at keeping my temper. One step out of line in all that time and I would have been gone."

The ex-captain bent down, picked up a stone and hurled it hard against a tree. Then he turned back to Danton and smiled wryly, "Doesn't mean I don't have a temper. Just means I control it."

Danton watched him steadily and finally let out a long breath, "Harkell, you're an impressive bastard. After our riotous evening the other night, I know you're fun and perceptive and quick-witted. And you obviously have cast iron self-control." He turned and began to walk again, signalling Harkell to fall in beside him. "Come on. I didn't really mean to come across so snakily about Stillwaters. She's above my touch too, you know. I said it dryly but I admit there may have been just a touch of acid in there. Probably more resentment at her attitude than a shot at you." He glanced at the sorcerer walking beside him and found Harkell's soft brown eyes trained on his face, studying him. Danton shook his head and smiled, "You have had to watch and learn, haven't you? If you took a path where no one would show you the way, I suppose you had to figure it all out yourself; how to act, what to say and do in all those structured, carefully choreographed court events." Danton gave him a friendly thump on the back, "That's no mean feat."

Harkell kept watching him, "No, perhaps not. But you don't like it, all the same. Do you?"

Danton stopped walking and turned to him, "Harkell, I will lay my cards on the table. I fear what an ambitious man like you wants with my prince. I don't want him used and his trust abused. He is too vulnerable and too important to have people using him for their own ends."

In the silence that followed, Harkell just looked at him. Danton suddenly smiled, "You and I are too much alike. I know what you're doing. You're trying to figure out what to say to make me trust you."

Harkell smiled slowly and nodded as they turned to continue along the path, "Yes I am. It doesn't mean I am not trustworthy, however."

"No, it doesn't. I have been in the same position myself. It does mean, though, that you don't have a glib cover story prepared which, I think, speaks in your favour since you are not stupid enough not to have foreseen the need."

Harkell grunted "I don't think that logic holds, much as I would like it to. Even if I am trustworthy I should still have foreseen the need to prove it. Perhaps you are wrong and I am stupid after all."

Danton chuckled, "Oh no, my friend. You are anything but. That's what worries me."

"Don't be worried, Danton," said Harkell impulsively, "I already have my heart's desire. Even as captain of the guard, I very rarely spoke with Prince Jarand and was even more rarely asked my opinion. Here, with Tarkyn, I could bend his ear all day if I wanted to. What else could I want that Tarkyn could give me anyway?"

"Wealth," said Danton shortly.

Harkell nodded, "True, I suppose. He did say he has hidden some of his valuables somewhere between here and Tormadell, but with his sense of direction I can't imagine he'll ever find them again." He gave a little smile. "It didn't seem to occur to him that any of us would need them."

Danton rolled his eyes, "Tarkyn hasn't a clue about money. Never had to bother with it. But in fairness, despite what I said at the beginning, you should be given some funds to support your family. I'll talk to Stormaway about it."

"You don't have to, you know. They will get by and, to be honest, I haven't done anything yet that deserves a salary. Every time I've tried to protect Tarkyn, I've got it wrong; first with the mountain lion, and then the other day with Waterstone. And then there was String's and my marvellous idea about freeing the Lost." He smiled ruefully, "Well, after that, I think I'm more of a liability than an asset."

"No, you're not. People just haven't given you enough information. That's all." Danton smiled, "That was a stunningly good idea; to challenge the whole concept of the Lost Forest. The execution just needed a bit of refining."

"Thanks. You know, that String character is pretty clever."

Danton laughed, "He certainly is. He spends his life thinking. So does Bean. Don't be misled by their lackadaisical air and the fact that they look like a pile of scrappy furs on legs. They are both as sharp as tacks."

"You don't seem to worry about them abusing your prince."

"Would you? They are happy with their life up in the mountains, far from politics and power. They just like the chance to be with the woodfolk. Tarkyn was an unwelcome, added extra from their point of view."

As he spoke, Danton came to a halt and looked around with a frown. He squatted down and ran his hand across the sand at the side of the path beneath a stand of scraggy bushes. His frown deepened, "Hmm. I'm sure this is where I found the tunnel in through the bushes. But there is no sign of it now."

Harkell looked around them, "How can you be sure it was here?"

Danton pointed to an old tree across the path that carried a large oval scar where, at some time in the past, a big branch had fallen off. "I particularly took note of that tree so that I could find it again."

"Hmm. Maybe she has gone or maybe she doesn't want you to find her again."

Danton straightened up, "Well, at least that will save me from arguing with her again."

"Very philosophical, Danton. Well done!"

Danton gave a short laugh.

"Maybe the entrance has moved," suggested Harkell.

Danton shrugged, "Maybe. In fact that is just the type of annoying thing she would do. But I'm not going to waste my time looking for it. Let's go back. Perhaps I'll come back later and see whether it has reappeared."

And when Danton returned on his own, later in the day, it had. He crawled through the bushes again, this time making no effort to conceal his presence. As soon as he was through the tunnel, he straightened up and looked around the clearing. A hesitant middle-aged man approached him.

"You are Lord Danton, I believe."

Danton gave a perfunctory bow, "I am. And you are…?"

"Who I am is of no concern to you. I am merely here to escort you to the lady."

But Danton had been learning from his prince, "Nevertheless, I would be honoured to know your name."

The sorcerer flushed with gratification, "I am called Caroman, my lord."

"I am pleased to meet you, Caroman. Am I to understand that the lady Stillwaters awaits my presence?"

"Yes, my lord. She thought she might see you this morning but unfortunately a difficulty presented itself." Caroman waved his arm, "If you please, come this way, sir."

Caroman led Danton around the edge of the clearing and up the side of the fountain. From there, they took a path back between the boulders into a small space surrounded by enormous rocks and hanging with flowering vines. A small patch of blue sky showed straight above them.

Stillwaters was seated at a small table set for two with fine china, crystal and silverware on a damask tablecloth. She inclined her head graciously in dismissal to Caroman before bending a smile on Danton and holding out her hand.

As Danton bent to kiss it, she said, "Good afternoon, my lord. I trust you have not eaten so much at lunch that you cannot join me for a light repast." She indicated the chair opposite her.

"No, I think I could manage a little more. It would be my pleasure to join you."

Danton sat down and smiled across the table at her. Today she was wearing an ice blue flowing gown and Danton registered with a slight shock that again her eyes were the colour of her gown, no longer kingfisher blue but ice blue. Despite her courtesy, the lighter colour made her eyes look even harder than yesterday. His eyes narrowed slightly as he studied her hair. It seemed to be a darker red today but perhaps that was because they were sitting out of the direct sunlight.

Stillwaters frowned, "Is there a problem, my lord? You seem a little preoccupied."

Danton waved his hand, "No, not all. I was just admiring the way your eyes match your dress."

Caroman returned and poured some sparkling wine into their glasses. Stillwaters ignored him while Danton nodded his thanks.

"I hear your prince has been throwing his weight around and disrupting an institution that has been working perfectly well for hundreds of years."

Danton eyed her, "From whose point of view has it been working well?"

"I have had no cause to question it. It has provided me with staff, and all the people within the Forest have been well cared for and have lived very long lives, much longer than if they had returned to the outside world. The guardians were quite happy with it until your presumptuous prince came along."

Danton took a sip of wine and said carefully, "I gather you are not pleased?"

Stillwaters shrugged, "As long as some people choose to stay, it is of little consequence."

"Do you have no care for the fact that people were forced to stay here against their will when they had committed no recognisable crime, some for hundreds of years?"

Stillwaters huffed, "Perhaps that is a little excessive for a slight lack of courage."

Danton's eyes crinkled, "You're in a huff because you didn't think of it yourself, aren't you? You realise now that there was an injustice right under your nose and you are chagrined that you allowed it to continue."

Her ice blue eyes drilled him for a moment, "You read too much into my reactions. And you are wanting me to be better than I am."

Danton could see that an injudicious reply to this remark would lay him open to attack. So he took his time in responding, "I do not yet know you well enough to have your full measure and so cannot say that I would want you to be better. In any case, I think it would be a presumption on my part to say that I wanted you other than how you are, no matter how well I knew you. What I would hope is that you are able to live up to your own expectations."

The blue eyes narrowed for a moment before she broke into a smile, "You sidestepped that one very well, my lord."

"Thank you. I try."

She sipped her wine, "And are you not curious about my disappearing path?"

Danton shrugged, "Not really. I just assumed that, if it had anything to do with me, you were just toying with me."

"Actually, it was more than that."

She waited while Caroman placed small dishes of delicately cooked salmon swimming in a herb butter sauce before them.

Danton smiled, "Tarkyn will be so jealous when I tell him of this. He has had nothing but woodfolk fare for months."

"I can give you all the details of the recipe so that you can tantalise him to the full." Stillwaters smiled, "If he could be bothered, he could make it himself." Seeing Danton frown, her smile broadened, "I know. It is not the role of a prince to cook his own meals. I love the way you are so ready to spring to his defence."

"Hmph. I don't see you cooking anything either," said Danton trenchantly.

Stillwaters waved an indolent hand, "Oh, absolutely not. I concur completely with Tarkyn. Food preparation must be left to others, if at all possible." She smiled tantalisingly, "It is not my role either."

Knowing full well that if he asked her what her role was, she would refuse to answer, Danton reverted to the discussion about the path. "So tell me why the path disappeared then."

She gave a tinkling laugh. "Oh, it was still there. I just placed a glamour on it so you couldn't see it. If you had persevered and trusted your memory, you could have felt your way off the path into the tunnel though the bushes. Once past the entrance, you would have been able to see it again."

Danton watched her carefully picking her way through her salmon and thought she was the most irritating, beautiful woman he had ever met. He wasn't at all sure that the beauty would be worth the irritation, though. "I see. I'm sure you enjoyed laughing at me trying to find it."

Stillwaters put down her cutlery and became serious. "No. I didn't laugh. I was actually regretful that I couldn't let you in, if you must know."

"And why couldn't you?" he asked, fully expecting to be refused an answer.

"Because Harkell was with you."

Danton frowned, "And what is wrong with Harkell? Are you afraid of him? Is there something I should know about him to protect Tarkyn?"

Stillwaters smiled, "No. Do not fear. Tarkyn is safe with him, as far as I know." She picked up her fork and took another small bite before saying, "But Harkell sees too much. He observes things other people miss. It would not suit me to meet him at the moment."

"What? Such as the fact that your eye colour changes each time I see you?"

Her smile broadened, "Oh, so that's what you were looking at, was it? Hmm, yes. A little fettish of mine, to match my eyes to my dress."

Danton put his head on one side. "You're lying. You didn't intend me to notice."

Immediately he had a wild cat on his hands.

"Lord Danton! How dare you speak to me like that?" She threw down her napkin and stood up at the table, her light blue eyes flashing as hard as diamonds. "I invite you here and serve you up an exquisite luncheon and you repay me by accusing me of lying."

Danton smiled quietly, "Come on. Sit down. You just don't like being caught out, that's all."

Stillwaters stood there rigidly, clearly uncertain what to do next in the face of Danton's non reaction.

Danton leaned over and took her hand, which she immediately snatched away.

"Don't touch me," she said frostily.

Danton stood up, "All right, if you would prefer it, I will go. But if I do, we both know that you will regret it and so will I."

Stillwaters hard blue eyes narrowed. "You are insufferably arrogant, Danton Patronell."

"No, I'm not. You're mixing me up with Tarkyn. I am just saying you will regret my departure because you did last time when you had said something unkind."

She drew herself up. "I didn't say anything unkind this time. You did."

"I'm sorry then. Perhaps I should not have phrased it so baldly." He raised his eyebrows at her and smiled, "But I'm afraid that I have no intention of lying to you. Some people I may lie to, but not you. So if you can't deal with the truth, then it may be better that I leave."

This caught her attention. Her body relaxed a little and she looked perplexed, "Why wouldn't you lie to me, if you would lie to others?"

Danton shrugged, "I only lie to achieve a particular purpose; usually if I am on some sort of fact finding mission. I do not lie to people I care about, except occasionally to spare their feelings. And so I would not lie to you."

Stillwaters dropped back into her chair, looking a bit dazed. "Do you care about me?"

Danton frowned a little as he sat back down, "Yes, I do. Is that so strange? Let's be clear. This is not an offer of marriage or anything like that. But I do care about you."

The beautiful wizard woman laughed, "No. I didn't think it was. And I wouldn't accept if it were."

Danton snorted, "I should think not, on a couple of hours' acquaintance" He shook his head, "You are the oddest person. Prickly as a thistle."

Caroman took this opportune moment to remove the plates and bring forth a roasted duckling glazed with honey and dried fruits, sitting on a bed of brown, crispy skinned vegetables. As he finished serving, he caught Danton's eye and gave him the slightest wink before straightening and retiring to some inner domain.

As Danton attacked his duck, he mused, "So what would Harkell notice that I might not?"

Stillwaters smiled, her good humour completely restored, "Obviously, since I wouldn't let him come, I am not going to tell you. And I hope you don't work it out for yourself."

"Blast you, Stillwaters. You are such a provocative woman. I don't know how anyone puts up with you."

She glanced at him before dropping her eyes to her plate. "No one does."

Danton studied her, trying to work out whether she was unhappy about this state of affairs. "You could come with us, if you no longer wish to be alone," he offered diffidently thinking, even as he said it, that she had already said she didn't want to meet Tarkyn yet. He waved his hand to pre-empt her objection. "No. Sorry. We've already covered this ground, haven't we? But the offer is there if you ever need it."

She looked up and smiled at him, "Thank you for your offer, Danton. It means a great deal to me but unfortunately I must refuse."

"I know. I don't know why you must refuse but I do know that you must."

At last, after they had eaten and talked their way through the duck, and the apple and blackberry tart that followed it, Danton regretfully laid his napkin on the table. "I have to go, you know. Tarkyn nearly killed me last time I was here with you."

"I know," said Stillwaters. "He can feel my presence. He is very powerful, you know; more so than any who have come before him. But don't worry. This time, I sent a message via the woodfolk to set his mind at rest." She smiled, "He will only be jealous this time, not angry."

Danton shook his head with a smile, "Last time he was actually scared for me but instead of saying so, conveyed his concern by bawling me out in front of everyone. He's a bloody menace sometimes."

"I'm glad you like him so much," said the wizard woman, reading between the lines. "He is so lucky to have you. I wish…" She waved her hand. "No. Never mind."

Danton stood up, took her hand and kissed it, saying, "Just remember. I do care about you and if you ever need me and can get word to me, I will come."

Stillwaters raised her eyebrows, "What about your precious prince? What if he needs you too?"

Danton smiled, "I could almost believe you were jealous. I can't answer that, except to say that Tarkyn has many to lean on and you seem only to have servants. I can only say that I would do my best."

"Before you go, there is one thing I need to say. I hope, if you like me, that you have not just taken a liking to my face. I would not want that."

Danton looked into her hard, light blue eyes and said, "So I would suppose. Since it is obvious to me that I have not yet seen how you really appear." He gave a wry smile, "I cannot promise to be able to deal with it when you do trust me with your true appearance, but I will try."

"Don't look so worried. I am not an ogre beneath this façade. But I am different from what you see now." She smiled at him, "Goodbye my friend. I will miss you. Don't come again before you go. I will miss you too badly if I get to know you any better."

Danton felt a lump in his throat, "Goodbye Stillwaters. I look forward to the time that we can meet again. I will try to think of what you said, not of how you look when I think of you. I too will miss you."

With that he turned on his heel and followed Caroman down the rocky path. When he reached the bottom, he looked back but could see no sign of her.

Chapter 31

Two days later, Tarkyn and his home guard left the Lost Forest. Just as they reached its borders, Moridan appeared before the prince on the path ahead of them.

"You might like to know, my young relative, that the challenge I had planned never came to fruition. The person concerned chose to confront it himself before I could set anything up."

"And who was this person?" asked Tarkyn.

"Waterstone."

Tarkyn gave a gentle smile, "It was the horse, wasn't it? He confronted it to repair our friendship."

Moridan looked at Waterstone who had come to stand beside Tarkyn. "I am glad my young relative warrants that level of courage from you but equally, I would be careful how often you stretch the bonds of friendship. One day you may ask too much of them and they may stretch beyond repair." He transferred his attention to include Tarkyn. "In the short time you have been in the forest, each of you has pushed the other too far. Be careful of one another. I know the depth of your friendship and know that the world would be poorer for the loss of it." He smiled as he faded from sight, "That is our final gift to you. Farewell."

Part 5: Boravar

CHAPTER 32

A huge war horse bearing a heavy, bearded sorcerer thundered through the night past sleeping villages and open fields until, just as the sky began to lighten, he reached the outskirts of the forest and was pulled back gradually until he stood, slick with sweat and trembling, near to exhaustion.

The sorcerer leaned forward and patted his neck, murmuring words of thanks and encouragement to him before urging him to a gentle walk. For another forty minutes, horse and rider made their way slowly along the dim forest trail, before the sorcerer dismounted and led his mount from the road, picking his way carefully through the dense foliage until finally he came to a clearing near a stream. He let the horse drink its fill. Then, even though he was near exhaustion himself, he took off the horse's saddle and rubbed him down with dry grass before making a great show of tethering it him firmly to a tree.

The sorcerer glanced around the surrounding area, noting the tangles of brambles and the light scattering of leaves across the floor of the clearing. He walked to the middle of the clearing and, squatting down, placed the back of his hand on the ground. Sure enough, a faint warmth still radiated up from the ground.

The sorcerer stood up in the middle of the clearing and slowly raised his hands above his head. Then he addressed the trees slowly in a deep, carrying voice.

"Please don't kill me. I need to speak to Prince Tarkyn. And I know only you will be able to find him." He took a deep breath and continued, "I'm sure by now there are at least a dozen arrows trained on me. Please, for the sake of the prince and for all woodfolk, shoot me down with a slingshot and tie my hands behind me. Then listen to what I have to say and convey it to the prince. If you must kill me then, so be it. As long as Prince Tarkyn is warned."

The sorcerer felt a sharp pain on the side of his head. Then everything went black.

When he came to, he was seated against a tree with his hands tied behind him and several coils of rope around his chest binding him tightly to the tree. As his vision swam back into focus, he realised his ankles were also bound. He heaved a sigh. *At least I'm alive*, he thought. He looked through the branches of the trees at the sun, now well up in the sky, and realised that he must have been unconscious for quite some time.

A scrawny old woodwoman pulled his head up by his hair and placed a cup to his mouth so that he could drink. Her green eyes glowered into his blue ones.

"Who are you and what do you want with Tarkyn?" she demanded. As an afterthought, she added, "I am Ancient Elm."

The sorcerer coughed as some of the water went down the wrong way. Instantly the woodwoman flicked back several feet watching him through narrowed eyes.

"Sorry," said the bound man when he finally caught his breath. "I just choked on the water. That's all. I can't do anything to anyone tied like this, I promise you."

"I think that is probably true. Tarkyn told the forestal woodfolk that he could not use magic with his hands tied behind him. So it must be true. We trust Tarkyn." Ancient Elm squatted down in front of him, "Who are you and what is so important that you would risk your life to contact him?"

"I am called Boravar. I have been living in the Forest of Yesterday Today and Tomorrow, the place you call the Lost Forest, for over one hundred years. A week ago, Prince Tarkyn released us all from the Forest, sorcerers and woodfolk alike, all of us who had been unable to leave."

Ancient Elm frowned, "How do you know of woodfolk? And knowing of woodfolk, why are you still alive?"

"I have lived side by side with woodfolk for decades in the Lost Forest. And to be allowed to leave the Forest knowing of you, I have sworn an oath of secrecy to Prince Tarkyn."

Ancient Elm stood up and walked over to a group of woodfolk who were looking on. There was a silence laced by expressions of doubt and disapproval.

After a few minutes, Ancient Elm returned and stood staring down at him. "How can we know we can trust you?"

Boravar tried to shrug but the ropes made the movement no more than a small muscle contraction. "I am not asking you to trust me. That's why I told you to tie me up. I just have to get word to Prince Tarkyn."

"We will probably kill you, you know," she said calmly.

Boravar nodded impatiently, "Yes, yes. I understand that. I knew that was probably the cost when I told you that I knew you were there. Just let me live long enough so that you can hear what Tarkyn needs to know."

Ancient Elm nodded, "Agreed. Go on then."

Boravar let out a sigh of relief and began, "King Kosar has found out that Prince Tarkyn will be arriving in this part of the woods soon. He is planning to trap him."

"What! Hold on. Back a bit. How did the king find this out?"

Boravar grimaced, "The sorcerers from the Lost Forest told people about their sojourn in the Forest and how Prince Tarkyn had released them. Everyone in the bars and taverns was agog to meet people from the Lost Forest. They wanted to know what it was like and where we had last seen it. And we told them."

Ancient Elm came forward and grabbed Boravar by the hair and yanked his head back against the tree. "And why, after Tarkyn had helped you, did you all turn on him and betray him?"

Boravar shook his head dolefully, even though his hair was still in Ancient Elm's firm grip. "We didn't know. None of us knew that Prince Tarkyn had been exiled. No one told us to say nothing of him and we were all singing his praises."

"And what about woodfolk? Did they tell everyone about woodfolk too?"

Boravar's eyes widened but he answered steadily, "No. Not a word did any of us breathe."

Ancient Elm yanked his head forward in disgust, before letting go and stalking over to the other woodfolk. A heated but silent discussion took place before she returned.

"So what do you know of this trap the king is planning to spring?"

"Tormadell is humming with Prince Jarand's defeat at Prince Tarkyn's hands. No word of woodfolk, though. They just think the Prince has a band of sorcerers with him in the woods and that he has developed new ways of using shields."

Ancient Elm nodded impatiently, "Go on."

"Hundreds of the King's troops are being sent ahead to infiltrate these forests. Then, in a week's time, the King will enter the forest with a small retinue, apparently to do some hunting. They are expecting Prince Tarkyn to confront the King as he did his brother and when he does, he will find himself surrounded by previously deployed soldiers of the King."

"Yes," said Ancient Elm dryly, "I think it might be helpful to forewarn our young prince, and all of us, if the woods are going to be swarming with sorcerers. Anything else?"

Boroavar grimaced as he wriggled to get comfortable and the ropes cut into him. "Only that they know the Prince can produce a spell while holding his shield up. I don't know what they are planning to do to combat that, but I'm sure they will be working on it."

"Hmph," Ancient Elm returned to the group of woodfolk and for the next half an hour, Boravar was completely ignored as they made plans for relaying the information and preparing woodfolk throughout the forest for the advent of such large numbers of sorcerers.

Finally Ancient Elm came back and stood staring down at him. "Tell me," she said at last, "Has your Prince Tarkyn ever injured a sorcerer and if so, why?"

Boravar bowed his head in embarrassment before remembering Tarkyn's demand that the Lost should not be ashamed. He brought his head back up and met the woodwoman's eyes. "Prince Tarkyn shot a sorcerer just below the knee who was hesitant in showing him the respect owed to him."

"And did it leave a scar?" she asked.

"Yes, it did. It left a mark like a small bull's eye. Three small concentric circles burnt into the skin."

Ancient Elm squatted down next to him and took hold of the bottom of his leggings. "May I look?"

Boravar rolled his eyes, "Yes. It was me and yes, you may look. Not that I can do anything to stop you anyway."

Ancient Elm raised her eyebrows, "I would not be so discourteous as to take advantage of your situation like that." She pulled up his leggings until the peculiar mark was revealed. A few of the other woodfolk gathered around to look too. "Hmph. Well, you are who you say you are. So that is something, I suppose." She pulled the leggings back into place and stood up. "So why would someone who has actually been injured by Tarkyn have any interest in saving him?"

Boravar frowned, "If I hadn't lived among woodfolk for so many years I would boggle in amazement at that question. Prince Tarkyn was kind enough to give me a minimal punishment for failing to give him due respect quickly enough, in a situation where he was almost being threatened by us. He could have had me flogged or crippled me for life if he had chosen to. Instead, all he did was send a short burst of power sufficient to knock my leg out from under me. It hurt badly at the time but the pain didn't last long." He took a minute to catch his breath, as the tightness of the ropes restricted his breathing. "Prince Tarkyn freed us all from the Lost Forest. Why would I turn on him?" He gave a slight smile, "In fact, as you can bear witness, I am willing to die for him."

Ancient Elm shook her head slowly from side to side in amazement, "What is it about that boy that inspires such extravagant devotion?" After a brief silent consultation with the other woodfolk, she turned back to the sorcerer, "We will untie you but you must not leave. If you should attack any of us, or attempt to leave, you will be killed without hesitation. If you try to hold any one of us hostage, we will sacrifice that person rather than sacrifice all of us." She glanced at the others, "Have I covered everything?"

"That *shturrum* spell," prompted a woodman in his late twenties, "I am Leaf Fall."

Ancient Elm turned back to Boravar. "At no time will you be able to see all of us, so the *shturrum* spell that Tarkyn uses to paralyse people will always leave some unaffected and able to kill you. Do you understand?"

Boravar nodded. "I can't do that spell anyway. Not that I expect you to believe me at the moment, but I can't. Very few people can."

"One final thing before we untie you. How did you find out about this plot? It can't be common knowledge or it would defeat the purpose of it."

"True." Boravar grinned, "I tracked down a great great grandson I discovered I had and found that he is in the King's Guard. Luckily, by the time I met him, I already knew about Prince Tarkyn's…predicament. So I feigned resentment at my punishment and showed him my scar." He grimaced, "Not really the best way to renew family relationships, starting out by lying to him. But maybe one day he will understand why I did it."

Leaf Fall and a small nimble woodwoman began to untie the ropes around Boravar as Ancient Elm asked, "And what is the mood among sorcerers in relation to Tarkyn?"

"Turbulent," said Boravar. "That's the only way I can describe it. It caused such a furore when we arrived and told the story of our rescue. You could see the man in the street was all for him but the official line was against him. So, I suppose the opinions expressed depended on who was listening. Beneath the surface there is a groundswell of support but I wouldn't want the prince to fall into the wrong hands. The official line is dogmatic and merciless."

"He will not fall into the wrong hands," said Ancient Elm firmly. "The woodlands are full of people willing to protect him." She hesitated for a moment then patted the big sorcerer on the shoulder before his hands were untied, "We thank you for warning us." She nodded to Leaf Fall and backed away before Boravar's hands came free. From a safe distance away, she offered him more to drink and some food.

Boravar smiled tiredly as he rubbed his wrists, "Mostly, now that I have passed on my message, I want to sleep. I'm exhausted. I don't know what you want to do about my horse. You can leave him tethered but his tracks may lead those who follow, to this clearing."

Leaf Fall shrugged, "Even if it does, they will not find us. They will find the horse but not us."

"But they will know a sorcerer is in the vicinity," said Boravar.

"Does that matter?" asked Ancient Elm. "Have you done anything to arouse suspicion?"

"Only if my great great grandson comes to visit me back in Tormadell. He may find it strange that I have left so soon after finding him…and if he follows those suspicions, that I have some so far so fast." He hesitated, "And I stole the horse."

Leaf Fall grimaced, "Risky, I think. For you. Not for us. I think we had better hide your horse and cover his tracks, at least while you sleep. Then we'll decide what to do next."

"Come this way, Boravar," said Ancient Elm, leading him through a narrow gap deep into the bramble patch. She waved her arm around, "You can sleep in here, safe from discovery. Put your mind at rest. Tarkyn has already been informed of what you have told us. We relayed the information straight away. Now all of us will work out what to do." She gave a slight smile, "It could be a long mind conference. With the threat from the sorcerers being so widespread, hundreds of us will be involved. I will let you know what we decide." Just as she was leaving, she turned back and said, "By the way, Tarkyn sends his thanks, and vouches for your character. None of us here is under oath to him but he is a forest guardian and a woodman, so we respect what he says."

Boravar was pleased, "I am honoured that the prince thinks well enough of me to vouch for me."

Ancient Elm rolled her eyes as she left, "You sorcerers!"

CHAPTER 33

"I know where we are," said Tarkyn triumphantly. "We are right back at the place where I recovered from my fall from the oak tree." He pointed to a huge tangled stand of brambles, "And my shelter is in there." He swung his arm around to his left, "And the river where we killed all those wolves and where I met the otter and the owl and the old man of the river is just down there. And the heron," he added as an afterthought.

"Who's the old man of the river?"

Tarkyn grinned at Harkell's confusion. "He's an enormous golden fish, I don't know what sort. I exchanged images with him last time we were here. This is where I first learnt that I could communicate with birds and animals."

"And where we discovered that Tarkyn was a forest guardian," said Waterstone. He smiled in reminiscence. "Stormaway and I were stunned, and Tarkyn was horrified. He thought that he couldn't be one, because he would have to be old and grey."

"Hmph," grunted Tarkyn. "I'll have you know I was more or less right about that. All the other Guardians started much later in life, they told me." He looked around at the bare trees and walked up to study one or two of them closely. "Look Waterstone. They are all beginning to bud and there is no sign of the damage to them."

In response to Harkell's frown of enquiry, Waterstone explained reluctantly, "Our oath to Tarkyn used to be tied to the forest's welfare. Early on, I was angry about something and when I behaved threateningly to Tarkyn, the forest suffered for it." He shrugged unhappily. "These particular trees may be all right, but many were damaged beyond repair."

"That was why I first gave Waterstone permission to attack me," said Tarkyn, with a wry smile. "To stop the damage to the forest."

Thunder Storm gave a deep chuckle, "And if you thought Waterstone was angry the other day, you should have seen him on the day the forest was damaged. Tarkyn had to use his *shturrum* spell and his shield to protect himself."

Harkell shook his head, "I'm amazed Tarkyn didn't just kill him out of hand, especially if it was early on in your acquaintance."

"Waterstone's anger was justified, Harkell." Tarkyn looked a little shame-faced. "When I saw my brothers for the first time since my exile, I inadvertently knocked out Sparrow with a mindblast of emotion."

"Oh. I see." Harkell lapsed into a thoughtful silence. After a while, he looked up to find Tarkyn watching him quizzically. He smiled in return, "Just trying to make sense of it all, really. The concept of justified anger is fine amongst most of the population. But I have never known anyone to escape punishment from a member of the Royal Family because his or her anger was justified, let alone be rewarded for it by being granted indemnity against future occurrences."

"But then, you have not known Tarkyn before," said Lapping Water gently.

"And Waterstone did not escape punishment, Harkell." Tarkyn shook his head ruefully, "Just as I am tied to Eskuzor's future, so is Waterstone tied to the welfare of the forest. When the forest suffered, so did he."

"And yet, the other day…" Harkell shook his head perplexed.

"The other day, I already had Tarkyn's permission. The rules had changed," explained Waterstone.

"No. That is not what I was going to say. I was going to say, 'And yet the other day, despite Tarkyn's generosity …'" Harkell's eyes flickered around the gathered woodfolk before waving his hand dismissively. "No. Forget it. I just don't understand well enough yet."

Waterstone frowned, "No. Go on. We will all learn better by discussing it."

Harkell took a deep breath, "Except for Stormaway and Danton, none of you has any experience of living around royalty. You have had a tiny taste of Jarand's style. That is the expected behaviour of the Royal Family. You have no idea how generously Tarkyn is behaving towards you all. Waterstone, you may have cringed with embarrassment at witnessing the Lost giving Tarkyn his due. But that is his due. He did not deserve to be taken down a peg or two by having a mistake exposed in public. He was not puffing up his consequence. That is his consequence."

Harkell's soft brown eyes flitted around his audience. He noticed Tarkyn had withdrawn and was sitting quietly against a tree, breaking pieces off a long stick. He could feel tension in the air but it was not threatening. As no one spoke, he continued, "And it nearly broke my heart to watch Tarkyn apologise to all of you to make the peace, when in truth, it was your lack of care for him that caused the situation in the first place." He waved a hand and said in exasperation, "Don't you see? He apologised to you when it was his right to do to you what Jarand did to me, for failing to serve him well." He waved his hand again, "And all this aside, how could you set up a young nineteen-year-old to face that level of public outcry?" He shook his head, "I'm sorry. I knew I should not have spoken. I feel too strongly about it to speak dispassionately."

There was a protracted silence. Harkell sat down on a stump, put his elbows on his knees and ran both hands through his hair but said nothing further.

"No. You should have spoken," said Tree Wind quietly. "Waterstone is right. We will learn better by discussing it. And I begin to see that, in the Lost Forest, watching people give Tarkyn that obeisance crystallised the dread we had all had in the past that we might have been required to do likewise."

Melting Snow's face lit with understanding, "That's right. And remember I said that in the Lost Forest, you will face your greatest fears and how you deal with them will determine whether you leave weaker or stronger."

Tree Wind nodded and gave a wry smile, "Well, I don't think we dealt with our fears very well in that instance. I don't know about individuals but I think the bonds between us have weakened and I hope, Harkell, that your brave words will begin to repair the damage."

She turned to the prince, "Tarkyn." She waited until he raised his eyes from his stick before continuing, "I realise now that, faced with the behaviours you could impose, we…I don't know …forced you into proving yourself. We allowed a very difficult situation to develop instead of giving you the support you deserve from, and are owed by, us. I apologise wholeheartedly." She smiled, "And not because I fear any retribution which Harkell says you could feel justified in meting out. I know you are not like your brother. But we all forget sometimes that it is only your choice that determines that you are not."

Tarkyn threw away his stick, "Tree Wind, I don't particularly want you to remember that all the time. I just want to know that I can depend on your support. After what happened in the Forest, I don't feel as sure of that as I did. In fact, I don't feel sure of it at all." He sighed, "I suppose what you did to me embodied my fear of betrayal, at least to some extent. I don't know whether dealing with it has made me weaker or stronger. I would say, on the whole, weaker. I feel less sure now, more concerned that I will make another oversight that will land me in a similar situation." He gave a wry smile. "Despite what Harkell said, I do know there was fault on my part and I should have realised what was going to happen. But I didn't. That's why I need to be able to depend on all of you. Sometimes I am strong, even fearsome, but I am not as strong or as clever or as knowledgeable as the sum total of all of us."

There was an out of focus silence while the woodfolk conferred. Then, as one, they placed their hands on their hearts while Tree Wind spoke for them, "Tarkyn, we re-avow our support of you. We will not wilfully withhold information from you in future or demand more of you than you are willing or able to give. And we will remind you rather than wait to see whether you remember, when it is important." She smiled, "Ancient Oak is right. You are a woodman, just as you are. No two of us are exactly alike. So we are all proud to have you as one of us, just as you are."

Tarkyn's face relaxed into a warm smile. "Thanks." He placed his own hand on his heart and let his eyes rove slowly over them; Rainstorm with a slight grin on his face, Lapping Water, her eyes shining, Summer Rain, serious as always, Waterstone meeting his eyes squarely, Ancient Oak smiling wryly, having supported Tarkyn staunchly throughout, Falling Rain, his gaze full of their shared memories, Sparrow trying to look solemn, Midnight, not really sure why he was doing it but happy to show his devotion to Tarkyn at any time of the night or day, Thunder Storm, Autumn Leaves and every single woodman and woman, all meaning something different and important to him. When he had acknowledged the gaze of every one of them, he said "I am deeply touched that, of your own free will, you should give me such a gesture, when I know you find it so unnatural." He grimaced, "I think every one of us was put through the wringer in some way in that blasted Forest. I can't say I'm looking forward to returning to it after my death." He gave a little smile, "So you and I will have to make sure I live to a ripe old age to avoid it as long as possible."

Chapter 34

It was not long after this that the first message came through from Ancient Elm. Several people picked it up but Waterstone had become the traditional go-between and so it was he who approached Tarkyn with the news. He did not look happy.

"Tarkyn, I'm afraid there has been another oversight," he shook his head, "which I'm sure could have been avoided if we had been working together properly." He put his hand on Tarkyn's shoulder, "All I can do is say that we are sorry."

"We have had enough recriminations. It is time to move on. We are where we are." Tarkyn patted Waterstone's hand and the woodman took his hand away. "So, what other vital piece of information did we miss?"

Waterstone grimaced, "None of the Lost realised that you had been exiled."

"Oh." Suddenly, Tarkyn's face split into a grin, "I wonder whether they would have been quite so obsequious if they had known."

Waterstone gave a short laugh, "I don't think it would have made the slightest difference. Whether I approve of it or not, you have amazing presence when you decide to use it."

Tarkyn gave a little smile of acknowledgement before asking, "So what has been the upshot of this oversight?"

"They have been singing your praises from pillar to post and letting people know where the Lost Forest was when they came out and therefore where you will be," said Waterstone in a rush.

"Oh good."

Despite himself, Waterstone smiled.

"And how do we know this?" asked Tarkyn.

"A sorcerer walked into the woods and gave himself up to the woodfolk. Well, actually, he rode into the woods but dismounted before letting the woodfolk know that he knew of their presence. As far as I can make out, he's that big fellow who did most of the talking, Boravar."

Tarkyn raised his eyebrows, "And has he survived the encounter?"

Waterstone shot him a glance, "Yes. So far. He is trussed up to a tree with hands tied behind him. At his request, apparently, so that he could get word to you."

"I see. Anything else?"

"They want to have some proof that we know him."

Tarkyn frowned, "Can't you just verify the images of him?"

"They are a long way away. Words travel better than images. By the time the image has been transferred through several people, it may have changed depending on each person's perceptions. He looks more or less like Boravar to me but I can't be sure."

"I wounded him, you know. There should be a mark on his leg; three concentric circles."

Waterstone looked at him frowning, "Out of everything that happened, you resorting to violence surprised me the most. I didn't think you would need to. I thought you would have been able to quell them, just with your presence."

The prince looked at him for a moment, "I could have, had I persevered. But to tell you the truth, I didn't have the patience to bother. I was feeling a bit rattled at the time and just wanted to get things sorted out quickly. I didn't do him any lasting damage, except for the little scar, and even that will fade over time." He frowned, "But we digress. What is the upshot of everyone knowing my whereabouts?"

"Well," Waterstone stopped and looked uncertainly at his friend, "Well, if we handle it properly, it will be to our advantage."

"I see," said Tarkyn in a voice that clearly said that he didn't see at all but wished he did by now.

"Your brother Kosar is setting a trap for you. He is sending hundreds of troops ahead to secrete themselves within the forest. Then he plans to enter the woods early next week, ostensibly on a hunting trip, using himself as bait to lure you into a position where his troops can surround you." The woodman watched Tarkyn anxiously for his reaction.

Tarkyn ran his hand through his hair and sighed, "Why do I struggle to be objective about this? It's not as though I don't know he's after me." After a moment, he pulled himself together, "Never mind. Go on. Anything else?"

"Boravar says they know you can hold your shield and do another spell at the same time. So he thinks they will be working out how to counter it."

A look of irritation crossed Tarkyn's face, "I shouldn't have been so keen to show Jarand, should I?"

Danton came in on this last remark and smiled reassuringly, "They would know anyway. Don't forget Journeyman. He would have told everyone when he returned. In fact, you knew that when you showed Jarand." He frowned, "Stop getting so down on yourself, Tarkyn. You don't usually overlook things, and you didn't with Jarand."

Tarkyn smiled wryly. "True," he said shortly and went on to talk with everyone about tactics.

But this little interchange, more than anything else, showed Waterstone the damage that had been done to Tarkyn's self-assurance.

CHAPTER 35

When Boravar awoke, he found a mug of berry juice and a plate of cold meat and dried fruits had been placed inside the shelter for him. He sat up and, propping his elbows on his knees, ran his hands back and forth through his hair to wake himself up. When eventually he wandered outside, he found his horse saddled up and tethered to a nearby tree. He inspected the saddlebags and discovered that they had been filled with provisions. There was no sign whatsoever of the woodfolk.

Heaving a sigh, he walked to his horse's head and stroked his nose. The horse tossed his head and nudged firmly at the sorcerer's pocket.

"Sorry, old fella. I don't have any treats for you." Boravar smiled fondly. "Just a minute." The burly sorcerer wandered over to a stand of succulent green grass and pulled up a few handfuls. He chatted quietly to the horse as he fed him, "I know you can get this grass yourself if I lead you over to it, but it's the best I can do at the moment."

The horse seemed quite grateful, nevertheless, and munched it contentedly. Boravar stroked the side of his neck and scratched him behind his ear. He gave him a couple of final pats and sighed, "Well, I guess that's it. I've delivered my message and they've disappeared on me. I suppose I return to Tormadell." He shrugged, "Fair enough, I suppose." He frowned, "Hmm, but didn't Ancient Elm say I wasn't to leave? But what happens if they have left me?" He glanced around the surrounding trees, pretty sure that someone would be watching him but unable to see any sign of them.

After a bit of thought, he untied the horse and led him over to where he could graze. Then Boravar sat down and waited.

And waited.

And waited.

By late morning, the enforced inaction was beginning to grate on him.

Suddenly a pattering voice spoke to him from somewhere above, "Don't look up. There is a lone soldier nearby. You had better have a story ready for him. We are sorry we left you for so long. We did not intend to be discourteous or to test you. We have been preoccupied with preparing for the advent of so many soldiers, especially if they mean to secrete themselves. That means that we have to go one level deeper, if you see what I mean. I think we'll be spending a lot of time in trees over the next week. We thank you for your warning."

"A pleasure."

"What's a pleasure? And who are you talking to?"

Boravar swung his head around to find a black clad soldier standing on the other side of the clearing. "It is a pleasure to be sitting here in these beautiful woodlands without any need to rush anywhere." He achieved a self-conscious smile, "And as to who I am talking to, I am talking to myself."

The soldier scowled at him, only half convinced, but since he had not had contact with woodfolk, he had not recognised Leaf Fall's voice for what it was. "Who are you?" he asked peremptorily, after a moment's scrutiny. "And where are you heading?"

"Sir, my name is Boravar and I am heading nowhere. As I said, I have no need to rush anywhere."

"Have a care, Boravar, you are beginning to try my patience." The wiry soldier moved with cat-like grace across the clearing to stand looking down appraisingly at the big sorcerer.

Boravar inclined his head in apology, "I did not mean to be obtuse. I am one of those who has recently returned from the Forest of Yesterday Today and Tomorrow. I have lost touch with my previous life and have not yet decided what I will do with myself."

The soldier raised his eyebrows, "Are you? That's interesting." In one fluid movement, he sat down cross-legged next to Boravar. "Let me introduce myself. My name is Petrand Closkaril."

Boravar inclined his head, "It is an honour, sir. You must be one of the elite. And are you also a lord?"

The elite guard's mouth quirked, "Of course. But I did not think it relevant to our exchange."

Boravar considered him thoughtfully, trying to work out whether the omission had been because he did not consider Boravar of sufficient importance to warrant a full introduction or whether the man was inclined towards egalitarianism.

Reading his thoughts, Petrand added, "My title matters at court. My name matters at work."

Boravar gave a slight smile, "I can see the logic in that. And, if I may ask, what is an elite soldier doing out here in the middle of the forest?"

The soldier's eyes narrowed as he tried to surmise the burly sorcerer's motivation for the question. It was well known that people from the Forest of Yesterday Today and Tomorrow felt grateful to Prince Tarkyn for their release. After a moment, he opted for partial honesty. "I am trying to track down the Rogue Prince. I have heard the talk of his return to this area and have been commissioned to find him."

He received partial honesty in return.

"I am not surprised," said Boravar. "I would have expected some response to all the new information being thrown around by the Lost sorcerers."

Petrand frowned, "Why do you call yourselves lost?"

With a jolt, Boravar realised that other people would not know the woodfolk name for the Forest of Yesterday Today and Tomorrow. "Because we were lost in that forest, some of us for decades and now we have found our way out…or rather Prince Tarkyn found a way to release us."

The elite guard folded his arms. "So presumably you could lead me to the place where you left this strange forest?"

Boravar bent down and picked up a couple of pebbles to fiddle with, to give himself time to think. He lifted his head to look at the soldier. "Yes, I possibly could. Two things I would say to you, though. Firstly, the Forest of Yesterday Today and Tomorrow will no longer be there and secondly it may already have moved by the time Prince Tarkyn left it several days after us."

Petrand raised his eyebrows, "And would you lead me to the Prince if you could?"

Boravar gave his head a little shake, "No. I would avoid leading you to him at all costs."

"What if I had you taken back into Tormadell and questioned?"

Boravar shrugged, "I cannot stop you, if that is what you choose to do. I can only hope that I would endure your torture. I would rather die than betray him." He tossed the little pebbles up and down and watched them for a moment before bringing his eyes back to the soldier's face. "Nevertheless, what I told you about the Forest is true. Its location moves. You need complicated wizardry to find it unless it decides to find you. And I honestly do not know whether the prince came back into this forest at the same place that we Lost sorcerers did."

Petrand studied him through narrowed eyes, "So, do you know where Prince Tarkyn is?"

Boravar gave a little smile, "In all honesty, I can say that I don't."

"That is what you would say though, isn't it?"

The burly sorcerer grimaced, "Probably. I might say that I know but won't tell you, but I suppose that would be a little foolhardy, wouldn't it?"

"Nearly as foolhardy as telling me that you wouldn't betray him."

Boravar tossed four stones up in the air and started to juggle them. After a while, he caught them all and looked at Petrand's surprise with a wry grin, "I had a lot of time to practice in the L… Forest of Yesterday Today and Tomorrow." He smiled, "I'll tell you what. If you like, I can tell you how to get to the place where we returned to this forest. For the reasons I just explained, I don't think it will help you but it might help me to avoid being tortured and it won't affect Prince Tarkyn." He shrugged, "Since I genuinely don't know where he is, that's the best I can offer, anyway."

"No, not quite the best you can offer. You can offer to come with me."

Alarm flared briefly in Boravar's eyes as he thought of the consequences of leaving the woodfolk.

Seeing it, Petrand's eyes narrowed, "What awaits me where you would send me? You are luring me into a trap." His mouth thinned, "But you have given yourself away. Wherever I go, I will take you with me for surety." His lips stretched into a humourless smile, "Now, would you like to rethink the directions you were about to give me?"

Boravar was big, heavy and strong but he was not naturally a fighting man. Assuming that the elite guard had other soldiers at his command, he offered no physical resistance, glumly resigning himself to death at the hands of the woodfolk once he left their firesite. He had, after all, already come to terms with dying to warn Tarkyn.

But after a moment, his natural sense of self-preservation asserted itself and urged him to make a one last-ditch stand. "Petrand, your training has made you unnaturally suspicious. How could I have set a trap for you when I did not expect to meet you?"

The elite guard shrugged, "You could have an ambush set up for anyone who comes that way under your directions."

"I could have an ambush set up for anyone who comes that way in my company," countered Boravar.

"Hmm. True." Petrand thought for a while. "Then we will have to make sure that your life depends on mine, won't we?" Before Boravar had time to respond, he asked, "How long will it take to reach this place?"

"Half a day, a day at the most, riding. Best part of two days walking."

Petrand nodded with satisfaction and drew out a small phial from within his black jacket. When he had taken out the stopper, he unsheathed his dagger and dipped the point of it carefully into the dark blue liquid inside. Then he calmly re-corked the phial and returned it to his pocket. In a sudden movement, before the big sorcerer knew what was coming, Petrand had scored Boravrar's forearm with the tip of his blade.

"There," said the elite guard calmly. "My insurance"

Boravar sucked at his arm as the blood swelled up along the cut. "What the blazes do you think you're doing?" he demanded between sucks.

"I have poisoned you," replied Petrand calmly. "Whether you take it in through your blood stream or your saliva matters little."

Boravar spat out as much of the blood as he could.

Petrand grunted, "Too late. You now have about five days to live. You see? I have been generous. I have built in some time for contingencies. When you have delivered me safely to see where your Forest disappeared, I will give you the antidote. Before that, if I die, so too do you."

"You have an over-inflated idea of your own importance," growled Boravar. "Why would I have any vested interest in killing you? If you fall, I have no doubt there will be other loyal guardsmen ready to take your place in the hunt for Prince Tarkyn."

Petrand raised his eyebrows, quite unmoved, "Perhaps. But I did not become an elite guard by taking unnecessary chances."

Boravar glowered at him as he stood up and went to un-tether his horse. "We had better go then." He thought of the woodfolk and muttered to himself, "Not that it is likely to make much difference to me, one way or the other."

The elite guard's hearing was acute. "And why not?"

Boravar glanced sharply at him as he hastily invented to cover his slip. "Because I do not yet have much to live for, in this new world in which I find myself."

Petrand watched him thoughtfully as the big sorcerer gathered the horse's reins and turned to walk with the soldier out of the clearing, "I see. And how long were you in that strange forest?"

"I am not completely sure but I think about one hundred and twenty years. King Lukazor was on the throne when I left."

The soldier's eyes widened. "So everyone you knew is no longer. And now, when you have been back for less than a fortnight, I have given you only five days to live." He shook his head and said spuriously. "It seems such a waste, doesn't it?"

Boravar grunted but did not reply.

A little further down the track, Petrand asked, "And do you have any descendants or relatives?"

The big sorcerer smiled slightly, "I have a great great grandson in the Royal Guard…Hmm, there might be another great in there, I'm not sure… which was a surprise to me since I was unaware that I had sired any children at all."

"Indeed? So were you a feckless man in your previous life?"

Boravar considered, "No. I would not say that. But I did not stay anywhere for long. I might have, if I had realised that I had fathered a child, but the Forest claimed me before I knew."

All the time they were talking, the space between Boravar's shoulder blades crawled in anticipation of an arrow in the back. After a while, when it didn't come, he realised that the woodfolk would wait to kill him at a time when they would not give themselves away. He breathed a small sigh of relief at his temporary reprieve.

"You seem a bit edgy," observed Petrand.

"Oh really?" said Boravar sarcastically, turning the tables. "No doubt you think I should feel calm about being poisoned." He glanced at his poisoner, "What symptoms should I expect? Will I gradually sicken or will it be sudden?"

"The poison takes a while to start taking effect. You might start to notice your vision blurring a little by the end of tomorrow. By the morning of the next day, you may begin to feel areas of numbness and find yourself a little clumsier than usual. But don't worry. We should be there before then, shouldn't we?" said the wiry soldier cheerfully.

Boravar trudged along in silence for a while, thinking that he was likely to be dead long before that, anyway. He had seen how rigidly the woodfolk adhered to their codes and he did not expect any mercy from them. Eventually he roused himself to ask, "How will you know that I have led you to the right spot?" Then he shook his head slightly at his stupidity in asking that question.

Petrand smiled, "Yes, not very clever, was it? But to answer your question; I am a skilled tracker. I should be able to find signs of so large a group appearing out of nowhere."

Boaravar nodded slowly, wondering if the prince's and his small group of sorcerers' tracks might also be visible. "Yes, that is true. You should. Provided we don't have a deluge between now and then." As he spoke, he decided that the woodfolk would obscure the prince's tracks and their own, leaving only the prints of the Lost sorcerers. He straightened and smiled, confident that the prince would be safe from discovery. "It should be all right."

Petrand looked at him but said nothing more until they broke sometime later for lunch. As Boravar rummaged through the saddle bags for some food, Petrand nodded at the horse and asked, "And how did you come to afford such a fine animal?"

Boravar had been dreading this question. The penalties for horse theft were severe. But he had had time now to concoct a reply, "In the Forest of Yesterday Today and Tomorrow, there was nothing to spend money on. So I left with my pockets full of the money I went in with. When I reached Tormadell, I discovered that my money is now regarded as antique coins. So I exchanged some of my coins for quite considerable sums. Hence the horse."

"I would almost believe you, Boravar, if the saddle weren't inscribed with the initials of one of my fellow guards."

"Blast it!" exclaimed Boravar without much heat. Still he offered the guard no violence and made no attempt to get away, sure that he would be dead soon anyway at the hands of the woodfolk. "It's true about the coins though," he said with a wry smile.

Petrand studied him, "Do you know, I don't think you are naturally dishonest. So there must have been a pressing reason for you to steal my friend's horse."

"What are you going to do about it?" asked Boravar resignedly.

"I don't know yet. Since you did not leave my friend stranded, the theft may not warrant the death penalty in this case." Petrand gave a delicate shrug. "Besides, if I say that I will take you back to stand trial, you may not consider it worth your while to continue to cooperate with me."

"On the other hand, you may say one thing now, and another when you have what you want anyway," observed Boravar dryly as he sat down to eat a bowlful of nuts and dried berries. He offered the bowl to the soldier. "Do you want some? I have more in the saddle bag if you do."

Petrand scooped a handful out of the bowl. "Thank you," he said with a smile. He sat down opposite the big sorcerer and watched him closely as he ate. "There is something not quite right here. I've poisoned you and now I'm considering taking you back to stand trial. Yet, having just said you don't trust my word, you offer to share your food with me?"

"I have not said I don't trust your word. You haven't given it to me. You have said that you will give me the antidote but you haven't given me your word on it."

"My point nevertheless stands. There is something unnervingly fatalistic about you."

Boravar had no intention of telling him the real reason for his fatalism. He shrugged and gave a slow smile, "Perhaps when, or should I say *if*, you ever reach the age of one hundred and forty-something as I have, you may begin to take things more in your stride."

"Hmm. You don't look that old. You don't look more than thirty. But even if you are that old, I don't think that is the reason. And why did you steal the horse?" The tight wiry guard waved his hand, "No. Don't bother coming up with another story. I'll just think about it myself for a while."

A few minutes later, he cocked his head at Boravar and said thoughtfully, "Whatever the reason, it no longer exists." Boravar tried to show no reaction but the soldier wasn't looking for one. "You were in such a hurry to get to these forests that you stole a horse but when I came upon you, you were taking your leisure and were in no hurry to go anywhere." He stared straight at the heavy sorcerer. "So whatever your mission was, you had accomplished it."

He slowly ate the rest of his fruit and nuts, deep in thought. Eventually, he raised his head, "You have a relative in the Royal Guard, do you not?" When Boravar nodded warily, he continued, "You came to warn the prince, didn't you? You know what is being planned. And now you are calmly leading me away from where he is based." He raised his eyebrows, "I applaud you. Not many people can lead me astray like that."

Boravar gave his head a little shake in amazement that the guard could get so close in his reasoning and yet end up with the wrong conclusion because of incomplete information.

Misinterpreting Boravar's reaction, Petrand said sharply, "There is no point in continuing with this farce. We will return forthwith to the clearing where I first saw you. Then… then I should be able to pick up his tracks from there." He frowned, "Hmm. Now what to do about you? By your own admission, you are a traitor, one of the Rogue Prince's sympathisers. By stealing that horse, you have willingly risked your life to bring him warning…"

You don't know the half of it, thought Boravar.

"Hmm. Now I am going to have to get word back to Tormadell that the prince has been forewarned. You are a pest, aren't you?" Petrand smiled in a friendly fashion. "I know you'll die in a few days anyway but you could get in my way far too much in the meantime. It does seem such a waste after so short a time out of that forest, doesn't it?" He shrugged, "But I'm afraid that's just the way it goes."

He stood up slowly and then, in one fluid motion, unsheathed his knife and flicked it straight at the unsuspecting sorcerer. Boravar reeled backwards, his shoulder searing with pain. He looked down to see the hilt of the dagger sticking out of the muscle just below his collarbone. He frowned slightly in surprise that Petrand had not killed him outright. As he braced himself for further attack, he realised that Petrand lay in a crumpled heap where he had stood, an arrow sticking out of his back.

A lithe figure swung down out of the trees, bow slung over his shoulder, and picked up an arrow that had landed on the ground near Boravar.

"Sorry I couldn't deflect his throw completely. Best I could do, I'm afraid," said Leaf Fall.

Despite the pain he was in, Boravar's eyes widened. "Did you hit his knife with your arrow?"

Leaf Fall nodded. "I couldn't put enough force into it, though, to knock it completely off target. Sorry about that."

Boravar sat down suddenly as physical and mental shock combined, and said in a dazed voice, "I thought you were going to kill me because I had left against your express instructions. I waited for an arrow in the back all morning until I realised you wouldn't risk exposure." He grinned weakly, "The last thing I expected was that you would rescue me." Gradually his face fell, "But now Petrand can't tell us the antidote and I will die slowly instead from his poison anyway."

"No you won't," said Leaf Fall bracingly. "We have his phial of poison, we have skilled healers and even more than these, we have our forest guardian. We won't let you die."

"But I think we had better do something about that dagger if you are to live long enough to get to the forest guardian." A bouncy young woodwoman with frizzy hair and twinkling eyes placed a wad of cloth to his shoulder, "Hi, I am Twig Snap but you can just call me Twig if you like."

Leaf Fall grinned at her, "She is looking pleased with herself because it has been her life's ambition to kill a sorcerer and finally the need has arisen."

Boravar's vision was starting to blur. He wondered whether it was the poison kicking in early or just loss of blood. With an effort he concentrated on the conversation and asked the woodwoman, "So were you hoping to shoot me too?"

Twig Snap laughed, "No. We knew you had no choice about leaving the clearing. We have been with you every step of the way."

She nodded to Leaf Fall, who carefully pulled out the dagger while she held the padding firmly over the wound. He rubbed pungent, powdered leaves into the wound, making Boravar gasp in pain.

"Sorry. It won't hurt for long. These leaves are anaesthetic and antiseptic," said Leaf Fall apologetically.

Twig Snap met the woodman's eyes briefly before saying firmly to the suffering sorcerer, "Now, Boravar, concentrate on what I'm saying." Boravar nodded weakly and did his best to listen. "Tarkyn asked us, and we agreed, to accept you as a friend of the woodfolk. We accept your word that you will not betray our presence, and acknowledge your courage in risking your life to warn us of the plot against Tarkyn."

Her voice wafted on, carefully distracting Boravar while Leaf Fall rubbed the leaf powder into and round the wound and then bound it tightly and fashioned a sling for the big man. Boravar felt himself slipping away. The world seemed to be fading into the distance. Then Twig Snap's insistent voice gradually brought him back.

"Boravar, you can't stay here. We are too close to the forest's edge. And you are much too heavy to lift."

He felt his cheeks sting as she slapped him sharply. He frowned, "Ow! What was that for?"

The bouncy woodwoman tugged at his other arm, "You have to get up. Come on. Get yourself up and we will help you onto your horse. It's not safe here. We have to go."

"All right. All right," grumbled the big sorcerer, forcing himself back to full consciousness. "You're a tough little thing, aren't you?"

He rolled onto his right side so that he could use his good right arm to push himself up, while the two woodfolk pushed him up from the back. Once up, he stood there swaying for a minute with the woodfolk holding him on either side to keep him from falling over.

"I don't feel too good," he said woozily. "Maybe I should just sit down for a while before we go."

"No!" chorused the woodfolk.

"Now, come on Boravar," urged Twig Snap. "Once you're up on your horse, you can rest."

"Good point." The powdered leaves, the poison and the loss of blood had combined to make him feel drunk. He swayed his way over to the horse and stood beside it looking up at the saddle. "Hmm. That's a long way up, isn't it? How am I going to get up there using only one hand?"

Leaf Fall looked around and spotted a tree stump a short distance away. "Lead your horse over there and you can step up onto that stump and from there onto your horse."

Boravar eyed the stump suspiciously and swayed. "I still have to get up onto the stump." He gave an unhappy little grunt, "And my shoulder is *hurting*."

"Boravar, you are pathetic," said Twig Snap severely. "I thought you were big and brave and strong."

Boravar raised his eyebrows rather clumsily, "That was before I was wounded. Now I am much smaller."

The sorcerer seemed to find this exquisitely funny. When the other two did not join him in his mirth, he pulled himself together, "Oh, all right. So serious, aren't we?" He tottered over to the stump, "I think I will have to mount from the wrong side. I will need my good right arm on the pommel of the saddle to haul myself up."

When they had lined the horse up next to the stump, Boravar made it up onto the stump by pulling himself up using the saddle and being pushed by two determined woodfolk. From there, still holding onto the pommel, he just swung his leg over and thumped down onto the saddle. The horse rolled its eyes and sidled, while Boravar went white as his arrival in the saddle jolted his shoulder.

"Oh! Ow! This is no fun at all." He swayed before collapsing forward over the horse's neck.

Only Leaf Fall's grasp on his right sleeve stopped him from toppling out of the saddle altogether. "Quickly, Twig. Get some rope. We're going to have to tie him on. I'll hold him while you tie."

Since woodfolk are not expert with horses, Boravar had ropes coming off him in all directions by the time they felt sure that he was securely fastened. They surveyed their handiwork critically.

Leaf Fall shrugged, "Not good for a quick getaway but at least he won't fall off." He took the horse's rein and began to lead it along the forest track, "Come on. We'd better get going. These woods are going to be swarming with sorcerers soon."

"What are we going to do about him?" asked Twig Snap, jerking her thumb in the direction of the dead soldier.

"Leave him where he is. You've got your arrow back. So there is nothing to give us away. Could have been brigands, for all anyone would know."

Suddenly a deep slurred noise began to emit loudly from the half conscious sorcerer.

Leaf Fall and Twig Snap looked at each other.

"Oh no!" exclaimed Twig Snap. "He's singing! Knock him out or gag him?"

"Knock him out, I think. At least until we get away from this track." Leaf Fall grinned, "Go on. You do it. I can see you're dying to."

Twig Snap grinned back and after taking careful aim with her slingshot, shot the wounded sorcerer neatly in the head. The singing stopped abruptly.

"What a lovely day you're having," observed Leaf Fall, smiling, "Two sorcerers in one day! Such a bloodthirsty little thing you are!"

"No, I'm not." Twig Snap looked a little hurt. When Leaf Fall just raised his eyebrows, she conceded, "Well, perhaps just a bit when it comes to sorcerers." She grinned again. "Actually, I am probably much more bloodthirsty than I ever get the chance to be… but only about sorcerers, of course. Anyway, both shots today were to protect that great hulk tied to the horse. So my motives were completely pure."

Leaf Fall put a fond arm around her shoulder. "Come on, Sis. Let's get our great hulk off into safety. These woods are going to be crawling soon and I think he may need our forest guardian's intercession. He's pretty far gone. Maybe there was more poison on that blade. Loss of blood doesn't account for his behaviour and neither do the symptoms described by that despicable man."

Chapter 36

For several hours, the two woodfolk led their charge through the deep woodlands, taking it in turns to cover their tracks as they went. Sometimes this slowed them up considerably because the horse left such deep, clear prints. When Boravar came round, they gave him water and tried to feed him but he complained of feeling sick and refused most of the food offered to him. As the light faded, they debated whether to stop for the night or keep going. In the end, the thought of getting Boravar down and then back up onto the horse persuaded them to continue.

But two hours later Boravar roused himself to say, "I can see why you have decided not to stop but I'm afraid you're going to have to. My bladder can't possibly last all night."

Leaf Fall and Twig Snap looked at each other.

"Blast it!" exclaimed Twig Snap unsympathetically. "What a nuisance you are!"

"Sorry," said Boravar meekly. "I'll try to do a better job of getting back up this time. I'm feeling a bit better than I was."

Leaf Fall peered at him through the dimness of late evening. "You don't look too good but maybe the shock has worn off."

A complicated half hour ensued. By the time Boravar was reinstated on his horse, he was sweating and shaky.

"Don't worry, Boravar. Sleep if you can," said Twig Snap more kindly. "We will reach the forest guardian and his home guard by morning."

Boravar subsided onto the horse's neck.

Through the long hours of the night they led the great horse with its sick burden unerringly through tiny woodland paths, always covering their tracks and resting as seldom as possible. In the early dawn, they stopped for a brief snack but the sounds of Boravar's laboured breathing made it an uneasy meal.

As they neared the home guard's firesite, Twig Snap said thoughtfully, "I wonder what this forest guardian is like?"

"Yeah, interesting. Ancient Elm is the only person I know who has met him."

"She seemed quite taken with him. She said he's huge… but he can't be bigger than this great hulk," said Twig Snap, jerking her thumb over her shoulder at Boravar.

"No, couldn't be. But someone told me that this Tarkyn character threw a woodman up into the air and the poor chap had nightmares for months. So we'll have to watch what we say to him."

Twig Snap's eyes narrowed, "He'd better not try anything on me. I will ping him with my trusty slingshot!"

Leaf Fall rolled his eyes. "No, you won't. You're not allowed to hurt forest guardians. Definitely not."

Twig Snap gave a cheeky grin. "I wouldn't hurt him, exactly. Just knock him out for a bit."

"NO!"

Twig Snap laughed, delighted to have wound her brother up.

Now, through the trees, they could see people moving around. They passed beneath Thunder Storm, standing lookout in the trees above them. They sent him a greeting before stopping just within the treeline to study their destination.

"Look," said Twig Snap quietly. "There are more sorcerers out there. Look, there's one with pale yellow hair and another with very dark brown hair."

"And over there, look at them. They have to be trappers. They're dressed like woodfolk trappers but bigger. None of them is as big as Boravar though."

Twig Snap folded her arms, "Well, I'm not going out there. There are sorcerers everywhere. Look. There's another one in a long green robe."

"He looks quite old." Just then the man in question turned around and a look of recognition crossed Leaf Fall's face. "Oh, that's Stormaway. I know about him. He does the trading for us."

Twig Snap frowned, "So which one's the forest guardian?"

A quiet laugh came from above them, "None of them. Our prince tends to be a late riser." Thunder Storm swung down to land next to them, "Don't worry. They're all quite harmless – well, not harmless exactly, especially Danton and Stormaway – but none of these sorcerers has ever threatened us."

"Hmph." Leaf Fall absorbed this information for a minute before asking, "And what about this guardian of the forest? What is he like? Besides being lazy."

Thunder Storm chuckled, "Yes, he is lazy, in our terms. Doesn't do anything he doesn't feel like doing. Never cooks. Gathers firewood and makes cups of tea as the mood takes him. Never makes his own shelter. Never does lookout duty." He laughed, "And we wouldn't want him to. He wouldn't be able to stand still long enough to be reliable!"

Twig Snap's eyebrows rose in astonishment, "Stars above! What a liability!"

"You poor things!" sympathised Leaf Fall, "I didn't realise how much you were having to put up with from that oath."

Thunder Storm shook his head, smiling, "He's all right. He makes up for it in other ways."

"I think that's very brave of you," said Twig Snap earnestly.

"Thanks. I'll tell him."

Leaf Fall's eyes widened in alarm, "No, Don't. We don't want to make him angry."

Thunder Storm realised that they were truly worried. He glanced up at Boravar, bound and unconscious on the horse behind them, "Would you rather that I asked Summer Rain to come here first? Then you can come out when you feel ready."

The siblings looked at each other and by common agreement, nodded. "We could do with some help getting him down though," said Twig Snap. "He's awfully heavy."

"Not sorcerers," added her brother hastily.

Thunder Storm smiled reassuringly, "Okay, not sorcerers." He hesitated, "But you will have to meet them sooner or later. We won't collude with you against them."

He found himself being scrutinised by two pairs of green eyes as Leaf Fall and Twig Snap assimilated this small rent in woodfolk unity. Thunder Storm understood their reaction, "No, my friends, I am not choosing them over you. But equally, I will not side against them, just because they are sorcerers. They too are my friends."

Summer Rain, Autumn Leaves and Running Feet appeared suddenly amongst them. Running Feet raised his eyebrows. "Snakes alive! Look at these ropes. They're everywhere. The poor man can't move a finger," he said, as he and the others set about untying the ropes and lowering the heavy sorcerer to the ground.

Twig Snap chortled, "Yes he can. But he kept sliding sideways. So then we would have to tie another rope on in another direction." She became serious. "He's not very well, you know. A special kind of sorcerer called an elite guard poisoned him… and stabbed him."

"Hmm, nasty things, elite guards," said Running Feet lightly. He nodded at the blonde sorcerer. "Danton over there is one of them."

When Twig Snap and Leaf Fall looked fearfully at one another, Thunder Storm intervened, "Stop it, Running Feet. These two are scared of sorcerers as it is. Don't worry. He is just like us. Has the skills to hurt people but doesn't necessarily use them." He thought for a moment, "In fact, he hasn't hurt anyone in the months he has been here, even under severe provocation."

When they looked queringly at him, Thunder Storm replied with a grunt of laughter, "Rainstorm."

Their faces lit with understanding.

"Yes he has," said Running Feet, "You've forgotten. He killed those two mountainmen."

"Well," said Twig Snap in a small voice, "Now that we have delivered our charge, we might just head off." She stood up and brushed off her hands, "Coming, Leaf Fall?"

"No, no, no. Don't go," Running Feet put his arm around her shoulder. "Danton wouldn't hurt a fly normally. Those mountainfolk deserved everything they got. They bashed up our forest guardian to within an inch of his life."

"What! We didn't hear about this. I think we have a bit of catching up to do." Leaf Fall turned to his sister, "We can't go yet. We have to explain what happened so that we can help Boravar." He reached into his pocket and pulled out the phial. "Here, Summer Rain. This is what was used to poison him."

The healer lifted up the phial to look at it against the light. She took out the stopper and sniffed, "I need to talk to Stormaway." She looked at Twig Snap, "Will you be all right if I call Stormaway over here? He's only half sorcerer. He does have woodfolk blood in him too."

Twig Snap looked a little panicky, "I might stand back in the trees a bit."

"Good idea," said Leaf Fall instantly, "I might just come with you." With a flick, the two of them were gone.

Thunder Storm shook his head, "We forget, don't we, how frightening we once found sorcerers?"

Stormaway joined Summer Rain in studying the phial of poison. "What has been done so far?"

Thunder Storm sent a mental question to the two rescuers, "Leaf Fall has rubbed a willow compound into the wound and bound it. Nothing other than that. Boravar wouldn't eat much, said he felt sick."

At their feet, Boravar stirred. He blearily opened his eyes "I can't see properly. Everything is blurry." He frowned in concentration as he peered up at Thunder Storm, "Don't I know you?" His gaze travelled to Running Feet and Summer Rain. "And you. You're with Prince Tarkyn, aren't you?" He let his eyes shut and his head drop back. "We must have made it." He gave a little smile. "What a great pair they are. They must have walked all through the night. Where are they? Are they all right?" He became restive and started rolling his head from side to side. "Twig Snap, Leaf Fall, where are you?" Panic-stricken, the ailing sorcerer became more and more insistent. "Why have you left me? What's happened to them?"

Twig Snap flicked back into view on the other side of Boravar from Stormaway and knelt down beside him. She placed her hand on his chest, and said softly, "It's all right. We're here. Leaf Fall's here too."

Boravar opened his eyes and breathed a sigh of relief, "I thought you had gone. I can't see properly, you know. You're all foggy."

"I think we are going to need Danton," Stormaway was saying. "If this fellow who hurt Boravar is an elite guard, then Danton may know what is in this poison."

As Boravar felt Twig Snap start to pull her hand away, he thumped his big hand down clumsily over hers, "Don't leave me. Please." He added in what he thought was a whisper, "I'm a bit scared. I don't like everything being blurry."

Twig Snap glanced at Stormaway and at the approaching Danton, and nodded reluctantly. "Okay. I'll stay."

Danton had been forewarned about the two woodfolk's fear of sorcerers. So when he arrived, he sat down opposite Twig Snap, rather than looming over her, and smiled disarmingly. "Hello, I'm Danton. I hear you two saved Boravar from an elite guard. You must be pretty good…But then, most woodfolk are pretty good when it comes to arrows and slingshots. I don't have anything like your finesse with a slingshot." He grinned up at Thunder Storm, "Do I?"

Thunder Storm smiled back. "There's a bit of room for improvement," he said dryly.

Twig Snap still knelt rigid with tension, her hand trapped under Boravar's.

Danton put his head on one side, "Would it help you to know that I have sworn not to hurt any woodfolk?"

"No. Running Feet said you killed two mountainmen."

Danton gave a rueful smile, "True. I did. But that was under Tarkyn's express orders." He shrugged, "But you have killed an elite guard, haven't you? So we are not so different."

Twig Snap narrowed her eyes. After a minute she said firmly, "I have not undertaken not to harm any sorcerers."

"No one is asking you to. But what say we each undertake not to hurt the other?" suggested Danton.

"What about my brother?"

Danton raised his eyebrows, "Of course I include him in this." He smiled at Leaf Fall. "You agree?"

They both nodded warily.

"So now that we have established the ground rules," said Danton, "can you tell me about this elite guard? You don't happen to know his name, do you?"

Leaf Fall frowned, "Petrand… Petrand…?"

"Closkaril," supplied Boravar hoarsely.

"Hello Boravar," said Danton cheerily. "You were looking a bit better last time I saw you. So you met up with Petrand Closkaril, did you? Not someone who should have been allowed to learn those skills, in my opinion. Slippery as a snake. Influential family - meant some of his worst misdemeanours were conveniently overlooked." He grinned at Twig Snap, "I felicitate you, on removing one of the world's nastier characters from the face of the earth."

Twig Snap stared back at him stonily.

Danton hitched a breath and turned back to Boravar, "So tell me what happened. Did he dip the tip of his knife into this little phial and then cut you with it?"

"Hmm." Boravar was beginning to fade again.

So Danton looked to Leaf Fall for his next answer, "Did you notice whether Petrand wiped the blade before returning it to its sheath?"

Leaf Fall thought for a minute, "No. I don't think he did."

Danton grimaced, "Hmm. Then Boravar will have got an extra dose when Petrand threw the knife at him." He shook his head. "Not good, I'm afraid," he mouthed at Twig Snap. "How long did Petrand give him?

"Five days," answered Twig Snap. "And that was about twenty four hours ago."

Danton shook his head, "He hasn't got four days left. I've seen the effects of this poison before. I would say he only has a few hours."

"Do you know the antidote?" asked Leaf Fall anxiously.

"I do, but it's complicated. Didn't Petrand have another small phial on him?"

Leaf Fall looked stricken, "We didn't look. We just brought this one."

"Do you still have his dagger?"

Leaf Fall nodded and produced it from his belt.

Danton smiled in thanks and moving slowly so as not the frighten them, he examined the hilt, pushing and prodding the carving on it until, suddenly, the top of the hilt sprang open. With a grunt of satisfaction, Danton tipped another small phial into his hand.

"That's ingenious," said Twig Snap. "Blast it! If we'd known, we could have helped him hours ago."

But as Danton shook the phial and then unstoppered it, a frown gathered on his face, "This is empty." He looked up at the woodfolk, his eyes glittering with anger. "That bastard never had any intention of letting Boravar live. He had run out of antidote."

The siblings looked panicky. "Now what are we going to do?" demanded Twig.

"Hmm, just a minute," said Danton, rising. "You stay here with him. I'll have a chat with Summer Rain and Stormaway."

After a few minutes of serious discussion, Danton returned to sit quietly on the other side of Boravar. "We have a slight problem… well, a couple actually. I know the ingredients needed for the antidote. Summer Rain and Stormaway are off to rummage through their herbs to find most of them. Then there are a couple of plants that they will need to gather from the woods around here. So we can deal with that. Some woodfolk have already headed off to look for them. But there is one ingredient we don't have. Every elite guard makes his own poison using a few drops of his own blood. Then, only an antidote containing his blood will work." Danton shrugged, "We can do the rest but we don't have any of Petrand's blood. The antidote won't work without it." He paused, "How far away is Petrand's body?"

Leaf Fall shook his head, "Too far. We have been travelling since lunchtime yesterday. Even if someone galloped on that horse there and back, it would take them until at least midnight, maybe longer. Some of the paths were very narrow and they wouldn't be able to travel fast all the time."

Danton shook his head, "Too long. And we can't start brewing the antidote until we have it."

"I might be able to help," came a small voice. Danton and Leaf Fall both looked at Twig Snap who seemed unaccountably embarrassed. She gave her frizzy hair a defiant shake and then looked Danton resolutely in the eye. "I didn't clean my arrow." She glowered at her brother, daring him to laugh. "I kept it as it was, as a sort of trophy."

Leaf Fall beamed at her, "Good girl! Thank goodness for bloodthirsty little sisters."

Her eyes narrowed, "Well, go on then. Get it out of my quiver. I can't move because this big galoot won't let go of my hand."

"Which one is it?"

"I don't know. It's one of those fletched with crow's feather."

After a couple of wrong guesses, Leaf Fall withdrew an arrow, still sticky with blood, well up the shaft. "Yuk, Twig Snap! You'll make your whole quiver stink, leaving it like this!"

"Will it be enough?" she asked anxiously, ignoring her brother.

Danton's eyes twinkled at her but he answered seriously, "Yes. Thank you. It doesn't take much." As he stood up, his mirth overcome him and he added with a grin, "It never occurred to me until now that I could end up as somebody's trophy."

"Well, don't you forget it!" snapped Twig Snap.

"No ma'am," said Danton with a small bow. As he walked away, he heard Leaf Fall berating his sister's cheekiness.

When Danton was sure that Stormaway and Summer Rain knew exactly what was required to brew the antidote, he returned to sit beside Boravar.

Twig Snap rolled her eyes, "Not you again. Why can't one of the woodfolk look after Boravar?" A spark of anger flashed in Danton's eye and Twig Snap knew she had touched a nerve. Suddenly she was contrite, "Sorry Danton. You didn't deserve that. If I have come to like Boravar, I guess I should give you a chance too."

"I didn't like Petrand any more than you did," said Danton quietly. "He just happened to be doing the same job, but not in the same way."

Twig Snap put her head on one side, "But you have poison too, don't you? How would you use it?"

Danton gave a slight smile, "In much the same way as you use your slingshot. I would knock someone out with it if I needed to search their house or their person and then use the antidote to revive them. I would have used a bigger dose in the first place but administered the antidote within a relatively short time."

Twig Snap explained how Petrand had used it, saying finally, "He used it as a means of control. Poor Boravar had to cope with knowing he was the walking dead." She chuckled, "Actually, he thought he was dead anyway because he thought we would kill him once he left our firesite without our permission."

"He still may be. He won't last until the antidote is brewed. We will have to ask Tarkyn to give him some life force to tide him over." Danton looked from one to the other of them, "Will you be all right if I get Tarkyn?"

"Maybe you'd be better off with more space around Boravar to work in," said Twig Snap, nervous again. She tried to pull her hand away but a little smile played around Boravar's mouth and his grip on her hand tightened. "Boravar," she said sternly, "If you weren't so sick, I'd bite your hand and then you'd let go. For future reference, I have very sharp teeth." Boravar's smile broadened but he still didn't open his eyes.

Twig Snap waved her other hand, "Come on then. Bring on your Forest Guardian. But just make sure you tell him that he is not to throw me up in the air."

"She is a feisty little thing, isn't she?" said Danton admiringly.

Leaf Fall shook his head fondly, "Nightmare."

A few minutes later Tarkyn walked towards them, rubbing his face to wake himself up.

Leaf Fall whistled, "He's tall, isn't he? But not as heavy as Boravar, I think. Look at his hair. It's *black*… and awfully long. Look! It's half way down his back." He leant over to Boravar and whispered, "Hey Boravar. I thought all sorcerers would have blue eyes like you. But they haven't. They're all different. This one with the black hair has eyes like an eagle's. And Danton's are like the sky in the evening. Amazing."

"Shh, Leaf Fall. They might hear you," whispered Twig Snap, digging her brother sharply in the ribs.

Hearing the last of this exchange, Tarkyn smiled, a little bemused, "Hello. I gather you two are the heroes of the hour. You must be exhausted. Has anyone thought to give you any food or a cup of tea?" he asked, sending a speaking glance to Running Feet. "I am Tarkyn Tamadil."

"Now Tarkyn," said Danton, speaking severely. "You are not to throw Twig Snap up into the air."

Tarkyn blinked but recovered quickly, "Well, I couldn't possibly manage it while her hand is being held by our sick friend here. If I lifted her up, she would have Boravar dangling from her arm and that would probably dislocate her shoulder. Very messy!"

Twig Snap frowned at him uncertainly, "Are you being funny?" she said after a moment.

"I hope so," replied Tarkyn. "And I hope you don't really think I'm about to toss you up into the air."

"You did it to someone once before though, didn't you?"

"Not toss, exactly." He cast a complicit glance at Running Feet. "I would never be so untidy."

Running Feet grinned, "Tarkyn lifted me up and then put me down. In fact he's done it to me three times now."

Twig Snap's eyes widened "*Three times?* He's lifted you up three times?" Suddenly she rounded on Tarkyn and demanded, "Why do you keep picking on Running Feet?"

Tarkyn did not like her tone of voice and withdrew a little. "I'll let Running Feet explain, if he wants to. I think I had better pay some attention to our sick friend here."

He turned his attention to Danton who said, "I don't think you should go into him, as you have done with some other people. I am worried you might absorb some of the poison." The blond sorcerer gave a self-conscious smile, "I don't really know how your healing works, but if you can just give him the strength to fight the poison for the time being, that should be enough. If it looks like he needs something further, we can reconsider. Is that all right?"

Stormaway and Summer Rain came over to add their opinions while Running Feet had a mind conversation with Twig Snap.

"I don't think you should deal with that knife wound yet, just in case you knit some of the poison into the repair work," said Stormaway. "Wait until we have cleansed his system."

"Danton is right. Just give him the strength to survive until we have the antidote ready," added Summer Rain.

Tarkyn sat down, put his hand on Boravar's shoulder and closed his eyes ready to concentrate. Just as he drew a deep breath, he felt a small hand tapping him on the arm. He opened his eyes to find Twig Snap staring anxiously up at him. "Sorry. I'm a bit quick off the mark sometimes… Just do your best for Boravar. Please?"

"I will," said Tarkyn quietly and closed his eyes. He let his life force flow in, making sure that it was all one way and that nothing came from Boravar into him. After a few minutes, he stopped the flow and opened his eyes. He found Boravar's blue eyes looking up at him. "Hello Boravar. Is that any better?"

"It is, although everything is still foggy, Your Highness." Some of the colour had returned to his face and his breathing was less laboured. The burly sorcerer struggled to sit up but fell back, breathing hard, "I'm afraid I cannot rise to give you your due, Sire. Please forgive me."

Tarkyn was shocked, "No, Boravar. Lie still. You must preserve your strength to fight the poison. You have already given me my due with your courageous actions to bring us warning of the king's plan. You have our deepest thanks."

Boravar gave a small smile of satisfaction and closed his eyes. As he started to drift off again, Twig Snap tried to extract her hand. Boravar opened his eyes again, "Please stay, Twig Snap." He released his grip on her hand enough so that she could pull away if she wanted to. Then he smiled gently up at her and closed his eyes.

Twig Snap left her hand where it was and thumped his good shoulder with her other hand, "Boravar, you are such a baby. How am I going to eat breakfast with one hand?"

Keeping his eyes closed, Boravar's smile broadened, "You'll manage somehow."

"And you may have forgotten, but Leaf Fall and I haven't been to sleep yet. How can you expect me to sit here all day waiting for this antidote when I'm exhausted?"

"You can put your head on my shoulder and go to sleep if you want to. I'm sure I'll make a good pillow."

Twig Snap huffed, "You are quite impossible. Now, do you want something to eat? I think you should have a drink, if you can manage it." She looked across at Tarkyn uncertainly, "Will you help me to lift him up enough to have a drink?"

"Of course I will."

Between them and Leaf Fall, Boravar's head was raised and a cup of warm tea put to his lips. He opened his eyes to drink the tea but closed them again as soon as he was lying back down.

"Why do you keep your eyes shut all the time?" asked Twig Snap

Boravar gave a wry smile, "It makes me feel sick having everything out of focus. And I don't really want to throw up."

"Very wise," she said tartly, "If you start vomiting, I shall be making a very quick exit."

But Tarkyn, watching her, suspected that nothing would drag her from Boravar's side.

CHAPTER 37

Twig Snap lay curled up sleeping peacefully, her left hand tucked firmly under Boravar's hand and her head on his big shoulder. It was actually a bit too high to be a perfect pillow but it was good enough.

Suddenly she was jolted awake. As she opened bleary eyes, her momentary reaction was to recoil in shock at the sight of the huge sorcerer but even before she could pull her hand away, she remembered where she was and wondered what had woken her.

Another jolt juddered through Boravar. She peered anxiously at him and noticed that there was a blue tinge around his lips. When another jolt shook him, her mind screamed for help.

Tarkyn arrived at a flat run almost immediately. Twig Snap didn't have time to wonder how he had responded so fast.

"Something is wrong. He keeps jolting. Please, help him. Please." Twig Snap's eyes were misted with tears.

One look at Boravar was enough to tell Tarkyn that the man was on the edge of death. Without waiting for instructions, Tarkyn threw himself down to sit beside Twig Snap and placed his hand on Boravar's shoulder.

"Tell them I've gone in," he said briefly before closing his eyes and taking a deep breath.

Tarkyn's essence flowed down his own arm and into the dying sorcerer. Boravar's whole system was seizing up. His heart gave an occasional almighty thump but the gaps between pulses were far too long. His lungs dragged in ragged breath but only with great effort, and the strength to keep doing it was fading. Tarkyn had no idea how the poison worked or even what it was doing to cause Boravar's body to shut down. All Tarkyn could think of doing was to take over, to fuse his own body with Boravar's and use his own functions to give strength and rhythm to Boravar's.

For a moment, Tarkyn left Boravar so that he could focus into his central core. He became aware of his own slow, measured breathing and his steadily beating heart. Then he delved deeper until he felt the life force that drove and orchestrated him. He steadied himself then gathering his strength and his knowledge of himself, he rode a surging wave of his essence down through his arm and into Boravar. Like a tidal wave, Tarkyn's essence flowed through Boravar's beleaguered body, taking suppleness and vigour into every straining cell, driving Tarkyn's own rhythm into Boravar's straining organs. Tarkyn felt his own system check as it came up against the resistance of the stiffening muscles of Boravar's heart and lungs. He forced a deep breath and dug deeper into his own well of life force. Bringing into play every last part of himself, he overrode the resistance and imposed his own rhythm on Boravar's body.

Inevitably, with that level of confluence, his mind connected with Boravar's. Boravar was frightened and confused. He had been straining to fight for each breath and now, suddenly he felt as though he had been caught in a deluge, as a huge river of power and life swept through him, assuming total control of him.

"Don't be afraid, Boravar," said Tarkyn's mind, flowing inside his own. "I will only stay until your body is recovered. Until then, we share the same breath, the same heartbeat, the same life. We will live or die together. You are only overwhelmed by my power now because my body was strong while yours was seizing up from the poison. Give it time. When the deluge calms, you will realise that we are sharing the same life force."

"It feels very strange," said Boravar's mind softly. "It feels as though I am outside looking in. This is not how my body feels. I don't breathe like this and my heart usually beats harder…Funny. I didn't even know I knew that about my heart and breathing until they were different."

"Sorry. That's the best I can do. The life force that drives your own heart and lungs is too weak. I have had to impose my own across both our bodies."

"And what about the poison? Can you fight it?"

Tarkyn's words came through calm and sure, "I don't know how to… and I don't think Danton or the others know enough about how it works to tell me. Life force alone will not defeat it. We must wait for the antidote."

"Sire, you must not risk your life for me," A wave of consternation emanated from Boravar's mind.

"Too late, I'm afraid. I told you before. We live or die together. We must put our faith in Danton, Stormaway and Summer Rain, and hope that my life force is enough to sustain us until the antidote is prepared."

Boravar subsided, dazzled by the sacrifice that Tarkyn was risking.

In the world outside, Twig Snap and others who had gathered, watched in consternation as Tarkyn slumped over the inert sorcerer, his pallour fading before their very eyes, to match that of Boravar's. With a sudden start, Boravar's chest heaved as Tarkyn took his deep breath and then the big man started to breath slowly and evenly in time with Tarkyn. Stormaway and Danton glanced at each other, then carefully lifted Tarkyn to lie flat beside Boravar with his hand still in contact with the big man's shoulder. Twig Snap stepped over Boravar to sit on the other side of him, without removing her hand from his grasp.

"What has happened?" she asked anxiously.

Stormaway looked at her severely, "Our forest guardian, who is also an impetuous young man, has joined his own life force with Boravar's to keep him alive."

Twig Snap's face crinkled up, "That's good, isn't it?"

Stormaway suddenly realised the minefield he would enter if he said that Tarkyn's life should not be risked in such a cause. He gave her a rueful smile, "Yes. That is good. That is what makes our forest guardian great."

"But the antidote will still not be ready for some time," said Summer Rain, less concerned for Twig Snap's feelings, "And we cannot afford to lose Tarkyn."

"Well, I cannot afford to lose Boravar. So we are even, aren't we?" snapped Twig Snap. Even as she said it, she realised what she had said and threw a defiant glance at her brother.

Leaf Fall smiled gently back at her and came over to sit beside her. He patted her arm, "Don't worry, Sis. Boravar will be all right. You'll see. Tarkyn is strong and has powers beyond other people. He will get them through."

"Hmph." grunted Stormaway, "Although you have no idea what you're talking about, you have raised a good point." He gestured to the people around him. "Come on, you lot. We have to move these two so that we can put Tarkyn's hand against a tree."

As the people around him rushed to follow his instruction, he turned to Leaf Fall and explained, "Tarkyn can replenish his strength through the trees, and the life force of the forest is immeasurable."

Within Boravar's head, he heard Tarkyn chuckle, "Oh Boravar, I am going to be in such trouble when we finally emerge from this. I can feel Stormaway and Summer Rain's displeasure from here. But your feisty little woodwoman has just put Summer Rain in her place. She's fallen for you, you know, Boravar."

Boravar felt slightly overwhelmed at having a casual conversation with a prince but did his best to respond, "She's a little viper, my lord. Smacked me around the face to wake me up enough to get me on the horse after I'd been stabbed. Knocked me out to stop me singing. Threatened to bite me, punched me in the shoulder. And all in the space of twenty four hours when I'm sick and wounded." A wave of humour and dawning realisation wandered through their joined minds, "Oh dear. And I love her to bits for it. What does that say about me, I wonder?"

Laughter rippled between them. After a while Tarkyn said, "But on the other hand, she did kill your assailant, heave you up onto that enormous horse - twice, from what I hear. Not to mention trussing you up like a chicken so you wouldn't fall off. And she has braved the proximity of several sorcerers, which she finds very frightening, to stay by your side and keep hold of your hand for hours on end."

There was a distinct smile in Boravar's voice, "No wonder I love her."

Tarkyn smiled in return, "You do realise she will be an absolute menace to live with?"

A hint of uncertainty entered Boravar's voice. "Do you think you can fall in love in one day? It seems a bit preposterous."

"I have two things to say to that. Firstly, it was a very long day. And secondly, I don't know what a person who is over one hundred and forty years old is doing asking a nineteen year old for advice."

"But Sire! You are not just any nineteen year old."

"Oh yes I am, when it comes to affairs of the heart. I'm a rank amateur."

Boravar chuckled. Then he thought about it all and chuckled more and more. "Oh dear, Sire. I am very confused. I don't feel old – well, I did with the poison coursing through my veins – but I don't usually. I look and feel like a thirty year old. I have my doubts about my mental age. If it were really one hundred and forty it would be non-existent because I'd be dead. It's probably more than thirty but nothing works the same in the lost forest. I wonder how old Twig Snap is?"

"A bit older than me, I'd say," said Tarkyn. "Maybe early twenties?"

"So there you are. We'd have an age gap of something in the vicinity of one hundred and twenty years. Funny sort of basis for a marriage, wouldn't you say?"

"Yes, very. And you're a sorcerer and she's a woodwoman with a fear of sorcerers. No logic in it at all." Tarkyn laughed, "You'll just have to make the best of it, won't you?"

And more uncertainties came, "She might fall out of love with me in a hurry when she finds I'm not weak and wounded anymore."

"She might. But she will have seen you when you first entered the forest. You have set yourself up as a rather romantic figure, you know, willing to sacrifice yourself to save your prince."

A small feeling of hurt wafted through the ether.

Tarkyn was instantly contrite. "No Boravar. I did not intend to mock you. I can't thank you enough for what you did. But that level of courage and dedication is bound to be attractive, and rightly so." Tarkyn sent a wave of kindness and understanding. "Twig Snap has seen you at your strongest and at your weakest. You have seen the best and possibly the worst of her." Despite his best intentions, he chuckled, "No. Actually, I don't think you've seen the worst of her yet."

Boravar chuckled in return, "She is a little vixen, isn't she?" After a moment he asked, "Do you not like her, Your Highness?"

"Whether I like her or not should not be relevant to your decision. But actually, I do like her. She is most intriguing."

After a long silence, Boravar said, "Sire, I am having these strange sensations. Are you sharing them?"

"Such as?"

"I can smell moss and pine forest. I can hear little streams burbling through the trees. I can feel the moisture of dew and the dampness of the soil beneath us, full of life."

Tarkyn smiled, "That is the forest coming to our aid. Stormaway has sensibly put me into contact with a tree. I am truly a forest guardian, you know."

"Sire, I never doubted it."

"Perhaps not. But I did at first. Here is the power of the forest guardian, all around you. You and I are connected to the whole life of the forest." Tarkyn breathed a sigh of relief, "We can last indefinitely now. The poison cannot possibly quell the might of the whole forest."

To the people watching, Tarkyn and Boravar slowly but surely turned green.

"Oh no!" exclaimed Sparrow, "I hate it when he does that. He looks so mouldy."

Midnight, who hadn't seen Tarkyn turn green before, crept over to him and sat hunched up and worried, in the angle between Tarkyn's arm and shoulder. He kept stroking Tarkyn's arm as though he might be able to wipe the green off.

"What's happening to them? Are they dying?" asked Twig Snap, her eyes widening in panic.

Lapping Water came over to stand looking down at Tarkyn. "Don't worry, Twig, that's a much better colour than the one before. The forest is sustaining them. The colour will fade over time when Tarkyn lets go of the tree."

After a moment, she sat down beside Midnight. Lapping Water could not take either of Tarkyn's hands but she sat near enough so that if he was at all aware, he could feel her against him. She stroked the little boy's hair comfortingly and smiled reassuringly at him when he looked at her. Once she had his attention, she sent him images of strength flowing from the tree making Tarkyn better. She gave a little smile. "They might be a bit more boisterous and cheery than usual when they first wake up though."

Twig Snap rolled her eyes, "Just what I need, a jolly green giant. He was enough of a handful yesterday when he was drunk on poison and loss of blood."

"You have played your part, Twig Snap," said Autumn Leaves with spurious kindness. "We can look after him from here, if you have had enough of him."

"Don't be mean to her," said Lapping Water, looking up at Autumn Leaves. "You know she wants to stay with him."

"No I don't," snapped the little woodwoman. "He forced me to."

Lapping Water just raised her eyebrows and smiled at her.

Twig Snap frowned ferociously, "Why would I want to stay with him? He's a sorcerer and it's well known that I hate sorcerers. Ask anyone."

"It's true. She does," put in her brother. He glanced at Twig Snap and gave a cheeky little grin, "At least, she did." He ducked sideways, skilfully avoiding a punch swung at him by his embarrassed sister. When he was sure it was safe, he put an arm around her shoulders. "Sis, it's no good pretending. Everyone heard you say you can't afford to lose him. Just admit it. You're mad on him."

"*But he's a sorcerer,*" she hissed between clenched teeth. "Woodwomen don't love *sorcerers*. Just let it be. When he wakes up, he'll go away and that will be that."

"Haven't you heard, Twig Snap?" asked Lapping Water gently. "I am betrothed to Tarkyn."

Twig Snap's eyes grew round. "*No!* Are you?" Her eyes flickered around the assembled group, looking for signs of disapproval. Instead, she found smiles of support.

"All of us, woodfolk and sorcerers alike, are very happy for them," said Waterstone gently. "And would be for you too, if that is what you chose to do."

Twig looked down at her big, unconscious hulk. She screwed up her face, "Well, I don't know. I'll have to think about it. He's a bit older than me."

Her brother chortled. "A *bit*? He's over a hundred years older than you."

"Well, he doesn't act it," she snapped. "He's the soppiest thing I've ever met."

"And exactly how many people have you met who have just been stabbed and poisoned?" asked Leaf Fall. "That may have some bearing on it."

"He was not stoic," she replied primly.

Leaf Fall smiled, "No, I grant you, he was not. But he didn't fall apart. He was just honest."

"Hmph." Twig Snap glanced around at everybody and sniffed, "Anyway. I will make my own decisions in my own time. So you can all just get on with whatever you were going to do."

Waterstone grinned, "We were all going to stand around and watch and worry about Tarkyn and Boravar, until the antidote was ready."

"Oh."

It was more than an hour later that Stormaway and Summer Rain finally brought forth a small cup full of a thick, dark green liquid. Stormaway shrugged, "I know it's more than we need but we couldn't make a smaller quantity, if we wanted to get the proportions right."

"Now Danton, we are unsure whether to give it only to Boravar or also to Tarkyn now that he has joined their life forces. So what we need to know is whether there would be a detrimental effect if we give it to Tarkyn if it turns out that he has no poison in him."

Danton thought hard, "Some of the ingredients destroy the actual poison and some of the ingredients counteract its effects. Those that counteract the effects would sharpen his focus and improve his reactions and coordination. Might make him a bit speedy for a while."

"The mind boggles, Danton!" exclaimed Waterstone. "Tarkyn can be bad enough just with the effects of the forest in him."

Danton gave a distracted smile, "I'm not sure about the other ingredients though. If they have nothing to counteract, would they become destructive? I don't know."

"Hmm" Stormaway thought through all the ingredients they had put into the antidote. "There is nothing in this that is toxic in itself. Anyway, my best guess is that Tarkyn's blood does not contain any poison. He has joined his life force with Boravar but not his body fluids. I think when he separates from Boravar, his body will be clear of poison."

"I don't know," contradicted Rushwind. "Remember, I gave Tarkyn the sickness through my hand on his shoulder."

The wizard nodded, "So you did. Hmm. Maybe we had better give it to both of them, just to be on the safe side."

Amid nods of agreement, Stormaway instructed people to lift Boravar and Tarkyn up enough to be given the antidote, taking care not to break the connection between them.

Tarkyn and Boravar together experienced the antidote entering their combined systems. It did not take long before they could feel the harsh resistance in Boravar's organs fading away. Almost immediately it was followed by a confused arrhythmia as Boravar's own rhythms tried to reassert themselves.

"Time to go. I'll fix your stab wound later," said Tarkyn. "I'll see you outside."

Before Boravar could reply, Tarkyn pulled out slowly and, by focusing on his own heart beating and the breath in his own lungs, drew back into himself.

When he was completely back in his own body, he waited for a few moments, feeling the ground beneath him, one of his hands on Boravar's shoulder, the other against the rough bark of a tree. Then he became aware of a warmth in the crook of his arm and another larger warmth pressing gently against his side. He peered through half open eyes to see what they were. When he realised it was Midnight and Lapping Water, he threw his arms around the two of them in one swift movement. Then he used them both to haul himself into a sitting position, grinning broadly as they ended up in a tangled heap on his lap.

"Hallo," he said cheerily, "I'm back. Did you miss me?"

Lapping Water laughingly disentangled herself. "You are a menace, Tarkyn Tamadil. You've had poor little Midnight beside himself with worry again. I'm not sure that he thinks green suits you."

"And I certainly don't," chimed in Sparrow as she jumped into the middle of them.

Tarkyn laughed and grabbed her within the circle of his arms too. "And how's Boravar?" he asked.

Everyone quietened down as they turned to look at the still-quiescent big sorcerer.

Tarkyn's eyes widened in alarm, "Is he all right? Should I go back in?"

Summer Rain shook her head, "I don't think there is cause for alarm. He is just giving himself time to readjust to his own breathing and his own heart rate. After all, his body has been under attack for over twenty-four hours now and for the last hour completely lost its own rhythms. Normally, he would be dead by now. I think he's just getting to know himself again before he ventures forth into the world around him."

Even as she finished speaking, his eyelids twitched. A few moments later, he opened his eyes and blinked a few times. "Oh good. I can see clearly again." His blue eyes swivelled to find Twig Snap's anxious green ones staring down at him. He gave her a slow warm smile, "Hello Twig. Thanks for staying with me."

As he gave her hand a gentle squeeze, her eyes filled with tears. She punched him hard on his good shoulder and said between sniffs, "Don't you ever do that to me again, you big galoot." With that she pulled her hand out from under his and flicked off into the woods.

Boravar shook his head in bewilderment, "What did I do?"

Amidst understanding laughter, Leaf Fall explained kindly, "She's just distraught. It was a long tense wait. She doesn't want everyone to see her crying. Don't worry. I'll go after her and calm her down."

"No," said Boravar firmly. "I will." He gave a rueful smile, "At least I will, if someone can help me up. I'm not sure how strong I am yet and

I don't want to crash down on top of His Highness if I lose my balance. That would be poor thanks indeed."

Many willing hands came to his aid and after standing still for a moment to test his balance, Boravar bowed to Tarkyn, "Excuse me Sire. I will be back shortly." Then he took a deep breath and headed off after Twig Snap.

He found her sitting against a tree with her head on her arms, sobbing her heart out.

"Go away. Leave me alone," she spat out.

But Boravar knew she would have heard him coming and could have avoided him had she wanted to. So instead, he sat down beside her and pulled her against him with his good right arm. Then he ran his hand through her frizzy hair in slow rhythmic strokes.

"You have very cute hair, you know," he said as he kissed the top of her head. "It suits your personality."

"What?" she demanded between sniffs. "All over the place?"

He gave a deep chuckle, "Something like that."

Suddenly she buried her face in his chest and flung her arm around him, "I was so frightened you wouldn't make it," she said in a muffled voice. "I don't know what I'm doing, caring about a sorcerer. I'm all confused."

Boravar's grip tightened around her, "And I don't know what I'm doing falling in love with someone who spends more time bashing me up than anything else."

Twig Snap raised her head at this, "I don't. I was trying to be kind to you." When Boravar shook his head smiling, a little worried frown appeared on her brow, "Are you? Falling in love, I mean."

Boravar smiled warmly down at her, "I think fallen is a better word. Yes, my little minx. I love you to pieces."

Twig Snap considered, "Well, that's a funny thing, isn't it?"

"Why?"

"Because that's how I feel about you as well." Suddenly, it was as though the sun had come out from behind the clouds as Twig Snap beamed up at him. "Oh Boravar. I love you to death and back." She leaned against his chest and gurgled. "In fact, I just have!"

Boravar gave a grunt of laughter, "Thank you little one, for standing by me, amongst all those scary sorcerers. You were very brave, I hear." At her look of query, he explained, "The prince and I have been talking." He patted her back, "Come on. Are you ready? Let's go back." He smiled, "I have a lot of thanking to do."

Part 6: The King's Gambit

CHAPTER 38

"You are obviously courageous, Boravar," said Rainstorm casually. "So how did you come to be stuck in the Lost Forest?"

"*Rainstorm!*" Tarkyn frowned furiously at him, "You do not ask questions like that, especially in front of everyone. That is Boravar's private business."

"Whoops, sorry." Rainstorm's eyes shone with unrepentant laughter.

Boravar, sitting with his hand tucked into Twig Snap's, watched the interchange between Tarkyn and Rainstorm and glanced at Harkell for his reaction. Harkell gave a slight smile and shrugged.

After giving it a bit of thought, Boravar said to Rainstorm uncertainly, "Your behaviour would suggest that you do not respect His Highness as you should. And yet… " He shook his head, trying to figure it out, "And yet… I think you do."

Rainstorm nodded smiling, "Of course I do." He couldn't resist a mischievous glance at Tarkyn before adding, "but only because he respects me too."

Boravar nodded slowly and said seriously, "Yes, I can see that." Suddenly his heavy face lit with a smile, as he met Tarkyn's eyes, "The more one gets to see past your role to the person behind it, the more one respects you."

The woodfolk all stared at him incredulously.

"What?" demanded Waterstone, "Even more than all that palaver in the Forest?"

Boravar shrugged, "Different kind of respect."

Waterstone nodded firmly, "I see what you mean. In that case, I agree with you completely."

"I will tell you my fear," said Boravar suddenly. "In fact, I had better tell you, if it turns out that I stay with you for any length of time." He took a deep breath, "I have a fearsome temper and I am afraid of hurting someone when I am in a rage." He glanced down uncertainly at Twig Snap who frowned but seemed otherwise unconcerned.

"Oh." said Rainstorm in a small voice. "Didn't realise what I was dealing with when I asked, did I?" Being Rainstorm, however, he made a quick recovery and asked another question, "So, have you ever actually hurt someone?"

Boravar nodded unhappily. "Yes. When I was young, maybe around your age, I was bigger and heavier than the others and they used to take delight in teasing me about it. One day, they just took it one step too far and I rushed at the ringleader and threw him to the ground." Boravar looked steadfastly at the ground. "He hit his head on a sharp rock as he fell backwards. He didn't die but he never fully recovered. His speech was slow and he shambled instead of walking." He lifted his head, "In some ways it was worse than if he had died. He was a constant reminder of what I had done, facing me every day in the village. And it was a constant reminder to everyone else as well. In the end I left, just before my seventeenth birthday. For years I travelled around, never able to settle, always afraid that I would lash out again and destroy someone else's life. Eventually, I found myself in the Lost Forest."

He felt Twig Snap squeeze his hand but didn't look at her.

Rainstorm took a breath and, glancing at Danton, said resolutely, "I did that, you know." In response to Boravar's querying frown, he continued, "When Danton first arrived among us, he didn't like how we acted around Tarkyn and tried to tell us off." The young woodman shrugged, "Well, I completely lost my temper and rushed at Danton, just as you did, and sent him flying. He is a better fighter than I am but Danton was under orders from Tarkyn not to retaliate, which I had completely forgotten. Even when Tarkyn ordered me to stop, I just kept hitting Danton and threw him down again." He glanced at Tarkyn with a rueful smile, "In the end, Tarkyn had to use his *Shturrum* spell on me. I've never been more mortified in my life." He gave a little shudder as he looked back to meet Boravar's eyes, "The only difference between us is that there was no rock where Danton fell."

In the silence that followed, Tarkyn and Waterstone glanced at each other, thinking of the fight they had had the other day, and exchanged a little smile as they decided not to mention it.

"Anyway, Boravar, how long is it since your rage overcame you?" asked Tarkyn.

Boravar thought carefully and a smile began to dawn on his face, "Over one hundred and twenty years, Sire."

"So, it would be reasonable to assume that you have learnt to manage it then?" Tarkyn smiled in return, "Perhaps you could put your fear to rest now."

"You don't scare me at all," said Twig Snap firmly, "no matter what you did in your misspent youth."

"I am pleased to hear it, my little feisty one." Boravar chuckled, "I suspect, if anything, it will be the other way around and I will be scared of you."

"No," said Leaf Fall cheerily. "She's all right. You just have to learn to duck and dodge."

The laughter that followed this left Twig Snap looking a little uncertain. Boravar said nothing more but gave her hand a reassuring squeeze. When she glanced up at him, she found him smiling warmly down at her. She gave a little sigh and leaned in against him.

Boravar returned his attention to Rainstorm, "I can see why His Highness respects you," he smiled, "even if you are a hothead."

"Oh, I'm not anymore," said Rainstorm airily.

This pronouncement was met with a great deal of mirth.

Rainstorm scowled, "What? I'm much less belligerent than I was. Lapping Water said so."

"Yes, that is true. You are." Tarkyn laughed, "And you are so much older now than back in those days when you attacked Danton, aren't you? What? Two months?" He shook his head, smiling, "Rainstorm, I will grant that you haven't attacked anyone recently and you are certainly easier to get on with, but you are the most brazen person I have ever met." Seeing the beginnings of a hurt expression on Rainstorm's face, he hurried on, "No, Rainstorm. That is not a criticism. It is your greatest strength and all of us benefit from it. You have helped me on several occasions, Lapping Water, Danton, Harkell and now Boravar… and probably others I don't know about."

Rainstorm glanced uncertainly around the group. "I am *trying* not to be a hothead."

Tarkyn chuckled, "So am I. And I think you're succeeding better than I am at the moment."

"Well, you have more pressure on you than I do," he conceded handsomely. After a moment's hesitation, Rainstorm smiled shyly, "And thanks for what you said."

He was then inundated with people from all sides reiterating Tarkyn's words.

In the midst of this conversation that he couldn't hear anyway, Midnight came trotting over and tugged on Boravar's sleeve. When he had the big sorcerer's attention, Midnight tugged at the bottom of the sorcerer's leggings with an enquiring expression until Boravar allowed him to see the mark on his leg just below the knee. Midnight peered closely at it and then used signs and facial expressions, to ask whether it hurt. Boravar frowned uncertainly at him before doing a series of gestures to show that it had hurt but was now all right. The little boy patted the big sorcerer's leg comfortingly before subsiding to think about it.

"He's a cute little fellow, isn't he?" whispered Twig Snap. "Funny colouring."

Boravar smiled, "You don't need to whisper. He can't hear. Midnight is half woodman and half sorcerer. His mother is here somewhere. You probably know her. Hail? One of the trapper woodfolk. " When Twig Snap nodded, he added, "But he is Prince Tarkyn's ward and spends most of his time with him."

Twig Snap frowned, the light of battle igniting in her eye, "Odd sort of arrangement. What's he doing keeping Midnight from his mother?"

"There are some pretty dark things in Midnight's past. Not that he's done, but that have been done to him." He smiled disarmingly at his little firebrand, "If you ask His Highness, be nice about it. He rescued Midnight from being abused and neglected, I gather."

Twig Snap's eyes narrowed. "You're not trying to tell me what to do, so early in our relationship, are you?"

It was at this point that Boravar realised that the roles of men and women in sorcerer and woodfolk relationships were quite different. But, unlike Tarkyn, he was happy to accept the woodfolk version. "I was advising you. Perhaps I should have phrased it better. It's up to you whether you take any notice. But if you are too aggressive with His Highness, he will withdraw and you will have no chance to get to know him. Besides, he doesn't deserve it."

"Hmph. Fair enough. Now you mention it, it has happened to me once already." Twig Snap smiled. "I do like you – as well as love you, I mean. You notice things about people that I might miss."

Boravar gave her a slow smile, "I've had years to learn about people, you know. I'd have to be a very slow learner not to have picked up one or two things by now."

At this point, Midnight regained Boravar's attention and drew a line through the air from his fingertip to Boravar and shook his head uncertainly. Boravar, understanding this to mean that Midnight shouldn't send a shaft directly at a person, shook his head in emphatic agreement. Midnight then drew a line from the end of his finger towards a rock at the edge of the clearing and put his head on one side. Boravar nodded.

Much to Boravar's confusion, Midnight then raised his shield. At first, the dark green dome attracted little attention from the rest of the group because Midnight often played with the other children using his shield. But when a shaft of dark green light streaked across the clearing to shatter a large rock with a loud report, all conversation ceased. Twig Snap and Leaf Fall jumped a mile and needed a great deal of mental reassurance not to flick into hiding.

Midnight, of course, hadn't heard the noise and calmly looked around at Boravar for approval. Boravar could only stare at him. Gradually, the little boy realised that everyone had stopped what they were doing and were staring at him. With a growing sense of dread, Midnight backed away, still within his shield, ready to run for cover.

"Uh oh. He's about to do a runner!" exclaimed Tarkyn. Instantly, his bronze shield slammed down over Midnight's, while he sent the little boy reassurances.

Midnight stood uncertainly, not knowing what he had done wrong and frightened by everyone looking at him. Tarkyn came around to stand in front of him and sent an image of Midnight releasing his shield and standing still. Although still frightened, Midnight put his faith in Tarkyn and complied. Tarkyn released his own shield and scooped the little boy up into his arms.

"Come here, rascal. No one's going to hurt you or get cross with you," crooned Tarkyn, matching images to words, as he stroked the little boy's back until he felt the tense little muscles begin to relax. Once he was sure that Midnight was back on an even keel, the prince held him away from him and sent an image of what Midnight had done, with a query attached to it.

Midnight immediately looked worried but nodded reluctantly.

Tarkyn smiled reassuringly at him and asked him to do it again. Midnight brightened and pushed himself out of Tarkyn's arms and onto the ground. He raised his shield and sent another shaft of dark green power at the damaged rock, cracking it even further. Then he looked at Tarkyn for his reaction.

"Look at that!" exclaimed Tarkyn, smiling proudly and applauding. "He can do two spells at once."

Midnight beamed at him.

Harkell looked thoughtful. "Has he ever sent out a shaft of power before?"

"I don't think so." Tarkyn looked around the group until he spotted Sparrow. "Have you seen him do that before?"

"No. He's only ever used his shield to play."

"And has he ever seen you send forth a shaft of power other than when you used it on Boravar?" asked Harkell.

Tarkyn frowned, trying to remember, "I hardly ever use it. The last time I used it was at the Great West Road to protect that sorcerer family and that was before I met Midnight." His brow cleared. "Oh no, that's right. He would have seen me driving Journeyman and his eight sorcerers down the path near the mountainfolk's firesite. I used it then."

"But you had your shield up then, too," put in Danton.

Harkell smiled wryly. "I am fairly sure that Midnight thinks he can only send a shaft of power when he has his shield raised, if he has learnt by watching you."

"We are going to have to spend some time training this boy, Tarkyn," said Stormaway sternly. "He is a fast learner and is figuring it out for himself, even if he has got it a little wrong. We need to make sure he knows when and how he can use his powers."

"He did come and ask me about my leg," said Boravar. "He wanted to check his understanding that he shouldn't aim at people in case he hurt them. But from what you're saying, he could just as easily have decided that if His Highness could do it, so could he."

Tarkyn looked at Boravar for a moment. "I'll have to be more careful around him, won't I, if he is copying me?" He tousled Midnight's hair, "He's a good little fellow. It would be terrible if he did something wrong by mistake. And he's shaping up to be very powerful. Not easy to manage in one so young." He looked at the wizard, "Stormaway, can you undertake his training? You might like to teach me a few tricks while you're at it."

Stormaway gave a slight bow, "It would be my pleasure, my lord."

When they had all resumed their seats and conversations were once more flowing, Harkell came over to sit beside the prince. "Sire, I have been thinking about how the enemy could counteract your ability to fire your power through your shield." He grimaced, "And I think you have just shown us how… more or less."

Tarkyn frowned, "Explain."

"Another sorcerer could place his shield around you and your shield."

"Yes, but if he stayed within his shield, I could attack him and if he stayed outside his shield, the woodfolk could attack him."

Harkell shook his head, "That's what I first thought. But it suddenly dawned on me. What happens if two sorcerers place their shields over yours? Three domes over each other? The two enemy sorcerers could stand next to each other and one of them place their shield over yours while the other placed their shield between themselves and any external attack."

"Hmm. Danton, Stormaway, listen to this. Boravar, you might as well join in as well." Tarkyn looked worried.

Rainstorm strolled over and sat down to join in, "This isn't another sorcerers only party, I hope?"

Tarkyn smiled at him, "No. Feel free to join us. We were just discussing a magical problem, that's all."

"In that case," said Rainstorm, "You had better include String and Bean. They are the best at solving any kind of problem."

"Come on, tell us all," said Waterstone, determined to make sure that the split between sorcerers and woodfolk did not re-open. "Just because we can't use magic like you, doesn't mean that we can't come up with ideas. After all, String, Bean and Harkell can't do half the things you can, either."

"You're right, Waterstone," said Tarkyn disarmingly. "After all, the discussion has already included the role that woodfolk could play."

"Well, good then," grunted Waterstone.

"So, if everyone wants to join in, I'll explain the problem," said Tarkyn, thinking wryly how far things had come. When he had first become a woodman, holding a joint discussion on the use of magic had stirred up major resentment among some woodfolk.

When he had finished, Autumn Leaves leaned forward, "I see. So one sorcerer, with his shield over yours, is easy to deal with. But two shields over yours means that neither you nor we can attack the sorcerers between the two shields."

"Ooh. That is tricky, isn't it?" String's eyes shone with interest.

"Yes, very," agreed Bean. "What about contacting people or animals mentally? You can do it through your shield, can't you?" When Tarkyn had nodded, he continued, "And you can contact Midnight through his."

"True." Tarkyn looked around, "No chance of a cup of tea and a snack while we're discussing this, is there?" With an impish grin, he returned his attention to Bean while a couple of woodfolk rolled their eyes and set about making tea for everyone. "But I couldn't contact the bloodhounds through Journeyman's shield, could I?"

"Couldn't you?" asked Bean. This was new information for String, Bean and Harkell.

"Well, that's no good then," drawled String. "You couldn't call on your raptor friends in that case."

"And even if you could," added Harkell, "they wouldn't be able to hurt a skilful shield wielder."

Waterstone frowned, "Well, at least these sorcerers between the two shields wouldn't be able to hurt Tarkyn, would they?"

Danton shook his head. "No. They could gradually force him to move in a direction they chose but it would be a slow process."

"They could outlast him though, couldn't they? Especially if there were many of them. They could take it in shifts to keep two shields up over a long time."

"What about you two?" asked Rainstorm, looking at Danton and Stormaway.

Danton shrugged. "We can't penetrate another's shield or even our own, for that matter. I suppose we could place our shields over the others but it would just create an impasse really."

Rainstorm chuckled, "Then they could place two more shields over you with the sorcerers safely between them. It would look like a domed rainbow."

String shook his head, giving a perfunctory smile, "But in the end, there will be more of them."

"So Tarkyn," said Bean, "what can you do to get out of it?"

"I don't know."

Harkell stood up and put his hands on his hips. "I think we should try it. If everyone could stand over there around the edge of the clearing… And Tarkyn, if you wouldn't mind, could you stand near the centre, just to one side of the firesite?"

Intrigued, Tarkyn and the woodfolk complied.

"Now, Tarkyn, if you could raise your shield and Danton, place your shield over the outside of Tarkyn's." Once this was in place, Harkell continued, "Now Stormaway, you stand next to Danton and raise your shield over the top of yourselves and the other two shields."

Harkell stood back and grunted in satisfaction. He waved his arm around like a showman. "And here we have our prince trapped by two sorcerers who are themselves impervious to attack."

Suddenly Tarkyn dropped his shield. At the looks of surprise, he shrugged, "No point. Danton can't attack me through his shield anyway. And I don't have to concentrate on keeping it up."

"True," said String slowly. "But you still can't attack him, can you?"

"No."

"Can you send images to the woodfolk or animals through Danton and Stormaway's shields?" asked Bean.

After a minute of strained concentration, Tarkyn shook his head. "No. I can't get through their shields." He smiled, "You can all hear my voice though. So I could call for help."

"You may be able to call," replied Waterstone, "But there is nothing we can do against sorcerers' shields."

"Except perhaps try to distract them" suggested Tree Wind.

String's face lit up. "How about sending a message to animals in the ground below you, where there is no shield?"

"Hmm, worth a try, I suppose." Tarkyn closed his eyes and concentrated for a couple of minutes.

Suddenly a small rabbit pushed up through the ground next to Danton. It looked around in bewilderment, sat down and scratched itself amid gales of laughter.

"Very scary, Tarkyn," said Lapping Water, grinning.

Tarkyn grinned back, "Thanks."

"It might work if there were a snake nearby," said String in high dudgeon.

Tarkyn smiled kindly at him, "Yes, it might, String, if we happened to be directly above a snake hole. But, unfortunately, my images don't seem to travel very far through solid ground." He laughed, "But I think Danton's shield is wavering under the effects of all this hilarity. So you never know. Even a rabbit might work."

Danton promptly sobered up and straightened his shield.

A thoughtful silence descended before Danton suggested, "Well, you could blast the ground as you did with Journeyman and his sorcerers."

"I could," agreed Tarkyn, "but there are no horses to panic this time and you could just step back and increase the circumference of your shield."

"Can you translocate?" asked Rainstorm.

"Not through other sorcerers' shields."

"Hmm. I think you're stuffed then," said Blizzard baldly.

"It would seem so," agreed Tarkyn wryly.

Behind the prince, Harkell took a deep breath. Suddenly, the ex-captain of Jarand's guard flicked up his deep purple shield. In a voice dripping with derision, he said scathingly, "So now at last, I have found a way to defeat you. Not so high and mighty now, are you, *Your Highness?*" He drew a seedpod from his pocket, "Contrary to what I told Rainstorm, I can keep up my shield indefinitely. And I have in my hand a seedpod from my garden in Montraya." His sneering voice grated on Tarkyn's ears. "And yes, I can translocate from within my own shield."

Rainstorm's eyes widened with shock and hurt. "You lied to me."

But the young woodman's reaction was nothing compared to Tarkyn's.

"How *dare* you betray your oath to me?" roared the prince. A shockwave of anger and outrage at Harkell's betrayal blasted outwards and knocked everyone sprawling. Danton, Stormaway and Harkell's shields disappeared as they lost their footing. In a flash, Tarkyn had flung his shield around Harkell, imprisoning him.

Harkell picked himself up and bowed low with his hand on his heart, "And there you have it, Your Highness. The solution to your dilemma."

As he straightened, Tarkyn frowned at him. "Put your shield back up," he snapped.

"Certainly, Sire." Harkell waved his hand and reinstated his shield.

Tarkyn just stood staring at him.

After a couple of minutes, Harkell's shield began to waver.

"Keep it up," said Tarkyn shortly.

"Yes, Your Highness." Signs of strain began to show on Harkell's face.

Still Tarkyn waited. The purple shield wavered and went out as Harkell slumped to the ground.

"Hmph," grunted Tarkyn. He turned to Danton. "What do you think? Faking it?"

Danton shook his head uncertainly. "No. I don't think so."

"Hmph," said Tarkyn again. "All that proves is that he lied about being able to keep his shield up indefinitely." He nodded to a few woodfolk who were standing by with hemp to bind Harkell's hands as Tarkyn dropped his shield.

The prince shook his head slowly from side to side as he stood looking down on the captain who now sat awkwardly with his hands bound behind him. "Oh, Harkell! What have you done? How can I ever trust you after this?"

"Quite easily," drawled String. "To start with, why would Harkell translocate with everyone watching him when a real traitor would leave quietly when everyone was asleep?"

"Yeah," came in Bean. "And I bet you that seedpod comes from around here somewhere." He raised his eyebrows at Harkell who merely nodded.

Waterstone picked up the seedpod that had fallen to the ground beside Harkell. He inspected it, turning it over in his hands, looking closely at its stem. He gazed around the clearing until he spotted what he was searching for. He took it over to a low lying bush and squatted down, running his hand along the lower branches. With a grunt of satisfaction, he placed the end of the seedpod's stem into a small scar on the branch.

"Autumn Leaves, Summer Rain. Have a look at this." When they had inspected it, he asked them, "You agree?" When they both nodded, he turned to the prince, "The seedpod comes from this bush, in fact, from this very branch."

With a glance at Danton, Tarkyn waved his hand at the woodfolk standing nearby. "Untie him." he said shortly and turned away. After taking a few paces, the prince turned suddenly on Harkell who had stood up and was now rubbing his wrists. With his voice vibrating with anger, Tarkyn said, "No matter how little you think of rank and no matter how strong your motivation, don't you ever speak to me like that again."

Harkell bowed low, hand on heart. "I apologize wholeheartedly, Your Highness… I would not have…"

Tarkyn waved his hand dismissively. "I don't want to hear." The prince spun on his heel and strode from the clearing.

Danton and Waterstone looked at each other and then at Harkell.

"Don't worry," said Waterstone kindly, "I expect he's just churned up. He has a bad history with betrayal. He'll get over it."

Danton shook his head admiringly. "You have a lot of nerve, staging that. Tarkyn could have killed you."

Harkell gave a slight smile. "He could have but he's had lots of chances to kill enemy sorcerers and hasn't." He shrugged, "Besides, I didn't think he'd throw away his oath to me so easily." His smile broadened, "His reflexes are amazing, though. It's great to watch him in action."

String frowned. "Well, I think he's being a bit churlish. After all, you did find a way for him to escape."

Harkell shrugged, "Oh well. I can console myself with knowing that I have tried my best to serve him truly." He smiled wryly, "But he is, after all, Jarand's brother. I suppose blood will out from time to time. At least Tarkyn's nice most of the time."

"Harkell!" came Tarkyn's voice from the edge of the clearing behind him. Harkell blushed from his neck to the tips of his ears. He rolled his eyes at Danton and Waterstone and cringed. "Oh no!" he mouthed, before turning on his heel to face his liege and bowing. "Yes, my lord?"

"Come with me." Tarkyn walked off towards the river without waiting for Harkell's response.

When they were out of earshot but no doubt still beneath the surveillance of the lookouts, Tarkyn threw himself down against a rock where he could look out over the river and gestured for Harkell to do likewise.

"I suppose I deserved that," observed Tarkyn.

Harkell blew out a sigh of relief. "Not really, sire. I did push the boundaries pretty hard. I think it would have tried anyone's tolerance."

Tarkyn ran his hand through his hair and smiled, "You were revolting, Harkell. I have not heard such derision since Sargon and Andoran had me bound and were herding me towards Tormadell to claim the reward."

"I'm sorry, Sire. I just wanted to make sure you reacted strongly."

Tarkyn grunted, "I certainly did that." He scooped up a handful of pebbles and began to skim them across the water, one by one, as he talked. "But Harkell, more than anything, I was upset when I thought you had betrayed me. I really like you – and I thought you liked me also. This is not to do with prince and liegeman. This is as you see it, man to man." He raised his eyes to Harkell. "I'm sorry if I behaved like my brother."

For the first time since he had known him, Harkell looked totally flustered. "Oh no, Sire, don't think that. You are nothing like your brother."

Tarkyn's eyes shone with laughter. "Yes, I am, Harkell. With the best will in the world, I am still like Jarand and Kosar sometimes. They are my heritage and my upbringing. I cannot leave that behind completely." As Harkell went to speak, Tarkyn put up his hand to stop him. "Two things I wish to say, Harkell. Firstly, thank you for your courage and secondly, do start calling me Tarkyn again. No amount of formality will wipe your tone of voice from my mind but I know you did it in service of me." He gave a friendly smile, "You are quite hopeless at shields, aren't you?"

Harkell grinned, "Absolutely useless, just as I told Rainstorm."

"And can you translocate?"

Harkell shrugged, "I doubt it. I've never actually tried."

"Well, all I can say is, you can definitely act!"

The ex-captain nodded, "Oh yes. Years in Jarand's service. Prevarication becomes a way of life. Though I would have to say that was the most difficult piece of acting I've ever done."

"Hmm" Tarkyn picked up another flat pebble and sent it spinning across the water, "Could I ask you to be as straightforward with me as you possibly can be? I know there may be times when we are among outside sorcerers and it would be expedient to have a cover story but other than that, can you just be straight with me?"

Harkell looked stricken. "I always have been, Sire – Tarkyn."

Tarkyn finally got to the point. "If you joke with others about my behaviour, will you, at some stage, include me too? It happens too often that people talk about me, instead of to me." Tarkyn waved his hand, "I don't mind if you and everyone else talk about me behind my back. I'm used to it. But if there is a real problem, I would like to know about it."

Harkell smiled slowly. "And you may talk about me to your heart's content, if you are so inclined. But likewise, if there is a problem, let me know." Suddenly he grinned, "Of course, you don't know my brother. So you won't know when I start acting like him."

The prince chuckled.

As they rose to return to the firesite, Harkell said, "The training has only just begun, you know, Tarkyn. Now you have to learn to produce that shockwave of anger at will."

Tarkyn sighed. "My life's work; trying to control my feelings in one way or another."

Harkell smiled. "Don't complain. You have the most effective feelings I've ever seen. It's a great secret weapon that the opposition could never predict."

Tarkyn gave a little smile. "Hmm. That's the first time anyone has thought of my unruly feelings as an asset. I'd better get on with it and practice then, hadn't I?"

CHAPTER 39

But when they returned to the clearing, they found everyone in turmoil. Woodfolk were wandering around looking distracted and Boravar was sitting in a gloomy heap against a tree, head in hands. "What is it? What's wrong?" asked Tarkyn anxiously.

Waterstone glanced across at Boravar, "I'm afraid your confrontation with Harkell has frightened off Twig Snap and Leaf Fall. They've disappeared."

"Oh no!" Tarkyn walked over to the distraught sorcerer who scrambled to his feet and bowed. "I am so sorry, Boravar. I didn't think. They're not used to us, are they?"

"It was intense enough for those of us who are," said Rainstorm dryly. "We woodfolk are not used to people getting so angry and shaking everyone about with their reactions. Even Waterstone's not as scary as that."

"Yes. I understand. Point taken," said Tarkyn irascibly. "But making me feel bad is not going to bring back Twig Snap and Leaf Fall. We have to find them."

Waterstone shook his head, "We've tried, but they have closed their minds off. They have well and truly gone to ground."

Tarkyn thought for a minute. "I should be able to find them. I can find Midnight when he has closed his mind off."

"But she has deserted me already at the first sign of trouble." Boravar shook his head dolefully. "I should have known it wouldn't work. I was a fool even to consider it."

"But even if I do find them," said Tarkyn, ignoring this, "how are we going to catch up with them?"

"I wouldn't bother, if I were you." said Boravar sadly. "What's the point? She's made her choice."

"Come on Boravar," said Tarkyn bracingly, giving the big sorcerer a couple of hearty slaps on the back, "Snap out of it! Give her a chance! I expect she's scared stiff after seeing our little display at close hand when she has never met sorcerers before."

Boravar flushed. "I beg your pardon, my lord," he said stiffly. "I did try to run after her, but she is a woodwoman and when she doesn't want to be caught, she won't be."

"True. So now we have a woodfolk problem. How do we catch two woodfolk who don't want to be caught?" Tarkyn looked around him, "Any ideas? From woodfolk or sorcerers."

"Have they taken the horse?" asked Bean. When Waterstone shook his head, Bean grimaced, "Pity. Tarkyn could have asked the horse to bring them back." He subsided into a thoughtful silence.

"I suppose if you can locate them, we could ask woodfolk they are heading towards to try to intercept them," suggested Rainstorm dubiously. He shrugged, "If they are willing to be found and if they will listen."

"Why don't we start by locating them? Then we will have a better idea of the extent of the problem," suggested String.

"Hmm, agreed," Tarkyn sat down where Boravar had been sitting and closed his eyes. He let his mind wander out into the woods around him. He found Midnight playing marbles with Sparrow and the other children. He sent them a little greeting on his way past that made them stop playing, look around and smile. As he spread out into the woods, it occurred to him that he should be trying to sense the fear emanating from Twig Snap and Leaf Fall. Almost immediately, he began to home in on an intense emission of fear, distress, and confusion from quite close by. The forest guardian sent forth waves of calm and friendship, gradually surrounding the two woodfolk with his strength.

Twig and Leaf Fall had not experienced the forest guardian's projected warmth before and they gradually let down their guards as his sureness enveloped them. Then Tarkyn sent them images of Harkell and himself talking down by the river, resolving their differences. He sent waves of apology for frightening them and images of Boravar's misery. Finally he sent a wave of invitation and further friendship and reassurance.

As he opened his eyes, he found Boravar's anxious blue eyes watching him intently.

"Have you found them, Your Highness?"

Tarkyn gave a wry smile, "Yes. They are fairly close by. They are not far beyond the lookouts, arguing about what to do. I have tried my best but I am not sure that it will be enough. Perhaps you might like to go with someone to seek them out."

Boravar nodded and looked uncertainly around the group.

"I'll come with you, Boravar," said Thunder Storm, "since I was the first person they met this morning when they arrived."

"And I will also accompany you, if you like," offered Running Feet. "After all, Twig Snap was very keen to champion my cause."

"I would offer," said Tarkyn. "But I feel I am the cause, not the cure at the moment, even though I have allayed their worst fears."

Boravar thanked them as soon as they left the clearing. "It is kind of you to offer to help when you hardly know me."

Thunder Storm glanced up at him, "You are welcome, but we are also helping our kin. We don't want to leave them frightened and distressed." He stopped walking, "Just a minute, I will tell them we're coming."

Boravar gave a little smile, "I'm sure they will have heard me by now."

Thunder Storm grinned, "Possibly. But I want to reassure them and stop them from flicking further away."

As they drew nearer, they could hear Twig Snap saying firmly, "I'm going back. Do what you like. You can stay here if you want to."

Boravar's face tightened. "She's leaving," he whispered.

"I'm not going to stay here without you. Don't be so cranky. I'll come back with you," retorted Leaf Fall. "Are you all right now?"

"I don't know. I must be mad, to have even let the idea of teaming up with a sorcerer cross my mind. They're all so big and scary."

Just as Boravar's face fell even further, a little voice behind him said, "But here I am, anyway."

The large sorcerer swung around to find Twig Snap, arms confidently flung out on either side but belied by an uncertain smile on her face. She was immediately enveloped in a big, bear hug.

"I thought you said you were going back," said Boravar, smiling at her as he let her go. "I thought…"

Twig Snap frowned in confusion, "I did. Going back to here."

"Oh. I see. Oh, good. I thought it had been all too much for you and we'd never see you again."

"It was terrifying," said Leaf Fall unequivocally. "We've never seen a sorcerer up close until we met you. Forty-eight hours ago we were scared to death of you. Then we finally overcame our fear and came to sit at a firesite with…what?…six of them and suddenly a quiet discussion turns into an earthquake and a pyrotechnic nightmare." The woodman ran his hand through his hair. "How do we know it won't happen again?"

Thunder Storm grimaced, "Tarkyn's feelings often knock people over. Sometimes it is his happiness or relief that does it, not just anger. He's harmless really. He wouldn't hurt a fly."

Twig Snap's eyes narrowed, "Oh yes, he would. He hurt Boravar in the Lost Forest."

"But he also saved Boravar's life today and put his own at risk to do it," Running Feet pointed out.

"He's totally unpredictable which means he's dangerous," pronounced Twig Snap. "Friend one minute, assailant the next."

Boravar shook his head smiling, "No, Twig. I can predict him. I think, as you get to know him, you will be able to predict him too. You do realise that Harkell knew exactly how Prince Tarkyn would react when he believed that Harkell had betrayed him? It was entirely predictable."

"And what about when he hurt you?"

"I behaved aggressively towards a prince of the realm and did not acknowledge his rank." Boravar shrugged, "I won't make that mistake again."

"Hmph," Twig Snap crossed her arms. "Hmph. That doesn't make sense. None of these other sorcerers are putting so much effort into being deferential to him."

Boravar shrugged unhappily, "I don't know, Twig. I just know what he expects of me. Maybe they are all nobility. I don't know enough about them."

While they were absorbed in this discussion, Thunder Storm was relaying it to the other woodfolk who in turn shared it with Tarkyn.

Tarkyn sighed and turned to his friend, "Waterstone, will you come with me? I think I need to address this, if Boravar is staying. My one moment of impatience has come back to haunt me." He grimaced, "Twig Snap is right. I can't insist on a different set of behaviours from Boravar alone. I should never have wounded him."

Watertsone patted him on the back, "And we should never have put you into a situation where you were so beset on all sides. But you did and we did. So let's go and sort it out together."

As Tarkyn and Waterstone approached, Boravar bowed low. "I think, Your Highness, that Twig Snap and Leaf Fall are willing to return with us."

Twig Snap stood there, arms folded, "I hope you're not expecting us to do that," she said belligerently.

Her brother rolled his eyes and, although he did not bow, looked apologetic.

Tarkyn smiled and sat down on a nearby log so that he didn't loom over them. "No, Twig Snap. You are not beholden to me in the same way that Boravar and the home guard are."

"No one else does it," she said baldly, a martial light in her eyes.

Waterstone gave a quiet cough, "That's not quite true. I don't know whether you were still there at that point, but when Harkell stood up after Tarkyn's anger had bowled him over, he bowed also." He gave an apologetic smile, "And Danton is renowned for bowing. We all make fun of him for it."

"I haven't seen String or Bean do it," she persisted.

Waterstone glanced at Tarkyn before replying, "No. They are not used to royalty, and their manners, I believe, are a bit rough and ready. You'll find, however, that Stormaway bows from time to time."

"But not all the time," she stated flatly.

"No, not all the time, Twig Snap," answered Tarkyn quietly. "And the woodfolk, almost never."

"So why Boravar?" she insisted.

Boravar was looking acutely uncomfortable. "Twig, please, let it go." He turned to the prince. "Your Highness, I do not need to know why. It is your prerogative to require different behaviours from different people, as you see fit. We are not all the same and do not all hold the same relationship with you."

Tarkyn turned to the woodwoman, "He is right, you know, Twig Snap. Not just about me. What he says applies to everyone, don't you think? You wouldn't expect me to behave in the same way as Leaf Fall, for instance. If I tried to be as familiar with you as he is, I think you would warn me off very quickly, wouldn't you?"

Twig Snap considered him through narrowed eyes before reluctantly conceding his point. She still looked dissatisfied but after glancing at Boravar, decided not to pursue the subject.

Tarkyn smiled slightly, "But nevertheless, I will answer your question." He shrugged, "The answer is simple. Before today, I have only had dealings with Boravar in public, in formal situations where my role as prince was of paramount importance. Today, he and I came to know each other more closely in a couple of hours than many people would in a lifetime. We shared the same life rhythm, the same expectations of living or dying…"

"So…" interrupted Twig Snap.

Tarkyn held up his hand, "Patience. I haven't finished. When I wounded Boravar, I was beleaguered on all sides and largely unsupported." He gave a wry little smile, "I freely admit that I could have turned the situation without hurting anyone. In retrospect, I wish I had. It is not my usual practice to hurt people."

"It is your right, Your Highness," said Boravar earnestly.

"Yes. Maybe so. But not the behaviour I expect from myself and not something of which I feel proud." Tarkyn ran his hand through his hair. He glanced at the three woodmen of his home guard, uncertain how to continue.

Waterstone came to his rescue, but the argument he presented surprised Tarkyn. "Boravar, the open gestures of respect that you gave to Tarkyn also reflect our feelings for him." Tarkyn blinked. Waterstone smiled warmly at his bloodbrother, before making a slight modification, "Well, more or less. But he realised long ago that gestures like that would embarrass us and damage the true respect we have for him."

Tarkyn was now able to pick up the thread, "And so, Boravar, I will not require them from you either, while we are within my forests and far from court unless, perhaps, you come at the head of a delegation as you did last time."

Boravar bowed low, "Thank you, Your Highness."

As Twig Snap frowned and went to speak, Tarkyn glanced at her and pre-empted her by saying, "It takes sorcerers a while to get used to the idea." He smiled, "You may also address me as Tarkyn, Boravar, except on formal occasions."

"Thank you, Y..S… Hmph. This will take a bit of getting used to, Your Highness. I think I will take my time, if you don't mind."

Tarkyn laughed, "It is not an instruction, Boravar. It is a permission. You may choose to use it or not, as you will." The laughter on his face faded as he turned to the two new woodfolk, "And to you two, I owe an apology. It was very careless of us to use any magic at all when you were so new to our company." He thought for a minute, "Perhaps you would feel better if we showed you some of our magic carefully?"

Twig Snap stepped behind Boravar and peeked out around him, "Go on," she said.

Tarkyn quietly produced his orb of light. Then he changed it to the apparition of bronze flame. He nodded at Twig Snap, "It's not hot. You can put your hand through it, if you want to."

Twig Snap stayed firmly where she was but Leaf Fall came forward and waved his hand quickly through it. "He's right, Twig. Not hot at all."

"This would be," said Tarkyn as he sent a small fire ball onto the ground that set a few leaves blazing. "There are other things I can do but let me show you the special skills of the forest guardian. Waterstone, can you find me a suitable stick please while I concentrate on something else for a minute?"

Once Waterstone had returned with a green stick, Tarkyn demonstrated how he could grow a small sapling from it.

After that, nothing happened for a little while. Then, to everyone's surprise, a badger trundled past Boravar to Tarkyn and butted his leg with its nose. Tarkyn smiled and began to pat it with long sure strokes. After a minute, he raised his head, "You are very privileged, you know. This is the first time I have ever asked an animal to come to me just to show someone my powers. But this badger and I have met before. When I first discovered that I was a forest guardian, she came to me and allowed me to pat her to calm me down. But she is brave to come into the midst of so many people, don't you think?"

"And why have you made an exception this time?" asked Twig Snap quietly.

"Because you have been brave enough to come into the midst of a group of sorcerers and we have frightened you. So I feel I owe you something. You see, all the other woodfolk who have met me… or us… met us in a large group of woodfolk who out-numbered us. You two are on your own. I know you know the woodfolk of the home guard but they are all used to us, and you are not. So, I can imagine you have felt a little isolated. I suppose I do this to acknowledge your courage."

Tarkyn looked down as the badger snuffled at his hand. "Ooh dear. I think she's hungry. Does anyone know what badgers eat?"

"I have a bit of dried fruit in my pocket," said Leaf Fall. "You could try that."

"Ok. Just a minute." Tarkyn sent a brief image to the badger and received permission. "Go on, Leaf Fall, you try it. Just move slowly and hold it out in your hand." Even as he said it, he realised that woodfolk would know how to avoid startling animals. "Sorry. I'm sure you know how to do it. Go on."

Leaf Fall moved forward slowly and held out his hand. The badger sniffed at his offering and then snapped it out of his outstretched fingers. Leaf Fall jumped back in fright and so did the badger. They stared at each other for a moment before the badger, close to Tarkyn's side, calmly began to chew the dried fruit.

"What about you, Boravar?" asked Thunder Storm as they all watched the badger. "What can you do?"

Boravar smiled gently. "I might wait until the badger has gone to show you. I don't want to frighten her."

"Is it so scary?" asked Running Feet.

Boravar chuckled, "No more scary than… Tarkyn's. Not that he has shown you the worst he has. But I think anything would scare the badger and so I will wait."

A few minutes later, by mutual consent, the badger trundled off into the undergrowth.

"Well, go on then," urged Twig Snap.

Boravar waved his hand and produced a beautiful peacock blue shield around himself and the two new woodfolk. He smiled, "This is what a shield looks like on the inside. You can touch it if you would like to. It won't hurt you. It just keeps you on one side of it."

Twig Snap and Leaf Fall gingerly ran their hands up and down the surface. On the outside, Running Feet and Thunder Storm, after a moment's embarrassed hesitation, did the same.

Tarkyn raised his eyebrows. "Haven't you two ever felt a shield?"

Running Feet gave an embarrassed smile, "No. We have never liked to ask. It's very interesting, isn't it? A bit buzzy, if you know what I mean."

After a moment, Waterstone casually put his hand out to feel it too.

When they had had enough of feeling the sheild, Boravar removed it. "I can send shafts of power, like His Highness, but not while holding up my shield. And I am quite good with light. I'll show you."

With that, Boravar created a soft white orb of light like Tarkyn's. Then he threw it up into the air, where it hung at the height of the treetops. Next, he created a blue light and sent it up to hover beside the white one. Red, green, purple and orange lights were created in quick succession. When they were all hanging in the air above them, Boravar waved his hand and brought them down to hover before him. He sent them spinning in a circle before catching them, one by one, and then juggling with them. After a while, he extinguished each one with a gentle pop until there were none left.

He smiled shyly around at the rapt faces. "Years to practise in the Lost Forest."

CHAPTER 40

A week later, the King rode into the forest along the Great West Road accompanied by a small retinue of fellow hunters and attendants. In all, the party numbered no more than twenty. After several miles, the party turned off onto a smaller path and a few of the attendants began to scout around for signs of game. Before long, the air was filled with squawks and shrieks of alarm as pheasants and woodcock were flushed out to become easy targets for the King and his companions. By not one glance or murmured word could anyone discern that the King's party was anything other than what it appeared to be.

In the twilight, the King's retainers erected a small pavilion among the trees and set about preparing a feast of game birds while Kosar and his companions drank fine wine and regaled each other with recollections of their finer shots. The darkness gradually closed in and the fire threw huge shadows dancing into the trees. Now and then, one or another of the lords would involuntarily glance up into the branches and as the night wore on, their conversation gradually became stilted and forced.

"I think we have had all the hunting we are going to get today," said Kosar ambiguously as he stood up. "We will try again tomorrow. I bid you good night."

Everyone stood up and bowed. The King retired to his tent, leaving his companions to sleep around the fire and to keep watch. His manservant attended him but when he made to leave, Kosar ordered him to remain. "I think I will sleep better if I know you are keeping watch by my side."

His manservant Farlowe bowed, not betraying by the slightest sign that he too was tired and had also been riding all day. "As you wish, Your Majesty."

The King slept fitfully, his dreams unsettled and full of Tarkyn. Every now and then, he would wake with a start, his mind wandering between justifying his actions against Tarkyn to envisaging every possible eventuality and the measures he had taken to combat them. In the morning, he awoke heavy-eyed and bad tempered. His manservant, circles under his eyes and grey with fatigue, brought him a basin of scented water to splash on his hands and face before rising.

Just as he was reaching for a towel, the King's ablutions were disturbed by the sounds of shouting and excitement outside. A young lord appeared at the opening in his tent and bowed, "Your Majesty, I believe our quarry has been spotted."

Kosar grabbed the towel and demanded, "Where?"

"Not far from here, Sire. Perhaps a quarter of a mile away. It seems he may have been trying to get close to your person, Your Majesty, just as you predicted. The soldiers are in hot pursuit. I expect their arrival at any time."

"Excellent." Kosar rubbed his face vigorously. "Leave me. I will come out shortly to await the arrival of my errant brother."

The lord bowed and withdrew while Farlowe removed the water basin and towel.

When he was dressed, Kosar looked at his manservant's haggard face and decided to send him away, "Smarten yourself up, man. Send me in someone who can attend to my needs with more energy than a slug. I am ready now for Tarkyn's arrival."

As the manservant reached the door of the tent, the king called after him, "Bring me a cup of tea and then find yourself somewhere to sleep. I will expect you by my side when we are ready to leave. I do not wish for another to attend me unless I must."

Farlowe bowed low, a smile splitting his tired face, "Thank you, sire."

The manservant stepped outside the tent and crumpled to the ground.

"Oh, for heaven's sake, Farlowe! Could you not have told me you were so tired?" exclaimed Kosar, careless of the fact that Farlowe would have been disciplined severely if he had shown any reluctance to carry out his orders, no matter how unreasonable. He strode to the tent's doorway. "You will be no good to me exhausted."

Kosar emerged into the cool morning air and found himself surrounded by inert guards. Reeling with shock, he whipped his head around at a movement in his peripheral vision. The person of his nightmares, long black hair framing those startling amber eyes, was walking towards him surrounded by a bronze haze. With a flick of his hand, Kosar raised his own shield, dark red like his twin's. Fear flickered in his eyes as he remembered the devastation left behind by Tarkyn in the Great Hall. But hugging to himself the knowledge of his carefully deployed troops, he was able to meet his fearsome younger brother with some semblance of calm.

Tarkyn nodded to him, "Good morning, Kosar." He gestured towards some logs near the fire. "Shall we be seated?"

The king frowned, "I had heard that you had forgotten your manners with Jarand but I did not expect your discourtesy to extend to your monarch."

"I am not being discourteous. In fact, I was about to offer you a cup of tea, made with my own fair hands," said Tarkyn with a smile. "I'm sure you could do with one after such a restless night."

"You are remarkably cold blooded, Tarkyn, to be able to sit among a dozen corpses and partake of tea. But then you are a mass murderer, are you not?"

As Tarkyn's smile froze on his face, his anger hit Kosar like a punch in the chest, forcing him to take an involuntary step backwards. "Have a care, Kosar. The reason those people died was that I lost my equanimity."

Kosar's eyes widened, "What was that?"

Tarkyn's eyes glittered with anger. "That was my displeasure. I cannot always keep my feelings to myself." Taking a breath to calm himself, Tarkyn waved his hand impatiently. "Don't look so worried, Kosar. Although you may deserve it, I have no intention of hurting you." Tarkyn indicated the bodies strewn around him, "None of your friends or retainers will suffer any lasting ill effects. None of them is dead, I assure you. You may check if you like."

"I do not need your permission to see to my friends, if I choose to," snapped Kosar.

Tarkyn raised his eyebrows, "Isn't that what I just said?" He picked his way between the scattered bodies towards the fire. "Come and sit down," he repeated, with a slight edge to his voice.

The king's face suffused with anger and he stood rooted to the spot with outrage. "How *dare* you speak to me like that?"

But since his encounters with Jarand and the old forest guardians, and his falling out with his woodfolk, Tarkyn had become less forgiving. He swung around to confront his brother, "Kosar, I am sovereign in these forests, not you. I am sure you know that and, unfortunately for you, so do I. So let's have a little less of the histrionics and a little more sensible discussion…Unless you would like me to insist that *you* pay your respects to *me*?"

"Whoo-hoo" mind-chortled Rainstorm to Waterstone in a nearby tree. "Even if I'm not a sorcerer, I know that was a very cheeky thing to say to a king."

"You will pay for this, Tarkyn. You will rue the day you were born." Kosar's voice trembled with rage.

Tarkyn stood with his hands on his hips and gave Kosar time to calm down before replying, "If you stop to think for a moment, you will realise that I have carefully engineered this encounter so that I don't show you up in front of your following. When they awake, they will not know I have been here unless you tell them yourself. The choice is yours."

Kosar couldn't help a glance into the surrounding woodlands.

Tarkyn shook his head, "I'm afraid the surrounding trees are full of my people, not yours. I think you will find your troops are in hot pursuit of another person who looks a lot like me. No doubt they will return in the fullness of time to report their failure." He gestured again towards the logs, "So, you can relax without losing face and talk to me." Tarkyn lifted a huge iron kettle off its tripod over the fire and poured two cups of tea. He left one for Kosar and took his own to sit on the far side of the fire. He bent his head and breathed in the aroma of the tea. "Very nice," he said appreciatively. "From the southern coasts, I would say. I haven't had tea like this for a while. Perhaps I should organise to procure some."

"I am pleased you like it," said Kosar frigidly. He stalked over reluctantly and sat on a log, ignoring his cup of tea. "Since you obviously have a reason for seeing me, perhaps you had better explain yourself in the short time you have, before you are surrounded."

Tarkyn nodded slowly and sipped his tea. "I have come to warn you."

Kosar frowned, "Are you threatening me?"

"No, not at all," Tarkyn looked surprised, "It is not against me that I am warning you. I am warning you against yourself and Jarand."

"First of all, before I listen to you, why? What do you hope to gain from this?"

"There's that devious sorcerer mind again for you," said Autumn Leaves silently to Falling Rain, watching from high in an old oak.

"I hope to gain a lasting, prosperous peace for Eskuzor," said Tarkyn, with a slight grin, knowing he sounded presumptuous.

Kosar frowned, "That is my job, not yours. I cannot imagine that it is any concern of yours, particularly since you have forfeited your place in our society."

Rainstorm frowned, "His tone of voice is nicer but his words are crueller."

Waterstone nodded agreement.

"Kosar, were you tutored well in the history of magic?" asked Tarkyn, in an apparent non-sequitor.

Kosar nodded impatiently. "Of course I was. I am the king, for heaven's sake. I have been trained for this role all my life."

"Just asking," returned Tarkyn mildly. He sipped his tea. "Then, in that case, have you heard of forest guardians? It is quite possible that you haven't. I think only wizards steeped in learning generally know of them. I certainly didn't, until recently."

Kosar's eyes narrowed, "The name rings a faint bell. I think we are supposed to have had an ancestor who was one. But people make up so much rubbish about our family, you can't believe any of it. Hmm. From what I remember, I think they are part of our folk lore from centuries ago, you know, figures in some of our fairy tales." He snorted in derision. "That's right. They were supposed to be able to talk to animals. Ridiculous. You see? The classic stuff of fairy tales; talking animals."

Tarkyn smiled weakly in response, thinking that this line of approach was rapidly becoming impassable. Suddenly, a huge golden eagle swooped down and landed next to him on the log. He wasn't sure why she had arrived since she couldn't have understood what Kosar had said. Perhaps the tone of the conversation was enough to alert her to Kosar's attitude and the fact that Tarkyn needed some support. He shook his head slightly, thinking that there was more to these huge birds of prey than he had realised. She tilted her head to fix him with her gimlet eye and Tarkyn received a clear image of her flying over to land on Kosar's right shoulder.

"Kosar, trust me. Drop your shield. I give you my word I won't hurt you."

"Don't be ridiculous. Of course I'm not going to trust you. Whether you meant it or not, and I will allow there is some doubt about that, your power caused the deaths of countless people and destroyed one of the great icons of our city. I have no intention of trusting you." Kosar folded his arms and stared stolidly at him.

Keeping his feelings severely in check, Tarkyn relayed the problem of the shield to the eagle, who came up with a modification.

"Brace yourself, Kosar. This eagle is coming over to you. She will land on top of your shield. This should be interesting."

Tarkyn nodded and in three slow flaps of its great wings, the eagle covered the short distance to Kosar. The king couldn't stop himself from ducking as she glided in to land directly over him, less than a foot above his head. The shape of the shield dinted slightly but held, as her great talons dug in. Kosar looked up straight into the burning golden eyes of the predator and straightened slowly, barely daring to breathe but determined not to be cowed. Eventually he asked quietly and slowly, "And will this animal go away if you ask it to?"

Tarkyn gave a slight smile, "Probably. But I would watch your tone of voice, if I were you. Perhaps she could watch us from the roof pole of your tent. I'll see." When he sent the image with a query, the great bird shrieked to make it clear that she was the one deciding, then took off and glided up onto the roof of the tent.

Kosar sat there stunned. Drawing a slightly ragged breath, he stood up and retrieved his tea from beside the fire with hands that trembled. He took another deep breath, sat back down and drank his tea. Then he glanced up at the enormous eagle, perched on the top of his tent before bringing his eyes back to rest on his younger brother.

"Did you ask that eagle to come to you?" he said finally.

Tarkyn shook his head, "No, but I did agree that she might land on your shield and I asked her to fly up onto your tent."

"I see." Kosar gave a faint smile, "So the animals don't actually talk after all, then."

"No. Not in words." The guardian of the forest smiled slowly and unconsciously, a sense of his power radiated from him. "And I would not have asked that majestic eagle to perform for you. I have too much respect for her. But she chose to come and was willing to work with me to show you."

There was a long silence.

"Hmm. I had heard rumours that you had become powerful, more powerful than even the mayhem you left behind you, might have suggested," said Kosar at last. "I believe you can perform more than one spell at a time too. Is that true?"

"Yes. But I did not come here with the intention of impressing you with my power. Far from it."

"But you *are* one of these guardians of the forest, I gather?"

Tarkyn nodded, deadly serious. "I am. In fact I am the Guardian of Eskuzor."

Kosar's mouth set in a hard line. "Obviously I was right after all. You are a rogue sorcerer. Clearly, you are completely deluded. And that, combined with your power makes you a very dangerous individual." Kosar stood up and began to pace. After a few turns back and forth, he stopped in front of his brother and began to speak slowly and carefully to him, "Now, Tarkyn, listen to me. *I* am the king. That means that *I*, not you, have the responsibility for Eskuzor. If anyone is the guardian of Eskuzor, it is I."

As Tarkyn went to speak, Kosar held his hand up and continued in a gentle voice as though talking to a four year old. "Now, I know you could talk to that eagle but that doesn't give you the right to run Eskuzor. In fact, it doesn't give you the right to any say in her affairs at all. It just means you have an interesting little party trick." He smiled patronisingly at Tarkyn. "Do you see?"

Tarkyn spluttered with laughter. "Yes, thanks for that, Kosar. I do see. But although I may be your junior by seven years, I have now grown up and am now nineteen. I too have left fairy stories far behind me." Tarkyn stood up to face his brother eye to eye, "All right, forget the guardian angle. Let us just say that that is for me to know and for you to ignore. And I completely agree with you. I am no threat to you. Eskuzor is your responsibility. That is why I have come to talk to you."

Kosar frowned, "Oh no. You may concede that Eskuzor is mine but you are definitely a threat. Anyone with as much power as you and holding the sovereignty of these vast forests at the centre of Eskuzor is a threat. No two ways about it. Especially when you have already been declared an enemy of the crown."

Tarkyn ran his hands over his face and sighed, "Kosar, listen to me. I do not want the throne of Eskuzor. But if *you* want to keep it, you had better look to your people. They need your protection and leadership. Jarand is agitating against you. He is gathering troops in the southwest. Two days ride along the Great West Road and you will come to his encampment."

"He is helping me to fight lawlessness."

"He *is* lawlessness. He press-gangs villagers and farmers into joining his ranks. People across the country are attacked by renegades whom you do nothing to quell. He pretends to fight for you while he derides your leadership and prepares to fight against you."

Kosar stared at Tarkyn through narrowed eyes, "How do I know you are telling the truth? Why would you support me rather than Jarand? After all, it was my final say that had you branded as a rogue sorcerer."

Tarkyn waved his hand, "I don't care about either of you. Don't you see that? I care about the people of Eskuzor who may die in a civil war. I want you to act to stop it. It may already be too late but at least you can try."

Kosar shook his head slowly, "I never did understand you, Tarkyn. What attraction do these people hold for you? Have we neglected your education so sadly that you have learnt nothing? They are here to serve us. In return we look after them. But if the affairs of state dictate that we must fight, then fight we shall. And every man, woman and child that I need will fight in my army." He smiled. "But thank you for warning me. Now I can gather my forces and give Jarand a good hiding. That will put him back in his place. I don't think I will hang him. Life would be too dull without the prospect of another fight with Jarand somewhere on the horizon. Besides, I don't think it would look good, would it, removing *all* of my siblings? People might begin to think there was something fundamentally wrong with the Tamadils. And we can't have that, can we?"

Tarkyn ran his hand dispiritedly through his hair, overwhelmed by the impossibility of the task and turned away to sit once more on a log. He drank the rest of his now cold tea to settle himself before saying in a low voice, "Kosar, I give you fair warning. I will not allow this to happen. If you ride against Jarand with an army of people whom you are willing to sacrifice to sort out your squabbles, I will intervene. And the next time, I will not knock your retainers out first. I will hold you to account in front of your whole army."

Kosar stood up, "Tarkyn, you may have the odd unusual power and may even be one of these fairytale forest guardians, although honestly, I doubt it. But whatever you are, you are not the king and you are not my master. You are merely some piddling little dictator calling the shots to a bunch of trees and a few birds." He smiled derisively, "Just not that scary, really." He waved his hand, "As one small concession, I will send for Jarand and ask him to justify his actions. Perhaps you are at least right in saying that he and I should work together to get rid of marauders and brigands."

Tarkyn smiled sadly, "You mean me, don't you?" He took a breath, "Kosar, Jarand is undermining you on all fronts. When did you last have a building project completed according to plan? Have you ever stopped to wonder where all the complainants come from? Or are you too busy dealing with them to think? When did you last have time to review the state of your troops?"

"ENOUGH!" roared Kosar. He took a breath to rein in his temper and repeated more quietly, "Enough. You have made your point." The king stood in silence, frowning at him as he tried to work him out. Eventually he said, "No matter what you do to support me, I will not pardon you, you know. You have caused far too much damage and killed far too many people for me ever to be able to justify it."

For a minute Tarkyn frowned with concentration and then said, "Kosar, I am now doing what I did in the Great Hall. I have evoked enough anger within myself to make my shield reflective. If you fired a shaft of power or an arrow at me now, it would rebound and quite possibly kill you. But if you do nothing, nothing will happen."

Even as he spoke a lone arrow flew from within the trees, hit his shield and speared back into the woods. Tarkyn smiled wryly, thinking that his time with Kosar was beginning to appear more like a play than a conversation, with his supporters putting actions to words.

When Kosar just stared at him, Tarkyn pressed his point, "Don't you see, Kosar? I didn't attack anyone. Everyone around me attacked me and then died by their own hands."

"But you didn't control it."

Tarkyn spread his hands, "It had never happened to me before. And no one ever took the time to teach me about magic."

Kosar was startled, "Didn't they? Hmm. Well, I must admit I'm surprised to hear that. I would have expected our mother to do a better job of organising your studies." He shook his head. "But it wouldn't have helped anyway. A reflective shield is unheard of."

"Then how could you expect me to have known how to control it?"

"Tarkyn," said the king gently, "I cannot have you back, no matter how well you plead your cause."

Tarkyn bent down and picked up a stick. He sat himself down and proceeded to demolish it, for a while ignoring his brother. Halfway through, he looked up, "I am not pleading my cause, Kosar, although I would like you to have a truer picture of me. And I know I could never come back because basically," here he shrugged and gave a little smile, "I am too popular." Seeing Kosar's outraged expression, his smile turned to a grin. "Come on Kosar, admit it. That's why you had me arrested in the first place, wasn't it?"

Kosar was not prepared to respond to this statement.

So after Tarkyn had broken off a few more pieces of his stick he continued, "And I will also tell you this, even though you will probably not believe it: I have never had any designs on your throne. You are not my twin and I have no wish to be like you, or to have what you have. The contest is, and always has been, just between you and Jarand."

Kosar thought through all the justifications he had dreamt his way through during the night and struggled to find any of them that continued to hold. But he also knew that he could never afford to lose face by sanctioning Tarkyn's return.

As he went to speak, Tarkyn held up his hand, "Don't Kosar. Don't reply. I know what you are bound to say, whatever you really think, and I don't want to hear it."

Eventually Tarkyn stood up, ready to leave. "One more thing, Kosar. About twelve years ago, Stormaway held a prisoner in his rooms at the castle. What do you know of this?"

The king's voice hardened, "What I know is that our father felt the need to protect you. He bequeathed these forests to you and bound the agreement so tightly in legalese and magic that only main force could change it. And I am not such a fool that I would expect to win a battle against a horde of people born and bred in the forests. I might try to capture you but I would not come against you and these people in open warfare… especially after what happened to Jarand and even more so, after today."

"Would you like to meet some of these people since they live within the borders of your kingdom?"

Kosar shrugged, "Not particularly. I will leave you all to live in your happy little fantasy among the trees." His face darkened. "I endure this state of affairs because I must. But I give you fair warning, Tarkyn. Should you step out of the forests or make one false move, my men will be waiting and if you are captured, I will show you no mercy."

"As long as we are all clear on where we stand, brother," replied Tarkyn tightly. "I think we have spoken enough. Your men will be regaining consciousness soon and I don't want to be here when they do."

"No. You had better run to safety, little brother," said the King with a sneer.

"I was more concerned that I would have to knock your men out again, actually," answered Tarkyn, then gave himself a mental kick for indulging in one-up-manship. He smiled, "Sorry. That was a cheap shot." He shrugged and spoke quietly but firmly, "Just know, Kosar, that I have the best interests of Eskuzor at heart. If ever you need me to help you with her welfare, I will. But conversely, if I feel you are acting against her best interests, I will intervene."

Kosar frowned in perplexity, "I never really knew you, did I, Tarkyn? I just thought you were a little softy. You used to embarrass yourself and all of us with your wild displays of emotion when your whipping boy was punished. And you were always such a goody two shoes. And now, here you are, facing down the King of Eskuzor, completely unfazed by the knowledge you must surely have by now, that the woods are rife with my soldiers. Your presumption and audacity are breath-taking."

Out of the corner of his eye, the king spotted one of his men stirring, but even as he determined to keep Tarkyn talking, the man suddenly keeled over again. Tarkyn glanced at the man and then at Kosar. "Please don't punish them, Kosar. They had no hope against my people."

The King raised his eyebrows haughtily, "They have failed me signally and must bear the consequences."

"There's that look," said Rainstorm silently to Waterstone.

Tarkyn considered him, "Kosar, if you pretend to them that they succumbed to some malady, I will not gainsay you. But if you choose to admit to them that I gained the upper hand, and punish them too severely because of it, I will be quite happy to come forward and humiliate you in front of them." When Kosar looked mutinous, Tarkyn continued steadily, "These are my forests and this is my jurisdiction. I would not like to see them unduly punished."

Although his tone was friendly enough, both of them knew that he would back his words with deeds.

The King waved his hand dismissively, "I was right in that, at least. You are a softy. Mark my words, Tarkyn. You cannot afford to be lenient with these people. In this particular instance, I can see that it would be in my own best interests to do as you suggest. But take a word of brotherly advice. You will find yourself in serious difficulties if you do not maintain a strict regime of discipline and due punishment among your tree dwellers." He shrugged, "I don't know why I'm telling you this because, in the end, it will be to my advantage if they overthrow you." He gazed around the surrounding trees and shrugged. "Actually, perhaps it would make little difference to me as long as you stay out of my affairs. No one could find them to govern them, anyway."

Tarkyn smiled, "That is a good way of looking at it. And hopefully, I *will* be able to stay out of your affairs. Good luck Kosar." He grinned, "If you ever need me, just come into the woodlands and call out. Sooner or later, word will get to me."

"Goodbye Tarkyn." Kosar hesitated before adding, "Might I remind you, in the interests of fairness, that this is not a truce. If I can capture you, I will."

Tarkyn's grin faded. "And if…" He waved his hand, "Never mind. It has all been said. Goodbye Kosar."

As the forest guardian turned and walked away into the trees, the huge golden eagle lifted slowly from her perch on the tent pole and glided above his head before flapping her wings ponderously to lift herself up through the trees and into the skies above.

Chapter 41

In a nearby part of the forest, Stormaway pounded along a narrow track, looking for all the world like Tarkyn from the back, long black hair streaming out behind him. A score of soldiers were in hot pursuit, calling ahead to their comrades hidden in the bushes to intercept. But unbeknownst to them, the woods on either side of Stormaway's pre-planned path were littered with unconscious sorcerers.

Stormaway reached a part of the forest where the path bent sharply to the right. As soon as he was out of sight of his pursuers, he stepped behind a bush, changed his appearance to blend with the soldiers and doubled back to join the rear of their ranks.

The soldiers rounded the corner and stared ahead at the empty path.

"Blast him! He must have slipped off into the trees. Why has no one intercepted him?" exclaimed an officer. "Spread out. He can't have got far."

From behind came the sound of more troops catching up to join the chase. They too were directed to join the search. As they scoured through the trees, they began to find unconscious sorcerers.

Cries of consternation filled the air and the soldiers re-grouped on the path carrying their fallen comrades. The officer put his shield up over them all. An air of dread settled on them and they looked nervously around themselves.

"Captain Sotrian, that is why no one intercepted him. He has killed them all," said a young soldier tightly. He looked around fearfully, "He is a madman. How did he do it? And why didn't he kill us too?"

In the trees above them, outraged woodfolk restrained themselves from correcting the soldiers' view of their prince.

Captain Sotrian shook his head, "I don't know. I can't begin to imagine how his mind works. But if that is so," replied the officer slowly, "the woods on either side of the path behind us, all the way along, must be littered with corpses." He squatted down and took a closer look at the soldiers laid out on the ground. He felt for a pulse in one inert soldier's neck and gave a grunt of relief, "This one, at least, is still alive. The Rogue Prince may not always have aimed well enough. Check the others."

It soon became apparent that all of the soldiers were alive. The captain scratched his head. "Well, that is a very strange thing. Surely he would have aimed properly some of the time, no matter how out of control he is. Just chance would dictate that he would hit truly sometimes."

Stormaway stood well back and resisted the temptation to enter the debate.

An old campaigner stood up from where he had been leaning over his fallen companions and said, "There is no chance involved in this, sir. They have all been hit with clinical precision, with skill far beyond our own. He may be a madman but he has not intended to kill any of us and his level of skill is astonishing… and terrifying."

The captain, who was young but from an influential family, glanced nervously around the trees. "And now he is somewhere out there waiting for me to drop my guard." He managed to produce a reassuring smile for his troops, "But don't worry, I won't."

"Sir," asked the old campaigner, mulling over events, "If he is so skilful, how did he make the error of letting us see him? And when you think about it, he can't have knocked out all those soldiers on the way past. He must have knocked them out *before* he ran down this way with us in hot pursuit."

The captain's eyes narrowed as he considered the old timer's words. "Hmm. I don't think he could have done all of this alone. I gather he has some sorcerers with him in the woods." He shook his head. "He must have trained them all up to be this skilful."

"But my point is, sir, that he had already prepared this path. He has deliberately led us this way, away from the king."

The captain's face blanched. "Oh my stars, Cobal, you are right! The king is in danger." He looked at the inert bodies laid out around him on the ground. "We'll have to leave these men. If what you say is true, they are safe enough." He shrugged, "But even if they aren't, our first duty is to the king. I will keep my shield up so that we can return unscathed to protect our liege."

As they turned back up the track in double quick time, Stormaway resigned himself to going with them. Because of the numbers of troops that had been deployed to catch Tarkyn, they did not all know each other. So he felt quite safe from detection. But it had not been part of his plan to return to the king's campsite and by the time they arrived there, he was out of breath and feeling his age.

The captain found the king seated near the fire in the midst of a bleary company of men, all giving their heads a little shake, grimacing with pain and then rubbing their hands over their faces, trying to give the appearance of some level of alertness. The king was paying little attention to their efforts, merely waiting patiently for them to pull themselves together.

In fact, he had been mulling over whether or not he should accede to Tarkyn's demand that he be lenient with his bested followers. Since the trip had already become an unmitigated disaster, his troops knowing that he had seen Tarkyn seemed to be almost irrelevant. In the end, the deciding factor was that Kosar did not want the world to know that Tarkyn, and not he, was sovereign of the forests and that was a trump that Tarkyn could use if Kosar insisted on punishing his followers.

As he saw the troops arrive, all shielded by a yellow haze, Kosar asked sharply, "What has happened that you have felt the need to raise your shield? You are supposed to be on the offensive, not the defensive."

The captain bowed low, "Your Majesty, I am relieved to find you safe. Might I suggest that it would be wise for you to raise your shield?"

"Why?" barked the King.

"The woods are full of unconscious soldiers, Your Majesty. The Rogue Prince has downed our troops wholesale. But he has not killed a single one of them. Even though he is the enemy, sir, one must admire such skill." The captain took a breath, aware that he walked on thin ice with his last statement. "But he did not manage to attack us, Your Majesty. So we returned to protect you, as soon as we realised the danger."

If Kosar was rocked by this evidence of his brother's far-reaching power within the forest, he didn't show it. He bit off the scathing remark he would have liked to make and instead demanded, "And where is my errant brother? I understood that you went in pursuit of him. I was expecting his delivery to me under guard."

Captain Sotrian glanced at his men before replying, "I beg your pardon, Your Majesty, but we lost sight of him. We scoured the trees on either side of the path but could not find him. It was then that we found the injured troops. Suddenly we realised that we had been deliberately led away from you."

"And in you absence, my renegade brother came here."

The captain's eyes widened. Every soldier and courtier went still. Ignoring their reactions, Kosar stared at him through narrowed eyes, "And how do you think I should reward such service as you have given me?"

The captain put his hand on his heart and went down on one knee. His troops followed suit behind him. "Your Majesty, whatever punishment you wish to give me, I will accept wholeheartedly. I realise that I have failed your expectation."

Kosar spoke coldly, "Of course you will accept it, Captain. That was never a consideration." He surveyed the soldiers before him for long minutes, letting them dread his retribution. Finally, he said, "At least you realised your priority was to ensure my safety and I can see that you acted as well as you could have, in the circumstances. You may all rise." He waved his hand and snapped, "Remove that ridiculous shield, Captain. You cannot protect me while you are protecting yourselves."

The officer looked chagrined and immediately waved away his shield, "I beg your pardon, sir. I had not thought."

"Now, go back and gather the fallen troops," ordered Kosar. "I want everyone assembled on the road near here in two hours' time. We return forthwith to Tormadell."

The captain hid his surprise by bowing, "Yes, Your Majesty. Your will is my command."

As soon as he and his troops had left, the King turned to his courtiers. "So, I hope you will be ready to ride in two hours. It is clear that we cannot capture Tarkyn within these forests." He glared at them all, "In fact, to all intents and purposes, he captured us. But for reasons I have yet to fathom, he chose not to kill any of us."

"But he is a rogue, isn't he, Sire?" asked one of his lords uncertainly.

"To all intents and purposes, yes," replied the king firmly. "He is excessively powerful, has no loyalty to his king, is unpredictable and in some ways, deluded." With the evidence staring them all in the face, he conceded, "He does not seem to be inherently evil but on the other hand, he does not have full control of his powers." He glanced around at all of them, "There is no doubt in my mind that he is extremely dangerous."

Part 7: Kosar and Jarand

CHAPTER 42

It was the end of a long day of feasting to welcome Prince Jarand back to Tormadell after several months' absence. The last of the guests had finally left amid florid gestures of gratitude and fealty. The vaulted ceiling of the great banqueting hall still seemed to ring with the laughter and chatter of a hundred voices.

Slowly the quiet returned and only the discreet footsteps and quiet murmuring of the servants clearing away the remains of the repast intruded on the silence.

The two brothers sat at the end of the long central table, one at the head and the other on his right hand side. The auburn of their hair matched perfectly as their heads bent together in quiet discussion. They both had their hands wrapped around heavy pewter goblets that were girded with a raised pattern of leaves circling cut garnets. Both brothers chose garnets above all other stones, even rubies, because they reflected the colour of their magic most exactly.

As one brother raised his grey eyes from the wine to contemplate the other, he could have been looking at himself. The only difference lay in the thin band of gold inlaid with silver filigree that Kosar always wore around his head to ensure that others could differentiate them and give each his correct due. A day of conviviality and drinking had relaxed them and, in addition, they had not seen each other for a while, so their differences had not yet resurfaced to mar their commonalities.

From fear of retribution, not one word of either brother's encounter with Tarkyn had crossed the lips of a single diner, sorely though it had tried their self-control. And only now that they were alone, did the brothers themselves allude to it.

Kosar looked at his brother with a little smile playing around his lips, "So, Jarand, I hear our little brother immobilised eighty of your men and took you hostage before their very eyes. How hideously embarrassing for you!"

Tarkyn, of all topics, united them in a common cause and so Jarand was able to take Kosar's remark in good part. He smiled wryly, "Yes. Not my finest hour, I would have to say. But you don't know the half of it."

Kosar leaned forward. "Really? Of course, I have so far only heard through my network. So, what happened?"

Jarand's eyes narrowed as he weighed up whether to broach the subject of the woodfolk. In the end, his need to share his experience overrode any caution. "You will be as astonished as I was to learn that we now have two more brothers and a niece in our family." Jarand then sat back and smiled as Kosar looked thunderstruck.

When he regained the power of speech, he demanded, "What do you mean? Tarkyn said nothing of this to me! What utter nonsense!"

Jarand's smile broadened. "No. I'm afraid not, brother. Tarkyn has allowed himself to become bloodbrother to one of these woodfolk - you know of woodfolk?"

When Kosar nodded shortly, "Not what they call themselves, but I do know of their existence."

Jarand suppressed a pang of disappointment that he hadn't surprised his brother with this knowledge too, as he continued with what he was saying. "His bloodbrother rejoices in the name of Waterstone. Our other brother is called Ancient Oak, I believe."

"Good heavens! What bizarre names! And the niece?"

"Her name is Sparrow. She was quite lacking in social graces. I think they must be a very crude people." He waited while Kosar signalled a servant to refill their goblets. When he had taken a sip of the deep ruby wine, he added, "There was one other I met: an arrogant young fellow called Rainstorm. He seemed to specialise in rudeness." He paused. "Unfortunately, I was not in a position to do anything about it and had to rely on Tarkyn's intercession which, in fairness, he did provide. But all in all, most unsatisfactory, to be frank."

Kosar glanced at him and then dropped his eyes to contemplate his wine. After a few moments, he reached out and took a savoury cheese biscuit from a basket on the table and broke it between his fingers. "I myself did not find Tarkyn's courtesy overwhelming." The king was not going to admit anything that might lead to the belief that Tarkyn had treated him with less deference than Jarand.

Jarand's eyes glittered angrily at the memory. "No. In fact I found him extremely insolent, but he did intervene with this Rainstorm character."

"In what way was he insolent?" asked Kosar casually.

Janrand knew this had now become a competition over who had been treated with more respect. But having come this far, he replied shortly, "He did not bow to me and sat down while I was still standing." Then his anger overcame him. "Outrageous! His behaviour was absolutely outrageous, Kosar. He treated me as an equal!"

"And yet here we are, you and I, conversing as equals," said Kosar gently, delicately twisting the knife of his superior rank.

But however much their inequality grated on Jarand, he accepted it, at least for the time being, as an unavoidable fact of life. "That may be so, Your Majesty, but I accorded you your due without question when I first arrived. Tarkyn did not accord me mine."

Having asserted himself, Kosar was able to concede, "No. I regret to say I had a similar experience and, without wishing to rub salt into wounds, it is of even greater significance when he does not accord due reverence to his king."

Jarand raised his eyebrows. "Indeed it is. I think you were right to arrest him. I had my doubts at the time but I had not fully realised how strong he had become." He waved his hand, "Not in terms of magical power - although that too is worrying – but in terms of his personal assurance." Jarand shook his head, "I always thought he was so unquestioningly compliant."

Kosar sighed. "I think he was. I think we may have uncaged a tiger. Information from all my sources now leads me to believe that, until he was arrested, he had no thought of challenging me. Others may have wanted him to challenge me, but not Tarkyn himself."

"And does he now?" asked Jarand.

Kosar frowned in perplexity. "Apparently not. Not if I can believe what he says."

Jarand snorted derisively, "Well, he's hardly likely to come straight out and say, 'Oh by the way, ready your defences because I'm coming for your throne,' is he?"

Kosar gave a distracted smile but was unconvinced. "You know, I don't think Tarkyn is as devious as your average sorcerer. In fact, incurably honest, as I remember him. One of his greatest failings."

"So why has he gone to all that trouble to talk to each of us when he could have stayed away with far less risk to himself and his associates?" Jarand reached into a bowl, selected a walnut and cracked it carefully with a fine silver nutcracker. He looked slyly at his brother, "No doubt he has said things to each of us to set us at odds with each other."

Kosar carefully sidestepped the implied question and got in first with his own. "So do I presume he spoke disparagingly of me? Come on, as your brother and your king, I am asking you, what did he say?"

But Jarand's loyalty to Kosar as his king only went as far as public acknowledgement. So he had no intention of being unduly honest unless it suited his cause… and he had had plenty of time to think on the long journey from Montraya.

"Tarkyn was not so much disparaging as pitying – no, perhaps sympathetic. Yes, I think sympathetic is a better word. He seemed to know from his sources which, by the way, have Stormaway Treemaster at their core unless I'm very much mistaken, that the affairs of the realm press heavily on your shoulders and he expressed some uncertainty about your ability to cope."

There was enough truth in this and enough resonance with what Tarkyn had said to Kosar for the king to become very angry in response. "How dare he? His attitude is insufferable. I'll have him horsewhipped. I'll hang him from the highest gallows. How dare he pass judgement on my kingship?" The fact that everyone in the land passed judgement on his governance behind closed doors did not even enter his mind.

Jarand sighed theatrically, "Would that you could have him horsewhipped and hanged, Kosar. But as he was quick to point out, he is now beyond the law."

As Kosar sat fuming, Jarand pressed home his advantage. "And I bet I can guess what he said about me." Jarand picked out the kernel of his walnut and broke it in half and ate one half neatly and slowly before continuing, "Let me see. He has probably blown the encampment I have in the western side of the forest out of all proportion and what else? That I have been press-ganging people into military service." Jarand shrugged disarmingly. "In fact, he was probably right about the latter. I had been running a recruitment drive to assist you in your fight against lawlessness and Tarkyn alerted me to the fact that some of my officers had become too zealous and harsh in the pursuit of their duties." He ate another morsel of walnut before adding, "But you will be pleased to know that I have addressed that."

"And this encampment of which you speak?"

Jarand waved his hand dismissively. "It just grew up out of nowhere. It began as a place of sanctuary, so to speak, for travellers we had rescued from brigands on the Great West Road but it has really got out of hand. People are so lazy. Because we provide them with food and shelter, however rudimentary, many of them have lingered. Even as we speak, the travellers who have overstayed their welcome are being escorted along the

Great West Road either towards their destination or back towards their homes. I really can't afford to keep them indefinitely."

Kosar who was, after all, steeped in sorcerer politics, was only partially convinced by this disarming little speech. "I thank you, Jarand, for the support you are giving my subjects. I think, when you return to Montraya, I will travel along the Great West Road with you and visit this encampment of yours to show my gratitude for your fine works."

Jarand inclined his head, "It would be an honour, sire."

Kosar patted his hand firmly but condescendingly, "I think it only fair that you should receive all the recognition you deserve."

Jarand's blood discreetly boiled.

CHAPTER 43

It was not until the following day that the conversation continued. The royal brothers were standing on a stone balcony overlooking the castle's training grounds watching men at arms practising their skills.

Kosar nodded down at a group of archers who were being put through their paces by Captain Sotrian. "That is the only good thing that has come out of my foray into the forest in search of Tarkyn. The skill of his followers has inspired my men to work on their own accuracy."

Jarand raised his eyebrows in surprise, "I did not find these woodfolk particularly impressive. It was clever use of a sorcerer's shield in the main that caused havoc with my men, not woodfolk. Not one of my men was killed, with the notable exception of my captain, of course. But that was my doing, not Tarkyn's or his woodfolk's."

Kosar nodded understandingly and forebore to mention that he had been manoeuvred by Tarkyn into refraining from punishing his men. After a minute or two during which he weighed up the wisdom of telling Jarand too much, Kosar said, "I suppose I cannot be sure whether it was sorcerers or these woodfolk who so efficiently knocked out my men. But I can tell you this; I had highly skilled soldiers, many of them elite guards, deployed throughout the forest ready to ambush Tarkyn when I arrived. Not of one of them reported sighting Tarkyn, his sorcerers or anyone else. Not only that, but at least seventy men were carefully and quietly knocked unconscious."

Jarand waved a hand in disgust. "Bloody Tarkyn! Why can't he just kill them as you or I would? He is so pretentiously moral."

Kosar gave a short laugh. "Perhaps. Or perhaps he does not want to justify our retribution. But you're missing the point here. How many of your men can reliably knock people unconscious without giving themselves away or inadvertently killing the odd one here or there?"

Jarand thought for a moment, "Not many, I suppose, when you put it like that. Perhaps none." He shrugged, "On the other hand, it mostly does not concern me if a miscreant is killed or maimed. If they have been targeted by my men, they probably deserve whatever they get."

Kosar rolled his eyes, "Jarand, again you are missing the point. The point is that whoever they are, Tarkyn has at his disposal a small army of people unmatched in marksmanship and camouflage. My seventy men are only alive because Tarkyn chose not to have them killed. And I suspect that every one of the six hundred men I deployed could have been picked off, had it suited our brother." The king shook his head. "You mark my words. The woodlands are no longer safe for sorcerers."

After a short pause Jarand gave an uncomfortable little cough, "Kosar, much as I like to concur with you on all matters but particularly on matters concerning Tarkyn, I cannot, in this instance, see that your logic holds. If, as you suppose, Tarkyn could have killed off your six hundred soldiers but didn't, even when they were part of a clear act of aggression against him, surely it holds that he is even less likely to harm them if they go into the woods on peaceful business."

"I do not like my men's lives being subject to Tarkyn's beneficence whenever they venture into the forests. It does not sit well with me at all," said the King flatly.

"No. I should think not," agreed Jarand. "It is *your* kingdom, after all."

"Hmph. Exactly," grunted Kosar, staring steadfastly at the soldiers training below.

But Jarand knew Kosar inside out and he caught the underlying lack of conviction in his words. His eyes narrowed, "What's going on, Kosar?"

But Kosar also knew how to keep Jarand at bay. He turned on him and said forcefully, "There are times when it doesn't feel as though it's my kingdom at all; my youngest brother running amok in the forests in the centre of the kingdom and you, up to all sorts of intrigue and subterfuge down in the south west. That does not leave me with much of the kingdom on which I can depend."

Jarand just stared at him. He was on dangerous ground with the king speaking like that. It was a very short step from this to an open accusation of treason. After a fraught silence, he drew a breath and said urbanely, "I am grieved that you should find my service in any way lacking. My efforts to subdue lawlessness on your behalf have no doubt ruffled a few feathers. I would be interested to know the source of these accusations."

"I'm sure you would, brother, but my sources are my own." The king shrugged, having successfully diverted his brother's attention from the sovereignty of the forest. "Besides, I am not accusing you of anything. There are merely rumours. As you say, probably disgruntled sorcerers who have felt the strong arm of your law enforcement." But even as he said it, he realised wryly that the source was Tarkyn and that he trusted his source. Tarkyn might be misguided or mistaken but he had never known him to be deliberately dishonest.

As Kosar digested this uncomfortable little truth about his maligned brother, the queen mother appeared in the doorway at the end of the balcony. She was a vision of frothy white lace, flanked by two ladies in waiting in similar but less ornate attire. As the trio approached the royal brothers, the two ladies in waiting dropped low curtsies while the queen mother made more of a gesture than a curtsey.

"My dears, it is lovely to see you together, enjoying each other's company. It is so rarely that we have time to spend together as a family."

"And this is obviously not one of those times," said Kosar with an irritated glance at his mother's retainers.

"My dear, Lady Jirriel and Lady Mirallee share my every secret. They are completely trustworthy."

Kosar inclined his head in acknowledgement. "I am pleased to hear it, mother. And yet they will not share mine." He nodded his head curtly and turned to walk away.

His mother placed a restraining hand on his arm which he looked down at with raised eyebrows. She whipped it away, but said, "No, stay, if you will, Your Majesty." She waved her hand, "Leave us, ladies. I will see you at luncheon."

Once they were gone, she turned to her sons and sighed with exasperation. "How are you ever going to produce heirs if you will not take wives?"

"Mother," said Jarand, "The need for heirs is a long way off. Neither of us has any intention of dying young."

"Neither did your father, and he was only in his early forties when he died." For a moment a shadow passed across her face but with a visible effort she brightened and said, "But at least he left thr…two fine sons behind him."

"You see?" said Kosar dryly. "It is just as well your women have left us…and I would not like to think that you discussed Tarkyn with your ladies, no matter how trustworthy you find them."

"But dear, I cannot help but discuss him. Everyone is talking about him again." She smiled uncertainly at him, "You see, I am honest with you, Kosar." After an appreciable hesitation, she looked from one to the other of them. "I know you have both met with him recently. Word of it is everywhere. And I know, Kosar, that against everything I believed about him, apparently he had designs on your throne. So I completely accept that you had to curtail him. But I was just wondering… Is he all right? How does he look? Is he much changed?"

"You tread on very thin ice here, Mother. You come close to expressing sympathy for a traitor." Kosar glanced at her sardonically, knowing she couldn't help herself.

Sure enough, she immediately became flustered, "No dear, no. I support you completely. You know I do. I was just wondering. That was all."

Kosar and Jarand looked at each other. By mutual consent, Jarand spoke first. "He is well, mother, but he is much changed."

Their mother put a hand to her face, "No! Don't tell me. Is he starved and ragged, with no one to turn to?"

"No Mother," replied Jarand dryly. "Stop being melodramatic. He is disgustingly healthy. His clothes are not the finest I have ever seen but they are adequate."

"*Barely* adequate. I would not call them a gentleman's attire. Rather rough and ready but warm enough, mother. You need not fear for his physical wellbeing," Kosar raised his eyebrows, "unless of course we catch him."

His mother gave a little wave of her hand as if to dismiss this unpleasant fact. "So, in what way has he changed, my dears?"

Kosar considered, "I suppose you could say he has grown up."

"That alone does not account for his lack of manners." said Jarand dryly.

"But my dears, he is probably angry with you. You can't really expect him to be nice about it, can you, even if your actions were justified."

"It is a little more than that, mother." Kosar turned from her to lean on the balcony and look out over the courtyard, "He behaves as though he were of equal or even higher rank. His behaviour is beyond arrogance or presumption. He has an assurance and a disregard for our status, my status, which is quite confounding."

The queen looked a little startled, "Good Heavens! That does not sound like him at all. He was always meticulous in observing the expectations of his and everyone else's roles." She gave a delicate little shrug, "Still, if he is no longer part of our hierarchy, I suppose the expectations have also changed. But you know, dears, I would have expected him to become less sure of himself after losing his place in our society. Besides which, I would have thought that he would be ashamed of himself for the disaster he left in his wake. I always found him very contrite in the past when he'd done something wrong."

"That was just to protect his whipping boy, mother," said Jarand scathingly. "It just goes to show how important it is to keep people under control. Who knows how he would have turned out if we hadn't had Danton as hostage to his good behaviour."

Kosar gave a little cough, "I think you are forgetting, brother, that he has turned out to be a hunted felon and so, arguably, could not have turned out worse."

Jarand waved an impatient hand, "You know what I mean. Anyway, he might have wreaked havoc earlier without Danton to punish."

"Yes, true, especially with that tendency towards disrespect that he obviously has. You noticed that Danton left precipitously after Tarkyn's exit? Do you think he feared punishment or do you think he went in search of Tarkyn?"

"The latter," said Jarand with certainty. "It was Danton's shield that held my troops while Tarkyn spoke with me. So I know he is with Tarkyn."

The king looked thoughtful, "What is it about our brother that warrants such extravagant loyalty?" he pondered, unknowingly echoing Ancient Elm's words. "Why would Danton throw away a perfectly good career in the palace guards and a life at court to go and live in exile in the forest?"

The Queen sighed, "I know what you mean, my dears. Sadly, much as I hate to say it, you were right to get rid of Tarkyn. He was becoming far too popular."

Kosar's eyebrows twitched together. "Mother! I hope you are not saying that to your ladies."

The Queen's eyebrows arched delicately, "Give me a little credit. It is not my custom to stir up ill feeling against you. You have a hard enough job as it is." She tripped over to the balustrade and waved down at Captain Sotrian who bowed and waved his hat gallantly before returning to his soldiers' training.

"Mother! You are such an outrageous flirt. That man is far too young for you!" Jarand tried to look severe but failed in the face of the laughter in his mother's eyes.

She put her hand on his arm, "Don't be silly, dear. Just a bit of fun. Anyway, it's his father I'm more interested in" She sighed gustily, "Sadly, he is happily married and I'm afraid I am decorous enough not to try my hand at an affair with a married man."

The king frowned at her, "I should hope so. You could wind up in all sorts of politically compromising situations if you did that."

The queen mother smiled sunnily, "That's what I meant; wary of intrigue. Decorous sounds better though, don't you think?"

"Yes, mother, it does. It makes it sound as though you harbour a few morals in that lace covered bosom of yours. Completely deceiving, of course."

The spoilt, pretty woman laughed, "Oh Kosar, how unkind! I do have a few morals, you know. I just try not to let them inconvenience me too often."

He raised his eyebrows, "And I understand that you did not inconvenience yourself to the extent of providing Tarkyn with any education in magic. Rather an oversight, wouldn't you say?"

His mother looked flustered, "Oh dear, I did mean to, you know. But there are always so many dramas when you two are under the same roof. And you know, dears, I did have to keep the peace so much between you when you were younger. It took up all my time…That and the odd chat… and liaison…and of course there were always so many social events to organise…and if not them, then there were official events."

"You do realise mother that, had Tarkyn known how to control his magic, those people may not have died and we might still have the Great Hall?" said Kosar.

"And then he'd have been safely tucked up in jail and you wouldn't have had all this gossip to contend with, would you, dears?" she said lightly. "Oh dear. Naughty me!"

The king frowned at something in her tone, "Mother, have a care. I would almost think you sympathise with him."

"Darling, a mother's love cannot just extinguish when her son does something wrong. But since he must be punished, I would prefer him to be safe and well, out in the woodlands somewhere, rather than rotting in one of our dreadful jails." She gave a little shudder, "Bedsides, it would be so unseemly for a member of the royal family to be reduced to such squalor. Not at all good for our image, dear."

She was such a flighty character that Kosar was not sure which factor weighed more heavily with her, although her tone inclined him towards the second. "You do realise, mother, that if I get the chance, I will bring Tarkyn back and have him hanged?"

The Queen picked at the lace on her sleeve. After a moment she raised her eyes, all laughter gone, "Yes dear, I do realise that. It grieves me more than I could ever express. That is all I will say about it. I keep my feelings about this very private. My ladies have no idea how I feel and never will. You have your kingdom to run and must do so, as you see fit." She gave a wan smile, "And now my dears, I think I must take a rest. I will see you this evening."

The twins watched in silence as she walked quietly along the balcony and out through the door on the end, all her usual exuberance in abeyance. After a moment, they turned in unison to lean once more on the balcony.

"Whew! That was a bit of a leveller, wasn't it?" breathed Jarand.

Kosar heaved a sigh. "I know you wish you were king, Jarand. But there are times when it is not an enviable position." He picked off a flake of peeling paint from the balustrade, "You know, I don't think I ever talked properly to Tarkyn before the other day? He was always too young and I was always swamped with intrigue and affairs of state. I sorely underestimated him."

"So too did I… which is not to say that I like his attitude." Jarand shrugged, "Anyway, you would have had to remove him sooner or later. He is much too strong. That's why we got rid of him when we did." He clapped his brother on the shoulder, "You …*we* …did the right thing, you know."

The king turned to his brother, "Trouble is, Jarand, we didn't get rid of him. He's out there in the forest and, as long as he stays there, unassailable. There is a growing groundswell of support for him. Those blasted sorcerers came back from the Forest of Yesterday Today and Tomorrow singing his praises to all and sundry. I should have had them all horsewhipped or had their tongues cut out when they first arrived. Too late now."

"Hmm," Jarand gazed out across the courtyard to the far fields beyond the castle wall, drumming his fingers as he thought. Suddenly he snapped his fingers, "You know, we could use those sorcerers from the Forest of Yesterday Today and Tomorrow. Imprison them and threaten to hang them for treason. If you want to lure Tarkyn out of the forest, there is your way to do it." Jarand leaned back and gave a predatory smile.

"He really annoyed you, didn't he?" Kosar thought for a minute. "He angered me too, very much so. But he also intrigued me. There is something quite impressive about him and, strange as it may seem, I'm beginning to believe that he actually doesn't want to be king." He shook his head in amazement, "After all, he has had each of us isolated and surrounded by his men, and yet did not harm either of us." He looked at Jarand, "Besides, these Lost sorcerers are almost folk heroes and to be honest, I'm not sure that it will do my popularity much good at the moment to drag them in… or to hang Tarkyn, for that matter." Even as he said it, he realised that anything that made him less popular would be to Jarand's advantage. "It's a good idea. Tarkyn is definitely too soft for his own good and I'm sure would try to rescue them. I will keep a very close eye on them so that I can close in on them if I find that Tarkyn is playing me false."

"You are just pandering to our mother," said Jarand with the slightest sneer.

"Perhaps, but I don't think so." He blew out a deep breath and said firmly, "Anyway, that is my decision for the time being."

"But am I permitted to lure him out of the forest to make him stand trial in Montraya?"

Kosar surprised himself by saying, "No. Not just now." He covered his reaction by saying, "I think it only fair that your popularity is also left untarnished for the time being."

Jarand blinked in astonishment at his brother's concern but inclined his head in acceptance, trying to work out as he did, how he could use his idea to his own advantage without directly disobeying the king.

Chapter 44

Twig Snap's eyes grew round. She gestured to Leaf Fall who had just arrived to join her where she sat under a tree chatting to Autumn Leaves. "Look Leaf Fall! See that man over there? That's Falling Rain. You know? The one who was exiled for betraying us to the sorcerers."

Leaf Fall glanced at her in some amusement. "Yes, but it turns out he didn't really, Twig. That's why he's back."

Twig Snap gave a huff of exasperation, "I know that. He's still famous though." She gave a little grin, "Just not infamous anymore." She raised her eyebrows, "And just think! He's been all on his own for *years*. The poor man! How sad. And he didn't even deserve it."

"Yes, it is sad that he lost all that time with us," said Autumn Leaves gravely. "And even more so the time with Tree Wind. They were to be wed, you know."

"Really? And what happened? Did Tree Wind find someone else?"

Autumn Leaves smiled, "No. She could never forget Falling Rain even though it seemed that there was no prospect of him returning." He gave a little chuckle, "She made life very hard for Tarkyn for a long time after he arrived."

Twig Snap screwed her face up in thought. "But have I got this all wrong? Wasn't Falling Rain sent into exile a long time ago? Tarkyn couldn't have been very old then. What did he have to do with it?"

"No, you are right. Tarkyn had nothing to do with it at all. He just inherited our dislike of the Tamadils and our resentment at having to serve them. But Tree Wind's loss was the greatest and so too was her resentment." Autumn Leaves shrugged, "There was some justification for her attitudes. After all, even if he didn't instigate it, the main purpose of imposing the oath was to provide Tarkyn with protection."

"Still, I suppose as soon as you realised he was a forest guardian, you all gave him your full support anyway, didn't you?" said Leaf Fall confidently.

Autumn Leaves glanced at the younger woodman. "Some of us did. But not all, by any means and even those of us who did support him, have doubted him and clashed with him sometimes." The heavy woodman nodded his head slowly as he thought about it, "Now you put it like that, I realise that if he had been a born woodman, our support for him as a forest guardian would have been far more unquestioning."

"But if he had been born a woodman," put in Waterstone, sitting down to join in the discussion, "he would never have been so autocratic."

"And we wouldn't have had that blasted oath confusing the issue," added Autumn Leaves.

"So, is he really as lazy as Thunder Storm says?" asked Leaf Fall.

Waterstone looked stunned, "Who? Tarkyn?" He gave a grunt of laughter. "No. He's not lazy. He just does as he chooses. Completely different." He nodded at Twig Snap. "You saw him in action. When the need arises, he achieves more in a few minutes than we could achieve in a lifetime." He grinned, "He just doesn't bother himself with the mundane things in life unless it takes his fancy. He keeps telling us that being a prince means being a drain on everyone around you, but don't believe him for a second. He gives us back a hundredfold anything we do for him."

A puzzled little frown appeared on Autumn Leaves' face. "What's made you wax so lyrical all of a sudden? I'm not saying I don't agree with you. I probably do. But you are usually the first to take him to task, not to sing his praises."

Waterstone shook his head regretfully, "You see? Moridan was right. I spend too much time getting up on my high horse and berating Tarkyn. I never behave like that to you, do I?"

Autumn Leaves gave a slight smile, "No, but you are not my older brother. And you do give him support when he is troubled that no one else can give."

"I know I do. And I would never want to lose that." Waterstone bent down and picked up a couple of small dusty pebbles to fiddle with. "What Moridan said is really worrying me."

"What did he say?" asked Twig Snap.

"He told Tarkyn and me to be careful not to strain the bonds of friendship too hard, in case they break." Waterstone threw away the pebbles, put his elbows on his knees and ran his hands distractedly though his hair. "And when I look back I can see that I have, much more than Tarkyn has. I get angry with him too often and too much."

"From what I saw of him with Harkell before we flicked into hiding, I would say that's a fairly dangerous occupation," said Leaf Fall.

Waterstone sent him an impatient glance, "No, he doesn't usually meet anger with anger. He is just as likely to take everything I say to heart and to withdraw into himself."

Twig nodded knowingly in agreement.

"Why don't you talk to him about it?" asked Autumn Leaves.

"What's to say? I've already said I'm sorry." He waved a hand, "That's what I do. Rip into him about something, then as often as not discover I'm wrong and apologise. But it's just not good enough."

"It's not all one way," said Autumn Leaves quietly. "Tarkyn can be very disdainful when he's angry." He glanced at Leaf Fall. "He never threatens anyone physically but he does have a knack of making people feel very small. But it is not Tarkyn's anger that strains the friendship with Waterstone." He waved a hand as he tried to explain, "Tarkyn has an inbred belief in his superior status and although as a rule, he tries to avoid it, sometimes he rams it down Waterstone's throat…and ours."

Leaf Fall and Twig Snap looked a little uncertain.

Waterstone smiled wryly. "For instance, in the Lost Forest he required all the Lost woodfolk and sorcerers to pay homage to him and worse than that, I had to stand beside him as his brother. It was ghastly." He shrugged, "Then there was the time we met up with Falling Rain and forgot to introduce him to Tarkyn… And I think probably the worst time was when he had rescued you, Autumn Leaves, and when we tried to remonstrate with him for going into danger without us, he told us that that he would dictate to us or not as he chose, but *he* would not be dictated to by anyone." A spark of anger flashed in the woodman's eyes. "He can be quite insufferable at times."

Autumn Leaves patted his knee, "Now, don't go winding yourself up, Waterstone. You know he does the best he can. And despite what he said then, he often does as others request. You just have to be careful how you phrase it." He thought for a minute before adding, "And other than the incident with Falling Rain, his behaviour has usually sprung from his wish to support others, not himself."

Waterstone eyed him belligerently for a moment before letting out a gusty sigh. "I just can't let it go. No more than he, can I foreswear the values I was brought up with."

"No one wants you to, Waterstone," said Autumn Leaves gently. "Not even Tarkyn's relative Moridan, I'm sure, and certainly not Tarkyn. Your strong belief in treating people equally is what made you look after Tarkyn in the first place. He knows that we think differently and have to accept his authority against our better judgement. He just maintains his own beliefs in the midst of us and generally tries to make them as unobtrusive as he can, without abandoning them completely."

Twig Snap snorted, "There's nothing unobtrusive about Tarkyn or his values. He's the most vibrant person I've ever met."

"I agree with Twig Snap," said her brother, "As soon as he deigns to make an appearance in the morning, that's it. Everything revolves around him.

Waterstone chuckled, "He doesn't mean it to. He takes it as a matter of course that he will be provided with breakfast when he appears but other than that, he doesn't expect everyone to stop what they're doing to gather around him. And let's face it. In the short time you have been here, he has been called upon to heal Boravar and then to meet up with his brother the king. We all had a vested interest in both of those activities but Tarkyn was pivotal to them." Waterstone waved his hand and gave another chuckle, "Who am I trying to fool? You're right. He is at the centre of nearly everything. I remember Autumn Leaves and myself trying to back up Tarkyn's statement that he had no intention of ruling us by showing Rainstorm images of us working together."

Autumn Leaves smiled, "Didn't work at all. In every situation he was exerting his authority to some extent. It comes as naturally as breathing to him."

"Even when everyone has a fair say, which is, I must admit, most of the time, it is because Tarkyn has chosen that to be the way things will run."

A glance of consternation passed between Twig Snap and Leaf Fall.

"How sad," said Twig Snap quietly, "that any woodfolk's independence is held hostage to this one man's good humour. I know ours is not, but it must be very hard for you."

Waterstone and Autumn Leaves exchanged glances and chose not to mention that there was a time when all woodfolk had unknowingly had their service to Tarkyn tied to the welfare of the forest.

"Is there nothing that can be done to release you from this situation?" asked Leaf Fall.

Autumn Leaves smiled, "Do you know, you are the first people not bound by the oath to talk to us about how we are managing with it. Everyone else just treated us like second class citizens when we gathered for the ceremony for Tarkyn to become a woodman."

"Is that how you feel?" asked Twig Snap, her little face puckered up with worry.

His smile broadened, "No, Twig Snap. We might have, at that stage, if Tarkyn had forced us to show him respect overtly in front of everyone else. But now, if anything, I would say we feel more privileged than others that we are able to share in the creation of legends that will be told to our children for generations to come."

Waterstone gave a warm smile, "Despite his drawbacks, none of us would choose to lose Tarkyn." He grimaced, "No. That statement is not strong enough. It's more than that. He has thrown his heart and soul into our cause; saving the entire woodfolk nation from the curse, bringing Falling Rain back from exile, organising the rescue of Golden Toad and his family, destroying the storm that threatened to herd us onto high ground, saving the forest from that rampant infection and releasing the forest from the oath…"

"And saving me," added Autumn Leaves.

Twig Snap smiled, "And Boravar."

Waterstone waved a hand, "And other things besides. You saw what he is like. He didn't think twice about the risk to himself. He just threw himself into keeping Boravar alive." The woodman smiled, "I suppose what I'm getting around to saying is that we can handle being bossed around a bit because he gives us so much in return. "

Twig Snap studied him, "You meant it when you said he gives you back a hundredfold anything you give to him, didn't you? I thought you were exaggerating at the time but I can see you really meant it."

"And you may come in from the outside and think he is strong and sure, and he is in many ways, I suppose. But you should have seen the fear on his face when he realised that he would have to summon a shade and exert dominion over him to release our people from the curse. But he did it. No one else in the whole world, literally, could have done it. It had to be him and so he did it. But he was scared to death of it." Waterstone wagged his finger, "Now, *that* is true courage."

Autumn Leaves looked at him, "You know Waterstone, I think you may nearly be ready to go and talk to him. You have more than an apology to say to him now, don't you?"

Waterstone's face lit in a broad smile, "Autumn Leaves, you're a genius! I think I'll find a flask of wine and a couple of mugs and bear him off to the river for a chat."

CHAPTER 45

Twenty minutes later, with a small rucksack filled with supplies slung on his back, Waterstone stomped over to Tarkyn and said, "Come on, young one. We need to talk."

Tarkyn raised his eyebrows and threw an apprehensive grimace at Danton and Harkell, with whom he had been talking, before standing up and following his woodbrother without question.

"I saw that," said Waterstone briefly over his shoulder as they walked down to the river.

Tarkyn grinned. "Sorry. I'm just waiting to see what I've done wrong this time."

Waterstone grunted but said nothing further until they had seated themselves in their time honoured place against the rocks looking out over the river. The reeds swayed in the soft breeze of early spring and the branches overhead were covered in buds that had not yet unfurled. A pale yellow sun failed to provide any real warmth but its clear light brightened colours and sent sparks of silver flashing off the surface of the rippling water.

"Come on then. What have I done?" asked Tarkyn, watching a small grebe bobbing up and down in the middle of the river.

"Nothing," said Waterstone, as he busily unpacked his rucksack and spread out a flask of wine, two cups, and various nuts and fruits in a couple of bowls. When he had finished, he looked up and smiled, "No, nothing at all. Nothing bad, anyway… and a huge amount that is very good."

Tarkyn turned to regard his woodbrother, his brow furrowed in a puzzled frown.

"Tarkyn, remember that time when you were upset, just before we rescued Golden Toad from the encampment?"

Tarkyn nodded uncertainly.

"Well, remember I said that I had chosen to have you as a brother and that I would never let you go?"

Misunderstanding where this was heading, Tarkyn's stomach turned over in dread. Seeing Tarkyn's face tighten, Waterstone rushed on, "No, no, no. I'm not about to say I've changed my mind. What I *am* about to say is that I want to make totally sure I keep my word. I don't want to let you go. This has nothing to do with the oath. You know that, don't you?"

Tarkyn nodded.

"Tarkyn, what Moridan said scared me. I don't want to lose your friendship and I don't want you to lose mine." Waterstone handed his adopted brother a cup of wine, "Here."

"Thanks." Tarkyn took a sip of wine, watching Waterstone over the rim of the cup.

Waterstone did not seem to mind that Tarkyn was saying very little and ploughed on regardless. "I didn't just want to apologise again. That seems a bit pointless. But, I don't know...I just want to make sure the firm foundation of our friendship is still in place, and if not, to repair it." The woodman eyed Tarkyn who was still not responding. "I have just finished talking to Leaf Fall and Twig Snap about some of your achievements and Autumn Leaves and I were more or less saying how proud we are, to be part of a legend unfolding. And it occurred to me, well to Autumn Leaves actually - since I had said to him that I wanted to talk to you but didn't know what to say – that I should tell you how impressed and proud I am of you. I even told them what courage you showed when you faced the shade of Pipeless, to fight for our cause." He gave a wry smile, "I seem to spend much too much time focussing on your shortcomings… as witnessed by your reaction to me asking to speak to you."

Finally a smile spread slowly across Tarkyn's face. "Thanks Waterstone. It means a great deal to me – not that you are impressed by what I've done – but that you have made the effort to make sure that things are well between us." He waved his hand, "I already knew what you thought about those achievements you're talking about, because you were with me every step of the way, supporting me. You mightn't have made a huge fuss about it but you have always given me acknowledgement...and often on a much deeper level than anyone else… when you helped me to gather my resources to heal myself after the mountainfolk attack , for instance, and when I was reeling from Stormaway saying he had given me to you." His eyes crinkled with laughter over the rim of his cup as he took another sip. "Don't worry. I don't think of you as an ogre. I only reacted like that because one is rarely pulled aside to be praised and you were so business-like about it."

"Hmph. Well, that's all right then."

"And whatever you do, please don't start thinking of me as my achievements. I am who I am, regardless of all that. And you, Waterstone, know who that is more than anyone else."

Waterstone sipped his wine and after a noticeable pause, asked, "Do I? I'm not sure that's true anymore."

A worried little frown appeared on Tarkyn's face. "*I* think you do. Why are you unsure?"

Waterstone flicked a quick glance at Tarkyn before looking steadfastly away across the river. "Because other people have shared so much more with you now, than I have. You shared all those memories with Falling

Rain. You've shared your whole life rhythm with Boravar. You have so many people from your own background now who have a more intuitive understanding of you than I have."

"You're not jealous of them, are you? Not one of them could replace you."

Waterstone gave a little smile, "Thank you. I feel honoured you say that because they are all fine people." He thought for a minute. "No. I am not jealous. I am glad to see you with so many true friends… but I confess that I am a little envious." He took a little breath and screwed up his courage to ask, "Do you think…? I mean, would you mind…? I mean, would you…"

Tarkyn watched him with his head on one side, with a little smile playing around his mouth, "Would I what? Come on, ask me. I promise I won't eat you."

"Would you consider sharing some of your memories with me?"

"What? Haven't I ever done that?" Tarkyn looked thunderstruck. He thought hard for a minute. "Yes I have. Remember? When you were checking that none of those parasites had gone into my brain."

"Not memories from your life among sorcerers."

"No, you're right. I never have, have I?" Without hesitation, he asked, "What would you like to see?"

Waterstone's face relaxed into a smile, "Are you giving me completely free access?"

Tarkyn smiled, "Yes, my friend. You did it for me. But be gentle with me."

The woodman thought for a minute, "Maybe I need to see something that will make me understand your attitudes better…Maybe some formal occasion. I wouldn't mind seeing that Great Hall you destroyed, the one that Kosar referred to as an icon. And maybe what it's like inside a palace." He grinned, "You realise I have never even been inside a permanent building. The closest I have ever come to it was when I stood outside the window of Lord Tolward's house."

Tarkyn laughed, "Waterstone, I have so shamefully neglected your education. You have taught me all about woodfolk and I have given you nothing in return."

"It's not quite that bad. You have talked about it. I just don't know what it looks like."

"Come on then. Look into my eyes and I will show you."

Good as his word, Tarkyn gave his friend a guided tour through the long corridors of the palace, detouring to show him his bed chamber, the huge public dining hall, the smaller family dining room, Danton's room, the parlours, the reception rooms and the throne room. *All the people I pass, bow and keep their eyes down. Here are the stables and kitchen garden, and just a quick look into the kitchen on the way past.* "Cook tried to hide it but she used to get very uncomfortable if I stayed too long." *Only in the kitchen and the stables, do people straighten up and converse with me but it is clear, even without words, that their conversation is stilted and self-conscious. From there I wander past the fountains and through the ornate gardens that surround the palace.* As his memories neared the huge wrought iron gates, flanked by guards, that gave passage through a high thick stone wall, Waterstone signalled a halt.

He gave a dazed smile, "Tarkyn, this is amazing. I can't begin to tell you how astonishing it all is." He reached for the flask. "I think we'd better have a drink to recover." After a few minutes he said, "That waterfall that runs upside down is intriguing. I have never seen one anywhere in the forest that doesn't run from top to bottom."

"It's not natural, Waterstone. The engineers have forced fast flowing water into increasingly small pipes until it has enough strength to flow up into the air." Tarkyn gave a little smile. "I don't actually know how it works but it's something like that."

"And everything seems to have sharp corners and all the surfaces seem to run either straight across or straight up. Not like the forest. Trees have all sorts of angles in them and so do our shelters." Waterstone looked down at himself, "And so do we."

Tarkyn laughed. "This is great fun. Come on. Are you ready? Let me show you the Great Hall."

Waterstone took a deep breath, "Okay. Go on."

Tarkyn took him along an avenue lined with carefully matched, pruned elms. *At the end is an enormous stone building, its portico held aloft by large stone pillars and flanked by bronze statues. Flags fly from every corner of the building, fluttering in the breeze. As I approach the building, men and women fall back and bow deeply, waiting until I pass, to straighten. When I glance back over my shoulder, they sink once more until I turn away.*

"This was to celebrate my brothers' twentieth birthday," explained Tarkyn. "I must have been thirteen."

Watertone's eyes grew round. "You were only thirteen and they treated you like that?"

Tarkyn smiled, "Always, Waterstone. From when I first appeared in public as a boy of four years old. That, at least, is my earliest memory of it."

"Huh, Harkell was right, wasn't he? You weren't demanding anything unusual from the sorcerers of the Lost Forest, were you?"

Tarkyn shook his head, "No. But I must admit it was strange that the Lost woodfolk were also keen to greet me like that."

Waterstone eyed the prince, wondering how much to say. In the end he simply decided to say what he was thinking. "Yes. That is what distressed me the most. You sorcerers are welcome to act strangely among yourselves but the fact that the woodfolk fell in with it was most disturbing."

"Hmm," Tarkyn thought for a minute, "Maybe it sprang from their dealings with the two sorcerer forest guardians or from years of talking to the Lost sorcerers. Or perhaps from the mysterious lady wizard. From what Danton said, she is quite exacting in her expectations."

"True. Most of them had been in the Forest for a long time, long enough to have their behaviours moulded, I suppose," he said dubiously, sending a worried glance at the prince.

Tarkyn held up a hand, "No. Don't even think it. I have no plans to mould anyone's behaviour."

"If you say so, I believe you." Waterstone's face relaxed into a smile, "I'm glad you're so transparent. It does make things easier, doesn't it? Especially when sorcerers are reputedly so devious."

"Hmph. Do you want to see the Great Hall or not?"

"Yes. Go on."

Tarkyn glanced at him, "Do you want to see it being destroyed after my brothers passed sentence on me?"

Waterstone studied him, "I would like to see inside this building but I do not need to see any more of your unpleasant memories than you wish to show me. I already know what happened."

"Thanks Waterstone. I will just show you the hall as it was then, on my brothers' twentieth birthday."

Tarkyn showed him the vaulted ceilings, the huge carved pillars and the enormous wooden dais on which stood the heavy table behind which his brothers had sat when they passed sentence. *Garlands of flowers and ribbons are hung on every wall. The hall is filled with courtiers. Both men and women are dressed in bright colours but women wear sweeping dresses while the men wear leggings and brightly coloured surcoats over loosely fitting shirts. Everyone's clothes are adorned with lace, embroidery and jewellery.* Waterstone studied the variety of eye and hair colour with fascination. Tarkyn's memory glanced sideways and Waterstone saw a blond haired adolescent standing respectfully at Tarkyn's right elbow.

"There's Danton!" said Waterstone excitedly. "Wow! Look at his outfit. It's an absolute work of art! Look at all that lace. It must get awfully dirty when you're eating. Look! The sleeves flop down over his hands. And the colour! It's a soft version of his eye colour. What amazing dyes you must have. Hmm. I think his might be derived from blackberry but it's marvellously consistent. No darker or lighter patches anywhere that I can see… What were you wearing?"

The memory flicked back to Tarkyn's bedchamber. *My manservant finishes tying back my hair. My black hair and amber eyes are accentuated by my surcoat of deep gold embroidered in black. A black sash crosses my chest diagonally, held in place by a large bronze brooch. Beneath the surcoat, I am wearing a black shirt trimmed with black lace on the cuffs and throat.*

"Stars above Tarkyn! That's a brilliant outfit. Far and away the best of all those people in the hall. No wonder your brothers had to get rid of you. Very sophisticated colours for one so young, I would have thought. They make you look very powerful." Waterstone gave a wry smile, "Probably a bit of an error, given your brothers' temperaments."

"Definitely, I would say." Tarkyn gave a short laugh. "Danton and I put so much thought into designing my clothes. On reflection, they are probably a bit ostentatious but we thought they were marvellous at the time."

I move my hand forward to rub a smear off the lower corner of the mirror.

As Tarkyn's hand came into view in front of him, Waterstone realised he was looking at a reflection.

"Oh! That's a mirror. Of course it is. How else could you have a memory of yourself face on? I have only seen small mirrors that Stormaway has brought back for us. It's enormous! Everything about your past home is enormous."

Tarkyn gave a slight smile and returned to his memory of the Great Hall.

Suddenly the crowd stirs and all eyes turn to the front door. Two men, identical except for a gold band around one's head and different coloured sashes, enter the Great Hall, one a few steps behind the other. They are both dressed in deep claret. Just behind them walks an auburn headed woman, dressed in lacy white, embroidered in dark claret, clearly the mother of the twins. The entire crowd bows deeply. A feeling of warmth and pride emanates from me.

For a while, Waterstone studied the trio that had just entered. Suddenly, he waved his hand, "Enough Tarkyn, enough. I can't take in any more." He smiled, shaking his head, "I can't thank you enough for showing me that. It was truly wonderful. I presume that is your mother?" When Tarkyn nodded, he continued, "She has the same colouring as your brothers. They take after her and you take after your father, I gather?"

Tarkyn smiled ruefully, "Yes. I'm afraid so. Once my father died, I was the odd one out."

"And why didn't you enter with them? It was obviously a planned entrance, so why weren't you with them?"

"It wasn't my birthday."

"It wasn't your mother's either. I think you threw them into the shade, that's why. They wanted to make sure all eyes were on them," said Waterstone firmly.

Tarkyn spluttered with laughter. "I don't think I was grand enough to draw attention away from the King, even in my marvellous gold and black. Not at thirteen."

Waterstone smiled at Tarkyn's unfeigned modesty.

Tarkyn's smile faded, "No, if you really want to know, I think they saw me as a bit of an afterthought. Mother, of course, always wanted to be at the forefront of anything that was going on but I was quite a bit younger than my brothers and often side-lined. My entry into the Great Hall on this occasion was rather like an appetiser before the main course." He thought for a minute, "I often wondered if perhaps they didn't really like my father and saw too much of him in me."

Waterstone was shocked, "Surely not your mother, though?"

"No. She loved him even though it had been an arranged marriage. But remember I told you? She couldn't stand up to my brothers. So if they chose not to include me, she could not gainsay them."

Waterstone gazed out across the river. After a minute, he said, "You know, even then we were already under oath to you but you knew nothing about it. And you were already liege of these forests." He looked at Tarkyn, "Hmm. But Kosar knew, didn't he, about the forests?" He spun a pebble out across the water. "Perhaps that is why he side-lined you."

"Then Kosar is a fool," said Tarkyn with unaccustomed venom. "If he had kept me by his side, I might never have found out… And even if I had, I would willingly have consigned them into his care, if he had asked. He was my king and older brother and I would have done anything for him."

Tarkyn picked up a large pebble and threw it with such force that it spun right across the river to hit a tree on the far bank and rebound into the water.

Waterstone gave Tarkyn one of his warm strong smiles, "Yes. Kosar was a fool. He should have worked with you and your power instead of trying to subdue you. You have such passionate loyalty. Perhaps, in your sorcerer's world of intrigue, he was unable to believe that such straightforward devotion could exist. I can only be glad that it is now woodfolk, and I suppose Eskuzor, that have claimed your loyalty."

The stormy look gradually faded from Tarkyn's face. "This is a harder path though, Waterstone. It is much easier to be loyal to one person who can tell you what to do."

Waterstone's smile broadened, "Don't kid yourself, Tarkyn. You are too much of a force to be reckoned with, ever to be content under the direction of one man. You were born to face a larger challenge."

Tarkyn sat back, folded his arms and smiled, "You see, Waterstone. That's what I meant when I said you acknowledge me. You give me faith in my strength. And without you, I couldn't be half as strong."

Suddenly Waterstone grinned, "Well, here's one piece of acknowledgement you probably won't like. That was an astonishing feat to knock down that big building I saw in your memories!"

"Thanks," said Tarkyn dryly. "But actually, it was the combined force of a troop of guards that destroyed it. My shield just provided the pivot for their power."

The woodman's eyes twinkled, "So modest!"

Tarkyn laughed, "Stop it! Whether the guards or I achieved it, the destruction of that beautiful building is not something I am proud of."

"No. It was an amazing structure. I'm not sure that I think it was beautiful. I do not see beauty in hard lines and sharp uncompromising angles. But the statues and the paintings and the stone carvings were evidence of great craftsmanship and it is sad to lose so much fine work." Waterstone looked at Tarkyn for a minute, "Would you mind if I shared some of these images with other people? Falling Branch and Rainstorm have a heritage of craftsmanship and would be very interested to see these works."

Tarkyn thought carefully through what he had shown Waterstone before answering. "You may share any or all of it. None of it is particularly personal." He gave a grunt of laughter, "I don't think I would have shown this to everyone too early in our acquaintance. They were intimidated enough by me as it was, without seeing the outlandish place I come from."

Waterstone grinned, "Yes. Your world is truly astonishing. And yet it is only a few days walk from here."

"But behind huge stone walls and scores of guards. They are just as impenetrable to us as we are to them."

For a few minutes, they sat in companionable silence, drinking their wine and watching a flock of ibis wheel across the afternoon sky and disappear into the trees further down the river.

"Tarkyn," said Waterstone quietly, "There is one other thing I would like you to show me, if you wouldn't mind. Could you show me what happened when you defied your father to protect Danton from the whipping? Although in some ways I hated Markazon, I also respected his dedication and would like to see the softer side of him that you knew." He looked down and picked up a couple of pebbles, "You don't have to, only if you feel all right about it. After all, I know what happened. But I would just like to see it."

Tarkyn smiled warmly at his friend, "I could hardly pass up the chance of showing you what I loved about my father. No one else has the slightest interest in it." He took a breath and gazing into Waterstone's eyes, retrieved the memory of his confrontation as a seven-year-old with this father.

I watch as Old Laramar swings his arm back ready to whip Danton for the misdemeanour we committed together. My father is standing grimly between Laramar and me, to prevent my interference. Taking a deep breath, I throw up my shield and hold a sharp piece of the broken vase against my forearm. "I tell him that I will cut my arm each time the whip comes down on Danton's back." *As he glares at me, I can feel my heart beating hard in my chest. He orders me to remove my shield and to behave.*

Tarkyn did not bother to translate his father's words at this point in the silent image, since Waterstone could see what the king was saying.

I stand rock still, quailing inside, hoping desperately that my father will let Danton go unpunished. But he calls my bluff and turns away from me to order Old Laramar to flog Danton.

"Having come this far, I could not back down or Danton would have paid dearly for my defiance." *As the whip lands on Danton's back, I grit my teeth and drag the sharp piece of porcelain along my arm. I can feel the sharp pain as it cuts, but keep my eyes on my father.*

"I say, 'As you choose, father.'" Tarkyn gave a faint smile. "I thought that sounded rather grown up, at the time."

My father whips his head around to stare at me and his eyes widen. As the second stroke lands, I cut my arm again. "I am so intent on my father that I feel detached from my body and barely feel the second cut. I don't realise that blood is now dripping from my arm." *As Old Laramar raises his arm again I tense, ready to cut myself again but my father orders him to stop and waves him away. Then my father, his face dark with anger, lowers over me and roars at me.* "He yelled that he could order my death and Danton's for defying him."

My stomach turns over at the danger I have placed Danton in and I am almost frozen with fear while I try to find a way out. Eventually I bow low. When I straighten to face him once more, my knees threaten to give way beneath me. "I told him that we had only broken a vase and that I was trying to protect Danton. I told him how hard I tried to behave well but that I just wasn't able to be perfect."

I start to cry, alone within my shield, still clutching the sharp piece of vase; vaguely aware and a bit frightened that my arm is dripping blood onto the clean, polished floor. My father just scowls at me. After a few moments, he realises Danton is watching us and orders him out.

My father walks away from me. He turns and stands by the long drawing room window, silhouetted against the light, with his hands on his hips, just staring at me. After what seems like an age, he finally asks quietly, "And will you remove your shield now, my son?"

I nod and drop my shield. Still he doesn't move. Now that Danton's danger has passed, I am rooted to the spot with fear, tears trickling down my face. My father walks over to me and pulls out his handkerchief. Without a word, he takes the piece of vase out of my hand and throws it away across the room. Then he raises my arm and binds it. When he has finished, he lifts me up and swings me onto his knee as he sits down in a big padded armchair. As soon as he is holding me, my tears redouble and I let go completely. He just holds me and lets me cry myself out.

He looks down at me, his amber eyes glowing in the late afternoon light. "You put us all to shame, my son." *He smiles at me and I try to understand what he means as he keeps speaking.* "This is when he says, 'You are the best of us but you will suffer for it. And in the end, you must be the one to bring hope to our nation and save us from ourselves.'"

For a while, he sits there in silence, holding me and thinking. Then suddenly, he swings me off his knee and stands up. He glowers down at me, "Now, I want no more scenes and disobedience." *When I nod unconvincingly, he smiles slightly and gives his head a little shake,* "I will ensure that your friend no longer suffers in your stead. In future, you will both be brought to book together." *He frowns,* "Now, will you undertake to do as I ask?"

I nod. "I told him I was sorry."

My father shakes his head, "No, you're not. You would do it again, wouldn't you?"

I stare up at him for a moment before replying. "No, sir. Not if Danton might lose his life over it. I would have to find another way."

My father smiles broadly and shaking his head, gives me a big final hug before striding off, leaving me standing alone in the gloomy drawing room next to the pool of my own blood.

Waterstone shook his head smiling. "You're as feisty as each other, aren't you?" His smile faded. "You must miss him terribly."

Tarkyn merely nodded, his eyes glassy with unshed tears.

"He knew your worth, Tarkyn," said Waterstone gently. "And he was not as rigid as I thought… Looking back, I suppose he did make a few concessions to us, just as he did to you. It's just that he behaved so aggressively, that we didn't really notice them."

Tarkyn sniffed and wiped a hand across his eyes. "If you would like to see it, I will show you one other occasion with my father that meant a lot to me. I was pretty young, I think. About five."

Kosar and Jarand, young adolescents, are kicking a ball around. Now and then, they grudgingly include me. When they do, they kick the ball with a little more force so that I have no hope of controlling it and have to run after it and bring it back. They exchange looks of mirth every time this happens. Suddenly their faces tighten and I look around to see my father coming out of the shade into the sunshine with a look of fury on his face.

"He told them that they had to include me properly and that their behaviour did not befit princes... or something like that." *He ruffles my hair and stays to join in for a while, helping me to retrieve the ball and giving it to me to kick back to the twins. He speaks shortly to them as he leaves.*

"What did he say?" asked Waterstone.

"He said, 'Don't let this one go the way of the other'." Tarkyn slowly shook his head, "I've never thought about those words before. I just remembered what he did. But they are strange, aren't they? They don't make a lot of sense."

"Maybe they had already scared off Danton or one of their friends?" suggested the woodman.

Tarkyn gave a whimsical little smile, "No Waterstone, you're not thinking. Friends or courtiers wouldn't have been allowed to be scared off. They would have had to stay at the princes' pleasure and take anything Kosar and Jarand dished out, whenever they felt like it."

Waterstone gave a shudder, "Oh Tarkyn, your family is hideous."

Tarkyn's face fell. "No they're not. Well, the twins are fairly awful but the rest of us are okay. Mother and Father and I have never taken delight in teasing or hurting people."

"No, as long as they behaved themselves!" Waterstone saw Tarkyn begin to close off and added hurriedly, "No, no. Don't take offence. From what I know of you and your parents, you did not delight in hurting people. And your family can't be too bad because they have bred a fine son in you. It is just that your laws and protocols demand that people are hurt from time to time, and your family over the generations has condoned it."

The woodman winced, knowing that once again they were on rocky ground. He concentrated steadfastly on the pebbles on the ground in front of him, sorting through to find one with attractive colouring to keep himself busy. After a bit of thought he looked up and asked, "Would you like to see my parents?"

"I would love to, Waterstone, especially since they are also my parents." Tarkyn grimaced, "I can't imagine they would have been too happy about having a sorcerer as a son though." He looked at Waterstone, "Could you have had me as a bloodbrother if they had not approved?"

"Hmm. Possibly not." Waterstone gave a quirky smile, "I would just have had to work on them until they agreed. I'm sure they would have, once they came to know you. It's a shame they died so young. They didn't ever get the chance to meet you." The woodman sighed, "They were very close, you know. After my father died of pneumonia during a particularly bitter winter, my mother just seemed to pine away. I sometimes wonder if perhaps she had some sort of an illness herself. She became thinner and thinner and finally just faded away altogether." He pulled himself together, "Anyway, let me show them to you. Ancient Oak and I have just been out on one of my first hunting trips. Ancient Oak was still too young to hunt himself but he came with me to watch."

As Tarkyn looked into Waterstone's eyes, he saw the hard closed face of a middle aged woodman melt into a welcoming smile. *I hold up a brace of rabbits and bask in my father's approval.*

"Well done, Waterstone." My father takes the rabbits from me, inspecting them until he finds the arrow wounds. "And why did you choose to use arrows rather than slingshot? Slingshot would have damaged the fur less."

"I am more accurate with arrows over longer distances and I wanted to make sure I brought back something for dinner."

"Fair enough, at this stage. And you have retrieved and cleaned your arrows, I presume?"

As I nod in response, my mother joins my father in admiring my booty. She has gentle eyes and a kind soft face, which dimples when she smiles.

She raises her eyebrows and says, "Now Waterstone, I am sure you wiped them at the time," A certain dryness in her voice tells me that she is not even sure of that, "but you have not yet had time to wash those arrows properly. Now, off you go and clean them thoroughly. You go with him, Ancient Oak."

Waterstone broke off the memory and laughed, "Looks are deceptive. My mother was much stricter than my father."

"Your father looked quite severe when he wasn't smiling."

"I know. He had rock hard principles but he understood kids. He just carried sadness on his face."

"Why?" asked Tarkyn, glancing at Waterstone to make sure he wasn't prying too much.

"There were a couple of miscarriages between Ancient Oak and me." The woodman shrugged, "I don't know. There may have been other reasons I didn't know about as well. But I know he took the loss of those unborn children very hard."

Tarkyn looked at his friend appraisingly then smiled, "I can see where you get your strength and your warmth from. Both your parents, in different ways, show that same firmness and kindness that you have."

Waterstone smiled his thanks and fell into an abstracted reverie, gazing out across the river and thinking about his past. After a protracted silence, he heard the sounds of Tarkyn standing up and looked up to see him walking to the water's edge to stand staring down into the dappled depths.

After a few minutes, Tarkyn said quietly, "Come here. Slowly."

Waterstone moved soundlessly to stand beside him. When he looked down into the water, he saw an enormous golden fish rising to the surface. He felt a nudge against his mind and when he opened it, images of the river bed, its flowing plants, little insects skittering over its rooftop and fish flitting from one hiding spot to the next flooded in. Slowly the images faded and were replaced by towering trees looming over bushes and grasses, with glimpses of small birds and insects flying from cover to cover, a small hedgehog burrowing through the undergrowth and a tawny owl sleeping high above them. The image swung slowly up the path until it showed the woodfolk and sorcerers gathered in the clearing accompanied by a sense of calm and contentment. Then all images faded as the golden fish sank back into the deep water.

Woodman and sorcerer looked at each other and smiled.

Chapter 46

Falling Rain looked up from feeding his egret to find Autumn Leaves bearing down on him with the two new woodfolk in tow.

"Hi Falling Rain," said the heavy woodman as he sat down quietly next to him, "Twig Snap and Leaf Fall wanted to meet you."

Falling Rain looked a little askance at them and nodded briefly as they sat down.

"She is a beautiful bird, isn't she," murmured Twig Snap. "Do you have a name for her?"

Nothing Twig Snap said could have mellowed Falling Rain faster. He gave a little smile, "Her name is Elsie. I reared her from a chick."

"And how does she manage in other birds' territories as you move about?" asked Leaf Fall.

Falling Rain shrugged, "It depends. Usually they will leave her alone if she keeps clear. She can usually find somewhere to fish but if not, we feed her. There's a particularly stern grey heron on this stretch of the river but Tarkyn has met it before and has made peace with it on Elsie's behalf. So it grudgingly allows her to fish here."

Twig Snap's eyes shone, "How wonderful, to have a forest guardian who can help you with something like that."

Falling Rain considered her for a moment before saying slowly, "Yes, it is. After such a hideous beginning, it turns out that having Tarkyn foisted upon us was not so bad after all."

"It wasn't great for *you*, though, was it?" Twig Snap shook her head, "Twelve years. That is such a long time to be away from your kin." She gave him a friendly smile, "Anyway, I just wanted to say, 'Welcome back.'" Suddenly she grinned, "It's really quite exciting to meet someone as famous as you!"

"*Twig Snap!*" Her brother rolled his eyes in embarrassment. "Sorry about her. She can't help herself."

Twig Snap swung at him but, as usual, failed to connect as he dodged cannily out of her way.

A large shadow loomed over them and they looked around to see Boravar walking over to join them. "Well dodged," said Boravar with a grin, "I can see you're going to have to give me some lessons." He immediately scored a small backhander in the stomach as he sat down. "Oof! Just as well my stomach has a bit of padding."

Twig Snap ignored this remark and said, "Boravar, this is Falling Rain. You know, the one who was banished because everyone mistakenly thought he had betrayed the presence of woodfolk."

"I *did* betray woodfolk," said Falling Rain tightly. "The mistake was in thinking that I could have avoided it."

"And how long did you spend in exile then?" asked Boravar.

"Twelve years."

Boravar smiled cheerily, "Oh! So not too long then."

"Boravar!" A small fist punched into his stomach. "Don't say that! Twelve years is ages."

"Oof! Again! One hundred and twenty is more," replied Boravar with a grin.

Twig Snap frowned at him. "You weren't all on your own. Falling Rain couldn't talk to anyone in all that time."

"Hmm. That would definitely make it tougher." Boravar looked as if he might have said more, but had decided against it.

Falling Rain knew what he was thinking, though. "But at least I had people I knew to come back to, didn't I?"

Boravar's smile went a little crooked. "Yes. Everyone I knew died long ago." After a moment, he heaved a sigh, "And now I have to make do with this little madam." The heavy sorcerer's face split into a grin. In an unexpectedly lightning fast movement, he caught Twig Snap's fist in mid flight and tucked her hand under his arm. He smiled down at her as she subsided against him. When he was sure she was happy, he raised his eyes, "So Falling Rain, who have you come back to, or was there no one in particular?"

The returned woodman glanced at Autumn Leaves, "I was affianced to Tree Wind but I was banished before we could wed."

"Oh dear!" sighed Twig Snap. "So what are you going to do now? Are you still in love with her? From what Autumn Leaves was telling us, it sounds like she is still in love with you."

Falling Rain's eyes narrowed, "As you have just finished pointing out, I have had no one to talk to for twelve years. So I am not accustomed to thinking things through in such a public forum."

Twig Snap glanced around her. "There are only four of us."

Before he could stop himself, Falling Rain's eyes flicked to Boravar.

"I'll go." Boravar drew his legs up, ready to rise.

But Falling Rain waved an impatient hand, "No, don't go. You're a fellow exile, after all. I'm just still not used to sorcerers completely. Anyway it's not particularly you that's the problem. It's the fact that four is a lot more than none… and I hardly know three of you."

Twig Snap waved her free hand casually, "Well, this can be how you get to know us better."

"*Twig Snap!*" hissed her brother, "Leave the poor man alone!"

Twig Snap glanced at her brother and then back at Falling Rain. "Sorry," she said, with a little sigh, "I just get carried away sometimes," and leant in against Boravar.

Suddenly Falling Rain's face split into a grin, "Twig Snap, you are such a character. You are nearly as fearsome as Tree Wind."

Autumn Leaves' eyes gleamed in appreciation. "Yes, Tree Wind is very strong, isn't she?"

"Mind you," added Falling Rain, "she doesn't go around hitting people as you do, but she is very forceful in her opinions and her actions."

"And she did hold Tarkyn down with an arrow to his throat, as I recall." Autumn Leaves smiled as four pairs of eyes swivelled to stare in astonishment at him. "Yes, quite feisty."

"Did she?" Falling Rain gave a short laugh and said fondly, "That's my girl!" After a few moments he asked Autumn Leaves, "Has she changed much over the years?"

"Yes, a bit," admitted Autumn Leaves. "She felt very bitter about what happened and she became harder and more remote. She has fierce loyalties, and for twelve years her loyalty to woodfolk and her loyalty to you have been in conflict."

"No wonder she became a bit remote then," said Boravar.

"And why do you ask Autumn Leaves these questions?" asked Twig Snap quietly. "Have you not seen her yourself since your return?"

"Yes, of course I have. I spend most of my time with her. But I am just not sure whether I am seeing what I expect to see from knowing her twelve years ago or whether I am seeing her as she is now."

"You *have* had a long time thinking on your own, haven't you?" remarked Boravar dryly.

"Falling Rain," said Autumn Leaves gently, "In essence, they are one and the same."

"Very well. I will accept that. But am I?" Falling Rain fed another little titbit to Elsie before looking up and asking, "Am I still the person I was twelve years ago? I have lived a very different life from the rest of you over that time. I am not used to crowds and sharing my thoughts with others any more. I need time on my own. How can I have that if I marry?"

"Wouldn't Tree Wind understand and leave you alone sometimes, if that is what you need?" asked Twig Snap. "Have you talked to her about it?"

Falling Rain shook his head. "No. I haven't talked to her. Because as soon as I do, I am more than halfway to committing myself and I know she will bend over backwards to assuage my doubts." He ran his hand through his hair, "And I really don't know if I can manage to share my life so closely with someone."

"If it helps," said Autumn Leaves, "I don't think Tree Wind would be able to live all the time in someone's pocket. She too is fiercely independent."

"You see? That's just it. When Tree Wind last knew me, I wasn't fiercely independent. I have grown to be, out of necessity...but I wonder if she realises how much I have changed?"

Boravar smiled warmly at him, "You don't strike me as fiercely independent. You strike me as someone who has become used to living alone and is still struggling with his resentment. And in the midst of all these people, you still feel very lonely… don't you?"

Falling Rain met the sorcerer's gaze for several long seconds before saying slowly, "And you Boravar, have spent a very long time studying people, haven't you?"

"Yes, my friend, I have."

Falling Rain concentrated on stroking his egret as he said, "Yes, I feel hurt and angry and I don't know what to do about it because none of these people deserve my anger. I would have done the same as they did." He sighed, "My head agrees with them but my heart doesn't. And until I can sort that out, I can't marry Tree Wind."

No one spoke and after a minute he continued, "Tarkyn and I had a ferocious mental slinging match when I first arrived back and that has cleared the air between him and me. But I hated him with such a passion that it was easy to do that." When he saw Twig Snap and Leaf Fall's eyes widen, he added, "Don't worry. I soon realised I was targeting the wrong person and it was his father, not he, that deserved my ire." He chuckled, "And now, out of everyone, I probably feel closest to Tarkyn, amazingly enough."

Falling Rain gave Elsie a final stroke and shrugged, "But I don't hate everyone else and I can't just start railing at them. That is not, and never has been, my style. So what do I do? I am left feeling resentful and alone among my kin."

"Hmm," said Autumn Leaves thoughtfully, "I think we have not given you enough care, my friend. It is good that our doughty little friend here insisted on coming over and talking to you. Thank you, Twig Snap. Even if we don't yet know what to do to solve it, at least knowing we have a problem is a good start."

Boravar smiled to himself at Autumn Leaves' natural assumption that if one woodman had a problem it was everyone's to sort out.

"Maybe you should talk to Tarkyn about it if you feel closest to him," Autumn Leaves was saying.

"Mmm, maybe. I know he's our forest guardian but he's only young. Why should he know what to do?" asked Falling Rain.

Boravar chuckled, "That's what he said to me when we were talking about Twig Snap here. Don't worry. He will tell you if he doesn't think he has anything to offer."

"Don't underestimate him, Falling Rain," said Autumn Leaves, "He has had to deal with more resentment than anyone I have ever known. He should be an expert by now." He smiled, "He dealt with your resentment of him pretty effectively. We were amazed when you two returned. Left as arch enemies, returned best of friends a couple of hours later."

Falling Rain shook his head at the memory, "Phew! What we went through to achieve that! You have no idea… It was *torrid*." He smiled, "All right, I'll talk to him. I can't lose anything by it."

"And I'll talk to the others and see if we can come up with any ideas," said Autumn Leaves cheerfully.

"No." Falling Rain said firmly. "I agreed to talk to you four. That was it. I don't want everyone discussing me any more than they already do."

Autumn Leaves looked totally nonplussed. "But how can we help you then?"

Falling Rain waved his hand, "You four can talk among yourselves or with Tarkyn or me. That's it. If you talk to anyone else, I will consider it a breach of trust."

"What? Not even Waterstone?" asked Autumn Leaves in bewilderment.

"*Particularly* not Waterstone. He was one of the four who sent me away."

"Who were the others?" asked Twig Snap.

"Running Feet, Creaking Bough and Thunder Storm. It wasn't their decision. It was a community decision but I most strongly associate it with them because they are the ones who stood there and told me to go."

"I don't think there is much we can do if we can't talk to anyone else," said Autumn Leaves, totally at sea. "How can we rally them around to support you?"

"I don't want them rallying around and treating me as though I have something wrong with me." Falling Rain was becoming impatient. "Leave it be. I will talk to Tarkyn." He stood up and walked off across the clearing. After a moment, Elsie took off and glided into a tree to be near him.

CHAPTER 47

Stormaway lay back napping against a tree. Suddenly he was startled awake by the shriek of a black hawk rending the air as it dive bombed a fat wood pigeon high above the treeline. The pigeon managed to swerve out of its way with a hair's breadth to spare. As the hawk swooped around for a second pass, the pigeon angled downward, beating its wings furiously in an effort to reach the cover of the forest canopy. Just as it seemed certain that the pigeon couldn't make it in time, an arrow streaked up from the trees to cut the air between them, just catching a breast feather of the hawk. The hawk screeched in alarm and pulled out of its dive, giving the pigeon the breathing space it needed to reach the safety of the woods.

A ripple of conjecture swept through the clearing. Tarkyn and Waterstone looked at each other and, by mutual consent, packed up and headed back up the path to join the others. It was not the battle between the pigeon and the hawk that was so unusual. It was the fact that someone had intervened in it.

With the aid of mind talking, it did not take long to establish that the marksman had been Thunder Storm. Someone else went aloft to relieve him from lookout duty so that he could come down into the clearing and explain his actions.

Thunder Storm swung down out of the trees to find himself surrounded by perplexed woodfolk. Before anyone could ask him, he answered the unspoken question, "Someone asked me to. Someone sent a strong, almost desperate request to save the pigeon. There wasn't time to argue. So I did."

"Brilliant shot, Thunder Storm," said Rainstorm appreciatively. "To save the pigeon without hurting the hawk? Brilliant!"

"Thanks," said Thunder Storm briefly, not really focused on his prowess.

Tree Wind put her hands on her hips, "So who asked you? Tarkyn?"

Thunder Storm glanced at Tarkyn with a slight smile, "No. There were words." He ran his hand through his hair, "No. I don't know who it was. It was a very brief message and besides that, I don't think I recognise the mind."

At this point in the proceedings, the plump wood pigeon flew into a nearby tree and began to coo loudly. Stormaway rose to his feet and gave a self-conscious little cough, "Ahem. This will be for me, I believe."

With the whole company watching, he walked quietly out of the clearing towards the wood pigeon. The bird did not fly away as he neared it but waited calmly while he removed a small piece of parchment from a ring around its leg. A message delivered to Stormaway, in itself, was not unusual. But the connection with mind speech was.

The wizard walked nonchalantly back into the clearing and asked, "Does anyone have some seeds to give this little fellow? He has flown a long way and could do with a snack."

Everyone started talking at once. Amid the uproar, Stormaway raised his eyebrows, his eyes twinkling and asked mildly again, "Seeds? Does anyone have any seeds?" When Creaking Bough brought some forward, he said cheerfully, "Perhaps the children might like to feed it. It is quite tame, you know."

When the seeds had been dispensed to Sparrow, Midnight and the others, Thunder Storm said severely, "I think you owe us an explanation, Stormaway."

Tarkyn frowned at his old retainer, "Do I take all this to mean that you can mind talk?"

A wide smile appeared on the wizard's face.

Tarkyn's brow wrinkled in thought, "But you said…"

"Yes?" asked Stormaway spuriously, with a grin on his face.

"Blast you, Stormaway! You're as slippery as an eel!"

The wizard let out a whoop of laughter, "Oh Tarkyn, my boy! When will you learn that you can't trust a word I say?"

Waterstone stomped up to him and put his hands on his hips, "Do you mean to tell us, Stormaway Treemaster, that you have lived among us on and off for twelve years and been able to hear all our mind talking without us ever realising it?"

Before Stormaway could answer, a cry of anguish ripped across the clearing from behind him, "You bastard! You knew all along that I'd been banished because of you. And you did nothing about it!" Falling Rain, his face a rictus of pain and hatred, drew his bow, pulled an arrow from his quiver, and sent it on its murderous way before anyone could stop him.

But several people were able to stop the arrow before it reached its target. Leaf Fall's knife spun in from the left, Thunder Storm's arrow streaked in from the right and Tarkyn's bronze ray speared in from beside Thunder Storm, while Danton's shield slammed down over Stormaway. Two arrows and a knife clashed together in a flash of bronze light and a little heap of white ash trickled to the ground.

Almost immediately Tarkyn's bronze shield slammed down over Falling Rain.

There was a shocked silence.

Then Leaf Fall said inconsequentially, "My mother gave me that knife."

"Sorry," said Tarkyn shortly.

Another silence ensued.

Inevitably, when no one else moved, Tarkyn took charge, "Right. We have two issues. What to do about Falling Rain and what to do about Stormaway?" He stood squarely before his wizard and said clearly, "Stormaway, for the rest of today, you will answer everyone truthfully. Not just me. Everyone. Is that clear? That is a direct order."

As Stormaway put his hand on his heart and bowed slightly, Tarkyn asked, "Did you knowingly allow Falling Rain to go into exile?"

"No, Your Highness. It is as I told you. I knew nothing of his exile until you returned to the forest."

"But you do have the ability to mind talk. So how do you explain this?"

"Sire, I have never used it until today. For my father's sake, I kept my mind closed so that no one would realise that I was of woodfolk descent. I have never listened into, nor sent, mind messages." He gave a sad little shrug, "It was something I was going to ask my great nephews to work on with me but the wood pigeon's plight drove me to try it today. I was surprised it worked."

Tarkyn cast his gaze around the gathered woodfolk, "Are you satisfied? Does anyone have any further questions of Stormaway?"

"Why did you not ask us about it earlier?" asked Autumn Leaves. "It has been over a month since you revealed that you were a woodman."

Stormaway shrugged, "I have been trying to master it myself. I am not used to taking instruction these days. But until the need was urgent today, I was unable to break through the barriers that I myself erected so long ago. I'm sorry. I did not mean to hold myself aloof from my new family but I have worked alone for a long time. I am used to being self-sufficient."

Tarkyn glanced at Autumn Leaves to see whether he had any more questions. When the woodman put his hand up and gave a shake of his head, Tarkyn turned his attention to Falling Rain.

"Falling Rain, I have placed my shield around you, both to protect others and to keep you from flicking into hiding. I do not understand woodfolk law enough to know what should happen in this situation and, as you know, I will not impose sorcerer law on woodfolk any more than I have to. So, I will leave it to woodfolk to confer. However, you are my friend and in order to support you, I will come within my shield with you."

So saying, Tarkyn walked over to Falling Rain, who was looking pale with shock, and swept a larger shield around the woodman and himself before extinguishing the one that held just Falling Rain. Then he turned to stand beside Falling Rain and waved his hand to indicate that he was relinquishing control.

As Danton flicked his shield from around Stormaway, an intense mind conference began among the woodfolk with Stormaway, from time to time, being consulted.

Tarkyn bent a little to whisper in Falling Rain's ear, "Can you tune in to what they're saying?"

The woodman shook his head dismally, "Not through your shield. Besides they would be excluding me."

"Oh Falling Rain. I am so sorry this has happened." After a moment Tarkyn glanced sideways and asked, "What is the usual punishment for a murderous attack?"

The woodman heaved a long shuddering sigh. "Banishment. It's banishment. Not for life but for a matter of years." He looked up at Tarkyn, "But this time, when I am banished, that will be it. I will never return. I couldn't go through this again."

The sorcerers and woodfolk had seated themselves in a semicircle around the outside of the translucent bronze shield but were still conferring among themselves. So Tarkyn and Falling Rain sat down inside the shield.

After a few minutes, Falling Rain said, "I was going to come and talk to you about how bad it feels. I can't stop resenting the fact that everyone sent me away even though I agreed with them." He shrugged disconsolately, "It doesn't really matter now, does it? No point in resolving a situation that will not continue anyway."

Suddenly everyone stood up and Waterstone took a step forward. He nodded at Tarkyn and waited until he and Falling Rain also rose to their feet.

"Your Highness," began Waterstone, strictly formal, "although we thank you for allowing us to pass judgement according to our laws for a crime against a woodman, it is also a crime against a sorcerer and therefore you too must have a say."

The prince nodded his head in acknowledgement. "Thank you. But as far as I understand it, although woodfolk do not wantonly kill sorcerers, when they do kill them, there are no consequences. Is that correct?"

"Sire, until recently, that has indeed been the case. But now that we have sorcerers living amongst us, these laws will need revision. It is one thing for Twig Snap to kill Petrand Closkaril and quite another if she were to fire her arrow at Danton, for instance."

The prince nodded slowly, "I see your point." He took a step away from Falling Rain and said formally, "This being the case, I reserve the right to challenge your judgement if I do not agree with it. Furthermore, if you are unable to convince me that your judgement is just for all parties, I reserve the right to overturn it." He paused, "Are you in agreement with this?"

After a very short mind conference, Waterstone nodded agreement.

Tarkyn turned to Falling Rain, "If I must pass judgement, I can no longer support you. Who would you choose to have by your side?"

Falling Rain said quietly, "Boravar." As a ripple of surprise ran through the company, the woodman added with an edge of bitterness, "If the woodfolk community is passing judgement on me, then none of them can support me."

There was a short delay while Boravar exchanged places with Tarkyn and erected his own peacock blue shield to stand within, beside Falling Rain.

"I am honoured that you chose me to support you." After a moment, Boravar gave a little smile, "Well, at least we know one thing. You will never be exiled for as long as I have been."

Falling Rain folded his arms and grunted in a bitter laugh, "Perhaps not, but it will be to the end of my days, for I will not return, no matter what length the sentence."

They were interrupted by Waterstone clearing his throat to gain their attention. He waited until they were facing him before saying, "Falling Rain, as you have heard, we will give you our judgement and then His Highness will either ratify it or modify it." He paused, "Unlike the last time you were banished, this time there can be no doubt that you have committed a crime against woodfolk. You might argue that Stormaway is in fact, and has lived most of his life as, a wizard-sorcerer. But not only is he a woodman by birth, he also lives under our protection. In fact, he has been instrumental in saving our nation from the curse that would eventually have undermined our nation's integrity, in rescuing woodfolk from the sorcerers' encampment and in dissipating the storm that threatened to flood us."

Running Feet stepped forward to stand beside Waterstone and looked around at Stormaway who was standing a little to one side before taking over the pronouncement. "Saying that, he was also the architect of your unwilling betrayal of woodfolk to the outside world, and the unwitting cause of your exile." He turned back to stare firmly at Falling Rain. "You loosed your arrow before the full facts had been made known and your justification, although in any case insufficient to commit murder, turned out to be incorrect."

Thunder Storm stepped forward, "Before we give you our judgement, do you have any questions or any statement that you would like to make?"

Falling Rain stared back, stony-faced. "No."

And then the last of the four who had banished him last time stepped forward. "You are lucky that the intercession of others prevented you from injuring or killing your intended victim. This circumstance, although not of your doing, has lessened the sentence." Creaking Bough took a deep breath. "Our judgement is that for your attempted murder of Stormaway Treemaster, you should be exiled for six years."

Falling Rain bowed his head as tears sprang to his eyes. Boravar put his heavy arm across the woodman's shoulders.

"However," continued Waterstone, "you have already served out more than that sentence unjustly. So, we contend that your debt has already been paid and you are free to stay among us." As Falling Rain raised his tear-streaked face in surprise, Waterstone indicated Tarkyn, "His Highness must now have the final say."

Tarkyn glanced at Stormaway who gave a slight nod, before pronouncing, "I waive all rights of appeal. I agree wholeheartedly with the woodfolk's decision."

A quiet cheer went up.

Suddenly Waterstone gave a warm smile, "Falling Rain, we have missed you dreadfully and it will take more than an attempted murder to drag you from us again. I can only hope that this judgement will in part repay the wrong done to you by us, all that time ago."

The time for formality was over. As Boravar dropped his shield, Waterstone gave a short laugh and added, "I wouldn't make a habit of trying to kill people if I were you, though."

Falling Rain tried to laugh and thank them through his tears but, as the pain that had been crushing him finally overcame him, he broke down completely. Tree Wind rushed forward and threw her arms around him. Boravar kept his arm across his shoulders and a bevy of woodfolk pressed in around him, murmuring encouragement, welcome and regret. Accustomed as he was to being alone, giving a public emotional display was the last thing Falling Rain wanted to do, but slowly the warmth and true concern of his woodfolk soothed him and he cried himself to a standstill. He was left feeling ragged with spent emotion but, at long last, part of his kin again. When he finally raised his head, he found Tarkyn watching him from across the clearing.

As soon as he met Tarkyn's eyes, the prince walked over and stood on the outskirts of the huddle of people around Falling Rain and said loudly, "Excuse me. Make way. Forest Guardian coming through."

The woodfolk looked around at him smiling at his silliness, as they made a path for him to reach Falling Rain. As soon as he was able to touch him, he placed his hand on Falling Rain's shoulder, "You look exhausted. This will do more for you than one of Summer Rain's hideous tonics." As Summer Rain looked around from in the midst of the crowd, Tarkyn said cheerily, "Oops. I forgot that she's your sister."

Summer Rain, humourless as ever, replied seriously, "Tarkyn is right. If he is willing to give you some of his strength, you take it."

Falling Rain just smiled and closed his eyes as a warm, soothing stream flowed from his shoulder around his entire body. All too soon, the stream of power stopped but Falling Rain felt as though his body had come back into focus and that he was ready to face life again. "Thanks Tarkyn and thanks everyone." He extricated himself gently from the people around him and rubbed his face with his hands. "I suppose my eyes are still red. Are they?"

Tarkyn put his head on one side, "Not too bad, considering. I probably got rid of some of it for you." He leant forward and said *sotto voce*, "But I wouldn't worry too much if I were you. There's not a soul here who doesn't know you've been crying your eyes out. So there's no one left to hide it from anyway."

Falling Rain gave a grunt of laughter, "Thanks!" He gave his face a final rub and said briskly, "Right. I'm off." With that, much to everyone's surprise, he strode across the clearing to stand facing Stormaway. "I owe you an apology. What can I say to a man I have just tried to kill, but that? You have my word I won't try to harm you again. I will not make excuses, but suffice it to say that at last the bubble has burst and I am feeling differently about things now. I appreciate that you did not demand retribution. I saw the woodfolk, and Tarkyn, consult you before the final decision. So thank you."

"Falling Rain, I am more sorry than I can say for the fate that befell you. When I first heard of it, I was not particularly moved by it but that was before I came to know you. I bear you no grudge for what happened today. It was completely understandable. In your eyes, I have done you a great wrong." Stormaway gave a wry smile, "Forgiving you for today is just a small token towards repairing the damage my actions have caused to your life."

Falling Rain just looked at him. "Hmph, I don't know what to say."

Stormaway's smile widened, "Nothing else needs to be said. We are each in the other's debt but I feel that, while your debt to me is paid out, I still owe you something. So, if you ever need help, know that you can call on me."

Falling Rain blinked, "Thank you."

Stormaway waved his hand, "Go on. Go off and be with your friends. You have a lot of catching up to do and maybe now you will be able to do it."

Chapter 48

Soon after Falling Rain had left him, Stormaway found himself surrounded by Tarkyn, Danton, Waterstone, Autumn Leaves, Thunder Storm and Lapping Water. Hoping that the contents of the message were going to be discussed, Harkell strolled over to join them.

"Were you happy with that, Stormaway?" Waterstone was saying, "I know we have had our differences in the past, but I want to make sure you feel that we supported you sufficiently."

"I was given an opportunity to have my say and did not take it," said Stormaway. "Further punishment to that young man on my behalf would not have sat well with me at all." He gave a smile, "And I am overwhelmed that I have four people to thank for saving my life."

Thunder Storm gave his deep chuckle, "There wasn't time, uncle, for a debate about who would do the honours."

"But now Stormaway," said Tarkyn, "You might like to share with us the contents of that little piece of parchment."

"Yes Sire, I would."

When the assembled group looked at it, they realised that the parchment had grown to several times its original size.

Tarkyn pointed at it, "How did you do that? The pigeon couldn't possibly have carried something that large."

"Precisely, Tarkyn. That's why it had been minimised." Stormaway looked a little smug, "I merely returned it to its original size. Perhaps I will show you how at another time. Now, do you want to know the contents?"

A slight impatience in Stormaway's voice made Tarkyn's eyes narrow, but on balance he let it pass and nodded agreement.

The wizard waved the parchment, "The king and Prince Jarand have spent some time together over the last few days. Several of Kosar's servants are in my pay and I have a particularly subtle device that carries sounds through a small vent in the ceiling of the balcony into a nearby room so that all their conversations can be best overheard when they think that no one is near them." Stormaway gave a grunt of satisfaction and looked around him for approbation before continuing, "And it was on the balcony that Jarand suggested that the Lost sorcerers should be rounded up and imprisoned to lure you out of the woods, Your Highness."

A wave of consternation issued forth from everyone, although the prince's reaction was the only one that rocked everyone gently backwards where they sat.

"This is dire news, Stormaway. We can't allow those poor sorcerers to suffer on my behalf after they have already endured exile for so long."

Stormaway smiled, "Sire, your sentiments do you credit. Sadly, your reaction is just as Jarand and Kosar expect." As Tarkyn went to speak, the wizard held up his hand, "Sire, it is not as dire yet as you might expect. Kosar has vetoed the idea for the time being. He told Jarand that he was concerned that such actions may damage his popularity. Even more interestingly, he forbade Jarand to try to lure you out to stand trial at this stage, saying that he was protecting Jarand's popularity too."

Danton frowned, "That is truly bizarre. Kosar would normally be delighted if Jarand's popularity were compromised."

Stormaway peered down at his parchment before raising his head and smiling, "Sire, I believe that you have impressed both of your brothers although they did not like your attitude."

As Tarkyn coloured faintly, Waterstone clapped him on the back, "There you are. That's quite an achievement."

"And reading between the lines," added Stormaway, "I suspect that Kosar is using you as an intelligence source."

"Ah. So he doesn't want you removed from the picture at least until he has checked out what you have said about Jarand." Harkell looked thoughtful, "Jarand, however, is not a fool and he will be doing his utmost to ensure that he covers his tracks until he is ready to move."

Stormaway looked up from studying the missive, "When Jarand returns to Montraya, the king plans to travel with him as far as the encampment to inspect it. Jarand told him it was a rescue centre for attacked travellers."

"And indeed, with very little effort, that is how it will appear." Danton grimaced. "And then your credibility in Kosar's eyes will be shot to pieces, Tarkyn."

"Oh, I don't know," said Stormaway, "I bet Kosar is having all roads from Tormadell watched to see whether Jarand sends out a messenger. The king, also, is not a fool. If he has given Jarand forewarning, he will be watching for a reaction."

Autumn Leaves shook his head, "I can't even begin to imagine myself being so mistrustful of Thunder Storm. How can two brothers, especially twins, behave like that to each other?"

"More than that, how could they treat their younger brother as they did?" said Waterstone acidly.

Danton shrugged, "It's the power. That's all they really care about. Even if Kosar heeds Tarkyn's advice to ensure that his people are safe from brigands, he will only do it to secure his position, not out of love for his people."

"So what should we do in all of this?" asked Lapping Water. "Do we concentrate on warning the Lost sorcerers or do we travel to the encampment in case a fight breaks out between Jarand and Kosar?"

Harkell smothered his surprise that a woman was entering into a tactical conversation but Lapping Water caught his expression before he could hide it and delicately raised her eyebrows at him. He gave a rueful grin, "I beg your pardon, Lapping Water. I struggle enough with women bearing arms, let alone formulating tactics. I do not mean to be offensive."

Lapping Water laughed, "Don't worry. I understand that sorcerers view some things differently. I can assure you that if Tree Wind were not looking after Falling Rain at the moment, she would be at the forefront of these discussions."

"Yes, now that you mention it, I'm sure she would." Harkell gave a small bow and said formally, "I can do no more than say I'm sorry."

Lapping Water frowned suddenly, "I hope you are not bowing because of my association with Tarkyn."

"No, I was merely according you a sorcerer courtesy that often accompanies an apology." Harkell grinned, "But now that you mention it, I will be sure to bow lower and be twice as vigilant not to offend you in future." He laughed as Lapping Water's composure deserted her and she went red with embarrassment. "No. I promise I won't, Lapping Water. I will respect your expertise and ignore your potentially elevated position. How's that?"

Lapping Water glanced at Tarkyn to find him smiling at her discomfort. He sent her the image of him saying, 'This was never going to be easy, was it?' She returned his smile and gave her head an almost imperceptible shake.

This little interchange was not lost on Harkell, however. "I'm sorry, Lapping Water. I did not mean to tease you. Well, I did, but I'll stop now." He firmly returned the focus to their discussion, "It would be interesting to know how many men Kosar intends to take with him to the encampment. He may be placing himself in a vulnerable position if he takes too few and yet virtually declaring war on his brother if he takes too many. Whatever he does, I think we may need to be near the encampment. The situation there could become quite volatile. Any idea how long Jarand plans to stay in Tormadell?"

Stormaway checked his message, "Hmm. There's nothing here about it but as a general rule, he stays at least two months. It's not really worth the effort of bringing his retinue if he stays less time and his stay in Tormadell gives him the chance to catch up with the threads of intrigue and weave a few more. It is also important for his plans to be seen by the public, supporting his brother."

"And what about the Lost sorcerers?" asked Waterstone. "We can't just leave them to their fate."

Autumn Leaves looked as though he was about to say something scathing but, after a brief hesitation, said with a sheepish grin, "No. We can't."

Harkell's soft brown eyes rested on Autumn Leaves for a moment. "For whose sake? Tarkyn's, or the sorcerers'?"

Autumn Leaves shrugged, "Both."

Harkell gave the woodman a slight smile before continuing, "I think we will have to warn them and make sure they lay low until this has blown over,"

"And where *can* they lay low?" asked Tarkyn. "These poor people have only just returned to the homes and families they left, some of them decades ago. We can't have them here with us. There are too many of them."

"I'm glad you said that, Tarkyn," said Thunder Storm approvingly. "Much as we'd like to help, we can't conceal too many sorcerers in our midst, if danger threatens. Those we have with us now already make it more difficult." He nodded at Harkell and Danton, "No offence intended. Just fact."

"None taken." replied Danton, "The sorcerer way of life has never been predicated on concealment in the way that yours has. I think we will have to relocate the Lost sorcerers to different parts of Eskuzor. From what Boravar said, most of them seem to have funds. So they will be all right, away from their families for the time being. But how do we get word to them and sneak them away if the king's men are watching them?"

Stormaway's eyes narrowed as he thought through his resources. "In the main, I think my network can handle it," he said slowly, "But I may need Boravar's assistance to make sure we have reached all of them. I'll let you know if I need help."

Danton frowned, "Stormaway, how do you afford to maintain such a network? They can't all be doing it out of loyalty to Tarkyn. There were many months where his support was extremely low and yet I suspect your network remained intact."

Stormaway gave an embarrassed little cough. "Ahem, that is so, Danton. I will see whether I can gain more detailed information about Kosar's intentions."

"Not so fast, Stormaway," said Danton. "You have not answered my question."

Stormaway looked around the group and grimaced, clearly reluctant to explain. When they all just waited, he sighed and waved a hand, "I use the commission from trading woodfolk goods."

"What?" Tarkyn raised his eyebrows in surprise, "Don't you keep that for yourself?"

Stormaway spread his hands disarmingly, "Very little, Your Highness. My needs are few. My life's work is, and always has been, the future of woodfolk and Eskuzor. Everything I have and do, goes into that."

Tarkyn shook his head, "Stormaway, your generosity and dedication overwhelm me. I know little of money, but I do know that it should be I, not you, who funds all of this. If you ever need anything, just ask and I will retrieve some of my hidden jewellery to provide you with funds."

Danton glanced sideways at Harkell and grinned.

Catching the look, Tarkyn folded his arms, frowning. "*What* is so funny?"

 Danton waved his hand, "Nothing, Sire. Nothing at all." Then he and Harkell went into whoops of laughter. Finally Tarkyn's forbidding expression dampened their hilarity. Danton wiped his eyes and said, "I'm sorry, Tarkyn. It's just that, strictly speaking, you should be paying all of us but don't. And also, I wonder whether you could ever find your way back to your hiding place, anyway."

Remembering Nightwind's words, Tarkyn realised that he was now in a rather tricky situation discussing money while woodfolk listened in who would be offended if they were offered payment.

After a moment's thought, he swept his arm around to include everyone, "As you can see, I have no need of wealth within the forest. Neither does any other woodfolk, for we all support each other. However, both of you, Danton and Harkell, have families outside the forest who may need some financial support. If that is the case, let me know. Stormaway, if I tell you where I have hidden my jewellery, can you organise to have some of it retrieved and sold, if the need arises?" As he remembered where he had hidden it, a grin spread across Tarkyn's face. "No, actually, now that I think about it, only I can retrieve it."

"And why is that, Sire?"

"I hid it behind an eagles' nest high on a cliff face and it didn't occur to me until now… I expect the eagles only tolerated me getting so close because I am a forest guardian." He chuckled, "And even then they were pretty scarey. Given the protectiveness that seems to have developed among these raptors, I don't think they would let anyone else take what they know to be mine."

Danton snorted, "Just as well we're not desperate to be paid then."

Stormaway gave a slight bow, "I will be happy to provide the funds myself, Your Highness."

"No Stormaway, you are already doing more than you should. But I would appreciate it if you could cover it for the time being…on the condition that you render me a strict account… And that is an order." The prince wasn't sure but he thought he saw a flicker of chagrin in Stormaway's face.

Tarkyn turned specifically to the woodfolk, "I hope you know that what is mine is yours, if you ever need it. So the offer is, of course, open to you as well." He shrugged, "I just can't imagine that you'd ever need it."

Stormaway gave a little cough, "While we're on the subject, might I suggest that Danton and Harkell may need money for their own needs, not just their families', if they ever choose to leave the forest or even to venture forth temporarily."

Tarkyn waved his hand dismissively, "Stormaway, I'll leave you to sort that out but if either of you has any need of money, talk to me about it. I mightn't think of it myself." Tarkyn heaved a sigh, "I think that is about as much as I can manage on the topic of money. I suspect finance may be another area of my education that my mother ignored. She has never concerned herself with the cost of things. So she probably didn't see it as important for me to know either. My father would have, I suspect, but…" He shrugged and looked at the two sorcerers, "So. Are you satisfied with that arrangement?"

There was heightened colour in Danton's face, "Sire, I hope you don't think I was trying to force the point. I am not by your side for the money I might make."

Tarkyn smiled, "I know that, Danton. And you, Harkell. And I thank you both, which to me means a lot more than any money I could give you."

At this point, Waterstone, after going briefly out of focus, sent Tarkyn a request to see him alone.

CHAPTER 49

Waterstone made their excuses pleading an issue with the children. Since Tarkyn was often drawn away by the exploits of his little charge, no one thought twice about their departure but as soon as they were out of earshot, Tarkyn turned to Waterstone, "Why all the subterfuge? It does not sit well with me to deceive our friends."

"I know it doesn't, but I will explain as we walk." Waterstone led them up the hill towards the place where Stormaway and he had first realised that Tarkyn was a forest guardian.

As they came closer, Tarkyn could hear the sounds of a heated discussion taking place. When he frowned a query, Waterstone answered, "Because Boravar and the trappers are with them, they are speaking out aloud."

Comprehension dawned, "Oh, I see. Nice of them." He raised his eyebrows, "So, what's going on?"

"Tree Wind and Falling Rain have decided to marry, now that Falling Rain feels truly back among us."

Tarkyn beamed, "Oh good. I'm so pleased. But why all the arguments then?"

"They are arguing over who should marry them. Traditionally, the oldest person present performs the ceremony. But in this case, it is Stormaway, followed by Summer Rain. Summer Rain can't do it because she is Falling Rain's sister and it needs to be someone unrelated to either party." Seeing a hint of scepticism flit across Tarkyn's face, Waterstone amended his last statement, "At least, not in the immediate family."

"So, who is next oldest?"

"I think either Falling Branch, Golden Toad or possibly Rushwind." He thought for a moment, "No, I think Golden Toad is older than Rushwind." He glanced at Tarkyn, "But the problem is that if we overlook Stormaway, he and his family will have every right to feel offended. On the other hand, Stormaway is half sorcerer and the architect of Falling Rain's misfortune." He gave a wry grin, "Not to mention the fact that Falling Rain has just tried to kill him."

"Ooh dear. This is a pickle, isn't it?" said Tarkyn thoughtfully. "I can see why you wanted to get me away without Autumn Leaves and Thunder Storm's knowledge. What about Creaking Bough? Where is she in all of this?"

"Right in the middle of that discussion up ahead of us," said Watersrtone tartly. "But she accepts that we need time to sort it out before we talk to Stormaway and his nephews about it."

As they entered the clearing, Tarkyn searched out Falling Rain and walked straight over to him and enveloped him in a bear hug, "Congratulations, my friend. I am so glad you feel right enough to marry." He pulled away from Falling Rain and turning to Tree Wind, smothered her in a big hug in her turn. "And you too, my worthy antagonist. Congratulations. I am so pleased for both of you."

As he stepped back, Falling Rain asked, "So, will you marry us?"

Without a moment's hesitation, Tarkyn said, "No. I will not."

Falling Rain was bewildered. "But why not? I thought you were my friend."

"I am your friend, Falling Rain. And nothing would give me greater pleasure than to marry you."

"So why not?"

"It is not my place to do so. I am not the eldest amongst us." The prince waved his hand around at the group gathered there. "And I have no intention of overturning woodfolk traditions any more than I have to. I can understand that giving the task, the honour, to me would solve your dilemma but it would create a new one." He paused, "Would I then be expected to perform all marriage ceremonies, thus destroying an age old tradition? Or would the next marriage be presided over by the eldest as tradition requires, thus insulting then, the people you are wishing to avoid insulting now?"

Tree Wind's eyes gleamed. "He's not bad, this prince of ours, is he Falling Rain? He could so easily use our request to enmesh our need for him within our society and yet he holds back." She smiled at him, "Thank you. You have not solved our dilemma but you have at least prevented us from making a fundamental error."

"Perhaps I can still help you with your dilemma but in a different way," suggested Tarkyn. He shrugged, "I don't know. It is difficult for me because I feel strongly for you two but I have also come to feel strongly for Stormaway." He came to a decision, "I will advocate for Stormaway but at the end, if you are still unhappy, and in truth I expect you will be, I will undertake to send him off to oversee the rescue of the Lost sorcerers. Or, if you wait long enough, he will inevitably decide to take himself off as he does from time to time."

Creaking Bough shook her head, "No Tarkyn, that will not do. Whatever is decided here, I cannot be expected to withhold information from my family." She shrugged, "Besides, Stormaway, whatever else he is, is not a fool. He knows our traditions by now and he would know why Falling Rain's marriage was held in his absence whether that absence was decreed by you, or chosen by him."

"And he would understand and accept it," said Tarkyn quietly. "And yet he too has a lonely past behind him, Falling Rain, and I feel sorry that his isolation should continue after he has done so much for woodfolk and for me."

A murmur of dissension arose but as Waterstone put his hand up, they quietened to listen to him. "Under pressure from Danton and a few of us, Stormaway has just admitted that all the money he gained from working for us as an intermediary has been spent on Tarkyn's and our behalf to maintain his intelligence network. All of his hard work as an agent, selling our goods, has been done to support our future and that of Eskuzor." He turned to Falling Rain, "I know you have been caught up in the middle of his machinations, but if you think about it, all he did wrong was to use mindpower on you to find out where we were, so that he could ensure that Tarkyn came to us. If he had not been trying to protect his father's reputation and we had been more forthcoming, he would have prevented your exile."

"Yes," came in Tree Wind dryly, "And then all he is left responsible for, is the sorcerous oath that threatened the forest and removed our independence."

"On the other hand," retorted Waterstone, clearly beginning to lose patience, "over time, we and our descendants would all have been corrupted by that dreadful curse without Stormaway's knowledge and assistance. Not to mention, the hundreds he saved from the sickness that laid us low, and the storm. I wouldn't have Sparrow, and many of you wouldn't have your friends and relatives but for his intercession. And now we find he has worked unremittingly on our behalf, not caring if we thought he was lining his own pockets at our expense, as long as he ensured our wellbeing and that of Tarkyn."

"That may be so," responded Falling Rain slowly. "But while I can logically accept your arguments, it is not you who has lost twelve years of life among woodfolk, twelve years of Tree Wind and with it, the chance to have children. Twelve years means that Tree Wind has now passed child bearing years."

Waterstone bowed his head, "I beg your pardon, Falling Rain. Your loss has been great. I will say no more on the subject."

"But I will," said Tarkyn firmly. "I will not advocate further for Stormaway. But I will advocate on your behalf, Falling Rain, and on yours, Tree Wind." He took a deep breath, "Do not let the past rule your future. No matter what recriminations you heap onto Stormaway and no matter how hard you hold on to the injustice done to you, nothing will bring back those twelve years. All of us acknowledge what a tragedy it has been for you, but we also cannot change what has happened. Whatever you decide to do, start from now and move forward with what you have. Don't let your future life be too badly marred with regrets for what might have been."

As he saw a tense glance pass between the two woodfolk, he held up his hand, "No. I am not saying forgive and forget. And I'm not saying that you should accept Stormaway to marry you. Like all of us, he must accept the consequences of his actions. I am simply saying that you need to let go and move on. "

Suddenly Bean spoke up, "Is it the oldest woodfolk or the oldest person who should marry them?"

"Why?" asked Tree Wind suspiciously.

"Because I think you will find that String is older than Stormaway and possibly I am too. But String is older than me, so my age is irrelevant."

"Ooh. That has put the cat among the pigeons," whispered Waterstone to Tarkyn as a furore broke out around them, "because I suspect some of the reluctance about Stormaway is that he is only half woodfolk but no one likes to mention it."

"He is no less woodfolk than I am," protested Tarkyn. "In fact, he is more so."

"Hmm. Your status cannot be compared to anyone else's because you were offered membership of the woodfolk as an unprecedented honour. Stormaway's claim is by blood through a parent who betrayed our oath of concealment."

Tarkyn rolled his eyes. "Oh my stars! This is all too much for me. I'm leaving. You can sort it out amongst yourselves."

Just as he turned to go, Boravar said quietly to the company, "I think you will find that I am the oldest by some sixty to eighty years. But I am not woodfolk, even though I intend to marry one of you."

"Oh my stars!" said Tarkyn again, in an undertone to Waterstone. "It just gets worse by the minute. What's Boravar's status going to be then, when he marries Twig Snap?"

Waterstone placed a restraining hand on Tarkyn's arm. "Don't go. You need to be party to this if it concerns the future of some of your sorcerers… and as a woodman."

The prince sighed. "True, I can't abdicate responsibility altogether, can I? It must be a community decision though, not mine. And does it have to include all woodfolk or just those in our company?"

"This is a fundamental decision, deciding on whether to initiate someone as a woodman if he marries a woodwoman. I think we will need widespread consensus," said Waterstone thoughtfully.

"Well, before you all go off into a long distance mindconference, can I just say three things? Firstly, don't decide to allow Boravar to join the woodfolk simply for the convenience of sorting out Tree Wind and Falling Rain's marriage because you will be setting a precedent for future similar situations. Secondly, as a woodman, will he be permitted to go into sorcerer society provided he is sworn to secrecy or will his oath of concealment also include himself?" Tarkyn smiled apologetically, "I only ask because that has been an issue for me and it will restrict Boravar's freedom and reduce his usefulness to me, and therefore to all of us, if he is not permitted to go forth."

"And thirdly?"

"And thirdly, what happens if Boravar and Twig Snap split up before the year is out or even after they are married?"

"Woodfolk marriages do not split up," said Waterstone unequivocally. "However, I take your point and will raise it." So saying, Waterstone went out of focus, as did all of the woodfolk, leaving String, Bean and Boravar to chat with Tarkyn.

A surprisingly short time later, Waterstone came back into focus, his face tense with anger.

"What's wrong?" asked Tarkyn.

"Those bastards! Every other group of woodfolk, except for the mountainfolk amazingly enough, have said that since we have allowed the problem to develop, it is up to us to sort it out. They are shocked at the number of sorcerers we now have among us, about our two half breeds, Midnight and Stormaway, and they are extremely unhappy about the upcoming marriages between sorcerers and woodfolk. So much so, that Twig Snap's people won't let her return to them if she marries Boravar."

"And Lapping Water?"

"You have already been accepted as a woodman and are the forest guardian. So they will accept your marriage to a woodwoman, but they are not as happy as I could wish." Waterstone began to pace back and forth in agitation, "The trouble is that we have not kept them all up to date on the developments as they occurred. So everyone is reacting as the mountainfolk did when they first saw the trappers and Stormaway with you and Danton. And now there is also Harkell and Boravar."

"Your communication system is patchy, to say the least," said Tarkyn scathingly.

"Be fair, Tarkyn," interjected Tree Wind. "We were out of range on the other side of the mountain and we were beyond communication in the Lost Forest. Almost as soon as we arrived within reach of other people's minds, Boravar's warning came through. Since then, we have been preoccupied with protecting you and woodfolk from an invasion of soldiers into the forest. We have only just had time to take stock now."

Tarkyn sighed and ran his hand though his hair, "This is disastrous. I do not want you people isolated from other woodfolk because of the presence of me or other sorcerers. It would be grossly unfair and divisive. I know what my immediate reaction is, but you may not agree with it."

"What is it?" asked Waterstone warily.

"I want to bring every woodman and woman together who has sworn the oath to me and make them start fulfilling their commitment. I am sick of you people having to fulfil the oath on behalf of hundreds of people who just sit back and criticise you. It is not good enough." A thought struck him, "In fact, do they even know that the forest is no longer ransom to their acquiescence?"

"No, they don't," said Tree Wind. "Stormaway revoked his spell on the other side of the mountain. So everyone else thinks the forest is still in danger if they don't uphold the oath." She shrugged, "Not that it should make any difference if their honour is worth anything."

"Tarkyn, what are you going to ask them to do when they get here?" asked Waterstone, with a tightly controlled voice. "We don't want to be sent away and replaced like some of those inconsequential servants in your past. I hope, I really hope, that that is not what you mean to do."

Tarkyn stared at him and, for a frisson of time, everyone held their breath. Then Tarkyn broke into a smile, "Of course it's not. And thanks for not jumping down my throat, although I would have preferred it if the thought had never even crossed your mind. Still, I suppose the paranoid mind could take my words the wrong way."

"So how were you planning on them fulfilling their commitment?" asked Thunder Storm evenly.

Tarkyn looked around in surprise, "Oh hello. You and Autumn Leaves are part of this discussion too, are you?"

"Of course. With decisions as weighty as this being made." Thunder Storm folded his arms, "Well?"

The prince waved his hand around, "To be honest, I don't know. I suppose I was mainly thinking of giving them a serious talking to about their attitudes towards you and me, and maybe getting them used to the other sorcerers. I did say it was only my immediate reaction, you know, not necessarily something I was going to put into action. In terms of fulfilling their commitment, I was thinking more of them *helping* you, not *replacing* you." He shook his head, "After all we have been through together, surely you know that no one else could replace any of you, and I certainly wouldn't want to find myself amongst a bunch of strangers again as I did when I first arrived."

Autumn Leaves looked from Waterstone to Tarkyn, "Well done, you two! A week or two ago, that would have led to a blazing row.

Waterstone and Tarkyn exchanged smiles and said in unison, "We're trying."

Rainstorm glanced at them before saying, "Well, if you want my opinion…" Hurrying on in the face of a few blank stares, he continued, "I think you should include everyone, not just those under oath if you want to get them used to sorcerers. After all, everyone supports our forest guardian to some extent now. And when you think about it, we all worked together when the king came into the woods, whether under oath or not. And secondly, if they are all being snaky and saying it is our problem, then that gives us free rein to make the decisions ourselves on behalf of all woodfolk … and frankly, we are in the best position to do it because we know more about sorcerers than they do."

Gradually tense faces relaxed into smiles. Tarkyn clapped the young woodman on the back, "Ah Rainstorm. Where would we be without you?"

"And thirdly," added Autumn Leaves, "None of us has any particular wish to share the *onerous* task of fulfilling the oath. I think we all regard it as a privilege rather than an imposition at this stage." He swept a look of enquiry around the woodfolk who nodded in agreement.

"Privilege might be too strong a word," said Waterstone dryly, "But life's too interesting with you around, Tarkyn, for us to quibble over a little thing like the oath."

Tarkyn laughed, "Waterstone, I can always depend on you to bring me back down to earth." But he knew that, for Waterstone who hated the oath, this was a handsome concession. He waved his hand, "So, let's leave the rest of them out of it for now. As Rainstorm has suggested, you discuss the issues among yourselves. I suggest you consider every possible scenario not just the present one where Boravar is the oldest. Remember, at some time in the future the oldest person could be a sorcerer you have not yet met whom you don't like. When you have reached your decision, I reserve the right to express my opinion before it is finalised. Agreed?"

Waterstone's eyes gleamed in appreciation at how deftly Tarkyn had reminded them not to set a precedent based on their present conundrum, while avoiding any reference to Stormaway in front of Autumn Leaves or Thunder Storm.

It took most of the afternoon for the woodfolk of the home guard to decide that the oldest person present, regardless of background, should be the celebrant for a marriage. The main argument for this was that it was too complicated to draw any clear line between sorcerers and woodfolk with full blood, half blood and honorary woodfolk among them. They decided that if someone was accepted as part of their community, even if temporarily, they should be accorded the same considerations as everyone else.

Once the decision was made, Rainstorm's eyes shone with mischief. "This will wind them all up," he said with some satisfaction.

"True," agreed Thunder Storm, "But if our fundamental tenet is equality, then it is the only fair decision."

"And what about Boravar's status or otherwise as a woodman?" asked Tarkyn.

Thunder Storm waved his hand dismissively. "We'll worry about that later. He won't become a woodman until he marries Twig Snap, if at all. So we have a year to think about it and we've had about as much discussion as we can manage in one sitting… If you don't mind, that is," he added as an afterthought.

Tarkyn's eyes gleamed in amusement, "No, I don't mind, thank you for asking. I suspect you are going to need a few of these sessions to sort out new rules to address the issues created by sorcerers living with you."

The prince wondered whether his woodfolk realised how closely the home guard was beginning to parallel the king's court, jealous of their privileged position and, in consultation with him, making decisions on behalf of the wider population. On the whole, he did not think it boded well for the woodfolk nation but at the moment, he did not know how to curtail it without making them feel that he wanted to disperse the home guard. In hindsight, he realised that accepting the offer made by the other woodfolk in a fit of pique, to decide on their behalf, could be the harbinger of a whole new way of woodfolk governance unless he, Tarkyn, took steps to prevent it.

Chapter 50

The wedding of Falling Rain and Tree Wind took place two weeks later when the rising of the moon would be late in the evening. Representatives from the forestals, harvesters, gatherers, mountainfolk and wanderers came together to celebrate their marriage and the unusually large numbers bore testament to the woodfolk's wish to welcome Falling Rain back into the fold.

The intervening weeks had been spent on bringing all woodfolk up to date with the events that had occurred since Tarkyn had left with the home guard to rescue Golden Toad and his family from the encampment. As they became more cognisant of the contributions made by the sorcerers to the welfare of the woodfolk nation, their attitudes had mellowed but the full breadth of their acceptance was yet to be tested. Remembering Leaf Fall and Twig Snap's trepidation when they first arrived, the home guard had spent some time on working out the best way to introduce so many sorcerers to the visiting woodfolk.

When the visitors arrived on the day before the ceremony, the sorcerers made themselves scarce until the newcomers had settled in. Once the woodfolk had eaten their evening meal and were sitting at their leisure around the firesite, Tarkyn finally felt the time was right to emerge. From the shadows beyond the firelight, he gazed around at the assembled woodfolk, noting the presence of Ancient Elm from the gatherers, Dry Berry and Dripping Rock from the mountainfolk, and Raging Water from the forestals plus many others he had never met.

A hush fell over the assembled woodfolk as he walked out from the shadows, tall and imposing despite his woodfolk clothing, glinting amber eyes framed by his long black hair. But as he entered the full light of the fire, the first unnerving impression of him was diluted by the realisation that he was holding a young woodchild on his hip.

Waterstone rushed in to cover any awkwardness by saying, "Hello, Tarkyn." He waved his arm round the gathering. "For those of you who have not yet met him, this is my bloodbrother, Tarkyn Tamadil, Prince of Eskuzor and Guardian of the Forest."

Tarkyn gave a shallow bow, "Good evening. I am pleased to meet you. And even more pleased to see old faces that I already know." He glanced down at his little charge who was clinging anxiously to him in the face of so many new people scrutinising him. He gave him a reassuring smile before looking up, "And this is Midnight. You have no doubt heard of him by now. He can't hear you but he can receive images if you get his attention first."

Even as Tarkyn noticed the surreptitious glances being cast at Falling Rain for his reaction, the returned woodman strode over to join Tarkyn and Midnight at the edge of the firelight and put his arm around the prince to draw him forward, "Come and join us. We were just about to broach the second flagon of fine wine brought by the mountainfolk to celebrate the occasion."

Tarkyn smiled broadly, "It would be a pleasure."

After perhaps an hour, when the newcomers were becoming inured to his presence, Tarkyn glanced at Waterstone to gauge his opinion then raised his voice enough to gain the attention of the whole group. "So, as you are aware, there are several more sorcerers residing with the home guard at the moment; six more to be precise." He cast his eyes around his audience. "Do you feel ready to meet them?"

A few mutters of disquiet arose but Raging Water said gruffly, "Come on. Bring them on, young one. I know you wouldn't let them hurt any of us. So I can't imagine we have anything to worry about."

Tarkyn grinned cheekily, "Quite right Raging Water, and three of them don't possess any attacking powers of any note, anyway." He thought about Harkell and added, "At least, not magical ones."

In a carefully orchestrated sequence, Hail introduced the trappers, explaining how much they had helped her, Autumn Leaves and Thunder Storm introduced their uncle whom many knew anyway through trading, Waterstone introduced Danton, and Tarkyn introduced Harkell, each giving a brief rundown of what the particular sorcerer had done to help woodfolk or Tarkyn.

Finally, Twig Snap stood up nervously and cleared her throat, "And finally, I would like to introduce Boravar, my future husband, who risked his life to bring word to Prince Tarkyn of an impending attack." Despite her best intentions, she couldn't stop herself from throwing a defiant glance at Ancient Elm and others from her group. She took a breath and ran her hand through her frizzy hair to push it off her face. "He has lived for over one hundred and twenty years with both woodfolk and sorcerers in the Lost Forest. As such, he is the oldest among us and will perform the marriage ceremony tomorrow."

Ignoring the smattering of disapproving frowns and a few quiet mutters, Tarkyn gave her a smile of approval which she returned with a little complicit grin.

As Boravar's bulky form emerged from among the trees, several people gasped. Someone could be heard to whisper in consternation, "Stars above! How much bigger do they get?"

Boravar smiled and gave a slight bow, "Not much bigger than this, my friend."

The six sorcerers stood in a row and, glancing at each other to get their timing right, bowed simultaneously to the gathered woodfolk. When they straightened, they were all smiling.

Tarkyn waved a hand at them, "Ask us any questions you would like to." He grinned, "As Twig Snap noticed, yes, we do have differing eye and hair colours. Stormaway and Midnight are the only sorcerers we know of, who have green eyes. This, of course, is because of their woodfolk heritage. We also have different types of powers. I am not going to go through them all, but feel free to ask any of us about them." He became more serious, "All of the sorcerers here are trusted by me and by the home guard. I am not suggesting for a moment that you should trust other sorcerers you may see within the forest. As woodfolk, our pledge of secrecy remains in force and I am not expecting you to extend the trust you give these people to any other sorcerers." He looked around, "Is everyone happy with that?" When there were no objections, Tarkyn tweaked his finger to indicate that the sorcerers should disperse to sit among the woodfolk.

With the determined help of the home guard, the woodfolk gradually began to include the sorcerers in their conversations and to talk to them about their adventures over the mountain and in the Lost Forest.

CHAPTER 51

In the late afternoon of the following day, Falling Rain and Tree Wind stood before Boravar on the bank of the river, facing each other with their hands linked. Tree Wind's hair was threaded with blossom and both of them wore garlands around their necks woven from grasses, leaves and flowers.

Shafts of deep yellow with motes of dust swirling within them, shone through the trees on the far side of the river to bathe everyone in an eerie golden light. Trees that had been covered in buds two weeks before were now sprouting forth with light green crinkly leaves, the woods were peppered with white and pink blossoms, and the woodlands rang with birdsong.

Despite his protests that he had seen more woodfolk marriages than anyone else, Boravar had been relentlessly drilled and knew to the syllable what was required of him. He smiled reassuringly at the two of them standing nervously before him and began:

"Falling Rain and Tree Wind have formed an intention to wed and this desire has stood the test of time." Not by a flicker, did the big sorcerer betray how excessive the time had been in their case. "Today, at their request, we will bind them to live together, to protect each other and to care for each other, for the rest of their lives."

Boravar nodded at Waterstone who came forward wielding a small sharp dagger. Tree Wind turned her left hand palm upwards and Falling Rain presented his right palm. Boravar took the dagger from Waterstone and said, "This is your last chance to turn back. Are you both sure?"

Tree Wind and Falling Rain looked at each other, gave a slight smile and nodded.

Boravar took the joined hands closest to him and lightly scored their palms diagonally from their forefingers so that when their hands came together, the cuts lay on top of each other.

"As their blood mingles, Tree Wind and Falling Rain become one family and will share their ancestors and descendants."

He waited for a few moments before continuing,

"Now, we bind them by the trees of the woodlands..."

At Boravar's gesture, a rope of leafy vines was wound around the wrists of their cut hands, binding them together.

"... by the soil beneath their feet,"

Running Feet came forward with a wooden bowl into which Boravar dipped his thumb before smearing each of their foreheads with a streak of red earth.

"… by the water that runs through the forest."

Boravar knelt down bedside the river and dipped his left hand into the water. Then using his hand as a cup, he wet the fingers of his right hand and smeared each of their cheeks with water.

"And finally, their union will be steeped in the goodwill of their kindred and friends, both woodfolk and sorcerer."

Tree Wind and Falling Rain turned to face the audience still bound together by one hand but free to return gestures of affection with the other. Every person present took their turn to come forward and hug or pat the bride and groom. Many offered gifts, either on their own behalf or for a group, and left them to one side. Some had nothing to give but among woodfolk, that did not matter. Summer Rain and Tarkyn came forward together.

"My gift will come to you over the coming months, long after this ceremony is over," said Tarkyn. He grinned mysteriously and moved on after hugging them.

Summer Rain gave them a perfunctory hug. "I, too, am a party to this gift. I wish you well, my brother and my new sister,"

When his turn came, Rainstorm threw his arms around them both, then shyly held out a tiny pair of carved egrets hanging on two pieces of leather thonging. "Falling Branch thinks I can't do anything but I have done my best for you."

"Oh, Rainstorm . They're beautiful," breathed Tree Wind. She glanced at Falling Rain, "Could we wear them now, do you think?"

Falling Rain glanced at Boravar for approval before nodding. Rainstorm went pink with pleasure that his gift was so appreciated and placed his egrets reverently over each of their heads.

At the very last, when everyone else had gone past, Stormaway walked up to them. He did not presume to hug them but gave each of their arms a pat. He glanced around to ensure that no one was in ear shot but Boravar, who was still overseeing the proceedings. "Tree Wind and Falling Rain, when you were discussing two weeks ago who should preside over your wedding, you forgot that I can now pick up mind talking." As a pall of embarrassment settled on the bride and groom's faces, Stormaway waved his hand dismissively, "No. Don't feel badly about it. I would just like to say that I appreciate the effort you put into trying not to offend me. I would have completely understood if you had thrown it in my face." He gave a little smile, "And now, I have a very special gift for you." He handed Tree Wind a phial of clear liquid, faintly tinted with blue. "No one can give you back your twelve years. But I can give you back your fertility. The life force of the forest guardian and the knowledge and skill of Summer Rain will ensure your child's growth within you." He smiled, "Think well before you use it. You will have a babe in arms at an age when most people's children are becoming independent. But at least the choice is yours."

"Oh Stormaway! Thank you." Tree Wind flung her arm around the old wizard's neck and hugged him while Falling Rain patted his back from the other side.

Stormaway was mightily embarrassed, "Well, harrumph. Glad you like it." He grimaced at Boravar, "So come on, man. Get on with it." He disentangled himself as quickly as he could and withdrew to one side.

Boravar flung his arms wide, "And now that everyone has given this union a token of their goodwill, I now pronounce that you are husband and wife." He beamed at them. "You have until the rising of the moon to eat and drink yourselves silly. Only after that, may you remove the vines binding you together. Then you will be escorted to the wedding shelter that has been prepared in a private clearing close by. For seven days and nights, you may not contact anyone, but all your needs will be provided for and lookouts will be posted to protect you." The burly sorcerer engulfed them in a huge bear hug. "Congratulations, my friends!"

When he straightened, he said, suddenly a little shy, "And now, my gift to you."

In the gathering darkness, he murmured "*Lumaya*," to produce a globe of pure white, then another. He sent them up to hang high in the air above their heads. A murmur of disquiet ran through the visiting woodfolk that was quickly dispelled by their neighbours.

Keeping his concentration on his display, Boravar produced balls of blue, gold, red, orange and purple in quick succession and sent them up to weave in and around the two white spheres. Then the coloured spheres followed each other around the periphery of the crowd, swooping down from time to time, to make the more faint-hearted woodfolk duck. Boravar chuckled quietly as he sent them soaring back up to weave in and out of the branches of the trees before returning to circle the two white globes. Then, slowly the circle of balls widened and the white globes descended.

"Hold out your hands," murmured Boravar, resisting the temptation to reassure them that it wouldn't hurt.

Trustingly, Tree Wind and Falling Rain each held out their unbound hands and were rewarded by a white globe landing gently on each palm. Boravar stepped back leaving the pair of them surrounded by a descending circle of coloured spheres. With a final sweep of his arm, the sorcerer sent the coloured balls swirling up into the trees to extinguish with faint pops high in the branches of the overhanging trees.

Then the intensity of the white globes increased until their light radiated out to brighten the whole clearing.

"Throw them up," whispered Boravar.

Tree Wind and Falling Rain did as they were asked and the bright white globes flew up and arced outwards before falling in a scatter of white sparks over either side of the crowd. Then the darkness of the evening enveloped them.

An awed "Wow" rose quietly from the crowd.

Boravar smiled shyly, "Just a little something I learned in the Lost Forest. Years to practice, you know."

Part 8: Orolan

CHAPTER 52

Midnight lay on his stomach deep within a dense bush, watching his mother between the gaps in the lower branches. He knew the signs and knew she was packing up to leave. What he didn't know was whether she would expect him to go with her and whether Tarkyn would let her take him.

If she didn't want to take him, he would feel hurt but relieved. If she did want to take him and insisted on it, and Tarkyn let him go, he would run away. Midnight didn't analyse why he would run away. He just knew that if Tarkyn let him go, he wouldn't want to be with anybody.

As he watched, Hail finished packing up and walked over to where Tarkyn was sitting. She asked to speak privately with him and he moved away from the others with her. Midnight watched as they discussed his future. He could see each of them look around from time to time, searching for him. Their discussion became more heated until finally Tarkyn raised his hand and dropped it, in resignation.

Midnight didn't wait. He wriggled backwards out of the bush and took off, his chest tight with contained misery. He ran blindly through the woods, dodging around bushes and jumping over logs, oblivious to where he was going, just desperate to get away from Tarkyn's betrayal of him.

Finally, he ran through a small copse of young poplars before wriggling his way deep into a thicket of hazel and holly. He was scratched mercilessly by their thorns and spikes as he pushed through but took perverse pleasure in the pain, somehow feeling that he deserved it. Then he curled up in a small ball, closed his eyes, and tried to block out the world.

He spent an hour in abject misery before he felt something soft butting at his hand. He pushed it away but it persisted. He opened his eyes and found himself face to face with a small brown rabbit, its little nose twitching in trepidation as it waited for his next move. Midnight blinked and, moving his hand very slowly so as not to frighten it, began to stroke it. Its fur felt warm and velvety beneath his fingers. Gradually, as he became engrossed in patting the rabbit, he unknowingly let down the barriers to his mind.

And at last Tarkyn, waiting patiently on the outside of the thorny bushes, was able to make contact with his little charge.

Now that the little boy's mind was open, Tarkyn sent him waves of caring and reassurance, but Midnight retaliated with disbelief. Midnight sat up within the thorny bushes, picked up the rabbit and put it gently in his lap. He kept his eyes on it and comforted himself by stroking it.

Tarkyn tried again. He sent Midnight an image of his mother packing up and waiting to say goodbye to him. But Midnight misinterpreted the image and thought that Tarkyn meant that she was waiting for him to go with her. So he responded with an image of himself walking away with his mother while Tarkyn laughed and looked relieved as he waved goodbye.

Tarkyn frowned in bewilderment and after a moment, showed himself with his hand on his heart and then a query accompanying the image of himself laughing at Midnight's departure. Midnight sent his memory of Tarkyn looking resigned after talking to Hail.

As comprehension dawned, Tarkyn sent a firm request for Midnight to look at him. There was a fraught minute while Midnight considered refusing. He knew Tarkyn would have his way in the end but he weighed up whether it was worth the effort to make Tarkyn be more forceful first. With a little sigh, he reluctantly raised his eyes from the rabbit to meet Tarkyn's.

Tarkyn was then able to use a combination of gestures and images to explain that his resignation had been because of his failure to persuade Hail to stay, not because he accepted that Midnight would accompany her. He then explained emphatically that Hail was angry with him because he wouldn't let Midnight go with her.

The little boy dropped his eyes back down to the rabbit, but gradually a smile grew on his face until he was grinning from ear to ear.

Tarkyn, watching him, said to himself, "Yes, young one. We both actually want you… and maybe now, you have finally realised it." He sent a query asking whether Midnight was ready to come out yet.

Midnight nodded, put the rabbit down carefully and began to push his way back out through the spiky foliage. But without the impetus of the strong emotion that had driven him into the depths of the bushes, he was much more aware of the sharp leaves and thorns and found that he couldn't force himself to be scratched like that again. He grinned sheepishly and let Tarkyn know that he was stuck.

Tarkyn shook his head, smiling ruefully at him. He drew his knife from his belt and began to hack away at the outside branches, planning to cut a path out for Midnight.

"I'd just burn it, if I were you," said Ancient Oak calmly, suddenly at his elbow. "You'll cut yourself to shreds on those thorns and spikes."

Tarkyn managed not to whip his head around in surprise but it took a conscious effort to turn his head slowly. "Hello. Where did you spring from?"

"I saw you head off in search of Midnight and thought you might need some help if he was upset." Ancient Oak gave a little smile, "I didn't expect the help to involve pruning holly and hawthorn though. Go on. Use your magic."

Tarkyn smiled at him, "Very well, I will. But I don't think I'll use a fireball. The whole thicket might go up in smoke then. I'll just use shafts of power to break off branches instead of cutting them. That will save me from scratching myself to bits. How about that? Does that meet with your approval?"

Ancient Oak grinned, "Yes thanks. Although I think you should use that "*Liefka*" spell to move the branches away once you've cut them down so that we don't stand on them. Those thorns can sometimes go straight through soft leather."

Tarkyn raised his eyebrows. "Anything else?"

"No. That should do it, I think." The woodman laughed, "Well, perhaps one more thing…You might get Midnight to help you from the inside."

Tarkyn frowned quizzically at his woodbrother. "Do you like walking on thin ice?"

Ancient Oak shrugged, smiling to take any sting out of it, "I don't mind, as long as the water's not too deep. After all, the worst that could happen is that if I push you too far, you'll get angry."

Tarkyn stared at him for a moment as he digested this before giving a grunt of laughter, "Hmmph. So we'd better get on with it then, hadn't we?"

He carefully aimed a shaft of bronze at a low holly branch and broke it off at its base. Then he nodded at Midnight and sent an image of the little boy doing the same thing with his green magic. Midnight grinned and sent a neat green shaft into the nearest low hawthorn branch, dropping it cleanly to the ground. Tarkyn smiled his approval as he intoned, "Liefka," and levitated the holly branch away. He frowned uncertainly at Midnight, knowing Midnight couldn't use speech to cast spells.

Midnight asked Tarkyn to repeat his spell. Once he had watched Tarkyn move the holly branch further away, Midnight focused furiously on his branch of hawthorn, holding his hand above it. Then he gradually raised his arm and the branch rose from the ground. Following the movements of the little wood sorcerer's arm, the hawthorn branch moved through the gap to the outside and floated across the ground to join Tarkyn's holly branch to one side. With a little flick of his hand, Midnight broke contact with the branch and it fell to land on top of the holly.

Midnight returned his attention to Tarkyn and smiled broadly as the prince and the woodman applauded. Giving the rabbit a final stroke, Midnight turned over and slithered on his stomach through the gap they had made, into Tarkyn's waiting arms.

As he held Midnight, Tarkyn looked over the little boy's head to Ancient Oak, "Look at him. The poor little fellow has cut his back to ribbons... and his shirt. They're bloody nasty, those spikes. See these dark marks. I think some of the spikes may have broken off in his back. Summer Rain will need to take a look at him." He sighed as he stroked Midnight's head, "Ah young one. When will you learn that I won't abandon you?"

As though in response to Tarkyn's words, Midnight heaved a shuddering sigh of contentment and leaned his head in, hard against the nape of Tarkyn's neck.

Ancient Oak smiled. "He's learning. Every time you bring him back, you convince him a little more."

As they headed back towards through the copse of young poplars, Tarkyn stopped and looked around. "These are the trees I planted to cover up the wolves' remains a few months ago."

"Are they?" Ancient Oak studied them with interest, "All still flourishing. Good, isn't it? Have you told Midnight about it? You could show both of us how you and Stormaway loosened the soil for the hole and how you planted the poplars."

"If you would like me to. We have time. Hail isn't leaving until tomorrow morning now." Tarkyn wandered over to sit on the little cairn of rocks at the edge of the clearing that they had noticed last time they were here.

But as soon as he touched the cairn, a sound like the tolling of a deep bell rang through the forest and a turquoise net of magic slammed down around him. "Oh no! This cairn is warded. Go, Ancient Oak. Fetch Stormaway!"

Even as Ancient Oak flicked out of sight, Tarkyn heard hoofbeats converging on him from several directions. He focused on Midnight and tried to explain that he should think of himself as a sorcerer in the upcoming confrontation. He sent a picture of the little boy with woodfolk and shook his head. Then, as he followed this with a picture of Danton, Harkell and himself, he pointed at Midnight nodding.

In response, much to Tarkyn's amazement, Midnight shifted his colouring through Danton's blonde hair with purple eyes to Harkell's dark brown hair and eyes to Tarkyn's black hair and amber eyes, attached to a calm query. After a moment's hesitation, Tarkyn opted for Harkell's colouring, reasoning that it was closest to Midnight's own. Tarkyn felt Midnight's twinge of disappointment that he hadn't chosen his own colouring for Midnight but before he could address it, the first riders appeared at the edge of the clearing.

They threw themselves off their horses and ran to stand in a belligerent circle around the imprisoned prince. Tarkyn stood up very slowly, holding Midnight protectively, wishing that he too could disguise his colouring.

Shocked looks of recognition passed between some of the riders but no one spoke or moved. The reason became apparent when a second lot of riders arrived and the crowd parted to allow a tough, stocky man through, to stand facing the prince with his hands on his hips. The man's face was lined and his thinning hair was pulled back into a grey wispy ponytail. Light brown eyes studied the prince.

Tarkyn took a long slow breath to steady himself before saying coolly, "No doubt you will show me the courtesy I am due in your own time."

He heard a whisper somewhere behind him, "Dog's teeth! It really is the prince."

Their captain produced a flourishing bow, "It is an honour, Your Highness. Unexpected, but an honour nevertheless."

His company followed suit.

"You may rise," said Tarkyn after a moment, "And perhaps you would honour me by introducing yourselves."

Their captain's eyes narrowed, "You're a cool customer. I'll say that for you. My name is Orolan. We are brigands, working the forest along the Great West Road. Turning a quick profit in any way we can." He folded his arms again, "And you have just triggered the alarm on our stash."

Tarkyn smiled, "Oh, is that what it was?" He frowned, "But we came this way a few months ago and I'm sure that someone must have touched these stones then – in fact, I'm sure they did – and nothing happened then."

Orolan shrugged, "No goodies hidden here then. We'd just spent them all. No point in warding an empty space."

"I see." Tarkyn paused, "As you can no doubt tell, I had no intention of raiding your '*goodies*', as you call them. In fact, I had no idea they were even here."

"But you do now."

The prince nodded, "True, I do now. That knowledge, however, does not change my intentions."

"And what exactly are your intentions, Your Highness?" asked Orolan with a slight sneer.

Tarkyn raised his eyebrows, "I'm sorry. I do not see that that is any of your business."

"Since I have you as my prisoner, I would say that your future is every bit my business." He leered at the prince, "You're worth a lot of money to the right people."

Tarkyn sat back down. "Your courtesy is beginning to wear very thin," he observed mildly.

"Courtesy is one thing, Your Highness. Business is quite another."

The prince looked down at the little boy pressed hard into his chest. He stroked his head, appearing to ignore the brigand captain completely. "Hmm, Midnight, how shall we play this? Shall we destroy their goodies while they watch? Shall we knock them all out, tie them up and leave them to their fate? Or shall we negotiate?" Tarkyn raised hard eyes to engage Orolan and said in a voice, now edged with impatience, "Orolan, to be the captain of such a large group of men, you must be reasonably astute. Have you not heard of my encounters with my brothers? And can you seriously imagine that I travel unaccompanied through the woodlands?"

Orolan and his men glanced uncertainly around themselves. But the captain was not easily intimidated. After a moment, he returned his gaze to Tarkyn, "You are not overwhelming me with your numbers, Your Highness. We know these woods and we have just ridden in from all sides. You have no army waiting in the wings. You are bluffing… and not very well, at that."

Tarkyn repressed his anger at being doubted and merely asked, "So, before I take any actions, what are your intentions?"

Orolan scratched his head, "As I see it, I have two options open to me. Either I can arrange for one of my men to take a message to one of your men demanding a ransom for you… or I could hand you over to the king and earn the reward, and possibly a pardon." He gave a short laugh, "Although I'm not sure that we'd really want a pardon. Might restrict our activities too much, hey lads?"

There was a general rumble of laughter that Tarkyn ignored.

"So, your motives are purely financial, then?"

Orolan waved his hand, "Oh yes, my lord. I don't hold you any particular grudge against you and I am no loyal supporter of the king. I will take whatever path is most profitable."

"Then I suggest you release me unharmed and I will leave your treasure intact."

Orolan shook his head regretfully, "No, Your Highness. That is not how I see it at all. If you are not prepared to co-operate, we will leave you in that little turquoise cage until we get word to the king. When we have received payment, we will tell him where you are and he can collect you."

As the brigand captain turned to leave, several things happened at once. The outer ring of brigands dropped like stones. The horses, startled by fast flying sharp stones hitting their chests or backs, reared and lunged, many of them breaking away to gallop off through the woods. And within the turquoise cage, Tarkyn rose and turned, still holding Midnight with one arm. Then, using his other hand, the prince blasted the rocks off the cairn, sending them flying to land against the further edge of the turquoise net, revealing a deep cavity filled with ill-gotten gains. As Orolan whipped his head back around in shock, Tarkyn sent an intense fireball into the cavity, burning its contents into a molten mass.

Orolan's eyes burned with fury, "You bastard! That took us months to collect!"

Tarkyn looked down his nose at the stocky brigand and spoke scathingly, "*Never* speak to a prince of the realm like that. Now, release this ward or the rest of you will also fall."

In response, the brigand defiantly raised a smoky grey shield over himself and his men.

Tarkyn waved his hand dismissively, "Fine. Let's do this the hard way then." He raised his voice slightly. "Stormaway, Danton, Boravar, come here. The others of you, stay hidden and ready."

The three sorcerers emerged and bowed.

"Danton and Boravar, I want you two to get yourselves up into the boughs of that overhanging tree so that you have a good angle. Then I want you to circle your shafts of magic around the outside of their shield… as you did with Stormaway to loosen the stake in the encampment, Danton. Remember?"

"And what are you hoping to achieve by that?" sneered Orolan, hands on hips.

Tarkyn just stared at him disdainfully and waited.

"What are you hoping to achieve by that, *Your Highness*?" he repeated, modifying his tone as little as he could, to get away with it.

"You can either wait to find out, or negotiate," said Tarkyn.

"You can't touch us. We'll wait," replied the captain, full of bravado.

Tarkyn turned his back on him so that he could talk privately with Stormaway He looked at the wizard and found himself gazing into nondescript brown eyes. "Well?" he murmured, "Can you get rid of this thing?"

"It is a wizard's work, Your Highness. It would be easier for the wizard concerned to remove it."

"And where is this wizard? Do you know?"

"Just a minute, I'll see." Stormaway closed his eyes and placed his hand on the outside of the turquoise net. After a few moments, he opened his eyes suddenly and pointed to a scruffy little man seated beside the brigand captain within the shield. He grimaced, "Unfortunately, he is safely tucked up within that shield, Tarkyn. Make sure no one hurts him in the mayhem to come."

Tarkyn raised his eyebrows, "And if they do?"

Stormaway waved his hand impatiently, "If they do, I'll have to study my books and figure something out. Or it might just fade if he dies… but I'm not sure. It's not as bad as a curse though. Another wizard can remove it. It just takes time." He nodded at Midnight, "But I think your little fellow there could do with some food and some salves in the near future." He smiled at Midnight, "Clever little lad, isn't he? Look at those eyes… and with no training at all."

By now, Boravar and Danton had levitated themselves into the tree. As their shafts of peacock blue and aqua began to circle the shield, their magics thrummed each time they crossed each other.

"Increase the intensity," shouted Tarkyn above the noise.

Gradually the thrumming grew louder until it was beating against the ears of the onlookers. Within the smoky grey shield, the brigands were holding their heads, cowering down against the onslaught of sound. Then the ground beneath them began to tremble as the bindings holding together the particles of soil slowly disintegrated under the force of the vibration. Within minutes, they were sinking into the loosened soil. Screams of fear rent the air until, in the midst of the chaos, Orolan finally waved his hand and removed the shield.

"Stop!" he yelled. "We throw ourselves on your mercy."

At a nod from Tarkyn, Boravar and Danton withdrew their shafts of power. A blissful silence fell.

The dishevelled brigand captain shoved the wizard in the back and pushed him up out of the soil to scrabble on his hands and knees until he landed, sprawled in an untidy heap before Tarkyn, his robes wrapped awkwardly around his ankles.

"Orolan, no doubt you will want to join him," said Tarkyn coldly.

His face shuttered with resentment, the brigand captain crawled up out of the dirt and threw himself on his face before the prince.

"Your wizard's name?" snapped Tarkyn.

The captain lifted his head to reply.

"Do not presume to raise so much as a finger until I give you permission," barked Tarkyn.

"Keepsafe Stonemaster, my lord," mumbled Orolan, his mouth taking in dirt as he breathed. He began to cough.

Tarkyn ignored him and turned to the wizard. "So Keepsafe, I believe you have a job to do. You may rise, very slowly. One false move and you will be shot down without compunction. Are we clear?" As the wizard disentangled himself from his robes and stood up, Tarkyn addressed his liegeman, "Danton, place your shield over this lot until we can concentrate on them."

The scruffy little wizard now stood, bowing obsequiously, hand on heart.

"Remove this ward of yours. Now! You should have done it as soon as you saw who I was."

"Yes, Your Highness." The wizard muttered under his breath and waved his hand. A bright turquoise flash erupted from his fingertips and the turquoise cage disappeared. He bowed again, "However, I believe my life would have been forfeit had I done so, Your Highness."

"You have chosen yourself a harsh master, wizard."

Keepsafe glanced at the brigand captain still lying in the dirt beside him. "That is so, Your Highness. Although generally, I would say he is fair. It is not unreasonable for a leader to expect loyalty from his men."

The prince turned his attention to the brigand captain, "You may now rise, Orolan. Turn and look at what your greed and stubbornness have done. Half of your men have been shot, most of your horses have decamped and the rest of your men are at the mercy of me and my m… followers." He sent a private, laughing apology up to Lapping Water and Twig Snap for his near slip. "What do you think I should do with you?"

The brigand captain turned back to the prince and considered carefully before replying, "If I had turned the tables on someone who had been planning to take me in for a reward, I would either send them away with a flea in their ear or…"

Tarkyn raised his eyebrows sardonically, "By which I presume you mean a severe beating, not a friendly telling off?" When the brigand nodded reluctantly, the prince merely said, "Go on."

He shrugged and grimaced, "Or I could hand them in for the reward instead," He waved his hand, "Or kill them."

"And have you ever been in that position?" asked the prince.

The captain shook his head, "No Sire. I can't say that I have."

"So what do you think you would do?"

A wry grin split through the dirt on the brigand's face. "To be honest with you, Your Highness, I am struggling to consider this objectively."

Tarkyn addressed the scruffy wizard, "Keepsafe, if you need it, I will give you my protection but I need an honest answer. Does your captain keep his word?"

Keepsafe glanced at his captain before replying, "Yes, Your Highness. If he did not, the men would not follow him."

"I see." The prince reached a decision. "Boravar, bind their hands behind them and tie them to the tree over there. Take shifts with Danton in maintaining the shield so that each of you can take part in the discussion that I will have, away from these people. Orolan and Keepsafe, I will return with my decision within the hour." As he turned to leave, he said quietly to Danton, "Wider shield, I think. You need to cover the shot brigands too, you realise?"

Danton grinned, "Yes. Good point, Sire."

As soon as he was out of sight, Tarkyn asked for Summer Rain and Hail to come to him. He reached the firesite to find all signs of woodfolk obliterated. He sighed, "Where can we sit and talk?"

Woodfolk flicked to stand in a huddle around him.

"Don't worry, Tarkyn," said Waterstone, "Now that they're all immobilised, we can stay here. If you give us one of your handy little fireballs, we'll have a fire rekindled in no time." He clapped Tarkyn on the back, "And thanks for remembering to consult us before you made your decision."

Tarkyn grinned, "It seems only fair. After all, I needed all the help I could get to find my way out of that sticky situation."

He handed Midnight over to Hail so she could hold him while Summer Rain extracted any thorns and put salves on his back. "Hail, your little son is very powerful. I think he has the makings of a wizard, like his father. He can change his eye and hair colour, you know. He is quite amazing. He needs to stay with Stormaway and be trained."

As he hesitated to continue the conversation in front of everyone, Hail said tightly, "But look what's happened. He got all upset and hurt himself."

"Hail," said Tarkyn gently, "He ran away to hide when he thought that I had resigned myself to letting him go with you. He does love you, but somehow, his whole faith in people has come to depend on me keeping my promise to him that I would always look after him. If he is to learn any trust, I must hold to my word." He smiled warmly at her. "If it's any consolation, I can tell you that I won't find it hard. I love that son of yours to bits."

Perhaps some of Tarkyn's feelings leaked out, because Midnight swivelled his head around to give him a confiding smile.

Tarkyn smiled back and spread his hands, "The choice is yours, Hail. You are welcome to stay with us and remain close to your son. If you go, perhaps we will come up into the mountains again and seek you out when things have settled down here. But no matter what, Midnight stays by my side."

Hail glanced around at the surrounding woodfolk and saw sympathy but no support in their eyes. She grunted, "I am too solitary to last for long in such a large group. At least this time when I leave him, I know Midnight will be cared for properly." Suddenly her face relaxed into a smile, "Thank you, Tarkyn, for all you have done for both of us. I know you love him, but I also know he is a handful and your patience with him has exceeded all bounds. You are very kind to him. Midnight is lucky to have found you."

"Thanks," muttered Tarkyn, colouring with embarrassment to the amusement of those around him.

"Now, Your Highness," said Stormaway firmly, "Do you think you could get back to being a prince so we can sort out this problem with the brigands?"

Tarkyn blinked a couple of times to pull himself together. He rubbed his hand across his forehead, "Sorry. Where were we?"

"We have about forty brigands under Danton's shield and two tied to a tree," Autumn Leaves summarised promptly.

"And we're helping you decide whether to let them go, kill them or turn them in for the reward," added Rainstorm.

"I'll go for killing them," said Twig Snap with relish. She raised her voice to overcome the murmurs of protest, "After all, that's what would have happened to Tarkyn if they'd turned him in."

"Lot of bodies to clean up," said Leaf Fall thoughtfully.

Twig Snap rolled her eyes, "You always have some objection."

"Do you trust what the wizard said, Stormaway?" asked Tarkyn.

"A wizard does not have to work for someone like that, unless he wants to. He could easily evade him and return to the towns if he wanted to. I trust what he says."

Tarkyn thought for a moment, "And the requirements of protocol, Stormaway? After all, Orolan did threaten a Tamadil."

"There is no doubt in my mind that he must be punished, Your Highness," said Stormaway unequivocally. "If he is allowed to get away with it, the next person will find it easier to threaten or harm you. The Royal Family must remain sacrosanct."

"Oh dear, this is where your family has an institutionalised sanction to hurt people, isn't it?" said Waterstone.

"So what would you do to someone who threatened to take one of you in and sell them?" asked Tarkyn sharply.

"What? A sorcerer?" asked Waterstone.

"Whoever."

"I'd kill a sorcerer before they left the forest," stated the woodman without hesitation. "But that would be to keep our presence secret as much as anything."

Tarkyn rolled his eyes in impatience, "Yes, but what if one of your own tried to kidnap one of you and make money out of them?"

Waterstone shrugged, "It wouldn't happen. We don't need money like that."

"Fine." Despite his good intentions, Tarkyn was becoming angry, "So, although you would kill a sorcerer who threatened one of you, I am being unreasonable, am I, if I want to punish someone who has threatened to sell me off to be hanged?"

Waterstone narrowed his eyes but managed to stay calm, "No. That is perfectly reasonable. What is not reasonable is to punish someone to keep your family sacrosanct when half of them are blatantly immoral. It's the underlying principle that's wrong."

And here they were again, squared off over their fundamental difference in beliefs.

Tarkyn glared at Waterstone as he mulled over what had been said. Finally he drew a deep breath, "All right. To appease you, I will make the punishment of this man purely personal. It will be for actions against me, personally, as a prince of Eskuzor, not as a crime against my family. Will that satisfy you?"

"It would be better if it were just for crimes against you personally and leave the prince angle out."

The prince shook his head, "No, it wouldn't. I cannot lose myself in your principles. My rank and my entitlement to due courtesy matter to me. It is an integral part of who I am. When he offends, he offends against me, the prince, as well as against me, the man. He knows that and so do I. If I do not insist upon recognition of that, he will think of me merely as a fellow outlaw. And if I can't accept equality with you people, I certainly can't accept it with common felons. It would be insulting to *you*, if nothing else."

A slow smile appeared on Waterstone's face. "Tarkyn, my brother, thank you for taking the time to present that convoluted argument. I am constantly amazed at the way you can turn facts to suit your purpose. It is very kind of you to puff up your consequence to protect *our* consequence."

Tarkyn laughed, "The pleasure is all mine." He looked around, "So, are we agreed that we let them go, but only after Orolan receives his punishment? And I intend to swear them all to my service in case we should need them in the future. Stormaway, I want you to find a way to bind their oaths as you did the woodfolk's, but not," he added hurriedly in the light of shocked faces, "to the welfare of the forest, of course."

As a babble of outrage broke out, Tarkyn raised his hand, "No, it is not the same at all. You are honourable people. The binding spell was never needed in your case and was insulting. These people are thieves and brigands, preying on innocent sorcerers for their livelihood. To say the least, we do not share the same standards of honour. I have no reason to trust them and so, since they live in our forests and the opportunity has arisen, I will bind them to my will."

The woodfolk shook their heads in disgust.

"What for?" demanded Autumn Leaves. "So they can be slaves to your every whim? So that they can be marched into your brothers' battles, to be killed in the first line of fire? Think what you are doing, Tarkyn. You are contriving total power over these people. Even your brothers do not do that."

Tarkyn went white. Without another word, he turned on his heel and strode back to the imprisoned brigands.

It was Boravar's shield that now held the brigands. Those who had been shot were slowly recovering and rubbing their heads. As he arrived, Tarkyn waved his hand, "Release them. All but Orolan. Bring him before me."

Boravar rushed to do the prince's bidding, wondering what had caused the tight set of his mouth and the dangerous glitter in his eyes. He waved away his shield, untied Keepsafe and brought Orolan to stand before the prince, hands still tied behind his back.

Then the big sorcerer took one step back and bowed, "As you requested, my lord," and received a slight wave of one hand as acknowledgement.

Tarkyn kept his eyes fixed on the brigand captain in front of him. "Look at me, Orolan." As the man raised his eyes, Tarkyn said, "Now, really look at me. I, like you, am a man with people who depend on me for their welfare. That little boy you saw earlier would be devastated if he lost me. The woman I am to marry would be sad to lose me and so would my friends and supporters. Orolan, I am fighting for Eskuzor, not with swords or arrows, at least not at the moment, but with words and guile. My brothers, unless they change their ways, will bring Eskuzor to her knees. I cannot allow that to happen."

In the silence that followed, Orolan gradually bowed his head.

"Look at me," said Tarkyn sharply. "Face what you would have thrown away. From your words, you seem to care only for money. Is there nothing or no one that you care for?"

"Your Highness, I care for my men and I care for their families. I would fight to my last breath to protect them," said Orolan quietly. After a slight hesitation he added, "And I thank you for not killing them."

Tarkyn ignored his gratitude to continue his conversation. "And beyond that?"

"Beyond that, there is nothing. Nothing but hardship, injustice and punitive rule by a weak king on one side of the kingdom and a sadistic prince on the other."

"And what do you know of me?" asked Tarkyn, his face becoming less rigid as he concentrated on the brigand's words.

Orolan took a deep breath and went to speak but thought better of it, "Your Highness, you have me at a disadvantage. I do not think it would improve my health to tell you my true thoughts."

Tarkyn's voice was silky with threat, "And yet I think you must take your chances. Not only that, but I will have Danton and Stormaway standing by to tell me if they think you are lying. I think your health will prosper better with the truth."

Orolan swallowed, "As you will, my lord." He licked his lips, "I have only seen you from afar before now and heard the rumours. That is all I have had to go on, until today."

"That, then, is what I would like to hear." Tarkyn nodded to Boravar to get the man a drink.

"Sire, as a younger man, you were considered to be aloof, and meticulous in the observance of protocols and customs. Occasionally word came through from people closer to you that you were fair and courteous and had a dry sense of humour, but always you kept your distance."

Orolan paused to accept the water offered by Boravar. "Thank you, my lord. As you grew older, your magical prowess, especially in tournaments, became widely known and your unswerving courtesy, in stark contrast to your brothers' disdain, gained you quite a following."

As the bound man hesitated, Tarkyn prompted him firmly, "Whatever you were going to say, say it."

Orolan cleared his throat, "It did not seem to me, Your Highness, that you were *involved* in the lives of those around you with the possible exception of a few close friends. But that is only conjecture."

"Go on."

"Since you won the Harvest Tournament, of course, there has been rumour after rumour. I think it is generally accepted now that you are not a rogue sorcerer but rumours of your power are growing… and after today, if I have anything to do with it, they will grow even further."

"You won't," said Tarkyn shortly.

Orolan swallowed, "Do you want me to go on, Your Highness?" When Tarkyn nodded briefly, the brigand continued, "I don't think people know what to make of you, Sire. Although there is a groundswell of support for you, it is rumoured that you will not support a coup. You have flexed your muscles with both of your brothers, so to speak, but have left them and their men unharmed. It is as though you are saying, 'I have the power to take your throne if I want it but at the moment, I'm just thinking about it.' "

Tarkyn raised his eyebrows, "And you dared to try to take this man of whom you speak, prisoner? Did you not consider the rumours that you have just told me?"

Orolan gave a wry grimace, "To be honest, Your Highness, you didn't look all that fearsome, holding that little boy in your arms. And you were trapped inside Keepsafe's cage." He shrugged, "I guess I decided the rumours must be exaggerations."

Tarkyn gave a feline smile, "But now, of course, you realise that they were, at least in most respects, true."

Orolan bowed his head, "Yes, Sire."

"Orolan, look at me." Tarkyn waited until they were once more eye to eye. "You are right in most of what you say. But I do not want Eskuzor's throne. I want her to be well governed by my brother, the king. And I am working to protect the people of Eskuzor against the possibility of civil war. I do not want to enter the lists and make it a three way war. Do you understand that?" When Orolan nodded, Tarkyn gave a faint unnerving smile, "And so I flex my muscles to make my brothers aware that the common people have a supporter.

"And now, Orolan, we come to the punishment you are due for threatening me. At court, it would unquestionably be death. You understand that, don't you?"

Orolan cleared his throat, "Yes, Your Highness."

Tarkyn waved his arm around him, "But out here, in my forests, my word is law. And so I give you two choices. You can either swear your allegiance to me of your own free will, dependant only on your honour. In this case, you will be branded in the soft part of your left side under your arm where no one will inadvertently see it. Alternatively, I can bind your oath to the welfare of your wizard friend here. In your stead, he will be given a small brand, causing only minimal pain, on the inside of his wrist. If you waver in your loyalty to me, he will feel pain through this brand, not you. But if you stay true, neither of you will have to endure any real pain."

"And if I do not wish to swear my allegiance to you?"

Tarkyn stared at him for a moment before breaking into a smile, "To be honest, the thought had not crossed my mind; partly because, as my friends will tell you, I am extremely arrogant, and partly because I believed that you cared about your people."

"And what will you do to my people if I do not swear my allegiance?" asked the brigand tightly.

Tarkyn waved his hand "No. That was not a veiled threat. I meant that since I am working for people like you – not brigands exactly, but people who have been maligned – I thought you would want to support me. However, obviously, I made a mistake. I do not want your oath under duress. So the same punishment will apply whether you swear an oath to me or not. You will be branded under your arm." He looked around, "Where's Harkell?"

As Harkell appeared, Tarkyn asked, "Firstly, since you have been too severely punished yourself, is this reasonable?"

"Absolutely, my lord. If it were my decision, I would kill him without hesitation for his intended treatment of you."

"Thank you. Secondly, since you know something of these things, can you fashion a brand for me?"

"Anything in particular?"

"No. I will leave the shape entirely to you. How long will it take?"

Harkell thought for a few moments, "If I may be permitted, I will use your knife hilt which has your crest on it. Then all we need is a very hot fire. It should take less than half an hour." He turned a feral smile on Orolan, "You can just sweat it out waiting. Perhaps you might like to consider how to treat His Highness the next time you meet him, if you are so lucky."

"Thank you, Harkell," said the prince repressively. "While you're about it, make sure that there are no children near here. Boravar, when the coast is clear of children, remove the brigand's shirt and string him up with his hands above his head. Over that branch should do. Make sure his feet are flat on the ground."

The prince turned to the host of brigands waiting in surly silence. "This is not a public spectacle for your entertainment. Take your weapons and leave. I will send your captain to follow you when I deem fit."

A rough voice called out, "We don't want to leave our captain."

"I am not giving you the choice. When I mete out punishment, it is not for public consumption. Now go."

And with angry grumblings, the brigands picked up their weapons, eyeing their captain as they left.

It seemed an eternity before Harkell reappeared, carrying the dagger by its blade, which was swathed in thick padding. The hilt was glowing red.

"Thank you, Harkell. I'll take that."

"But Your Highness…"

"No Harkell. This task is mine. It is between Orolan and me only. I would like everyone else to leave."

After some awkward fumblings, the blade was transferred in its wrapping to Tarkyn's hands. When no one was left in the clearing, Tarkyn walked over to the brigand and said, "I respect your courage that you did not allow your wizard to take your punishment."

Orolan glared at the prince. "It was not courage, Your Highness. It was the desire to keep my free will."

"Then I hope you put your free will to better use in the future."

With no further warning, Tarkyn pressed the red hot hilt, hard against the side of the man's upper ribs. A raw cry of pain issued from the tied man's throat. Tarkyn held the hot metal in place as the flesh sizzled for a slow count of three, then let the knife hilt drop.

Without a word, Tarkyn cut through Orolan's bonds with a flash of bronze magic, lowered him carefully to the ground and disappeared into the woods.

"Someone else attend to him now. I have done my part," he said curtly as he strode straight through the clearing and down to the river, without looking at anybody.

He threw himself down against a rock, drew his knees up and linked his arms across them. Then, letting out a long shuddering breath, he slowly lowered his head to rest on his arms and tried to forget the smell of burning flesh.

CHAPTER 53

Some time later, Tarkyn felt a gentle hand on his shoulder. Wishing tiredly that people would leave him alone, he looked up to see who it was.

"Hello," said Lapping Water, stroking his hair. "That was hard, wasn't it?"

Tarkyn nodded his head morosely. "Yes, it was. Bloody hard. Injuring a helpless man…"

Lapping Water came around and sat down in front of him, a little distance away, with her back against another rock. After a moment, she said quietly, "Autumn Leaves is sorry for what he said."

"Bloody Autumn Leaves can tell me that himself, if he is so contrite," snapped Tarkyn. He waved his hand angrily, "Anyway, you all agreed with him."

"You're just angry because, once he pointed it out, you agreed with him too, didn't you?" Lapping Water pushed her soft brown hair back off her face and smiled. "You must have, because you went straight out there and did the opposite to what you said you were going to do." She started to place pebbles in a row from darkest to lightest, keeping her eyes firmly on what she was doing. "I expect you feel a bit embarrassed, do you, being reined in so publicly when you got a bit carried away with your own power?"

After a short silence, she risked a quick glance to see how her words had been received and found Tarkyn smiling at her, "Lapping Water, you are a horrible woman, and deserve to die!"

As the woodwoman grinned with relief, the prince held his hand out.

"Come over here," he said quietly. When she complied, Tarkyn wrapped his arms around her and buried his face in her hair for a moment before propping his chin on her head and murmuring, "Thanks."

The woodwoman nestled into his arms and looked up at him, "It must be hard, having all that power. It's not just your own power. You have Stormaway's and Danton's, ours, everyone's. You're bound to make mistakes sometimes."

Tarkyn gave a grunt of laughter, "I don't know. It's pretty hard to make mistakes with all of you lot keeping me in line."

She smiled at him, "I'm glad you listened."

They lapsed into a companionable silence, watching the coots and moorhens gliding in amongst the reeds.

"Oh blast," said Lapping Water suddenly. In response to Tarkyn's frown of enquiry, she gave a rueful smile, "You're wanted. That Orolan fellow wants to speak to you before he goes."

Tarkyn raised his eyebrows, "I haven't given him permission to leave yet. He can just wait until I'm ready to see him."

Lapping Water grinned, "I love it when you're supercilious… as long as it's not at me."

It was well over an hour later that Tarkyn finally decided to grace Orolan with his presence.

The brigand captain was sitting against a tree, shirtless, with a bandage wrapped around his chest. He looked up as Tarkyn arrived and hastened to stand and make his bow.

"Thank you for seeing me again, Your Highness," he said, wincing as he straightened. "From your response to my request, I fear you thought that I was about to leave without your permission, but such was not the case. I remember very clearly you saying that I would be sent to follow my men when you deemed fit. I merely wished to ensure that I might see you before you sent me away." The brigand's tone was respectful, almost obsequious.

"Well, I am here. What do you wish to say to me?"

"My lord, I wish to pledge you my allegiance."

Tarkyn frowned in confusion, "And what has brought about this change of heart?"

Orolan gave a slight smile, "I never said that I wouldn't. I merely asked what would happen if I wouldn't."

"Hmm, so you did. I jumped the rest of the way myself, didn't I?"

"Yes, my lord." The brigand shrugged, "But I do prefer to offer it to you when there is no threat of punishment left hanging in the air."

"Even after I myself branded you?"

"Particularly after that, my lord. You did not humiliate me in front of my men and you did not force them to endure it. You were no more brutal than you had to be, even though you could have justified killing me." Orolan dropped to one knee and placed his hand over his heart, gritting his teeth against the pain. "Will you accept my oath of allegiance, Your Highness?"

Tarkyn nodded gravely, "I will."

"Then I vow to be your man, body and soul, until the end of my days. You should have had me killed, but didn't. So my life is yours, to do with as you will."

Tarkyn glanced into the trees, knowing woodfolk were everywhere listening. "I thank you, Orolan. In return, I will support you and come to your aid, if you request it and I am able. However, I will not support you to steal from innocent folk and I may intervene to protect them. You may rise."

"Your Highness, my oath is my men's oath. So you can count all of us as loyal." Orolan held out a small silver pendant, inlaid with mother of pearl. "If ever you have need of us, use this to contact us. Your wizard will know what to do."

Tarkyn held it up and studied it, wondering at its properties. After a few moments, he looked at the brigand, "Orolan, before you go, tell me what you know of Jarand's encampment. Is it filled with your victims?"

Orolan choked on hastily suppressed laughter. "I beg your pardon. No, Your Highness. We are not so ruthless nor so numerous that we could fill such a place. Most of our victims are relieved of most, but not all, of their money and allowed to go on their way. We do not make it our intention to kill or injure people, although of course there are times when we do."

"So, are there many gangs like your own?"

Orolan shook his head, "Not so many. Certainly none so big."

"And what do you know of soldiers disguised as brigands that we intercepted near the encampment a couple of months ago?"

In answer, Orolan spat on the ground in disgust.

Tarkyn raised his eyebrows in distaste and unconsciously took a step backwards.

The brigand grinned, "I beg your pardon, my lord. I can see that, despite your exile, you are not used to rough ways."

"Hmm. So, to be more specific…"

"To be more specific, Your Highness, those bastard soldiers disguise themselves as brigands to prey on families. As often as not, they kill off the womenfolk and children so that their fellow soldiers can then take the distraught men under their wings to join their ranks at the encampment. You'll notice that there are far greater numbers of men than women at that encampment."

The prince's face tightened with shock. He raised his voice, "Harkell. Stormaway. Danton. Here! Now!" As Harkell arrived, Tarkyn turned on him, "What do you know of this practice? Did you condone it?"

Harkell's soft brown eyes glittered with anger. Before he could calm himself enough to answer politely, Stormaway intervened, "If you remember, Your Highness, even the patrol from the encampment knew nothing about them. They were as shocked as we were. I would doubt that Harkell, far away in Montraya, had any knowledge of it."

Tarkyn stared at Stormaway before transferring his gaze to Harkell. He ran his hand through his hair and sighed, "I'm sorry Harkell. Knowing you as I do, I should not have suggested that you would be complicit in such a practice."

Harkell gave a stiff, shallow bow. "Apology accepted, Your Highness."

Laughter lit Tarkyn's eyes, "Oh Harkell, with a temper like yours, how did you survive for so long with my brother?"

A reluctant smile tugged at the side of Harkell's mouth, "It was… difficult, my lord." Suddenly he grinned, "But luckily for me, nothing delighted Jarand more than goading people and then watching them struggle to contain their ire."

A faint blush of embarrassment heightened Tarkyn's colour. He lifted his hand and dropped it again, "What can I say? I apologise for my brother's behaviour."

Danton, seeing Tarkyn's discomfort, took over the conversation. "Orolan, what else do you know of these gangs? Do they have a base away from the encampment? What are their numbers? Do they have magically strong sorcerers among them?"

"Whoa. Whoa. Take it slowly." The brigand captain's cockiness was beginning to return, "And who might you be, my young buck?"

"I am Danton Patronell, Lord of Sachmore," replied Danton frigidly, still angry at this man for his previous attitude towards Tarkyn. "And you would do well to remember it."

Disappointment flitted across Orolan's face as he produced a florid bow, "I beg your pardon. I did not realise I was surrounded by nobility. His Highness gave the impression that he had broadened his acquaintanceship. But of course, I should have realised that his concern for us hoi polloi would only be from a distance."

Tarkyn raised his eyebrows, "And do you now regret your oath?"

Orolan shrugged, "A little, but I will honour it nevertheless… I accept that a prince, even in exile, must have his court of nobles around him. It is the way of the world." He waved his hand and gave a sad little smile, "Just for a few moments there, I let myself get carried away." He gave a formal bow and said, with just a hint of irony, "We are honoured, Your Highness, that we commoners figure at all in your dealings with your brothers."

Tarkyn sent an image to Waterstone, asking him to send forward all of the sorcerers in the home guard. Once they were all standing in a circle around the brigand captain, Tarkyn said quietly, "Orolan, let me present the sorcerers of my home guard to you. To all intents and purposes, these people are the sorcerers of my court in exile. Lord Danton, you know. Harkell, ex-captain of Prince Jarand's Royal Guard. His family are blacksmiths, I believe. String and Bean, trappers of indeterminate origins," Tarkyn grinned at them as he said it. "Boravar, sorcerer of the Lost Forest and before that…?" The prince frowned, "What were you before that, Boravar?"

"My family were farmers, my lord, with a small holding of fifty acres, eighty miles south of Tormadell. I myself, as I have mentioned before, was a drifter."

Tarkyn nodded his thanks and moved on to Stormaway, "And this is Stormaway Treemaster, once wizard to my father and now to me."

Orolan bowed, his face wreathed in smiles, "It is truly a pleasure to meet you all. You have rekindled the feeble flame of my hope for Eskuzor's future." After a moment, he asked, "And what of the little boy I saw you with, my lord?"

Tarkyn smiled, "He is nowhere near old enough to form part of my court but for your information, his father was a wizard and his mother is a trapper. I look after him because his mother is often away."

Tarkyn felt a wave of applause from the woodfolk for his half-truth until Orolan exclaimed, "How extraordinary! A woman trapper. There can't be too many of them around. And is she part of your court when she is not in the mountains?"

Tarkyn merely nodded, feeling that he was beginning to get out of his depth.

Stormaway flicked him a smile and rescued him. "So Orolan, now that you have satisfied yourself of Prince Tarkyn's good intentions, could you perhaps answer Danton's questions about these pseudo-brigands?"

Orolan shook his head smiling, "This is the oddest situation I have ever been in; where a prince actually takes the time to convince me of his goodwill. Me, a common bandit. Wait til I tell the others. They'll think I've gone mad." He gave a little cough, as he saw Stormaway becoming impatient. "Right. Now about these soldier bandits. I can show you where their base is if you like, or I can give you directions. It's in a large house just beyond the forest edge. As for numbers, it's hard to say. They work in shifts, you see. They all work legitimately in the encampment as far as I can work out, and do their pseudo-brigand work on the side… Pseudo-brigands; good description, I'll coin that one, if you don't mind." He gave a little chuckle to himself. "Anyway, my best guess is that there are about forty of them; sixty at the outside. Problem is, they're never all there at the same time. So it would be hard to capture them all, if that's what you were planning."

Tarkyn smiled wryly, "I don't think we know what we're planning at this stage. But we can't let it continue, whatever we do about it… And their magic?"

"There are a couple of officers who might have a few power shafts to their name but most of them are just your general soldier types. Nothing special that I've noticed. Just swords and arrows like the rest of us."

"Thank you, Orolan," said Tarkyn. "Give Stormaway, Danton and Harkell the rest of the details. I have had enough for one day. After that, you may leave when you are ready. Boravar, where is his shirt? Can you find it and give it back to him? Thanks. Farewell Orolan. I suspect we will meet again."

"I hope so, my lord. And when we do, I will not again treat you with disrespect. Not because of your rank or your hot iron or even my oath, but because of your treatment of me." Orolan bowed with a flourish, "Until next time, Your Highness."

Tarkyn nodded briefly and strode off into the trees.

Chapter 54

"Obviously, the officers are Sargon and Andoran, aren't they?" said Danton. "After all, the bandits we intercepted near the encampment mentioned Andoran. So, naturally, Sargon will be up to his neck in it too. It's just the sort of underhand, devious activity they would relish. Tricking their fellow officers at the encampment and no doubt raking in an extra income for it." He poked a stick viciously into the red coals of the fire. "We should have killed them while we had the chance, Stormaway."

Stormaway shook his head, "No we shouldn't have, Danton. We had a job to do. We had to make sure Golden Toad, Rushwind and Ibis Wings were safe first."

Danton sighed, "I know. But now Andoran and Sargon are still alive and killing off innocent women and children."

The evening had closed in and everyone was sitting around the fire mulling over the events of the day. For perhaps the tenth time, Midnight appeared on the outskirts of the company, this time gesturing that he needed a drink of water.

Midnight's scratches had been repaired by the combined ministrations of Summer Rain and the forest guardian, but he was still churned up after the run-in with the bandits and at the prospect of his mother leaving. Every time he was put to bed, he would find a new reason to come back out.

Tarkyn sighed and held out his arms, "Come here, young one. Come and sit in my lap. You may go to sleep here."

Midnight padded sheepishly into the middle of the crowd and climbed onto Tarkyn's lap. He snuggled up into a little ball and, heaving a great sigh, nestled his head on Tarkyn's shoulder. Almost immediately his eyelids began to droop.

"There is a time to be firm and a time to be kind," said Creaking Bough, with a gentle smile. "Midnight has been through a lot today and will lose his mother again tomorrow. Let him stay up and feel safe. Look, he's nearly asleep already."

Tarkyn breathed a little sigh of relief that his instinct to keep Midnight with him was being sanctioned by someone more experienced than he in the art of parenting. He was always acutely aware that his behaviour with Midnight was under the constant scrutiny of the woodfolk around him who had children. And whether they said anything or not, he often second-guessed their opinions. In general, however, he followed his instincts, erring always on the side of kindness with the little boy who had had such a hard start to his life.

"Yeah, he's all right usually," said Hail gruffly, coming to sit beside Tarkyn and stroke her son's head. "He's turning into a pretty good kid, actually."

Midnight, as though he understood what she'd said, smiled sleepily at her.

Summer Rain frowned. "You know, that's the second time today that Midnight has reacted to something someone has said. Remember, Tarkyn? He turned around and smiled at you earlier today when you said you loved him to bits."

"Hmm. He can't be picking up facial expressions because he had his back to me. Maybe he can hear the tone of voice but not the words?"

Summer Rain shook her head. "I don't think so. He doesn't react to sudden noises."

Stormaway leaned forward and considered the little boy across the fire from him, "I would say that he is picking up feelings, just as Tarkyn does. He shows no understanding of words or sound at all."

"Maybe you should teach him to read, Stormaway," suggested Rainstorm. "Isn't that a way of saying words that he can see?"

Danton smiled at him quizzically, "I thought you said, quite dismissively as I remember, that reading was a sorcerer thing. What's a woodman doing suggesting it?"

Rainstorm waved his hand, "Well, to start with, Midnight is half sorcerer anyway but more importantly, he can't communicate like we can. So he needs another way to do it. His images and gestures aren't bad but there are definitely limits to them. And we all do our best but each of us uses whatever gesture we think of at the time. Poor Midnight is probably receiving half a dozen gestures for the same thing from various people."

"Learning to read won't do his communication much good if none of you can read anyway," pointed out String.

"Oh yes, it will," said Stormaway, "If he is to learn advanced magic, he will need to be able to read the great tomes. I shudder at the thought of trying to interpret that great mass of work into signs and images. Just reading it out aloud would be bad enough. Besides, if he has something complicated to say, then one of the sorcerers can read it out for woodfolk." The wizard rubbed his hands together, "Excellent idea, Rainstorm. I will begin teaching him to read tomorrow."

"And perhaps, we should put a bit of work into all using the same hand signals," suggested Tarkyn. "If we were consistent, we could expand our repertoire. If we all had the same gestures for things, we wouldn't have to keep pointing at them."

"We don't have to, anyway. We can use an image," said Blizzard.

"Sorcerers can't," retorted String.

"Whoops! Sorry, I forgot." Blizzard scratched his head, "Yeah. It must be hard to talk to him just gesturing."

"It is," said Bean. "It is very frustrating. I've known Midnight for years and we still struggle to understand each other."

"I will work on developing one set of hand signals as I teach him to read. Then I'll let you all know what we have devised, so you can use them too," Stormaway offered. The wizard eyes lit up in anticipation. "This should be an interesting little project."

"Well, don't let it distract you from helping us to find a fitting end for Sargon and Andoran," said Danton. "I think some of your nasty concoctions could come in handy again."

Stormaway looked mildly offended, "Danton, dear boy, I think my poor brain can just *possibly* manage more than one thought in a day."

Danton grinned, "Can it? Well, that's a pleasing surprise."

Several people blinked at Danton's unexpected over-familiarity with the wizard, but Stormaway explained mildly, "Danton and I spent a couple of harrowing days together in that encampment. Talk of Andoran and Sargon has made us remember it." He gave a reminiscent chuckle, "Yes. We had quite a bit of fun coming up with ways of punishing those two, since we weren't allowed to kill them. Powdered stinging nettles rubbed into their bedclothes, as I recall."

"Hallucinogens in the wine, and something else quite nasty in their water supply." Danton grinned. "With any luck, they had a distressing few weeks." Suddenly he scowled, "Deserved every last bit of it, the bastards, for what they did to Tarkyn."

A few puzzled people around the fire, who had not been there for Tarkyn's capture, mistreatment and subsequent injury, were filled in quietly or mentally by their neighbours.

"But these two nasty pieces of work, Andoran and Sargon, must be working *for* someone, mustn't they?" asked Bean.

"Yeah. No advantage for them in killing off women and children unless they are being paid, as far as I can see," agreed String.

Bean nodded, "Over and above the booty."

"I suspect most of this booty finds its way into Lord Davorad's pockets to finance the encampment," said Stormaway, "although no doubt our pseudo-brigands get a cut."

"This is the most devious ploy I have ever heard!" exclaimed Autumn Leaves. "Now let me get this clear in my poor straightforward woodfolk mind; Andoran and Sargon rob people, kill off their families to make them susceptible to the sympathy of the encampment patrols. The patrols then bear them off to join their ranks in the encampment where the victims then live unknowingly off the profits from their own goods that have been stolen from them."

Harkell chuckled, "We'll make a sorcerer of you yet."

Autumn Leaves raised his eyebrows, "No. Don't bother, thanks. It's not something I aspire towards."

There was an uncomfortable silence.

But even as Harkell drew breath to respond, the woodman waved his hand apologetically, "Sorry. That sounded unkind, didn't it? I think I'm just a bit rattled at the moment. Sorcerers' values are so different from ours."

Tarkyn considered having it out with Autumn Leaves but, on balance, decided to leave it for a less public forum.

Harkell, however, had no such qualms, "I hope you are not implying that any of us sorcerers here would devise or carry out any such a reprehensible scheme?"

Autumn Leaves glanced around at every sorcerer before answering, "No. But I think you are all *capable* of devising similar schemes, with the possible exception of Boravar."

Boravar huffed, "Hmph. I don't know whether to feel flattered or offended by that."

With a small sigh, Tarkyn threw caution to the winds and entered the lists, "Autumn Leaves, remember in the cave where we first met String and Bean? You conceded that woodfolk, too, have a dark side. You keep it in check, but it is still there." He waved his hand, "It is the same for all of us. Maybe today, my dark side surfaced when I wanted to control those brigands. You obviously thought so. At the time I thought I could justify it, but I suppose most evil acts can be justified by their perpetrators." Sitting with Midnight curled up on his lap, the prince looked anything but evil as he stared steadfastly down, stroking the little boy's hair to cover his embarrassment, "But even if I have horrified you, please don't paint the other sorcerers here with the same brush. The fault was mine, not theirs. They are not in the same position as I, and do not share my family's heritage."

Tarkyn was so intent on Midnight that when a hand came down on his shoulder, he jumped. He looked up to find that Autumn Leaves had come around the fire to him. As soon as he had Tarkyn's attention, Autumn Leaves squatted down in front of him, keeping his hand on his shoulder. "Tarkyn, it is true that your intention horrified me, but not for one second did I think of you as evil. It was as I said. You just hadn't thought it through enough." He gave the young prince a warm smile, "And you justified my faith in you."

"You didn't sound as though you had faith in me."

"Tarkyn, had I not trusted you, I could never have said what I did to you. And none of us felt obliged to disguise our reactions, as Harkell has had to do in the court of your brother."

"True." Tarkyn slowly broke into a smile. "And I suppose you think that's good, do you? Being able to tell me off, as the mood takes you?"

Autumn Leaves smiled back, "Yes, very good. Especially when you take notice. You're doing well, young one. And we are right behind you."

The prince smiled wryly and glanced across at Stormaway, "And what do you think, Stormaway, of a Tamadil being taken to task by his companions?"

"Now that I have the measure of your companions' attitude to you, I approve if it's done judiciously. I only wish your father had listened as you do, when I raised issues with him."

Suddenly Tarkyn grinned, "And after all that, the brigands have sworn to support me of their own free will."

Autumn Leaves gave the prince's shoulder a final pat before standing up. "You should have had more faith in yourself."

Tarkyn blinked, "What? Not arrogant enough for you?"

Autumn Leaves just laughed and headed back to sit down on the other side of the fire.

"So now all we have to do," said Harkell, once he was sure the air had been cleared, "is find a way to curtail the activities of those sorcerers who have allowed their darker side to take over."

Danton leaned forward to throw another branch on the fire. "Stormaway, what happened to those disguised soldiers we captured who had attacked the family on the Great West Road? The last we saw of them, Sergeant Torgan was taking them back to the encampment to be questioned."

Stormaway answered, "They were questioned closely about their activities and I was questioned about what I had seen. But in the end, it was felt that there was not enough evidence, so they were allowed to go free with a half-hearted warning." The wizard shrugged, "In truth, it was fairly flimsy evidence on which to base the hanging of eight men. So I can't be sure whether the disguised soldiers were being protected by the camp's authorities or not."

"I suppose you realise that, even now, the only evidence we have of the nature of their activities is the word of the captain of a rival band of brigands?" pointed out Lapping Water tartly.

Rainstorm smiled, "Didn't like him much, did you?"

"No, but that is beside the point."

"You're right," agreed Harkell. "And it would help his gang, if we eliminated a rival group for him, wouldn't it?"

"Yes, it would. But we have seen for ourselves that disguised soldiers are attacking families of travellers," said Rainstorm, "even if we have not seen the deliberate slaughter of women and children."

"Exactly," exclaimed Danton vehemently, "And I think it is outrageous that people who are being paid to protect the public are actually robbing and killing them. Let me at them. I'll soon show them what I think of them betraying their soldiers' honour."

"And I'll be right behind you," said Twig Snap enthusiastically. "I would be honoured to lend you my support."

Leaf Fall rolled his eyes, "What she means is she can see the opportunity to knock off a few sorcerers.

"Just ignore your brother." Danton smiled at her, "I am overwhelmed that you would deign to accompany me, a dastardly elite guard, at all."

"Before you two bloodthirsty wretches go forth and wreak havoc," said Tarkyn dryly, "we had better consider the effect that wiping out a whole company of soldiers may have on the rest of the encampment. We don't really want hundreds of soldiers scouring the woodlands looking to avenge their fallen companions."

"But we can't sit back and do nothing about it," protested Autumn Leaves.

Tarkyn was moved, "Never did I think I'd see the day when you would actually care about what happened to sorcerers."

"Very funny! Whatever manner of people they are, their children should be protected from wanton killing."

Tarkyn raised his eyebrows. "Not their women?"

Autumn Leaves snorted, "Their women should be able to look after themselves."

"Hmm," murmured Tarkyn to fill in time while he pondered what to say in response. Finally he said, "I expect neither the men nor the women are able to stand up to armed trained soldiers ambushing them."

"Strange, isn't it?" mused Autumn Leaves. "Only some of your sorcerers are trained in use of arms but they fight among themselves. On the other hand, every woodman or woman is trained but we only use it against outsiders..." He gave a wry smile, "...or for hunting."

"*Anyway*" intervened Danton firmly, to get back onto the topic, "You're right, Tarkyn. We will have to be careful not to incite retribution. We'll have to make sure that our motivation is clear to those who might seek revenge." He thought for a minute. "Andoran and Sargon told us Lord Davorad was financing the encampment but whether Jarand is aware of his recruitment tactics, I don't know."

"And even if Jarand does know, he may not be able to stand up to Davorad without the risk of losing his support," said Stormaway.

"Or he may be complicit in it." Tarkyn stared firmly into the fire and suppressed a sigh. "I hope he's not."

Waterstone flicked a sympathetic glance at Tarkyn, remembering the pride in the prince's memory of his brothers' entry into the Great Hall. "We can either stop this practice ourselves, or get word to Jarand or Kosar about it. Perhaps when they realise what's happening, they may put a stop to it themselves."

"If Jarand realises that Kosar may find out, he will have to put a stop to it, whether he loses Davorad's support or not," added Tarkyn dryly.

"So how do you want to play this, Tarkyn?" asked Autumn Leaves.

The prince pondered for a minute, "There would be no point in me confronting this Lord Davorad character, since he seems to have his eggs placed firmly in Jarand's basket. He won't change anything until he has discussed it with Jarand first." He shook his head. "No. We will have to intervene either higher or lower than him."

"And I presume," asked Harkell. "that intervention at a higher level involves talking and intervening lower means killing?"

"Hmm. That sounds about right," Danton's purple eyes gleamed in the firelight. "There would be no point in trying to talk to Andoran and Sargon. They don't have consciences to appeal to. Only threats would have any effect but they would test whether our threats were genuine anyway. So we might as well just kill them and be done with it."

"And what of their followers?" asked Waterstone.

"They may have had limited choice in the matter, if Andoran and Sargon are their commanding officers," answered Harkell.

Waterstone considered the ex-captain for a moment before saying, "And would you have shot down defenceless men, women and children, if your commanding officer had ordered you to?"

Harkell stared at the woodman for long moments, making onlookers uneasy that Waterstone had overstepped the mark.

Waterstone, however, ignored them and prompted him to reply, "Well?"

Harkell drew a breath and said slowly, "I would like to think that I would not have. But in the heat of battle, who knows what a person might do. And what if the safety of my own family had been held against me as surety?" He shook his head slowly, "Life cannot always be measured neatly into black and white. If I had refused, I would have been signing my own death warrant. I could countenance that. I wouldn't like it, but I could choose it, if I had to. But signing the death warrants of my own wife and children to save someone else's?" He shrugged, "I just hope I never have to make that choice."

A slow smile spread across Waterstone's face, "The forest guardians in the Lost Forest were right. You *are* strong and true. You did not rush to your own defence with empty words."

"I do not need to defend myself. I have done nothing wrong," replied Harkell firmly. "But I would ask you in return, how many hapless, innocent people have you killed who have inadvertently seen you?"

Waterstone pointed to himself, "Me personally? None. It almost never happens. But anyone who has, has my full support and we collectively share the responsibility for it."

"How convenient for you, not to have to live with your own individual conscience," said Harkell silkily.

As the woodman's face suffused with anger, Tarkyn interceded firmly, "Waterstone, Harkell. Enough. We will be fighting each other soon instead of the opposition, if you don't desist."

Stormaway stood up to pour himself another cup of tea. He looked around to see whether anyone else would like one, before resuming his seat. "Whatever we do, we will have to tell Jarand about it and give him the chance to sort it out himself, or at least to take credit for it. Otherwise, if you tell the king, you are undermining Jarand even further when he may not even be a knowing party to it."

"Yeah, that's right," said Bean. "And all you've done so far is undermine Jarand in Kosar's eyes."

"True," chimed in String. "Despite what you say about supporting neither brother, you have effectively been taking Kosar's side... Don't worry," he added, as he saw Tarkyn frown, "We understand why. Supporting Jarand would lead to civil war."

Danton however, was not to be distracted, "But how long will it take to get word to Jarand and then for him to intercede, assuming he believes you? And how many more people will be killed in the meantime?"

Tarkyn gave a little smile, "Danton, you may go forth with Twig Snap and whoever else wants to go with the two of you, and kill or capture as many of these reprobates as you choose. Just make sure that you find some proof, or someone, to back up the word I send to Jarand. I would suggest taking Andoran and Sargon alive to stand trial."

Danton was stunned, "You're not coming with us?"

Tarkyn shook his head, "No my friend. Not this time. There are other things to consider: the safety of the Lost sorcerers, getting word to

Jarand of the reasons for your attack and preparing for Kosar's visit to the encampment." He smiled at his childhood friend, "And if I remember rightly, I was criticised for not having enough faith in you, Waterstone and others once before. So I leave it to those of you who wish to go, to plan and execute your own campaign. The rest of us will follow you more slowly and meet up with you in the vicinity of the encampment in readiness for the twins' arrival." The prince let his gaze travel slowly around the firesite, "I trust that meets with everyone's approval?"

An intense mind talking silence suddenly erupted into a hubbub of chatter as the woodfolk overcame their initial reaction to include the sorcerers in their discussions.

CHAPTER 55

Four days later, Danton lay on his belly in the undergrowth next to Twig Snap, watching the comings and goings around a large rundown farm house that lay a stone's throw from the edge of the forest, on the northern side of the Great West Road. Of the sorcerers of the home guard, Danton was the only one who had chosen to come on this venture. Boravar and Stormaway were too occupied with trying to rescue the Lost sorcerers, Harkell was working on tactics for the upcoming confrontation at the encampment and the trappers had no inclination towards intentional violence. Most of the woodfolk who had chosen to come were those who had witnessed the damage caused to Tarkyn, both physically and mentally, by Andoran and Sargon.

On the other three sides of the building were fields with only an occasional bush offering any sort of cover. In the woods nearby, two sorcerer lookouts lay dead, a hole in each one's back the only evidence of the arrows that had struck them down. One guard patrolled slowly back and forth across the front of the house but his open position had so far saved him from attack.

Dusk was gathering as a relaxed group of men clad in rough workmen's clothes sauntered along a dusty track that emerged from the forest a hundred yards to their left, passing a couple of dilapidated outhouses before arriving at the back door of the house, talking and laughing amongst themselves. Many of them were burdened with well stuffed backpacks. Danton's mouth set in a hard line as he watched them, knowing from woodfolk-relayed messages that these same men had, less than an hour before, ambushed and killed off most of a small family, leaving only the distraught father and another man alive; wounded, but not permanently incapacitated.

"Look at them!" he whispered fiercely, "Not a sign of distress or guilt in any of them."

"I think we should just kill them all and be done with it," replied Twig Snap quietly.

Murmurs of agreement issued from the surrounding darkness.

Danton held up his hand, "Just wait. We have to know where Andoran and Sargon are. If we kill only a couple of men, Andoran or Sargon will throw up his shield over the rest of them and we will be unable to attack further. And from then on, they will be on their guard." His teeth showed white in the darkness as he grinned evilly, "And we want to capture those two alive… As much as anything, *I* want them to know what they are dying for."

Just as he finished speaking, a red-haired officer strode into view. Danton's heart missed a beat. "That's Andoran. Now where's Sargon?"

"Didn't Orolan say that these people work in shifts? Surely the other officer would be at the encampment now?" asked Lapping Water.

Danton scratched his chin in thought, "I don't know. When we were there, Andoran and Sargon went off together on duty for a full day."

"But that could have been on legitimate duties, couldn't it?" pointed out Autumn Leaves. Seeing that Danton was still unwilling to commit himself to action, the woodman continued, "I agree that we should be cautious. I will send everyone an image of what Sargon looks like and we will locate him before we make a move."

"Thanks Autumn Leaves. Andoran and Sargon are both powerful sorcerers. So they have lethal shafts of power and strong shields. They are everything you expected all sorcerers to be; magic wielders using their powers for combat," he grunted, "…and as you and Tarkyn have both experienced, vicious and ruthless."

"Petrand Closkaril was like that too," said Twig Snap in a small voice.

"I know, Twig, I know." Danton looked at her, and gave a warm smile, "But you know now that we're not all like that, don't you?"

Twig Snap gave a tiny sigh and lowered her head onto her hands, "I miss Boravar."

"Twig Snap, you are pathetic," said Leaf Fall, with laughter in his voice, "What happened to the feisty, independent sister I grew up with?"

"Hmph, I'm still here. Otherwise I wouldn't have come while he stayed with Tarkyn…But I still miss him."

At this point, Autumn Leaves brought them back to the job at hand, "Word has just come through. A patrol has picked up the injured travellers and is taking them back to the encampment. Sargon is the captain of the patrol."

"Those bastards!" spat Danton under his breath. "They are working in concert."

"Of course they are," said Waterstone, who had just crawled in from further back to join them. "From what everyone says, they are virtually joined at the hip. So… do you think they have a way of communicating with each other, or is it all pre-planned?"

Danton thought for a minute, "I think the location of the attack must be pre-planned. After all, don't forget that Sargon is at the head of a legitimate patrol. It would look a little suspicious if he received a message each time to tell him where to find a group of attacked travellers."

"I presume they swap roles and at other times, Sargon attacks while Andoran discovers the victims and recues them," said Autumn Leaves. He gave a little shudder, "I suspect they enjoy the violence."

"They certainly relished belting Tarkyn and humiliating him as they force marched him through the forest," growled Waterstone.

"And they were unnecessarily savage in the way they knocked me out," added Autumn Leaves.

"So I gather." Danton took a deep breath, "Right. So now we have verified Orolan's story and we know more or less how they are operating. So what do you want to do; attack both groups immediately, while Andoran and Sargon are both out of the encampment, or wait until their next sortie?" Danton looked around him, "How many are in the patrol? Do we have enough people?"

"There are six soldiers on horses, two of them holding injured men before them in their saddles. And there is Sargon." Autumn Leaves wriggled to get a sharp stick out of his side. "I'm assuming that we don't want to kill the patrol soldiers or the traveller victims?"

"No. They haven't done anything wrong, as far as we know," replied Running Feet. "We don't even want to knock off Sargon, do we?" He jerked his thumb sideways at Danton, "Our benign sorcerer here wants to let out a bit of his dark side on Sargon and his fellow miscreant. Don't you?"

The whites of Danton's eyes flashed in the dark as he glanced at the woodman, "Don't you? After what they did to Autumn Leaves?"

Running Feet nodded reluctantly, "I suppose so. They certainly deserve it."

The doubt in his voice prompted Danton to ask, "What do you think I am planning to do?"

Running Feet shrugged, "I don't know. But I've heard about these terrible tortures they use on the king's prisoners. I don't really want to be a party to that sort of cruelty, no matter what they've done."

Danton dropped his head on his hands in mock despair, "Stars above! Save me from untrusting woodfolk! What have I ever done that would make you think I was going to indulge in that sort of wanton cruelty? All I said was that I want them to know why they are going to die."

Running Feet relaxed and patted Danton cheerily on the back, "Sorry Danton. But just the fact that that sort of torture exists means that I don't know what to expect from sorcerers."

Danton lifted his head and smiled ruefully, "I can see why Tarkyn ends up negotiating everything with you. It's a full time job assuaging your fears. So let me follow in my liege's footsteps. Once we have captured

Sargon and Andoran, we will decide between us what to do with them. Agreed?"

Autumn Leaves smiled, "We'll make a woodman of you yet. Of *course*, we will decide among us. That is what we always do."

"That's all very well for you to assume that, but if I am the one confronting them, how will I know what you all think? I can't mind talk and I'm the only sorcerer here."

Autumn Leaves shrugged, "Don't worry. One of us will come down and stand in the shadows so we can talk to you. It won't really matter if they see us since they are going to die anyway." He gave a little chuckle, "I notice you didn't mind that notion of becoming a woodman, even after I was so rude about the possibility of me becoming a sorcerer."

"I wasn't brought up fearing woodfolk as you were, fearing sorcerers. Anyway..." Danton cleared his throat, "Anyway, are we moving, or staying here and talking?"

Lapping Water glanced at him, knowing that wasn't what he had been going to say, but deciding to let it go. After a brief mind conference she said, "We'll move now."

Within minutes, three miles away, four patrolmen suddenly slumped in their saddles. Even as their horses sidled in alarm and alerted the other patrolmen, they too were hit with deadly accuracy. Hearing the unsettled movements of the horses, Sargon looked back to find himself in charge of a troop of unconscious soldiers, slumped over their horses' necks or gradually toppling sideways to the ground. He had just registered that even the rescued travellers were unconscious when he felt a sharp pain in his head and everything went black.

The attack on the house was not so straightforward. They had seen at least sixteen sorcerers entering the house and didn't know who else was already inside. And there were only eight woodfolk and Danton ranged in the trees outside. Their plan of action was to kill or knock out anyone who ventured outside so that they didn't have to deal with the whole company at once. The risky part was dragging the fallen men out of sight before another group emerged. But as the minutes ticked by and no one emerged, they changed their plan.

"We can't wait much longer," murmured Waterstone. "They will be changing their lookouts over soon and they will either find their bodies or realise they are missing. Not only that, the patrol will be expected back at the encampment soon and the alarm will be raised when they don't arrive. Can we flush these men out into the open somehow? We don't really want to go into a house unless we have to."

"Stormaway gave me a little gauze bag of some concoction to make their fire smoke and smell. I was hoping that we could slip it into their woodpile…but they don't seem to have one. Maybe they just collect wood from around about when they need it." Danton dug around in his pocket until he found it and held it up. "Here it is. We just need some way of introducing it into their fire."

"Down their chimney," said Twig Snap promptly.

Danton frowned, "Is anyone a good enough shot in the dark to send an arrow up in an arc and then down the chimney? Then we could attach Stormaway's little concoction to the tip of the arrow."

"Brilliant, we are. Magic, we're not," answered Autumn Leaves trenchantly. "If we miss, the arrow will land on the roof and alert them."

"Fine. Just asking."

Twig Snap tapped Danton's arm. "You are, though," she said. "Can you make things float through the air like Boravar does?" When the sorcerer nodded, she smiled, "There you are then. You can just float this little bag up over the chimney and then let it go."

"I can, but I will have to be careful that they don't see the light of my magic. The aqua shaft of magic lifting Stormaway's concoction through the air will glow quite conspicuously in the dark."

Twig Snap's brow wrinkled, "But Boravar didn't have a shaft of magic going from him to his balls of light."

"They were an illusion, Twig. This little bag of tricks is real." Danton rose silently to his feet. "If I move around so that I'm in line with the back door, it should be okay. There are no lights coming from the back windows, only from the front. I'll do a quick circuit of the house to check. I'll get rid of the guard at the front of the house while I'm at it."

Danton slipped quietly down the small slope and moved silently across the open ground until he was pressed up against the farmhouse wall. Even the keen eyes of the woodfolk struggled to pick him out, his black attire blending into the shadows. Like a wrinkle in the shadows, he slid along the wall and out of sight around the corner.

Minutes later, he reappeared and, after a quick glance around, emerged from the cover of the shadows to make the quick dash back to the safety of the forest.

"They are all in the large front room where the fireplace is," reported Danton. "There are sixteen of them, as we thought, plus Andoran." He pushed back his black scarf and ran his hand back and forth through his hair as he spoke, "One slight problem though. They are just as likely to leave the house through the front door if we smoke them out."

"Any cover around that side?" asked Autumn Leaves.

Danton shook his head, "Not much. The odd bush, that's all. I had to drag the guard several yards to find enough cover to hide his body. Anyway, we don't have enough people to cover both entrances with only eight of you. If we split up into two groups, and then the bandits all go out one way, that will be at least seventeen of them to four of you if I am still down near the house somewhere. Two to one is fine when surprise is on our side. Four to one isn't."

A mind talking silence greeted this. After a couple of minutes, Waterstone said, "And if we block one door somehow, that will alert them that something is wrong, won't it?"

Danton grimaced, "I would have thought so."

"What else did Stormaway give you? Anything handy?"

Danton opened his pack and rummaged inside it. He brought out two more small bags, "These are for infecting their water supply but that is a bit too slow for what we want." He drew forth a couple of small cylinders. "Hmm. These might be helpful. They are incendiary devices. You light them and throw them up. They will make a huge noise and light up the sky for a moment. Good for diversions."

"Or to lure them out of the house…although then they will be warned that something is up," said Waterstone.

"Is the front door open?" asked Twig. When Danton nodded, she continued, "Why don't we throw these devices of yours in through the front door so that one lights up with a huge noise in amongst them, and the other does it just inside the door. Then all the bandits should come haring out the back door, all confused and frightened."

"…where we will be waiting for them," finished Autumn Leaves. "Good idea, Twig."

"Who wants to go down and throw them in then?" asked Danton, meticulously consulting at every step.

Waterstone patted him on the back, "I think we'll leave the workings of a sorcerer's device to the sorcerer amongst us, if you don't mind. Off you go." As Danton stood up, the woodman added, "Make sure you don't get between the bandits and our arrows at any stage."

For several minutes, the woodfolk watched the house in silence, bows strung and arrows notched ready to attack. Suddenly, a brilliant light blazed forth through the windows of the house and a loud crack rent the air. On its heel, a second wave of light and another explosion issued from nearer the front door. As predicted, men streamed forth from the back door, shouting and pushing one another out of the way. As soon as they were all out and the woodfolk could clearly see Andoran, they fired two volleys in quick succession and dropped everyone but the red headed leader. But even in the midst of the chaos, Andoran's reactions were quick and he threw his red shield over himself before any of the woodfolk had time to fire a third volley.

Danton worked his way along the shadowed walls of the house and, when he reached the back of the house, poked his head around the corner, checking to see whether there were still any arrows flying. He spotted Andoran in his shield and pulled back into the shadows to think. Suddenly he became aware that sharp, cold steel was poking into his side. Someone had slid a dagger up under his shirt and was pressing its point into his flesh. As he tensed up to spring away from the knife, a deep voice murmured in his ear, "I wouldn't do that, if I were you. I'm sure my arm can move faster than your whole body."

"I doubt it." Danton whirled away from the blade and dropped like a stone to land on his shoulders throwing his legs up to kick the knife out of the man's hand. In one fluid movement, he rolled over backwards and back onto his feet, drawing a knife from his belt and sending it flying into his assailant's shoulder as he became upright.

"Aagh!" The man cried out in pain and sank to the ground, clutching his shoulder.

Danton glanced around to check that Andoran was still standing within his shield before bending over the wounded man.

"So where did you come from then?" he asked the wounded man as he grasped the hilt of his knife still embedded in the man's shoulder. "Everyone from inside came out of the back door."

The man rolled his eyes in pain, "Aagh. Don't. I will answer. I... I was outside taking a leak. I couldn't see the guard and was just beginning to look for him when chaos erupted."

"I see."

Danton applied vertical pressure on the knife hilt, to force the man up onto his feet. The man scrabbled up, clutching at Danton's hand and gasping with pain, as the knife moved within the wound in his shoulder.

"Put your hands out to either side," ordered Danton coldly. "You have eight arrows trained on your back. If you move, you die." Leaving the knife sticking out of the man's shoulder, Danton patted the man down and extricated three more daggers which he pocketed about his own person. He glanced again at Andoran, "The same applies to you. If you drop your shield, you will be shot down."

"You are slipping, Danton. I can remember when your aim was deadly accurate," said Andoran, his hands on his hips, and a slight smile on his face. There was nothing wrong with his courage, only his morals.

"It still is, Andoran. I hit where I aimed."

"And why do you keep Maragan alive when you have slaughtered the rest?"

Danton shrugged, "Someone has to explain to Jarand what you have been doing. In case you and Sargon cannot bring yourselves to do it, this man is my backup." As he spoke with Andoran, he was ripping strips off the bottom of the man's shirt to form padding and a bandage.

"Oh for heaven's sake, Danton! Don't be such a fool! Why would Prince Jarand want to know about it, assuming you know what it is. Then he would have to do something about it and that would not suit him at all, I can assure you. You will not find favour in his eyes in that way."

"I do not want his good opinion," replied Danton.

A sly understanding crept into Andoran's eyes, "You want free run of the Great West Road, don't you? You obviously have a well-trained band of brigands in the trees over there and you want it all for yourselves." Still within his shield, Andoran sauntered over to the back steps of the house and sat down. "Well, I'm sorry to disappoint you, my friend, but there are other bands of robbers out there, not just us."

It slowly dawned on Danton that Andoran had no idea that Tarkyn was involved at all. He concentrated for a minute or two on slowly extracting the dagger and binding the man's shoulder before answering, "Why would I need to take you to Jarand if I just wanted to clear out my rivals?"

A puzzled frown appeared on Andoran's forehead, "Hmmm. Good point. If not for money or influence, what other reason could there possibly be?"

Danton's intention to answer was interrupted by the sound of approaching horses. He glanced at Maragan whose face was white and sweaty from pain, "I'm sorry but I'm going to have to bind your hands behind you. I don't know what magical skills you possess." When the man looked sickened at the prospect of having his injured shoulder dragged back, Danton hesitated and after a moment's thought, waved at the trees and pointed to the man's temple and tapped it.

Out of the darkness, a small stone flew towards them, bare inches from Danton, and dropped the man to the ground.

Andoran raised his eyebrows, "That's impressive. You were so sure of your men's aim that you didn't even flinch."

Danton gave a slight smile, "They are not my men. They are the people I travel with."

In the shadows behind him, the sound of water running over pebbles formed the words, "Make sure Andoran stays outside. Then we can outlast him. You might need to put your shield over his, if he tries to run. Three horses approach; one carries Sargon, trussed up, and the other two horses are riderless. We are looking after the two victims. We may need their evidence. Creaking Bough will bring the horses to the edge of the trees for you. I will stay here so you can communicate with us."

Danton smiled, "Thanks." He moved away from the side of the house to stand before the red shielded sorcerer. "Andoran, if you attempt to go into the house, we will smoke you out." He reached behind the sorcerer and closed the door. "If you attempt to run, I will throw my shield over yours. And if you stay, eventually, you will go to sleep." He waved his hand, "But keep your shield up, by all means. While it is up, you cannot attack me. And if you drop it, your fate will be the same as Maragan's."

"You are very clinical, Danton," said Andoran in mild reproof. "You used to be more fun."

Danton glanced at him but did not bother rising to the bait. Instead he walked to the point where the path emerged from the trees to meet Creaking Bough as she arrived with the horses.

"Hello Danton. I think Sargon is beginning to come around. But don't worry. His hands are securely tied behind him...Not a very comfortable way to ride a horse, I wouldn't think."

"Hi Danton," rumbled a deep voice out of the darkness behind the horses. "You're doing a fine job there. As soon as we can get Andoran out of his shield, we can head off."

"They don't realise I'm with Tarkyn, Thunder Storm. Do you think I should tell them?"

After a tiny mind talking silence, Creaking Bough replied, "I don't see why not. Jarand and Journeyman already know and we are not planning on letting these three loose."

"But although Autumn Leaves thought you people would be safe to show yourselves to Andoran and Sargon because they are going to die anyway, I've been thinking about it and I don't. They could talk to any number of people before they die, if they are to stand trial. So I think you should stay hidden." As he spoke, Danton took the reins of the three horses and glanced up at Sargon to check that he was still unconscious.

Thunder Storm patted him on the back, "I'm impressed. You're holding to our oath of secrecy better than we are. I think you're right. I'll let the others know."

Danton nodded his thanks as he took the reins from the woodwoman. He led the three horses nearer to the back door of the house and tied them to a hitching post, making sure that they were not between Andoran and the woodfolk watching from the trees. Danton saw Andoran's eyes widen and a little of his bravura slip when he realised that it was Sargon trussed up on the horse. "Hoping for a last minute rescue from your friend here, were you?" he asked sardonically.

Andoran glared defiantly at Danton, "Some of us have stayed loyal to each other, even if you have chosen to go your own road with your own exclusive team."

Danton gave a little grunt of laughter, "As I said before, they are not my team. I am merely permitted to travel with them... and even that is an honour. But you're right about them being exclusive...It is almost impossible to join their ranks. Only one person has ever done it and he is far greater than I."

Andoran frowned, "And who is this great person that can so far outstrip a lord?" Suddenly light dawned, "Oh no! Don't tell me! You've been with the prince all along, haven't you? You conniving little weasel!" After a moment's thought, he nodded approvingly, "Good move on your part. From what I hear he is beginning to gain influence again. If he succeeds in usurping his brothers, you'll have placed yourself very well." His eyes narrowed, "You always were a crafty one with politics."

Danton folded his arms and looked down at Andoran, still sitting nonchalantly on the steps within his red shield. "Andoran, I know this is beyond your comprehension, but I sought out Tarkyn because I care for him. As far as I know, he has no wish to be king. But wherever he goes, I will follow and support him. He has always had, and always will have, my undivided loyalty."

Andoran leaned in closer and said very quietly, "I understand completely. You have to say that, don't you? They're all around us listening."

Danton just stared at him for a few moments before shaking his head ruefully, "Andoran, I would be half inclined, if not for your shield, to belt the living daylights out of you for that remark. But in the end, what would be the point? You have no concept of the things I care about." His face hardened, "But I will never forgive you for what you did to Tarkyn." He looked around as a groan issued from the back of one of the horses.

Sargon had opened his eyes and was staring at them, trying to work out where he was and what was happening. He tried to sit up but, with his hands tied behind him, found it too difficult in his befuddled state and slumped back down onto the horse's neck. Danton walked over and, grasping the man's shoulder, pushed him upright.

"Hello Sargon."

Sargon's eyes flickered around the clearing, taking in Andoran in his shield and the dead men strewn across the open ground. He cocked an eyebrow at Andoran, "Rumbled?"

Andoran shrugged, "Afraid so. I'm not sure on whose authority. I explained to Danton here that Jarand would not really want to know.

Apparently Danton has taken up with Tarkyn but why an outlaw would have any interest in our activities other than to take them over, I don't know." He grimaced, "Of course, there is the other little matter Tarkyn may have taken exception to."

"What?" Sargon frowned, trying to convey meaning without words, "You mean...? How could anyone know? We stayed out of view, if you remember."

"You stayed out of Tarkyn's view. But other people saw you," said Danton. "And for that alone you will die, let alone the rest."

"Oh come on, Danton," cajoled Sargon. "Be reasonable. Tarkyn was branded a rogue sorcerer. We were merely doing our public duty and bringing in a wanted felon."

Danton looked at him with blatant dislike, "Whatever else he is, Tarkyn is a prince of the royal line of Tamadil. It was never your right to punish him or to treat him with anything less than respect. But more than that, Tarkyn was your friend and without a second thought, you betrayed him."

Sargon rolled his eyes, "Danton, Tarkyn was a moralistic prig. We put up with him because he was a prince. I'll grant you he was nice to us and even funny sometimes, but he never let his guard down. He was never just one of the lads. He kept his distance and you could always feel his eyes on you, judging what you were doing. You could never get up to any real fun when he was around."

Danton swept his arm around the clearing, "If this is your idea of fun, I'm not surprised."

"Oh stop it, Danton. You know what I mean."

Danton smiled ruefully, "Yes, I know what you mean. And you, knowing that, might begin to understand that Tarkyn would not stand by and allow your nefarious activities to continue."

"What? Even though he is nothing more than an outlaw? What right does he have to interfere?" demanded Andoran.

Danton smiled, knowing the concept of forest guardian would be lost on them. "He has the right of might, if nothing else. And on his behalf, we have defeated you. He is as upright and honest as he always was and will no more countenance foul play now, than he ever did." Even as he said it, he remembered Orolan and wondered at Tarkyn accepting him and his brigands.

"Pompous, self-righteous prig, that's what he is," spat out Sargon. "Rigid as the day is long."

Danton's eyes narrowed, "Have a care Sargon. There is only so much I will put up with."

"You were happy to slag off at him when we saw you in the encampment," said Andoran, hoping to show Danton up in front of his hidden followers.

"Absolutely true. I did talk disparagingly about Tarkyn, but although I may have hidden it from you, I was not happy about it." Danton gave a reminiscent smile. "Neither were the people I travel with, as I recall." He became more business-like. "Now, Andoran, as you can see, the game is up. So, will you give up and accompany us or do we have to wait it out until you can no longer keep yourself awake and your shield slips? I can assure you that the people watching us from the trees will quite happily take shifts at keeping watch and sleeping. So there is no doubt we will outlast you."

Andoran thought for a moment, "I will agree to accompany you but will keep my shield raised."

"In that case, you and I will walk. I'm not having you on horseback in your shield. I will lead Sargon's horse and leave the other two behind. My companions can bring Maragan along later if we need him." Danton backed up to the corner of the house and said quietly into the shadows, "Do you agree? I can't lift Maragan up onto a horse on my own and you can't come out to help me."

"Agreed, but at least sign of trouble, we will knock out Sargon again," replied Waterstone quietly. "Be careful. Even if you tell them that we are shadowing you, they will still feel as though it is two of them against one of you. They are almost certain to try something."

Danton nodded, "I will be on my guard."

But it was more than physical danger that he would need to guard himself against.

CHAPTER 56

Dear Jarand,
Word will reach you soon that a small company of your soldiers has been slaughtered. Disguised as bandits they have been preying on travellers along the Great West Road, robbing them and leaving only the men alive to serve in your army.
I do you the credit of believing that you know nothing about this. As I have no vested interest in drawing the king's attention to your soldiers' shortcomings, I will deliver their leaders, Andoran and Sargon, to you, rather than to Kosar, so that you may question them and mete out your own justice.
I think you will find that there are one, possibly two more companies of these soldiers who are in league, preying on innocent travellers. I also think it is highly likely that your friend Lord Davorad may have knowledge of this.
What you do about it is your choice, with one proviso; this practice must stop. I'm sure that you would agree with me on this point.
Your brother,
Tarkyn.

Jarand looked up from the letter, his eyes blazing with rage. Any retainer nearby unconsciously straightened up ever further and tried to melt into the background.

"Send Journeyman to me," he snapped at the nearest page.

The boy fled, relieved to have a reason to leave Jarand's presence.

When the wizard arrived, Jarand waved away his other retainers before thrusting the letter into his hands, "Look at this!" he demanded. "My upstart younger brother has taken it upon himself to kill off some of my men. I should drag his name through the mud."

Journeyman coughed "Yes Sire, although I think you have already done that."

Jarand paced up and down in agitation, "I will not brook this sort of interference. I will scour the woodlands and kill off every last one of them, if I have to."

"It is indeed very presumptuous of him, Your Highness, but at least he did not take his information straight to Kosar…and I think it would be *unfortunate* if you were to divert vast resources at a time when you are gathering your forces."

Jarand rounded on the young wizard and stood glaring at him, hands on hips, "So what are you suggesting? That I allow my younger brother to dictate to me?"

Journeyman gave another nervous cough, "He seems to think that you would agree with his actions, Your Highness."

Journeyman did not know whether Jarand had already been cognisant of his soldiers' banditry but was inclined to think he had been. Jarand, on the other hand, was not sure how much Journeyman might say to the king, particularly under duress, if it came to it. And so they fenced with one another.

"That is not the issue here, Journeyman. The issue is that he is using the threat of telling Kosar to ensure my compliance with his own moral stand."

"Perhaps you could pre-empt him by going to Kosar yourself. You could lay the blame for the banditry at Tarkyn's door and the bodies of your soldiers can bear witness to your efforts to quell him," suggested Journeyman.

Jarand held the wizard unnervingly in his gaze for a long moment before finally heaving a sigh. "I like your thinking, Journeyman. But having met with Tarkyn and knowing that Kosar too has met up with him, I know that neither of us would believe that of him." His eyes narrowed, "No. What I need is a way of controlling him. Have you tracked down any of the Lost sorcerers yet? I think we need a couple of them to act as surety for Tarkyn's compliance. Even if we don't lure him in to be brought to trial, at least I can use them to barter for his co-operation."

Journeyman gave a slight bow. "It has been difficult, Your Highness. Someone else has also been searching for them. But we managed to snatch away two women just hours before another interested party came looking for them."

Jarand raised his eyebrows, "Indeed? And who else is interested in them?"

The wizard shrugged, "I can only imagine that it is the king, Your Highness. After all, he did say he might resort to using the Lost sorcerers as bait later, if the need arose."

"True. I had not expected him to act so swiftly, however." Jarand walked over to an ornately carved sideboard and poured himself a glass of red wine from a crystal decanter as he thought. "Hmm. So what is Kosar proposing to do with all these Lost sorcerers, I wonder? Perhaps he too wishes to ensure Tarkyn's compliance."

Journeyman who was still smarting from his own defeat at Tarkyn's hands, replied, "I cannot imagine that either of you would be willing even to consider the demands of a mere wanted felon."

Jarand's hard grey eyes held the wizard's gaze, "Do not overstep yourself, wizard. There is nothing 'mere' about Tarkyn. He is my brother and a prince and it is not for one such as you to dismiss his worth."

Journeyman bowed, "I beg your pardon, Your Highness." He restrained himself from pointing out that it had been the twins' actions that had made Tarkyn a felon in the first place. Instead he said obsequiously, "But however worthy His Highness, Prince Tarkyn, may be, you still outrank him and should not be answerable to him."

"True. So you have my thanks for finding the two Lost sorcerers who will provide me with the means of binding my impertinent younger brother's will to mine." He sat down decisively at a finely made desk inlaid with mother of pearl. He took a draught of his wine before setting down the glass at his elbow. "Bring me pen and paper. If we attach a letter to the pigeon that brought me Tarkyn's missive, I'm sure it will find its way back to him."

Chapter 57

Dear Tarkyn,

I thank you for your efforts on my behalf. I was shocked to hear that soldiers under my ultimate command had so badly abused their position of trust. If you deliver the ringleaders to my encampment, I will ensure that a public example is made of them.

In return, you will be pleased to know that I have rescued two young women whom I believe were victims of the Forest of Yesterday Today and Tomorrow and who have been finding life difficult in Tormadell. So, as a gesture of good faith, I have taken them into my keeping.

I do not expect any recompense for this but merely hope that it will herald the beginning of a new era of cooperation between us.

Your brother,

Jarand.

"**B**oravar, Harkell, read this!" Tarkyn virtually threw the letter at them as they hurried over to join him.

Boravar glanced at Harkell and cleared his throat, "Perhaps if you read it out…"

After the slightest of hesitations, Harkell straightened the page, ready to read it. "Good idea! Then woodfolk can hear its contents too…if that is all right with you, Tarkyn."

Tarkyn waved his hand in consent. Once the letter had been read out there was a short, shocked silence.

"He's not very subtle, is he, Tarkyn?" observed Rainstorm.

"No. He's not. And I can hear the smugness in every line." Tarkyn smacked his palm against a tree, "Blast it! And we were so close. Didn't you say we have nearly everyone rounded up and accounted for?" he asked Boravar and Stormaway.

Boravar glanced anxiously at Tarkyn before dropping his eyes and mumbling, "Yes Sire, nearly but not all. I'm sorry. We are doing our best. There are such a lot of them, you see, and so widespread. It has taken Stormaway's network quite a while to locate them and…"

"Boravar, stop." interrupted the prince gently. "I am not angry with you. I know you are doing your best. We have just been unlucky and now must work out what we will do about it."

Rainstorm chuckled, "So a new era of cooperation is out of the question, I suppose."

Tarkyn flicked him a glance and didn't even bother replying. "Stormaway, these women. Do you know who they are?"

"I think I do, Your Highness," replied Boravar, anxious to make amends. "There are only five of the eighty that we have not yet located. Two of these are sisters, Caroya and Loressa. When Stormaway's people went to their address, they were told that the sisters had left only hours before." He shrugged, "I would say it was them, Sire."

Tarkyn raised his eyebrows, "And the other three?"

"A husband and wife, with the wife's younger brother, Sire."

"And do we know their whereabouts?"

Stormaway cleared his throat, "We have encountered a similar problem with them, Your Highness. They are reported to have left shortly before my people arrived."

Tarkyn ran his hand through his hair, "And since Jarand did not mention them, I think we can surmise that Kosar has taken them as surety or bait. Oh wonderful!"

"Tarkyn, I can see that your brothers may think you have a particular connection with these people because you rescued them from the Lost Forest," said Harkell. "But in truth, they are no more or less important than the hundreds of sorcerers who people your brothers' prisons."

"Or who walk the streets, for that matter," put in Summer Rain. "They could take anyone and hold them as surety for your cooperation. And there are Danton's and Harkell's families."

Tarkyn frowned, "So what are you saying? That we shouldn't rescue them?"

Summer Rain shook her head. "No, I am simply pointing out that if you take the risk, or ask us to take the risk of rescuing these sorcerers, there are hundreds to take their place."

Stormaway looked at her thoughtfully. "She's right, you know." His eyes turned to meet Tarkyn's. "Your Highness, imagine if I came to you and said that Jarand had abducted a family travelling along the Great West Road and was holding them until you gave yourself up, or complied with his requests, or whatever it was that he wanted…Would they matter any less than these Lost sorcerers?"

Tarkyn glanced at the big sorcerer. "They might to Boravar."

"Your Highness…"

"Boravar!… and Stormaway!" exclaimed Tarkyn impatiently. "Will you please stop being formal with me? I reiterate; I am not angry with you. We are all trying to work this out together."

Boravar and Stormaway looked at each other and relaxed into grins.

"Sorry, Tarkyn," said Boravar. "I didn't realise I was doing it. So, to answer your question, the Lost sorcerers probably do mean more to me. They are the only people I know in this new world, besides all of you. But in essence, Summer Rain and Harkell are right. If we rescue the sisters, there are hundreds to take their place….and both of your brothers can arrest people at will."

Even as they spoke, another pigeon flew into a branch near Stormaway and cocked its head at him.

"Excuse me," Tarkyn's wizard retrieved the parchment from the little bird's leg and with a muttered incantation, restored the letter it had carried to full size. After a moment, he raised his head, "I'm afraid your surmise was right. This missive is from Kosar."

Tarkyn frowned, "Before I read it, may I ask; how do they know where we are, to deliver these messages? Jarand's I can understand, because he sent it back with the same pigeon that delivered our message to him, but Kosar…?"

Stormaway gave a little cough, "I took the liberty of sending this pigeon with a message to the king, saying that he could use it, should he ever wish to contact you." Looking a little worried, the wizard added, "After all, you did tell him to come into the forest and shout, if he ever needed you and I couldn't help thinking that that wasn't very well thought out."

Tarkyn gave a slow smile, "That wasn't very clever, was it? You see? That's why I need people helping me. Thanks Stormaway." He dropped his eyes and began to read:

Tarkyn,
I understand that you have a close association with the Lost sorcerers, many of whom seem to have disappeared in recent weeks. So it will relieve your mind a little to know that I have under my care, three of them who were finding life in Tormadell rather stressful.
Of course, it is a natural part of my role to support those of my subjects who are needy but I hope this gesture of good faith will provide us with the basis for a better working relationship.
Kosar

Tarkyn handed it without comment to Harkell to read out.

Rainstorm, as usual was irrepressible, "So now you have to manage a better working relationship in a new era of cooperation! You should be able to do that…except that, from your brothers' points of view, the two are mutually exclusive."

Tarkyn grunted, "Well, from my point of view, I'd be happy to have both, if that was what they really meant."

String and Bean who had been mumbling between themselves as they sat nearby against a tree, wandered over to join in.

"At the moment, it is quite easy to manage," observed Bean nonchalantly.

"Yep," agreed String, "But it is likely to escalate in the future if we don't find a way to curtail it now."

"And what's so easy about managing the present situation?" asked Stormaway.

Bean shrugged, "Just send each of the letters to the other brother with a little note to say that you're looking forward to working with both of them."

The trappers broke into broad grins, as String added, "Yep. That should put the cat amongst the pigeons."

Rainstorm, who was quickest to see all the implications, roared with laughter, while the others talked it through more fully before smiles began to appear on their faces.

Tarkyn smiled broadly, "Our scruffy geniuses have done it again,"

"I think it is genii," said String quietly.

"I think I don't care." replied Tarkyn flippantly. He looked around at everyone, "So are we agreed? I will have to tear the top part off Jarand's so that Kosar does not see the reference to the pseudo bandits but other than that..." When they all nodded, Tarkyn chortled, "I wish I could see their faces when they get this."

"You can, Tarkyn," said Rainstorm. "You can link with the pigeon. Then we could all see too."

Tarkyn hesitated, "It is not very respectful."

"Of what? Their privacy or their rank?" asked Rainstorm trenchantly.

Tarkyn grimaced, knowing he was on difficult turf. "Both. But probably, more their privacy. I don't know that I feel good about setting up the king and the heir to the throne as laughing stocks. But more importantly, I wouldn't want anyone to give me a difficult piece of news in front of a large unseen audience, whatever my rank."

Ancient Oak quietly gave his support, "In the same way that you don't like your conversations being shared mentally with others, without your knowledge." He nodded, "I can accept that."

Tarkyn smiled his gratitude, "Exactly the same principle. I can't do to someone else something I don't like having done to me."

Rainstorm scowled, "Well, that's nonsense for a start. You are quite happy to order other people around but don't like to be on the receiving end." The feisty young woodman folded his arms and stared defiantly at Tarkyn.

The prince returned his gaze, not angry but simply wondering how to handle him. Eventually he gave a slight smile, "You're right of course, Rainstorm. That argument did sound good though, didn't it?"

Rainstorm's eyes narrowed as he considered whether he was being made fun of. When he decided he wasn't, he breathed out and shrugged, "Well in all fairness, you issue as few orders as you can, presumably because you don't like it yourself."

"It's not quite the same. I don't like it because no one has the right to order me around."

"That's exactly how we feel too," returned Rainstorm quickly. "But we've just learnt to put up with it because we have to."

Tarkyn waved his hand and sighed, "Can we stop this now please? This is old ground. We have agreed to disagree."

Suddenly Rainstorm took a mental step backwards and realised that he was holding up proceedings. "Sorry Tarkyn. I didn't mean to badger you." He smiled, all belligerence gone, "And I can see that I wouldn't necessarily want to set up Ancient Oak, for instance, to be ridiculed unknowingly…It's up to you," he conceded magnanimously, "After all, they're your brothers."

"Thank you," replied Tarkyn gravely, with a lurking twinkle in his eyes. "Well, shall we do the deed? Pen, paper and two pigeons, if you please, Stormaway."

CHAPTER 58

It was only a two hour walk to the gates of the encampment but during that time Andoran and Sargon badgered Danton incessantly. "You know, Danton, I was very impressed when you managed to become an elite guard. It was the first...in fact, possibly the only thing you have ever done without Tarkyn at your side. Yes, I remember you had to go off on training camps and leave your precious prince behind." Andoran nodded understandingly, "I imagine that must have been quite hard for you. Was it?"

Danton glanced around at him, "Yes. As a matter of fact, it was. Especially the first time."

"I'm sure it was. After all, you have grown up together, haven't you? And always you in Tarkyn's shadow." Sargon smiled, "You know, when we met up with you at the encampment, I thought, 'Good old Danton. Now, at last that Tarkyn has gone, he will be able to become his own man'. Still, I admire such loyalty. Independence is a small price to pay, to know you are giving such fine service. And I'm sure Tarkyn appreciates you, doesn't he?"

After a blissful but short silence, Andoran started up again, "Still I hope, since he has had you by his side for so long now, that he doesn't take your presence for granted. Does he?"

"No, he does not," replied Danton hotly. He thought for a few minutes about their recent shared experiences before reiterating more slowly, "No. He does not."

A few minutes later, Danton sighed as Andoran began to talk again, "And this exclusive group you travel with...It must feel a bit isolated, does it?... if your liege is accepted and you are not."

"No," replied Danton. "I am not the only one travelling with them who is not one of them...But in my case, it is only my association with Tarkyn that permits me even to travel with them. So I suppose everything I do is interpreted in terms of my value to Tarkyn by everyone who knows me."

Sargon sighed gustily, "I think that's so sad. Don't you?"

"What?"

"To have no identity of your own."

Despite his best intentions, the sorcerers' constant questioning was beginning to get under Danton's skin. "I do have an identity of my own. I am an elite guard and Tarkyn is not. I appreciate fashion, clothing, dalliance and court intrigue far more than Tarkyn does."

"But I bet, even though you have spent your life with him and for him, he would not consider you his equal."

Danton snorted, "No. Of course not."

"So what sort of friendship is that? Sargon and I have always been equal partners in everything we do." Andoran shrugged, "You may not always approve of what we've done but at least we have devised it together. It must stifle you not to be able to act on your own ideas without consultation or permission all the time."

After a few moments, Danton conceded, "There have been times when Tarkyn has been a little constrictive or overly controlling. But he is improving."

"Well, that's good then," said Sargon heartily. "One day you may have as much freedom to follow your own path as the rest of the population. And make your own decisions. Could be a long time coming though."

Danton glared at him, "Have you thought that I might not want that freedom? That I might be happy having my decisions made for me? After all, that is all I have ever known."

Andoran shook his head, "You say that, Danton, but I know you. You are not the apathetic type. You could not have made it through the training to become an elite guard if you were. Despite your horrendous upbringing, you have a spark of independence in you. You have far more value in your own right than just being Tarkyn's shadow. Surely you have met people who value you for who you are, quite apart from your value to Tarkyn?"

Danton thought for a few minutes. He thought about Summer Rain caring about his safety at Lord Tolward's house. He thought about the wizardess he had met in the Lost Forest saying that he was worth risking the future of Eskuzor for. He thought of his conversations with Waterstone and finally he remembered Tarkyn saying that he had saved him from the whippings because he cared for him, not as a matter of principle.

He smiled gently, "Yes, I have."

"So, why don't you shake the dust of Tarkyn off your feet and go your own way?"

Danton shook his head ruefully. "It won't work, Andoran. All of those people who care for me, care for Tarkyn also. To betray Tarkyn, which I would never do anyway, would be to betray all my friends as well." He shrugged, "You may be right. Tarkyn may be too much at the centre of my universe but he has earned his place there through his actions, not by his birthright. I would die before I betrayed him."

"Well," sighed Andoran philosophically, sweeping his unruly red hair out of his eyes, "It was worth a try."

"And now we have only imprisonment, torture and hanging to look foward to," said Sargon morosely. "And, to make it worse, I have such a sore head from being knocked out." He swayed a little in the saddle before righting himself with an effort. "Don't worry. Just felt woozy for a minute there."

Suddenly Sargon swayed alarmingly to one side, threatening to fall out of the saddle altogether. Danton made a grab for him but as he found himself with his arms full of Sargon, Andoran dropped his shield and sent a shaft of red power spearing towards him. With a desperate yank, Danton managed to twist Sargon between him and Andoran even as the shaft of magic split the air. The shaft hit the outside of Sargon's shoulder and deviated slightly in its path to graze the side of Danton's head. The smell of burning hair filled the air. Danton collapsed to the ground, Sargon falling on top of him. Andoran dropped where he stood, hit by a woodfolk slingshot. A second slingshot made sure that Sargon was unconscious as woodfolk converged on the scene from all directions.

Two woodfolk bound Andoran's hands while the rest concentrated on extracting Danton from beneath the weighty body of Sargon. When they laid the blonde headed sorcerer out, they could see immediately that Sargon's weight had snapped his wrist. His face was white; his lips and the shadows under his eyes were blue.

"He's been hit by one of these hideous sorcerer shafts," said Twig Snap with an anxious frown. "How deadly are they?"

Waterstone shook his head, "I don't know. From what I've pieced together, the sorcerer can vary its strength. They rarely seem to kill first time, from what I've seen. But I expect Andoran gave it everything he had. Saying that, he was probably tired from holding up his shield for so long."

Twig Snap bent down, put her ear to Danton's mouth, then placed her hand on his chest. She shook her head, looking panicky, "I don't know. I don't know if he's breathing. I can't feel anything."

"Oh no," breathed Autumn Leaves. "All of our healers are back with Tarkyn. We need their help... If we all transmit the images together, perhaps we can make it across the distance. Tarkyn was able to connect to the mouse from far away. We'll aim for Tarkyn, Summer Rain and Stormaway. Quickly."

Eight minds joined together then threw their thoughts through the forest searching for the others of the home guard.

In the quiet of the sleeping campsite, Rainstorm and North Wind, being teenagers and the only ones not yet asleep, suddenly sat up and bellowed, "Tarkyn, come quick." They transmitted the images they had received around to everyone, waking them indiscriminately.

Everyone tumbled out of their shelters into the clearing, children crying at having been woken so suddenly. As soon as Tarkyn emerged, everyone converged on him.

"Danton. Did you see? He's not breathing. He's been hit by one of your magic shafts." Rainstorm's voice rose in panic, "He might be dead."

Tarkyn grasped him by both shoulders. "Rainstorm. Be strong. For me…and for Danton." Rainstorm took a deep shuddering breath and nodded. "Now, show me the images. See if you can connect us all to the others with Danton. Some of you, use words. But remember, I can't hear what you're saying. When I know where to send my mind, I will try to go into Danton. Meanwhile, Summer Rain and Stormaway, you help them with more conventional forms of healing. Let's go."

Tarkyn sat down with his bare back against a tree with Midnight and Sparrow, whom he had volunteered to look after in Waterstone's absence, on either side of him. He closed his eyes, and connected firstly with the minds around him. Then drawing a deep breath, he rode the wave of their thoughts across the miles in between, until he had connected with Waterstone and the anxious group looking down at Danton. He took another slow breath as he strained his mind, feeling for Danton's.

He had never been able to connect with an unconscious mind before, let alone across such a distance. But on the other occasions, he had not known where they were. This time his target was right in front of the minds he was connected to.

Slowly he became aware of a cold, faint spark flickering uncertainly, almost guttering from the shock of the magic wave that had swamped it. Tarkyn slid his mind in gently, feeling tentatively around until with the faintest of tremors, his mind connected with Danton's. The blonde sorcerer's mind was filled with darkness, no sense of the outside world or of his own body. Tarkyn wondered frantically which part of Danton's mind controlled his breathing but had no idea where to look. Instead, he visualised the rise and fall of Danton's chest and tried to will him to take a breath. The little cold flame seemed to be fading before his very eyes. Suddenly, the light flickered slightly brighter before fading again.

A voice said in the world outside Tarkyn. "We are breathing for him. We are trying to get him to do it himself. Follow our rhythm."

"His heart?" croaked Tarkyn. "What about his heart?"

"The same, Tarkyn, as the breath, but a different rhythm. Follow our rhythms if you can."

The little light flickered brighter again as air was forced into Danton's lungs. Tarkyn changed his images of Danton's chest rising and falling to fit in with the rhythmic flickering of the light. From this distance, Tarkyn couldn't send any of his healing force into the ailing sorcerer.

Suddenly an image appeared of his force going into the tree behind him through the forest to the place where Danton lay.

"Put Danton's hand on a tree," said Sparrow clearly to those around her.

Tarkyn refocused on Danton's mind and sent him all the strength and care that he could. He sent memories of their years together and wrapped the little cold flame in his warmth, careful not to smother it. He let his mind flow down Danton's arm and through his hand until it had touched the tree outside. Then Tarkyn pulled back and, keeping one part of his mind carefully wrapped around the weak flame of Danton's mind, transferred his attention to his own back, using his contact with the tree behind him to send his power driving into the trees, down through the roots and subterranean streams. Deep in the bowels of the earth below the forest, Tarkyn knew his sense of direction would never be able to lead him to Danton. So he transmitted the feeling of Danton's mind and hand, and his own mind's touch on the distant tree into the forest.

For long minutes, nothing happened. Then he felt his power being dragged away from him as the mighty forest pulled it over the miles to the point where his mind had touched the tree. His essence drew out of him into one long thin wire.

Suddenly with a faint jolt, the extremity of his power hit Danton's hand and stopped. He vaguely realised that for his power to go further and to reach into Danton, he would have to risk letting go of the injured sorcerer's mind. Tarkyn was too thinly stretched to do both. Taking a long slow breath, he withdrew his mind slowly from Danton's, wishing him goodbye and good luck as he went. Then Tarkyn surrendered his mind, his consciousness and his whole being to the might of the forest.

In the clearing around Tarkyn, Midnight and Sparrow sat stalwartly on either side of him, looking anxiously at his ghastly white pallor that was slowly taking on a green hue, and listening to his slow shallow breathing.

"You stay with him, you two," urged Rainstorm. "He needs someone to anchor on, when he goes this deep."

A little distance away, Stormaway and Summer Rain were orchestrating events at the other end of the mindlink, showing Waterstone and Autumn Leaves how to keep Danton's heart and lungs going until, or if, he could take over himself.

Then, slowly, when all hope was fading, Danton began to turn faintly green. It was not Tarkyn's strength that entered Danton's body. It was the slow sure strength of the whole forest. Tarkyn was too dissipated across the miles to have any consciousness left at all. And because it was so slow, it took another hour before the weak flame of Danton's mind was able to take over his own breathing and pulse. As soon as Danton looked as though he would survive, mind messages went back to the clearing where Tarkyn leant, now as green as Danton, against the tree.

A short debate between Summer Rain and Stormaway concluded that the risk to Tarkyn was too great to continue healing Danton from this distance. Not only that but the recent fracas with the pseudo-bandits had given rise to an urgent need for Danton and the woodfolk with him to leave the proximity of the encampment, and to immerse themselves deeper into the forest. So, in consultation with both groups, they removed Danton's hand from the tree and set out to bring Danton back, still unconscious but at least breathing independently, so that Tarkyn could compete the healing when he arrived.

Once the course of action was settled, Stormaway came over to stand looking down at the quiescent Forest Guardian. He shook his head. "He has really gone far away this time. I just hope we can get him back." He transferred his gaze to Midnight and Sparrow. Using words, images and gestures, he asked, "You two, you have been touching him the whole time, haven't you?" When they both nodded solemnly, Stormaway said, "I want you both to call him back. Do it strongly and slowly. Don't be afraid if he doesn't come straight away. Just be strong and sure and keep calling him. Can you do that?"

Sparrow and Midnight looked at each other before nodding at Stormaway.

Stormaway walked over to Rainstorm and said quietly, "Can you stay with them and encourage them. It could take up to an hour, I think. And when he starts coming round, don't let them go away or make any fast movements until he is fully back with us. Do you understand?"

"I'll stay with you," said Ancient Oak firmly. "Maybe the four of us can put our minds together to call him back."

"Try it," replied Stormaway. "Just don't let the children lose their physical connection with him."

Within the network of the forest, Tarkyn's mind had become part of a huge expanse, equally aware of running streams, trees waving gently in the night breeze, twisting tree roots deep underground, small rodents scurrying across the forest floor, and a myriad of bushes, vines and grasses swaying and rustling as night creatures pushed through them, and eddies of air ruffled their foliage.

Every now and then, a tiny pull was exerted on him from one particular place. There was something different about it. It had a warmth, a faint familiarity that came only from that one point in the forest. Gradually, curiosity drew his mind towards it to work out what was so different about it. As his mind began to focus on it, he began to hear a repeated noise accompanied by a repeated unworded beckoning, unlike the wind in the trees or the babbling of the streams. The noise resolved itself into two sounds being repeated over and over again. Slowly he realised that the sound was both in his mind and outside.

After a while, he let his attention wander off to other parts of the woodlands. But the insistence of the beckoning eventually drew him back. As he came closer, he felt a new sensation and remembered his sense of touch. Once he had remembered that, he could feel his body again still leaning against the tree, feel the rough bark against his back and small hands resting on his arms. Now he knew once more where his body was and who was waiting patiently for him. He let his mind drift briefly, back through the forest bidding it farewell and making sure he had disentangled himself from it before, with a final surge, he resurfaced and opened his eyes.

Four faces leaning in on him, broke into smiles.

"Tarkyn, my brother. It is good to see you back with us again." Ancient Oak grasped his hand, his voice husky with emotion. "You have been gone for a very long time."

Rainstorm grinned at him, "Stars above Tarkyn! These poor kids have been calling you for close to an hour and sitting here for well over two. They are absolute heroes."

Tarkyn smiled at them, still feeling dazed. "Hello, you two. It was your insistence that drew me back. Without Sparrow's voice and Midnight's urging, I would never have known where to come back to. In fact, I would not even have known that I owned a body." Realising that Sparrow's face was wet with tears of relief, he put his arm around her and drew her into a hug. "Sorry I frightened you." When he looked at Midnight, he could see that the little boy's face was white with strain. "And you. Come here, little one. Thank you both very much." He smiled at Rainstorm and Ancient Oak, "And you two."

Suddenly as he remembered why he had gone in the first place, a look of fear crossed his face, "Danton?"

"Danton lives, Tarkyn," said Stormaway, coming over to stand beside Ancient Oak. "But he has a long way to go. He is still unconscious but at least he is now breathing independently. His wrist is badly broken. We have explained how to set it temporarily but they are bringing him away from the encampment and back here to safety and your healing."

Tarkyn breathed a sigh of relief. "Oh. A broken wrist. That's nothing. The main thing is that he is alive. We came so close to losing him. The spark of his mind was almost out when I went in. It was only because you started the breathing for him that it didn't go out altogether." After a moment he asked, "And what about that bastard Andoran? And Sargon? Where are they?"

"They are tied to the gates of the encampment, with a bag of booty tied beside them in an attempt to incriminate them. Hopefully, Jarand will send word tomorrow that they must be tried. Unfortunately, with Danton out of action, there was no one to write an account of their activities for the camp commander." Stormaway shrugged, "To be honest, with Danton's life hanging in the balance, Andoran and Sargon's fate tended to fade into insignificance."

"And who sent me the image of my power going from this tree through the forest to Danton?" asked Tarkyn.

Stormaway frowned. "I assumed you thought of that yourself."

"No. I was too preoccupied with Danton's mind at that stage."

"You should know," piped up Sparrow. "He was sitting right next to you. I picked it up too. That's why I told everyone to put Danton's hand against a tree."

Midnight looked up from where he was drawing patterns in the dirt with a stick, to find everyone's eyes on him. Safe within the circle of Tarkyn's arm, he didn't flinch back but met their gazes calmly. In answer to a query from Tarkyn, he nodded with a little smile. Then his face broke into a grin as Tarkyn gave him a huge squeeze and the others ruffled his hair and smiled their thanks at him.

"You know," said Rainstorm, only half joking, "possibly your greatest single achievement as forest guardian, has been to make sure that Midnight did not become a force for evil."

Tarkyn grunted, "Don't take the credit from this little fellow. Despite all the evil done to him, he has never been more than pesky in return."

"That could well have changed over time," said Stormaway.

"*I* think his innate good character would have prevailed," returned Tarkyn. He gave Midnight a squeeze, "Wouldn't it, Rascal?"

Stormaway shrugged, "Perhaps. But now, we will never know..."

"*I* know," said Tarkyn gravely, with absolutely no basis for his statement other than his care for Midnight.

Stormaway actually rolled his eyes. "Heart-warming but naive, Your Highness."

Tarkyn laughed. Suddenly, his head fell back against the trunk of the tree, "Ooh. I feel a bit odd. I can still hear the rippling waters of subterranean streams and the footsteps of a hundred small animals upon the floor of the forest…"

"Tarkyn!" said Stormaway sharply. "You must move away from that tree. You must break your contact with the forest until you have closed your own boundaries completely. Now!" The wizard gestured to Rainstorm and Ancient Oak to help him, "We need to get him away from any contact with trees and into bed so that he can recover."

Tarkyn waved his hand, "No. I must go to Danton. Danton needs me."

Sparrow and Midnight had moved out of the way while Ancient Oak and Rainstorm heaved Tarkyn to his feet.

Stormaway walked with them as they headed towards Tarkyn's shelter, "Tarkyn, you cannot help Danton until you are stronger yourself. He is out of danger. He will endure until you are ready. You must gather your own resources first."

Tarkyn managed to bring his eyes into focus to glare at his retainer, "Have a care Stormaway. You are coming perilously close to dictating to me."

"Then so be it, my lord. As your physician, I am laying down the law to protect your health. You will ignore me at your peril," replied Stormaway with no hesitation whatsoever.

Tarkyn frowned. Stormaway had learnt the dangers of trying to dictate to his young but forceful charge, and recently his advice had been couched in suitably respectful tones. Therefore, Tarkyn sat up and took notice when Stormaway risked his ire so emphatically. Now he just had to find a way to back down gracefully, when his mind felt as though it was full of grasses swaying before the wind, and leaves shimmering in the moonlight. In the end he simply smiled and transmitted the images in his mind to those around him, "I will concede. You are right, Stormaway. I have to get the forest out of my head."

Part 9: Danton's Rise

CHAPTER 59

Sargon sat with his eyes closed, taking in information about his predicament before he opened them. He could feel his hands tied behind his back and a slight tug informed him that he was bound to a wooden structure behind him that creaked slightly when he pulled. Even more than the pain on the side of his head, his left shoulder still hurt badly where Andoran's strike had glanced off him on the way through to Danton. He gradually opened his eyes and found himself in the darkness of a moonlit night, face to face with his red haired friend, tied beside him to the gate of the encampment. Even as he watched him, Andoran groaned and opened his eyes to meet Sargon's.

"Ugh. Bloody Danton! We nearly made it." Andoran groaned again, "Ooh, my head's sore."

"*Your* head's sore. What about mine? I was hit twice and you hit my left shoulder. It's killing me!"

"Quick reflexes, that Danton. Dragged you across in front of him as a shield." Andoran grunted in satisfaction, "Not quick enough, though. I still hit him, right on the side of the head. I gave that strike everything I had. I can't imagine he survived it. Pity about his friends. We would have got away without them." He swivelled his head to see what was pushing up against his left side. His eyes widened, "Oh shit, Sargon. They've tied the booty from our last raid next to us. Quick! Think! How are we going to explain our way out of this one?"

Behind them they could hear the rhythmic steps of approaching soldiers, then the heavy jovial voice of Sergeant Torgan, "Good heavens. What have we here? Look what the cat dragged in. We were just on our way to look for you, Captain Sargon. Where's the rest of your patrol?"

Dragging his strength together, Sargon frowned and snapped, "Sergeant, that is no way to address a senior officer."

"Sorry, Captain. But the question still remains; where is your patrol?"

Sargon shook his head, "I don't know. We were attacked and our horses were stolen. I was knocked out so I don't know what became of my men or the travellers we rescued."

Sergeant Torgan turned to the men behind him, "Right, you lot. Fan out and look for them. Take care. There are obviously armed men in the area. Four of you, stay here and help me with these two."

The sergeant and his men untied Andoran and Sargon from the gate. But Torgan had spent many hours talking to Stormaway while he had resided in the encampment and had learnt of their questionable reputation. So, under his direction, the soldiers left Andoran and Sargon's hands bound behind them.

Once they were standing, Andoran drew himself up to glower down at the sergeant. "What is the meaning of this? Why have you not released us?"

Torgan stood stolidly before him, "Because there is some explaining to do and if all is well, you will receive my humblest apologies. But if all is not well, then I must protect my men from your power."

"But we are officers in your own army," protested Sargon.

"Which makes this very awkward for all of us. But I do not feel that I have the authority to decide the meaning of this situation." As Torgan turned them towards the encampment he added, "But I will do you the courtesy of rousing Captain Guerion rather than making you wait until morning."

Meanwhile, his men were sorting through the sack of booty that had been tied to the gate beside Andoran. "Sergeant, this looks like a traveller's belongings. Look, sir. Jewellery, money, a couple of good silver goblets…"

As Andoran went to speak, Torgan held up his hand, "No, don't tell me. I don't want to know. Wait until you can speak to Captain Guerion."

Andoran's eyes glittered with anger, "Sergeant, I insist that Lord Davorad be summoned so that I can make a formal complaint."

Torgan shrugged, "I will convey your wishes to Captain Guerion but I think it is Colonel Charford who will decide what to do."

Andoran and Sargon were marched firmly but not unkindly into the encampment and deposited on chairs in a large tent. They were given water and were then left to sit and wait for Captain Guerion to appear. It was not long before the men of Sargon's patrol arrived and were also escorted into the tent. The two injured travellers were assisted in to join them and given food and water while they waited.

Twenty minutes later, a trim, middle aged man entered the tent flanked by Sergeant Torgan. There was not one wispy grey hair out of place on the Captain's head and his uniform was immaculate. He carried himself with the casual authority that comes from years of experience and there was nothing to betray that half an hour before he had been sound asleep. He put his hands on his hips and surveyed the throng of people gathered before him.

With the time at two hours after midnight, he said, "Good morning," with only the faintest dryness in his voice.

Sargon nodded affably, "Good morning Guerion. We apologise that you have been disturbed but this buffoon will not release us. No doubt you will do so now and we can all go to bed and make the best of what is left of the night."

"Perhaps I will," replied Guerion. "But unlikely, I think. It is not up to me to decide such things. I am merely here in a fact finding capacity until the camp commander returns. Since men under your command have previously come under suspicion, Andoran, I think I must proceed with caution." He looked around, "Would anyone like to tell me what happened?"

Once the natural reaction of everyone to talk at once had been quelled, one of Sargon's soldiers glanced at his companions before replying, "We were riding back to the encampment with these two," here he indicated the travellers, "when four of the soldiers around me suddenly blacked out and slumped on their horses. Then I felt a pain in my head and next thing I knew, I was lying on the ground with the others lying all around me."

Captain Guerion raised his eyebrows, "I see. And I believe that all but one of the horses were found, tethered to nearby trees. Is that correct?" When he had received confirmation from one of his own soldiers, he continued, "And what makes this even more peculiar is that we have here a small sack of valuables that was found at the gateway to the encampment." He nodded at the two travellers, "Do these belong to you?" He gestured for one of his soldiers to take the sack over to the injured men to show them its contents.

One of the men rummaged through the valuables in the sack before nodding, "Yes, sir, Captain. These are our things. Look sir, I can prove it." He drew out a locket, "This is…was my wife's. It has a strand of my hair in it." He faltered to a standstill. After a moment, he brushed the back of his hand over his face as his eyes misted with tears. "We were on our way to my wife's parents place to celebrate their thirtieth wedding anniversary." He shook his head, "I don't think I'd have the heart for it now."

"I am sorry you lost those you love, sir," said the captain quietly. "We will do whatever we can to help you." He turned back to Andoran and Sargon. "So, Andoran, what were you doing outside the encampment. You are not in uniform, I notice."

"No, I was off duty." Andoran shook back his red hair and gave a wry smile. "I thought I would go out and meet Sargon coming in, to tell him about a new card game that has just started up. I wanted him to hurry back to catch the start of it."

"And what happened to you?"

Andoran shrugged disarmingly, "To be honest, I'm not really sure. Much the same as happened to the patrol by the sound of things. And I woke up next to Sargon, tied to the gate."

"With these ill-gotten gains beside you," stated the Captain with no particular heat. "Hmm. So would you like to explain that to us?"

Andoran shrugged, "I have no idea how they came to be there…or why."

Sergeant Torgan cleared his throat, "Can I just say, Captain, that whoever has done this, has used the same technique that was used to knock out our border guards when the horses were stolen and the same technique that was used a couple of months ago to knock out those soldiers who were disguised as bandits that we apprehended on the Great West Road."

"Yes, thank you. That had occurred to me also. And that group of soldiers was under Andoran's command, as I recall… although Andoran himself was incapacitated at the time."

"Yes sir. I believe so."

Andoran frowned, "I thought we had cleared that up. Those men were disguised as bandits in order to investigate the activities of brigands in the area."

The Captain nodded a brief acknowledgement as he tapped his front teeth with his forefinger, "Hmm. Interesting." He whirled on Sergeant Torgan and asked suddenly, "And do we think that the bandits who killed this poor man's kin are the same people who knocked out our patrol and the disguised soldiers on the Great West Road?"

Torgan glanced uncertainly at his men before bringing his eyes back to meet the Captain's, "I wouldn't have thought so, sir."

Captain Guerion began to pace slowly and thoughtfully back and forth. "So, that would mean we have a group of bandits out there preying on the travellers and another group who rescued the booty from these bandits, knocked out an entire patrol and Andoran, without killing anyone, and returned the booty." He shook his head, "None of this makes sense. We need more information. Is anyone else missing from the encampment?"

Although he was not looking directly at them, the Captain did not miss the look that passed between Sargon and Andoran at this question. He forbore to comment on it and instead, issued orders for a roll call.

It took a good couple of hours to work out who should be in the encampment and then to organise soldiers to check off the occupants of the tents against their expectations. Only when all the men had reported back to Captain Guerion, did it become clear that twenty soldiers were missing.

"Right, Sergeant Torgan! These men must be found. I don't care whether they are off duty or not. I want a systematic search made of the surrounding area, working your way gradually outwards from the encampment."

"In the darkness, sir?"

"Yes. Dawn is at hand. So it will not be dark for long. Besides, you might struggle to find one man in the dim light but twenty should be hard to miss unless they are deliberately hiding, in which case they could be miles away by now anyway." As the men left to carry out his orders, Captain Guerion turned to Andoran and Sargon, "I am sorry for this. It could be a long wait. I can offer that you exchange your bonds for imprisonment within someone's shield, if you prefer." When they nodded, he produced a knife that he placed carefully in Sargon's hands before stepping back and waving to one of his more magically powerful soldiers to place his shield over the suspect pair.

When they had freed each other, Andoran stood up, rubbing his wrists and pacing the short distance within the orange shield. He frowned and looked down at his arms, "Look at this! I have scratches all over me. Whoever did this must have dragged me through holly and hawthorn."

"I'm the same," responded Sargon.

Captain Guerion shook his head, "But despite that, whoever did this, didn't kill you when they could have. Now why would that be, I wonder?"

"I must say I'm amazed at that myself," replied Andoran, although he clearly remembered Danton saying that he would be given over to be questioned so that his squad's activities could be exposed.

Three long hours passed before the search spread wide enough to find the deserted house on the edges of the forest, its back door guarded by a pile of dead men. With no one alive left to protect it, the house passively revealed its secrets. Uniforms and bandit disguises hung side by side in dressing rooms. These could have been explained away by clandestine operations to capture the real bandits. But the cupboards, filled with jewellery, money, silverware and other valuables provided incontrovertible evidence that the soldiers had themselves been engaged in highway robbery.

CHAPTER 60

It was almost dawn before the woodfolk with Danton felt that they were far enough away from the encampment to be safe. They had hoisted the injured sorcerer up onto the horse, glad that he was not conscious to feel the jolting on his broken wrist. Throughout the journey, Danton had not so much as stirred.

While most sorted out shelters, two were posted as lookouts and Autumn Leaves and Running Feet led the horse off, to tether it well away from their chosen firesite before backtracking to make sure its tracks had been obscured. The woodfolk were so worried about Danton that they made sure that two people stayed with him at all times; one to keep constant check on his breathing and the other to make sure the first stayed awake. Everyone was dog tired after the long hours of lying in wait, the sorties with the sorcerers and then their long-winded, desperate efforts to keep Danton alive.

Those who slept woke to a windy, profoundly grey day. They sat hunched against the cold around a cheerless fire.

"We can't go yet," said Waterstone. "We have to give the others a chance to sleep first. And we don't want to split into smaller groups in case the sorcerers react badly to our gift of Andoran and Sargon."

"I agree," replied Lapping Water. She stood up and poured cups of tea before adding, "And I think Danton should travel in easy stages, if at all."

"Hmm. Maybe we should just wait here and let Tarkyn do the travelling," suggested Creaking Bough, as she accepted a cup from Lapping Water.

Waterstone shrugged, "We'll see. From what I gather, Stormaway and Summer Rain have decided that he needs time to recover after spreading himself too thinly through the forest to reach Danton last night."

"Can't he just put his hand on a tree?" asked Creaking Bough.

Waterstone shook his head, "No, apparently Tarkyn became too much a part of the forest last night and needs time to make sure his own boundaries are firm before he draws on the forest's strength again."

Thunder Storm gave a gentle snort, "Of course, how anyone knows what they are talking about, I have no idea. Stormaway seems to make it up as he goes along."

"Very true." Waterstone smiled, "But he must have felt quite strongly about this because I gather he risked a stand up row with Tarkyn in order to make him stay put for a while... Tarkyn did take over an hour to return to his body last night, you know. I think they were nearly as worried about Tarkyn as we were about Danton."

Autumn Leaves ran his hand tiredly through his hair, "These sorcerers… They take a lot of work, don't they?"

"They certainly do at the moment," conceded Thunder Storm. "But usually you can't fault Danton. He takes his fair share of everything we do. And in the attack against Andoran and Sargon, he did more than anyone."

"He did." Lapping Water sipped her tea. After a moment, she asked, "Did you hear what he was saying to Andoran yesterday?"

"About our exclusive membership, you mean?" Running Feet reached over to a pile of wood to grab another branch for the fire. "Yes. And his belief that we only allow him to travel with us because of his value to Tarkyn… Hmm. I wonder if that's true?"

"Of course it's not true," exclaimed Autumn Leaves hotly. "We don't weigh up the value of people like that."

"And yet," persisted Lapping Water, "what right would Danton have to stay with us, if for some reason, Tarkyn were no longer with us?"

"He wouldn't want to stay with us," replied Autumn Leaves. "He would want to go with his liege."

Lapping Water folded her arms. "You are dodging the issue. What if Tarkyn died? Then what? Danton would feel bereft. Would we then kick him out because he could be of no more use to Tarkyn? And is that truly all we think of him? "

Finally, she had Autumn Leaves backed into a corner.

"No. Of course it's not," he answered. "How could we turn away someone who has shielded us against the shade of Pipeless and against the people of the Lost Forest? …someone who risked his life and reputation to help us rescue the captured woodfolk from the encampment?"

"And worked with Tarkyn to turn back Journeyman and his posse?" added Running Feet.

"And how egalitarian are we if we only accept a prince as one of us but not his liegeman who has supported us every inch of the way?" pursued Lapping Water.

Autumn Leaves recoiled under the barrage. "I don't know why I am scoring the brunt of your argument. After all, I'm the one who said to him, 'We'll make a woodman of you yet.'"

Lapping Water gave a sad smile, "But he knew you were saying that rhetorically. Remember? He said, 'I wasn't brought up fearing woodfolk as you were, fearing sorcerers.' Then he said, 'Anyway,…' and trailed off. I think he was going to say, 'Anyway, I can't be one of you.' That's certainly what he told Andoran and Sargon.

"Hmph. You're right, Lapping Water," said Watersone, entering the conversation. "You know, Danton has become one of my best friends. We used to be forever sniping at one another about whose people should take precedence with Tarkyn but now we actually work together to protect Tarkyn from the pressure of having to be all things to all people." He frowned, "You know, all his life Danton has been taken for granted, not so much by Tarkyn, but by everyone else who engineered his employment as Tarkyn's whipping boy from the age of eight years old. And I hate to say it, but I think we have fallen in with Danton's assumption that he is of little account. It never even occurred to me until now to consider whether he should be granted membership of our community."

"And when you think about it," continued Running Feet, "he has added his power to Stormaway's and Tarkyn's to protect us over and over again. Now, for different reasons, both of them are woodmen. But he is not."

"And clearly he has no expectation of being offered that privilege," added Lapping Water.

Silence fell while they thought it through. Eventually Autumn Leaves said, "We will have to get a general consensus on it. That could be quite difficult when many people have not been there to see what Danton has done for us."

"Then we will have to argue forcefully on his behalf," said Waterstone firmly.

Chapter 61

Autumn Leaves and Thunder Storm were in the shelter with Danton when he first showed signs of coming round.

Autumn Leaves grasped his hand and leant over him as his eyelids fluttered. "Hello Danton. It's all right. We're here. You're safe," he murmured.

A slight crease appeared between Danton's eyebrows. He didn't open his eyes but Autumn Leaves saw his whole body gradually tense up.

Autumn Leaves glanced at Thunder Storm before continuing his litany, "Don't worry. You are safe. No one is going to attack you. Andoran and Sargon are far from here. Your wrist is broken. That is the pressure you can feel on your left arm. Just relax. As soon as you are ready, we will give you something to eat and drink."

Danton's body gradually relaxed but the frown didn't disappear. He slowly opened his purple eyes and gazed up at Autumn Leaves. Then he closed them again and shook his head fretfully from side to side before suddenly reopening them and asking faintly, "Who are you?"

Autumn Leaves recoiled as his whole perspective on the situation changed. Suddenly he, a woodman, was in the presence of a dangerous sorcerer who, without prior knowledge of him, might decide to attack.

Thunder Storm put a restraining hand on his brother's arm and took over. "Hello Danton," he rumbled in his deep soothing voice, "How are you feeling? Feeling a bit confused, are you? Don't worry. You've been hit by a sorcerer's power ray but you are over the worst of it now. You remember Autumn Leaves, don't you?"

Danton half shook his head and frowned harder, "Maybe. I don't know. I'm not sure."

"Don't worry, Danton. It will come back to you. And I'm Thunder Storm, in case you've forgotten me as well. There are a few more of us outside. You know all of us. You are among friends. So don't fret. Just give yourself time to recover. It will come back to you when you've been awake a bit longer."

Autumn Leaves' voice appeared in Thunder Storm's head saying dryly, "You're making it up as you go along, just as much as Stormaway does."

Thunder Storm gave a mental chuckle, "Oh, much more than Stormaway. At least he is learned in healing and magic." Aloud, he said, "Here Danton, have something to drink."

Between them, they raised Danton enough to drink.

"Do you want be propped up or stay lying down?" asked Thunder Storm, but one look at Danton's strained face answered his question for him. "No. I think lying down for a while longer."

The blonde sorcerer breathed a sigh of relief as he was lowered back down. He lay with a frown puckering his forehead, as he tried to make his fuzzy mind work. He did not feel threatened by these people but equally he did not feel safe because he didn't know where he was or who they were. There was something else he didn't know, but every time he came close to it, his mind shied away. He heard the two voices talking above him.

"Danton. Are you all right? Has he passed out again, do you think?" rumbled the deeper voice.

Danton made an effort and managed to give his hand a little wave. He felt so heavy and tired.

"Look. He can hear us," came the rustling voice. "I think he just needs to rest still."

A while later, Danton opened his eyes to find two new people leaning over him. He frowned, trying to chase memories that flitted through his mind. His purple gaze moved anxiously from one to the other, "Do I..." He coughed, his throat parched.

When Lapping Water and Waterstone had given him a drink, Danton ventured, "I know you, don't I?"

Lapping Water smiled, "Yes, Danton. You do. And everyone here knows you. We have been looking after you since the sorcerer Andoran hurt you with his magic."

Danton thought carefully for a minute, "And how many of us are here? And are we safe now?"

Waterstone smiled strongly, "There are thirteen of us, including you: the eight of us who were with you when we attacked the house and the other four who dealt with Sargon's parol. And yes, we are safe here, Danton. We are deep within the forest where none but other woodfolk can find us."

"Hmm." Danton mulled this over. Then he made a decision, "I think I would like to come outside. Is it safe for me to do that? I want to see everybody. I need to get my bearings."

"Are you sure? You are still very weak," said Lapping Water.

Danton became fretful, "Yes, I must come outside. I must. Please. You will have to help me but I have to see everyone."

In answer to a mind call from Waterstone, Autumn Leaves and Thunder Storm turned up to help carry Danton. Danton gave them a faint smile. "Hello. That's handy that you two showed up right now. Could you help to get me outside?"

Waterstone and Autumn Leaves' eyes met.

"Something not quite right here," came Thunder Storm's thoughts. "He's forgotten about mind talking."

Lapping Water listened in but made no comment, "Come on Danton. Maybe when you see the others, everything will fall back into place."

Once outside, they laid him up against a tree, swathed in warm cloaks. He still had dark hollows under his eyes, his face pinched with pain and unhealthily pale. His purple eyes scanned slowly back and forth around the small gathering of woodfolk. Every now and then a flicker of panic would cross his face.

Creaking Bough brought him some thin soup and helped him to drink it. "There is some more comfrey in that soup Danton. Your arm is wrapped in a comfrey and willow compound but I'm sure it is still quite painful."

Danton merely nodded briefly in acknowledgement.

Twig Snap leaned over to whisper to her brother, "Now that is stoic," not realising that Danton was concentrating hard to hold himself together against the severity of the pain.

Leaf Fall smiled at her, "You don't want stoic. You are quite happy with your soppy sorcerer just the way he is."

Twig Snap grinned.

When he had finished the soup, Danton thanked Creaking Bough and said, "I think I will just sit here quietly and watch, if you don't mind."

The woodwoman patted his arm. "Good idea. Give yourself time to get your thoughts straight."

Because he was with them, the woodfolk meticulously spoke out loud to include him. Only when he was napping did they use any mind talk. But even though he felt safe with them, for a reason he couldn't fathom, Danton was desperate to cover up the extent of his memory loss. So, between catnaps, he listened carefully and re-learnt everyone's names. From what they were saying, he tried to piece together what had happened and where they were going.

From time to time, one of the woodfolk would come over and make sure he was all right and give him more to drink but they didn't press him to talk. By mid-afternoon, the need to stretch and to relieve himself prompted Danton to throw back his coverings and stand up. This was a little awkward using only one hand but quite manageable. He waved away any offers of assistance and stood quietly for a few moments while his head pounded in response to the exertion, before heading a little way off into the trees.

When he returned, he picked up his cup and walked straight over to the fire. With a slight smile, he said, "Waterstone, could you please pour some tea into this? At a push, I could do it myself but I'm likely to splash boiling water all over the place at the moment if I try to aim for a cup on the ground."

"Of course," Waterstone eyed him as he poured the tea into his cup. "Feeling any better? How's the head?"

"It's all right as long as I don't make any sudden movements. Thanks." Danton placed his cup on the ground and sat down next to Waterstone. "How urgently do we need to get back to the others? I think I'm up to walking as long as we rest every now and then."

Waterstone looked at him a little strangely. "You can go on the horse. I don't think anyone expects you to walk until you are more fully recovered."

"Oh." *Blast*, thought Danton, *Got it wrong the first thing I say.* "I didn't know there was a horse." He frowned, "We don't usually have horses… do we?"

"No Danton," replied Lapping Water. "You're right. We don't. This is a sorcerer's horse that we took to carry you on when you were unconscious. He's still tethered a short distance from here. So you will be able to ride him again. We just have to be careful to obliterate his tracks as we go."

"And it is not too urgent that we return to Tarkyn," put in Autumn Leaves. "The main urgency revolved around getting you to him so that he could heal you, especially when you were still unconscious. We have set your broken wrist under instruction from Stormaway and Summer Rain but it would be better if Tarkyn could repair it."

Danton nodded abstractedly, trying to work it all out. "Oh, well, that's all right then, isn't it?" After a few moments' thought he said, "Do you think we could wait until tomorrow morning to leave? I don't want to hold everyone up but I do still feel a bit wrung out. Still, if you put me up on a horse, I expect I could manage if we have to leave now."

Waterstone looked quizzically at him, "I'm not surprised you feel wrung out. I have never known anyone come closer to dying than you did last night. No need to rush. I think we could all do with a rest after the events of yesterday."

After a slight hesitation while Danton worked out that he couldn't be expected to know what happened when he was unconscious, he said, "I'm a bit vague about what happened. Can you tell me?"

"After Andoran hit you, you stopped breathing. We had to take turns in giving you our breath for ages…and keeping your heart going… for well over an hour." Waterstone patted him on the back. "We really thought we'd lost you, Danton. It was so scary. Eventually, the strength of the forest saved you…with Tarkyn's help."

Danton raised his eyebrows. "Did it?" He placed his hand against a nearby tree and nodded casually, "Oh yes. Now you mention it, I can feel its strength." He was busy concentrating on the tree and so missed the woodfolk's looks of astonishment. "Hmm. There's a storm coming in an hour or two. So it probably isn't a good idea to head off now, if we don't need to, is it?"

Waterstone blinked at him, "Bad storm, is it?"

"No. Not awful. But we'd just be better out of it than in it." Gradually, Danton realised that everyone had stopped what they were doing and were staring at him. "What? What have I done?"

That question, more than anything else, showed them how confused Danton really was.

"Danton, no one can predict the weather from touching a tree." said Waterstone gently. "Perhaps you can feel the breeze on your face and it is making you think of storms."

Danton looked around at the sea of concerned faces and took his hand slowly away from the tree. "Perhaps that is what it was," he said slowly. In his mind, he could see distant trees bending as a heavy wind rushed through them. He knew the storm was coming but he wasn't prepared to uphold his view against a group of strangers, particularly when he was trying to blend in and appear normal.

An hour later, the late afternoon sky darkened as the first of the storm clouds rolled into view. Danton stood up, "I think I will head off for a rest in my shelter. I don't want to have to run through the rain." He leant his hand against the tree for balance as he looked up at the darkening sky. "I'll come back out to join you for dinner in a couple of hours. It will have passed by then."

As he lay down in his shelter, the first heavy drops of rain fell.

CHAPTER 62

When he awoke, Danton could hear the occasional drip of water falling from leaves above his shelter but the storm had moved on. It was nearly dark but he could just make out a figure sitting in the corner. He studied him through half closed eyes until he worked out who it was.

"Hello Waterstone. What are you doing in here?"

The woodman emerged from the shadows to sit closer to the sorcerer. "Hello. I am just keeping an eye on you. None of us knows much about head injuries and even less about the effects of sorcerers' magic. So we want to make sure you are all right."

A flicker of panic crossed Danton's face as he remembered how confused he still was.

Waterstone frowned, "What is it?"

Danton considered telling Waterstone but the thought of fully confronting the void in his mind made his stomach turn over. Instead, he opted to tell him of the flashbacks he was having. "I keep seeing a flash of red spearing towards me. And a face filled with hatred behind it. Then it goes black. It replays over and over again." But at least it stops me from thinking about anything else.

"That's Andoran hitting you with his magic," said Waterstone. "Don't you recognise him?"

Danton did not want to lie to this man but he couldn't face a discussion about his memory. So he said, hazarding a guess, "I think it is his expression that makes him look so different. I wouldn't have seen that expression on his face before, would I?"

"No. Probably not." Waterstone considered him in silence for a while before saying gently, "Danton, I can tell that all is not as it should be with you. Don't feel you have to cover it up. But also, don't feel that you have to talk about it until you are ready. Just tell me, tell us, that you don't want to reply. We will understand."

Danton breathed a sigh of relief. "Sorry." Another flicker of panic crossed his face, "It's too frightening. I just can't deal with it yet."

Waterstone restrained himself from asking what 'it' was and said quietly, "When you are ready, we will be here." His tone became brisker. "So, are you coming out to join us for dinner?"

As he helped Danton up and out of the shelter, he relayed their conversation to the others, adding mentally, "I'm not sure how much Danton remembers but I suspect, not as much as he's is pretending to.

Just fill in his knowledge when he needs it without commenting on his lack of memory."

"Another seat of the pants medical decision," chortled Thunder Storm in his mind.

"Any better ideas?" asked Waterstone dryly.

"No. Go with that for the time being."

The conversation that evening wandered through plans for the summer, the recent wedding of Falling Rain and Tree Wind, and their run-in with Andoran and Sargon. For the most part, Danton listened and learned but then he asked a question that stopped everyone in their tracks.

He had been frowning as he listened to the tales of banditry and murder that had taken place along the Great West Road. Finally, he said slowly, thinking he was safely on objective political ground, "I can see that this is very wrong, and unfortunate for those sorcerers who use the Great West Road. But I don't see why we are concerning ourselves with the fortunes of sorcerers. Why don't we just stay deep in the woods and mind our own business and let them mind theirs?"

There was a silent chorus. *He thinks he's a woodman.*

Hard upon that came the realisation that Danton must have no idea who Tarkyn was either. Despite the woodfolk's best intentions, the conversation jolted to an abrupt halt.

Danton looked around at the silent faces, panic growing inside him. "Oh no! What have I said wrong? I didn't mean to sound hard-hearted. It's just that sorcerers have all that powerful magic. Look what happened to me."

Waterstone was the first to recover, "Yes. They are certainly difficult to deal with. I think we will have to be more careful in future. But I think the discussion about why we concern ourselves with sorcerers might be better dealt with another day, Danton. The answer is long and complicated, and too much for this time of night."

A flash of comprehension crossed Danton's face as he realised that Waterstone was protecting him from delving too deeply. "Oh. I see. Thanks."

After this, the conversation was kept strictly to the immediate practicalities of bedding down for the night, posting new lookouts and planning for the onward journey on the morrow. After a short debate it was decided that although Danton did not need anyone to stand vigil over him, Waterstone would bed down in the same shelter as a precaution.

CHAPTER 63

By the time the bodies of the twenty soldiers and the contents of the house had been returned to the encampment, Colonal Charford had been summoned back from his furlough by an emphatic but courteous letter from Captain Guerion.

Colonel Charford was tough. Unlike Guerion, he knew the secondary reason for the encampment was to gather forces to back Jarand's quest for the throne but his commitment to restoring law and order was genuine. He demanded loyalty and discipline from his men and he had already had words on a few occasions with Andoran and Sargon about their casual attitude. He was not a party to Andoran and Sargon's little scheme and would not have wanted to be.

Consequently it was an outraged camp commander who confronted the two miscreants.

"So, you two, this is how you serve your prince and country, is it?" barked Charford. "Preying on hapless travellers whom you have been paid to protect? In all my years of soldiering, I have never come across such perfidy."

Sargon protested, "But why do you include me in this? I was on patrol when this last group of travellers was robbed. I found the survivors and was bringing them back to the encampment when we were attacked."

Andoran threw him a glance of pure derision but in fact, for all their faults, each of them was loyal to the other and they both knew that if Sargon could talk his way out of it, he would be in a better position to help Andoran escape.

However, the Colonel was not so easily misled. "You may drop the play-acting, Andoran," he said scathingly. "I know perfectly well that you two are as thick as thieves about everything. If one is in it, then so too is the other." He turned to the soldier who was holding his shield over them, "I have no intention of wasting unnecessary manpower on such vermin. They deserve no such courtesies from us. I want ten men around them with arrows or power shafts at the ready. Then you may release your shield and retie their hands. They have besmirched the name of Prince Jarand's forces and will hang for it." Gesturing to Captain Guerion to accompany him, the Colonel walked from the tent saying as he went, "Send word to Lord Davorad for his authorisation. I expect he will want to witness this, to set an example for the men. Prepare the hanging for dawn, the day after tomorrow."

Once outside the tent Colonel Charford turned to Torgan and Guerion, "This hidden group who knocked out Andoran, Sargon and the patrol without killing them; do we think they are responsible for the deaths of those twenty men at the deserted farmhouse?

Torgan shrugged, "If not them, who? But I don't know. This group has never killed before, as far as we know."

The Colonel raised his eyebrows, "Perhaps they were as outraged as we are. Or perhaps there was disagreement among thieves. But if that is the case, one faction was far more skilful or prepared than the other." He nodded at Guerion, "Your opinion?"

Captain Guerion scratched his head then smoothed his hair back into place before replying. "If one were being generous, one could surmise that this group, whoever they are, put Sargon's patrol out of action while they attacked the corrupt soldiers…This would imply two things. Firstly, that they are averse to killing innocent people and secondly, that they are virtually on our side. " He shook his head, "But why did they not kill the disguised soldiers that they left for us to find by the roadside last time?"

"Perhaps they left them to our justice and when those soldiers were allowed to go free, took the law into their own hands this time," suggested Torgan, carefully keeping his voice respectful.

"And how does that explain the raid on our encampment when the horses were stolen?" asked Colonel Charford. "Since the guards were knocked out then in a similar fashion to Sargon's patrol, I'm assuming they are somehow connected."

Torgan gave a slight smile, "Maybe they are not *always* on our side."

The Colonel gave a grunt of laughter, "You may be right, Sergeant Torgan. Perhaps they are only taking our part in clearing out these vermin among us, to protect themselves and their own nefarious trade, as much as anything. But why did they attach Andoran and Sargon to our gates with the booty? Why not just kill them with the others? Or are these two, in fact, not involved?"

The three of them lapsed into silence while they thought about it. Eventually, Sergeant Torgan cleared his throat before suggesting, "Perhaps they wanted to make sure we knew about it. Perhaps they wanted us to have Andoran and Sargon as proof of what was happening… so that we could question them."

The Colonel waved away that suggestion, "But the contents of the house bear clear witness to it."

"Maybe they didn't realise that." Torgan shrugged, "And would we have found the house if Andoran and Sargon hadn't been delivered to us? If we hadn't been trying to solve a mystery, we may not have searched so assiduously for the missing men. After all, men decamp from here all the time."

"Good point, Sergeant. I think these people, whoever they are, want to see us mete out justice to these two. And I think you're right, Sergeant. They have provided these two as proof and they are expecting us to question them, uncover the full extent of their activities and then hang them." Captain Guerion sighed. "This whole affair sickens me, Colonel. After all, who is to say that all the accomplices are dead? There may be many more within our ranks who were a party to this practice."

The Colonel scowled, "Take Andoran and Sargon to a tent on the north side, away from the travellers and new recruits. Then, I want answers from them. I want to know who else is involved and I want this camp cleansed."

Chapter 64

It was nearly midnight when Lord Davorad; cold, angry and tired rode into the encampment, his white clothes spattered in mud. He waved away offers of food but grabbed a glass of red wine that he slugged down in one draught before demanding to see the prisoners. As he strode across the breadth of the encampment, his white cloak flying behind his stocky figure, and a gaggle of anxious attendants in his wake, Colonel Charford and Captain Guerion fell in beside him.

"So tell me," barked Davorad, "What have these wretched men told you so far?"

Colonel Charford shook his head, "Very little, sir. They were insistent on speaking to you first. Personally, I believe the evidence of the bandit's house condemns them anyway, but I want to make sure that there are no other soldiers involved. We cannot have these sorts of activities among the ranks. It must be stamped out." He hesitated, "Because they were so insistent that you would wish to see them, I have not yet used any forms of inducement on them. I have told them they will hang the day after tomorrow but of course, that will require your endorsement. There is plenty of time in the interim to force the truth out of them, if they refuse to cooperate."

"You have done well, Colonel and have my complete support, and that of the Prince. In fact, Prince Jarand has somehow got wind of this situation and is sending some of his troops up from Tormadell to support our quest for justice." He glanced sideways at the Colonel, "Much as we value his support, I need hardly emphasize that the perceived need for his intervention does not reflect well on our operations. So, I am pleased that you have the situation in hand. However, I believe we must await the arrival of the Prince's troops so that they may oversee, or at least witness, the hanging. I understand they are due to arrive sometime on the day after tomorrow. So I suggest we reschedule the hanging for the day after that. Give the troops time to get their bearings and settle in first."

Colonel Charford felt his stomach tighten at the thought of the Prince finding his service inadequate. Knowledge of Captain Harkell's fate after the Prince's encounter with his brother had spread far and wide through the Prince's service. "Of course, my lord. It will make no difference if we delay the hanging by one day."

They came to a halt outside a large white tent.

"Here we are, sir," said Charford, holding back the flap to let Lord Davorad inside.

Davorad stopped. "They are bound, are they not?" When the Colonel nodded, he continued, "Then I will see these men on my own in the first instance. They obviously harbour some groundless belief that I will support their cause. Until they see me alone, with no witnesses, they may continue to harbour that belief. As soon as I can put paid to that idea, the sooner your men will be able to extract the information they need. Agreed?"

The Colonel frowned a little uncertainly, as he nodded.

"Agreed?" repeated the lord sharply.

Colonel Charford snapped a salute, "Yes sir."

"Good. Take your men out and withdraw with them until I call for you. Stay within view of the doorway and within earshot of a shout. Clear?" Without waiting for a response, Lord Davorad entered the tent and stood in silence until the guards left.

As soon as he was alone with Andoran and Sargon, he shouted, "You men are a disgrace to your uniforms. Do not expect any quarter from me." He strode over and slapped Andoran and Sargon, one after the other, across their faces before slamming his hand down hard twice on a table. Outside, a discreet distance away, the guards glanced uneasily at each other at the sounds emitting from the tent.

As Andoran and Sargon grimaced with pain, Davorad leaned forward and hissed, "What on earth were you idiots doing, getting yourselves caught like that? And I suppose all the spoils have been confiscated, have they? Blasted pests, you are."

He straightened up and roared, "I will not allow this reprehensible behaviour to flourish in my encampment," before leaning forward and demanding quietly, "What have you told them?"

Andoran and Sargon shook their heads. "Nothing, my lord."

"Not yet," added Andoran.

"What do you mean, not yet?"

Andoran shrugged, "It depends on what they do to us and what inducement we have to stay quiet."

Davorad belted Andoran hard across the face and slammed the table again for extra effect. Then he hit Andoran again from the other direction. Despite the charade, the groans that could be heard by the guards were real. Andoran glowered at Davorad from beneath his shock of red hair, blood running from a cut on his lip. To his annoyance, he found his vision was beginning to blur.

"I will give you one chance," hissed Davorad, "in return for which you will keep your mouths shut about our arrangement. Because Jarand is sending troops to see justice done and to make an exhibition of you, I cannot kill you and I cannot allow you to escape before they arrive."

With malicious glee, he hit Sargon across his face, bloodying his nose before giving the table another good belting. Then he bellowed, "Take that, you dogs! Betraying your honour like that! You should hang your heads in shame!"

Davorad held up a tiny, wickedly sharp dagger before pushing it out of sight down the back of Sargon's trousers. "My men will guard you closely. If you attempt to escape before Jarand's troops arrive, you will be given no quarter. I want nothing to tie my visit to your escape. But once you are under Jarand's guard, you may take your chance."

He raised his voice again and roared, "Now, you *will* tell me who else was involved or your last days on earth will be a sea of pain."

He smiled, "Once more, I think," and backhanded each of them hard across the face before pulling his gloves out of his belt and whacking them on the table with a loud thwack. He raised his eyebrows and smiled even more broadly, "That was a good one. I should have thought of that before." He leaned in and whispered, "You will have to betray a few men to show good faith." He shrugged, "Take your pick. It doesn't matter who is sacrificed as long as my name is kept clear."

He straightened up, eyed the battered men and said in a conversational but carrying voice, "Yes, very satisfactory, I think. So, are we clear? You will tell them who else was involved. And do not expect another visit from me."

With that, he tucked his gloves back into his belt and strode out of the tent without a backward glance.

CHAPTER 65

Early the next morning, Danton and Waterstone were woken by the sound of hoofbeats. They scrambled out of the shelter in time to see Tarkyn, mounted on Boravar's great warhorse, and Ancient Oak, mounted on a beautiful bay mare, cantering into the clearing. Midnight was perched in front of Tarkyn, and Sparrow in front of Ancient Oak.

As they pulled up their horses, Danton dragged Waterstone behind a tree, "Oh my stars!" he exclaimed, "That's a sorcerer out there. What's he doing with woodfolk? Do you think he saw us?"

Waterstone grasped the panic-stricken sorcerer's arm, "Danton, Danton. Be calm. Not all sorcerers are bad."

Before he could say any more, Tarkyn appeared around the side of the tree, towering over them. "Danton, my friend. I am so glad to see that you are up and about." Tarkyn's intention of hugging his friend in greeting was halted by the alarm that flared in Danton's eyes. Tarkyn stopped dead, "Danton, it's me. Tarkyn."

Danton threw Waterstone a look of reproach, "You forgot to mention that your healer friend was a sorcerer."

Waterstone carefully placed his arm around the back of Danton to keep him from running off. "Danton, it's all right. We would not allow you to be placed in a dangerous situation. Tarkyn is quite safe."

As Waterstone glanced apologetically at Tarkyn, Danton twisted away from him and made a dash for the nearby trees. Without a second thought, Tarkyn murmured "*Shturrum*," dropping Danton in his tracks.

Waterstone rolled his eyes, "Oh good. That will reassure him then."

But Tarkyn was already moving to squat beside his friend, grasping his arm gently just above the broken wrist as he waved away the spell. "Danton. I do not know why you fear me suddenly, but I give you my word I will not hurt you. I have come to heal you, not to hurt you." He frowned in confusion at the fear in Danton's eyes, "Danton, don't you know me? I am your lifelong friend."

A look of consternation swept across Danton's face before his eyes rolled up in his head and he blacked out completely.

Waterstone came to stand beside them. "Well, that could have gone better," he said prosaically.

Tarkyn straightened up and stood with his hands on his hips looking down at Danton. "What did I do to make him fear me?" he asked eventually.

"Nothing, Tarkyn. You did nothing wrong." He clapped the young sorcerer on the back. "Come on. Let's move him to somewhere more comfortable. There are twigs and rocks sticking into him everywhere here. Then you can at least repair his wrist before he wakes up. I'll explain as we go."

Tarkyn gave him a slight smile, "You'd better greet that daughter of yours first. She's dying to see you. Send someone else to deal with Danton and I'll see you in a minute." He waved his hand, "On second thoughts, I'll just move him myself."

Muttering "*Ka liefka*," the sorcerer prince lifted Danton into the air and drew him carefully along to land gently on a flat spot at the firesite.

As soon as he had released the spell, Lapping Water walked up and put an arm around his waist, "Hello. Creating havoc as soon as you get here, I see."

Tarkyn put his arm around her and kissed her in greeting, "Yes. Looks that way."

Tarkyn did not waste time on giving or receiving explanations, preferring to take the opportunity to repair Danton's arm while the blonde haired sorcerer still lay unconscious. As soon as the mending was complete, Ancient Oak and he were deluged with questions.

"Where did you get the other horse?"

"Why are you travelling with so little protection?"

"How's Boravar?"

"How are our children?"

"Orolan lent us the bay," replied Tarkyn. "Boravar and the children are all fine. We took a slight chance so that we could get here more quickly." He added sardonically, "Because I had cooperated with Stormaway's *request* that I wait to gather my forces, I was *permitted* to travel light to make up time."

Ancient Oak chuckled, "There is only so far you can push an anxious liege lord, we discovered."

"And why did you bring Sparrow and Midnight?" asked Creaking Bough.

Tarkyn smiled sheepishly, "Because I had undertaken to look after Sparrow and I always keep Midnight with me."

Ancient Oak looked around, "So now that we have satisfied your curiosity, it's time you satisfied ours. What on earth is going on with Danton?"

"He's lost his memory," said Leaf Fall baldly.

"It's worse than that," put in Lapping Water. "He thinks he's a woodman. He's completely confused."

Tarkyn raised his eyebrows, "And how did he come to that miscomprehension?"

Waterstone shrugged, "He woke up among us and assumed he was one of us. We only realised late last night. I don't know what's happening to him but he isn't ready to deal with it, whatever it is. So much so that he has been desperately pretending to us that he knows what's going on when, in reality, he is struggling to keep his head above water."

Tarkyn frowned, "But does he know who you are?"

"He knows our names," said Autumn Leaves slowly. He thought back over the events of the day before. "He didn't know who I was when he first came round, though." The woodman hit his knee in realisation. "Oh the silly bugger! He doesn't have a clue who we are. He has just sat there and carefully learnt everyone's names so he could pretend he did. After all, how could he know who we are, if he thinks he is one of us? He's trying to figure out his past."

Waterstone shook his head, "No. I think he is trying to fit into his present as he finds it, and trying to avoid the fact that he can't remember his past. That's what he's so scared of. He doesn't know who he is."

Tarkyn shook his head as he looked down at his friend, "Poor Danton. And look! His blonde hair is all singed and blackened in the spot where he was hit." He leaned forward, "And he has a scar. Oh well. That's the least of his worries. His hair will grow back over it in time."

"Hmph. I don't think he has figured out yet that his hair isn't light brown and his eyes aren't green," said Thunder Storm. "I fear for him. I really do. We will have to handle this carefully."

"What do you suggest?" asked Tarkyn.

Waterstone gave Tarkyn a sympathetic smile. "I don't think you should go into his mind with him fearing you as he does at the moment."

"Can you heal his mind, even if you did?" asked Thunder Storm.

"I don't know. I certainly don't know how to, but I could give him the strength to help him to heal himself, if it's just physical."

Beneath their gazes, Danton began to stir.

"Tarkyn," said Waterstone, "I think you should withdraw to the other side of the fire until we can reassure him. Do you agree?"

"Yes, yes, I agree," he replied tetchily. After a moment, the prince smiled wryly, "Now I know how Danton felt when he searched for me all those months and I greeted him with suspicion."

Waterstone swept his arm around, "At least you have all of us. Danton didn't."

"He does now, though," said Lapping Water firmly.

Tarkyn glanced from one to the other, sensing an undercurrent in that exchange that he was not a party to. Any question he might have had was forestalled by a groan emitting from Danton. So he removed himself quickly to sit with his arms linked across his knees on the other side of the fire.

Waterstone made sure he was leaning over Danton, blocking the view of Tarkyn when the blonde sorcerer first opened his eyes. "Hi Danton. We lost you again for a while there."

Danton blinked to clear his vision and then frowned, "Something's changed." He looked down at his arm. "My arm has stopped hurting. It was hurting quite badly before. I could hardly sleep last night. And now the pain's gone." He dropped his head back, "How strange."

Waterstone smiled, "No, it's not. Tarkyn healed it for you."

Alarm flared again in Danton's eyes. Waterstone was glad that his body was blocking Tarkyn's view.

"Now that I've seen him," whispered Danton confidingly, "every time you say that name, it's like a big gong going off in my head. He scares the life out of me."

Lapping Water smiled at him, "I don't think it's Tarkyn you are scared of it. It is what he represents."

"Ooh. Hello." Danton swivelled his head, "Oh. We're out near the fire, are we? I thought we were in my shelter." He returned his gaze to Lapping Water, "I don't understand. What do you mean, what he represents?" Suddenly panic flashed in his purple eyes, "No. Don't bother answering that. I don't want to know."

After a glance around at the assembled group, Waterstone drew a deep breath and took the plunge, "It's all right, Danton. *We* know who you are. We know you have forgotten, but the knowledge is safe with us… and with Tarkyn."

Danton just stared at him, horror struck. Suddenly he scrabbled up into a cross-legged seating position and began to rock backwards and forwards, hugging his arms around himself, "Oh no! That's what I forgot! That's the worst thing I forgot. I don't remember anything much, you know. I don't who you are, you realise?"

Waterstone nodded, "We know. It's all right, Danton. We know."

Danton continued as though he hadn't spoken, "But what I really forgot was that I don't know who I am. I didn't want to remember that, you see. It's a bit too worrying. It was easier to deal with the fact that I didn't remember who you were."

Creaking Bough walked slowly over to him and offered him a cup of tea.

"Here, Danton. Don't panic. We will help you to get your memory back." She placed one hand on his back and waited until he had stopped rocking and unwrapped his arms. Then she handed him the cup before squatting down next to him and stroking his back in long slow calming movements. "Your name is Danton, you know. It is Danton Patronell in full."

Danton eyed her sideways as he sipped his tea. "My name is not a sound of the forest like yours…is it?"

"No, Danton. It is not."

"I don't think I like where this is going," he said querulously. "I think that is enough information for now."

After a while, Autumn Leaves began gently, "Danton, I know you remember the sorcerer who attacked you. He was evil, wasn't he? But not all sorcerers are like him. What about the families that travel the Great West Road? They are just ordinary folk like us." He threw a wry smile at Tarkyn as he continued, "We have many friends now who are sorcerers. You remember only the worst of them but there are many others."

"What about Midnight?" suggested Thunder Storm. "Maybe he would be a good introduction."

Sparrow and Midnight skipped over together from where they had been playing to stand in front of Danton. Danton looked from one to the other of them over the rim of his cup but said nothing.

"Hello Danton. I'm Sparrow. Remember me? I'm Waterstone's daughter. Ancient Oak and Tarkyn are my uncles."

Danton frowned in confusion.

"And this is Midnight. He's my friend and he's a sorcerer…well, a half-sorcerer, anyway."

In response to a mental prompting from Sparrow, Midnight waved his hand in greeting. When Danton didn't respond, the children looked at each other, uncertain what to do next.

After a minute, Midnight pointed to himself, Sparrow and Danton and then wrapped his hands around each other in his gesture for friendship.

"He is telling you that we are your friends, Danton, and you are ours," said Sparrow. "You and I played in the snow together when we were sad? Remember? When I was missing Dad and you were missing Tarkyn."

At last Danton roused himself to reply, "I'm glad we are friends. And Midnight seems a friendly little fellow, even if he is a sorcerer."

Sparrow looked at him a little strangely, "But you are…"

"*Thank you* Sparrow," intervened Waterstone. "Enough. Off you go and play now."

As the children left, Danton smiled sadly up at Waterstone, "It's all right. I may have absolutely no memory but I'm not stupid, you know. I'm a sorcerer, aren't I?"

Waterstone let out a breath and smiled warmly, "Yes, Danton. But we all love you, regardless of whether you are a sorcerer or a woodman."

Danton gave a whimsical smile, "Well, it must be true that you think not all sorcerers are bad, because you have all been very kind to me." He put down his cup and put his hands over his head, "Ow. My head hurts. It is too full of too many thoughts and I don't know how to stop them."

Gradually he became aware of a stream of warmth, calm and strength flowing gently into his mind, slowly soothing its turmoil. Seeing his puzzled frown and discovering its cause, Waterstone smiled, "That, if I am not mistaken, is the work of Tarkyn."

Danton glanced at Waterstone, "And this Tarkyn...he is someone like me, isn't he? A sorcerer. So do I have amber eyes?"

Waterstone's smile broadened, "No Danton. Yours are purple. I would not say you were alike, any more than Thunder Storm and I are alike but yes, you are both sorcerers."

"Oh. And he said he was my lifelong friend, didn't he? I remember him saying that, just before I blacked out. That's what shocked me so much. A sorcerer being my lifelong friend didn't fit with anything I had already worked out." Danton rubbed his hands back and forth across his face. "Ugh. This is so hard." Suddenly he reached a decision and sat up. "Well, where is he, this Tarkyn? I had better not neglect him if he is my friend and has come especially to heal me. At the very least, I need to thank him for what he has done."

Waterstone moved to one side, revealing Tarkyn sitting on the other side of the fire.

"I am here, Danton." Tarkyn spoke quietly, in a tone of voice that said he would always be there if Danton needed him.

Danton took a breath and resisted the temptation to look away. After a moment, he gave a little smile and said, "Pleased to meet you."

A slow grin spread across Tarkyn's face. "I suppose that is how it must seem to you. And do you know who I am?"

"Oh yes," replied Danton confidently, glad to be on safe ground. "You're their best healer. There are two other healers, Stormaway and Summer Rain. But you are the best."

Tarkyn nodded slowly, wondering how on earth to proceed. "Actually, they know more than I do, but I have a special healing power that neither of them possesses."

"...which has something to do with the forest. Correct?" Danton smiled, pleased to be able to show how much he had already picked up.

"Correct."

"If I place my hand against a tree, I can feel that power," confided Danton. "I don't know that I can draw on it, but I can feel it."

"Danton predicted the arrival of a storm last night," said Autumn Leaves dryly.

Danton glanced at Autumn Leaves, "They don't believe me but we shall see. I will try it from time to time and see if it works."

Tarkyn frowned in incomprehension, "See if what works?"

"Feeling what is happening in other parts of the forest through my hand on the trunk of a tree."

"What? Everything? Or just big things?"

Danton smiled self-consciously and shrugged, "I don't really know. I've only tried it once…well twice actually. I predicted when the storm would arrive and then I checked how long it would last. But it was all part of the same thing, if you know what I mean."

Tarkyn was beginning to realise how much respect usually underlay all of Danton's interactions with him and he found it unsettling to have Danton speaking to him so casually.

"Anyway," Danton was saying, "I gather I owe you my thanks…and my friendship, by the sounds of things. I'm sorry I don't remember you. But you're in good company. I don't remember any of these fine people either." He frowned, "But it seems a bit worse really, doesn't it, if we are lifelong friends…" He pondered for a minute, "So how did we meet? Do we come from the same village? Did I learn healing too?" He gave a shy smile, "I feel so foolish, asking all these questions but how else will I learn who I am?"

Tarkyn hesitated. He really didn't want to tell Danton that his father had virtually sold him to the palace to be used as Tarkyn's companion and whipping boy. "Danton, my friend. I think there are some questions that are better left unanswered. There are some things in your past…our past…that are better left to surface on their own, over time."

Danton's face fell, "But how can I find out who I am?"

"I will undertake to tell you, if your memory does not recover, but not now. Why don't we concentrate on talking about who you and I are now?"

Danton waved his hand dismissively, "Well, I know who you are. But I must say I have no idea why either of us is living with the woodfolk, if we are sorcerers."

"The short answer is that I have been exiled and you, loyal friend that you are, came to find me."

Danton's eyes grew round, "Wow. Exiled! What did you do?"

Tarkyn looked beseechingly at Waterstone. At the moment, he couldn't bring himself to tell Danton who he really was. He felt that Danton had enough to cope with, without dealing with how to behave around royalty. "I was set up, Danton, and during my escape from custody, several guards were killed." As he saw Danton's eyes widen, he added hastily, "But none by my direct hand."

Danton cocked his eye at Autumn Leaves and gave a little grimace as though to say, 'Did you know about this?'

Autumn Leaves grinned, "It's all right, Danton. We know all about Tarkyn's past."

"Everyone does," added Lapping Water.

"Hmm," Danton gave Tarkyn a cheeky little grin, "Must have been quite a scandal then."

"You could say that," said Tarkyn dryly.

"Hmm, you must have really pissed someone off to set you up like that. Pinched someone's patient, did you?"

Tarkyn gave his head a little shake, struggling to keep up with Danton's misapprehensions. "Uh no. It was more that someone thought I might be going to steal something"

"Stars above, Tarkyn! Setting you up on a mere suspicion is a pretty ruthless reaction, I would have thought. What sort of people are we dealing with here?"

"Ruthless people," said Waterstone firmly, "with a lot to lose. Now come on, young man. Stop hounding Tarkyn. You don't need to know everything straight away."

"Oops, sorry. It's just that I have so much I need to re-learn." He glanced at Waterstone, "Can I just say one more thing to Tarkyn?" When Waterstone nodded, Danton took a breath and said very seriously, "You say you are my lifelong friend and although I don't remember that, I do know you healed my arm and that, two days ago, you and these people between you, saved my life. So I would just like to say that whatever you have done and whoever comes looking for you, you can count on me as your friend."

Tarkyn blinked in bemusement, feeling as though he had just been bestowed a gift of charity. "Thank you Danton. That is very kind of you."

Danton smiled benevolently, "Don't mention it." He let his eyes wander around the company, the smile gradually fading from his face, "And now, I might just retire for a little while. My brain needs time to think."

CHAPTER 66

A scrabbling noise at the doorway of his shelter alerted Danton to someone's arrival just as the brush screening was pulled back. "Danton, may I come in?"

Danton rolled over to see Twig Snap's anxious face, outlined by her frizzy hair, in the doorway. "Yes, of course you may."

He sighed heavily, preparing to pull himself together to be sociable.

Twig Snap came close and sat down cross legged next to him, "I can see you are very despondent that it turns out you are not a woodman. But it is not so very bad. I am planning to marry a sorcerer, you know. His name is Boravar and you helped to save his life."

"Did I?"

Twig Snap nodded and went on to tell him about it.

Danton ran his hand through his hair, "Your Boravar may be nice but this Petrand character sounds ghastly. It seems that for every nice sorcerer there is a bad one."

Twig Snap gave a little smile, "Well, to tell you the truth, before I met Boravar, I hated all sorcerers with a passion. My life's ambition was to kill one. But now I know several sorcerers whom I like a great deal, you being one of them."

"Just as well you like me, by the sound of things," said Danton dryly.

Twig Snap chuckled, "Yes, it is, isn't it?"

Danton face clouded over again, "But Twig Snap, from what I've seen of you woodfolk and Tarkyn, woodfolk seem much friendlier and easy going. Are all sorcerers like Tarkyn?" He scratched his head. "I don't know. He seems friendly enough but there is an aura of power around him. He seems more reserved, somehow, than you people. I almost get the feeling that there is some danger attached to him" He frowned, "It's hard to explain... but for all his avowals of goodwill, I think it would be dangerous to cross him."

Twig Snap thought carefully before answering. Outside, they had reached a mutual consensus that it should be left to Tarkyn to explain who he was, when the time was right. Finally she replied, "I don't think you could say that Tarkyn is a typical sorcerer. For a start, he is far more powerful than most sorcerers." Twig Snip gave herself a little pat on the back for the ambiguity of that remark. "And you're right. You wouldn't really want to cross him but saying that, he is one of the kindest people I know. And he worries about everyone. And he risked his life for you two days ago and on at least one other occasion, I gather. And for Boravar."

"He is a dedicated healer, isn't he?"

"Yes, among other things. But give yourself time to get to know him. He can be intimidating on first acquaintance but you could not ask for a more passionate, caring friend."

Danton raised his eyebrows, "Is that right? Then I should count myself privileged that he considers me his friend, I suppose."

Twig Snap smiled, "Don't worry. I was scared witless when I first met him. He can be quite formal when he's not sure of his ground but he becomes more easy-going when he gets to know you." She leaned forward and patted his hand, "And don't worry about what sorcerers are like. It only matters what you are like."

"No. Not true. It matters a great deal to me what sorcerers are like if I have to live with sorcerers and not woodfolk," retorted Danton.

"Oh Danton, you can stay with us as long as you like. We all agreed that, even before we knew that you had lost your memory."

Danton's face relaxed into a smile, "Did you? Oh good. That makes it easier then, if I don't have to rush off and learn how to fit in with a whole new group of people."

Twig Snap tugged on his arm, "Come on. Come outside and be with us all. I'm afraid the down side of woodfolk is that we are very sociable. So you will never last for long, mooning around on your own." Just as she headed towards the doorway, she turned back and said, "Oh, and one more thing that you might find interesting. Lapping Water is going to marry Tarkyn. So he can't be too bad."

Twig Snap emerged with a little smile of triumph, and a mind message saying, "Mission accomplished!"

Danton emerged behind her to find Ancient Oak waiting for him, "Danton, can you help me find a safe place to tether the three horses, so we can feed them and brush them down? I suspect you have more knowledge of horses than I do."

From then on, for every hour of the day, there was a task waiting for him, not too strenuous but always with someone, so that he didn't have time to think too hard or to wander off on his own and become morose. By nightfall, he was almost legless with fatigue. As Running Feet asked him to accompany him to collect some wood, Tarkyn intervened, "I think that will do. Danton is not yet fully recovered. Let him sit with me for a while until dinner is prepared."

Danton watched Running Feet head off with Lapping Water instead, feeling a little guilty.

Seeing his expression, Tarkyn said, "Don't feel badly, Danton. Unlike me, you always pull your weight. No one wants you to overtax yourself but they do want to make sure you feel included." Tarkyn picked up a stick and started breaking bits off the end of it. He looked up at him to find Danton's eyes on him with a puzzled frown on his face. Tarkyn smiled, "Do you remember this? I have always done it."

"Maybe. It seems familiar."

"Danton, the rest of our company will join us here in two days' time. Before they arrive, I would like to spend some time on my own with you tomorrow. Will you agree to that?"

"I'll see how I feel in the morning. I don't want to stray too far from these people. I feel safe with them." Seeing Tarkyn look taken aback, Danton gave a slight smile, "What would I normally say?"

Tarkyn grimaced, "What you would normally say isn't relevant at the moment, for a host of reasons. But to assuage your fears, if you will agree to spend some time with me, I will agree not to take you beyond the view of the lookouts."

"I'm sorry. I didn't mean to suggest that I mistrust you. Obviously the woodfolk hold you in high esteem and you have been my friend for years, apparently. And yet there is something about you that unsettles me. It is almost as though you hold life and death in your hands." He shrugged, "Perhaps it's because you are a healer. Or perhaps I feel safer with the woodfolk because they are the people who were here when I first woke up and they seem more familiar. But I will agree to go with you. It would be churlish of me not to, when you have done so much on my behalf."

"Thank you," replied Tarkyn unable, for the life of him, to keep a certain dryness out of his voice.

"I've upset you now. I can tell."

"No, not exactly. But let's just say that you are not the only one struggling with your lack of memory."

Danton smiled, "Huh. I suppose not."

Later in the evening, Waterstone pulled Tarkyn aside, "So when are you going to tell him? You will have to do it before the others arrive. Even now it is hard to maintain."

"I will tell him tomorrow sometime. But first, I want to spend time with him before he knows." Tarkyn grasped the woodman's arm in excitement, "Don't you realise? He is possibly the first person I have ever met, who doesn't know who I am. For everyone else, even you, I am inextricably linked with my role."

"String and Bean didn't know who you were."

"Only for a few minutes. But Danton is so confused, he hasn't a clue."

Waterstone frowned, "Be careful Tarkyn. I can see you or him getting hurt in all this. What if he doesn't like you? All those years you spent with him could turn to bitter dust."

"Yes, possibly." The prince thought for a minute, "No they won't. They still stand, quite separate from this. Our previous friendship is based on shared experiences but it is very much the friendship of lord and liegeman. Tomorrow, I may find out how someone really reacts to just me and sow the seeds of a new, more equal friendship at the same time."

Waterstone blinked, "Tarkyn! That doesn't sound like you."

Tarkyn laughed. "I didn't say equal, I said more equal. There are limits." He chuckled, "I don't know whether you've noticed, but Danton has been treating me with a casualness that would shock him to the core, if his real self knew he was doing it."

"And is it shocking you?"

"Yes. A bit…well, quite a lot actually," answered the prince, incurably honest. "But it has made me realise how careful Danton usually is around me. And I'm not sure that I still want that… at least not to the same degree."

"Well, whatever you do, be careful with him. Don't let him learn a new reality and then make him realise that he has it all wrong again. I don't think he'd cope. He's right on the edge as it is."

"I would not put my interests before Danton's in this instance. I know, in the normal course of events he would expect me to, but I promise you, I will not toy with his mind." Tarkyn looked at the woodman and frowned, "I shouldn't have to tell you that."

Waterstone smiled reassuringly at him, "You don't. I'm just anxious about him, that's all. We all are."

"With just cause." Tarkyn gave a wry smile, "To be honest, I have no idea how I'm going to broach the topic of my identity, and his, with him. And will he remember anything of the expectations of royal etiquette? I presume he has forgotten his whole life at court along with the rest." The prince patted Waterstone on the back, "But don't worry. I will make no demands on him until he is well again." He chuckled, "Even if my poor royal soul is shocked to the core by his cavalier treatment of me."

Waterstone just smiled and shook his head.

CHAPTER 67

"Where is that brother of mine?" shouted Kosar. "I want him here! NOW!" The King waved a missive that had just been borne to him on the leg of a fat wood pigeon. "How *dare* he disobey me?"

Servants went running in all directions to find the king's brother. Into the mayhem, the queen mother entered, watching the rushed departure of so many servants with faint amusement.

"You two fighting again, are you?" she asked, with a twinkle in her eye. "You know, I always naively thought that the pair of you would grow out of it. "

"Mother! This is no laughing matter. Jarand has gone against my express wishes. He has gone too far this time."

"Come on, tell me. What is the problem, dear?"

Kosar stabbed at the letter with his forefinger, "This! This is the problem." He flicked the torn letter at his mother with its attached note which read:

Dear Kosar,

I write to express my gratitude to you.

I am so pleased that you have graciously condescended to look after those people from the Forest of Yesterday, Today and Tomorrow. You will be delighted to know that Jarand, too, has taken their plight to heart and is providing for some of them.

It occurs to us that you might expect us to take the Lost sorcerers off your hands. Unfortunately we believe it would be a futile gesture on our part, since all of the Lost sorcerers, their friends and associates know that they can trust you with their friends' welfare. We are also aware that, being a man of generous nature, there are so many more people whom you could easily visit with your munificence in the future. Such generosity can only be admired and I would not dream of interfering with it.

It is heart-warming to see that both you and Jarand are looking forward to working more closely with me. I will feel much more secure about Eskuzor's future if the three of us are willing to develop a relationship that can lead us into a new era of cooperation.

(Tarkyn had chuckled to himself as he had penned that last phrase and read it out to Rainstorm.)

Your brother
Tarkyn.

The queen mother put her hand to her cheek as she handed back the letter, "Oh my! How our little Tarkyn has grown! He could be a visiting monarch from the tone of his address." Kosar flicked her a suspicious glance, wondering whether she knew about the sovereignty of the forests, but she met his eyes guilelessly. "What is it, dear?" she asked. "I can admire his writing style without supporting him against you, you know."

Kosar was saved from replying by the appearance of his brother who bowed stiffly in the doorway and did not enter until the King nodded his consent.

"I believe you wished to see me, Your Majesty?"

Before replying, the king turned to his mother and said, "I beg your pardon, ma'am, but I am afraid I must discuss this with my brother in private."

Kosar waited until his mother and the servants had departed before thrusting Tarkyn's letter under Jarand's nose.

"What is the meaning of this?" he demanded. "I stated explicitly that the Lost sorcerers were not to be used to lure Tarkyn into custody."

Jarand scanned the letter briefly, noting that the reference to the doings of Andoran and Sargon had been removed, but not knowing by whom. "And I have not done so, Sire."

"Don't talk rot, Jarand! Your letter clearly states that you have taken two Lost sorcerers into your keeping."

"That is true, Sire, but not with the intention of luring Tarkyn out of the forest as you so clearly proscribed. I merely felt that a gesture of goodwill was needed on my part to show him that I too have the best interests of Eskuzor at heart." Jarand drew forth a similar letter from his inside pocket. "And I believe you are also wishing to demonstrate your charity towards these people. Very kingly of you, Sire."

Kosar became almost apoplectic with rage, "How dare he share the king's private correspondence to him with a third party?"

Jarand coughed, "I could say much the same myself."

"Is nothing sacrosanct?" fumed Kosar.

"Apparently not, Your Majesty."

"Oh, stop being so formal, Jarand," said Kosar irritably. "There is no one here to hear you."

Jarand gave a nod of acknowledgement, knowing that Kosar would have been just as displeased if Jarand has used his name without permission.

Suddenly Kosar gave a bark of laughter. "Huh! So, our little brother has outwitted the pair of us, hasn't he? By showing each of us the other's letter, he has cancelled out any advantage either of us may have hoped to gain."

Jarand raised his eyebrows, "And he has made it clear that he is not as soft as we thought he was and will not, in fact, make any attempt to rescue these Lost sorcerers."

"His logic for that is impeccable, though, isn't it? That we could turn round and take any number of hostages in their place."

Jarand walked to the window and looked out over the palace gardens, "I don't think he would naturally act so logically. He is too passionate for that. I think he is taking heed of some very canny advisors."

"Quite possibly." Kosar read through the letter again, "And look at this! He is threatening us with a public outcry if we do anything untoward with these Lost sorcerers." He waved his hand disparagingly, "Well, that threat is so much hot air, as far as I'm concerned. My popularity is quite sufficient to withstand a minor scandal like that."

"Oh yes. So too is mine," agreed Jarand.

"However,…" they chorused and stopped.

Kosar folded his arms and frowned, "However, I can see no point in holding on to these Lost sorcerers anyway."

"Well no. Exactly my thoughts."

Kosar scowled, "That blasted brother of ours has us behaving like a pair of marionettes. It will not do, Jarand."

"No. It most certainly won't." Jarand's eyes sparked as he thought about Tarkyn's thinly veiled demand for him to sort out the soldiers who had been preying on travellers. Thinking of the torn letter, he wondered if Tarkyn had, despite his word, sent Kosar word of his soldiers' activities. After a bit of thought, he decided to cover himself by raising the subject himself.

"By the way, Kosar, I should draw your attention to the fact that a small troop of my soldiers will shortly be leaving Tormadell to ride ahead to my encampment. Although they will naturally apprise everyone of your imminent arrival in order to prepare for such an honour, they are more particularly charged with sorting out a small disciplinary matter that has arisen."

"Is that so?" The dryness of Kosar's tone made it clear that he thought the disciplinary matter was just a cover. Tarkyn had kept his word, after all.

"Yes, Kosar. It *is* so. Two of my officers and some of their men have been indulging in a little banditry of their own on the side, I believe. Naturally, they will be dealt with harshly."

This revelation had an unexpected consequence, "On my word, Jarand! Tarkyn was more accurate than I realized. If lawlessness has spread to soldiers, there must be a serious problem out there." He nodded approvingly. "You do well to act hard and fast. This must be stopped at all costs." Kosar looked thoughtful, "Hmm. I can see that I will have to gather widespread reports on the criminal activities around the nation."

Jarand cursed himself for having unnecessarily brought to Kosar's attention something that had now fired his interest in quelling lawlessness. '*Blast Tarkyn!*' he thought savagely, "*If I'm not careful, he will undo everything I have been working towards.*"

To Kosar he produced a slight bow, and said, "I would be honoured to assist you."

Chapter 68

The sun streamed through the trees on the following morning. Not a leaf moved. Woodfolk and sorcerers were sitting around the fire, finishing off their breakfast. The grass around them was still damp with dew and shining droplets hung from the leaves.

Danton placed his hand casually against a tree and said with a little grin, "No storms on the horizon. So we won't get wet." After a moment, he added, "Hmm, interesting. There is a column of mounted soldiers just turning off a large road onto a smaller track in that direction." He nodded towards the west.

"That will be near the encampment," said Running Feet.

Tarkyn decided to take Danton at his word, "Hopefully, that will be Jarand's soldiers riding to sort out Andoran and Sargon and the bands of soldier-bandits." Seeing the uncertainty in Danton's eyes, he added, "We sent Prince Jarand a letter alerting him to what was happening among his troops so that he could address it. We didn't want it to appear that we were slaughtering his soldiers indiscriminately."

Danton's eyes narrowed as he thought this new information through. "Well, I hope this Andoran and Sargon are still there, when these troops arrive."

"So do I," said Running Feet. "We left them tied with their booty but they are such slippery eels they may find a way to talk their way out of it anyway."

"Especially if they are clandestinely working for someone higher up," added Tarkyn.

"They will get their just deserts this time, one way or another," said Waterstone with grim certainty. "We are very angry about what they did to you, Danton," he glanced at Tarkyn, "...and to Tarkyn... and Autumn Leaves. It took a lot of restraint on our part not to kill them there and then."

Tarkyn nodded approvingly, "I can imagine it did. You all did very well!"

Lapping Water saw Danton look at Tarkyn a little strangely after this exchange, "Careful Tarkyn," she said, "I think your wig is slipping, so to speak."

Tarkyn looked around at his liegeman and smiled, "Come on Danton, we had better get going before things get too complicated around here."

Danton nodded, "Right. I'll just finish my tea and we can head off. If you get together a few things to take with us for lunch, I should be ready by the time you are."

There was the slightest moment where everyone stilled with shock before the conversation rolled on. Tarkyn's eyes narrowed but luckily Danton was peering into his cup and by the time he looked up, Tarkyn had himself in hand.

"I will sort out the lunch for you, Tarkyn," said Lapping Water, realising that Tarkyn probably had no idea how to put a lunch together, not to mention wouldn't want to. "Perhaps you should make sure your little Midnight knows where you are going."

"Thank you," said Tarkyn briefly. He stood up and walked a little way from the fire before signalling to Midnight. Immediately the little boy responded by running over and jumping up into his arms. Tarkyn smiled down at him and sent him images to explain what was happening and that he would be back in a few hours. As Midnight pushed out his bottom lip and threatened to make a scene, Tarkyn quietly placed his hand on his heart and then tapped his finger on the end of the Midnight's nose with a warm smile. Midnight huffed but eventually placed his hand on his heart and gave a reluctant smile in return. Tarkyn gave him a big squeeze and set him down. He looked up, "Little one will cope until I get back. Are we ready?"

Lapping Water presented him with a full rucksack as Danton shook out his cup before standing up. "Right. Let's go."

As they strolled through the trees and out into a small bright meadow, Tarkyn said, "I thought you might like to relearn some of your sorcerer skills and perhaps revise your elite guard training. After all, you are a very powerful sorcerer and one of the best fighters in the kingdom."

Danton raised his eyebrows, "Am I? Hmph. Well, after seeing what that Andoran did with his fighting prowess, I'm not sure that I think that's a good thing."

"You are not like Andoran, Danton. Think about it. All those woodfolk back there know how much power you have and yet feel quite safe with you among them." Tarkyn smiled at him, "And in the past, you have used your power to protect them." He hesitated before saying, "We have all come to depend on your support in one way or another."

"Have you? Hmm. Well, that's nice." Danton gave a little smile, "I can't be too bad then."

Tarkyn chuckled, "No, not too bad at all…although you can't trust what I say. I'm your oldest friend. So I'm bound to be prejudiced."

Danton looked at him, "So, if you're a healer, are you any good at fighting?"

Before he could help himself, Tarkyn exploded with laughter. "Whoops. Sorry." Danton just waited, frowning quizzically until Tarkyn had recovered himself sufficiently to say, "Sorry Danton. You just caught me by surprise." He grinned, "Yes, I'm not too bad." He managed to become a little serious. "But you're better with knives and tracking and camouflage. I haven't had elite guard training as you have. In fact I never use any weapons except magic. I have practised a bit with the woodfolk's slingshots but I can't see the point really, when I can just use my power."

"So why don't we have a duel then? That would be fun, wouldn't it?"

"Do you know what you're doing with your magic?" asked Tarkyn.

Danton grinned, "No. No idea. So you'd better show me first."

Tarkyn thought back, "As I recall, the last time you practised using your power, you displayed all the subtlety of a charging bull. Rainstorm was trying to coach you to vary your power so that you could knock people out without killing them but with minimal success."

"Oh. So, a duel might be a bit dangerous then?"

"Nothing a good shield couldn't fix," replied Tarkyn flippantly, "But let's firstly spend a bit of time reminding you what you can do."

Tarkyn perched the rucksack under a tree and then moved to stand a few yards from Danton.

"Firstly, a shield." Tarkyn swept his hand around him and enveloped himself in a bronze haze.

Danton's eyes narrowed, "There's something about that colour. It's important for some reason."

"Well, I am the only person who has magic this colour and you found me by seeing it in the clouds. So, if nothing else, it is important to you because it is my magic's colour," suggested Tarkyn.

Danton frowned, "Not that sort of important." He waved his hand, "Oh never mind. Right. Now, I'll try."

Danton waved his hand and produced his aqua shield. He looked around himself in distaste, "Oh, your shield's a much stronger colour than mine. Aqua! Yuk!"

Tarkyn laughed, "There's nothing you can do about it. You're born with it. I don't mind it. It's quite a fresh, peaceful colour. Mine looks muddy half the time."

Danton put his hands on his hips in disgust, "I don't want to look fresh and peaceful if I'm in the middle of a fight. What sort of message is that giving my opponent?" When Tarkyn couldn't answer for laughing, Danton raised his eyebrows and demanded half-seriously, "Stop standing there guffawing, and get on with teaching me how to do one of those power rays that nearly killed me."

Tarkyn blinked and then smiled to himself at the shock of being addressed so peremptorily, "Oh my word, Danton. You don't know what fire you are playing with," he murmured ambiguously. "Very well, let's move on. Release your shield and wait here for a minute."

Tarkyn found a few rocks and set them up along the top of a fallen tree. When he returned to Danton, he said, "Now, watch this." He murmured, "*Fierspa!*" and sent a bronze shaft wafting through the air to move a small rock a few inches backwards but not off the log altogether. "Now that is a gentle ray of power. See if you can do it. Just think of a little trickle of power releasing through your hand."

Danton promptly sent forth a fearsome stream of aqua that knocked a good sized rock flying.

Tarkyn rolled his eyes, "Stars above Danton! I said a trickle, not a deluge. You're an absolute menace!"

"It's quite fun though, isn't it?" Danton's eyes were shining with excitement.

"Yes, I have to admit it. Power is fun." Gradually a grin spread across Tarkyn's face, "Come on then. Let's have some fun and see who can send a rock the furthest."

In rapid fire, they sent one rock after another hurtling off the log into the grass behind. When Tarkyn's final turn came, he took a quick breath, and sent a mischievous glance at Danton as he focused his full power onto the last hapless rock. The rock shot up on a bronze stream, arcing through the air, to land with a distant thunk somewhere within the tree line.

Danton raised his eyebrows, "Wow! That was a great shot." He turned eyes brimming with laughter on Tarkyn, "You have been holding out on me, Tarkyn. You're miles more powerful than I am."

Tarkyn grinned, "It's more a matter of focus. And maybe you're still weak from your injury…"

Danton snorted, "Huh! You don't believe that for a minute."

"No. True, I don't." Still smiling, Tarkyn patted Danton on the back, "But I do know that you shouldn't expend too much power while you're recovering. So perhaps we had better have a short break before I show you any more."

As they sat picking their way through a selection of dried fruits, Danton said, "Twig Snap was right, you know. She said you became more easy-going once you had relaxed with someone. You're quite good fun actually. I didn't expect that when I first saw you."

Tarkyn brushed the last of the dried fruit from his hands, glancing at Danton, "Remember today in times to come. For reasons you will understand later, it is a very special day for me… and I think, for you."

Danton stared at him, "What are you talking about? You've come over all melodramatic on me. It's certainly a special day for me. If I don't get my memory back it's the second, no, the *third* day of my life, as far as I'm concerned. When I have so few of them to remember, every day is momentous."

"I can't imagine that you won't get your memory back. It has to be in there somewhere. Do you remember anything at all?"

Danton's face tightened as he tried. Finally he shook his head, "No. You see, between me and the rest of my life is that horrendous vision of that hate-filled sorcerer spearing his bright red magic straight at me."

"Well," reasoned Tarkyn, "the blast can't have wiped out all your memory because that vision of Andoran comes before you were hit, doesn't it?"

Danton's face lit up, "Yes. Yes, it does. Maybe I will get my memory back, after all."

"Later on, I will give you some strength to help your mind to heal, if you like."

"Why not now?"

Tarkyn looked at his friend for a long time while he worked out what to say, "Because you and I have a lot of complications, not all of our making, between us. I just wanted the chance to see what sort of friends we could become without the preconceptions we grew up with."

Danton frowned, "And if I don't get my memory back, were you planning on telling me these preconceptions at any stage?" He did not sound pleased.

Tarkyn gave a gentle smile, "If you remembered me, you would know that I wouldn't be dishonest with you. I haven't been so far. I just haven't told you everything yet. I undertake to do so by the end of today." He shrugged. "Well, not everything. We have a lifetime of shared experiences to get through, but the main things I will tell you."

"That gives you a lot of power, doesn't it? Holding all that knowledge about me and choosing when and what to divulge?"

Tarkyn threw his hands up, "I beg your pardon. I did not see it that way. I will tell you everything you want to know straight away, if that is your wish."

Danton considered Tarkyn for several long seconds before eventually replying, "No. I must admit I am agog with curiosity about this complicated past of ours, but I can see that, for some reason, it matters to you to have this time where the past has no hold on us. And once I know about it again, there will be no going back, will there?"

"No. Although I am hoping that some of what we gain here today will carry forward into the future."

Danton shook his head, "You are too obscure for me. I will give you until we break for lunch. Until then, you can teach me all about our magic. Agreed?"

Tarkyn nodded, although his stomach tensed at Danton's authoritative tone. "Agreed. It's your memory. So you may call the shots...at least until lunchtime." With that, he muttered, "*Ka Liefka!*" and levitated the rucksack up into the air to land on a stump a few yards away.

Danton raised his eyebrows, "Ooh. That's interesting. Does that work on anything?"

"Pretty much. It takes more energy to lift heavier objects though."

Danton gave a wicked little grin, "Let's see how this goes, then." With a flourish, he pronounced, "*Ka Liefka!*" and shot Tarkyn ten feet into the air.

"Whaa! Blast you, Danton! Try for a little subtlety!" Tarkyn then lifted Danton, not quite as speedily, into the air until they were face to face ten feet above the ground.

"That was a bit feeble! No excitement at all in rising up so slowly."

"On the other hand," said Tarkyn dryly, "If I lifted you up too quickly, you might have taken fright and dropped me."

Danton chortled, "Good point." The blonde sorcerer looked down and around him. "Now what do we do? We are each in the other's power."

"It's a bit dangerous, actually." Tarkyn thought for a moment, "If you maintain your focus on holding me up, I will deposit you on the branch over there. Then you can do the same for me. Agreed?"

When they were both safely in trees, Tarkyn said, "Right. You can let go now. Now I'll show you how to lift yourself. *Ma liefka!*"

Tarkyn floated out into the open space beside the tree and waited for Danton to join him.

"So, can we chase each other?" asked Danton cheerfully.

Tarkyn laughed, "No reason why not, but be careful not to lose your focus. Stay fairly close to me in case something goes wrong. After all, your mind has been blacking out lately."

"True. Off you go then. I'll count to five and come after you." Danton dipped as he began to concentrate on counting, "Whoa. I see what you mean about keeping focus."

As soon as Danton came after Tarkyn, it was clear that he could move more quickly through the air than Tarkyn. Tarkyn stayed out of his reach by dodging sideways or vertically but it was not long before Danton caught him.

Suddenly, a large hawk swooped over them, checking to see that Tarkyn was not in trouble. Immediately Danton lost focus and plummeted.

"*Ka liefka!*" yelled Tarkyn, lifting Danton just before he hit the ground. Holding him in the air, Tarkyn descended slowly and landed them both gently on the ground.

Danton sat down, looking pale and shaken. Tarkyn sat next to him and offered him a drink.

"It's all right, Danton. I wouldn't have let you fall. I wouldn't have let you hold yourself up if I couldn't be sure that I could protect you. Your mind is too uncertain at the moment."

Instead of being grateful, Danton was angry. "You might have mentioned that earlier. And that bloody bird? That has something to do with you, hasn't it?" He shook his head in irritation as he tried to catch his fleeting thoughts, "I remember a huge eagle owl flying past us once and a whole bevy of eagles and hawks, gathered around you keeping people away from you." He shook his head again "No. It's gone. Blast!"

Tarkyn smiled ruefully, "I'm sorry Danton. I'm afraid that hawk was just checking whether I needed help."

Danton studied him, "So is this part of our complicated past?"

"No. This is more a part of our complicated present." Tarkyn took a breath, "I am a guardian of the forest. That is why I have such healing powers and why the forest protects me."

"I see," said Danton, clearly not seeing at all.

Tarkyn spent some time explaining the role and powers of a forest guardian.

"You have quite a lot of responsibility then, don't you?" commented Danton. "So that's why the woodfolk support you to sort out sorcerers… because you're supposed to be keeping an eye on the whole of Eskuzor, not just the forests. Is that right?"

"Yes. And if we don't stop civil war from erupting, it will end up invading the forests."

"So who's going to fight this civil war? Who is spearheading each side?"

Tarkyn looked at him and blinked, "You really have lost your memory, haven't you? Every last bit of it!"

Danton scowled, "Don't be mean. I'm doing my best. I get flashes now and again but that's about it."

Tarkyn patted him on the back, "Sorry Danton." He studied his liegeman, "I suppose, in order to answer that question, I am going to have to tell you who I am and how you fit into it all."

"Well, go on then. I've been dying to hear this all morning."

Tarkyn sighed. "The two protagonists of this civil war we are trying to head off are Kosar, King of Eskuzor and his twin Prince Jarand."

"And?"

"They are my brothers."

"Oh. I see," said Danton slowly. A little smile began to play around his mouth. "Well, that's interesting then, isn't it?" He waved his hand, "Just give me a minute. I need to think this through." After some careful consideration, he said, "You're pretty casual for a prince, I would have thought. Still, that would explain why you came across as so much more reserved than the woodfolk." After still further thought, he added sympathetically, "Hmm. That does make it hard for you then, doesn't it? I bet both your brothers think you're on the other one's side. Families are always like that, aren't they?"

Tarkyn goggled at him, at a complete loss on how to proceed.

"And so how do I fit into all of this?" asked Danton casually.

Tarkyn recovered himself enough to say, "You are my liegeman."

"Well, obviously. So, I presume, are all the woodfolk. I don't think that really answers my question."

The prince sprang to his feet and started pacing. In his mind, he had expected that their little game of equality would stop as soon as he revealed his true status to Danton. Tarkyn had been willing to concede a little, but true equality had never been part of his plan. And now he had no idea how to re-impose his expectations without pulling rank hard, and losing all the goodwill he had built up during the morning.

Danton watched him pacing up and down for a few minutes before asking, "What is so bad that you are so uncomfortable with telling me?"

Tarkyn turned and waved his hand, "I can't begin to explain it to you. It seems that a man without a memory lives outside the social mores of society. You seem to have no idea of what is owed your prince and liege lord."

"Well, how could I? Anyway, you're the one who has set up the expectations. I only have your behaviour to go by, you realise," retorted Danton crossly. "You're still the man you were half an hour ago. Knowing your heritage doesn't alter that. But if the rules of engagement have suddenly changed, tell me. I'm not a bloody mind reader, you know."

Tarkyn frowned, "Danton. You never used to be so irritable. Is this how you used to treat your fellow officers?"

"Oh for heaven's sake, Tarkyn! How would I know? All I can say is that I've never been this confused before, either." He scowled up at Tarkyn, "And now I can tell you're not happy with me and I have no idea how I'm supposed to act." He ran his hand through his hair and brushed the scar. "Ow! My life is becoming a total nightmare."

Tarkyn was instantly contrite. He threw himself down next to Danton and put his arm around his distressed liegeman. "I'm sorry, Danton. I told Waterstone I wouldn't impose any expectations on you until you are well again and I will keep to my word. I suppose I am just shocked at how little it matters to you that I am a member of the royal family when both of our lives until now have revolved around that fact."

Danton looked sideways at him, "I can't see why it matters. Being the guardian of the forest sounds much more important to me."

"If I didn't know better, I'd say you'd been talking to Rainstorm. That's exactly what he would say."

"There you are then."

Tarkyn smiled, "But woodfolk have never been part of sorcerer society nor acknowledged the authority of the royal family, whereas sorcerers do without question." The prince thought about Orolan's behaviour and what Waterstone had said about an institutionalised right to punish people and added, "At least, there are severe consequences if they do question it."

Danton frowned and pulled away, "Is that a threat? I can see now why I thought you held life and death in your hands."

Tarkyn looked at him in surprise, "No Danton. No, I was merely giving you a little sociology lesson. I told you; I won't place any expectations on you until you are well."

"So, everything changes, does it, when I get my memory back?"

Tarkyn scratched his head in perplexity, "Stop being so antagonistic. Everything will change then because you will remember how you have always acted around me…and it is not how you are acting now." He held up his hand, "And before you take issue with me again, let me say that the whole point of this morning was to give us a chance to begin a more equal relationship than we have had before…and for me to enjoy the company of someone who didn't know I was a prince."

"I am tempted to take umbrage at being used for your enjoyment and yet I think perhaps your wish to change the nature of our relationship weighed just as heavily with you." Danton gave a big shrug, "Ah well, let's forget all of that, shall we? It seems I have a moratorium until I get back my memory. So I think I will make the most of it. You don't mind if I call you Tarkers, do you?"

Tarkyn's eyes flashed, "Yes. I most certainly do." He belatedly realised that Danton was grinning hugely at him.

His liegeman laughed, "I may know you're a prince now, but I still don't know the limits and I suspect it may be fun finding out."

Tarkyn was visited by a vision of a huge, out of control puppy. He smiled wryly, "You will be interested to know that you have been testing my limits almost constantly since I arrived."

"Have I? And yet, I had you marked as someone who did not like to be crossed."

"I don't. But you have had enough to deal with. So even though your behaviour has unsettled me and even shocked me at times, I have stomped on my natural reactions."

Danton looked at him, "And your natural reactions would be… to do what?"

"To get angry. To tell you in no uncertain terms what I am prepared to put up with." A glimmer of laughter shone in Tarkyn's eyes, "And I suspect the woodfolk would tell you that I am naturally arrogant, haughty and disdainful. So I suppose some of that would show up in my dealings with you."

"Actually no woodfolk has told me any such thing. In fact, Twig Snap said no one could want for a kinder, more passionate, caring friend than you."

Tarkyn flushed with pleased embarrassment. "Did she?"

Danton nodded, smiling at the prince's reaction. Then he gave a short laugh, "But she agreed that you didn't like to be crossed." He lay in the long grass on his side, his head propped up on his hand, watching Tarkyn. After a minute he said, "You realise I may not get my memory back at all? Then you will be stuck with a liegeman who I suspect you think is not treating you with enough deference. What would you do then? After all, you have undertaken not to impose any expectations in that case and I have the strong impression that you are a man of your word."

Tarkyn shook his head a little in amazement, "Danton, my friend, you would not know yourself, if you met yourself at the moment. In answer to your question, I said I would not *impose* my expectations but I did not say that I would not let you know what they are. If, once you know them, you still choose to go your own way, I can see two courses of action open to me."

"Which are…?"

"Either I change my expectations or shun your company."

"Ugh." Suddenly, Danton went pale and clutched his stomach.

Tarkyn leant forward, frowning with concern. "What is it?"

"I just felt as though I had been punched in the gut." He smiled wryly, "I think you must be more important to me than I realised."

Tarkyn smiled reassuringly, "Danton, I have no fear that it would ever come to that. The whole point of today is for me to change how we work together," he waved his hand, "…but perhaps not quite as much as this."

Danton rolled over onto his back to lie looking up at the sky and chewing on a stalk of long grass. After a minute, he said, "Okay, now that I am totally clear, or as clear as I can be in the circumstances, I'll stop being belligerent." He glanced at Tarkyn, "I don't actually have a vested interest in making you feel uncomfortable. I like what I have seen of you today. The woodfolk obviously care for you and, judging by my gut reaction a minute ago, you and I must share some deep connection. So why don't you just let me know when something I do upsets you and we can sort it out as we go along?"

Tarkyn's face relaxed into a smile. "Thank you." The prince stretched himself sideways out on the ground, with his head propped on his hand facing Danton. "You know, the other night, when the last of your life was flickering and threatening to go out, I suddenly realised how much you meant to me and how devastated I would have been, had you died." He waved his hand, "And now, I am a stranger to you…and to a lesser extent, you are a stranger to me. Hmm, no. You are not a stranger but I am seeing parts of you that I have never seen before."

"But at least you know who I've been. I don't know anything about either of us."

And so, at last, the prince sat up, linked his arms across his knees and began to talk. "You came to me when you were eight and I was six. You were always so much older and wiser in my young eyes…and yet I held the authority. And you were kind and patient with me, beyond what was expected of you by my retainers…at least that is what I like to think… but I do think it was true. For my part, I thought I had never abused my authority, but now that I see you unfettered by our past, I realise how much deference I always took for granted." He gave a rueful smile, "After all, I was just a child and I suppose I ordered you around mercilessly. That's what everyone expected me to do and no one would have been there to take your part." He glanced with unusual shyness at Danton, "But, to tell you the truth, I absolutely hero-worshipped you and so I did my utmost to protect you from the unkindness of those around us."

Danton eyed him and then looked away into the trees, "Funny sort of relationship. Uneven in both directions."

"Yes, I suppose so. As we grew older, the gap between us seemed to narrow in terms of age but widened in terms of rank. But as I began to take more part in public life, you were there by my side, supporting me. You were always the one who kept me informed about the latest court intrigues. You could go to so many places that I could not. When a prince enters the room, everyone stops talking. But a lord has entree to every salon without becoming the immediate centre of attention."

Danton grunted, "I'm a lord, am I? The woodfolk forgot to mention that."

Tarkyn laughed, "That's because they don't care."

"Hmm. And here we are now, in the middle of a forest. What on earth did you do to get yourself arrested? I would have thought a prince could get away with nearly anything."

"A shaft of my power went wide in the final of the Harvest Tournament and knocked one of the spectator stands. My brothers used it as an excuse to get rid of me."

"The *final* of a *tournament*? You are a dark horse, aren't you? A tournament fighter, no less. No wonder you laughed your head off when I asked you whether you could fight! And did you win?"

Tarkyn laughed, "Yes. I beat the sorcerer who injured you."

Danton nodded approvingly. "Excellent!" After a minute, the other half of what Tarkyn had said, sank in. "Did you say your *brothers* used it as an excuse? Oh, I see. In fact, now I think about it, it's obvious, isn't it? Only the King could exile a prince. So those ruthless people Waterstone was talking about are your brothers, I take it?"

When Tarkyn nodded, Danton asked, "So were they just quicker off the mark than you? Would you have done them, if they hadn't done you first?"

Tarkyn eyes flickered with anger, "Do you mean, am I just as ruthless as them but a bit stupider?"

Danton held up his hand, "No. Don't tell me. I've overstepped the mark, haven't I?"

"It is not that so much. It is more that I am offended that you might think me so lacking in integrity." Tarkyn shrugged, "But since, to all intents and purposes you have only just met me, I suppose you cannot know my calibre. And although I would like to think my integrity shines forth on first meeting, clearly it doesn't."

"In answer to that, I should point out to you, Tarkyn, that integrity tends to shine most strongly out of the most accomplished con artists." Danton gave his head a little shake, wondering from where he had dredged that knowledge.

Tarkyn laughed, "Good answer. For your information, you are very astute when it comes to intrigue."

Danton sat up and swivelled to face the prince, "So, at the end of all this, where do you and I stand now? Unless I'm much mistaken, I can see no signs of hero worship in you any longer." He gave a grunt of laughter, "So where did I go wrong? Or did you just grow up?"

Tarkyn smiled. "No. You did nothing wrong, my friend. As you say, I just grew up. But now, when I nearly lost you, I realised that you were more of a brother to me when I was growing up, than my own brothers were, and I have never stepped out of my role enough to acknowledge that." He waved his hand, "So, I suppose I just wanted to tell you that and to say how glad I am that you survived."

A slow smile spread across Danton's face. "Yesterday, when I first saw you, I thought I was a woodman. Then I discovered that I was a sorcerer and didn't know where I belonged. But now?... Now I understand. I belong with you, don't I? I have belonged to you ever since I was eight years old."

The prince frowned in consternation, "I do not own you, Danton. You are your own man. But you are sworn to me as my liegeman and when our paths separated and all the world shunned me, you stayed true to me. And although there are now woodfolk and other sorcerers I trust, you are the only person who grew up with me." He gave a wistful smile, "I would almost say we belong together as brothers do, but in my case, at least on one side of my family, that is such a fraught statement. So instead I will say; we belong to each other not only through fealty, but also through years of mutual experience and friendship."

Danton breathed a deep sigh of relief. "I think I will be able to manage this maelstrom of uncertainty, if I know that."

Chapter 69

Andoran and Sargon waited for darkness on the third night before making any effort to free themselves. They still felt groggy from the effects of Davorad's charade and now, their hands were numb and stiff from days of being bound. So it took several frustrating attempts before Andoran was able to extract the tiny knife from where it had been thrust into the material inside the back of Sargon's trousers.

They had listened carefully for hours to learn the pattern of the new guards. They waited until they heard the guard walk slowly past the side of the tent before Andoran manoeuvred himself behind Sargon's hands to start cutting through the thick rope that bound them. It was a slow process. The knife, although sharp, was very small and Andoran's hands were clumsy and behind his back. By the time the guard was walking back up the other side of the tent, Andoran had managed to cut through only one strand. He gave a grunt of irritation and moved back to his original position in case the guard popped his head in on the way past, which he did randomly, as far as Andoran and Sargon could work out. It took four more of the guard's circuits for Andoran to free Sargon and another three for Andoran's hands to be cut loose.

The next time the guard popped his head in, Andoran was waiting beside the doorway. Fighting his clumsiness, the red-headed tournament sorcerer clamped one hand over the guard's mouth and slit his throat with the wicked little knife he held in the other. Nodding to Sargon to follow him, Andoran carefully peered through the tent's lacing before venturing forth into the night.

But Colonel Charford had not reached his position by chance alone and he had no intention of leaving his future career in the hands of Jarand's troops. So, as Andoran and Sargon slipped out of the tent and flitted from one shadow to the next towards the perimeter of the encampment, two watchers sent warning of their passage to encampment guards on the perimeter and to Colonel Charford himself.

Andoran and Sargon found their exit from the camp remarkably easy to accomplish. The guards seemed to be preoccupied with something a little further up that neither of them could see. Thanking their lucky stars, they ran as swiftly as their stiff legs would carry them into the shelter of the forest and when they had put a decent distance between themselves and the encampment, sat down under a tree to catch their breath.

But the encampment guards were not the only ones who had mounted an extra watch on the two miscreants.

Suddenly, from the darkness of the trees above them, came the deep rumble of thunder, "For what you did to our kinsman, we give you this."

Out of the darkness, two small stones hurtled with deadly accuracy to crack the bridge of each sorcerer's nose.

"Aagh!" Both Andoran and Sargon cried out in pain and clasped their faces.

The deep voice seemed to reverberate around them. "And for what you did to our forest guardian, we give you this."

Before they could recover enough to even consider raising their shields, two slightly larger, sharp stones hit them hard in their sides and a sickening click signalled the cracking of two ribs.

Andoran and Sargon each whipped one hand from their bleeding noses to clutch at their sides.

The perimeter guardsmen stationed among the trees, couldn't for the life of them see where the missiles were coming from. They stood rooted to the spot with fear as the thundery voice boomed again, "And for what you did to our elite guard, we have already taken our revenge."

As the echoes of the thunder died away, everyone on the ground waited for the next missile. But none came.

Then the deep voice issued forth once more, almost in a sing song rhythm, "Is your vision blurry or can't you tell in the dark? Are your movements clumsy or is it only from the ropes? ...... Do you know the symptoms of an elite guard's poison?"

Then very quietly, came a soft sighing of wind though grasslands, "Andoran and Sargon. There is nowhere to run to. Nowhere to hide. You carry your death within you."

For a moment, all was silent. Then the soft voice wafted through the air for the last time, "Sorcerers of the encampment, you may take back your prisoners."

Charford, Guerion and Torgan stood within the trees with their men around them, taking in the eerie encounter. As the last words died away, the Colonel gave himself a mental shake and without hesitation, walked out into the open to stand before Andoran and Sargon. He knew that his men would need his example to overcome their fear of what they had just witnessed.

"Take these men back," he said matter-of-factly. "Guerion, Sergeant Torgan, stay here with me please."

When his soldiers had dragged the groaning prisoners away, Colonel Charford raised his voice enough so that it would carry into the nearby trees. "I don't know who you are, but I would like to thank you before we return, for your assistance in bringing these men to justice and for putting an end to an infamous practice. If, as I suspect, you yourselves are brigands, you will get no quarter from me in future encounters, but on this occasion, we appear to be united against a common foe. You have my assurance that these men will hang at dawn. I bid you good evening."

With a curt nod at his officers to accompany him, the Colonel turned on his heel and headed back to the encampment to make sure that justice was meted out.

CHAPTER 70

Thunder Storm chuckled, "You should have seen their faces. Actually, I can show everyone but Danton."

"I think you should re-enact it, Thunder Storm. Tarkyn and Danton need the sound effects. And you do your bit too, Grass Wind. Your voice sounded so spooky. It was brilliant," said Leaf Fall enthusiastically.

"And I was able to indulge in my favourite hobby," said Twig Snap cheerfully, "Which is firing at sorcerers…*bad* ones, that is," she added hastily.

Thunder Storm smiled, "It won't be as effective in the daylight but we'll do our best."

Using Waterstone and Ancient Oak to play Andoran and Sargon, the events of the night before were re-enacted for the benefit of the sorcerers among them.

As the small audience applauded, Danton exclaimed, "Stars above! And you were worried about *me* torturing them!"

"How did you know that?" asked Running Feet shortly.

Danton was taken aback, "I don't know." He shook his head as though to sort out his thoughts, "I just did."

"So when did you administer Danton's poison?" asked Tarkyn.

Waterstone glanced at Tarkyn, unsure how he would react. "Before we tied Andoran and Sargon to the gate of the encampment. We disguised the cuts by surrounding them with a lot of other scratches. We knew *you* wanted them to be kept alive to give evidence but *we* wanted them dead after what they'd done to Danton…and to you and Autumn Leaves. We'd had enough. And we didn't want them coming back later to hurt someone else." He shrugged, "So we compromised."

"So, is that what you meant when you said, 'They will get their just deserts this time, one way or another'?" To Waterstone's relief, Tarkyn grinned, "Brilliant! I, too, was worried that they would wriggle out of it somehow. Well done! That was a great idea."

But Danton, watching the woodfolk's faces relax, turned to Tarkyn and asked, "What was everyone worried about?"

Tarkyn looked around at the gathered woodfolk and smiled, "Two things, I suspect. One, that they had come perilously close to disobeying my wishes and they are, after all, under oath. And two, that I have a tendency to want to oversee important decisions and can become a little… *agitated,* if I am not consulted."

"Hmm. Interesting," said Danton thoughtfully.

Before Danton could say anything further, Twig Snap's head suddenly went up and her face split into a broad smile, "Listen! I can hear Borovar coming."

"And Stormaway, and String and Bean and Harkell," added Autumn Leaves with a grin.

Twig Snap waved her hand. "Obviously. But I'm only interested in Boravar…See you," she said with a cheeky grin as she flicked out of sight to greet her beloved as he neared the firesite.

Leaf Fall shook his head, "I've never seen anyone more besotted."

Autumn Leaves gave him a friendly clap on the shoulder, "Your sister does nothing by halves, does she?"

All the woodfolk turned their gaze towards the eastern side of the clearing waiting for the appearance of those Tarkyn had left behind. Tarkyn threw Danton a wry glance, knowing that he too would not yet have heard anything, before joining the woodfolk in watching expectantly.

As soon as he thought their attention was fixed, Danton stood up quietly and crept into the trees to watch the new arrivals in peace. Of course a sorcerer rarely makes a move without woodfolk being aware of it, so Waterstone sent Tarkyn a brief image to let him know but, by mutual consent, they let him go.

From within the trees, Danton watched the newcomers' arrival, straining his mind to catch any glimpse of memory. Tarkyn and the woodfolk had told him about the sorcerers as part of their efforts to jog his memory and to re-teach him his life. So he knew their names and as they appeared, was able to fit each name to a person.

When Stormaway appeared, he suddenly remembered standing in a tent with him, rubbing green powder into bedding. But even as he struggled to make sense of it, it was gone. Danton nearly stamped his foot with frustration. His eyes widened when the great bulk of Boravar came into view, holding hands with little Twig Snap who bounced along, all smiles, at his side.

As Danton watched them talking, he decided that he himself was most similar to the dark haired Harkell, an officer by background like himself. Danton saw Harkell's eyes flickering around the clearing, checking out the surroundings and possibly looking for him. Danton knew that he would have to go out and meet them all soon but he just wanted to get his bearings as best he could, first.

Suddenly, a young woodman was standing at his elbow, looking out into the clearing with him, "Hi Danton. You don't remember me, but my name's Rainstorm." He nodded at the people gathered around the firesite. "So what do you think of them all? Boravar's huge, isn't he? And see the woodwoman standing next to Stormaway? That's Summer Rain. She's a healer too. So now that you have Stormaway, Tarkyn and Summer Rain on your case, you should be right in no time."

Danton glanced at him and smiled, "Hello Rainstorm. Pleased to meet you. Tarkyn tells me I share your views about forest guardians."

Rainstorm raised his eyebrows, "Do you? In what way?"

"I think they're more impressive than princes."

"*Do you?*" The woodman stared at him in astonishment. "That's amazing. You'll be amazed yourself, when you get your memory back."

"Why?"

"Because you think the sun shines out of Tarkyn, just because he's a prince."

Danton shook his head, "No. I'm sure you're wrong. I'm sure I would like Tarkyn for more than just being a prince. Tell me I'm not such a toadeater."

Rainstorm laughed. "No. No, you're not. I did think you were, when you first arrived but we didn't really understand your customs then." He thought about it for a few moments, "No, you do like Tarkyn... a great deal, I think. You just act like a toadeater."

A shadow of uncertainty crossed Danton's face, "Oh dear," he said fretfully, "What if I don't like myself when I remember who I am?"

It was then that Rainstorm realised how unwell Danton still was. "Sorry Danton," he said gently. "I didn't mean to upset you. It's just your funny sorcerer customs. We all like you tremendously. I'm sure you will too."

Suddenly Waterstone appeared at his other side, frowning, "I hope this young ratbag is not upsetting you, Danton."

"Oh come on Waterstone, be fair," protested Rainstorm. "I don't usually upset people even if I do take a few chances."

Waterstone nodded at Danton, and sent a mind message to say that Danton looked upset. A silence ensued around Danton while the woodmen on either side of him had a quick altercation.

Judging the content of their conversation purely by their expressions, Danton smiled slightly and said to Waterstone, "Don't worry. Every second thing people say to me at the moment unsettles me because I have to readjust all the information I already know, to fit it in." His smile broadened, "If you two have finished arguing, perhaps we should venture out and greet the others."

The two woodmen looked guiltily at each other.

"Oops," said Rainstorm, breaking into a grin.

Despite their best intentions to the contrary, the newcomers crowded around Danton the moment he emerged, all anxious to see how he was, to greet him and tell him how glad they were that he had survived. Danton stood in their midst with a dazed grin on his face, thinking that his life seemed to be full of very kind, friendly people. And the whole time he could feel Waterstone's and Rainstorm's arms laced across his back in silent support.

Gradually, an expectant silence fell as they waited for Danton's response to their many questions. He took a quick breath, "Thank you for your warm welcome. I am beginning to have high hopes that I will like myself when I remember myself," he couldn't resist glancing at Rainstorm as he added, "even if I am a bit of a toadeater." Danton chuckled at the wave of protest that this produced.

When they were quiet again, Danton continued, "Just to save you wondering; I am sorry but I don't recognise any of you except for the odd fleeting image, and if I know anyone's name it will be because someone has told me or I have heard someone else addressing you." He smiled wryly, "I feel like a rank beginner in the midst of experts. Everyone of you knows more about me than I do…and everyone knows more about you than I do."

Harkell smiled at him, "It must feel rather odd, being welcomed so effusively by a group of strangers."

 "Actually, that's all I've ever known." Danton gave a wry smile, "I've been surrounded by friendly strangers ever since I woke up three days ago. So I'm beginning to get used to it."

Stormaway made his way to the front, "And has Tarkyn given you any of his healing force yet?"

Danton waved his arm, "Oh yes. See? My wrist is completely repaired."

"But what about for your memory?"

Danton nodded, "We tried last night but so far, nothing. I'm feeling stronger, though."

"Hmph." Stormaway looked thoughtful. "I can see you're going to be a bit of a challenge, young man." He gave a distracted smile, "Just give me an hour or two to settle in and unpack my things. I need to put together a few ingredients and then I'll come back to you. Summer Rain, perhaps you might like to assist me in an hour's time?"

"I would be pleased to, Stormaway. Meanwhile, I might give our young friend a restorative tonic to complement Tarkyn's healing. I have prepared something to strengthen his circulation after his episode of non-breathing."

Tarkyn who was standing at the back of the throng, folded his arms and smiled, his eyes twinkling with fellow feeling. Danton frowned quickly in suspicion but had no time to think before Summer Rain produced a small flask and offered it to him.

"Thank you," he said gravely before swallowing it down in one swift gulp. "Aaaah!" Danton shook his head from side to side, "That tastes terrible!" As he pulled himself together, he saw Tarkyn grinning hugely in the background. He narrowed his eyes before turning to the woodwoman and saying pointedly, "Oh, I do beg your pardon, Summer Rain. That was rude of me, wasn't it? I'm afraid the piquancy of the flavour was a little more than I had anticipated."

Rainstorm shouted with laughter, "I take it all back. You are a toadeater."

Danton put his hands on his hips and smiled down at Summer Rain. "Are they always this rude to you? I don't know why you put up with it."

Summer Rain patted Danton on the arm, "What a dear boy you are! Yes. They are always scathing about my tonics... but they always accept them when they need them. My reward is in watching them get better." She leant in slightly and said *sotto voce*, "If they are excessively rude, I believe they find the tonics even more unpalatable the next time they need one." Then she gave the faintest conspiratorial smile and a final pat to Danton's shoulder, "Now, young man, I must go and settle myself in, so that I can assist Stormaway. I will see you later on."

As Danton smiled in her wake, he realised he was surrounded by a bemused silence.

Rainstorm frowned, "Did she just crack a joke?"

Autumn Leaves screwed his face up in thought, "Hmm, I wouldn't bet on it. She never has before. I think perhaps I'll be a little more circumspect in future about how I receive her tonics."

Now that she was safely out of earshot, Danton shrugged, "I wouldn't bother, if I were you. They couldn't taste any worse than the one I just had."

"Oh, I see. Different story now that she's left," observed Rainstorm tartly.

"At no stage did I say that I liked the taste." Danton smiled and added casually, "Anyway, I was really just giving one in the eye to Tarkyn who was laughing at me from the back row."

"Interesting," said Harkell slowly, unconsciously speaking for everyone. His eyes darted from Danton to Tarkyn and back again. "I can see that our reunion will be full of surprises."

Danton glanced at him, understood the inference but decided to let it ride.

Chapter 71

It was not until the early afternoon that Stormaway was ready to work with Danton. He had consulted at length with Tarkyn and Summer Rain at various times, both singly and together, and various herbs had been requested and sought in the surrounding woodlands. Now, finally, he was ready.

The old wizard drew Danton aside and walked a little way with him to a nearby clearing, sat down on a mossy log and gestured for Danton to sit close to him.

Stormaway rummaged around in his tattered old satchel and brought forth several small, stoppered bottles and some little sachets filled with a variety of herbs, plants and flowers. He spread them out carefully on the top of the stump at the end of the log. When all was in readiness, he turned to Danton.

"These bottles and sachets contain your past." He waved his hand, "Not your real past, of course, but the smells of your past. There is nothing that more strongly evokes a memory that the smell of it. Tarkyn, Summer Rain and I have brought together combinations of ingredients to recreate the odours that accompanied various times in your sojourn among the woodfolk and your life in the castle and at court."

Danton looked warily at the array of bottles and sachets. Now that the time had come, he felt nervous about what he would discover. He glanced at the wizard. "So what do we do first?"

"Hmm. To be honest, this is new territory for me. My feeling is that we should start with more recent memories and gradually work our way backwards. But who knows? Perhaps when you regain one memory, you will regain everything at the same time." He gave a reassuring smile, "I think we should at least be prepared for that possibility." He studied Danton for a moment, taking in his clenched hands and tight face. "Do you feel up to this?"

"Yes. It's just that it is unnerving to have my life facing me in a row of bottles."

Stormaway gave a grunt of laughter before asking, "Do you want someone to be with you?"

Danton shook his head, "No. I don't want the people involved watching me while I react to my memories of them, when or if those memories return." He gave a shy smile, "I remembered a scene with you in it but when I tried to grab hold of it and learn more, it faded. If you have it in one of your bottles, perhaps we could start there."

"I thought you just finished saying that you didn't want the people you were retrieving the memories about, present."

Danton shrugged, "I did, but from the small flash I saw, it didn't seem like a complicated relationship between us. Besides, I think you are old enough and wise enough to be objective about my reactions whereas I suspect Tarkyn, for instance, isn't."

Stormaway raised his eyebrows, "That was a remarkably perceptive comment for one so close to Tarkyn."

"You're confusing the past with the present. The person you are talking to now has only known Tarkyn for a little over two days."

"Hmm," Stormaway went into a reverie for a minute or two, staring abstractedly at Danton. Then he gave his head a little shake and said, "All right. Let's start where you suggested. Tell me what you can of the scene you remembered."

Danton shrugged, "There's not much to tell. Just you watching me, rubbing some green powder into bedding. That's it."

Stormaway's eyes lit up, "Ah yes. That was when you and I infiltrated the encampment. You were rubbing ground nettles into Andoran and Sargon's bedding, as I recall. We were determined to cause the terrible twosome as much discomfort as we could, short of killing them." He picked up one of the sachets and frowned, "Now, just a minute. I may need to modify one of these to create the cocktail of smells that was inside that tent."

After a few minutes of fiddling, the wizard sprinkled smatterings from two of the sachets on a flat dish and added a few drops of water. "Dampness brings out the aromas," he explained. "There. Now try this." He handed the dish to Danton and said, "Close your eyes, breathe in the scent and think about the image you just described to me."

As the young sorcerer inhaled Stormaway's concoction, Andoran and Sargon's quarters appeared strongly in his mind. He remembered the footsteps passing outside the tent that had made Stormaway and him pause and he remembered the devious plans for poisoning Andoran and Sargon that they had devised and were in the process of carrying out. Slowly, as he explored either side of the image, he remembered working with Stormaway to free the stake that held the imprisoned woodfolk and drinking with the terrible twosome, while he tried to mask the sounds of the woodfolk's activities outside as they had rescued their kin. Suddenly everything went black and he thought he had lost the memory, but then he saw himself in the forest, his hands bound behind him, facing the questioning of Waterstone and then Tarkyn.

Danton pulled his head back away from the scents. When he opened his eyes, they were glittering with anger. "How long ago was this?"

Stormaway thought for a moment, "Not long. Perhaps three months ago."

"So much for lifelong friendship then," spat out Danton.

"What? What have you remembered?" asked Stormaway.

"Having my loyalty doubted by Waterstone and Tarkyn." He grunted. "Waterstone, I can understand, if he had only known me for a matter of weeks, but Tarkyn…"

"Did you stay with your memory until the situation was resolved? You were angry then and you are angry now. So perhaps if you try to remember the rest…"

Reluctantly, Danton closed his eyes and brought back the memory of sitting with his hands tied, spitting his outrage at being doubted and refusing to cooperate with Waterstone. Then he remembered how anxious he had been to please Tarkyn and how much resolve it had taken to confront Tarkyn with the consequences of his mistrust.

I meet Tarkyn's gaze squarely, even though my stomach is knotted with fear. "If you punish me, when I have given you nothing but loyal service, your behaviour will be no better than your brothers'. The reason for your behaviour may be different, but the effect will be the same on the people you hurt."

Tarkyn lets out a low whistle and shakes his head, his face white with anger. Never before have I angered him like this. "Danton, you forget yourself. I think woodfolk society has affected your sense of propriety more than I expected. I can't believe you just had the temerity to say that to me."

He stands up and glowers down at me, ordering me to stand. I try my best to comply but it is difficult with my hands tied. Tarkyn grabs me and drags me roughly to my feet. "Turn around," he snaps. As I feel the ropes fall from my wrists behind me, he orders me to turn and face him.

I force myself to meet his burning amber eyes, my heart beating hard in my chest.

He says flatly, "You are free to go."

It feels like a death knell to me. I don't know what to do, so I just keep staring at him.

"I said, Danton, you are free to go."

I screw up my courage to respond, as calmly as I am able, "I heard you, my lord. And I thank you for your trust. But I have no wish to leave you, Sire."

Tarkyn raises his eyebrows haughtily. "Indeed? And what should I think of someone who is prepared to serve such a corruption as myself?"

I sense that I have a reprieve. If he were determined to send me away, he would not have asked a question. I take a breath and tell him the truth, "You should think of him as a loyal friend and liegeman who is willing to stake his life on his belief that your integrity will overcome your fear of betrayal."

"Even though I am no better than my brothers?"

I should have realised that his anger springs partly from hurt. "I did not say that, my lord. I said your actions against me would make it seem that way." I take a moment to gather my thoughts. "All three of you fear betrayal, but in you, it is counter-balanced by your care for people. In your brothers, it is fed by their obsession with power." I become aware that my wrists are stinging as the circulation returns and I rub them as I talk. "My lord, for you, betrayal means personal pain. For them it is merely a counter move in a political game. You care for people. They care only for power."

I can see hurt and confusion on his face and know that he needs me to steady him.

I drop to one knee to bow, hand on heart, and give him my faith. "And that is why, my lord, you are the only true hope for the future of Eskuzor and why I will serve you to the end of my days."

When Tarkyn next speaks, his voice is husky with emotion, but all anger is gone. "Please rise, Danton. I am honoured by your loyalty and your service. I will do my best to justify your faith in me."

And I know he will do his best, because he always does.

This time when I face him, I can see that he is back on an even keel. He gives a wry smile, "As to being the hope of Eskuzor, I think not. As you have just said yourself, I have no aspirations to enter into a game of power with my brothers." He smiles at Ancient Oak and Waterstone, "…. any of my brothers."

Danton pulled himself back to the present, "Whoa. He's fearsome, isn't he? He hasn't acted like that with me at all, this time around." A warm smile spread over his face, "But, he's manageable. And in remembering that, I can feel the strength of our connection with each other." He scratched his head, "But I don't understand. How could someone who now professes to be my lifelong friend, and from that memory, clearly is, doubt me like that?"

Stormaway took a deep breath and said gently, "Danton, I need to explain the context of this. These events took place only weeks after Tarkyn's own brothers had betrayed him and only a couple of weeks after Andoran and Sargon, whom he had also counted as friends, had tried to drag him back for the reward. Tarkyn's whole world had been destroyed by people he had trusted. And there you were, consorting with the enemy, and even though I knew how distasteful you found Andoran and Sargon's company, Tarkyn's fragile trust in you, or in anyone for that matter, was stretched to breaking point."

As Danton looked half convinced, Stormaway pressed home his advantage, "Just imagine if Waterstone, whom you have only known for three days in your present state, suddenly tried to kill you. What would that do to your faith in everyone else?… And that is only after three days. What if that was after a lifetime of being in the same family?"

Danton nodded slowly, "Yes. I suppose I can see that. Still, I must admit I still feel offended."

"Don't be, Danton. Just remember that Tarkyn feels responsible for the safety and welfare of the woodfolk and he can afford to take less chances than most. And, when you think about it, he released you purely on the basis of your words without any other evidence."

"True. I suppose he did." Danton waved his hand, "Never mind. Let's move on. If each of these scents takes this long to discuss, we'll be here for weeks."

Stormaway considered him for a moment before selecting a little green bottle which he held to the light and then removed the cork and sniffed before handing it to Danton. "Try this one."

Danton closed his eyes and took in a deep breath filled with the smell of heather, woodsmoke and pine. Suddenly, he was high on a mountain, surrounded by the aqua of his shield, with Sparrow next to him. As he looked around he realised that his shield was protecting hundreds of woodfolk who were all watching Tarkyn sitting quietly beside an old gnarled tree with one of the trappers by his side with his hand on his shoulder. Suddenly a huge spectre erupted from the tips of Tarkyn's fingers to stand glowering over him. Danton saw Tarkyn scrabble to his feet and flick his shield up just before a blast of wizard fire engulfed him. Then he watched as Tarkyn drew himself up and demanded obeisance from the giant towering above him. Danton could see the strain on Tarkyn's face and how much the effort cost him. And with a feeling of great pride, Danton watched as the spectre bowed to his prince's will.

Danton opened his eyes, misty with tears. "I remember. At least, I remember that. And I remember how I felt about Tarkyn. Such strength, to face that spectre." He waved his hand, "Just give me a minute." As he closed his eyes, memories of their time in the forest came flooding back. A kaleidoscope of memories swirled through his mind; watching helplessly as Tarkyn had writhed in agony from the aftermath of fighting off the virus, Tarkyn's disdainful dismissal of the mountainfolk's first efforts at reconciliation and Danton's own subsequent beating at their hands. He remembered Tarkyn passing judgement on him for hitting Waterstone and dressing him down when he had first arrived among the woodfolk. And he remembered countless occasions where he had bowed and woodfolk had smirked at him. Then he remembered when he had angered Tarkyn with his behaviour towards Harkell and had not been allowed to straighten from his bow.

When Danton opened his eyes, they were not shining with the admiration of Tarkyn that Stormaway had anticipated. The young sorcerer looked squarely at Stormaway, "He doesn't mind humiliating me, does he?"

Stormaway was shocked. For a moment he stared at Danton, speechless. Then he asked, "How far back do you remember?"

Danton shrugged, "Only in the forest, so far. And, I suspect, only parts of that."

Stormaway hurriedly grabbed for another small bottle, "Here. Try this one. This is from your time in the palace. It is filled with the scent of beeswax and furniture polish, the perfumes of court ladies and the aromas of exquisite cooking spices."

Danton eyed him suspiciously, "I do not want to be indoctrinated into thinking that Tarkyn's treatment of me is acceptable. It is not."

"But twice he has jeopardised his life to save you," protested Stormaway.

"For that, I thank him. Nevertheless it does not give him the right to treat me so disparagingly. If I had saved his life, I would not expect to be able to treat him like that."

When Danton was adamant in refusing the proffered bottle, Stormaway tried a new tack. "Tell me what you have remembered so far."

When Danton had finished, Stormaway sprinkled the contents of another sachet on a dish and dampened them. He offered it to Danton, "Here. These are the scents of the clearing where you and Tarkyn fought off the posse of sorcerers who came in pursuit of Tarkyn. I promise you, it is not the smells from the palace. I will not betray your trust."

Danton accepted the dish slowly and bent over it to sniff it gingerly. Then his eyes widened with fear as he remembered standing beside Tarkyn facing the edge of the clearing, as bloodhounds and mounted sorcerers pushed into view through the undergrowth. He replayed the whole episode in his mind, smiling at the airborne antics of Tarkyn firing shafts of power as he clung to Danton's back, and reliving the camaraderie of fighting off such a huge challenge together.

He raised his eyes and grunted with laughter, "Huh. Well, maybe there is some basis for this professed friendship of his."

"Do you remember Lord Tolward's house?"

Danton thought hard but eventually shook his head.

Stormaway selected another little bottle, "Here. Try this."

As the scent wafted up his nostrils, Danton remembered peering in the window at the injured children, fighting with Lapping Water to enlist Tarkyn's aid, watching the lord and his retainers sink to their knees as Tarkyn entered and working with Tarkyn as he healed the children, protecting him within his shield when the family and farmhands became edgy.

"Hmph. He does have a dry sense of humour, doesn't he?" said Danton, remembering Tarkyn's remark that healing was a dangerous business.

As Stormaway looked enquiringly at him, Danton held up his hand, "No. No more for now. My brain is reeling." He stood up, "Thank you for your efforts. Perhaps later, we can do some more, unless I remember it all myself in the meantime."

CHAPTER 72

Stormaway watched him leave with some trepidation. He was not sure that a patchwork memory was much better than no memory at all and he was inclined to think that Danton had gained a rather skewed view of Tarkyn, if he did not have the years of court expectations to provide the backdrop to the prince's more recent behaviour.

Danton walked off into the forest away from the clearing and from any contact with either woodfolk or sorcerers. He found a soft mossy spot beneath an oak and sat with his head against its trunk, letting the memories of the forest reel around his head. It was not long before his brain tired from the excessive activity and he fell asleep.

When he awoke, he found himself lying on the mossy ground, with his head cushioned by a rucksack and a warm cloak thrown over him. After a few minutes, it occurred to him to look in the rucksack and he found that it contained some roasted venison, apples, dried fruits and a flask each of water and wine. He smiled and raised his voice to say thanks, knowing that a lookout would be nearby.

A slight rustle alerted him to the presence of someone else sitting a short distance away from him, leaning against the next oak.

"Hello," said Tarkyn.

"Hello." Danton considered the prince for a few moments, working out that he would already have spoken to Stormaway and would know Danton's reactions to the memories he had recovered. He would also be wondering how much more Danton had remembered and what conclusions he had drawn. He smiled, "Would you like to join me in a wine?"

Tarkyn inclined his head, "Thank you. I would."

With an inward smile, Danton remembered Twig Snap saying that Tarkyn became more formal when he was feeling unsure.

"Well, come over here then," said Danton cheekily "I can't chat to you from that distance away." He rummaged around in the rucksack. "Well, fancy that! There are two cups."

Tarkyn gave a slight smile as he rose and walked quietly over to stand above Danton, with his hands on his hips, "What a coincidence! If you lay out the cloak and spread the food out on it, we can sit on either side of it."

Danton knew that Tarkyn was very gently reasserting his authority but complied nonetheless. He smiled at Tarkyn as the prince folded his long frame into a cross legged seating position. Danton filled the two cups with wine and handed one to Tarkyn.

He held up his cup, "Here's to us."

Tarkyn clicked cups with him and took a sip, watching him over the brim of the cup.

Danton realised that he was deriving an unaccustomed sense of power from knowing where he stood better than Tarkyn did. For a moment he relished it before relenting, "I understand why yesterday mattered so much."

"Do you?"

"Yes. You were giving away your right to humiliate me, weren't you? You were changing the terms of our friendship. You knew that yesterday was the first time that I could look at you without seeing you through the veil of fear and adulation that surrounds the royal family."

Tarkyn nodded, "Yes. It has slowly dawned on me that I have been treating the woodfolk with more respect than you, simply because they demand it. And because of your upbringing, you would never have demanded it. And yet you deserve my respect just as much, if not more, because of our long association." He leant forward and picked up a chunk of venison, "You understand that this is more than just eschewing the trappings of deference. I gave you permission to be informal with me long ago…" he gave a slight smile, as he saw Danton about to protest, "which I keep to, except for the odd occasion when I lose my temper."

Danton gave a derisive grunt, "Tarkyn, I have spent a lifetime learning how to weather your moods. Just as you make allowances for Rainstorm and accept that his outbursts are more to do with him than you, so do I make allowances for you."

"Oh." For a moment, Tarkyn looked completely non-plussed. Then suddenly he grinned, "Well, that's good then, because despite my best efforts, I'm sure I'll lose my temper again sometime in the future, and give you the most horrendous setdown."

Danton chuckled, "I'm sure you will. But it might make it a little harder for you to maintain, if you know that I'm simply waiting for you to calm down."

Tarkyn frowned, "But does that mean that you don't take me seriously when I am displeased?"

"No, Tarkyn. Never fear. I care a great deal about fulfilling your wishes. And I think very carefully before doing anything that might displease you. I do not ignore the message. It is merely the delivery that one must sometimes insulate oneself against."

Tarkyn looked at his liegeman with dawning respect, "Danton, I have truly underestimated you." His eyes narrowed, "And are there other ways in which you manage me and my emotions?"

Danton's eyes twinkled, "Oh yes, Sire. After all, as you pointed out yesterday, I have always been two years older and wiser than you. And my life depended on knowing how to manage you."

"Hmph. I'm not sure that I'm very happy about this. It sounds as though you have been manipulating me all my life."

"If one does not have authority, one must find other ways." As the prince's eyes began to cloud with anger, Danton held up his hand, "Tarkyn, I have never used it to work against you and I never would. I have only used my knowledge of you to support you. If that were not the case, I would not be letting you know about it now."

"I didn't know what I was unleashing when I let you have your head yesterday, did I?"

Danton smiled with a calm assurance that Tarkyn found very difficult to accept, "If you give respect, you receive openness in return. I have never told you any of this before because I needed it to protect myself and to give myself some power in our relationship. However, if you grant me that power anyway, I no longer need to hide my advantages."

Tarkyn let out a long breath, "Now I feel the shoe is on the other foot. Have you had any respect for me at all, or have I just been a game to you?"

Danton frowned in consternation. "No, Tarkyn. Don't think like that. As you respect that black mountain lion, but found ways to manage it, so did I with you. I have always been devoted to you. You are the prince, not I. It means the earth to me that I have been privileged to serve a member of the royal family, but most particularly you. You are the forest guardian and the man who faced down the shade of Pipeless. I could never have done that, even if I had the power. My respect for you is boundless."

He smiled gently and put his hand on Tarkyn's arm. Tarkyn looked pointedly down at Danton's hand and his eyes narrowed, but he made no move to remove it from his arm.

"Tarkyn, if I had just stood in awe of you all those years, how could I have served you?" When Tarkyn didn't look up and didn't respond, Danton took his hand away and stood up. "Right. Fine. Let's go back to how we were, shall we? Obviously, you are unable to accept what you yourself started." Danton bowed low. "I beg your pardon for treating you with insufficient deference," he said with awful sarcasm and strode off, back to the clearing.

Inevitably, news of their altercation preceded Danton's arrival at the clearing. Assuming this, Danton rolled his eyes and slapped his thigh in irritation as he saw Waterstone approaching, "What a bloody idiot I am! I should never have been so open with him. It was too much of a shock for him. I assumed a level of maturity in him that is still lacking. Oh well, perhaps when Tarkyn finally grows up, we may actually become friends. Until then, I had better watch myself. I think I have overstepped the mark well and truly."

Waterstone's eyes gleamed with amusement. "Danton! So scathing, you are. I can't believe how much you've changed. I think that blast of magic did more than wreck your memory."

"Huh." Danton put his hands on his hips, "Well, I have most of my memory back now, I think. Enough to realise that I have been taken for granted right, left and centre. What's the point of me trailing along behind Tarkyn's coat tails? He obviously can't cope with the idea that I'm not some mindless vassal under his total control. You would think that having the power to imprison or execute me all my life would have been enough for him. But no! He is upset that I actually indulged in some independent thought and found ways to cope with his unruly behaviour. The man is a total menace."

"What did you mean, that you've been taken for granted right, left and centre?" asked Lapping Water quietly.

Danton stared at her. After a moment, he said rather unconvincingly, "Nothing. I meant nothing by it. Just that Tarkyn obviously prefers to underestimate me." He waved a hand. "Let's just leave it, shall we? This is between Tarkyn and me. If he can put up with the charade knowing the truth, then so too must I."

"Danton."

Danton rolled his eyes in irritation and swivelled into a low bow, "Yes, Your Highness?"

Tarkyn stood with his hands on his hips, looking down at his liegeman with a slight smile playing around his mouth, "Your sarcasm is noted. You may rise in your own time." He glanced around at the woodfolk, "Danton and I have some unfinished business to discuss. I would appreciate some privacy. So would you please recall the lookout from this side of the clearing? We will take our chances." He returned his gaze to Danton who was standing woodenly in front of him. "Danton, come with me."

"Certainly, Sire."

With a slight shake of his head, Tarkyn turned and, assuming that Danton was following, returned to the remains of their disturbed picnic. He sat down and gestured for Danton to do likewise. The prince refilled their cups with wine and handed one to Danton.

Danton pulled himself together enough to produce a courteous thanks.

Tarkyn eyed him and began, "So. Was that another example of manipulating me? Going off in a huff so that I would run after you?"

"No Sire. I did not expect you to follow me."

Tarkyn gave a grunt of sardonic laughter, "No. Judging by what you were saying about me, I think that must be true."

"I beg your pardon, Your Highness. I should not have spoken of you like that," said Danton stiffly.

The prince waved his hand. "Oh, put a sock in it, Danton." When Danton glared at him, Tarkyn continued, "The last sensible thing you said to me was, 'If I had just stood in awe of you all those years, how could I have served you?' And while I was thinking about that, you suddenly stood up and went off in a huff. Now *this* time, I forbid you to leave until I say so."

"Your will is my command, Sire."

"*Stop* it, Danton. I will get angry in a moment, if you continue. You have made your point loud and clear, not just to me but to anyone who would listen to you. I can only hope you were not as indiscreet when you served me at court."

Danton lips tightened. Then he said, in genuine remorse, "No Sire. I would never have betrayed your confidence like that and I am sorry I have done so now. I must admit I am a little quick to anger at the moment." He heaved a deep sigh and waited.

"Danton, may we try again please? You hit me with a whole new way of looking at our past and I wasn't able to adjust my ideas to it instantaneously. Given my difficulties in discerning duplicity and my history of being betrayed, a couple of minutes to digest the fact that you were not as ingenuous as I had thought, should not have been too much to ask."

At last Danton smiled, "I'm sorry. If you had, in fact, asked, I would have stayed. But you stayed silent while you thought and I feared that I had gone too far."

"You have only gone too far in that you have given me a glimmering of a world of intrigue and manipulation that I would rather not know about." Tarkyn sipped his wine before giving a faint smile. "Perhaps, as you say, I am not yet mature enough to deal with it. I don't like to think of you fighting for your life with subterfuge, simply because of my volatility. That is not a very comfortable thought."

"There was nothing comfortable about life at court, Sire. It was complicated and dangerous. Unbeknownst to you, I steered you through one intrigue after another. I am only sorry that I failed so signally at the end."

Tarkyn shook his head, "No, Danton. No one could have stopped my brothers. Sooner or later they would have got rid of me."

"I was beginning to suspect that." Danton scratched his blonde hair, "Only, I didn't know how to tell you."

"You mean, you knew I wouldn't have believed you, don't you?"

Danton grimaced, "There was always something charming, but at the same time potentially lethal, about having a charge as naive as you."

Tarkyn chuckled, "So, given that I am obviously never going to grow up enough to stop being naive, do you think you can bring yourself to be my friend, instead of just my liegeman?"

Danton grinned, "I have always been your friend, sire." He became more serious, "But I would indeed like to put our friendship on a stronger footing. In fact, now that we have come this far, I don't see how we could really turn back."

"No. Nor do I." Tarkyn hesitated, "Besides, you have changed, Danton. It is not just our time yesterday. You are more forthright, more sure of yourself, quicker to anger. A lot has changed. Perhaps when you stand outside of all societies, as you have over the last few days, it changes your perspective."

Danton nodded slowly, thinking about it, "I have never felt so alone, not even when I first came to the palace. Although I was surrounded by kind people, I had no connection with them, with my past or my future. It was like being surrounded by blackness. A lot of the everyday mundanities seem awfully irrelevant, when faced with that void. And I felt as though I was on the outside looking in. I still do, to some extent… because the memories are sitting alongside that experience. They haven't replaced it."

A companionable, thoughtful silence fell. Danton fiddled with a bit of venison before adding a piece of apple to it and eating it. He glanced up at Tarkyn a couple of times before saying, "You realise I made an absolute idiot of myself before you arrived, don't you?"

"No." Tarkyn frowned, "In what way?"

Danton waved his hand, "I assumed I was a woodman because I was surrounded by woodfolk when I woke up."

"What's so bad about that?"

"Well, it's such a privilege to be a woodman, isn't it? It's not just something you can take for granted. I mean, just think. You're the only sorcerer ever to be admitted into their ranks and you're a forest guardian, for heaven's sakes, and their sworn liege lord. Then I go and blithely assume that I'm one of them." Danton grimaced, "It couldn't be more embarrassing, actually."

"Danton, I'm sure they understand. After all, they all know that you didn't remember who they or you were."

"Hmm, I suppose so." He grunted in derisive laughter, "No wonder they went to such pains to introduce me gently to the idea that I was a sorcerer. At least at that stage, I didn't realise what a gaff I had made. It's only now that I have my memory back that I understand the enormity of my blunder."

Suddenly there was a rustling in the nearby undergrowth. Before thought, Danton found himself enclosed within Tarkyn's bronze shield.

"Who is there?" asked Tarkyn sharply.

As two little heads rose slowly above the tops of the bushes, Tarkyn waved away his shield. He smiled, "Hello, you two. So much for privacy. What are you doing here?"

Sparrow smiled shyly, "We've come to see how Danton is... and if he remembers me."

Danton smiled and held out his arms. "Yes. Yes, I do, Sparrow. And I remember playing in the snow with you when we were missing Tarkyn and Waterstone and Ancient Oak. Come on. Come and have a hug."

Sparrow ran to him, plopped on his lap and put her arms around his chest. "I'm glad you're back, Danton. We are particular friends, aren't we, after that day in the snow." She gazed up at him, "I was a bit upset, you know, when you didn't know who I was."

Danton smiled at her, "I'm sorry Sparrow. But I know now."

Meanwhile Midnight was sitting comfortably on Tarkyn's knee, helping himself to the leftovers of their picnic. Tarkyn tousled his hair, "Come on. Let's rejoin the others." He gave a short laugh and said with mock severity, "And you, Danton, can set about repairing my reputation that you besmirched so thoroughly, earlier on."

Chapter 73

As they walked back into the clearing, it was obvious that something important was happening. The sorcerers were gathered in a little cluster together chatting quietly among themselves, while most of the woodfolk were out of focus.

Tarkyn frowned and asked of no one in particular, "What's going on?"

String shrugged and smiled, "Nothing to do with us. Woodfolk business." When Tarkyn looked uncertain, he added, "Don't worry. We're not at odds with them. They're just in the middle of a conference with their kin, that's all." He looked at Danton, "So, how are you?"

"I am fine, if a little irascible." He smiled and clapped Tarkyn on the back. "And you'll be pleased to know that Tarkyn has now matured enough to enter my circle of close friends."

Harkell looked at him in astonishment, "You're a cheeky bugger, aren't you?"

Danton laughed, "I am merely making amends for what I said about Tarkyn earlier." He took his arm down, "I'm afraid, in a moment of chagrin, I underestimated him, for which I have apologised."

Harkell's eyes flicked back and forth between the two of them, taking in and analysing the change. After a moment he nodded, "I would not presume to comment on whether or not His Highness has matured, but certainly your friendship has." He considered Danton, "I suspect we will all have to make some adjustments."

Suddenly Danton found Rainstorm at his side.

"Danton, I know you have just returned, but would you mind coming for a walk with me?"

Danton threw him a puzzled frown but said willingly enough, "Of course." Flicking a quick grin and a shrug over his shoulder, Danton turned and followed the young woodman back out of the clearing and into the surrounding trees.

"There is a small stream down through this glade and past these old oaks," said Rainstorm. "Perhaps we could go for a wander down there."

Danton nodded but glanced curiously at Rainstorm out of the corner of his eye. The woodman was clearly, and unusually for him, nervous. Danton made no comment, deciding to wait until they reached the stream.

The oaks gave way to a row of weeping willows whose long branches brushed the surface of the shallow water. The stream chattered as it burbled its way beneath the willows and out over beds of smooth rounded pebbles. When they reached its bank, Rainstorm did not find somewhere to sit as Danton had expected, but stopped and turned to face him.

Danton frowned slightly, "Are you all right, Rainstorm? Can I do anything to help?"

Rainstorm relaxed a little but not completely, and smiled, "No. I'm fine. Just a little nervous, if you must know." He took a deep breath, "Danton Patronell, would you do me the honour of becoming my bloodbrother?"

Danton goggled at him. Then he waved his hand and began to turn away, "No. No. You mustn't do this."

Rainstorm looked stricken, "What have I done wrong?" He grabbed Danton's shoulder and pulled him back around, "Danton. What did I do? I thought we were friends these days." His face was burning with chagrin. "If you refuse me, then who would you accept as a bloodbrother or sister?"

Danton stood and looked at him, "Rainstorm", he said gently, "I would be more honoured than I could say to count myself your bloodbrother. That is not why I refuse."

"Why then?"

"Because it is only my mistake that has forced you into this. It is very kind of you but now that I have my memory back, I understand completely what a presumption I made by thinking I was one of you when I was confused. You cannot overturn hundreds of years of tradition just to ease my embarrassment. I can live with it, if you can."

Rainstorm's face relaxed into a smile, "No, Danton. We are not asking you to join us because of that. You're right. We wouldn't overturn hundreds of years of tradition just to ease someone's embarrassment. While you lay unconscious, Waterstone and Lapping Water and Autumn Leaves and the others all realised how much you have done for us and how little recognition you have received." He shrugged, "It is not only Tarkyn who, when faced with your loss, realised your worth." He bent over to pick up a stick and, with a complicit little grin, began to break bits of the end as Tarkyn habitually did. "And they heard what you said to Andoran about how exclusive we were and they realised you had no expectation of ever being included among us." He threw away the last of the stick and brushed his hands, unconsciously mimicking every movement of Tarkyn's. "Danton, in your own way, you have given us as much support as Tarkyn and Stormaway. We want you to become a woodman too." He glanced sideways at Danton, "And I would like you to be my brother, if you could stand it." He shrugged, "You could be Falling Branch's bloodbrother if you preferred, although I think he's nearly twenty years older than you. Then you'd be my uncle. But I would rather you were my brother."

Danton slapped Rainstorm on the shoulder and then grabbed him and drew him into an embrace. "Rainstorm, it would give me great delight to be your older brother. Then I can boss you around mercilessly."

Rainstorm grunted, "I wasn't thinking of that, exactly. But I'll take the chance if it means you will join us."

Danton's eyes were wet with tears when he pulled away. "Do you know, I have had no family since I was eight? I was never allowed to see them and I lost the desire to, when I found out that my father had given me away to further his own career. In recent years, I have visited them from time to time, but there is no closeness between us. I would like to have a father again."

As they turned and began to walk back to the clearing, Danton could hardly contain his excitement, "Do you know, when I first came to the forest, I missed the glitter of court dreadfully but now I am used to damp ground and basic fare and the company of trustworthy, kind, straightforward people. And I have grown to love it." He glanced sideways at Rainstorm, "And you. You have supported me when everyone else was embarrassed about me being flogged. And you blast your way into one awkward situation after another and resolve it. I will be very proud to be your brother," he chuckled, "even if you can't read and don't know what a ball is."

As they neared the edge of the clearing, Danton fell silent and then came to a complete halt just within the treeline. When Rainstorm looked at him enquiringly, he gave a little shrug, "I'm a bit embarrassed to go out there, actually."

Rainstorm grinned, "That's easily fixed."

Moments later, all the woodfolk converged on him and dragged him out into the open. The sorcerers stood in the background smiling. Then everyone, sorcerer and woodfolk alike, formed into a semicircle around Danton and Rainstorm. Falling Branch came to stand beside him, giving Danton a smile and pat of encouragement as he did.

Lapping Water walked out of the semicircle to stand before him. "Danton Patronell, you have supported us with your power, your friendship, your subterfuge and your protection, with no thought of reward. We would feel honoured to have you as our kin."

Danton's eyes shone, "The honour is all mine. I can't begin to express how much this means to me."

Lapping Water nodded at Rainstorm to come forward and stand beside her, facing Danton.

Rainstorm took a deep breath and said formally, "Danton Patronell, I offer you membership of my family that you may share with us the joys and trials of kinship and that we may call upon each other's strength in times of need. Do you accept?"

Danton was so overcome, he had to swallow and clear his throat before replying, "I am honoured by your offer and accept." He gave a watery, apologetic grin.

Lapping Water continued to be strictly formal. She withdrew her hunting knife from its sheath and held it up. "To establish a new blood tie, blood must be shared. Roll up the sleeve of your right arm. Now hold out your arm, palm upwards and stand opposite one another."

Lapping Water tested the edge of her blade with her thumb as she waited for them to roll up their sleeves, sending a quick, glance of appreciation for her knife's sharpness to Harkell. When they were ready, she drew her knife lightly along each of their arms, leaving long, shallow cuts in its wake.

Rainstorm and Danton grasped each other's arms near the elbow so the two long cuts lay over each other. Rainstorm smiled into his new brother's shining eyes and intoned, "We are now of one blood. My kin are your kin. My ancestors are your ancestors. I welcome you as a brother. Falling Branch and Sun Shower welcome you as their son and Raging Water welcomes you as a grandson."

Danton had seen Stormaway's inauguration and knew what to say. He cleared his throat and replied, "We are now of one blood. My kin are your kin. My ancestors are your ancestors. I welcome you as a brother and Falling Branch and Sun Shower as my father and mother, and Raging Water as my grandfather."

Lapping Water held out her arms, her blood stained knife still in one hand. "Danton Patronell, companion of the forest guardian and supporter of the woodfolk, is now a member of a woodfolk family and no longer an outsider." She dropped her arms and smiled, "Welcome to our nation."

And so Danton, who until now had lived his life in Tarkyn's shadow, was finally recognised by both woodfolk and sorcerers for his own worth. In the nearby encampment, two dead sorcerers hung, swaying in the breeze, and in far off Tormadell, twin brothers still plotted each other's downfall and prepared for a military showdown. But within the clearing in the woods, a young, blonde, passionate sorcerer had come into his own.

THE SCORCERER'S OATH – BOOK FOUR

THE WIZARDESS

Stormaway Treemaster extracted a small message from the leg of his favourite wood pigeon. He gave her a few grass seeds and tickled the back of her neck before turning his attention to the tiny parchment held between his forefinger and thumb. Stormaway, part woodman, part sorcerer, was an experienced wizard and needed little concentration to murmur the words that would reconstitute the parchment to its original size.

As he waited for the parchment to stabilise, he gazed abstractedly at Tarkyn, who sat under a tree on the edge of a clearing, his long black hair partly obscuring his face as he bent forward, deep in conversation with Harkell, ex-Captain of Prince Jarand's Royal Guard. Over the past months, Stormaway had watched his young liege mature from a meticulously courteous, aloof youth into a self-assured leader, friendly and more relaxed in the company of the straightforward woodfolk than he could ever have been among the sophisticated guile of the Court sorcerers. The old wizard felt a pang of regret as a fleeting expression on Tarkyn's face reminded him of his old friend, King Markazon, who had died so many years before.

Feeling the wizard's eyes upon him, Tarkyn looked up, his eyes brilliant amber just like his father's, and sent him a warm, understanding smile.

Blast the boy! grumped Stormaway to himself. *Too knowing by half.*

Seeing the wizard's frown, Tarkyn's smile faded. "I could feel your regret and caught a brief image of my father," he said by way of explanation. "I am sorry, Stormaway, if I remind you of my father but am not the man himself. I hope I do not disappoint you too much."

Stormaway was so flustered by this remark that he dropped the parchment and had to chase after it as the breeze caught it and threatened to send it up into the trees. As soon as he had snatched the parchment back into his safekeeping and had drawn breath, he gasped, "No sire!

You do not disappoint me. You have misconstrued my feelings entirely. I merely regret the loss of your father's company."

"After all, you must be such a youngster in Stormaway's eyes," said Harkell, softening his unnerving acuity with a disarming smile.

Tarkyn watched the betraying flush mount Stormaway's cheeks. "I see... " Suddenly he smiled at his wizard. "Well, I can't do much about that, can I? But although it will always be different, I think, I hope that we are developing our own friendship between us."

Stormaway smiled fondly at his young charge. "Yes, Sire. We are."

Faced with the depth of feeling in his usually stoic wizard's eyes, Tarkyn covered his embarrassment by letting his eyes wander down to the piece of parchment waiting disregarded in Stormaway's hands and raised his eyebrows.

With a jolt, Stormaway remembered what he was holding. He scanned it briefly before saying to the prince. "They're on their way, Sire. The king and his brother have left Tormadell and are heading towards the encampment."

Harkell nodded in grim satisfaction. "And so the game begins."

Jennifer Jane Ealey was born in outback Western Australia where her father was studying kangaroos on a research station, one hundred miles from the nearest town. Her arrival into the world was watched, unexpectedly, by their pet kangaroo who had hopped into the hospital. Having survived the excitement of her birth, she moved firstly to Perth and then Melbourne where she spent most of her formative years. She took a year off from studying to ride a motorbike around Australia before working as a mathematics teacher and school psychologist in England and Australia, a bicycle courier in London and running a pub in outback New South Wales.

She now lives in Melton, a country town just outside Melbourne, working by day as a psychologist and beavering away by night as a novelist. She has written two detective novels and has just completed *The Sorcerer's Oath*, a series of four fantasy novels, of which *The Wizard's Curse* is the second.